MYTHS
and
MOTIFS
in
LITERATURE

edited by

DAVID J. BURROWS
DOUGLASS COLLEGE

FREDERICK R. LAPIDES
UNIVERSITY OF BRIDGEPORT

JOHN T. SHAWCROSS
CITY UNIVERSITY OF NEW YORK

The Free Press
A Division of Macmillan Publishing Co., Inc.
New York

The Free Press
A Division of Macmillan Publishing Co., Inc.
866 Third Avenue, New York, New York 10022

Library of Congress Catalog Card Number: 72–90546
Printed in the United States of America

printing number
5   6   7   8   9   10

ACKNOWLEDGMENTS

Maud Bodkin: "Archetypal Patterns in Tragic Poetry" is from *Archetypal Pat-*
terns in Poetry by Maud Bodkin, published by Oxford University Press.

Leslie Fiedler: "Archetype and Signature" is from Leslie A. Fiedler, "Archetype
and Signature": First published in *The Sewanee Review,* LX, 2 (Spring, 1952).
Copyright © 1952 by The University of the South. Reprinted with the permission of
the author and the publisher.

Erich Fromm: "The Nature of Symbolic Language" is from *The Forgotten*
Language by Erich Fromm. Copyright 1951 by Erich Fromm. Reprinted by permission of Holt, Rinehart and Winston, Inc.

William J. Goode: "Family and Religion" is reprinted with permission of The
Macmillan Company from *Religion Among the Primitives* by William J. Goode.
Copyright 1951 by William J. Goode.

Sir James G. Frazer: "The Sacred Marriage" is reprinted with permission of
The Macmillan Company from *The Golden Bough* by Sir James G. Frazer. Copyright 1922 by The Macmillan Company, renewed 1950 by Barclays Bank Ltd.

Northrop Frye: "Fictional Modes" is from Northrop Frye, *Anatomy of Criticism*
(copyright © 1957 by PUP; Princeton Paperback, 1971), pp. 33–35. Reprinted by
permission of Princeton University Press.

The Mission Indians of California: "The Origin of the World" is from the
Journal of American Folklore, 19 (1906), 312–314. Reprinted by permission of the
American Folklore Society, Inc.

Ovid: "The Creation"; "The Four Ages"; "Jove's Intervention"; "The Story of
Lycaon"; "The Flood" are from Ovid's *Metamorphoses,* translated by Rolfe Hum-
phries. Copyright © 1955 by Indiana University Press. Reprinted by permission of
Indiana University Press.

iv

John Lennon and Paul McCartney: "Lady Madonna" Copyright © 1968 by Northern Songs Limited. Used by permission. All rights reserved.

John Barth: "Night-Sea Journey"—Copyright © 1966 by John Barth from *Lost in the Funhouse*. Reprinted by © permission of Doubleday & Company, Inc.

Ted Hughes: "Crow Blacker Than Ever" is from *Crow* by Ted Hughes. Copyright © 1971 by Ted Hughes. Reprinted by permission of Harper & Row, Publishers, Inc.

Ovid: "Europa" is from Ovid's *Metamorphoses*, translated by Rolfe Humphries. Copyright © 1955 by Indiana University Press. Reprinted by permission of Indiana University Press.

William Butler Yeats: "Leda and the Swan" is reprinted with permission of The Macmillan Company from *Collected Poems* by William Butler Yeats. Copyright 1928 by The Macmillan Company, renewed 1956 by Georgie Yeats.

James Joyce: "Araby" is from *Dubliners* by James Joyce. Originally published by B. W. Huebsch, Inc. in 1916. Copyright © 1967 by the Estate of James Joyce. All rights reserved. Reprinted by permission of The Viking Press, Inc.

Dylan Thomas: "Fern Hill" is from *Collected Poems* by Dylan Thomas. Copyright 1946 by New Directions Publishing Corporation. Reprinted by permission of New Directions Publishing Corporation.

A. E. Housman: "When I Was One-and-Twenty" is from "A Shropshire Lad"—Authorised Edition—from *The Collected Poems of A. E. Housman*. Copyright 1939, 1940, © 1959 by Holt, Rinehart and Winston, Inc. Copyright © 1967, 1968 by Robert E. Symons. Reprinted by permission of Holt, Rinehart and Winston, Inc.

Sean O'Faolain: "Innocence" is from *The Man Who Invented Sin* by Sean O'Faolain. Copyright 1948 by The Devin-Adair Company.

David Wagoner: "The Hero with One Face" is from *A Place To Stand*, by David Wagoner. Copyright © 1958 by Indiana University Press. Reprinted by permission of the publisher.

Kenneth Patchen: "What Is The Beautiful?" is from *Collected Poems* by Kenneth Patchen. Copyright 1943 by Kenneth Patchen. Reprinted by permission of New Directions Publishing Corporation.

William Butler Yeats: "The Land of Heart's Desire" is reprinted with permission of The Macmillan Company from *Collected Plays* by William Butler Yeats. Copyright 1934, 1952 by The Macmillan Company.

Allen Tate: "The Mediterranean" is reprinted by permission of Charles Scribner's Sons from *Poems* by Allen Tate. Copyright 1932 Charles Scribner's Sons; renewal copyright © 1960 Allen Tate.

Grey Cohoe: "The Promised Visit" is from *Design for Good Reading, Level D*, by Melba Schumacher et al., © 1969 by Harcourt Brace Jovanovich, Inc. and reprinted with their permission.

James Joyce: "An Encounter" is from *Dubliners* by James Joyce. Originally published by B. W. Huebsch, Inc. in 1916. Copyright © 1967 by the Estate of James Joyce. All rights reserved. Reprinted by permission of The Viking Press, Inc.

Homer: "Telemachus" is from *The Odyssey of Homer*, translated by W. H. D. Rouse. Copyright 1937 W. H. D. Rouse. By arrangement with The New American Library, Inc., New York, New York.

e. e. cummings: "my father moved through dooms of love"—Copyright, 1940, by e. e. cummings; Copyright, 1968, by Marion Morehouse Cummings. Reprinted from *Poems 1923–1954* by e. e. cummings by permission of Harcourt Brace Jovanovich, Inc.

Sylvia Plath: "Daddy" is from *Ariel* by Sylvia Plath. Copyright © 1963 by Ted Hughes. Reprinted by permission of Harper & Row, Publishers, Inc.

Pär Lagerkvist: "Father and I" is from *Modern Swedish Short Stories*, translated by M. Ekenberg. Reprinted by permission of Jonathan Cape Limited, London.

Delmore Schwartz: "In Dreams Begin Responsibilities" is from *The World Is a Wedding* by Delmore Schwartz. Copyright 1938 by New Directions, 1948 by Delmore Schwartz. Reprinted by permission of New Directions Publishing Corporation.

Ovid: "The Story of Orpheus and Eurydice" is from Ovid's *Metamorphoses*, translated by Rolfe Humphries. Copyright © 1955 by Indiana University Press. Reprinted by permission of Indiana University Press.

Durango Mendoza: "Summer Water and Shirley" is reprinted by permission from *Prairie Schooner*. Copyright © 1969 by the University of Nebraska Press.

D. H. Lawrence: "Snake" is from *The Complete Poems of D. H. Lawrence*, Volume I, edited by Vivian de Sola Pinto and F. Warren Roberts. Copyright 1923, renewed 1951 by Frieda Lawrence. Reprinted by permission of The Viking Press, Inc.

Alfred Hayes: "Joe Hill"—Copyright 1938, renewed and assigned © 1965, © 1970 by MCA Music, A Division of MCA, Inc., 445 Park Avenue, New York, New York 10022. Used by permission.

Homer: "Achilles" is from *The Iliad* by Homer, translated by W. H. D. Rouse. Copyright 1937 W. H. D. Rouse. By arrangement with The New American Library, Inc., New York, New York.

Aeschylus: *Prometheus Bound* is reprinted from *The Three Greek Plays*, translated and with introductions by Edith Hamilton. By permission of W. W. Norton & Company, Inc. Copyright 1937 by W. W. Norton & Company, Inc. Copyright renewed 1965 by Dorian Fielding Reid.

Georg Büchner: *Woyzeck* is reprinted by permission of Hill and Wang, a division of Farrar, Straus & Giroux. *Georg Büchner: Complete Plays and Prose*, translated by Carl Richard Mueller. Copyright © 1963 by Carl Richard Mueller.

Edwin Muir: "Oedipus" is from *Collected Poems* by Edwin Muir. Copyright © 1960 by Willa Muir. Reprinted by permission of Oxford University Press, Inc.

Conrad Aiken: "Morning Song from 'Senlin'" is from *Collected Poems* by Conrad Aiken. Copyright 1953 by Conrad Aiken. Reprinted by permission of Oxford University Press, Inc.

Robert Duncan: "Parsifal" is from *Bending the Bow*. Copyright © 1968 by Robert Duncan. Reprinted by permission of New Directions Publishing Corporation.

Dick Allen: "Rethinking a Children's Story" appeared in *Cimarron Review*, #4, June, 1968. Reprinted by permission of the author.

Langston Hughes: "God's Other Side" is from *Simple's Uncle Sam* by Langston Hughes. Copyright © 1965 by Langston Hughes. Reprinted by permission of Hill and Wang, Inc.

Woody Guthrie: "New Kittens" is from the book *Bound for Glory* by Woody Guthrie. Copyright 1943, 1968 by E. P. Dutton & Co., Inc., publishers, and reprinted with their permission.

Isaac Bashevis Singer: "Gimpel the Fool" is from *A Treasury of Yiddish Stories*, edited by Irving Howe and Eliezer Greenberg. Copyright 1953 by Isaac Bashevis Singer. Reprinted by permission of The Viking Press, Inc.

George Meredith: "Lucifer in Starlight" is from *Selected Poems* by George Meredith (Charles Scribner's Sons, 1897).

e. e. cummings: "in Just-spring"—Copyright 1923, 1951, by e. e. cummings. Reprinted from his volume *Poems 1923–1954* by permission of Harcourt Brace Jovanovich, Inc.

Gary Snyder: "Milton by Firelight" appeared originally in *Rip Rap*. Copyright © 1958, 1965 by Gary Snyder. Used by permission of Gary Snyder.

Harlan Ellison: "I Have No Mouth, and I Must Scream" appeared in *If: Worlds of Science Fiction* for March, 1967. Copyright © 1967 by Galaxy Publishing Corporation; all rights returned to Author, 1968. Reprinted by permission of Author and Author's Agent, Robert P. Mills, Ltd.

Edwin Arlington Robinson: "Miniver Cheevy" (Copyright 1907 Charles Scribner's Sons; renewal copyright 1935) is reprinted by permission of Charles Scribner's Sons from *The Town Down The River* by Edwin Arlington Robinson.

Claude McKay: "Outcast" is from *Selected Poems of Claude McKay*, by Claude McKay. Published by Twayne Publishers, Inc. Copyright 1953 by Bookman Associates, Inc.

Franz Kafka: "Unmasking a Confidence Trickster" is reprinted by permission of Schocken Books Inc. from *The Penal Colony* by Franz Kafka. Copyright © 1948 by Schocken Books Inc.

Delmore Schwartz: "The Heavy Bear Who Goes With Me" is from *Selected Poems: Summer Knowledge*, by Delmore Schwartz. Copyright 1938 by New Directions, © 1966 by Delmore Schwartz. Reprinted by permission of New Directions Publishing Corporation.

Theodore Roethke: "In a Dark Time"—Copyright © 1960 by Beatrice Roethke as Administratrix to the Estate Of Theodore Roethke; first published in *The New Yorker Magazine* from *The Collected Poems of Theodore Roethke*. Reprinted by permission of Doubleday and Company, Inc.

Ovid: "Adonis" is from Ovid's *Metamorphoses*, translated by Rolfe Humphries. Copyright © 1955 by Indiana University Press. Reprinted by permission of Indiana University Press.

Yuri Suhl: "The Permanent Delegate" is by permission of the author.

Yuri Suhl: "The Death of Helga Brunner" is by permission of the author.

Lerone Bennett, Jr.: "The Convert"—Copyright © 1963 by *Negro Digest*. Reprinted by permission of *Black World*.

Homer: "Circê" is from *The Odyssey of Homer*, translated by W. H. D. Rouse. By arrangement with The New American Library, Inc., New York, New York.

James Joyce: "The Boarding House" is from *Dubliners* by James Joyce. Originally published by B. W. Huebsch, Inc. in 1916. Copyright © 1967 by the Estate of James Joyce. All rights reserved. Reprinted by permission of The Viking Press, Inc.

Archibald MacLeish: "Calypso's Island" is from *Collected Poems 1917–1952*. Copyright 1952 by Archibald MacLeish. Reprinted by permission of the publisher, Houghton Mifflin Company.

Contents

Preface

AN ARCHETYPE is a model, or pattern, from which all other things of
a similar nature are made. Archetype critics are literary critics, or myth
critics, strongly influenced by the belief that primitive man is yet within
us and that myth, ritual, and poetry—found in the beginnings of every
culture—have the power to make us aware of the collective experiences
of the race. The archetype critic is concerned with the enduring patterns
and motifs and how these are reflected in literature.

It is the purpose of this book to describe a large group of commonly
accepted archetypes and to present them as they make their appearance
in various genres of literature. We hope that such a collection of archetypal motifs will enable the reader to deepen his appreciation for the
continuity and tradition of our literary heritage and will offer a useful
critical approach to the study of literature. Society, institutions, and
literature change; the human condition remains the same.

For it has been the editors' experience in various schools and situations that myth provides an important avenue for the student to see
beneath the surface of "story" to essential and lasting concerns of the
human race, to recognize the repetitions of man's history and the com-
monality of the human condition throughout man's life, and to realize
the craftsmanship of the author in weaving his creation with the very
stuff of all men's lives. The excitement that the mythic approach can
generate in establishing the interdisciplinary nature of the study of
literature—its links with anthropology, psychology, sociology, religion—
leads to enthusiasm for knowledge in these varied, but related, fields.

It is to Carl Jung (1875–1961), a Swiss psychoanalyst and disciple
of Sigmund Freud, that credit for the formulation of the archetypal is
usually assigned. In his book *Contributions to Analytical Psychology*,
Jung states that there are unconscious primordial images, inherent in
the structure of the brain, that are basic and central experiences (collective) of the human race. But whereas Freud stresses the uniqueness of
each personal unconscious, Jung believes that there exists a "collective
unconscious," a common pool of the experience of the race inherited by
each successive generation. It is, according to Jung's view, only the individual ego that is truly different from all others. Why, Jung asks, should
the psyche be "the only thing in the world that has no history beyond its
individual manifestation"?

Jung suggests that archetypes are primitive, preconscious, instinctual expressions that are universal and that they derive from the fact that men always undergo common and essential experiences. Naturalists have observed that animals pass on acquired habits such as mating, territorial aggressiveness, and leadership prerogatives; these experiences are available to each species as unlearned, or coded, patterns. According to Jung, man too is coded with the experiences of his past necessary for his survival. The code is the archetype, the "psychic residue of numberless experiences of the same type."

Though we are unable to know our unconscious life directly, the archetype, according to Jung, is an expression of this hidden life. These archetypes (the collective life of the race) find expression in dreams, myths, rituals, and art. And because archetypes are recurrent, succeeding generations are able to be emotionally moved by these archetypal projections of the collective unconscious.

It should be noted that Freud, when he spoke of art, directed his attention primarily to the artist rather than to the work of art. For Freud, art was the working out of the artist's psychic problems. Jung, by contrast, was primarily concerned with the work of art, for the work expressed an archetype, a typical manifestation of the experience of the race.

To allow the student to examine these important myths and motifs we have assembled in the present anthology a wide variety of literary works from various historical periods. In Part I we reprint essays that discuss the theory of archetypes and their importance to literature. In Part II we reprint myths of creation; we include a section on Mating with a Mortal, as many cultures and literatures depict unions of godlike beings with mortals; we include, next, a section on the fall from innocence (youth) to experience (maturity); and we follow this with literary selections that depict the theme of the journey, the quest, and the search for the father —all of which deal with the motif of the initiation into maturity. The cycle is completed with selections depicting death and rebirth.

In Part III we have brought together under separate headings a variety of archetypal characters—character types that appear with great frequency in folk material, myth, legend, and literature. Our list is hardly exhaustive, and the reader is encouraged to add to it. The section on heroes and antiheroes in Part III should be read with Northrop Frye's essay (in Part I) in mind, because his useful distinctions between religious heroes, secular heroes, representative heroes (GI Joe), and ironic (or anti-) heroes almost exactly parallels the development of the role of the hero in the chronological development of narrative literature.

It is our hope that the student using this book will come to appreciate his connectedness with the past and will recognize that this past is still relevant today. To achieve this end, we have brought together materials from the classical and biblical traditions, as well as folk materials, songs, and the literary tradition even now developing. Further, an extensive glossary of archetypal and psychological symbols, terms, and motifs is appended. The reader is urged to refer to these definitions and ideas frequently.

A word of caution. Acquaintance with an archetypal pattern is not sufficient for a full appreciation of a literary work. To understand, recognize, and discover an archetype may be helpful in understanding one source of enjoyment of a work, and it may also be helpful in relating a specific work to a tradition. But the reader must also recognize the "signature" (see Fiedler's essay in Part I) of the author in order to appreciate the vision and uniqueness of the individual as he contributes to our collective tradition.

DAVID J. BURROWS
FREDERICK R. LAPIDES
JOHN T. SHAWCROSS

Authors Represented
in the Present Collection

Aeschylus (525–456 B.C.), Greek tragic poet, known as "Father of Tragedy." Only seven plays are extant, including *Prometheus Bound* and the trilogy of *Agamemnon, Choephori,* and *Eumenides,* known as "The House of Atreus."

Conrad Aiken (1889–), important American poet and fiction writer. Among important poetic volumes are *Senlin: A Biography and Other Poems* (1918), *The Pilgrimage of Festus* (1923), *John Deth* (1930), *Preludes for Memnon* (1931), *A Letter from Li Po* (1955). He received a Pulitzer prize for *Selected Poems* (1929); his *Collected Poems* appeared in 1953.

Dick Allen, contemporary American poet, now teaching at the University of Bridgeport. Among his volumes of poetry is *Anon & Various Time Machine Poems* (1971).

John Barth (1930–), important American novelist. Among his works are *The Floating Opera* (1956), *The End of the Road* (1958), *The Sot-Weed Factor* (1960), *Giles Goat-Boy* (1966), and *Lost in the Funhouse* (1968).

Charles Baudelaire (1821–67), French symbolist poet, known somewhat infamously as author of *Les Fleurs du Mal* (1857).

Lerone Bennett, Jr (1928–), American author and editor. His *Before the Mayflower: A History of the Negro in America, 1619–1962* (1962), *What Manner of Man: A Biography of Martin Luther King, Jr.* (1964), *Confrontation Black and White* (1965), *The Negro Mood* (1964), *Black Power, U. S. A., The Human Side of Reconstruction, 1867–1877* (1967), and *Pioneers in Protest* (1968) are significant studies of the Black in America. Bennett is an editor of *Ebony* magazine.

Maud Bodkin (1875–), British author and educationalist. Ms Bodkin applied studies of anthropology and psychology to literature in *Archetypal Patterns in Poetry* (1934), *The Quest for Salvation in an Ancient and a Modern Play* (1941), and *Studies of Type Images in Poetry, Religion and Philosophy* (1951).

Georg Büchner (1813–37), German poet. His poetical dramas *Dantons Tod* (1835) and *Woyzeck* (1837) are charged with political and social criticism.

Grey Cohoe, contemporary American Indian author.

Stephen Crane (1871–1900), American journalist, fiction writer, and poet; his important works are *Maggie: A Girl of the Streets* (1893), *The Red Badge of Courage* (1895), *The Black Riders* (1895; poems), *George's Mother* (1896), *The Open Boat* (1898), *The Monster* (1899), and *War Is Kind* (1899; poems).

e[dward] e[stlin] cummings (1894–1962), important American poet; his volumes of poetry include *Tulips and Chimneys* (1923), *&* (1925), *XLI Poems* (1925), *is 5* (1926), *No Thanks* (1935), *95 Poems* (1958), and *73 Poems* (1963). He also wrote a novel, *The Enormous Room* (1922); a play, *him* (1927); and a travel diary, *Eimi* (1933).

Robert Duncan (1919–   ), American poet. Important volumes include *Heavenly City, Earthly City* (1947), *Medieval Scenes* (1947), *Poems 1948–49* (1950), *Song of the Borderguard* (1952), *Letters* (1958), *The Opening of the Field* (1960), *Roots and Branches* (1964), *Fragments of a Disordered Devotion* (1966), *Passages, 22–27* (1966), and *Bending the Bow* (1968).

Harlan Ellison (1934–   ), American author. His works include *Rumble* (1958), *The Deadly Streets* (1958), *Gentleman Junkie and Other Stories of the Hung-up Generation* (1961), and *Rockabilly* (1961).

Leslie A. Fiedler (1917–   ), critic and novelist, who has investigated the psychological and political bases of American literature in a number of important and controversial volumes, including *An End to Innocence, Essays in Culture and Politics* (1955), *Love and Death in the American Novel* (1959, 1966), *No! In Thunder: Essays on Myth and Literature* (1960), *Waiting for the End* (1964), and *Radical Sophistication* (1969).

Sir James G. Frazer (1854–1941), major British social anthropologist. His influential works include *Totemism* (1887) and *The Golden Bough* (1890–1915).

Erich Fromm (1900–   ), psychoanalyst and social philosopher. First a strong Freudian, Fromm, a native of Germany, altered his own emphasis to a consideration of social and economic factors as major in the development of the human mind. Among his well-known books are *Escape from Freedom* (1941), *Man for Himself* (1947), *The Forgotton Language, An Introduction to the Understanding of Dreams, Fairy Tales, and Myths* (1951), *The Sane Society* (1955), *The Art of Loving* (1956), and *The Heart of Man* (1964).

Northrop Frye (1912–   ), Canadian critic. A major critic of English literature, Frye has categorized mythopoeic forms in literature in *Fearful Symmetry: A Study of William Blake* (1947), *Anatomy of Criticism* (1957), *The Well-Tempered Critic* (1963), *Fables of Identity; Studies in Poetic Mythology* (1963), and *Return to Eden* (1965).

William J. Goode (1917–   ), sociologist. A professor at Columbia University, Goode is author of *Religion Among the Primitives, Methods in Social Research,* and *After Divorce.*

Woody Guthrie (1912–67), American folk singer and composer. Woodrow Wilson Guthrie performed on the guitar and sang his more than a thousand songs for generations of appreciative listeners. His message was social and political, consistently advancing the cause of freedom for the impoverished and minorities. His autobiography, *Bound for Glory*, was published in 1943.

Nathaniel Hawthorne (1804–64), major American novelist and short-story writer. His works include *Twice-Told Tales* (1837, 1842), *Mosses from the Old Manse* (1846), *The Scarlet Letter* (1850), *The House of Seven Gables* (1851), *The Snow-Image and Other Twice-Told Tales* (1851), *The Blithedale Romance* (1852), and *The Marble Faun* (1860).

Alfred Hayes (1911–   ), American novelist, playwright, and poet; author of the play *The Girl on the Via Flamina* (1954) and two volumes of poetry, *The Big Time* (1944) and *Welcome to the Castle* (1950).

Homer, Greek epic poet, alleged author of the *Iliad* and the *Odyssey;* the supposed facts of his life and works are disputed.

A[lfred] E[dward] Housman (1859–1936), British classical scholar and poet. His poetry appears in *A Shropshire Lad* (1896) and *Last Poems* (1922).

Ted Hughes (1930–   ), British poet. His works include *The Hawk in the Rain* (1957), *Lupercal* (1960), *Wodwo* (1967), and *Crow: From the Life and Songs of the Crow* (1971).

Lionel Johnson (1867–1902), British poet and critic, whose chief poetic works are *Poems* (1895) and *Ireland* (1897).

James Joyce (1882–1941), major Irish novelist; author of *Dubliners* (1914), *A Portrait of the Artist as a Young Man* (1915), *Ulysses* (1922), and *Finnegans Wake* (1939). Two volumes of poetry, *Chamber Music* (1907) and *Pomes Pennyeach* (1917), and a play, *Exiles* (1918), complete his literary output.

Franz Kafka (1883–1924), major German novelist (of Czech origin); works include *The Trial, The Castle, Amerika, In the Penal Colony,* and *Metamorphosis.*

John Keats (1795–1821), major British poet, among whose publications were *Poems by John Keats* (1817), *Endymion* (1818), and *Lamia and Other Poems* (1820).

Pär Lagerkvist (1891–   ), Swedish author of plays, poetry, and fiction. Lagerkvist, who lives in England, is best known for *The Dwarf* (1945), *Barabbas* (1951), *The Eternal Smile and Other Stories* (1954), *The Marriage Feast and Other Stories* (1955), *The Sibyl* (1958), *The Holy Land* (1966), and *Mariamne* (1968).

Dilys Laing (1906–60), poet born in Wales, who later settled with her husband and family in the United States. *The Collected Poems* (1967) contains all her poetry, some of which had been published in *Another England* (1941), *Birth Is Farewell* (1944), *Walk Through Two Landscapes* (1949), and *Poems from a Cage* (1961).

D[avid] H[erbert] Lawrence (1885–1930), major British novelist, short-story writer, poet, and critic, among whose works are *The White Peacock* (1911), *Sons and Lovers* (1913), *The Rainbow* (1915), *Women in Love* (1920), *Lady Chatterley's Lover* (1928, 1929 unexpurgated). The collected poems appeared in 1928.

John Lennon (1940–   ), musician and songwriter. Born in Liverpool, Lennon organized the Beatles, a popular musical quartet, in 1958. With Paul McCartney he wrote the major hits of the group and has been most influential in the musical and social scene in the last ten years.

Archibald MacLeish (1892–   ), major American poet and dramatist; best known for collections of verse like *Tower of Ivory* (1917), *The Pot of Earth* (1925), *Nobodaddy* (1926), *Conquistador* (1932, for which he received the Pulitzer Prize), and *Collected Poems 1917–1952* (1952, for which he received a second Pulitzer Prize) and for verse dramas like *Panic* (1935), *The Fall of the City* (1937), and *J. B.* (1958, for which he received another Pulitzer Prize).

Christopher Marlowe (1564–93), important British playwright and poet. His major plays were *Tamburlaine* (two parts), *The Tragedy of Dr. Faustus*, *The Jew of Malta*, and *Edward II;* his poems include "Hero and Leander" and "Come live with me and be my love."

Paul McCartney (1942–   ), musician and songwriter. Born in Liverpool, McCartney, who now works on his own, was a member of the Beatles, whose musical and life styles have been a strong influences on recent generations. With John Lennon, he created the hit songs identified with the group.

Claude McKay (1890–1948), Black American poet and novelist, originally from Jamaica. His works include *Songs of Jamaica* (1912) and *Harlem Shadows* (1932), poetic collections, and *Home to Harlem* (1928), *Banjo* (1929), and *Banana Bottom* (1933). He also wrote an autobiography, *A Long Way from Home* (1937), and a sociological study, *Harlem* (1940).

Durango Mendoza, contemporary Mexican-American author.

George Meredith (1828–1909), major British novelist and poet. His poems were published in 1851, in *Modern Love* (1862), in *Poems and Lyrics of the Joy of Earth* (1883), in *Ballads and Poems of Tragic Life* (1887), and others. *Last Poems* appeared in 1909. The best-known novels are *The Ordeal of Richard Feverel* (1859), *The Egoist* (1879), and *Diana of the Crossways* (1885).

John Milton (1608–74), major British poet and prose writer, whose *Paradise Lost* appeared in 1667 (ed. 2, 1674), *Paradise Regain'd* and *Samson Agonistes* in 1671, and minor poems in 1673.

Edwin Muir (1887–1959), important Scottish novelist, poet, and critic. His poetry includes *First Poems* (1925), *The Chorus of the Newly Dead* (1926), *Variations on a Time Theme* (1934), *The Voyage,* and *Collected Poems 1921–51* (1952).

Sean O'Faolain, contemporary Irish author. Among his works are *Midsummer Night Madness* (1932), *A Nest of Simple Folk* (1933), *Bird Alone* (1936), *Come Back to Erin* (1940), *The Vanishing Hero* (1956), *The Stories of Sean O'Faolain* (1958), and *The Talking Trees* (1970).

Ovid (43 B.C.–A.D. 18), major Roman poet, whose name was Publius Ovidius Naso. His influential works were *Amores, Heroides, Ars Amatoria,* and *Metamorphoses.*

Kenneth Patchen (1911–72), important American poet and novelist; poetic volumes include *Before the Brave* (1936), *First Will and Testament* (1939), *The Teeth of the Lion* (1942), *Cloth of the Tempest* (1943), *An Astonished Eye Looks Out of the Air* (1945), and *The Famous Boating Party* (1954). *The Journal of Albion Moonlight* (1941) is a major achievement in the novel form.

Sylvia Plath (1932–63), important American poet, wife of Ted Hughes. Her poetic output consists of *The Colossus* (1962) and *Ariel* (1966). She committed suicide while living in England.

Edgar Allan Poe (1809–49), major American fiction writer and poet. His short stories and poems have frequently been reprinted, including selected and "complete" editions. Poe has often been called the father of the modern detective story and was a major influence on the French symbolist poets.

Edwin Arlington Robinson (1869–1935), major American poet; works include *The Torrent and the Night Before* (1896), *The Children of the Night* (1897), *Captain Craig* (1902), *The Town down the River* (1910), *The Man Against the Sky* (1916), *Merlin* (1917), *Lancelot* (1920), and *Cavender's House* (1929). He received the Pulitzer Prize for *Collected Poems* (1921), *The Man Who Died Twice* (1924), and *Tristram* (1927).

Theodore Roethke (1908–63), important American poet; author of *Open House* (1941), *The Lost Son* (1948), *Praise to the End!* (1951), *The Waking* (1953, for which he received the Pulitzer Prize), and *Words for the Wind* (1958, for which he received the Bollingen Prize).

Delmore Schwartz (1913–66), important poet, critic, and prose writer; books include *In Dreams Begin Responsibilities* (1938) and *Summer Knowledge* (1959), both poems, and *The World Is a Wedding* (1948), stories. His verse play *Shenandoah* (1941) is a great achievement.

Isaac Bashevis Singer (1904–   ), novelist. Born in Poland, Singer has been a resident of the United States since 1935. Among his numerous works are *Satan in Goray* (1932) and *The Family Morkat* (1945), both of which first appeared serially in Yiddish, with English translations in 1955 and 1950 respectively; *Gimpel the Fool and Other Stories* (1957), *The Magician of Lublin* (1960), *The Spinoza of Market Street* (1961), *The Slave* (1962), *Short Friday and Other Stories* (1964), *In My Father's Court* (1966), *The Manor* (1967), and *The Estate* (1969).

Gary Snyder (1930–   ), American poet. His works include *Riprap* (1959), *Myths & Texts* (1960), *Hop, Skip, and Jump* (1964), *A Range of Poems* (1966), *The Back Country* (1967), and *Regarding Wave* (1970).

(M. A.) Yuri Suhl (1908–   ), author and poet. Born in Galicia, Suhl has lived in the United States since 1923; he is the author of *Ernestine L. Rose and the Battle for Human Rights* (1959) and *They Fought Back; The Story of the Jewish Resistance in Nazi Europe* (1967).

Allen Tate (1899–   ), important American poet, critic, and biographer. Poetry volumes include *Mr. Pope and Other Poems* (1928), *The Mediterranean and Other Poems* (1936), *Winter Sea* (1944), and *Poems, 1922–1947* (1948).

Alfred, Lord Tennyson (1809–92), major British poet and poet-laureate. His poems appear in many selected and collected editions and include *Poems* (1833, 1842), *The Princess* (1847), *In Memoriam* (1850), *Maud* (1855), and *Idylls of the King* (1859–72).

Dylan Thomas (1914–53), major Welsh poet, whose volumes were *Eighteen Poems* (1934), *Twenty-five Poems* (1936), *The Map of Love* (1939), *Deaths and Entrances* (1946), and *Collected Poems* (1962). He also wrote a play for voices, entitled *Under Milk Wood* (1953), and various prose works.

Vergil (70–19 B.C.), major Roman poet, whose name was Publius Vergilius Maro. His major works were the *Georgics,* the *Eclogues,* and the epic of the Roman people, the *Aeneid.*

David Wagoner (1926–   ), American poet and novelist. His poetic volumes are *Dry Sun, Dry Wind* (1953), *A Place to Stand* (1958), *The Nesting Ground* (1963), *Staying Alive* (1966), *New and Selected Poems* (1969), and *Working Against Time* (1970).

William Butler Yeats (1865–1939), major Irish poet and dramatist and a leader of the Irish Renaissance. His works have frequently been reprinted; see the *Collected Poems* (1950) and the *Collected Plays* (1952). He also wrote various prose works, such as *A Vision* (1925), an important work for an understanding of his poetry and plays.

1

ARCHETYPAL THEORY

For the literary critic, Jung's two important formulations are, as noted before, his discussions of a collective unconscious and his theory of archetypes. Maud Bodkin, a British psychologist and literary critic, used Jung's insights in her book *Archetypal Patterns in Poetry: Psychological Studies of Imagination* (1934). Widely read in diverse disciplines, Ms. Bodkin is eclectic, refusing to follow blindly the steps of Jung. She agrees with Gilbert Murray when she states that an archetypal pattern is that within us which "leaps in response to the effective presentation in poetry of an ancient theme." She disagrees with Murray (and Jung), who believed that the archetypal patterns were stamped or inherited structures of the brain. Ms. Bodkin suggests, instead, that possibly the archetypal patterns are culturally acquired; that is, the patterns are taught to and learned by successive generations. This suggestion is useful, as it seems to account for the cultural modifications that archetypes suggest in their various manifestations from culture to culture.

Like Jung, Ms. Bodkin recognizes that a collective unconscious and archetypal patterns will not render themselves to objective, scientific study. In her study she therefore relied upon the intuitive, collective responses of a number of readers of poetry whom she sampled to describe the archetypes in certain poems. Collective responses are those common to the readers sampled and demonstrably part of an archetypal pattern rather than, say, an ephemeral influence. Ms. Bodkin assumes that a collective response will validate a collective experience generated by the literature. The student should try to put the theory to the test with each of the items included in this anthology.

Northrop Frye, more concerned than Ms. Bodkin with making literary studies more exact, believes literature to be a sophistication of a basic group of formulas that derive from primitive cultures. Frye attempts to turn literary criticism into a social science by charting the basic categories into which any given literary expression will fit. Frye took two basic mythic patterns (monomyths), combined them, and explained in his *Fables of Identity: Studies in Poetic Mythology* (1963) that his categories contained four phases which corresponded to the four seasons; these categories represent general plots and are the very essence of all literature.

Another degree of sophistication for archetypal studies was added by Leslie Fiedler. This critic, upset by the habit of the "New Critics" of ignoring biographical facts as irrevelant, insists that the response of the artist to his archetypal material gives a unique stamp—the artist's "signature"—to the work. Thus, a study of a literary work provides useful insights into the individual psyche of the writer and at the same time into the archetypal nature of the materials of literature. According to Fiedler, a study of a writer's life is useful, for art combines the uniqueness of the writer (his signature) and the collective experience of the race (the archetype). For Fiedler, an archetype is a representation of any of the "immemorial patterns of response to the human situation in its most permanent aspects." Literature, Fiedler feels, has its beginning when the signature (the uniqueness of the writer, the *persona* of the artist) is imposed or stamped upon the archetype. Myth, by contrast, is archetype without signature.

Contemporary writers on archetypal theory, it is clear, have broadened the meaning of Jung's earlier formulations. Indeed, for the non-Jungian, an archetype may be merely a paradigm, a pattern or outline that accounts for a number of stories. Critics such as Fiedler and Richard Chase, paying little attention to the notion of the "collective unconscious," focus attention upon the archetype as a pattern representing a whole set of basic emotional experiences.

When we turn away from the speculations of the origins of archetypes and concern ourselves instead with myth, folklore, and literature, we observe that all cultures seem to share a basic system of symbols. In order to systematize these symbols, anthropologists have developed two "monomyths," large overall patterns that contain diverse myths and symbols. Other essays included here, such as Fromm's and Frazer's, will aid in understanding such symbolic language and the myths themselves. The two monomyths are the Seasonal Myth and the Myth of the Hero (or the Quest Myth).

The Seasonal Myth represents a cycle of human life patterned after the succession of the seasons. Life is viewed as a pattern of birth and youth (Spring), growth (Summer), fruition or maturity (Fall), and Death (Winter). This is, however, an endless cycle; though the leaves wither and die, the tree is "reborn" the following spring. The lake freezes, but it thaws and comes "alive" again in the spring. Man ages and dies but is reborn in an afterlife or in the likeness of his children. The king is dead; long live the (new) king.

In the second monomyth, the Myth of the Hero, the emphasis is upon the special qualities of the hero in his society. The hero usually is born under mysterious or unusual circumstances (virgin birth); he is the son of a great man or of a deity (Prometheus, Jesus); he is marked for greatness (a special sign); while still a young person he is often exiled or placed in harm's way so that he may be killed (Orestes, Moses, Hamlet, Snow White); he must prove his claim to a heroic role by a test or a trial (Arthur pulling the sword from the stone, Hercules and his tasks); he accomplishes great deeds for his people (Moses, Beowulf killing the monster); his death is often mysterious or ambiguous (Arthur goes off to Avalon, the Crucifixion of Christ). There is, finally, the suggestion that the hero is perhaps not dead, or that he may be reborn, or perhaps return at some future time of great need.

What both monomyths have in common is a cyclic pattern, from the advent of birth to maturity, death, and a real or symbolic rebirth. In our text we have not strictly followed either of these monomyths, preferring instead to borrow from each.

The essays included in Part 1 should direct the student to the substance of these monomyths and the ways in which they emerge in created literature, and at the same time they should aid in developing the viability of symbolism and symbolic language in communicating these age-old motifs of life. Further, such literary criticism as is illustrated in the analyses of Bodkin, Frye, and Fiedler offers not only approaches to understanding the literature reprinted here but also patterns for the student's own attempts to express his insights into the myths and motifs which undergird the literature he is reading.

Archetypal Patterns in Tragic Poetry

MAUD BODKIN

I

In an article, "On the relation of the analytical psychology to poetic art," [1] Dr. C. G. Jung has set forth an hypothesis in regard to the psychological significance of poetry. The special emotional significance possessed by certain poems—a significance going beyond any definite meaning conveyed—he attributes to the stirring in the reader's mind, within or beneath his conscious response, of unconscious forces which he terms "primordial images," or archetypes. These archetypes he describes as "psychic residua of numberless experiences of the same type," experiences which have happened not to the individual but to his ancestors, and of which the results are inherited in the structure of the brain, *a priori* determinants of individual experience.

It is the aim of our present writer to examine this hypothesis, testing it in regard to examples where we can bring together the recorded experience and reflection of minds approaching the matter from different standpoints. It is hoped that, in this way, something may be done towards enriching the formulated theory of the systematic psychologist through the insight of more intuitive thinkers, while at the same time the intuitive thinker's results may receive somewhat more exact definition.

My first illustration I shall take from an essay by Professor Gilbert Murray,[2] where the effect of great poetic drama is described in language somewhat similar to that of Jung. Gilbert Murray has been comparing the tragedies of *Hamlet* and of *Orestes*, noting the curious similarities between them, and how the theme that underlies them seems to have shown an "almost eternal durability." When such themes as stirred the interest of primitive man move us now, we say, "they will tend to do so in ways which we recognize as particularly profound and poetical" (p. 238). Gilbert Murray apologizes for the metaphor of which he cannot keep clear when he says that such stories and situations were "deeply implanted in the memory of the race, stamped as it were upon our physical organism." We say that such themes "are strange to us. Yet there is that within us which leaps at the sight of them, a cry of the blood which tells us we have known them always" (p. 239). And again: "In plays like *Hamlet* or

[1] Included in *Contributions to Analytical Psychology*, trans. H. G. and C. F. Baynes (Kegan Paul, 1928).

[2] "Hamlet and Orestes," in *The Classical Tradition in Poetry* (Oxford, 1927).

4

the *Agamemnon* or the *Electra* we have certainly fine and flexible character-study, a varied and well-wrought story, a full command of the technical instruments of the poet and the dramatist; but we have also, I suspect, a strange, unanalysed vibration below the surface, an undercurrent of desires and fears and passions, long slumbering yet eternally familiar, which have for thousands of years lain near the root of our most intimate emotions and been wrought into the fabric of our most magical dreams. How far into past ages this stream may reach back, I dare not even surmise; but it seems as if the power of stirring it or moving with it were one of the last secrets of genius" (pp. 239–40).

We have here an expression, itself somewhat imaginative and poetical, of an experience in the presence of poetry which we may submit to closer examination—and this in two ways. We may study the themes that show this persistence within the life of a community or race, and may compare the different forms which they assume; also we may study analytically in different individuals the inner experience of responding to such themes.

The inquiry is plainly of a subtlety and complexity apt to discourage at the outset those who prefer to avoid all questions that cannot be investigated in accordance with a strict technique. There is little possibility here for experiment, since the kind of emotional experience which it is desired to investigate cannot be commanded at will under test conditions. A profound response to great poetic themes can be secured only by living with such themes, dwelling and brooding upon them, choosing those moments when the mind seems spontaneously to open itself to their influence. We must take where we can find it the recorded experience of those who have such acquaintance with poetry.

To the present writer it appears, however, that it is by the study of such deeper experience that psychology at the present time particularly needs enrichment. We might almost say that academic psychologists have been routed by the attack of those medical writers who claim access to the deeper layers of the mind, just because the demand for exact verifiable results has held academic psychologists to the mere outworks or surface of the mind they set out to study. If inexactness of thought or one-sided emphasis has characterized the medical writers, this can be established only by following them along the obscure paths they have opened into the concrete human psyche, and bringing to bear, if possible, a wider ranging interest and a more exact and cautious scrutiny.

The student who seeks to explore the imaginative response of present-day minds to the great themes of poetry may profit by considering the work not only of the medical psychologists, but also of the anthropologists who have attempted to study scientifically the reactions of more primitive minds. In studying the reception by a people of new cultural elements anthropologists have made use of the term "cultural pattern" to designate the pre-existing "configuration," or order of arrangment, of tendencies which determines the response of members of the group to the new element. In discussing the value of our "conceptual explorations" of "the culture pattern concept," Goldenweiser [3] has noted its relation to the concept of form and system in the arts and cultural disciplines; and L. L. Bernard, in the same work, has undertaken a classification of different kinds of environment, distinguishing the psycho-social environment, which includes such systems of symbols as are preserved in books, and in which he says "psychic processes reach the highest type of their objectified development." Such stored symbolic content can at any time become effective in activating the corresponding patterns in the minds of members of the group whose collective product and possession the symbols are.

It is within the general field of anthropology or social psychology that I conceive the inquiry to lie which I am here attempting to pursue. I shall use the term "archetypal pattern" to refer to that within us which, in Gilbert Murray's phrase, "leaps in response" to the effective presentation in poetry of an ancient theme. The hypothesis to be examined is that in poetry—and here we are to consider in particular tragic poetry—we may identify themes having a particular form or pattern which persists amid variation from age to age, and which corresponds to a pattern or configuration of emotional tendencies in the minds of those who are stirred by the theme.

In Jung's formulation of the hypothesis, and in the more tentative metaphorical statement of Gilbert Murray, it is asserted that these patterns are "stamped upon the physical organism," "inherited in the structure of the brain"; but of this statement no evidence can be considered here. Jung believes himself to have evidence of the spontaneous production of ancient patterns in the dreams of fantasies of individuals who had no discoverable access to cultural material in which the patterns were embodied. This evidence is, however, hard to evaluate; especially in view of the way in which certain surprising reproductions, in trance states, of old material, have been subsequently traced to forgotten impressions of sense in the lifetime of the individual.

Of more force in the present state of our knowledge is the general argument that where forms are assimilated from the environment upon slight contact only, predisposing factors must be present in mind and brain. Whoever has experienced and reflected upon the attempt to convey an idea, especially an idea of intimate and emotional character, to a mind unprepared to receive it, will have realized that it is not mere contact with an idea's expression that secures its assimilation. Some inner factor must co-operate. When it is lacking, the experienced futility of attempted

[3] *The Social Sciences and their Interrelations,* edited by W. F. Ogburn and A. Goldenweiser (Allen & Unwin, 1928).

communication is the most convincing proof that it is, as Mr. F. C. Bartlett has said, "not fanciful to hold" that for the capture of objects complete, by the assimilative imagination, there must stir within us "larger
systems of feeling, of memory, of ideas, of aspiration." [4] Such systems may
be cultural patterns confined to a particular group at a certain time, or
may characterize a particular individual; but there are others of much
wider range. Our question is whether there are some whose "almost
eternal durability," in Gilbert Murray's phrase, justifies us in applying to
them the term archetypal, and renders them of special interest and importance to the student of psychology and of literature.

II

We come nearer to our particular subject in raising the question:
What is the distinctive advantage of having recourse to poetry for the
study of these patterns?

Such a theme as that discussed by Gilbert Murray existed as a traditional story in ancient Greece before Aeschylus, and in Northern Europe
before Shakespeare handled it. In that form it was already, as A. C.
Bradley says of another traditional theme, "an inchoate poem": "such a
subject, as it exists in the general imagination, has some aesthetic value
before the poet touches it"; "it is already in some degree organized and
formed." [5] Enriched by the poet's touch, the traditional story lives on in
our imagination, a memory with aesthetic value, but fading into formless-
ness, when, as perhaps now in the mind of the reader, the reference to
Orestes or to Hamlet excites only a faint recollection of what was once a
vivid poetic experience. When, therefore, we desire to examine psychologically the emotional pattern corresponding to a poetic theme, we may
sometimes avail ourselves of references to the mere tales recalled in outline, but for closer examination there is need that the actual poetic experience be recovered, since it is in the imaginative experience actually
communicated by great poetry that we shall find our fullest opportunity
of studying the patterns that we seek—and this from the very nature of
poetic experience.

In the writings of Professor Spearman, which have had so much
influence in the determining of psychological method, there are references
to imagination—one particularly to imagination as exercised in poetry [6]—
in which he asserts that imagination in its intellectual aspect does not
differ essentially from any other logical process in which new content may
also be said to be generated, as when, from a given term, say "good," and

[4] "Types of Imagination," *J. of Philos. Studies,* iii, part 9, p. 80.
[5] *Oxford Lectures on Poetry* (Macmillan, 1909), pp. 11–12.
[6] *The Nature of Intelligence and the Principles of Cognition* (Macmillan, 1927), pp.
334–36.

a knowledge of the nature of verbal opposition, we pass to the term, "bad." Such a treatment of imagination illustrates the kind of abstraction that makes psychology, to some thinkers, appear so unreal and empty a study. A student who is interested in imaginative activity as exercised in poetry cannot accept the view that its intellectual aspect can be separated from its emotional nature and covered by any such logical formula as Spearman proposes.

Of the three laws of cognition which Professor Spearman formulates it would seem to be the first which most nearly concerns the poetic imagination. This law is stated: "Any lived experience tends to evoke immediately a knowing of its characters and experiences." A note adds: "The word 'immediately' means here the absence of any mediating process." [7] It is perhaps within this mediating process, denied by Spearman, that we may find a distinctive place for imagination as exercised in poetry.

When psychologists have raised the question: How does lived experience come to awareness? they have usually been content to assert that it happens through introspection, and to leave to philosophers any further investigation of the question. It is here that difficulty has arisen between the academic and the medical psychologists; since the latter believe themselves to have discovered large ranges of lived experience, of conative character, of which introspection can give no account—a discovery that seems surprising to those who believe that in introspection we have direct access to the nature of our desires.

Professor S. Alexander,[8] examining the question as a philosopher, concludes that lived experience, which is of conative character—as distinct from sensations and images, the objects of the mind—can only be "enjoyed"; it cannot be contemplated. Introspection, he says, is "enjoyment" lived through, together with "a whole apparatus of elaborated speech" (p. 18), which causes the elements of the experience enjoyed to stand out in "subtly dissected form" (p. 19). "It is small wonder," he adds, "that we should regard our introspection as turning our minds into objects, seeing how largely the language which expresses our mental state has been elaborated in pursuit of practical interests and in contact with physical objects."

If this view is accepted, we see that the mediating process necessary before lived experience can come to awareness is the linking of such experience with actions and objects that affect the senses and can be contemplated, and with words that recall these objects in all their variety of human perspective. It is in the process of fantasy that the contemplated characters of things are broken from their historical setting and made

[7] *Ibid.*, p. 48.
[8] *Space, Time, and Deity* (Macmillan, 1920).

available to express the needs and impulses of the experiencing mind. The recent study of dreams appears to have made it certain that the bewildering sequence of the images thrown up by the sleeping mind is due to processes of interaction between emotional dispositions lacking the customary control. In individual waking fantasy, and in myth and legend, we have other sequences of images which emotional patterns determine, and which seem to us strange as dreams, when, repeating them in the words used also for the results of logical reflection, we are led to contrast these incompatible renderings of experience.

When a great poet uses the stories that have taken shape in the fantasy of the community, it is not his individual sensibility alone that he objectifies. Responding with unusual sensitiveness to the words and images which already express the emotional experience of the community, the poet arranges these so as to utilize to the full their evocative power. Thus he attains for himself vision and possession of the experience engendered between his own soul and the life around him, and communicates that experience, at once individual and collective, to others, so far as they can respond adequately to the words and images he uses.

We see, then, why, if we wish to contemplate the emotional patterns hidden in our individual lives, we may study them in the mirror of our spontaneous actions, so far as we can recall them, or in dreams and in the flow of waking fantasy; but if we would contemplate the archetypal patterns that we have in common with men of past generations, we do well to study them in the experience communicated by the great poetry that has continued to stir emotional response from age to age. In studying such poetry here, we are not asking what was in the mind of Aeschylus or of Shakespeare when he fashioned the figure of Orestes or of Hamlet, nor do we ask how these figures affected a Greek or an Elizabethan audience. The question is between the writer and the reader of this book: what do the figures of Orestes and Hamlet stand for in the experience communicated to us, as we see, read, or vividly recall the Greek or Shakespearian tragedy?

III

A preliminary difficulty, already touched on, must be considered in more detail. How can we secure that the experience communicated by a great play shall be present to us with such completeness and intensity that we can make adequate study of it?

A parallel question has been discussed by Percy Lubbock [9] in regard to the study of the form of a novel. Critical perception, he says, is of no

[9] *The Craft of Fiction* (The Travellers' Library, 1926).

use to us if we cannot retain the image of a book, and the book reaches us as a passage of experience never present in its completeness. The task of the reader, before he can criticize, is to refashion the novel out of the march of experience as it passed. The procession "must be marshalled and concentrated somewhere" (p. 15).

In watching a play adequately interpreted upon the stage, we find, perhaps more readily than in the silent reading of a novel, that the procession of experience is marshalled and concentrated at certain points; so that, recalling the images of these, we can look back upon the whole play as a living unity. The powerful emotional impression thus attained may persist while the play is read and recurred to again and again, and the individual impression clarified by comparison with the reflective results of critics and scholars. Central passages, while the play is thus lived with, grow ever richer in meaning, becoming intertwined with the emotional experience of one's own life.

Some such experience of *Hamlet* I must presume in the reader, since I cannot afford space to recall the play at all fully. I will venture, however, to refer to that passage in which for me the significance of the whole play seems most concentrated.

From the experience of seeing *Hamlet* performed some thirty years ago, there has remained with me the memory of the strange exaltation and wonder of beauty that attended the words of the dying Hamlet to Horatio:

> If thou didst ever hold me in thy heart,
> Absent thee from felicity awhile,
> And in this harsh world draw thy breath in pain,
> To tell my story.

This is one of the passages chosen by Matthew Arnold [10] as "touchstones" for poetry—passages possessing both in style and substance supreme poetic quality, the Aristotelian high truth and seriousness, beyond that of history or ordinary speech. I would suggest that this "high truth" of which Matthew Arnold speaks—like that character attributed by Lascelles Abercrombie to great poetry, "a confluence of all kinds of life into a single flame of consciousness"—belongs to the lines not as isolated, but as grown familiar in their setting—the unified experience of the play converging upon them and the incantation of their music carrying them ever deeper into the secret places of the mind that loves them.

One may make some attempt to analyse that "incantation," [11] or enchantment, in which rhythm and sound of words evidently play a part. It seems to me that the enchantment of the line, "Absent thee from felicity

[10] "The study of poetry," *Essays in Criticism,* 2nd series, 1889.
[11] Cf. Lascelles Abercrombie, *The Idea of Great Poetry,* 1925, p. 19.

awhile," is heightened by the later echoing of its sounds in the lines spoken by Horatio:

> Good night, sweet prince,
> And flights of angels sing thee to thy rest!

Against this music of heaven we feel more poignantly the contrast of the words, "in this harsh world draw thy breath in pain," that move, labouring, toward their goal in the words, "to tell my story." Through their power of incantation these words, as they fall in their place, seem to gather up all the significance of that struggle of a powerful impulse to action against an obscure barrier, all the impotent anger and perplexity, and longing for justification and release, that make up the story of Hamlet as Shakespeare tells it, and make also of Hamlet, and of these lines, a symbol for whatever such struggle and longing has tortured the mind that is responding to Hamlet's words.

IV

Before attempting to compare, with reference to underlying emotional pattern, *Hamlet* and the plays concerned with Orestes, we may consider briefly the study made of *Hamlet* by Dr. Ernest Jones.[12]

Dr. Jones, in exploring the nature of Hamlet's conflict, has to some extent followed the same line of inquiry that I am pursuing here. For what is it that the critic is actually doing when he traces the motives of a character in a play?

In projecting the figure of a man of a certain disposition and analysing the forces behind his behaviour, the critic is inevitably using the emotional experience which he himself undergoes in living through the play. Having experienced, as communicated by the speeches of Hamlet, a certain psychological movement in which a strong impulse to action is aroused, and again and again sinks back into apathy and despair—a movement which, while imaginatively experiencing it, the reader imputes to the fictitious speaker—afterwards, in reviewing the total impression so received, with analysis and synthesis of its successive movements, the critic discerns, so far as his thought does not deceive him, within the fictitious personality of Hamlet, the reflected pattern of the emotional forces that have operated within his own imaginative activity.

To Dr. Jones the conflict of Hamlet appears an example of the working of the Oedipus complex. Hamlet cannot whole-heartedly will the slaying of his uncle, because "his uncle incorporates the deepest and most buried part of his own personality." The repressed desire for the death of

---

[12] "A psycho-analytic study of *Hamlet*," included in *Essays in Applied Psychoanalysis*, 1923.

his father and the sexual enjoyment of his mother, persisting unconsciously from infancy, has produced an unwitting identification by Hamlet of himself and his guilty uncle, so that only at the point of death, "when he has made the final sacrifice . . . is he free . . . to slay his other self" (p. 57).

This psychological hypothesis, contributed by Freud and elaborated by Dr. Jones, has been welcomed by certain literary critics. Herbert Read, referring to the view of J. M. Robertson, that *Hamlet* is "not finally an intelligible drama as it stands"—that Shakespeare could not make a psychologically consistent play out of his barbaric plot and supersubtle hero—urges that however baffling to critics the play may have proved, nevertheless in experiencing it we are aware of a personal intensity of expression, a *consistent* intensity, giving the play a unity which the older academic critics lacked means to explore.[13] Dr. Jones's hypothesis, he considers, does serve to explain this acceptance by our feeling of any difficulties and incoherence which our thought may find. Using the terms I have suggested, we might say that the hypothesis of the Oedipus complex—i.e., of a persistent unconscious wish, hostile to the father and dishonouring to the mother, in conflict with the sentiment of filial love and loyalty—offers to our thought an emotional pattern which does correspond to the play of feeling stimulated during a full imaginative participation in the drama. Professor Bradley has spoken of *Hamlet* as deserving the title of "tragedy of moral idealism," [14] because of the intensity, both of idealizing love and of horror at betrayal of love, that we feel in Hamlet's speeches. He dwells upon the shock to such a moral sensibility as Hamlet's of witnessing the faithlessness of his mother and uncle; yet there seems a discrepancy between the horror and disgust that a sensitive mind might naturally feel at such faithlessness in others and the overwhelming disgust that Hamlet feels, at himself, his whole world and his attempted action, unless we realize that he feels the treachery of his mother and uncle echo within himself, and within the sentiment of loyal love to his father that is his strongest conscious motive. If, in reviewing the experience communicated by the play, we conceive a loyal love undermined, as it were, by a bewildered sense of treachery within as well as without, we must, I think, agree that the Freudian hypothesis does throw some light upon that intimate immediate experience which is the final touchstone of critical theory.

V

Perhaps the most important contribution that has been made by the Freudian theory of dream interpretation to the understanding of the emo-

---

[13] Herbert Read, *Reason and Romanticism* (Faber & Gwyer), p. 101.
[14] *Shakespearian Tragedy* (Macmillan, 1912), p. 113.

tional symbolism of poetic themes is that concerned with the "splitting" of type figures. In comparing the Hamlet story with the story of Oedipus, Dr. Jones asserts that both are variants of the same *motif*, but in one the father figure remains single, while in the other it is "split into two"—the father loved and revered, and the hated tyrannical usurper.

This assertion involves two elements of hypothesis:

1. The fundamental assumption—implied also by the statements of Jung and Gilbert Murray, with which this discussion opened—that these ancient stories owe their persistence, as traditional material of art, to their power of expressing or symbolizing, and so relieving, typical human emotions.

2. That the emotion relieved is in this case the two-sided—ambivalent —attitude of the son towards the father. Let us examine this latter hypothesis more closely.

It appears to be characteristic of the relation between father and son that the father should excite in the son both feeling of admiration, love, and loyalty, and also impulses of anger, jealousy, and self-assertion. The more the son learns to "idolize" his father, developing what Shand has called the "conscience of the sentiment," so that any muttering of jealousy or hostile criticism is suppressed as disloyal, the more acute will become the tension of the inner attitude. It is such an attitude that can find relief in imaginative activity wherein both the love and the repressed hostility have play. In the story of Oedipus, according to the Freudian hypothesis, a repressed persistent impulse to supplant the father and enjoy the mother finds expression in the first part of the action; then in the latter part, in the hero's remorse and suffering, appears the expression of the sentiment of respect and loyalty. In the Hamlet legend—as it appears, e.g., in the Amleth Saga—combined fear and hostile self-assertion against the father find expression through all the incidents of simulated stupidity, and secret bitter word-play, and at last in the achievement of the plotted slaying of the usurper; while at the same time the sentiment of love and loyalty is triumphantly expressed in that same act of filial vengeance. It is Shakespeare only who appears to have brought into the rendering of the ancient story the subtle factor of the division and paralysis of the will of the hero, by the intuitive apprehension that the impulse that drove his uncle against his father was one with that present in himself.

The story of Orestes may be considered as another example of the imaginative expression of the ambivalent attitude of child toward parent. In this story, as presented by the three great Attic tragedians, there is a wealth of material illustrating the manner in which inner forces of emotion may, through shapes created by imagination, become palpable to sense. But we must be content here to consider briefly only the outline of the story.

Considered as a variant of the Hamlet theme, its distinctive note is that the usurper upon whom the son's fierce self-assertion and craving for vengeance strike not alone the male kinsman, but also the queen-mother, who has betrayed, and with her own hands murdered the father. Therefore the moment of triumphant self-assertion, when the son has proved his manhood, and vindicated his loyalty upon his father's enemies, is also the moment when there awakens the palpable, pursuing horror of the outraged filial relation—since this enemy was also a parent, the mother of the slayer.

The conflict presented in the Orestes dramas is plainly concerned not directly with sex, but with combined love and hate of either son or daughter converging upon a parent figure which may be either father or mother. It is the enduring conflict between the generations which continues to find expression in the story, when more temporary questions—such as that between patriarchy and mother-right, which may have been present in Athenian minds—are no longer urgent. That this theme of conflict between the generations had great significance within the sensibility that found expression in Shakespeare's plays, is evident in the tragedy of *King Lear.*

In this drama the emotional conflict between the generations is communicated from the standpoint of the old man, the father who encounters in separate embodiment in his natural successors the extremes of bestial self-seeking, and a filial devotion. Bradley has noted how the play illustrates "the tendency of imagination to analyse and subtract, to decompose human nature into its constituent factors." [15] This mode of thought, he suggests,[16] is responsible for "the incessant references to the lower animals" which occur throughout the play. Thus Goneril is likened to a kite, a serpent, a boar, a dog, a wolf, a tiger. This analysing work of the imagination, separating the bestial and the angelic in human nature and giving them distinct embodiment, in the wicked daughters and Cordelia (and again in Edmund and Edgar, the cruel and the loyal sons of Gloucester), presents another instance of what we have already observed in the "splitting" of the father figure. The splitting in this play is from the point of view of the parent; as, in the Orestes or Hamlet story, it is from the point of view of the child. As, to the feeling of the child, the parent may be both loved protector and unjustly obstructing tyrant, and these two aspects find their emotional symbolism in separate figures in the play; so, to the feeling of the parent, the child may be both loving support of age and ruthless usurper and rival, and these two aspects find expression in separate figures, such as the tender and the wicked daughters of Lear.

[15] *Shakespearian Tragedy,* p. 264.
[16] *Ibid.,* p. 266.

VI

We have considered, so far, the emotional pattern corresponding to a particular theme—the conflict between the generations—which, though a recurring one, is by no means co-extensive with the realm of tragic drama. Can we identify an archetypal pattern corresponding to tragedy itself—its universal idea or form?

Gilbert Murray, taking the "essential tragic idea" to be that of "climax followed by decline, or pride by judgement," and attempting a closer analysis of this sequence, maintains that what is "really characteristic" of the tragic conflict is "an element of mystery derived ultimately from the ancient religious concepts of *katharsis* and atonement." [17] The death or fall of the tragic hero has in some sense the character of a purifying or atoning sacrifice.

In considering this conception we may first remedy an inadequacy that the reader has probably noticed in the previous discussion of the dramas of Hamlet and Lear, Orestes and Oedipus. We have so far ignored the royal status of the father and son concerned in the tragic conflict. Yet the kingly status has great significance for the feeling expressed in the play.

Consider, for instance, the tragedy of *King Lear*. "The master movement of the play," says Granville-Barker, is Lear's passing "from personal grievance to the taking upon him, as great natures may, of the imagined burden of the whole world's sorrow." [18] It is Lear's royal status that helps to make this movement possible. King Lear is at once "a poor, infirm, weak, and despised old man"—a father broken to tears and madness by his daughters' cruelty—and also in his sufferings a superhuman figure, one who can bid the "all shaking thunder strike flat the thick rotundity of the world" in vengeance for his wrongs. It is in part the associations with which history, and pre-history, has invested the name and image of king that make it possible for us, under the spell of Shakespeare's verse, to accept the figure of Lear as in this way exalted in his agony beyond human stature. His madness, his pitiful humanity, appear, according to that comment which Shakespeare puts into the mouth of an attendant, on behalf of all onlookers, "a sight . . . past speaking in a king." The word "king" is here, through its position in the play, loaded with a significance for the sources of which we must go far back in the story of the race and of the individual.

It is probably because, to the mind of the young child, the father appears of unlimited power that in the life-history of the individual

---

[17] *Op. cit.,* "Drama," p. 66.
[18] H. Granville-Barker, *Prefaces to Shakespeare* (1927), 1st series, p. 171.

imagination the figures of father and king tend to coalesce. Legends and fairy stories that reflect the feelings of more primitive people towards their king are interpreted by the child in the light of his own earlier feeling towards his father. In the case both of the child and of the primitive individual the same process seems to take place—an emerging of the consciousness of self from out a matrix of less differentiated awareness, which may be called collective or group-consciousness. The figures of both father and king tend to retain within those deeper levels of the mind to which poetry may penetrate, something of the *mana* that invested the first representative of a power akin to, but vastly beyond, that of the individual emerging into self-consciousness.

It is this supernatural aspect which the father-king of tragic drama has for the kindled imagination that is of importance when we try to understand the element of religious mystery which is characteristic of tragedy—plainly in the past, and, as Gilbert Murray holds, in some subtler fashion still in our experience today.

Upon this character of tragedy and the tragic hero it is possible, I think, to gain a certain fresh light from a consideration of the conclusions at which Dr. Jung has arrived through his study of fantasy figures appearing in personal analysis.

In *The Psychology of the Unconscious*, in the chapter entitled "The Sacrifice," he examines the symbol of the dying hero as it appears in individual fantasy, representing, according to his interpretation, an inflated infantile personality—a childish self that must be sacrificed, if the libido is to move forward into active life—and in a later work he discusses, under the title of the "Mana Personality," [19] a hero figure which he finds appearing with a richer content at late stages of analysis.

It is especially at times when barriers of personal repression are removed and images of "cosmic" character are arising freely, that the fantasy figure may appear of some great prophet or hero who tends to assume control of the personality.[20] If the conscious or practical personality is poorly developed there is the greater likelihood that it will be overwhelmed when such powerful images rise from the unconscious.

As a literary example of such a case, parallel to actual ones within his experience, Jung accepts H. G. Wells's story of Preemby,[21] "a small, irrelevant, fledgling of a personality," to whom is presented in dream and fantasy the figure of Sargon, King of Kings, in such compelling fashion

[19] *Two Essays on Analytical Psychology*, 1928, trans. by H. G. and C. F. Baynes, Essay II, ch. iv.

[20] An interesting autobiographical account of this condition may be found in the writings of E. Maitland (*The Story of Anna Kingsford and Edward Maitland and of the New Gospel of Interpretation*, 1st ed., 1893). See especially the passage where he describes the first arrival of the authoritative "presence," and the voice distinctly heard: "at last I have found a man through whom I can speak."

[21] *Christina Alberta's Father*, 1925.

that he is led to identify himself with it. Jung observes that here "the author depicts a really classical type of compensation," [22] and we may compare it with the type of compensation which occurs in connexion with what we have already considered as the ambivalent attitude towards a parent.

If, within the conscious life, in relation to a parent, only reactions of admiration and affection are recognized, while other reactions, of hostile character, excited within the brain, are repressed, it is these latter that tend to present in dreams a parent figure as object of violence or contempt. Similarly, if within the conscious life the personal self comes to be known only as "an onlooker, an ineffective speechless man," utterly insignificant; while yet, within the life that animates that particular brain, strong reactions are excited of sympathetic exultation and delight at imaginative representations of human achievement—as the little Preemby of Wells thrilled at "the mystery of Atlantis and of the measurements of the Pyramids"—then there may arise, as compensatory to the belittled self, the figure of a hero-self, or *mana* personality, fashioned, as it were, from the stuff of these imaginative reactions; just as the figure of the hated father was fashioned from the energy of the repressed hostility, in compensation for the over-idealizing love.

The Preemby of Wells's story is saved from his delusion, after many sufferings, by learning to think of his vision as of the spirit of man and its achievements—an inheritance belonging no more to him personally than to every other man. In the same manner every individual in whose fantasy such mighty ghosts arise, with their superhuman claims and relationships, must learn to distinguish such claims from those of the personal self; while yet the personal self may be enriched through the conscious experience of its relation to the great forces which such figures represent.

In this way, according to the view of Jung—by interpreting and giving conscious direction to the "pure nature-process" [23] of fantasy in which compensatory images arise—such fantasy can become instrumental to the purging of the individual will and its reconciliation with itself. Is it in some such fashion as this that tragic drama, deeply experienced, now or in the past, exercises the function of purgation or atonement in relation to the passions of the spectator? With this question in view, we may examine a little further the nature of the emotional experience of tragic art, still using the examples of *Hamlet* and of *King Lear*.

Professor Bradley, in examining the experience of tragedy, cites these dramas as examples of tragedies at whose close we feel pain mingled with something like exultation. There is present, he declares, "a glory in the greatness of the soul," and awareness of an "ultimate power" which is "no

---

[22] *Op. cit.*, p. 193.
[23] *Op. cit.*, p. 258.

mere fate," but spiritual, and to which the hero "was never so near . . .
as in the moment when it required his life." [24]

I quote these statements of Bradley, not, of course, as universally
acceptable, but as the attempt of one eminent critic to render his own
deeply pondered experience of tragic drama. The experience is rendered
in terms rather of philosophy or religion than of psychology. Can we
translate it into any more psychological terms? What is this spiritual
power, akin to the characters, and, in some sense, a whole of which they
are "parts, expressions, products"? [25] I would propose (following the
view set forth by F. M. Cornford) the psychological hypothesis that this
power is the common nature lived and immediately experienced by the
members of a group or community—"the collective emotion and activity
of the group." [26] This common nature can, in Alexander's phrase, be enjoyed, but never directly contemplated. As unfathomable to introspection, it is termed by Jung the Collective Unconscious—the life-energy that
in its spontaneous movement toward expression generates alike the hero
figures of myth and legend and the similar figures that, appearing in individual fantasy, may overwhelm the personal consciousness.

According to Bradley, the tragic exultation that we feel at the close of
Hamlet is connected with our sense that the spiritual power of which
Hamlet is in some manner the expression or product is receiving him to
itself. It would be this same sense that, as Bradley observes,[27] demands,
and is satisfied by, the words of Horatio, introducing, against Shakespeare's
custom, the reference to another life: "flights of angels sing thee to thy
rest." If, as I suggest, the spiritual power, which the philosopher analysing
his poetic experience is constrained to represent, be conceived psychologically as the awakened sense of our common nature in its active emotional
phase, then our exultation in the death of Hamlet is related in direct line
of descent to the religious exultation felt by the primitive group that made
sacrifice of the divine king or sacred animal, the representative of the
tribal life, and, by the communion of its shed blood, felt that life strengthened and renewed. Hamlet, though he dies, is immortal, because he is the
representative and creature of the immortal life of the race. He lives, as
he desired to live, in the story with which he charged Horatio—and us,
who, having participated in that story, descend from the poetic ecstasy to
draw breath again in the harsh world of our straitened separate personalities.

The insight of Nietzsche, who knew at once the intoxication of the

[24] *Oxford Lectures on Poetry*, p. 84.
[25] *Shakespearian Tragedy*, p. 37.
[26] F. M. Cornford, *From Religion to Philosophy* (Arnold, 1912), p. 78.
[27] *Op. cit.*, p. 147.

artist and the analytic urge of the philosopher, discerned the essential
nature of tragedy as a vision generated by a dance.[28] The dance of rhyth-
mical speech, like the dance of the ancient chorus, excites the Dionysian
ecstasy wherein arises, serene and clear, the Apollonian vision of the
imaged meanings the dancing words convey.

The painful images within the vision are at once intimately known
and felt, and also "distanced" like the objects in a far stretching landscape, "estranged by beauty." So far as the memory material used by the
imaginative activity comes from personal experience, it has undergone
"separation . . . from the concrete personality of the experiencer" and
"extrusion of its personal aspects"; [29] but experience is also used which
has never been connected with the personal self—as when, in *King Lear*,
Shakespeare causes the actor to "impersonate Lear and the storm together," [30] and in the storm "it is the powers of the tormented soul that
we hear and see." [31] Here, dramatist, actor, and spectator are using experience which was never personal, but shaped through previous apprehension of physical storms into which was imaginatively projected that
same impersonal emotional energy from which the daemonic figure of
the hero is now fashioned.

To the impersonal, "distanced," vision corresponds, in Schopen-
hauer's phrase, "a Will-free subject," one indifferent to the aims and fears
of the ego—not held to its private perspective.[32]

This felt release, and Dionysian union with a larger whole, would
seem to constitute that element of religious mystery—of purgation and
atonement—traditionally connected with the idea of tragedy.

VII

If now, summing up our results, we recur to the question: what determining emotional pattern corresponds to the form of tragedy? we may
answer first, in accordance with our earlier discussion, that the pattern
consists of emotional tendencies of opposite character which are liable

---

[28] See *The Birth of Tragedy*, Section 8.

[29] E. Bullough, "Distance as an aesthetic principle," *Brit. J. of Psychol.* v. part 2, p. 116.

[30] Granville-Barker, *Prefaces to Shakespeare*, p. 142.

[31] A. C. Bradley, *Shakespearian Tragedy*, p. 270.

[32] This character of the aesthetic experience is vividly expressed, in imaginative form,
in the lines of de la Mare:

> When music sounds, all that I was I am
> Ere to this haunt of brooding dust I came.

Here we have the felt contrast between the subject of the aesthetic experience—"all that
I was I am"—and the self that is bounded in space and time by the bodily organism—
"this haunt of brooding dust."

to be excited by the same object or situation, and, thus conflicting, produce an inner tension that seeks relief in the activity either of fantasy, or
of poetic imagination, either originally or receptively creative. The nature
of the opposed tendencies that find relief through diverse renderings of
the essential tragic theme, the death or fall of a hero, it is not easy to
describe at once with conciseness and adequacy. But we may attempt
this through the concept of an ambivalent attitude toward the self.

In the gradual fashioning and transforming, through the experience
of life, of an idea of the self, every individual must in some degree experience the contrast between a personal self—a limited ego, one among
many—and a self that is free to range imaginatively through all human
achievement. In infancy and in the later years of those who remain
childish, a comparatively feeble imaginative activity together with an
undisciplined instinct of self-assertion may present a fantasy self—the
image of an infantile personality—in conflict with the chastened image
which social contacts, arousing the instinct of submission, tend to enforce.
In the more mature mind that has soberly taken the measure of the
personal self as revealed in practical life, there remains the contrast between this and the self revealed in imaginative thought—wellnigh limitless in sympathy and aspiration.

Within what McDougall calls the self-regarding sentiment these contrasting images, and the impulses that sustain and respond to them, may
bring about persistent tension. The experience of tragic drama both gives
in the figure of the hero an objective form to the self of imaginative aspiration, or to the power-craving, and also, through the hero's death, satisfies
the counter movement of feeling toward the surrender of personal claims
and the merging of the ego within a greater power—the "community
consciousness."

Thus the archetypal pattern corresponding to tragedy may be said
to be a certain organization of the tendencies of self-assertion and submission. The self which is asserted is magnified by that same collective
force to which finally submission is made; and from the tension of the
two impulses and their reaction upon each other, under the conditions
of poetic exaltation, the distinctive tragic attitude and emotion appears
to arise.

The theme of the conflict between the generations—considered
earlier, in relation to Hamlet and Orestes, as corresponding to an ambivalent attitude toward a parent figure—is plainly related to this more general theme and pattern; since, as we saw, the same underlying emotional
associations cling to the images of father and of king. In experiencing
imaginatively the conflict of the generations, the spectator is identified
with the hero both as son, in his felt solidarity with the father and revolt
against him, and again, when, making reparation for the "injustice"

against his predecessor, he gives place to a successor, and is reunited with that whole of life whence he emerged.[33]

One or two points in regard to the argument may be briefly reviewed.

The question is sometimes asked whether the creative activity of the poet and the imaginative response of the reader are sufficiently alike, psychologically, to be considered together. Here I have been concerned primarily with imaginative response, and have not attempted to consider the distinctive activity of original composition. In so far, however, as the poet's work, e.g., a play of Shakespeare, does reveal his imaginative response to material communicated to him by others and by him to us, I have of course been concerned with the poet's experience.

The concept of racial experience enters the present essay in two ways: (1) all those systems or tendencies which appear to be inherited in the constitution of mind and brain may be said to be due to racial experience in the past. It is not necessary for our purpose to determine exactly the method of this "biological inheritance" from our ancestors. Of more importance for our purpose is the question concerning (2) the racial experience which we may "enjoy" in responding to that "social inheritance" of meanings stored in language which also comes to us from our ancestors, and wakens into activity the potentialities of our inherited nature. In such racial or collective experience as we have discussed in relation to tragic poetry, so far as there is reference to an experiencer, this seems to be not an individual, but rather that larger whole from which what we know as the individual, or personal, self has been differentiated, and which remains with us as the sense, either latent or active, of a greater power.

In the present paper it is maintained that racial experience in this sense is an important factor in the total experience of tragic drama, at the present day, as in the ritual dance from which drama arose. In regard to this question further examination of the imaginative experience can alone be decisive.

---

[33] Cf. the mystic saying of Anaximander, concerning the cycle of birth and death, wherein things "give reparation to one another and pay the penalty of their injustice," and the discussion of it by F. M. Cornford, *op. cit.* See especially pp. 8, 147, 176.

Archetype and Signature

(The Relationship of Poet and Poem)

LESLIE FIEDLER

I

A central dogma of much recent criticism asserts that biographical information is irrelevant to the understanding and evaluation of poems, and that conversely, poems cannot legitimately be used as material for biography. This double contention is part of a larger position which holds that history is history and art is art, and that to talk about one in terms of the other is to court disaster. Insofar as this position rests upon the immortal platitude that it is good to know what one is talking about, it is unexceptionable; insofar as it is a reaction based upon the procedures of pre-Freudian critics, it is hopelessly outdated; and insofar as it depends upon the extreme nominalist definition of a work of art, held by many "formalists" quite unawares, it is metaphysically reprehensible. It has the further inconvenience of being quite unusable in the practical sphere (all of its proponents, in proportion as they are sensitive critics, immediately betray it when speaking of specific works, and particularly of large bodies of work); and, as if that were not enough, it is in blatant contradiction with the assumptions of most serious practicing writers.

That the anti-biographical position was once "useful," whatever its truth, cannot be denied; it was even once, what is considerably rarer in the field of criticism, amusing; but for a long time now it has been threatening to turn into one of those annoying clichés of the intellectually middle-aged, proffered with all the air of a stimulating heresy. The position was born in dual protest against an excess of Romantic criticism and one of "scientific scholarship." Romantic aesthetics appeared bent on dissolving the formally realized "objective" elements in works of art into "expression of personality"; while the "scholars," in revolt against Romantic subjectivity, seemed set on casting out all the more shifty questions of value and *gestalt* as "subjective," and concentrating on the kind of "facts" amenable to scientific verification. Needless to say, it was not the newer psychological sciences that the "scholars" had in mind, but such purer disciplines as physics and biology. It was at this point that it became fashionable to talk about literary study as "research," and graphs and tables began to appear in analyses of works of art.

Both the "scholarly" and the Romantic approaches struck the antibiographists as "reductive"—attempts to prove that the work of art was *nothing but* the personality of the Genius behind it, or the sum total of its genetic factors. In answer to both heresies of attack, the anti-biographist offered what he came to call the "intrinsic" approach, which turned out, alas, to be another *nothing but* under its show of righteous indignation—namely, the contention that a poem was *nothing but* "words," and its analysis therefore properly *nothing but* a study of syntax and semantics. An attempt to illuminate a poem by reference to its author's life came therefore to be regarded with horror, unless it confined itself to an examination of his "idiosyncratic use of words"! This is not parody, but direct quotation.

By this time a generation of critics has grown up, of whom I am one, to whom the contention that biographical material is irrelevant to the essential "experience" of a poem was taught as the basic doctrine of all right-thinking readers. The word "experience" is important; it comes out of I. A. Richards at his most scientizing, and along with the "extrinsic-intrinsic" metaphor is a key to the anti-biographist point of view. It must be understood for what the word "experience" is being substituted: as an "experience," a poem is no longer regarded as an "imitation," in any of the received senses of the word; nor even as an "expression" in the Crocean sense; and above all not as a "communication." All three possible substitute terms imply a necessary interconnectedness between the art object and some *other* area of experience—or at least an essentially intended pointing outward or inward toward some independently existent *otherness*. This is distasteful to the anti-biographist, who shows the ordinary nominalist uneasiness at any suggestion that there are realities more comprehensive than particulars, to which words only refer.

An odd phenomenon is the support of a position to which nominalism is logically necessary, by many confirmed anti-scientizers and realists; they are betrayed into their ill-advised fellow-traveling, I think, by an excess of anti-Romanticism. It is no longer as fashionable as it once was to publicly anathematize Shelley and Swinburne, but the bias persists as a real force in current critical practice, and cuts off many, to whom the position would be temperamentally and metaphysically attractive, from Expressionism. What the modern sensibility finds particularly unsympathetic in some Romantic writing has been misleadingly called, I think, "the exploitation of personality"; it is rather a tendency toward the excessively "programmatic." Just as music and painting can be too "literary," so literature itself can be too "literary." In reaction against the programmatic, there are two possible paths: more deeply into and through the personalism of Romanticism to Expressionism; or outward and away toward the sort of "abstraction" achieved in cubist painting. As a matter of fact, there has been at work all along in our period an underground, and probably harmful, analogy between poetry and the plastic arts. A poem, the feeling has been, should be as "palpable and mute" not merely as an actual fruit, but as the fruit become pure color and texture of Picasso or Matisse. As pictures have become frankly paint, so should poems be frankly words. "A poem should not mean but be." There is the slogan of the movement!

It is a rather nice phrase in the limited context of MacLeish's little poem, but a dangerous full-blown aesthetic position. The notion that a work of art is, or should be, absolutely self-contained, a discrete set of mutually interrelated references, needs only to be stated clearly to seem the *reductio ad absurdum* which it is. Yet this belief in the poem as a closed system, "cut off" in ideal isolation, descends from the realm of theoretical criticism to practical criticism and classroom pedagogy (if not in practice, at least as an institutionalized hypocrisy) to become the leitmotif of the New Teacher: "Stay *inside* the poem!"

The narrative and dramatic poem, finally poetic drama itself, is assimilated to a formulation, even *apparently* applicable only to a lyric of the most absolute purity—and it becomes heretical to treat the work as anything but "words," to ask those questions which attest our conviction that the work of art is "real"; that in the poem, the whole is greater than the sum of its parts; that certain created actions and characters exist, in some sense, *outside* of their formalizations. How long was Hamlet in Wittenberg? How many children did Lady Macbeth have? In what sense does Prospero speak for Shakespeare? What developing sensibility can be inferred from the Shakespearian corpus and be called (what *else?*) Shakespeare? We cannot ask these questions in the dewy innocence with which they were first posed; we restate them on the second convolution, aware of all the arguments against them, and the more convinced that they are essential, and cannot be shelved any more than those questions about the ends and origins of existence which have also been recently declared "unreal."

Closely associated with the Richardsian experiential-semantic approach in the total, eclectic position of the anti-biographist is the psychological notion of the poem as the "objective correlative" or a complex of "objective correlatives" of emotional responses to the given world. Mr. Eliot's term is as elusive as it it appealing; but I am concerned here (Mr. Eliseo Vivas has elsewhere criticized it as containing some "nonintrinsic" contradictions) only with the adjective "objective" in one of its possible implications. Whatever its origins, Mr. Eliot seems to be asserting, a poem succeeds, as a poem, insofar as it is detached from the subjectivity of its maker. The poem is achieved by a process of objectification, and can be legitimately examined and understood only as an "object." This formulation leaves a somewhat second-best use for the biographical approach, as a way of explaining the particular badness of certain kinds of bad poems, e.g., Romantic verse and Shakespeare's *Hamlet*.

From this presumed insight follows the deprivation of the poet's right to explain his own poem, or at least the challenging of his claim to speak with final authority about his own work. Once realized, the argument runs, the successful poem is detached; and the author no longer has any property rights in what now belongs to the tradition rather than to him. And if, benightedly, he protests against some critical analysis or interpretation which seems to him wrong on the basis of his special biographical knowledge, he reveals that either his poem is not truly "successful," or even worse, that he has never read "Tradition and the Individual Talent."

There are, in fact, two quite different contentions, one valid, one invalid, confused in most statements about the poet as commentator on his own work. First it is asserted (and with real truth) that a poem may contain more meanings than the maker is ever aware of; and second (this is false, of course) that nothing the poet can tell us about his own work is of any *decisive* importance, because the poet cannot help falling into the trap of talking about his "intentions." But the notion of "intention" implies the belief that there is a somehow existent something against which the achieved work of art can be measured; and although this has been for all recorded time the point of view of the practicing writer, every graduate student who has read Wimsatt and Beardsley's ponderous tract on the Intentional Fallacy knows that we are all now to believe that there is no poem except the poem of "words."

The fact that all recognized critics have consistently spoken of intention shows merely that in the unfortunate past the writer about literature has often (unfortunately!) spoken more like the poet than the scientific semanticist. This regrettable looseness of expression we can only hope will be amended in the future, now that we have been duly warned. It is difficult not to be tempted by analogy. Why, we want to ask, can we properly laugh at the visiting dignitary in the high hat when he slips on the steps to the platform, because of the disparity between the entrance he *intended* and the one he achieved; and still not speak of a bathetic disparity between what a poem obviously aims at and what it does? On what respectable grounds can it be maintained that a poem is all act and no potentiality?

It is difficult to understand the success of the anti-biographist tendency in more respectable critical circles and in the schools, in light of its own internal contradictions. The explanation lies, I suppose, in its comparative newness, and in the failure of its opponents to arrive at any *coherent* theory of the relationship between the life of the poet and his work; so long as biographers are content merely to place side by side undigested biographical data and uninspired paraphrases of poems— linking them together mechanically or pseudo-genetically: "Wordsworth lived in the country and therefore wrote Nature poetry," or even worse, so long as notes proving that Milton was born in one house rather than another continue to be printed in magazines devoted to the study of literature, people will be tempted into opposite though equal idiocies, which have at least not been for so long proved utterly bankrupt.

A recent phenomenon of some interest in this regard is the astonishing popularity of such texts as Thomas and Brown's classroom anthology called *Reading Poems*—the very title reveals the dogma behind the books; in a world of discrete, individual "experiences," of "close reading" (a cant phrase of the anti-biographist) as an ideal, one cannot even talk of so large an abstraction as poetry. It is only "poems" to which the student must be exposed, poems printed out of chronological order and without the names of the authors attached, lest the young reader be led astray by what (necessarily irrelevant) information he may have concerning the biography or social background of any of the poets. It is all something of a hoax, of course; the teacher realizes that the chances of any student knowing too much for his own good about such matters are slight indeed; and besides, there is an index in which the names are revealed, so that unless one is very virtuous, he can scarcely help looking up the anthologized pieces. In addition, the good teacher is himself aware to begin with of the contexts, social and biographical, of a large number of the pieces. Frankly, that is why they make sense to him; and even when he admonishes the young to "stay *inside*" the poems, he is bootlegging all kinds of rich relevancies which he possesses because he is capable of connecting.

I cannot help feeling that the chief problem of teaching anything in our atomized period lies precisely in the fact that the ordinary student cannot or will not connect the few facts he knows, the slim insights he has previously attained, the chance extensions of sensibility into which he has been once or twice tempted, into a large enough context to make sense of the world he inhabits, or the works of art he encounters. It is because the old-line biographist fails to connect his facts with the works they presumably illuminate, and not because he does connect them, that he is a poor critic. And the doctrinaire anti-biographist, like the doctrinaire biographist before him, secure in pride and ignorance of the newer psychologies, makes worse the endemic disease of our era—the failure to connect. There is no "work itself," no independent formal entity which is its own sole context; the poem is the sum total of many contexts, all of which must be known to know it and evaluate it. "Only connect!" should be the motto of all critics and teachers—and the connective link between the poem on the page and most of its rewarding contexts is precisely—biography.

The poet's life is the focusing glass through which pass the determinants of the shape of his work: the tradition available to him, his understanding of "kinds," the impact of special experiences (travel, love, etc.). But the poet's life is more than a burning glass; with his work, it makes up his total meaning. I do not intend to say, of course, that some meanings of works of art, satisfactory and as far as they go sufficient, are not available in the single work itself (only a really *bad* work depends for all substantial meaning on a knowledge of the life-style of its author); but a whole body of work will contain larger meanings, and, where it is available, a sense of the life of the writer will raise that meaning to a still higher power. The latter two kinds of meaning fade into each other; for as soon as two works by a single author are considered side, by side, one has begun to deal with biography—that is, with an interconnectedness fully explicable only in terms of a personality, inferred or discovered.

One of the essential functions of the poet is the assertion and creation of a personality, in a profounder sense than any non-artist can attain. We ask of the poet a definition of man, at once particular and abstract, stated and acted out. It is impossible to draw a line between the work the poet writes and the work he lives, between the life he lives and the life he writes. And the agile critic, therefore, must be prepared to move constantly back and forth between life and poem, not in a pointless circle, but in a meaningful spiraling toward the absolute point.

To pursue this matter further, we will have to abandon at this point the nominalist notion of the poem as "words" or "only words." We have the best of excuses, that such terminology gets in the way of truth. We will not, however, return to the older notions of the poem as a "document" or the embodiment of an "idea," for these older conceptions are equally inimical to the essential concept of the "marvelous"; and they have the further difficulty of raising political and moral criteria of "truth" as relevant to works of art. To redeem the sense of what words are all the time pointing *to* and what cannot be adequately explained by syntactical analysis or semantics, I shall speak of the poem as Archetype and Signature, suggesting that the key to analysis is *symbolics;* and I shall not forget that the poet's life is also capable of being analyzed in those terms. We have been rather ridiculously overemphasizing *medium* as a differentiating factor; I take it that we can now safely assume no one will confuse a life with a poem, and dwell on the elements common to the two, remembering that a pattern of social behavior can be quite as much a symbol as a word, chanted or spoken or printed. In deed as in word, the poet composes himself as maker and mask, in accordance with some contemporaneous *mythos* of the artist. And as we all know, in our day, it is even possible to be a writer without having written anything. When we talk therefore of the importance of the biography of the poet, we do not mean the importance of every trivial detail, but of all that goes into making his particular life-style, whether he concentrate on recreating himself, like Shelley, in some obvious image of the Poet, or, like Wallace Stevens, in some witty anti-mask of the Poet. Who could contend that even the *faces* of Shelley and Stevens are not typical products of their quite different kinds of art!

The word "Archetype" is the more familiar of my terms; I use it instead of the word "myth," which I have employed in the past but which becomes increasingly ambiguous, to mean any of the immemorial patterns of response to the human situation in its most permanent aspects: death, love, the biological family, the relationship with the Unknown, etc., whether those patterns be considered to reside in the Jungian Collective Unconscious or the Platonic world of Ideas. The archetypal belongs to the infra- or meta-personal, to what Freudians call the id or the unconscious; that is, it belongs to the Community at its deepest, pre-conscious levels of acceptance.

I use "Signature" to mean the sum total of individuating factors in a work, the sign of the Persona or Personality through which an Archetype is rendered, and which itself tends to become a subject as well as a means of the poem. Literature, properly speaking, can be said to come into existence at the moment a Signature is imposed upon the Archetype. The purely archetypal, without signature elements, is the myth. Perhaps a pair of examples are in order (with thanks to Mr. C. S. Lewis). The story of Baldur the Beautiful and Shakespeare's *Tempest* deal with somewhat similar archetypal material of immersion and resurrection; but we recall *The Tempest* only in all its specificity: the diction, meter, patterns of imagery, the heard voice of Shakespeare (the Signature as Means); as well as the scarcely motivated speech on pre-marital chastity, the breaking of the fictional frame by the unconventional religious *plaudite* (the Signature as Subject). Without these elements, *The Tempest* is simply not *The Tempest;* but *Baldur* can be retold in any diction, any style, just so long as faith is kept with the bare plot—and it is itself, for it is pure myth. Other examples are provided by certain children's stories, retold and reillustrated without losing their essential identity, whether they be "folk" creations like *Cinderella* or art products "captured" by the folk imagination, like Southey's *Three Bears*.

In our own time, we have seen the arts (first music, then painting, last of all literature) attempting to become "pure," or "abstract"—that is to say, attempting to slough off all remnants of the archetypal in a drive toward becoming unadulterated Signature. It should be noticed that the *theory* of abstract art is completely misleading in this regard, speaking as it does about pure forms, and mathematics, and the disavowal of personality. The abstract painter, for instance, does not, as he sometimes claims, really "paint paint," but signs his name. So-called abstract art is the ultimate expression of personality; so that the spectator says of a contemporary painting, not what one would have said in the anonymous Middle Ages, "There's a *Tree of Jesse* or a *Crucifixion!*" or not even what is said of Renaissance art, "There's a Michelangelo *Last Judgment* or a

Raphael *Madonna!*" but quite simply, "There's a Mondrian or a Jackson Pollock!" Analogously, in literature we recognize a poem immediately as "a Marianne Moore" or "an Ezra Pound" long before we understand, if ever, any of its essential meanings.

The theory of "realism" or "naturalism" denies both the Archetype and the Signature, advocating, in its extreme forms, that art merely "describes nature or reality" in a neutral style, based on the case report of the scientist. Art which really achieves such aims becomes, of course, something less than "poetry" as I have used the term here, becoming an "imitation" in the lowest Platonic sense, "thrice removed from the truth." Fortunately, the great "realists" consistently betray their principles, creating Archetypes and symbols willy-nilly, though setting them in a Signature distinguished by what James called "solidity of specification." The chief value of "realism" as a theory is that it helps create in the more sophisticated writer a kind of blessed stupidity in regard to what he is really doing, so that the archetypal material can well up into his work uninhibited by his intent; and in a complementary way, it makes acceptance of that archetypal material possible for an audience which thinks of itself as "science-minded" and inimical to the demonic and mythic. It constantly startles and pleases me to come across reference to such creators of grotesque Archetypes as Dostoevsky and Dickens and Faulkner as "realists."

A pair of caveats are necessary before we proceed. The distinction between Archetype and Signature, it should be noted, does not correspond to the ancient dichotomy of Content and Form. Such "forms" as the structures of Greek Tragedy (*cf.* Gilbert Murray), New Comedy and Pastoral Elegy are themselves *versunkene* Archetypes, capable of being rerealized in the great work of art. (Elsewhere I have called these "structural myths.")

Nor does the present distinction cut quite the same way as that between "impersonal" (or even "nonpersonal") and "personal." For the Signature, which is rooted in the ego and superego, belongs, as the twofold Freudian division implies, to the social collectivity as well as to the individual writer. The Signature is the joint product of "rules" and "conventions," of the expectations of a community and the idiosyncratic responses of the individual poet, who adds a personal idiom or voice to a received style. The difference between the communal element in the Signature and that in the Archetype is that the former is *conscious*—that is, associated with the superego rather than the id. The relevant, archtypal metaphor would make the personal element the Son, the conscious-communal the Father and the unconscious-communal the Mother (or the Sister, an image which occurs often as a symbolic euphemism for the Mother)—in the biological Trinity.

It is not irrelevant that the Romantic movement, which combined a deliberate return to the archetypal with a contempt for the conscious communal elements in the Signature, made one of the leitmotifs of the lives of its poets, as well as of their poems, the flight of the Sister from the threat of rape by the Father (Shelley's *Cenci,* for instance) and the complementary desperate love of Brother and Sister (anywhere from Chateaubriand and Wordsworth to Byron and Melville).

Even the most orthodox anti-biographist is prepared to grant the importance of biographical information in the *understanding* of certain ego elements in the Signature—this is what the intrinsicist calls the study of an author's "idiosyncratic use of words." But they deny vehemently the possibility of using biographical material for the purposes of *evaluation.* Let us consider some examples. For instance, the line in one of John Donne's poems, "A Hymne to God the Father," which runs, "When thou hast done, thou hast not done . . ." would be incomprehensible in such a collection without author's names as the Thomas and Brown *Reading Poems.* Without the minimum biographical datum of the name of the poet, the reader could not realize that a pun was involved, and he could not therefore even ask himself the evaluative question most important to the poem, namely, what is the value of the pun in a serious, even a religious, piece of verse? This is the simplest use of biography, referring us for only an instant outside of the poem, and letting us remain there once we have returned with the information. Other similar examples are plentiful in Shakespeare's sonnets: the references to his own first name, for instance, or the troublesome phrase "all *hewes* in his controlling."

A second example which looks much like the first to a superficial glance, but which opens up in quite a different way, would be the verse "they'are but *Mummy,* possest," from Donne's "Loves Alchymie." Let us consider whether we can sustain the contention that there is a pun on *Mummy,* whether deliberately planned or unconsciously fallen into. Can we read the line as having the two meanings: women, so fair in the desiring, turn out to be only dried-out corpses after the having; and women, once possessed, turn out to be substitutes for the Mother, who is the real end of our desiring? An analysis of the mere *word* does not take us very far; we discover that the *lallwort* "mummy" meaning "mother" is not recorded until 1830 in that precise spelling, but that there are attested uses of it in the form "mammy" (we remember, perhaps, that "mammy-apple" and "mummy-apple" are interchangeable forms meaning "papaya") well back into Donne's period, and that the related form "mome" goes back into Middle English. Inevitably, such evidence is inconclusive, establishing possibilities at best, and never really bearing on the question of probability, for which we must turn to his life itself, to Donne's actual relations with his mother; and beyond that to the science of such relationships.

When we have discovered that John Donne did, indeed, live in an especially intimate relationship with his mother throughout her long life (she actually outlived her son); and when we have set the possible pun in a context of other literary uses of a mythic situation in which the long-desired possessed turns at the moment of possession into a shriveled hag who is also a mother (Rider Haggard's *She*, Hilton's *Lost Horizon*, and, most explicitly, Flaubert's *L'Education Sentimentale*), we realize that our original contention is highly probable, for it is motivated by a traditional version of what the psychologists have taught us to call the Oedipus Archetype. It should be noticed in passing that the archetypal critic is delivered from the bondage of time, speaking of "confluences" rather than "influences," and finding the explication of a given work in things written later as well as earlier than the original piece. Following the lead opened up by "*Mummy*, possest," we can move still further toward an understanding of Donne, continuing to shuttle between life and work with our new clue, and examining, for instance, Donne's ambivalent relations to the greater Mother, the Roman Church, which his actual mother represented not only metaphorically but in her own allegiance and descent. This sort of analysis which at once unifies and opens up (one could do something equally provocative and rich, for instance, with the fact that in two of Melville's tales ships symbolic of innocence are called *The Jolly Bachelor* and *The Bachelor's Delight*) is condemned in some quarters as "failing to stay close to the actual meaning of the work itself"—as if the work were a tight little island instead of a focus opening on an inexhaustible totality.

The intrinsicist is completely unnerved by any reference to the role of the Archetype in literature, fearing such references as strategies to restore the criterion of the "marvelous" to respectable currency as a standard of literary excellence; for not only is the notion of the "marvelous" pre-scientific but it is annoyingly immune to "close analysis." Certainly, the contemplation of the Archetype pushes the critic beyond semantics, and beyond the kind of analysis that considers it has done all when it assures us (once again!) that the parts and whole of a poem cohere. The critic in pursuit of the Archetype finds himself involved in anthropology and depth psychology (not because these are New Gospels, but because they provide useful tools); and if he is not too embarrassed at finding himself in such company to look about him, he discovers that he has come upon a way of binding together our fractured world, of uniting literature and nonliterature *without the reduction of the poem.*

It is sometimes objected that though the archetypal critic can move convincingly between worlds ordinarily cut off from each other, he sacrifices for this privilege the ability to distinguish the essential qualities of literary works, and especially that of evaluating them. Far from being irrelevant to evaluation, the consideration of the archetypal content of works of art is essential to it! One of the earlier critics of Dante says someplace that poetry, as distinguished from rhetoric (which treats of the credible as credible), treats of the "marvelous" as credible. Much contemporary criticism has cut itself off from this insight—that is, from the realization of what poetry on its deepest levels *is*. It is just as ridiculous to attempt the evaluation of a work of art *purely* in formal terms (considering only the Signature as Means), as it would be to evaluate it *purely* in terms of the "marvelous," or the archetypal. The question, for instance, of whether *Mona Lisa* is just a bourgeoise or whether she "as Leda, was the mother of Helen of Troy, and, as St. Anne, was the mother of Mary" is just as vital to a final estimate of the picture's worth as any matter of control of the medium or handling of light and shadow.

The Romantics seem to have realized this, and to have reached, in their distinction between Fancy and Imagination, for rubrics to distinguish between the poetic method that touches the archetypal deeply and that which merely skirts it. Even the Arnoldian description of Pope as "a classic of our prose," right or wrong, was feeling toward a similar standard of discrimination. It is typical and ironic that Arnold in a moralizing age should have felt obliged to call the daemonic power of evoking the Archetype "High Seriousness." Certainly, the complete abandonment of any such criterion by the intrinsicist leaves him baffled before certain strong mythopoeic talents like Dickens or Stevenson; and it is the same lack in his system which prevents his understanding of the complementary relationship of the life and work of the poet.

II

The Archetype which makes literature itself possible in the first instance is the Archetype of the Poet. At the moment when myth is uncertainly becoming literature—that is, reaching tentatively toward a Signature—the poet is conceived of passively, as a mere vehicle. It is the Muse who is mythically bodied forth, the unconscious, collective source of the Archetypes, imagined as more than human, and, of course, female; it is she who mounts the Poet, as it were, in that position of feminine supremacy preferred in matriarchal societies. The Poet is still conceived more as Persona than Personality; the few characteristics with which he is endowed are borrowed from the prophet: he is a blind old man, impotent in his own right. That blindness (impotence as power, what Keats much later would call "negative capability") is the earliest version of the blessing-curse, without which the popular mind cannot conceive of the poet. His flaw is, in the early stages, at once the result and the precondition of his submitting himself to the dark powers of inspiration for the sake of the whole people.

But very soon the poet begins to assume a more individualized lifestyle, the lived Signature imposed on the Archetype, and we have no longer the featureless poet born in seven cities, his face a Mask through which a voice not his is heard, but Aeschylus, the Athenian citizen-poet; Sophocles, the spoiled darling of fate; or Euripides, the crowd-contemner in his Grotto. The mass mind, dimly resentful as the *Vates* becomes *Poeta,* the Seer a Maker, the Persona a Personality, composes a new Archetype, an image to punish the poet for detaching himself from the collective id— and the Poet, amused and baffled, accepts and elaborates the new image. The legend asserts that Euripides (the first completely self-conscious alienated artist?) dies torn to pieces by dogs or, even more to the point, by *women.* And behind the new, personalized application looms the more ancient *mythos* of the ritually dismembered Orpheus, ripped by the Maenads when he had withdrawn for lonely contemplation. The older myth suggests that a sacrifice is involved as well as a punishment—the casting-out and rending of the poet being reinterpreted as a death suffered for the group, by one who has dared make the first forays out of collec- tivity toward personality and has endured the consequent revenge of the group as devotees of the unconscious.

In light of this, it is no longer possible to think of the *poète maudit* as an unfortunate invention of the Romantics, or of the Alienated Artist as a by-product of mass communications. These are reinventions, as our archetypal history repeats itself before the breakdown of Christianity. Our newer names name only recent exacerbations of a situation as old as literature itself which in turn is coeval with the rise of personality. Only the conventional stigmata of the poet as Scape-Hero have changed with time: the Blind Man becomes the disreputable Player, the Atheist, the incestuous Lover, the Homosexual or (especially in America) the Drunk- ard; though, indeed, none of the older versions ever die, even the Homer- *typus* reasserting itself in Milton and James Joyce. Perhaps in recent times the poet has come to collaborate somewhat more enthusiastically in his own defamation and destruction, whether by drowning or tubercu- losis or dissipation—or by a token suicide in the work (*cf.* Werther). And he helps ever more consciously to compose himself and his fellow poets—Byron, for instance, the poet par excellence of the mid-nineteenth century, being the joint product of Byron and Goethe—and, though most of us forget, Harriet Beecher Stowe! Some dramatic version of the poet seems necessary to every age, and the people do not care whether the poet creates himself in his life or work or both. One thinks right now of Fitzgerald, of course, *our* popular image of the artist.

The contemporary critic is likely to become very impatient with the lay indifference to the poetizing of life and the "biographizing" of poetry; for he proceeds on the false assumption that the poet's life is primarily "given" and only illegitimately "made," while his work is essentially "made" and scarcely "given" at all. This is the source of endless confusion.

In perhaps the greatest periods of world literature, the "given" ele-

ment in poetry is made clear by the custom of supplying or, more precisely, of *imposing* on the poet certain traditional bodies of story. The
poet in such periods can think of himself only as "working with" materials
belonging to the whole community, emending by a dozen or sixteen lines
the inherited plot. Greek myths, the fairy tales and *novelle* of the Eliza-
bethans, the Christian body of legend available to Dante are examples of
such material. (In our world a traditionally restricted body of story is
found only in subart: the pulp Western, or the movie horse opera.) In
such situations, Archetype and "story" are synonymous; one remembers
that for Aristotle *mythos* was the word for "plot," and plot was, he in-
sisted, the most important element in tragedy. That Aristotle makes his
assertions on rationalistic grounds, with no apparent awareness of the
importance of the Archetype as such, does not matter; it does not even
matter whether the poet himself is aware of the implications of his material. As long as he works with such an inherited gift, he can provide the
ritual satisfaction necessary to great art without self-consciousness.

A Shakespeare, a Dante or a Sophocles, coming at a moment when
the Archetypes of a period are still understood as "given," and yet are
not considered too "sacred" for rendering through the individual Signature, possesses immense initial advantages over the poet who comes
earlier or later in the process. But the great poet is not simply the
mechanical result of such an occasion; he must be able to rise to it, to be
capable (like Shakespeare) at once of realizing utterly the archetypal
implications of his material and of formally embodying it in a lucid and
unmistakable Signature. But the balance is delicate and incapable of
being long maintained. The brief history of Athenian tragedy provides
the classic instance. After the successes of Sophocles come the attempts
of Euripides; and in Euripides one begins to feel the encounter of Signature and Archetype as a *conflict*—the poet and the collectivity have begun
to lose touch with each other and with their common pre-conscious
sources of value and behavior. Euripides seems to feel his inherited material as a burden, tucking it away in prologue and epilogue, so that he
can get on with his proper business—the imitation of particulars. The
poem begins to come apart; the acute critic finds it, however "tragic,"
sloppy, technically inept; and the audience raises the familiar cry of
"incomprehensible and blasphemous!" Even the poet himself begins to
distrust his own impulses, and writes, as Euripides did in his *Bacchae*,
a mythic criticism of his own sacrilege. The poetry of the struggle against
the Archetype is especially moving and poignant, but to prefer it to the
poetry of the moment of balance is to commit a gross lapse of taste.

After the Euripidean crisis, the Archetypes survive only in fallen
form: as inherited and scarcely understood structures (the seeds of the
genres which are structural Archetypes become structural platitudes); as
type characters, less complex than the masks that indicate them; as

"popular" stock plots. The "Happy Ending" arises as a kind of ersatz of the true reconciliation of society and individual in Sophoclean tragedy; and the audience which can no longer find essential reassurance in its poetry that the superego and the id can live at peace with each other content themselves with the demonstration that at least Jack has his Jill, despite the comic opposition of the Old Man. Still later, even the tension in Euripidean tragedy and New Comedy is lost, and the Signature comes to be disregarded completely; poetry becomes either completely "realistic," rendering the struggle between ego and superego in terms of the imitation of particulars; or it strives to be "pure" in the contemporary sense—that is, to make the Signature its sole subject as well as its means.

Can the Archetype be redeemed after such a fall? There are various possibilities (short of the emergence of a new, ordered myth system): the writer can, like Graham Greene or Robert Penn Warren, capture for serious purposes—that is, rerender through complex and subtle Signatures—debased "popular" Archetypes: the thriller, the detective story; the Western or science fiction; or the poet can ironically manipulate the shreds and patches of outlived mythologies, fragments shored against our ruins. Eliot, Joyce, Ezra Pound and Thomas Mann have all made attempts of the latter sort, writing finally not archetypal poetry but poetry *about* Archetypes, in which plot (anciently, *mythos* itself) founders under the burden of overt explication or disappears completely. Or the poet can, like Blake or Yeats or Hart Crane, invent a private myth system of his own. Neither of the last two expedients can reach the popular audience, which prefers its Archetypes rendered without self-consciousness of so intrusive a sort.

A final way back into the world of the Archetypes, available even in our atomized culture, is an extension of the way instinctively sought by the Romantics, down through the personality of the poet, past his particular foibles and eccentricities, to his unconscious core, where he becomes one with us all in the presence of our ancient Gods, the protagonists of fables we think we no longer believe. In fantasy and terror, we can return to our common source. It is a process to delight a Hegelian, the triple swing from a naïve communal to a personal to a sophisticated communal.

We must be aware of the differences between the thesis and the synthesis in our series. What cannot be re-created as Plot is reborn as Character—ultimately the character of the poet (what else is available to him?), whether directly or in projection. In the Mask of his life and the manifold masks of his work, the poet expresses for a whole society the ritual meaning of its inarticulate selves; the artist goes forth not to "re-create the conscience of his race," but to redeem its unconscious. We cannot get back into the primal Garden of the unfallen Archetypes, but we can yield ourselves to the dreams and images that mean paradise regained. For the critic, who cannot only yield but must also *understand,* there are available new methods of exploration. To understand the Archetypes of Athenian drama, he needs (above and beyond semantics) anthropology; to understand those of recent poetry, he needs (beyond "close analysis") depth analysis, as defined by Freud and, particularly, by Jung.

The biographical approach, tempered by such findings, is just now coming into its own. We are achieving new ways of connecting (or, more precisely, of understanding a connection which has always existed) the Poet and the poem, the lived and the made, the Signature and the Archetype. It is in the focus of the poetic personality that *Dichtung und Wahrheit* become one; and it is incumbent upon us, without surrendering our right to make useful distinctions, to seize the principle of that unity. "Only connect!"

The Nature of Symbolic Language

ERICH FROMM

Let us assume you want to tell someone the difference between the taste of white wine and red wine. This may seem quite simple to you. *You* know the difference very well; why should it not be easy to explain it to someone else? Yet you find the greatest difficulty putting this taste difference into words. And probably you will end up by saying, "Now look here, I can't explain it to you. Just drink red wine and then white wine, and you will know what the difference is." You have no difficulty in finding words to explain the most complicated machine, and yet words seem to be futile to describe a simple taste experience.

Are we not confronted with the same difficulty when we try to explain a feeling experience? Let us take a mood in which you feel lost, deserted, where the world looks gray, a little frightening though not really dangerous. You want to describe this mood to a friend, but again you find yourself groping for words and eventually feel that nothing you have said is an adequate explanation of the many nuances of the mood. The following night you have a dream. You see yourself in the outskirts of a city just before dawn, the streets are empty except for a milk wagon, the houses look poor, the surroundings are unfamiliar, you have no means of accustomed transportation to places familiar to you and where you feel you belong. When you wake up and remember the dream, it occurs to you that the feeling you had in that dream was exactly the feeling of lostness and grayness you tried to describe to your friend the day before. It is just one picture, whose visualization took less than a second. And yet this picture is a more vivid and precise description than you could have given by talking *about* it at length. The picture you see in the dream is a *symbol* of something you felt.

What is a symbol? A symbol is often defined as "something that stands for something else." This definition seems rather disappointing. It becomes more interesting, however, if we concern ourselves with those symbols which are sensory expressions of seeing, hearing, smelling, touching, standing for a "something else" which is an inner experience, a feeling or thought. A symbol of this kind is something outside ourselves; that which it symbolizes is something inside ourselves. Symbolic language is language in which we express inner experience as if it were a sensory experience, as if it were something we were doing or something that was done to us in the world of things. Symbolic language is language in which the world outside is a symbol of the world inside, a symbol for our souls and our minds.

If we define a symbol as "something which stands for something else," the crucial question is: *What is the specific connection between the symbol and that which it symbolizes?*

In answer to this question we can differentiate between three kinds of symbols: the *conventional,* the *accidental* and the *universal* symbol. As will become apparent presently, only the latter two kinds of symbols express inner experiences as if they were sensory experiences, and only they have the elements of symbolic language.

The *conventional* symbol is the best known of the three, since we employ it in everyday language. If we see the word "table" or hear the sound "table," the letters T-A-B-L-E stand for something else. They stand for the thing table that we see, touch and use. What is the connection between the *word* "table" and the *thing* "table"? Is there any inherent relationship between them? Obviously not. The thing table has nothing to do with the sound table, and the only reason the word symbolizes the thing is the convention of calling this particular thing by a particular name. We learn this connection as children by the repeated experience of hearing the word in reference to the thing until a lasting association is formed so that we don't have to think to find the right word.

There are some words, however, where the association is not only conventional. When we say "phooey," for instance, we make with our lips a movement of dispelling the air quickly. It is an expression of disgust in which our mouths participate. By this quick expulsion of air we imitate and thus express our intention to expel something, to get it out of our system. In this case, as in some others, the symbol has an inherent connection with the feeling it symbolizes. But even if we assume that originally many or even all words had their origins in some such inherent

connection between symbol and the symbolized, most words no longer
have this meaning for us when we learn a language.

Words are not the only illustration for conventional symbols, although
they are the most frequent and best-known ones. Pictures also can be conventional symbols. A flag, for instance, may stand for a specific country,
and yet there is no connection between the specific colors and the country
for which they stand. They have been accepted as denoting that particular country, and we translate the visual impression of the flag into
the concept of that country, again on conventional grounds. Some pic-
torial symbols are not entirely conventional; for example, the cross. The
cross can be merely a conventional symbol of the Christian church and in
that respect no different from a flag. But the specific content of the cross
referring to Jesus' death or, beyond that, to the interpenetration of the
material and spiritual planes, puts the connection between the symbol
and what it symbolizes beyond the level of mere conventional symbols.

The very opposite to the conventional symbol is the *accidental* symbol, although they have one thing in common: there is no intrinsic relationship between the symbol and that which it symbolizes. Let us assume
that someone has had a saddening experience in a certain city; when he
hears the name of that city, he will easily connect the name with a mood
of sadness, just as he would connect it with a mood of joy had his experience been a happy one. Quite obviously there is nothing in the nature of
the city that is either sad or joyful. It is the individual experience connected with the city that makes it a symbol of a mood.

The same reaction could occur in connection with a house, a street,
a certain dress, certain scenery, or anything once connected with a
specific mood. We might find ourselves dreaming that we are in a certain
city. In fact, there may be no particular mood connected with it in the
dream; all we see is a street or even simply the name of the city. We ask
ourselves why we happened to think of that city in our sleep and may
discover that we had fallen asleep in a mood similar to the one symbolized
by the city. The picture in the dream represents this mood, the city
"stands for" the mood once experienced in it. Here the connection between the symbol and the experience symbolized is entirely accidental.

In contrast to the conventional symbol, the accidental symbol cannot
be shared by anyone else except as we relate the events connected with
the symbol. For this reason accidental symbols are rarely used in myths,
fairy tales, or works of art written in symbolic language because they are
not communicable unless the writer adds a lengthy comment to each symbol he uses. In dreams, however, accidental symbols are frequent, and
later in this book I shall explain the method of understanding them.

The *universal* symbol is one in which there is an intrinsic relationship
between the symbol and that which it represents. We have already given
one example, that of the outskirts of the city. The sensory experience of a

deserted, strange, poor environment has indeed a significant relationship to a mood of lostness and anxiety. True enough, if we have never been in the outskirts of a city we could not use that symbol, just as the word "table" would be meaningless had we never seen a table. This symbol is meaningful only to city dwellers and would be meaningless to people living in cultures that have no big cities. Many other universal symbols, however, are rooted in the experience of every human being. Take, for instance, the symbol of fire. We are fascinated by certain qualities of fire in a fireplace. First of all, by its aliveness. It changes continuously, it moves all the time, and yet there is a constancy in it. It remains the same without being the same. It gives the impression of power, of energy, of grace and lightness. It is as if it were dancing and had an inexhaustible source of energy. When we use fire as a symbol, we describe the inner experience characterized by the same elements which we notice in the sensory experience of fire; the mood of energy, lightness, movement, grace, gaiety—sometimes one, sometimes another of these elements being predominant in the feeling.

Similar in some ways and different in others is the symbol of water— of the ocean or of the stream. Here, too, we find the blending of change and permanence, of constant movement and yet of permanence. We also feel the quality of aliveness, continuity and energy. But there is a difference; where fire is adventurous, quick, exciting, water is quiet, slow and steady. Fire has an element of surprise; water an element of predictability. Water symbolizes the mood of aliveness, too, but one which is "heavier," "slower," and more comforting than exciting.

That a phenomenon of the physical world can be the adequate expression of an inner experience, that the world of things can be a symbol of the world of the mind, is not surprising. We all know that our bodies express our minds. Blood rushes to our heads when we are furious, it rushes away from them when we are afraid; our hearts beat more quickly when we are angry, and the whole body has a different tonus if we are happy from the one it has when we are sad. We express our moods by our facial expressions and our attitudes and feelings by movements and gestures so precise that others recognize them more accurately from our gestures than from our words. Indeed, the body is a symbol—and not an allegory—of the mind. Deeply and genuinely felt emotion, and even genuinely felt thought, is expressed in our whole organism. In the case of the universal symbol, we find the same connection between mental and physical experience. Certain physical phenomena suggest by their very nature certain emotional and mental experiences, and we express emotional experiences in the language of physical experiences, that is to say, symbolically.

The universal symbol is the only one in which the relationship between the symbol and that which is symbolized is not coincidental but intrinsic. It is rooted in the experience of the affinity between an emotion or thought, on the one hand, and a sensory experience, on the other. It can be called universal because it is shared by all men, in contrast not only to the accidental symbol, which is by its very nature entirely personal, but also to the conventional symbol, which is restricted to a group of people sharing the same convention. The universal symbol is rooted in the properties of our body, our senses, and our mind, which are common to all men and, therefore, not restricted to individuals or to specific groups. Indeed, the language of the universal symbol is the one common tongue developed by the human race, a language which it forgot before it succeeded in developing a universal conventional language.

There is no need to speak of a racial inheritance in order to explain the universal character of symbols. Every human being who shares the essential features of bodily and mental equipment with the rest of mankind is capable of speaking and understanding the symbolic language that is based upon these common properties. Just as we do not need to learn to cry when we are sad or to get red in the face when we are angry, and just as these reactions are not restricted to any particular race or group of people, symbolic language does not have to be learned and is not restricted to any segment of the human race. Evidence for this is to be found in the fact that symbolic language as it is employed in myths and dreams is found in all cultures, in so-called primitive as well as such highly developed cultures as Egypt and Greece. Furthermore, the symbols used in these various cultures are strikingly similar since they all go back to the basic sensory as well as emotional experiences shared by men of all cultures. Added evidence is to be found in recent experiments in which people who had no knowledge of the theory of dream interpretation were able, under hypnosis, to interpret the symbolism of their dreams without any difficulty. After emerging from the hypnotic state and being asked to interpret the same dreams, they were puzzled and said, "Well, there is no meaning to them—it is just nonsense."

The foregoing statement needs qualification, however. Some symbols differ in meaning according to the difference in their realistic significance in various cultures. For instance, the function and consequently the meaning of the sun is different in northern countries and in tropical countries. In northern countries, where water is plentiful, all growth depends on sufficient sunshine. The sun is the warm, life-giving, protecting, loving, power. In the Near East, where the heat of the sun is much more powerful, the sun is a dangerous and even threatening power from which man must protect himself, while water is felt to be the source of all life and the main condition for growth. We may speak of dialects of universal symbolic language, which are determined by those differences in natural conditions which cause certain symbols to have a different meaning in different regions of the earth.

Quite different from these "symbolic dialects" is the fact that many symbols have more than one meaning in accordance with different kinds of experiences which can be connected with one and the same natural phenomenon. Let us take up the symbol of fire again. If we watch fire in the fireplace, which is a source of pleasure and comfort, it is expressive of a mood of aliveness, warmth, and pleasure. But if we see a building or forest on fire, it conveys to us an experience of threat or terror, of the powerlessness of man against the elements of nature. Fire, then, can be the symbolic representation of inner aliveness and happiness as well as of fear, powerlessness, or of one's own destructive tendencies. The same holds true of the symbol water. Water can be a most destructive force when it is whipped up by a storm or when a swollen river floods its banks. Therefore, it can be the symbolic expression of horror and chaos as well as of comfort and peace.

Another illustration of the same principle is a symbol of a valley. The valley enclosed between mountains can arouse in us the feeling of security and comfort, of protection against all dangers from the outside. But the protecting mountains can also mean isolating walls which do not permit us to get out of the valley and thus the valley can become a symbol of imprisonment. The particular meaning of the symbol in any given place can only be determined from the whole context in which the symbol appears, and in terms of the predominant experiences of the person using the symbol.

Family and Religion

WILLIAM J. GOODE

Patently the psychoanalytic theory of religion is not universally correct which contends the religious structure is simply a projection of the parent-child relationship. Nevertheless, it is true that the relationship between man and the gods, spirits, or natural forces which he conceives to be sacred, is a social one. This fact is particularly obvious where the gods are conceived in symbolically familial terms such as those expounded by psychoanalysts, but it is true even in religious systems in which this is not the case.

Two facts are evidently correlated here. One is the social character of the religious forces, and the other is the fact of socialization within a family or kinship structure. The assumption of communication between social creatures, whether men or gods, the acceptance of some authority, indeed, the learning of all social behavior, occur within such a structure. That this learning primarily involves social objects is to be expected, even when those objects are sacred. The question of priority need not concern us here.

The main social function of the family, whatever its structure in a given society, is a composite one embracing several aspects of *creating new members of the society:* the reproduction, maintenance, status ascription, and socialization of the child. This also includes the old age and burial of a member of the society, the completion of the cycle. Like the society of which it is a part, the family achieves its results by enlisting the energies of its members, giving them security, affection, sexual gratification, etc.

These functions taken together require a structure which is not to be found in any other institution. It must be a *biological* grouping, since at least two of the participants are linked sexually; and some kind of biological relationship, real or assumed, exists between its members. However, this does not alone define the familial relationships or structure. In addition, the pattern must contain *economic* relationships, since the feeding and general care of the new members requires it, just as does the continued support of the adults. For the *ascription of status*, the members of the family must have a similar status, thus allowing considerable determination of such status by the mere fact of birth in a particular family. Furthermore, this pattern must be one of *long duration*, for the period of socialization in man is long, as is the period of dependence. Even though the adulthood and marriage of the children partly loosen the links between the participants in the structure, this period of common life, with its mutual habituation, gratifications, and conflicts, is nevertheless fundamental in the formation of the individual personality, as well as in the sentimental cohesion of all the familial members.

The chief points of relationship between this familial structure and religious activity are those of *status* and *sanctions*. The ramifications of status are of course many, involving such matters as birth, status ascription a well as the achievement of status, rites of passage and initiation, definition of various kinship positions, legitimacy, and certain aspects of marriage. Sanctions involve the socialization of the child, with reference to both secular and nonsecular matters, ritual and secular conformity and punishment, and so on. Or, in reciprocal terms: It is within the kin group that religious socialization occurs, and these learned sanctions in turn support much of the familial structure.

"An individual life, whatever the type of society, consists in passing successively from one age to another, and from one occupation to another." As a general rule, the most significant of such acts of succession or passage are set off by ritual and ceremony. The most important are usually birth, adulthood, marriage, and death. Such birth rituals seem to have as their chief function the announcement to the community of the existence of a child, and an acceptance of that announcement, as well as the familial acceptance of a delegated responsibility, the sustenance and socialization of the child. All societies seem to take note of birth in some manner. The passage of the individual *after* birth reflects the fundamental system of stratification, of status and role. A morally accepted and sanctioned pattern of action is to apply to each position in any society. The person who makes the passage is officially empowered by the ritual to fit the pattern of action, and the society *gives notice that it will expect that pattern.* It is a part of the common value system that just those statuses should exist, and that this person should occupy them or it. This becomes particularly relevant to the familial system, since any growth in the individual, i.e., change in a determinate direction, must mean a change in his familial relationships. In fact, these individual status changes reflect most immediately on the family, not the society. Any puberty or other passage ceremonies will explicitly change the status of the individual in the society at large, but the locus of primary experience and orientation for that individual will be his family or kin group. The social adjustments called for in the new status will mostly be made by the family, not the society, unless the individual is the only one of his class (e.g., a monarch). The society itself is little affected as a whole, since the process merely allows one generation to replace another. The structure, the systematized set of social relationships or elements, may for the most part stay the same. These remarks also hold in a broad way for the passage into puberty and adulthood, or marriage. Being social events, however, they receive some attention in the form of ritual. Since adulthood or puberty is so intrinsically related with sexual maturity and potential reproduction, the ritual is likely to reflect that fact by having reference in symbolic or explicit ways to the sexual organs and their use.

It must be remembered that it is *not the mere licensing of a sexual union* which makes marriage important, since in many societies a rather wide sexual freedom is allowed outside of marriage. Undoubtedly of more importance is the entrance of a new member into one familial or kin group, or the leaving of an old member. Yet even such changes are less important than the actual *creation of a complete family* which is implied by the union. This is suggested by the facts on illegitimacy and incest. It may now be taken as a truism that whatever the ideas of a given tribe about premarital sexual unions, even those lasting for a long time, no society allows indiscriminate *childbearing.* Malinowski states the principle in terms of fatherhood, by pointing out that ". . . no child can be brought into the world without a man, and one man at that, assuming the role of sociological father, i.e., guardian and protector, the male link between the child and the rest of the community." Malinowski might actually have gone further, by pointing out that a sociological mother is required as well as a sociological father. It is in these terms, then, that rituals relating to marriage have their significance, giving a stamp of approval to children and kinship beginnings. In a sense, that is, the society is validating and accepting future parents. Once accepted, the child must be socialized. This is a long process, of both an informal and a formal character. Skills must be acquired, and many value patterns must form the structure of his personality. Religious instruction is likely to be part of the child's daily life. He will be forbidden to touch sacred objects. He may be threatened by godly wrath if his actions are not proper. At major stages in his growth process, the transition may be marked by rituals, and at such rituals he will be given moral injunctions, emphasized by the sacred situation. He will earn the tabus of kinship, as well as those of religion, and come to accept their reciprocal supports unthinkingly. By the time he is an adult, they will be so much a part of his action pattern that passing them on to his children in turn will not need to be a rationally planned, "educative" process. His children will learn them from everything he does.

The exit of a human being from the tribe and his entrance into another state or world are the occasion of ritual, but it usually waits upon the definitive fact of death: complete lack of expected social response. This is a social definition of a physiological state. This type of social definition is common enough. However, it is understandable that death should have the social immediacy and finality of a "stubborn fact" far more than birth or puberty. Though in the case of birth there must be a recognition of something having entered this world, this need not be, and sometimes is not, considered human. The distinction is simple enough, since being human is a product of the socialization—"humanizing"—process, and before the child has formed a part of "humanity" it is possible to ignore its birth as having no social significance as yet. Although puberty rites presumably recognize a physiological fact, available evidence is clear that they do not necessarily occur contemporaneously with either reproductional or sexual maturity, coming much later or much earlier than either. But to the extent that the activities of the group are dependent on social interaction, death is inevitably and immediately noticed. The new-born child is first of all a *thing*, with few if any social expectations to meet at once. The man who has just died forces the group to recognize his new state, because there are such expectations, and he fails to meet them.

This does not mean, of course, that the dead individual immediately disappears from his family or society. Aside from the living memory of the dead, they often remain as part of the supernatural forces, even in societies which are not cases of "ancestor worship." In fact, practically every primitive religious system imputes both power and interest to the dead. It is significant that in spite of the wide disparity between the societies treated in this investigation, all of them consider the dead to figure largely among the sacred forces. This suggests two important questions. One of them is, Why is there a sacred funeral ritual? The other is possibly related to it, whence this power of the dead in these religions?

Death is rarely impersonal. It is a brute fact, and is inevitably recognized, but for clear reasons it is not a physiological fact alone. This is true, whether one thinks of the cause of death, the realm to which the dead go, or familial and group bereavement. As many others have pointed out, whatever our scientific preconceptions, we do not tend to think of the death of a loved one in terms of purely physical causation. The question stemming from our feelings is *Why?* not *How?* That is, we seek an anthroposocial explanation, one couched in terms of will and motivation, not physical process alone. Primary group interaction, and this is even more intensely true for close familial interaction, depends on a tight interweaving of personalities, sentiments, attitudes, cooperation, and ideas. One's whole personality is involved in the relationship. When one member leaves, the gap cannot be filled by another in quite the same fashion. All the daily expectations of action, sentiment, and thought are frustrated, and the emotional props based on the lost one are gone.

Two inferences may be drawn from this. One is that to prevent familial or group disorganization from becoming too widespread, there must be some techniques for bridging the emotional gap. This is perhaps the most important implicit function of the mortuary ritual. The other is that even when the dead are not themselves sacred, they are nevertheless related to the supernatural world. This is abundantly shown in the symbolism of the ritual.

The society enjoins particular types of mourning and funeral ritual. This means that at the moment of greatest preoccupation with one's own sorrow, the group forces those most concerned, the family, to take part in something which points beyond sorrow itself to other interests, social and sacred. The solidarity of the family has been temporarily broken by the removal of an integral part, and the collective mourning and ritual serve to realign the unity in an emotionally satisfactory and socially approved manner. Communal activity is required at a time when the emotional shock might otherwise lead to complete lack of action. Mourning and ritual adjust the individual to the reality of death. That is, there is a forced catharsis and a deviation of interest from sentiment to activity.

Certainly part of the reference of the dead to the sacred forces arises from the division of the universe into the day-to-day profane, impersonal phenomena on the one hand, and the sacred, moral, and supernatural on the other, wherein the dead clearly do not fall into the first category. Naturally, they are not necessarily identified with the sacred completely, but such a division leaves them more closely related to that supernatural system of forces than to the impersonal, prosaic ones. Let us look at these connections.

First of all, there is one of *common moral interest*. Both the gods or spiritual forces and the dead have considerable common cause in maintaining the traditional morals, particularly those of the familial group. This is not so completely true of the living members, who may also be motivated in this direction to the extent that they are adequately socialized, but whose own physiological, intensely individual, or immediate drives precipitate conflict with those *mores* from time to time. The dead and the spiritual forces may have passions of their own, if they are conceived anthropomorphically, but it is the passions and the moral actions *of the living* which they are interested in directing. Morality being, in all cultures, something which one is somewhat more interested in forcing on others than on oneself, there is again a break between the gods and the dead on the one hand, and the living on the other. Besides this link between the dead and the sacred, there is another in their common motivation *toward helping the group*. No society believes in spiritual powers which are even for the most part inimical. Although these forces are sometimes whimsical, mischievous, or even vengeful (for contravention of the *mores*), in the main their explicit task consists in helping the society with regard to food, fecundity, and health, as well as in more purely spiritual affairs.

A further relationship between the dead, the living and the sacredness of the mortuary ritual may be seen in the fact that the individual *comes from the dead*. This is true, of course, for any society, with or without an ancestral cult. More to home, the individual comes from the ancestors of the immediate family, for they are his ancestors, usually physiologically and always sociologically. Thus there is always a link with the dead, even the unknown dead. This is true for the dead whom one did know, for the links are based on both kinship and *Gemeinschaft*. Moreover, *everyone returns ultimately to the dead*. This does not exhaust, however, the possibilities of relations or occasions of respect, especially when clan solidarity insists so much on the unity of the living and the dead. *It is the dead who are great*. This is true from the rational point of view that numerically there will always be a larger number of great men in the past than at any given time in the present. But, more important, it is the judgment of the only members in the tribe who have seen both the old and the new, who have a rational advantage in maintaining this point of view, and who usually are in a dominant enough position to impose it on the rest: the old, generally the old men. Furthermore, the *dead are the personnel of the sacred myths, legends, and sacred beliefs*. In any society, the past great are respected, by definition, and to the extent that the society singles out members of past generations to whom tribute is to be paid. When this body of legend and sacred myths and beliefs is symbolized in a sacred well, as in the case of the Murngin, the possible implications are many and clear. All that is great and glorious in the past of the family or clan is collected there, and it then must follow that all of value in the present had to issue from that source. Whether symbolized as a sacred well or not, any society will at least implicitly recognize this circular process, in which all come from the ancestors and all become ancestors in turn. These general points may perhaps be clarified further by treating these societies in somewhat greater detail.

The Sacred Marriage

SIR JAMES G. FRAZER

THE SYMBOLIC MARRIAGE OF TREES

Often the marriage of the spirit of vegetation in spring, though not directly represented, is implied by naming the human representative of the spirit, "the Bride," and dressing her in wedding attire. Thus in some villages of Altmark at Whitsuntide, while the boys go about carrying a May-tree or leading a boy enveloped in leaves and flowers, the girls lead about the May Bride, a girl dressed as a bride with a great nosegay in her hair. They go from house to house, the May Bride singing a song in which she asks for a present, and tells the inmates of each house that if they give her something they will themselves have something the whole year through; but if they give her nothing they will themselves have nothing. In some parts of Westphalia two girls lead a flower-crowned girl called the Whitsuntide Bride from door to door, singing a song in which they ask for eggs. At Waggum in Brunswick, when service is over on Whitsunday, the village girls assemble, dressed in white or bright colours, decked with flowers, and wearing chaplets of spring flowers in their hair. One of them represents the May Bride, and carries a crown of flowers on a staff as a sign of her dignity. As usual the children go about from cottage to cottage singing and begging for eggs, sausages, cakes, or money. In Bresse in the month of May a girl called *la Mariée* is tricked out with ribbons and nosegays and is led about by a gallant. She is preceded by a lad carrying a green May-tree, and appropriate verses are sung.

SEX AND VEGETATION

When our rude forefathers staged their periodic marriages of the Kings and Queens of the May, or of the Whitsun Bridegrooms and Brides, they were doing something far more important than merely putting on a pastoral play for the amusement of a rustic audience. They were performing a serious magical rite, designed to make the woods grow green, the fresh grass sprout, the corn shoot, and the flowers blow. And it is natural to suppose that the more closely the mock marriage of the leaf-clad mummers aped the real marriage of the woodland sprites, the more effective was the rite believed to be. Accordingly we may assume with a high degree of probability that the profligacy which notoriously attended these ceremonies was at one time not an accidental excess but an essential part of the rites, and that in the opinion of those who performed them the marriage of trees and plants could not be fertile *without* the real union of the human sexes.

For four days before they committed the seed to the earth the Pipiles of Central America kept apart from their wives "in order that on the night before planting they might indulge their passions to the fullest extent; certain persons are even said to have been appointed to perform the sexual act at the very moment when the first seeds were deposited in the ground." The use of their wives at that time was indeed enjoined upon the people by the priests as a religious duty, in default of which it was not lawful to sow the seed. In the month of December, when the alligator pears begin to ripen, the Indians of Peru used to hold a festival called *Acatay mita* in order to make the fruit grow mellow. The festival lasted five days and nights, and was preceded by a fast of five days during which they ate neither salt nor pepper and refrained from their wives. At the festival men and boys assembled stark naked in an open space among the orchards, and ran from there to a distant hill. Any woman whom they overtook on the way they violated. In some parts of Java, at the season when the bloom will soon be on the rice, the husbandman and his wife visit their fields by night and there engage in sexual intercourse for the purpose of promoting the growth of the crop. Again, among the Fan or Pangwe of West Africa, the night before a man sows earth-nuts he has intercourse with his wife for the purpose of promoting the growth of the earth-nuts, which he will plant next morning.

The same means which are thus adopted to stimulate the growth of the crops are naturally employed to ensure the fruitfulness of trees. The work known as *The Agriculture of the Nabataeans* contained apparently a direction that the grafting of a tree upon another tree of a different sort should be done by a damsel, who at the very moment of inserting the graft in the bough should herself be subjected to treatment which can only be regarded as a direct copy of the operation she was performing on the tree. Among the Bagoda of Central Africa, a barren wife is generally sent away because she is supposed to prevent her husband's garden from bearing fruit. A couple who have given proof of extraordinary fertility by becoming the parents of twins are believed to be endowed with a corresponding power of increasing the fruitfulness of the plantain-trees, which furnish them with their staple food. Some little time after the birth of the twins a ceremony is performed, the object of which clearly is to transmit the reproductive virtue of the parents to the plantains. The mother lies down on her back in the thick grass near the house and places a flower of the plantain between her legs; then her husband comes and knocks the flower away with his genital member. Further, the parents go through the country, performing dances in the gardens of favoured friends, apparently for the purpose of causing the plantain-trees to bear fruit more abundantly.

In various parts of Europe customs have prevailed both at spring and harvest which are clearly based on the same crude notion that the relation of the human sexes to each other can be so used as to quicken the growth of plants. For example, in the Ukraine on St. George's Day (the twenty-third of April) the priest in his robes, attended by his acolytes, goes out to the fields of the village, where the crops are beginning to shew green above the ground, and blesses them. After that the young married people lie down in couples on the sown fields and roll several times over on them, in the belief that this will promote the growth of the crops. In some parts of Russia the priest himself is rolled by women over the sprouting crop, and that without regard to the mud and holes which he may encounter in his beneficent progress. In England it seems to have been customary for young couples to roll down a slope together on May Day. In some parts of Germany at harvest the men and women who have reaped the corn roll together in the field.

Again, the sympathetic relation supposed to exist between the commerce of the sexes and the fertility of the earth manifests itself in the belief that illicit love tends, directly or indirectly, to mar that fertility and to blight the crops. The Bahaus or Kayans, a tribe in the interior of Borneo, believe that adultery is punished by the spirits, who visit the whole tribe with failure of the crops and other misfortunes. Hence in order to avert these calamities from the innocent members of the tribe, the two culprits, with all their possessions, are put in quarantine on a gravel bank in the middle of the river; then in order thoroughly to disinfect them, pigs and fowls are killed, and with the blood priestesses smear the property of the guilty pair. Finally the two are set on a raft, with sixteen eggs, and allowed to drift down the stream. They may save themselves by swimming ashore, but this is perhaps a mitigation of an older sentence of death by drowning. Young people shower long grass-stalks, which stand for spears, at the shamefaced and dripping couple.

The Blu-u Kayans of the same region similarly imagine that an intrigue between an unmarried pair is punished by the spirits with failure of the harvest, of the fishing, and of the hunt. Hence the delinquents have to appease the wrath of the spirits by sacrificing a pig and some rice. When it rains in torrents, the Galelareese of Halmahera say that brother and sister, or father and daughter, or in short some near relations are having illicit relations with each other, and that every human being must be informed of it, for then only will the rain cease to descend.

In some parts of Africa, also, it is believed that breaches of sexual morality disturb the course of nature, particularly by blighting the fruits of the earth. Thus the Negroes of Loango suppose that the intercourse of a man with an immature girl is punished by God with drought and consequent famine, until the culprits atone for their sin by dancing naked before the king and an assembly of the people, who throw hot gravel and bits of glass at the pair. Similar notions of the disastrous effects of sexual crimes may be detected among some of the civilised races of antiquity, who seem not to have limited the supposed sterilising influence of such offences to the fruits of the earth, but to have extended it also to women and cattle. Amongst the Bavili of Loango, it is believed that if a man breaks the marriage law by marrying a woman of his mother's clan, God will in like manner punish the crime by withholding the rains in their due season. So too among the Hebrews we read how Job, passionately protesting his innocence before God, declares that he is no adulterer; "For that," says he, "were an heinous crime; yea, it were an iniquity to be punished by the judges: for it is a fire that consumeth unto Destruction, and would root out all mine increase." In this passage the Hebrew word translated "increase" commonly means "the produce of the earth"; and if we give the word its usual sense here, then Job affirms adultery to be destructive of the fruits of the ground, which is just what many savages still believe. Again, in Leviticus, after a list of sexual crimes, we read: "Defile not ye yourselves in any of these things: for in all these the nations are defiled which I cast out from before you: and the land is defiled: therefore I do visit the iniquity thereof upon it, and the land vomiteth out her inhabitants." This passage appears to imply that the land itself was somehow physically tainted by sexual transgressions so that it could no longer support the inhabitants.

It would seem that the ancient Greeks and Romans entertained similar notions. According to Sophocles the land of Thebes suffered from blight, from pestilence, and from the sterility both of women and of cattle under the reign of Oedipus, who had unwittingly slain his father and wedded his mother. The Celts of ancient Ireland similarly believed that incest blighted the fruits of the earth. According to legend Munster was afflicted in the third century of our era with a failure of the crops and other misfortunes. When the nobles enquired into the matter, they were told that these calamities were the result of an incest which the king had committed with his sister.

If we ask why it is that similar beliefs should logically lead, among different peoples, to such opposite modes of conduct as strict chastity and more or less open debauchery, the reason, as it presents itself to the primitive mind, is perhaps not very far to seek. If rude man identifies himself, in a manner, with nature; if he fails to distinguish the impulses and processes in himself from the methods which nature adopts to ensure the reproduction of plants and animals, he may leap to one of two conclusions. Either he may infer that by yielding to his appetites he will thereby assist in the multiplication of plants and animals or he may imagine that the vigour which he refuses to expend in reproducing his own kind will form as it were a store of energy whereby other creatures, whether vegetable or animal, will somehow benefit in propagating their species. Thus from the same crude philosophy, the same primitive notions of nature and life, the savage may derive by different channels a rule either of profligacy or of asceticism.

THE DIVINE NUPTIALS

Magical dramas designed to stimulate the growth of plants by the real or mock marriage of men and women who masquerade as spirits of vegetation have played a great part in the popular festivals of Europe, and based as they are on a very crude conception of natural law, it is clear that they must have been handed down from a remote antiquity. We shall hardly, therefore, err in assuming that they date from a time when the forefathers of the civilised nations of Europe were still barbarians. But if these old spells and enchantments for the growth of leaves and blossoms, of grass and flowers and fruit, have lingered down to our own time in the shape of pastoral plays and popular merry-makings, is it not reasonable to suppose that they survived in less attenuated forms some two thousand years ago among the civilised peoples of antiquity? Or, to put it otherwise, is it not likely that in certain festivals of the ancients we may be able to detect the equivalents of our May Day, Whitsuntide, and Midsummer celebrations, with this difference, that in those days the ceremonies had not yet dwindled into mere shows and pageants, but were still religious or magical rites, in which the actors consciously supported the high parts of gods and goddesses? May not the priest who bore the title of King of the Wood at Nemi and his mate the goddess of the grove have been serious counterparts of the merry mummers who play the King and Queen of May, the Whitsuntide Bridegroom and Bride in modern Europe? and may not their union have been yearly celebrated in a *theogamy* or divine marriage? Such dramatic weddings of gods and goddesses, as we shall see presently, were carried out as solemn religious rites in many parts of the ancient world; hence there is no intrinsic improbability in the supposition that the sacred grove at Nemi may have been the scene of an annual ceremony of this sort. No ancient writer mentions that this was done in the grove at Nemi; but our knowledge of the Arician ritual is so scanty that the want of information on this head can hardly count as a fatal objection to the theory. That theory, in the absence of direct evidence, must necessarily be based on the analogy of similar customs practised elsewhere. Some modern examples of such customs, more or less degenerate, were described above. Here we shall consider their ancient counterparts.

At Babylon the imposing sanctuary of Bêl rose like a pyramid above the city in a series of eight towers or stories, planted one on the top of the other. On the highest tower, reached by an ascent which wound about all the rest, there stood a spacious temple, and in the temple a great bed, magnificently draped and cushioned, with a golden table beside it. In the temple no image was to be seen, and no human being passed the night there, save a single woman, whom, according to the priests, the god chose from among all the women of Babylon. They said that the deity himself came into the temple at night and slept in the great bed; and the woman, as a consort of the god, might have no intercourse with mortal man.

At Thebes in Egypt a woman slept in the temple of Ammon as the consort of the god and, like the human wife of Bêl at Babylon, she was said to have no commerce with a man. In Egyptian texts she is often mentioned as "the divine consort," and usually she was no less a personage than the Queen of Egypt herself. For, according to the Egyptians, their monarchs were actually begotten by the god Ammon, who assumed for the time being the form of the reigning King, and in that disguise had intercourse with the Queen. The divine procreation is carved and painted in great detail on the walls of two of the oldest temples in Egypt, those of Deir el Bahari and Luxor; and the inscriptions attached to the paintings leave no doubt as to the meaning of the scenes.

At Athens the god of the vine, Dionysus, was annually married to the Queen, and it appears that the consummation of the divine union, as well as the espousals, was enacted at the ceremony; but whether the part of the god was played by a man or an image we do not know. We learn from Aristotle that the ceremony took place, not at the sanctuary in the marshes, but in the old official residence of the King, known as the Cattle-stall, which stood near the Prytaneum or Town-hall on the northeastern slope of the Acropolis. Its object can hardly have been any other than that of ensurng the fertility of the vines and other fruit trees, of which Dionysus was the god. Thus both in form and in meaning the ceremony would answer to the nuptials of the King and Queen of May. Again, the story, dear to poets and artists, of the forsaken and sleeping

Ariadne, waked and wedded by Dionysus, resembles so closely the little drama acted by French peasants of the Alps on May Day, that, considering the character of Dionysus as a god of vegetation, we can hardly help regarding it as the reflection of a spring ceremony like the French one. The chief difference between the French and the Greek ceremonies appears to have been that in the former the sleeper was a forsaken bridegroom, in the latter a forsaken bride; and the group of stars in the sky, in which fancy saw Ariadne's wedding crown, may have been only a translation to heaven of the garland worn by the Greek girl who played the Queen of May.

The marriage of Zeus and Hera was acted at annual festivals in various parts of Greece, and it is at least a fair conjecture that Zeus and Hera at these festivals were the Greek equivalents of the Lord and Lady of the May. Homer's glowing picture of Zeus and Hera couched on fresh hyacinths and crocuses, like Milton's description of the dalliance of Zephyr with Aurora, "as he met her once a-Maying," was perhaps painted from the life.

The sacred marriage of Zeus and Hera had, as was natural, its counterpart among the northern kinsfolk of the Greeks. In Sweden every year a life-size image of Frey, the god of fertility, both animal and vegetable, was drawn about the country in a waggon attended by a beautiful girl who was called the god's wife. She acted also as his princess in the great temple at Upsala.

Thus the custom of marrying gods either to images or to human beings was widespread among the nations of antiquity. The ideas on which such a custom is based are too crude to allow us to doubt that the civilised Babylonians, Egyptians, and Greeks inherited it from their barbarous or savage forefathers. This presumption is strengthened when we find rites of a similar kind in vogue among the lower races. Thus, for example, we are told that once upon a time the Wotyaks of the Malmyz district in Russia were distressed by a series of bad harvests. They did not know what to do, but at last concluded that their powerful but mischievous god Keremet must be angry at being unmarried. So a deputation of elders visited the Wotyaks of Cura and came to an understanding with them on the subject. Then they returned home, laid in a large stock of brandy, and having made ready a gaily decked waggon and horses, they drove in procession with bells ringing, as they do when they are fetching home a bride, to the sacred grove at Cura. There they ate and drank merrily all night, and next morning they cut a square piece of turf in the grove and took it home with them. After this, though it fared well with the people of Malmyz, it fared ill with the people of Cura; for in Malmyz the bread was good, but in Cura it was bad. Hence the men of Cura who had consented to the marriage were blamed and roughly handled by their indignant fellow-villagers. "What they meant by this marriage ceremony," says the writer who reports it, "it is not easy to imagine. Perhaps, as Bechterew thinks, they meant to marry Keremet to the kindly and fruitful Mukyléin, the Earth-wife, in order that she might influence him for good." This carrying of turf, like a bridge, in a waggon from a sacred grove resembles the Plataean custom of carting an oak log as a bride from an ancient oak forest; and we have seen ground for thinking that the Plataean ceremony, like its Wotyak counterpart, was intended as a charm to secure fertility. When wells are dug in Bengal, a wooden image of a god is made and married to the goddess of water.

Often the bride destined for the god is not a log or a clod, but a living woman of flesh and blood. The Indians of a village in Peru have been known to marry a beautiful girl, about fourteen years of age, to a stone shaped like a human being, which they regarded as a god (*huaca*). All the villagers took part in the marriage ceremony, which lasted three days, and was attended with much revelry. The girl thereafter remained a virgin and sacrificed to the idol for the people. They shewed her the utmost reverence and deemed her divine. The Blackfoot Indians of North America used to worship the Sun as their chief god, and they held a festival every year in his honour. Four days before the new moon of August the tribe halted on its march, and all hunting was suspended. Bodies of mounted men were on duty day and night to carry out the orders of the high priest of the Sun. He enjoined the people to fast and to take vapour baths during the four days before the new moon. Moreover, with the help of his council, he chose the Vestal who was to represent the Moon and to be married to the Sun at the festival. She might be either a virgin or a woman who had had but one husband. Any girl or woman found to have discharged the sacred duties without fulfilling the prescribed conditions was put to death. On the third day of preparation, after the last purification had been observed, they built a round temple of the Sun. Posts were driven into the ground in a circle; these were connected with cross-pieces, and the whole was covered with leaves. In the middle stood the sacred pole, supporting the roof. A bundle of many small branches of sacred wood, wrapped in a splendid buffalo robe, crowned the summit of the temple. The entrance was on the east, and within the sanctuary stood an altar on which rested the head of a buffalo. Beside the altar was the place reserved for the Vestal. Here, on a bed prepared for her, she slept "the sleep of war," as it was called. Her other duties consisted in maintaining a sacred fire of fragrant herbs, in presenting a lighted pipe to her husband the Sun, and in telling the high priest the dream she dreamed during "the sleep of war." On learning it the priest had it proclaimed to the whole nation to the beat of drum. Every year about the middle of March, when the season for fishing with the drag-net began, the Algonquins and Hurons married their nets to two young girls, aged six or seven. At the wedding feast the net was placed between the two maidens, and was exhorted to take courage and catch many fish. The reason for choosing the brides so young was to make sure that they were virgins. The Oraons of Bengal worship the earth as a goddess, and annually celebrate her marriage with the Sun-god at the time when the *sāl*-tree is in blossom, the roles of bride and groom being played by the priest and his wife.

At the village of Bas Doda, in the Gurgaon district of North-Western India, a fair is held on the twenty-sixth of the month Chait and the two following days. We are told that formerly girls of the Dhinwar class used to be married to the god at these festivals, and that they always died soon afterwards. (Of late years the practice is said to have been discontinued.) Among the Ewe-speaking peoples of the Slave Coast in West Africa human wives of gods are very common. In Dahomey they swarm, and it has even been estimated that every fourth woman is devoted to the service of some deity. The chief business of these female votaries is prostitution. In every town there is at least one seminary where the handsomest girls, between ten and twelve years of age, are trained. They stay for three years, learning the chants and dances peculiar to the worship of the gods, and prostituting themselves to the priests and the inmates of the male seminaries. At the end of their noviciate they become public harlots. But no disgrace attaches to their profession, for it is believed that they are married to the god, and that their excesses are caused and directed by him. Strictly speaking, they should confine their favours to the male worshippers at the temple, but in practice they bestow them indiscriminately. Children born of such unions belong to the deity. As the wives of a god, these sacred women may not marry. But they are not bound to the service of the divinity for life. Some only bear his name and sacrifice to him on their birthdays.

It deserves to be remarked that the supernatural being to whom women are married is often a god or spirit of water. Thus Mukasa, the god of the Victoria Nyanza lake, who was propitiated by the Baganda every time they undertook a long voyage, had virgins provided for him to serve as his wives. Like the Vestals they were bound to chastity, but unlike the Vestals they seem to have been often unfaithful. The custom lasted until Mwanga was converted to Christianity. In Kengtung, one of the principal Shan states of Upper Burma, the spirit of the Nawng Tung lake is regarded as very powerful, and is propitiated with offerings in the eighth month (about July) of each year. A remarkable feature of the worship of this spirit consists in the dedication to him of four virgins in marriage. Custom requires that this should be done once in every three years. It was actually done by the late king or chief (Sawbwa), in 1893, but down to 1901 the rite had not been performed by his successor. When the Arabs conquered Egypt they learned that at the annual rise of the Nile the Egyptians were wont to deck a young virgin in gay ap-

parel and throw her into the river as a sacrifice, in order to obtain a
plentiful inundation. The Arab general abolished the barbarous custom. It is
said that under the Tang dynasty the Chinese used to marry a young
girl to the Yellow River once a year by drowning her in the water. For
this purpose the witches chose the fairest damsel they could find and
themselves superintended the fatal marriage. A usage of the same sort is
reported to have prevailed in the Maldive Islands before the conversion
of the inhabitants to Islam. The famous Arab traveller Ibn Batutah has
described the custom and the manner in which it came to an end. He was
assured by several trustworthy natives, whose names he gives, that when
the people of the islands were idolaters there appeared to them every
month an evil spirit among the jinn, who came from across the sea in the
likeness of a ship full of burning lamps. The wont of the inhabitants, as
soon as they perceived him, was to take a young virgin, and, having
adorned her, to lead her to a heathen temple that stood on the shore, with
a window looking out to sea. There they left the damsel for the night,
and when they came back in the morning they found her a maid no more,
and dead. Every month they drew lots, and he upon whom the lot fell
gave up his daughter to the jinnee of the sea.

Ibn Batutah's narrative of the demon lover and his mortal brides
closely resembles a well-known type of folk-tale, of which versions have
been found from Japan and Annam in the East to Senegambia, Scandinavia,
and Scotland in the West. The story varies in details from people to
people, but as commonly told it runs thus. A certain country is infested
by a many-headed serpent, dragon, or other monster, which would destroy
the whole people, if a human victim, generally a virgin, were not delivered
up to him periodically. Many victims have perished, and at last it has
fallen to the lot of the king's own daughter to be sacrificed. She is exposed
to the monster, but the hero of the tale, generally a young man of humble
birth, interposes in her behalf, slays the monster, and receives the hand of
the princess as his reward. In many of the tales the monster, who is sometimes described as a serpent, inhabits the water of a sea, a lake, or a fountain. In other versions he is a serpent or dragon who takes possession of
the springs of water, and only allows the water to flow or the people to
make use of it on condition of receiving a human victim.

It would probably be a mistake to dismiss all these tales as pure in-
ventions of the story-teller. Rather we may suppose that they reflect a real
custom of sacrificing girls or women to be the wives of water-spirits, who
are very often conceived as great serpents or dragons.

Now, besides the King of the Wood, an important figure in the grove
at Nemi was the water-nymph Egeria, who was worshipped by pregnant
women because she, like Diana, could grant them an easy delivery. From
this it seems fairly safe to conclude that, like many other springs, the

water of Egeria was credited with a power of facilitating conception as well as delivery. The votive offerings found on the spot, which clearly refer to the begetting of children, may possibly have been dedicated to Egeria rather than to Diana, or perhaps we should rather say that the water-nymph Egeria is only another form of the great nature-goddess Diana herself, the mistress of sounding rivers as well as of umbrageous woods, who had her home by the lake and her mirror in its calm waters, and whose Greek counterpart Artemis loved to haunt meres and springs. The identification of Egeria with Diana is confirmed by a statement of Plutarch that Egeria was one of the oak-nymphs whom the Romans believed to preside over every green oak-grove; for while Diana was a goddess of the woodlands in general she appears to have been intimately associated with oaks in particular, especially at her sacred grove of Nemi. Perhaps, then, Egeria was the fairy of a spring that flowed from the roots of a sacred oak. This would explain the more than mortal wisdom with which, according to tradition, Egeria inspired her royal husband or lover Numa. When we remember how very often in early society the King is held responsible for the fall of rain and the fruitfulness of the earth, it seems hardly rash to conjecture that in the legend of the nuptials of Numa and Egeria we have a reminiscence of a sacred marriage which the old Roman kings regularly contracted with a goddess of vegetation and water for the purpose of enabling him to discharge his divine or magical functions. In such a rite the part of the goddess might be played either by an image or a woman, and if by a woman, probably by the Queen. If there is any truth in this conjecture, we may suppose that the King and Queen of Rome impersonated the god and goddess at their marriage, exactly as the King and Queen of Egypt appear to have done.

The legend of Numa and Egeria points to a sacred grove rather than to a house as the scene of the nuptial union, celebrated annually as a charm to ensure the fertility not only of the earth but of man and beast. Now, according to some accounts, the scene of the marriage was no other than the sacred grove of Nemi, and on quite independent grounds we have been led to suppose that in that same grove the King of the Wood was wedded to Diana. The coincidence suggests that the legendary union of the Roman king with Egeria may have been a reflection or duplicate of the union of the King of the Wood with Egeria or her double Diana. This does not imply that the Roman kings ever served as Kings of the Wood in the Arician grove, but only that they may originally have been invested with a sacred character of the same general kind, and may have held office on similar terms.

Our knowledge of the Roman kingship is far too scanty to allow us to affirm any one of these propositions with confidence; but at least there are some scattered hints or indications of a similarity in all these respects between the priests of Nemi and the kings of Rome, or perhaps rather between their remote predecessors in the dark ages which preceded the dawn of legend.

In the first place, it would seem that the Roman king personated no less a deity than Jupiter himself. For down to imperial times victorious generals celebrating a triumph, and magistrates presiding at the games in the Circus, wore the costume of Jupiter, which was borrowed for the occasion from his great temple on the Capitol; and it has been held with a high degree of probability both by ancients and moderns that in so doing they copied the traditionary attire and insignia of the Roman kings. They rode a chariot drawn by four laurel-crowned horses through the city, where everyone else went on foot; they wore purple robes embroidered or spangled with gold; in the right hand they bore a branch of laurel and in the left hand an ivory sceptre topped with an eagle; a wreath of laurel crowned their brows; their face was reddened with vermilion; and over their head a slave held a heavy crown of massy gold fashioned in the likeness of oak leaves. In this attire the assimilation of the man to the god comes out above all in the eagle-topped sceptre, the oaken crown, and the reddened face. For the eagle was the bird of Jove, and the face of his image standing in his four-horse chariot on the Capitol was in like manner regularly dyed red on festivals.

Thus, we may fairly assume that on certain solemn occasions Roman generals and magistrates personated the supreme god, and that in so doing they revived the practice of the early kings. To us moderns such mimicry might appear impious, but it was otherwise with the ancients. To their thinking gods and men were akin, for many families traced their descent from a divinity, and the deification of a man probably seemed as little extraordinary to them as the canonisation of a saint seems to a modern Catholic. The Romans in particular were quite familiar with the spectacle of men masquerading as spirits; for at the funerals of great houses all the illustrious dead of the family were personated by men specially chosen for their resemblance to the departed. These representatives wore masks fashioned and painted in the likeness of the originals: they were dressed in rich robes of office, resplendent with purple and gold, such as the dead nobles had worn in their lifetime: like them, they rode in chariots through the city preceded by the rods and axes, and attended by all the pomp and heraldry of high station; and when at last the funeral procession, after threading its way through the crowded streets, defiled into the Forum, the maskers solemnly took their seats on ivory chairs placed for them on the platform of the Rostra, in the sight of the people, recalling no doubt to the old, by their silent presence, the memories of an illustrious past, and firing the young with the ambition of a glorious future.

According to a tradition which we have no reason to reject, Rome was founded by settlers from Alba Longa, a city situated on the slope of the

Alban hills, overlooking the lake and the Campagna. Hence if the Roman kings claimed to be representatives or embodiments of Jupiter, the god of the sky and of the thunder, it is natural to suppose that the kings of Alba, from whom the founder of Rome traced his descent, may have set up the same claim before them; and, indeed, the Roman annals record that one of them, Romulus, Remulus, or Amulius Silvius by name, set up for being a god in his own person, the equal or superior of Jupiter. To support his pretensions and overawe his subjects, he constructed machines whereby he mimicked the clap of thunder and the flash of lightning. Diodorus relates that in the season of fruitage, when thunder is loud and frequent, the king commanded his soldiers to drown the roar of heaven's artillery by clashing their swords against their shields. But he paid the penalty of his impiety, for he perished, he and his house, struck by a thunderbolt in the midst of a dreadful storm. Swollen by the rain, the Alban lake rose in flood and drowned his palace. But still, says an ancient historian, when the water is low and the surface unruffled by a breeze, you may see the ruins of the palace at the bottom of the clear lake. This legend points to a real custom observed by the early kings of Greece and Italy, who like their fellows in Africa down to modern times may have been expected to produce rain and thunder for the good of the crops. The priestly king Numa passed for an adept in the art of drawing down lightning from the sky. Mock thunder, we know, has been made by various peoples as a rain-charm in modern times; why should it not have been made by kings in antiquity? At Rome the sluices of heaven were opened by means of a sacred stone, and the ceremony appears to have formed part of the ritual of Jupiter Elicius, the god who elicits from the clouds the flashing lightning and the dripping rain. And who so well fitted to perform the ceremony as the king, the living representative of the sky-god?

The conclusion which we have reached as to the kings of Rome and Alba probably holds good for all the kings of ancient Latium: each of them, we may suppose, represented or embodied the local Jupiter. For we can hardly doubt that of old every Latin town or settlement had its own Jupiter, as every town and almost every church in modern Italy has its own Madonna; and like the Baal of the Semites the local Jupiter was commonly worshipped on high places. Wooded heights, round which the rain-clouds gather, were indeed the natural sanctuaries for a god of the sky, the rain, and the oak. At Rome he occupied one summit of the Capitoline hill, while the other summit was assigned to his wife Juno, whose temple, with the long flight of stairs leading up to it, has for ages been appropriately replaced by the church of St. Mary "in the altar of the sky" (*in Araceli*). That both heights were originally wooded seems certain, for down to imperial times the saddle which joins them was known as the place "between the two groves."

If the kings of Rome aped Capitoline Jove, their predecessors the kings of Alba probably laid themselves out to mimic the great Latian Jupiter, who had his seat above the city on the summit of the Alban Mountain. Latinus, the legendary ancestor of the dynasty, was said to have been changed into Latian Jupiter after vanishing from the world in the mysterious fashion characteristic of the old Latin kings. The sanctuary of the god on the top of the mountain was the religious centre of the Latin League, as Alba was its political capital till Rome wrested the supremacy from its ancient rival. Apparently no temple, in our sense of the word, was ever erected to Jupiter on this his holy mountain; as god of the sky and thunder he appropriately received the homage of his worshippers in the open air. The massive wall, of which some remains still enclose the old garden of the Passionist monastery, seems to have been part of the sacred precinct which Tarquin the Proud, the last king of Rome, marked out for the solemn annual assembly of the Latin League. The god's oldest sanctuary on this airy mountain-top was a grove.

Since, then, we have seen reason to suppose that the Roman kings personated Jupiter, while Egeria is expressly said to have been an oak-nymph, the story of their union in the sacred grove raises a presumption that at Rome in the regal period a ceremony was periodically performed exactly analogous to that which was annually celebrated at Athens down to the time of Aristotle. The marriage of the King of Rome to the oak-goddess, like the wedding of the vine-god to the Queen of Athens, must have been intended to quicken the growth of vegetation by homoeopathic magic. Of the two forms of the rite we can hardly doubt that the Roman was the older, and that long before the northern invaders met with the vine on the shores of the Mediterranean their forefathers had married the tree-god to the tree-goddess in the vast oak forests of Central and Northern Europe.

Fictional Modes

NORTHROP FRYE

In the second paragraph of the *Poetics* Aristotle speaks of the differences in works of fiction which are caused by the different elevations of the characters in them. In some fictions, he says, the characters are better than we are, in others worse, in still others on the same level. This passage has not received much attention from modern critics, as the importance Aristotle assigns to goodness and badness seems to indicate a somewhat narrowly moralistic view of literature. Aristotle's words for good and bad, however, are *spoudaios* and *phaulos,* which have a figurative sense of weighty and light. In literary fictions the plot consists of somebody doing something. The somebody, if an individual, is the hero, and the something he does or fails to do is what he can do, or could have done, on the level of the postulates made about him by the author and the consequent expectations of the audience. Fictions, therefore, may be classified, not morally, but by the hero's power of action, which may be greater than ours, less, or roughly the same. Thus:

1. If superior in *kind* both to other men and to the environment of other men, the hero is a divine being, and the story about him will be a *myth* in the common sense of a story about a god. Such stories have an important place in literature, but are as a rule found outside the normal literary categories.

2. If superior in *degree* to other men and to his environment, the hero is the typical hero of *romance,* whose actions are marvelous but who is himself identified as a human being. The hero of romance moves in a world in which the ordinary laws of nature are slightly suspended: prodigies of courage and endurance, unnatural to us, are natural to him, and enchanted weapons, talking animals, terrifying ogres and witches, and talismans of miraculous power violate no rule of probability once the postulates of romance have been established. Here we have moved from myth, properly so called, into legend, folk tale, *märchen,* and their literary affiliates and derivatives.

3. If superior in degree to other men but not to his natural environment, the hero is a leader. He has authority, passions, and powers of expression far greater than ours, but what he does is subject both to social criticism and to the order of nature. This is the hero of the *high mimetic* mode, of most epic and tragedy, and is primarily the kind of hero that Aristotle had in mind.

4. If superior neither to other men nor to his environment, the hero is one of us: we respond to a sense of his common humanity, and demand from the poet the same canons of probability that we find in our own experience. This gives us the hero of the *low mimetic* mode, of most comedy and of realistic fiction. "High" and "low" have no connotations of comparative value, but are purely diagrammatic, as they are when they refer to Biblical critics or Anglicans. On this level the difficulty in retaining the word "hero," which has a more limited meaning among the preceding modes, occasionally strikes an author. Thackeray thus feels obliged to call *Vanity Fair* a novel without a hero.

5. If inferior in power or intelligence to ourselves, so that we have the sense of looking down on a scene of bondage, frustration, or absurdity, the hero belongs to the *ironic* mode. This is still true when the reader feels that he is or might be in the same situation as the situation is being judged by the norms of greater freedom. Looking over this table, we can

see that European fiction, during the last fifteen centuries, has steadily
moved its center of gravity down the list. In the pre-medieval period
literature is closely attached to Christian, late Classical, Celtic, or Teutonic
myths. If Christianity had not been both an imported myth and a de-
vourer of rival ones, this phase of Western literature would be easier to
isolate. In the form in which we possess it, most of it has already moved
into the category of romance. Romance divides into two main forms: a
secular form dealing with chivalry and knight-errantry, and a religious
form devoted to legends of saints. Both lean heavily on miraculous viola-
tions of natural law for their interest as stories. Fictions of romance dominate literature until the cult of the prince and the courtier in the Renaissance brings the high mimetic mode into the foreground. The characteristics
of this mode are most clearly seen in the genres of drama, particularly
tragedy, and national epic. Then a new kind of middle-class culture intro-
duces the low mimetic, which predominates in English literature from
Defoe's time to the end of the nineteenth century. In French literature it
begins and ends about fifty years earlier. During the last hundred years,
most serious fiction has tended increasingly to be ironic in mode.

Something of the same progression may be traced in Classical literature too, in a greatly foreshortened form. Where a religion is mythological
and polytheistic, where there are promiscuous incarnations, deified heroes
and kings of divine descent, where the same adjective "godlike" can be
applied either to Zeus or to Achilles, it is hardly possible to separate the
mythical, romantic, and high mimetic strands completely. Where the
religion is theological, and insists on a sharp division between divine and
human natures, romance becomes more clearly isolated, as it does in the
legends of Christian chivalry and sanctity, in the Arabian Nights of
Mohammedanism, in the stories of the judges and thaumaturgic prophets
of Israel. Similarly, the inability of the Classical world to shake off the
divine leader in its later period has much to do with the abortive development of low mimetic and ironic modes that got barely started with
Roman satire. At the same time the establishing of the high mimetic mode,
the developing of a literary tradition with a consistent sense of an order
of nature in it, is one of the great feats of Greek civilization. Oriental
fiction does not, so far as I know, get very far away from mythical and
romantic formulas. . . .

Additional Readings

CAMPBELL, JOSEPH. *The Hero With a Thousand Faces*. (New York, Pantheon, 1949).

CHASE, RICHARD. *The Quest for Myth*. (Westport, Greenwood, 1949).

GORDIS, ROBERT. "The Significance of the Paradise Myth," *The American Journal of Semitic Languages and Literatures*, Vol. 52 (1936).

FRAZER, SIR JAMES. *Folklore in the Old Testament*. (London, Longman's, 1918).

HARRISON, JANE. *Prolegomena to the Study of the Greek Religion*. (London, Macmillan, n.d.).

HAYS, H. R. *The Dangerous Sex: The Myth of Feminine Evil*. (New York, Putnam, 1964).

JAMES, EDWIN OLIVER, *The Ancient Gods*. (New York, Putnam, 1964).

KLUCKHOHN, CLYDE. "Recurrent Themes in Myths and Mythmaking," *Daedalus*, Vol. 88 (1959), 268–79.

RADIN, PAUL. *Primitive Religion*. (New York, Dover, 1937).

RAGLAN, LORD. *The Hero*. (London, Oxford, 1937).

REIK, THEODORE. *Ritual*. (New York, Norton, 1931).

RÖHEIM, GÉZA. "Eden," *Psychoanalytical Review*, Vol. 27 (1940).

SHAWCROSS, JOHN T. "*Paradise Lost* and the Theme of Exodus," *Milton Studies*, Vol. 2 (1970), 3–26.

VICKERY, JOHN B., ed. *Myth and Literature*. (Univ. of Neb. Press, 1966).

2

THE CYCLE OF LIFE

THE monomyth of the Cycle of Life developed from observation of the seasons, for the new year once began at March 15, roughly the time of the vernal equinox. The vernal equinox—that is, the time when the sun's orbit crosses the plane of the earth's equator so that daylight and night are of equal length, with daylight thereafter becoming longer—is, of course, the beginning of spring, symbolizing the rebirth of vegetation and consequently the birth of man. Spring became equivalent to man's youth; summer, his maturity and height of vigor; autumn, his older age and decline; and winter, his death. The attributes of the seasons —rain, sun, wind, snow, or warmth, cold, or light, dark—took on metaphoric meanings for man and his life. Seasonal observations, as well as the daily movement of the sun, involving sky, earth, sun, and rain and man's birth, growth, decline, and death were thus confounded in myth. While nature offered a metaphoric explanation of man's life, man's observations of birth as union of the sexes offered a metaphoric account of the creation of the world. Accordingly sun, sky, and rain became male images, and earth and sea became female images, the creation of nature resulting from the action of sun and/or rain on the earth. The American Indian account of the "Origin of the World" is an explicit example of this myth-making, but other items likewise reflect these myths. As the sun rose in the east, the east was indicative of birth; and since it set in the west, the west imaged death. But the sun disappeared into the sea, as it were, as it passed the horizon, which indicated a return to the mother (or to the womb), just as burial in the earth did. Woman as bearer of life is revered, but she is treated as the passive partner in creation (cold was thus one of her attributes) and is associated with water imagery (wetness thus being another) because of the amniotic waters of birth. Man as the projector of life has a more divine status through equation with the godhead in the sky; he is thus treated as the aggressive partner in creation (fire being man's attribute) and is associated with dryness. These symbols and image patterns recur throughout the mythic stories underlying the selections in this book. Barth's "Night-Sea Journey" is particularly notable for its use of the mythic patterns involving rebirth, the east and movement toward it, immersion in the sea and return from it, and the passage through darkness to light. (See also the Glossary under *Jonah myth* and *night sea journey*.)

One other pattern of creational myth should be mentioned: the sky god's mating with a mortal woman, who bears a child or children who in turn become important for man's history. Such myths reflect the belief in a messiah or savior or Christ who combines divinity and mortality. The offspring, however, do not always serve one or more of the threefold roles of prophet, king, and priest associated with the Christ, but rather may function as agents for the godhead's intentions concerning man. This mythic pattern is a less metaphoric statement of the sun and rain's union with earth: it is the godhead's descent from the sky to couple with one woman on earth. (Compare *Danäe* in the Glossary.) The Annunciation of the birth of Jesus sets the antitype for this myth in Western culture, the godhead appearing in some form, usually an animal. Examples in modern literature, not included here because of their length, include D. H. Lawrence's "The Woman Who Rode Away" and Robinson Jeffers' "Roan Stallion." The obverse of this mythic pattern is the legend that Belial, one of the rebellious angels against God, coupled with beasts or women to beget bestial and lecherous men.

Mythic patterns depicting the life of man in his struggle from birth to death with hopes of the rebirth implied by the cycle of nature center around man's initiation into what maturity is (encased religiously in confirmation rites), his accompanying loss of innocence through experience, the tasks imposed upon him to make him mature or worthy of assuming leadership among men or worthy of salvation, and the journey of life itself, often accompanied by the search for the key to rebirth or for the father (that is, God). Initiation involves a symbolic death (realized through pain as in circumcision or in battle) and the dissolution of idealistic beliefs (as seen in Hawthorne's "Young Goodman Brown"); he is reborn or translated into a new world of independent individualism, which allows the task, the journey, or the quest to proceed. A more specific myth of initiation is the death of innocence by experience, archetypally told in the story of Adam and Eve. Most frequently such experience is interpreted sexually; psychologically it may be the replacement of the father or mother by the wife or husband. The loss of innocence is thus the taking on of the knowledge of the means to life or the means to death (real or spiritual). Such initiation and experience maintains the cyclic nature of life through progeny, who in turn will follow the mythic pattern. The young boy in Joyce's "Araby" awakens into experience at the end of the

story by the recognition of his former idealization of life, with its appealing exoticism, and by the unrealized but felt understanding of its sexual
basis. He can only proceed to a journey and quest in reality to balance
his romantic journey in the story.

In most literary works the theme of the task is part of a larger narrative dealing with journey, quest, or the hero, for achievement of the task
makes one worthy of the journey or quest and is the result of a hero's
action. As in the three items included under this heading, the task is imposed upon a "hero" to prove that he is worthy to serve as a deliverer.
For example, Ferdinand in Shakespeare's "The Tempest" must prove
himself to Prospero by carrying and stacking wood; his successful dis-
patch of this mysteriously difficult task makes him worthy to be Miranda's
husband and to become the next Duke. (See also *Hercules* and *Jason* in
the Glossary.) The task may require the overcoming of an evil force, and
it is this (perversion) that the boy in Joyce's "An Encounter" conquers in
his journey to the Pigeon Works, which implies an annunciation of
divinity for those who reach it without mishap. (Joyce's involved imagery
recalls the dove of the Annunciation and thus predicates the boy's future
prophetic role.) As part of the quest, the task may involve the discovery
of treasure and the overcoming of its guardian; compare specifically
Hercules' eleventh labor and Yeats' play "The Land of Heart's Desire."
Journey is thus that voyage through life which will lead to rebirth,
whether of spirit or, in religious terms, of body and soul in an Edenic
afterlife; the quest emphasizes attainment of the symbol of such rebirth.
Poe's "El Dorado" becomes the Edenic world sought, while "The Promised Visit" by Cohoe delineates the search for the Self which will finally
unite the conscious and the unconscious.

The little poem "I saw a man" by Stephen Crane makes clear the
cyclic nature of the journey and quest throughout the life of mankind.
But alongside this cyclic myth (influenced by Greek concepts of time
and Platonic ideas as in *Timaeus*) is the linear myth of exodus, crystal-
lized in the Exodus of the Hebrews from Egypt. Hebraic concepts of
time are linear, and these stages of times are clearly shown in Kenneth
Patchen's "What Is the Beautiful?" With each generation, the myth says,
there is an exodus from the secure but stultifying life of the past, man with
each exodus coming to face new "wildernesses" to make himself worthy
of salvation. Each stage of history—that is, each generation—advances
nearer to the goal of salvation for mankind, but there is no returning
back upon time as in a cycle. Again the myth would seem to arise from
natural observation of birth from the security of the womb into the
wilderness which is life. Thus seen, the expulsion of Adam and Eve from
the Garden of Eden is an exodus. A clear example of the myth and its
source will be discerned in Joyce's *A Portrait of the Artist as a Young
Man.*

The Search for the Father theme is a more specific form of the quest theme, for the child leaves the mother's body only to return to the womb at death, but he returns in hope of reuniting with God the Father. His search in his lifetime is, therefore, to find the means to salvation, and this will be achieved by finding the Self. The search for the *animus* to balance the presence of the feminine *anima* within man is successfully completed by an understanding of the unconscious. Most cogent, perhaps, as examples of such search will be, on the one hand, Sylvia Plath's "Daddy" with its suicidal implications and, on the other, Pär Lagerqvist's "Father and I" with its transcendence of oppositions. All of the aspects of what we have here called "Becoming" are, like these latter two pieces, concerned ultimately with death and rebirth. And it is in attitudes toward death and rebirth that man conceives of the end of cycle, the eternal continuance of cycle, or the fusion of cycle and linear time when the Millennium occurs and the cycle of life ends to make way for eternity. Man's Hope, like that of Shakespeare's Hotspur in "1 Henry IV," is that "Time must have a stop."

The Divine Family:
Sky Father–Earth Mother

ALL cultures develop explanations of their origin. Most familiar to us is, of course, the Old Testament story of Genesis (the creation of the world out of nothingness by God in six days with a day of rest on the seventh); this is known as *creatio ex nihilo*. Creation has, however, been conceived of as developing out of the substance which is God, *creatio ex Deo*. Observation of human genesis through sexual activity is thus the basis for creation and fertility myths (compare *fertility rites* and *marriage* in the Glossary). The *divine father*, and thus Man, takes on concepts of good, of power and activity, and of the *hero* in the mythic world. In contrast is Woman, often seen as passive, like the earth itself. As most creation myths are developed by men, including that in the Bible, there is often an ambiguous attitude toward Woman. Often she is depicted as a source of evil (Pandora, Cybele, Eve) or trouble, just as the earth may at times become destructive. At other times her role as mother is associated with the fertility of the earth and fecundity. (See, on the one hand, *temptress* and *terrible mother*, and on the other, *earth mother* and *woman*.) Woman, then, is often seen as a defective man—a castrated male, a destroyer who sexually swallows men—or she may be seen as virtually the life principle itself—a symbol of fertility, growth, and womblike security. Molly Bloom in James Joyce's *Ulysses* is erotic and slovenly, but she does not seem to suffer the paralysis that affects her husband. Man has in some instances repressed erotic impulses —or is it fear of Woman?—by idealizing her into a nonsexual being, an ideal who should be approached but not touched, as in the courtly love tradition or in the emphasis upon the importance of the Virgin Mary in religious art of the medieval period.

The Origin of the World

THE MISSION INDIANS OF CALIFORNIA

Tamaiawot, the Earth, was a woman, the mother of all people. She was a person (atakh). Her feet were to the north, her head to the south. Dupash, the Sky, was a man. He was the younger brother of the Earth. All the people were born from the Earth. Some went this way, some that. At first they travelled together. They went from where they emerged to the end of the world and from there westward. The eagle (aswut) went in advance and they all followed. While they were all together they had one language. Then they began to separate. The whites went away. The people (Indians) were left. They still went on following the eagle as he flew. Where he stopped they slept. So the eagle went on and they followed him until they came to Nachivomisavo, "north in the San Bernardino Needles." As they went the people had been going singly, in a long row. When they slept at this place they all crowded together in a great pile. There was no room for them. Now they smelt each other there. They found that they did not smell good. Some of them did not like others. So they went in different ways and some of them came here. Before that they all had the same language. This original language was that of San Gabriel. Those who continued to speak this stayed at the place of separation.

Wiyot was the chief of the people. It was he who separated them at Nachivomisavo when they did not like each other. Wiyot was killed by the people. They quarrelled about life. Some of them said people should die, others said they should live and change. Wiyot tried to stop the quarrel but became tired of it. Then he said he would go away. He went to the sky. He is there now. Those who wanted people to die were Awaavit, fog, Tumihat, thunder (?), and Chebepe, wind (?). These three were wise and were doctors. Wiyot, however, knew most of all, and therefore some of the people did not like him. Many doctors wanted him killed. Those who made him die were Wakhaut, the frog, and Karaut, a red worm that lives in the mud. While Wiyot was alive all called him Wiyot. Now he has two names, Moila, the moon, and Wiyot. When Wiyot was dying he said: "I will teach no one. I will leave you all without telling you." Only to Chekhemal, a bird (probably the meadow-lark), he said: "When I die watch for me. I will come in the morning. Watch and tell all the people that I have not died." Then after Wiyot had died, in the morning Chekhemal chirped: "Moila Wiyot is coming." Then the people knew. Wiyot died at Tova near Maronge, north of the San Jacinto Mountains where the Serrano (Maringayam) live.

While Wiyot was sick Coyote was waiting to eat him. He watched. Wiyot said: "You see that Coyote constantly wants to eat me. When I die there will be a great fire far off in the east. Let Coyote be sent to bring that fire. All of you say that you have no fire. Then he will go. As soon as he goes, make a fire and burn me. If you do not do that he will eat me." Now when Wiyot died the people told Coyote: "You are the best runner. You can get it quickly. Go and bring the fire to burn Wiyot. Then when he is roasted you can eat a little." Coyote went running. He saw the fire ahead and kept on running but never reached it. Meanwhile they burned Wiyot. Coyote turned around, and saw the fire, and ran back. As he came he said: "Give me room. I want to see my father Wiyot." The people knew him and stood about the fire in a thick crowd. They would not let him inside. Then Coyote went back a distance, ran, jumped over them, and just as the heart of Wiyot was burning he seized it and ate it.

Not only people but all things were born from Tamaiawot. They all came from her belly: the sun, the stars, the rocks, the trees, and everything. The ocean is her urine. That is why it is salty.

The Creation

GENESIS, CHAPTERS 1 AND 2

CHAPTER 1

1 In the beginning God created the heaven and the earth.   2 And the earth was without form, and void; and darkness was upon the face of the deep. And the spirit of God moved upon the face of the waters. 3 And God said, Let there be light: and there was light.   4 And God saw the light, that it was good: and God divided the light from the darkness.   5 And God called the light Day, and the darkness he called Night. And the evening and the morning were the first day.

6 And God said, Let there be a firmament in the midst of the waters, and let it divide the waters from the waters.   7 And God made the firmament, and divided the waters which were under the firmament from the waters which were above the firmament: and it was so.   8 And God called the firmament Heaven. And the evening and the morning were the second day.

9 And God said, Let the waters under the heaven be gathered to-

gether unto one place, and let the dry land appear: and it was so.   10
And God called the dry land Earth; and the gathering together of the
waters called he seas: and God saw that it was good.   11 And God
said, Let the earth bring forth grass, the herb yielding seed, and the fruit
tree yielding fruit after his kind, whose seed is in itself, upon the earth:
and it was so.   12 And the earth brought forth grass, and herb yielding
seed after his kind, and the tree yielding fruit, whose seed was in itself,
after his kind: and God saw that it was good.   13 And the evening
and the morning were the third day.

14 And God said, Let there be lights in the firmament of the heaven
to divide the day from the night; and let them be for signs, and for
seasons, and for days, and years: 15 And let them be for lights in the
firmament of the heaven to give light upon the earth: and it was so.
16 And God made two great lights; the greater light to rule the day, and
the lesser light to rule the night: he made the stars also.   17 And God
set them in the firmament of the heaven to give light upon the earth,
18 And to rule over the day and over the night, and to divide the light
from the darkness: and God saw that it was good.   19 And the evening
and the morning were the fourth day.

20 And God said, Let the waters bring forth abundantly the moving
creature that hath life, and fowl that may fly above the earth in the open
firmament of heaven.   21 And God created great whales, and every
living creature that moveth, which the waters brought forth abundantly,
after their kind, and every winged fowl after his kind: and God saw that
it was good.   22 And God blessed them, saying, Be fruitful, and
multiply, and fill the waters in the seas, and let fowl multiply in the earth.
23 And the evening and the morning were the fifth day.

24 And God said, Let the earth bring forth the living creature after
his kind, cattle, and creeping thing, and beast of the earth after his kind:
and it was so.   25 And God made the beast of the earth after his kind,
and cattle after their kind, and every thing that creepeth upon the earth
after his kind: and God saw that it was good.

26 And God said, Let us make man in our image, after our likeness:
and let them have dominion over the fish of the sea, and over the fowl of
the air, and over the cattle, and over all the earth, and over every creeping thing that creepeth upon the earth.   27 So God created man in
his own image, in the image of God created he him; male and female
created he them.   28 And God blessed them, and God said unto them,
Be fruitful, and multiply, and replenish the earth, and subdue it: and have
dominion over the fish of the sea, and over the fowl of the air, and over
every living thing that moveth upon the earth.

29 And God said, Behold, I have given you every herb bearing seed,
which is upon the face of all the earth, and every tree, in the which is
the fruit of a tree yielding seed; to you it shall be for meat.   30 And

to every beast of the earth, and to every fowl of the air, and to every thing that creepeth upon the earth, wherein there is life, I have given every green herb for meat: and it was so. 31 And God saw every thing that he had made, and, behold, it was very good. And the evening and morning were the sixth day.

CHAPTER 2

1 Thus the heavens and the earth were finished, and all the host of them. 2 And on the seventh day God ended his work which he had made; and he rested on the seventh day from all his work which he had made. 3 And God blessed the seventh day, and sanctified it: because that in it he had rested from all his work which God created and made.

4 These are the generations of the heavens and of the earth when they were created, in the day that the LORD God made the earth and the heavens, 5 And every plant of the field before it was in the earth, and every herb of the field before it grew: for the LORD God had not caused it to rain upon the earth, and there was not a man to till the ground. 6 But there went up a mist from the earth, and watered the whole face of the ground. 7 And the LORD God formed man of the dust of the ground, and breathed into his nostrils the breath of life; and man became a living soul.

8 And the LORD God planted a garden eastward in Eden; and there he put the man whom he had formed. 9 And out of the ground made the LORD God to grow every tree that is pleasant to the sight, and good for food; the tree of life also in the midst of the garden, and the tree of knowledge of good and evil. 10 And a river went out of Eden to water the garden; and from thence it was parted, and became into four heads. 11 The name of the first is Pison: that is it which compasseth the whole land of Havilah, where there is gold; 12 and the gold of that land is good; there is bdellium and the onyx stone. 13 And the name of the second river is Gihon: the same is it that compasseth the whole land of Ethiopia. 14 And the name of the third river is Hiddekel: that is it which goeth toward the east of Assyria. And the fourth river is Euphrates. 15 And the LORD God took the man, and put him into the garden of Eden to dress it and to keep it. 16 And the LORD God commanded the man, saying, Of every tree of the garden thou mayest freely eat: 17 But of the tree of the knowledge of good and evil, thou shalt not eat of it: for in the day that thou eatest thereof thou shalt surely die.

18 And the LORD God said, It is not good that man should be alone; I will make him an help meet for him. 19 And out of the ground the LORD God formed every beast of the field, and every fowl of the air; and brought them unto Adam to see what he would call them:

and whatsoever Adam called every living creature, that was the name thereof.   20 And Adam gave names to all cattle, and to the fowl of the air, and to every beast of the field; but for Adam there was not found an help meet for him.   21 And the LORD God caused a deep sleep to fall upon Adam, and he slept; and he took one of his ribs, and closed up the flesh instead thereof;   22 And the rib, which the LORD God had taken from man, made he a woman, and brought her unto the man. 23 And Adam said, This is now bone of my bones, and flesh of my flesh: she shall be called Woman, because she was taken out of Man.   24 Therefore shall a man leave his father and his mother, and shall cleave unto his wife: and they shall be one flesh.   25 And they were both naked, the man and his wife, and were not ashamed.

The Creation; The Four Ages; Jove's Intervention; The Story of Lycaon; The Flood
(from Metamorphoses I, 1–373; trans. Rolfe Humphries)
OVID

My intention is to tell of bodies changed
To different forms; the gods, who made the changes,
Will help me—or I hope so—with a poem
That runs from the world's beginning to our own days.

THE CREATION

Before the ocean was, or earth, or heaven,
Nature was all alike, a shapelessness,
Chaos, so-called, all rude and jumpy matter,
Nothing but bulk, inert, in whose confusion
Discordant atoms warred: there was no sun
To light the universe; there was no moon
With slender silver crescents filling slowly;
No earth hung balanced in surrounding air;
No sea reached far along the fringe of shore.
Land, to be sure, there was, and air, and ocean,
But land on which no man could stand, and water
No man could swim in, air no man could breathe,

Air without light, substance forever changing,
Forever at war: within a single body
Heat fought with cold, wet fought with dry, the hard
Fought with the soft, things having weight contended
With weightless things.
                              Till God, or kindlier Nature,
Settled all argument, and separated
Heaven from earth, water from land, our air
From the high stratosphere, a liberation
So things evolved, and out of blind confusion
Found each its place, bound in eternal order.
The force of fire, that weightless element,
Leaped up and claimed the highest place in heaven;
Below it, air; and under them the earth
Sank with its grosser portions; and the water,
Lowest of all, held up, held in, the land.

Whatever god it was, who out of chaos
Brought order to the universe, and gave it
Division, subdivision, he molded earth,
In the beginning, into a great globe,
Even on every side, and bade the waters
To spread and rise, under the rushing winds,
Surrounding earth; he added ponds and marshes,
He banked the river-channels, and the waters
Feed earth or run to sea, and that great flood
Washes on shores, not banks. He made the plains
Spread wide, the valleys settle, and the forest
Be dressed in leaves; he made the rocky mountains
Rise to full height, and as the vault of Heaven
Has two zones, left and right, and one between them
Hotter than these, the Lord of all Creation
Marked on the earth the same design and pattern.
The torrid zone too hot for men to live in,
The north and south too cold, but in the middle
Varying climate, temperature and season.
Above all things the air, lighter than earth,
Lighter than water, heavier than fire,
Towers and spreads; there mist and cloud assemble,
And fearful thunder and lightning and cold winds,
But these, by the Creator's order, held
No general dominion; even as it is,
These brothers brawl and quarrel; though each one
Has his own quarter, still, they come near tearing

The universe apart. Eurus is monarch
Of the lands of dawn, the realms of Araby,
The Persian ridges under the rays of morning.
Zephyrus holds the west that glows at sunset,
Boreas, who makes men shiver, holds the north,
Warm Auster governs in the misty southland,
And over them all presides the weightless ether,
Pure without taint of earth.
                              These boundaries given,
Behold, the stars, long hidden under darkness,
Broke through and shone, all over the spangled heaven,
Their home forever, and the gods lived there,
And shining fish were given the waves for dwelling
And beasts the earth, and birds the moving air.

But something else was needed, a finer being,
More capable of mind, a sage, a ruler,
So Man was born, it may be, in God's image,
Or Earth, perhaps, so newly separated
From the old fire of Heaven, still retained
Some seed of the celestial force which fashioned
Gods out of living clay and running water.
All other animals look downward; Man,
Alone, erect, can raise his face toward Heaven.

THE FOUR AGES

The Golden Age was first, a time that cherished
Of its own will justice and right; no law.
No punishment was called for; fearfulness
Was quite unknown, and the bronze tablets held
No legal threatening; no suppliant throng
Studied a judge's face; there were no judges,
There did not need to be. Trees had not yet
Been cut and hollowed, to visit other shores.
Men were content at home, and had no towns
With moats and walls around them; and no trumpets
Blared out alarums; things like swords and helmets
Had not been heard of. No one needed soldiers.
People were unaggressive, and unanxious;
The years went by in peace. And Earth, untroubled,
Unharried by hoe or plowshare, brought forth all
That men had need for, and those men were happy,
Gathering berries from the mountain-sides,

Cherries, or blackcaps, and the edible acorns.
Spring was forever, with a west wind blowing
Softly across the flowers no man had planted,
And Earth, unplowed, brought forth rich grain; the field,
Unfallowed, whitened with wheat, and there were rivers
Of milk, and rivers of honey, and golden nectar
Dripped from the dark-green oak-trees.
                                        After Saturn
Was driven to the shadowy land of death,
And the world was under Jove, the Age of Silver
Came in, lower than gold, better than bronze.
Jove made the springtime shorter, added winter,
Summer, and autumn, the seasons as we know them.
That was the first time when the burnt air glowed
White-hot, or icicles hung down in winter.
And men built houses for themselves; the caverns,
The woodland thickets, and the bark-bound shelters
No longer served; and the seeds of grain were planted
In the long furrows, and the oxen struggled
Groaning and laboring under the heavy yoke.

Then came the Age of Bronze, and dispositions
Took on aggressive instincts, quick to arm,
Yet not entirely evil. And last of all
The Iron Age succeeded, whose base vein
Let loose all evil: modesty and truth
And righteousness fled earth, and in their place
Came trickery and slyness, plotting, swindling,
Violence and the damned desire of having.
Men spread their sails to winds unknown to sailors,
The pines came down their mountain-sides, to revel
And leap in the deep waters, and the ground,
Free, once, to everyone, like air and sunshine,
Was stepped off by surveyors. The rich earth,
Good giver of all the bounty of the harvest,
Was asked for more; they dug into her vitals,
Pried out the wealth a kinder lord had hidden
In Stygian shadow, all that precious metal,
The root of evil. They found the guilt of iron,
And gold, more guilty still. And War came forth
That uses both to fight with; bloody hands
Brandished the clashing weapons. Men lived on plunder.
Guest was not safe from host, nor brother from brother,
A man would kill his wife, a wife her husband.

Stepmothers, dire and dreadful, stirred their brews
With poisonous aconite, and sons would hustle
Fathers to death, and Piety lay vanquished,
And the maiden Justice, last of all immortals,
Fled from the bloody earth.
                                        Heaven was no safer.
Giants attacked the very throne of Heaven,
Piled Pelion on Ossa, mountain on mountain
Up to the very stars. Jove struck them down
With thunderbolts, and the bulk of those huge bodies
Lay on the earth, and bled, and Mother Earth,
Made pregnant by that blood, brought forth new bodies,
And gave them, to recall her older offspring,
The forms of men. And this new stock was also
Contemptuous of gods, and murder-hungry
And violent. You would know they were sons of blood.

JOVE'S INTERVENTION

And Jove was witness from his lofty throne
Of all this evil, and groaned as he remembered
The wicked revels of Lycaon's table,
The latest guilt, a story still unknown
To the high gods. In awful indignation
He summoned them to council. No one dawdled.
Easily seen when the night skies are clear,
The Milky Way shines white. Along this road
The gods move toward the palace of the Thunderer,
His royal halls, and, right and left, the dwellings
Of other gods are open, and guests come thronging.
The lesser gods live in a meaner section,
An area not reserved, as this one is,
For the illustrious Great Wheels of Heaven.
(Their Palatine Hill, if I might call it so.)

They took their places in the marble chamber
Where high above them all their king was seated,
Holding his ivory sceptre, shaking out
Thrice, and again, his awful locks, the sign
That made the earth and stars and ocean tremble,
And then he spoke, in outrage: "I was troubled
Less for the sovereignty of all the world
In that old time when the snake-footed giants
Laid each his hundred hands on captive Heaven.

Monstrous they were, and hostile, but their warfare
Sprung from one source, one body. Now, wherever
The sea-gods roar around the earth, a race
Must be destroyed, the race of men. I swear it!
I swear by all the Stygian rivers gliding
Under the world, I have tried all other measures.
The knife must cut the cancer out, infection
Averted while it can be, from our numbers.
Those demigods, those rustic presences,
Nymphs, fauns, and satyrs, wood and mountain dwellers,
We have not yet honored with a place in Heaven,
But they should have some decent place to dwell in,
In peace and safety. Safety? Do you reckon
They will be safe, when I, who wield the thunder,
Who rule you all as subjects, am subjected
To the plottings of the barbarous Lycaon?"

They burned, they trembled. Who was this Lycaon,
Guilty of such rank infamy? They shuddered
In horror, with a fear of sudden ruin,
As the whole world did later, when assassins
Struck Julius Caesar down, and Prince Augustus
Found satisfaction in the great devotion
That cried for vengeance, even as Jove took pleasure,
Then, in the gods' response. By word and gesture
He calmed them down, awed them again to silence,
And spoke once more:

THE STORY OF LYCAON

                    "He has indeed been punished.
On that score have no worry. But what he did,
And how he paid, are things that I must tell you.
I had heard the age was desperately wicked,
I had heard, or so I hoped, a lie, a falsehood,
So I came down, as man, from high Olympus,
Wandered about the world. It would take too long
To tell you how widespread was all that evil.
All I had heard was grievous understatement!
I had crossed Maenala, a country bristling
With dens of animals, and crossed Cyllene,
And cold Lycacus' pine woods. Then I came
At evening, with the shadows growing longer,
To an Arcadian palace, where the tyrant

Was anything but royal in his welcome.
I gave a sign that a god had come, and people
Began to worship, and Lycaon mocked them,
Laughed at their prayers, and said: 'Watch me find out
Whether this fellow is a god or mortal,
I can tell quickly, and no doubt about it.'
He planned, that night, to kill me while I slumbered;
That was his way to test the truth. Moreover,
And not content with that, he took a hostage,
One sent by the Molossians, cut his throat,
Boiled pieces of his flesh, still warm with life,
Broiled others, and set them before me on the table.
That was enough. I struck, and the bolt of lightning
Blasted the household of that guilty monarch.
He fled in terror, reached the silent fields,
And howled, and tried to speak. No use at all!
Foam dripped from his mouth; bloodthirsty still, he turned
Against the sheep, delighting still in slaughter,
And his arms were legs, and his robes were shaggy hair,
Yet he is still Lycaon, the same grayness,
The same fierce face, the same red eyes, a picture
Of bestial savagery. One house has fallen,
But more than one deserves to. Fury reigns
Over all the fields of Earth. They are sworn to evil,
Believe it. Let them pay for it, and quickly!
So stands my purpose."
                              Part of them approved
With words and added fuel to his anger,
And part approved with silence, and yet all
Were grieving at the loss of humankind,
Were asking what the world would be, bereft
Of mortals: who would bring their altars incense?
Would earth be given the beasts, to spoil and ravage?
Jove told them not to worry; he would give them
Another race, unlike the first, created
Out of a miracle; he would see to it.

He was about to hurl his thunderbolts
At the whole world, but halted, fearing Heaven
Would burn from fire so vast, and pole to pole
Break out in flame and smoke, and he remembered
The fates had said that some day land and ocean,
The vault of Heaven, the whole world's mighty fortress,
Besieged by fire, would perish. He put aside

The bolts made in Cyclopean workshops; better,
He thought, to drown the world by flooding water.

THE FLOOD

So, in the cave of Aeolus, he prisoned
The North-wind, and the West-wind, and such others
As ever banish cloud, and he turned loose
The South-wind, and the South-wind came out streaming
With dripping wings, and pitch-black darkness veiling
His terrible countenance. His beard is heavy
With rain-cloud, and his hoary locks a torrent,
Mists are his chaplet, and his wings and garments
Run with the rain. His broad hands squeeze together
Low-hanging clouds, and crash and rumble follow
Before the cloudburst, and the rainbow, Iris,
Draws water from the teeming earth, and feeds it
Into the clouds again. The crops are ruined,
The farmers' prayers all wasted, all the labor
Of a long year, comes to nothing.
                          And Jove's anger,
Unbounded by his own domain, was given
Help by his dark-blue brother. Neptune called
His rivers all, and told them, very briefly,
To loose their violence, open their houses,
Pour over embankments, let the river horses
Run wild as ever they would. And they obeyed him.
His trident struck the shuddering earth; it opened
Way for the rush of waters. The leaping rivers
Flood over the great plains. Not only orchards
Are swept away, not only grain and cattle,
Not only men and houses, but altars, temples,
And shrines with holy fires. If any building
Stands firm, the waves keep rising over its roof-top,
Its towers are under water, and land and ocean
Are all alike, and everything is ocean,
An ocean with no shore-line.
                          Some poor fellow
Seizes a hill-top; another, in a dinghy,
Rows where he used to plough, and one goes sailing
Over his fields of grain or over the chimney
Of what was once his cottage. Someone catches
Fish in the top of an elm-tree, or an anchor
Drags in green meadow-land, or the curved keel brushes

Grape-arbors under water. Ugly sea-cows
Float where the slender she-goats used to nibble
The tender grass, and the Nereids come swimming
With curious wonder, looking, under water,
At houses, cities, parks, and groves. The dolphins
Invade the woods and brush against the oak-trees;
The wolf swims with the lamb; lion and tiger
Are borne along together; the wild boar
Finds all his strength is useless, and the deer
Cannot outspeed that torrent; wandering birds
Look long, in vain, for landing-place, and tumble,
Exhausted, into the sea. The deep's great license
Has buried all the hills, and new waves thunder
Against the mountain-tops. The flood has taken
All things, or nearly all, and those whom water,
By chance, has spared, starvation slowly conquers.

Lady Madonna

JOHN LENNON AND PAUL McCARTNEY

Lady Madonna children at your feet
wonder how you manage to make ends meet.
Who finds the money when you pay the rent?
Did you think that money was heaven sent?
Friday night arrives without a suitcase
Sunday morning creep in like a nun
Monday's child has learned to tie his bootlace.
See how they'll run.
Lady Madonna baby at your breast
wonder how you manage to feed the rest.
See how they'll run.
Lady Madonna lying on the bed
listen to the music playing in your head.
Tuesday afternoon is never ending
Wedn'sday morning papers didn't come
Thursday night your stockings needed mending.
See how they'll run.
Lady Madonna children at your feet
wonder how you manage to make ends meet.

Night-Sea Journey

JOHN BARTH

"One way or another, no matter which theory of our journey is correct, it's myself I address; to whom I rehearse as to a stranger our history and condition, and will disclose my secret hope though I sink for it.

"Is the journey my invention? Do the night, the sea, exist at all, I ask myself, apart from my experience of them? Do I myself exist, or is this a dream? Sometimes I wonder. And if I am, who am I? The Heritage I supposedly transport? But how can I be both vessel and contents? Such are the questions that beset my intervals of rest.

"My trouble is, I lack conviction. Many accounts of our situation seem plausible to me—where and what we are, why we swim and whither. But implausible ones as well, perhaps especially those, I must admit as possibly correct. Even likely. If at times, in certain humors—stroking in unison, say, with my neighbors and chanting with them 'Onward! Upward!'—I have supposed that we have after all a common Maker, Whose nature and motives we may not know, but Who engendered us in some mysterious wise and launched us forth toward some end known but to Him—if (for a moodslength only) I have been able to entertain such notions, very popular in certain quarters, it is because our night-sea journey partakes of their absurdity. One might even say: I can believe them *because* they are absurd.

"Has that been said before?

"Another paradox: it appears to be these recesses from swimming that sustain me in the swim. Two measures onward and upward, flailing with the rest, then I float exhausted and dispirited, brood upon the night, the sea, the journey, while the flood bears me a measure back and down: slow progress, but I live, I live, and make my way, aye, past many a drownèd comrade in the end, stronger, worthier than I, victims of their unremitting *joie de nager*. I have seen the best swimmers of my generation go under. Numberless the number of the dead! Thousands drown as I think this thought, millions as I rest before returning to the swim. And scores, hundreds of millions have expired since we surged forth, brave in our innocence, upon our dreadful way. 'Love! Love!' we sang then, a quarter-billion strong, and churned the warm sea white with joy of swimming! Now all are gone down—the buoyant, the sodden, leaders and followers, all gone under, while wretched I swim on. Yet these same reflective intervals that keep me afloat have led me into wonder, doubt, despair—

strange emotions for a swimmer!—have led me, even, to suspect . . .
that our night-sea journey is without meaning.

"Indeed, if I have yet to join the hosts of the suicides, it is because
(fatigue apart) I find it no meaningfuller to drown myself than to go on
swimming.

"I know that there are those who seem actually to enjoy the night-sea;
who claim to love swimming for its own sake, or sincerely believe that
'reaching the Shore,' 'transmitting the Heritage' (*Whose* Heritage, I'd like
to know? And to whom?) is worth the staggering cost. I do not. Swimming itself I find at best not actively unpleasant, more often tiresome, not
infrequently a torment. Arguments from function and design don't impress
me: granted that we can and do swim, that in a manner of speaking our
long tails and streamlined heads are 'meant for' swimming; it by no means
follows—for me, at least—that we *should* swim, or otherwise endeavor to
'fulfill our destiny.' Which is to say, Someone Else's destiny, since ours,
so far as I can see, is merely to perish, one way or another, soon or late.
The heartless zeal of our (departed) leaders, like the blind ambition and
good cheer of my own youth, appalls me now; for the death of my comrades I am inconsolable. If the night-sea journey has justification, it is not
for us swimmers ever to discover it.

"Oh, to be sure, 'Love!' one heard on every side: 'Love it is that drives
and sustains us!' I translate: we don't know *what* drives and sustains us,
only that we are most miserably driven and, imperfectly, sustained. *Love*
is how we call our ignorance of what whips us. 'To reach the Shore,' then:
but what if the Shore exists in the fancies of us swimmers merely, who
dream it to account for the dreadful fact that we swim, have always and
only swum, and continue swimming without respite (myself excepted)
until we die? Supposing even that there *were* a Shore—that, as a cynical
companion of mine once imagined, we rise from the drowned to discover
all those vulgar superstitions and exalted metaphors to be literal truth:
the giant Maker of us all, the Shores of Light beyond our night-sea
journey!—whatever would a swimmer do there? The fact is, when we
imagine the Shore, what comes to mind is just the opposite of our condition: no more night, no more sea, no more journeying. In short, the blissful
estate of the drowned.

"'Ours not to stop and think; ours but to swim and sink. . . .' Because
a moment's thought reveals the pointlessness of swimming. 'No matter,'
I've heard some say, even as they gulped their last: 'The night-sea journey
may be absurd, but here we swim, will-we nill-we, against the flood,
onward and upward, toward a Shore that may not exist and couldn't be
reached if it did.' The thoughtful swimmer's choices, then, they say, are
two: give over thrashing and go under for good, or embrace the absurdity;
affirm in and for itself the night-sea journey; swim on with neither motive

nor destination, for the sake of swimming, and compassionate moreover with your fellow swimmer, we being all at sea and equally in the dark. I find neither course acceptable. If not even the hypothetical Shore can justify a sea-full of drowned comrades, to speak of the swim-in-itself as somehow doing so strikes me as obscene. I continue to swim—but only because blind habit, blind instinct, blind fear of drowning are still more strong than the horror of our journey. And if on occasion I have assisted a fellow-thrasher, joined in the cheers and songs, even passed along to others strokes of genius from the drownèd great, it's that I shrink by temperament from making myself conspicuous. To paddle off in one's own direction, assert one's independent right-of-way, overrun one's fellows without compunction, or dedicate oneself entirely to pleasures and diversions without regard for conscience—I can't finally condemn those who journey in this wise; in half my moods I envy them and despise the weak vitality that keeps me from following their example. But in reasonabler moments I remind myself that it's their very freedom and self-responsibility I reject, as more dramatically absurd, in our senseless circumstances, than tailing along in conventional fashion. Suicides, rebels, affirmers of the paradox—nay-sayers and yea-sayers alike to our fatal journey—I finally shake my head at them. And splash sighing past their corpses, one by one, as past a hundred sorts of others: friends, enemies, brothers; fools, sages, brutes—and nobodies, million upon million. I envy them all.

"A poor irony: that I, who find abhorrent and tautological the doctrine of survival of the fittest (*fitness* meaning, in my experience, nothing more than survival-ability, a talent whose only demonstration is the fact of survival, but whose chief ingredients seem to be strength, guile, callousness), may be the sole remaining swimmer! But the doctrine is false as well as repellent: Chance drowns the worthy with the unworthy, bears up the unfit with the fit by whatever definition, and makes the night-sea journey essentially *haphazard* as well as murderous and unjustified.

" 'You only swim once.' Why bother, then?

" 'Except ye drown, ye shall not reach the Shore of Life.' Poppycock.

"One of my late companions—that same cynic with the curious fancy, among the first to drown—entertained us with odd conjectures while we waited to begin our journey. A favorite theory of his was that the Father does exist, and did indeed make us and the sea we swim—but not a-purpose or even consciously; He made us, as it were, despite Himself, as we make waves with every tail-thrash, and may be unaware of our existence. Another was that He knows we're here but doesn't care what happens to us, inasmuch as He creates (voluntarily or not) other seas and swimmers at more or less regular intervals. In bitterer moments, such as just before he drowned, my friend even supposed that our Maker wished us unmade; there was indeed a Shore, he'd argue, which could save at least

some of us from drowning and toward which it was our function to struggle—but for reasons unknowable to us He wanted desperately to prevent
our reaching that happy place and fulfilling our destiny. Our 'Father,' in
short, was our adversary and would-be killer! No less outrageous, and
offensive to traditional opinion, were the fellow's speculations on the
nature of our Maker: that He might well be no swimmer Himself at all,
but some sort of monstrosity, perhaps even tailless; that He might be
stupid, malicious, insensible, perverse, or asleep and dreaming; that the
end for which He created and launched us forth, and which we flagellate
ourselves to fathom, was perhaps immoral, even obscene. Et cetera, et
cetera: there was no end to the chap's conjectures, or the impoliteness of
his fancy; I have reason to suspect that his early demise, whether planned
by 'our Maker' or not, was expedited by certain fellow-swimmers indignant at his blasphemies.

"In other moods, however (he was as given to moods as I), his theo-
rizing would become half-serious, so it seemed to me, especially upon the
subjects of Fate and Immortality, to which our youthful conversations
often turned. Then his harangues, if no less fantastical, grew solemn and
obscure, and if he was still baiting us, his passion undid the joke. His objection to popular opinions of the hereafter, he would declare, was their
claim to general validity. Why need believers hold that *all* the drownèd
rise to be judged at journey's end, and non-believers that drowning is final
without exception? In *his* opinion (so he'd vow at least), nearly everyone's
fate was permanent death; indeed he took a sour pleasure in supposing
that every 'Maker' made thousands of separate seas in His creative lifetime, each populated like ours with millions of swimmers, and that in
almost every instance both sea and swimmers were utterly annihilated,
whether accidentally or by malevolent design. (Nothing if not pluralis-
tical, he imagined there might be millions and billions of 'Fathers,' perhaps in some 'night-sea' of their own!) However—and here he turned
infidels against him with the faithful—he professed to believe that in
possibly a single night-sea per thousand, say, one of its quarter-billion
swimmers (that is, one swimmer in two hundred fifty billions) achieved a
qualified immortality. In some cases the rate might be slightly higher; in
others it was vastly lower, for just as there are swimmers of every degree
of proficiency, including some who drown before the journey starts, unable
to swim at all, and others created drowned, as it were, so he imagined
what can only be termed impotent Creators, Makers unable to Make,' as
well as uncommonly fertile ones and all grades between. And it pleased
him to deny any necessary relation between a Maker's productivity and
His other virtues—including, even, the quality of His creatures.

"I could go on (*he* surely did) with his elaboration of these mad
notions—such as that swimmers in other night-seas needn't be of our

kind; that Makers themselves might belong to different *species,* so to speak; that our particular Maker mightn't Himself be immortal, or that we might be not only His emissaries but His 'immortality,' continuing His life and our own, transmogrified, beyond our individual deaths. Even this modified immortality (meaningless to me) he conceived as relative and contingent, subject to accidental or deliberate termination: his pet hypothesis was that Makers and swimmers *each generate the other*—against all odds, their number being so great—and that any given 'immortality-chain' could terminate after any number of cycles, so that what was 'immortal' (still speaking relatively) was only the cyclic process of incarnation, which itself might have a beginning and an end. Alternatively he liked to imagine cycles within cycles, either finite or infinite: for example, the 'night-sea,' as it were, in which Makers 'swam' and created night-seas and swimmers like ourselves, might be the creation of a larger Maker, Himself one of many, Who in turn et cetera. Time itself he regarded as relative to our experience, like magnitude: who knew but what, with each thrash of our tails, minuscule seas and swimmers, whole eternities, came to pass—as ours, perhaps, and our Maker's Maker's, was elapsing between the strokes of some supertail, in a slower order of time?

"Naturally I hooted with the others at this nonsense. We were young then, and had only the dimmest notion of what lay ahead; in our ignorance we imagined night-sea journeying to be a positively heroic enterprise. Its meaning and value we never questioned; to be sure, some must go down by the way, a pity no doubt, but to win a race requires that others lose, and like all my fellows I took for granted that I would be the winner. We milled and swarmed, impatient to be off, never mind where or why, only to try our youth against the realities of night and sea; if we indulged the skeptic at all, it was as a droll, half-contemptible mascot. When he died in the initial slaughter, no one cared.

"And even now I don't subscribe to all his views—but I no longer scoff. The horror of our history has purged me of opinions, as of vanity, confidence, spirit, charity, hope, vitality, everything—except dull dread and a kind of melancholy, stunned persistence. What leads me to recall his fancies is my growing suspicion that I, of all swimmers, may be the sole survivor of this fell journey, tale-bearer of a generation. This suspicion, together with the recent sea-change, suggests to me now that nothing is impossible, not even my late companion's wildest visions, and brings me to a certain desperate resolve, the point of my chronicling.

"Very likely I have lost my senses. The carnage at our setting out; our decimation by whirlpool, poisoned cataract, sea-convulsion; the panic stampedes, mutinies, slaughters, mass suicides; the mounting evidence that none will survive the journey—add to these anguish and fatigue; it were a miracle if sanity stayed afloat. Thus I admit, with the other possibilities, that the present sweetening and calming of the sea, and what seems to be a kind of vasty presence, song, or summons from the near upstream, may be hallucinations of disordered sensibility. . . .

"Perhaps, even, I am drowned already. Surely I was never meant for the rough-and-tumble of the swim; not impossibly I perished at the outset and have only imaged the night-sea journey from some final deep. In any case, I'm no longer young, and it is we spent old swimmers, disabused of every illusion, who are most vulnerable to dreams.

"Sometimes I think I am my drownèd friend.

"Out with it: I've begun to believe, not only that *She* exists, but that She lies not far ahead, and stills the sea, and draws me Herward! Aghast, I recollect his maddest notion: that our destination (which existed, mind, in but one night-sea out of hundreds and thousands) was no Shore, as commonly conceived, but a mysterious being, indescribable except by paradox and vaguest figure: wholly different from us swimmers, yet our complement; the death of us, yet our salvation and resurrection; simultaneously our journey's end, mid-point, and commencement; not membered and thrashing like us, but a motionless or hugely gliding sphere of unimaginable dimension; self-contained, yet dependent absolutely, in some wise, upon the chance (always monstrously improbable) that one of us will survive the night-sea journey and reach . . . Her! *Her,* he called it, or *She,* which is to say, Other-than-a-he. I shake my head; the thing is too preposterous; it is myself I talk to, to keep my reason in this awful darkness. There is no She! There is no You! I rave to myself; it's Death alone that hears and summons. To the drowned, all seas are calm. . . .

"Listen: my friend maintained that in every order of creation there are two sorts of creators, contrary yet complementary, one of which gives rise to seas and swimmers, the other to the Night-which-contains-the-sea and to What-waits-at-the-journey's-end: the former, in short, to destiny, the latter to destination (and both profligately, involuntarily, perhaps indifferently or unwittingly). The 'purpose' of the night-sea journey—but not necessarily of the journeyer or of either Maker!—my friend could describe only in abstractions: *consummation, transfiguration, union of contraries, transcension of categories.* When we laughed, he would shrug and admit that he understood the business no better than we, and thought it ridiculous, dreary, possibly obscene. 'But one of you,' he'd add with his wry smile, 'may be the Hero destined to complete the night-sea journey and be one with Her. Chances are, of course, you won't make it.' He himself, he declared, was not even going to try; the whole idea repelled him; if we chose to dismiss it as an ugly fiction, so much the better for us; thrash, splash, and be merry, we were soon enough drowned. But there it was, he could not say how he knew or why he bothered to tell us, any more than he could say what would happen after She and Hero, Shore and Swimmer, 'merged identities' to become something both and neither. He quite agreed with me that if the issue of that magical union had no memory of the night-sea journey, for example, it enjoyed a poor sort of immortality; even poorer if, as he rather imagined, a swimmer-hero plus a She equaled or became merely another Maker of future night-seas and the rest, at such incredible expense of life. This being the case—he was persuaded it was— the merciful thing to do was refuse to participate; the genuine heroes, in his opinion, were the suicides, and the hero of heroes would be the swimmer who, in the very presence of the Other, refused Her proffered 'immortality' and thus put an end to at least one cycle of catastrophes.

"How we mocked him! Our moment came, we hurtled forth, pretending to glory in the adventure, thrashing, singing, cursing, strangling, rationalizing, rescuing, killing, inventing rules and stories and relationships, giving up, struggling on, but dying all, and still in darkness, until only a battered remnant was left to croak 'Onward, upward,' like a bitter echo. Then they too fell silent—victims, I can only presume, of the last frightful wave—and the moment came when I also, utterly desolate and spent, thrashed my last and gave myself over to the current, to sink or float as might be, but swim no more. Whereupon, marvelous to tell, in an instant the sea grew still! Then warmly, gently, the great tide turned, began to bear me, as it does now, onward and upward will-I nill-I, like a flood of joy—and I recalled with dismay my dead friend's teaching.

"I am not deceived. This new emotion is Her doing; the desire that possesses me is Her bewitchment. Lucidity passes from me; in a moment I'll cry 'Love!' bury myself in Her side, and be 'transfigured.' Which is to say, I die already; this fellow transported by passion is not I; *I am he who abjures and rejects the night-sea journey!* I. . . .

"I am all love. 'Come!' She whispers, and I have no will.

"You who I may be about to become, whatever You are: with the last twitch of my real self I beg You to listen. It is *not* love that sustains me! No; though Her magic makes me burn to sing the contrary, and though I drown even now for the blasphemy, I will say truth. What has fetched me across this dreadful sea is a single hope, gift of my poor dead comrade: that You may be stronger-willed than I, and that by sheer force of concentration I may transmit to You, along with Your official Heritage, a private legacy of awful recollection and negative resolve. Mad as it may be, my dream is that some unimaginable embodiment of myself (or myself plus Her if that's how it must be) will come to find itself expressing, in however garbled or radical a translation, some reflection of these reflections. If against all odds this comes to pass, may You to whom, through whom I speak, do what I cannot: terminate this aimless, brutal business! Stop Your hearing against Her song! Hate love!

"Still alive, afloat, afire. Farewell then my penultimate hope: that one may be sunk for direst blasphemy on the very shore of the Shore. Can it be (my old friend would smile) that only utterest nay-sayers survive the night? But even that were Sense, and there is no sense, only senseless love, senseless death. Whoever echoes these reflections: be more courageous than their author! An end to night-sea journeys! Make no more! And forswear me when I shall forswear myself, deny myself, plunge into Her who summons, singing . . .

   " 'Love! Love! Love!' "

Crow Blacker Than Ever

TED HUGHES

When God, disgusted with man,
Turned towards heaven,
And man, disgusted with God,
Turned towards Eve,
Things looked like falling apart.

But Crow   Crow
Crow nailed them together,
Nailing heaven and earth together—

So man cried, but with God's voice.
And God bled, but with man's blood.

Then heaven and earth creaked at the joint
Which became gangrenous and stank—
A horror beyond redemption.

The agony did not diminish.

Man could not be man nor God God.

The agony

Grew.

Crow

Grinned

Crying: "This is my Creation,"

Flying the black flag of himself.

The Divine Family:
Mating with a Mortal

MANY legends and stories relate the mating of a mortal with a deity. Through such a union, the mortal achieves something of the god-like, and the deity provides a knowledge or a child that partakes of divinity. Such a child becomes a mortal hero, a Christ figure; compare *Hercules, Danäe,* and *Semele.* Zeus, a divine father notorious for the eroticism that man has endowed Man with, often took the form of various animals to satisfy his lust, among them the bull who seduced Europa. The practice of Baal (bull, lord) worship in Phoenicia is probably connected with the masculinity, potency, and power associated with this animal. American literature, from Melville's Moby-Dick (a whale) through Norman Mailer's *Why Are We in Viet Nam?*, depicts this odd fascination with such creatures. Robinson Jeffers's "Roan Stallion" is a curious blend of both the Christian and Greek traditions as its central character (named California) has a mystical encounter with a magnificent and wild stallion, though she abhors sexual contact with her husband.

Europa
(from Metamorphoses, II, 830–875; trans. Rolfe Humphries)
OVID

And back in Heaven, he found his father waiting;
Jove had an errand for him, he did not say
Love was the reason for it, but simply told him:
"My son, my ever-willing faithful servant,
Be quick, glide back again, go down to Sidon,
You will find a herd, the king's, of cattle grazing
Along the mountains. Drive them to the sea-shore!"
There was no delay; the herd was quickly driven
From the hillsides to the shore, where the king's daughter
Used to go playing with her Tyrian comrades.
Do majesty and love go well together
Or linger in one dwelling? Hardly. Jove

Put down his heavy sceptre: the great father,
Great ruler of the gods, whose right hand wields
Triple-forked lightning, and whose awful nod
Makes the world tremble, put aside his might,
His majesty, and took upon himself
The form of a bull, went lowing with the heifers
Over the tender grass, showy and handsome,
The color of snow, which never a foot has trodden,
Never a raindrop sullied. The great muscles
Bulged on the neck, the dewlaps hung to the chest,
The horns were small, but every bit as perfect
As if a sculptor made them, and as shining
As any jewel, and the eyes and forehead
Offered no threat, and the great gaze was peaceful.
And the king's daughter looked at him in wonder,
So calm, so beautiful, and feared to touch him,
At first, however mild, and little by little
Got over her fear, and soon was bringing flowers
To hold toward that white face, and he, the lover,
Gave kisses to the hands held out, rejoicing
In hope of later, more exciting kisses.
Is it time? Not quite. He leaps, a little playful,
On the green grass, or lays the snowy body
On the yellow sand, and gradually the princess
Loses all fear, and he lets her pat his shoulder,
Twine garlands in his horns, and she grows bolder,
Climbs on his back, of course all unsuspecting,
And he rises, ever so gently, and slowly edges
From the dry sand toward the water, further and further,
And swimming now, with the girl, trembling a little
And looking back to the land, her right hand clinging
Tight to one horn, and the other resting easy
Along the shoulder, and her flowing garments
Filling and fluttering in the breath of the sea-wind.

The Annunciation

LUKE, Chapter 1

26 And in the sixth month the angel Gabriel was sent from God unto a city of Galilee, named Nazareth,   27 To a virgin espoused to a man whose name was Joseph, of the house of David; and the virgin's name was Mary.   28 And the angel came in unto her, and said, Hail, thou that art highly favoured, the LORD is with thee: blessed art thou among women.   29 And when she saw him, she was troubled at his saying, and cast in her mind what manner of salutation this should be.   30 And the angel said unto her, Fear not, Mary: for thou hast found favour with God.   31 And, behold, thou shalt conceive in thy womb, and bring forth a son, and shalt call his name JESUS.   32 He shall be great, and shall be called the Son of the Highest: and the Lord God shall give unto him the throne of his father David: 33 And he shall reign over the house of Jacob for ever; and of his kingdom there shall be no end. 34 Then said Mary unto the angel, How shall this be, seeing I know not a man?   35 And the angel answered and said unto her, The Holy Ghost shall come upon thee, and the power of the Highest shall overshadow thee: therefore also that holy thing which shall be born of thee shall be called the Son of God.

Leda and the Swan

WILLIAM BUTLER YEATS

A sudden blow: the great wings beating still
Above the staggering girl, her thighs caressed
By the dark webs, her nape caught in his bill,
He holds her helpless breast upon his breast.

How can those terrified vague fingers push
The feathered glory from her loosening thighs?
And how can body, laid in that white rush,
But feel the strange heart beating where it lies?

A shudder in the loins engenders there
The broken wall, the burning roof and tower
And Agamemnon dead.
                      Being so caught up,
So mastered by the brute blood of the air,
Did she put on his knowledge with his power
Before the indifferent beak could let her drop?

Becoming: Initiation

THE fall from innocence to experience usually incorporates a number of archetypal motifs. These motifs constitute an initiation into life. In literature, the theme of initiation focuses upon the youthfulness of the protagonist. In ritual practices among various cultures, this entrance into manhood is established by certain ceremonies or tests, such as the Jewish bar mitzvah or the tribal initiation in which a warrior is subjected to a series of tests (usually physical) to prove his manhood. Initiation involves pain, sexual experience, and an awareness of evil or death in the world; in myth these ideas are generally conflated. An important literary type that deals with the emergence of youth into adulthood is the *bildungsroman,* the first-person account of the life of the protagonist as a minor (as in Charles Dickens's *David Copperfield* or W. Somerset Maugham's *Of Human Bondage*). A special form is the *kunstlerroman,* the first-person account of the artist-in-the-making (as in D. H. Lawrence's *Sons and Lovers* or James Joyce's *A Portrait of the Artist as a Young Man*).

The Prodigal Son
LUKE, Chapter 15

11 And he said, A certain man had two sons: 12 And the younger of them said to *his* father, Father, give me the portion of goods that falleth *to me.* And he divided unto them *His* living.   13 And not many days after the younger son gathered all together, and took his journey into a far country, and there wasted his substance with riotous living. 14 And when he had spent all, there arose a mighty famine in that land; and he began to be in want.   15 And he went and joined himself to a citizen of that country; and he sent him into his fields to feed swine. 16 And he would fain have filled his belly with the husks that the swine did eat: and no man gave unto him.   17 And when he came to himself, he said, How many hired servants of my father's have bread enough and to spare, and I perish with hunger!   18 I will arise and go to my father, and will say unto him, Father, I have sinned against heaven, and before thee,   19 And am no more worthy to be called thy son: make

me as one of thy hired servants.   20 And he arose, and came to his father. But when he was yet a great way off, his father saw him, and had compassion, and ran, and fell on his neck, and kissed him.   21 And the son said unto him, Father, I have sinned against heaven, and in thy sight, and am no more worthy to be called thy son.   22 But the father said to his servants, Bring forth the best robe, and put *it* on him; and put a ring on his hand, and shoes on *his* feet: 23 And bring hither the fatted calf, and kill *it;* and let us eat, and be merry: 24 For this my son was dead, and is alive again; he was lost, and is found, And they began to be merry.   25 Now his elder son was in the field: and as he came and drew nigh to the house, he heard music and dancing.   26 And he called one of the servants, and asked what these things meant. 27 And he said unto him, Thy brother is come; and thy father hath killed the fatted calf, because he hath received him safe and sound.   28 And he was angry, and would not go in: therefore came his father out, and intreated him.   29 And he answering said to *his* father, Lo, these many years do I serve thee, neither transgressed I at any time thy command- ment: and yet thou never gavest me a kid, that I might make merry with my friends: 30 But as soon as this thy son was come, which hath de- voured thy living with harlots, thou hast killed for him the fatted calf. 31 And he said unto him, Son, thou art ever with me, and all that I have is thine.   32 It was meet that we should make merry, and be glad: for this thy brother was dead, and is alive again; and was lost, and is found.

A Voyage to Cythera

(trans. Frederick Morgan)

CHARLES BAUDELAIRE

My heart, like a bird, ahover joyously,
circled the rigging, soaring light and free;
beneath a cloudless sky the ship rolled on
like an angel drunk with blazing rays of sun.

What is that black, sad island?—We are told
it is Cythera, famed in songs of old,
trite El Dorado of worn-out roués.
Look, after all, it's but a paltry place.

—Isle of sweet mysteries and festal loves,
above your waters antique Venus moves;
like an aroma, her imperious shade
burdens the soul with love and lassitude.

Green-myrtled island, fair with flowers in bloom,
revered by every nation for all time,
where sighing hearts send up their fervent praises
afloat like incense over beds of roses

or like a ringdove's endless cooing call!
—Cythera now was but a meager soil,
a flinty desert moiled with bitter cries.
And yet, half-glimpsed, a strange shape met my eyes.

It was no temple couched in shady groves
where the young priestess, lover of flowers, moves,
her body fevered by obscure desires,
her robe half opened to the fleeting airs;

but as we passed, skirting the coast so near
that our white canvas set the birds astir,
we saw it was a three-branched gibbet, high
and black-etched, like a cypress, on the sky.

Perched on their prey, ferocious birds were mangling
with frenzied thrusts a hanged man, ripe and dangling,
each driving like a tool his filthy beak
all through that rot, in every bleeding crack;

the eyes were holes, and from the ruined gut
across the thighs the heavy bowels poured out,
and crammed with hideous pleasures, peck by peck,
his butchers had quite stripped him of his sex.

Beneath his feet, a pack of four-legged brutes
circled and prowled, with upraised avid snouts;
a larger beast was ramping in the midst
like a hangman flanked by his apprentices.

Child of Cythera, born of so fair a sky,
you suffered these defilements silently:
atonement for your impure rituals
and sins that have forbid you burial.

Ridiculous corpse, I know your pains full well.
At sight of your loose-hanging limbs I felt
the bitter-flowing bile of ancient grief
rise up, like a long puke, against my teeth;

poor wretch, so dear-remembered, in your presence
I felt each beak-thrust of those stabbing ravens,
and the black panthers' jaws—each rip and gash—
that once took such delight to grind my flesh.

The sky was suave, and level was the sea,
yet all was blood and blackness then to me,
alas! and my heart in this parable,
as in a heavy shroud, found burial.

On your isle, Venus, I saw but one thing standing,
gallows-emblem from which my shape was hanging . . .
God! give me strength and will to contemplate
heart, body—without loathing, without hate.

Young Goodman Brown

NATHANIEL HAWTHORNE

Young Goodman Brown came forth at sunset into the street at Salem village; but put his head back, after crossing the threshold, to exchange a parting kiss with his young wife. And Faith, as the wife was aptly named, thrust her own pretty head into the street, letting the wind play with the pink ribbons of her cap while she called to Goodman Brown.

"Dearest heart," whispered she, softly and rather sadly, when her lips were close to his ear, "prithee put off your journey until sunrise and sleep in your own bed tonight. A lone woman is troubled with such dreams and such thoughts that she's afeard of herself sometimes. Pray tarry with me this night, dear husband, of all nights in the year."

"My love and my Faith," replied young Goodman Brown, "of all nights in the year, this one night must I tarry away from thee. My journey, as thou callest it, forth and back again, must needs be done 'twixt now and sunrise. What, my sweet, pretty wife, dost thou doubt me already, and we but three months married?"

"Then God bless you!" said Faith, with the pink ribbons; "and may you find all well when you come back."

"Amen!" cried Goodman Brown. "Say thy prayers, dear Faith, and go to bed at dusk, and no harm will come to thee."

So they parted; and the young man pursued his way until, being about to turn the corner by the meeting-house, he looked back and saw the head of Faith still peeping after him with a melancholy air, in spite of her pink ribbons.

"Poor little Faith!" thought he, for his heart smote him. "What a wretch am I to leave her on such an errand! She talks of dreams, too. Methought as she spoke there was trouble in her face, as if a dream had warned her what work is to be done to-night. But no, no; 't would kill her to think it. Well, she's a blessed angel on earth; and after this one night I'll cling to her skirts and follow her to heaven."

With this excellent resolve for the future, Goodman Brown felt himself justified in making more haste on his present evil purpose. He had taken a dreary road, darkened by all the gloomiest trees of the forest, which barely stood aside to let the narrow path creep through, and closed immediately behind. It was all as lonely as could be; and there is this peculiarity in such a solitude, that the traveller knows not who may be concealed by the innumerable trunks and the thick boughs overhead; so that with lonely footsteps he may yet be passing through an unseen multitude.

"There may be a devilish Indian behind every tree," said Goodman Brown to himself; and he glanced fearfully behind him as he added, "What if the devil himself should be at my very elbow!"

His head being turned back, he passed a crook of the road, and, looking forward again, beheld the figure of a man, in grave and decent attire, seated at the foot of an old tree. He arose at Goodman Brown's approach and walked onward side by side with him.

"You are late, Goodman Brown," said he. "The clock of the Old South was striking as I came through Boston, and that is full fifteen minutes agone."

"Faith kept me back a while," replied the young man, with a tremor in his voice, caused by the sudden appearance of his companion, though not wholly unexpected.

It was now deep dusk in the forest, and deepest in that part of it where these two were journeying. As nearly as could be discerned, the second traveller was about fifty years old, apparently in the same rank of life as Goodman Brown, and bearing a considerable resemblance to him, though perhaps more in expression than features. Still they might have been taken for father and son. And yet, though the elder person was as simply clad as the younger, and as simple in manner too, he had an indescribable air of one who knew the world, and who would not have felt abashed at the governor's dinner table or in King William's court, were it possible that his affairs should call him thither. But the only thing about him that could be fixed upon as remarkable was his staff, which bore the likeness of a great black snake, so curiously wrought that it might almost be seen to twist and wriggle itself like a living serpent. This, of course, must have been an ocular deception, assisted by the uncertain light.

"Come, Goodman Brown," cried his fellow-traveller, "this is a dull pace for the beginning of a journey. Take my staff, if you are so soon weary."

"Friend," said the other, exchanging his slow pace for a full stop, "having kept covenant by meeting thee here, it is my purpose now to return whence I came. I have scruples touching the matter thou wot'st of."

"Sayest thou so?" replied he of the serpent, smiling apart. "Let us walk on, nevertheless, reasoning as we go; and if I convince thee not thou shalt turn back. We are but a little way in the forest yet."

"Too far! too far!" exclaimed the goodman, unconsciously resuming his walk. "My father never went into the woods on such an errand, nor his father before him. We have been a race of honest men and good Christians since the days of the martyrs; and shall I be the first of the name of Brown that ever took this path and kept—"

"Such company, thou wouldst say," observed the elder person, interpreting his pause. "Well said, Goodman Brown! I have been as well acquainted with your family as with ever a one among the Puritans; and that's no trifle to say. I helped your grandfather, the constable, when he lashed the Quaker woman so smartly through the streets of Salem; and it was I that brought your father a pitch-pine knot, kindled at my own hearth, to set fire to an Indian village, in King Philip's war. They were my good friends, both; and many a pleasant walk have we had along this path, and returned merrily after midnight. I would fain be friends with you for their sake."

"If it be as thou sayest," replied Goodman Brown, "I marvel they never spoke of these matters; or, verily, I marvel not, seeing that the least rumor of the sort would have driven them from New England. We are a people of prayer, and good works to boot, and abide no such wickedness."

"Wickedness or not," said the traveller with the twisted staff, "I have a very general acquaintance here in New England. The deacons of many a church have drunk the communion wine with me; the selectmen of divers towns make me their chairman; and a majority of the Great and General Court are firm supporters of my interest. The governor and I, too— But these are state secrets."

"Can this be so?" cried Goodman Brown, with a stare of amazement at his undisturbed companion. "Howbeit, I have nothing to do with the governor and council; they have their own ways, and are no rule for a simple husbandman like me. But were I to go on with thee, how should I meet the eye of that good old man, our minister, at Salem village? Oh, his voice would make me tremble both Sabbath day and lecture day."

Thus far the elder traveller had listened with due gravity; but now burst into a fit of irrepressible mirth, shaking himself so violently that his snake-like staff actually seemed to wriggle in sympathy.

"Ha! ha! ha!" shouted he again and again; then composing himself, "Well, go on, Goodman Brown, go on; but, prithee, don't kill me with laughing."

"Well, then, to end the matter at once," said Goodman Brown, considerably nettled, "there is my wife, Faith. It would break her dear little heart; and I'd rather break my own."

"Nay, if that be the case," answered the other, "e'en go thy ways, Goodman Brown. I would not for twenty old women like the one hobbling before us that Faith should come to any harm."

As he spoke he pointed his staff at a female figure on the path, in whom Goodman Brown recognized a very pious and exemplary dame, who had taught him his catechism in youth, and was still his moral and spiritual adviser, jointly with the minister and Deacon Gookin.

"A marvel, truly, that Goody Cloyse should be so far in the wilderness at nightfall," said he. "But with your leave, friend, I shall take a cut through the woods until we have left this Christian woman behind. Being a stranger to you, she might ask whom I was consorting with and whither I was going."

"Be it so," said his fellow-traveller, "Betake you to the woods, and let me keep the path."

Accordingly the young man turned aside, but took care to watch his companion, who advanced softly along the road until he had come within a staff's length of the old dame. She, meanwhile, was making the best of her way, with singular speed for so aged a woman, and mumbling some indistinct words—a prayer, doubtless—as she went. The traveller put forth his staff and touched her withered neck with what seemed the serpent's tail.

"The devil!" screamed the pious old lady.

"Then Goody Cloyse knows her old friend?" observed the traveller, confronting her and leaning on his writhing stick.

"Ah, forsooth, and is it your worship indeed?" cried the good dame. "Yea, truly is it, and in the very image of my old gossip, Goodman Brown, the grandfather of the silly fellow that now is. But—would your worship believe it?—my broomstick hath strangely disappeared, stolen, as I suspect, by that unhanged witch, Goody Cory, and that, too, when I was all anointed with the juice of smallage, and cinquefoil, and wolf's bane—"

"Mingled with fine wheat and the fat of a new-born babe," said the shape of old Goodman Brown.

"Ah, your worship knows the recipe," cried the old lady, cackling aloud. "So, as I was saying, being all ready for the meeting, and no horse to ride on, I made up my mind to foot it; for they tell me there is a nice young man to be taken into communion to-night. But now your good worship will lend me your arm, and we shall be there in a twinkling."

"That can hardly be," answered her friend. "I may not spare you my arm, Goody Cloyse; but here is my staff, if you will."

So saying, he threw it down at her feet, where, perhaps, it assumed life, being one of the rods which its owner had formerly lent to the Egyptian magi. Of this fact, however, Goodman Brown could not take cognizance. He had cast up his eyes in astonishment, and, looking down again, beheld neither Goody Cloyse nor the serpentine staff, but his fellow-traveller alone, who waited for him as calmly as if nothing had happened.

"That old woman taught me my catechism," said the young man; and there was a world of meaning in this simple comment.

They continued to walk onward, while the elder traveller exhorted his companion to make good speed and persevere in the path, discoursing so aptly that his arguments seemed rather to spring up in the bosom of his auditor than to be suggested by himself. As they went, he plucked a branch of maple to serve for a walking stick, and began to strip it of the twigs and little boughs, which were wet with evening dew. The moment his fingers touched them they became strangely withered and dried up as with a week's sunshine. Thus the pair proceeded, at a good free pace, until suddenly, in a gloomy hollow of the road, Goodman Brown sat himself down on the stump of a tree and refused to go any farther.

"Friend," said he, stubbornly, "my mind is made up. Not another step will I budge on this errand. What if a wretched old woman do choose to go to the devil when I thought she was going to heaven: is that any reason why I should quit my dear Faith and go after her?"

"You will think better of this by and by," said his acquaintance, composedly. "Sit here and rest yourself a while; and when you feel like moving again, there is my staff to help you along."

Without more words, he threw his companion the maple stick, and was as speedily out of sight as if he had vanished into the deepening gloom. The young man sat a few moments by the roadside, applauding himself greatly, and thinking with how clear a conscience he should meet the minister in his morning walk, nor shrink from the eye of good old Deacon Gookin. And what calm sleep would be his that very night, which was to have been spent so wickedly, but so purely and sweetly now, in the arms of Faith! Amidst these pleasant and praiseworthy meditations,

Goodman Brown heard the tramp of horses along the road, and deemed it advisable to conceal himself within the verge of the forest, conscious of the guilty purpose that had brought him thither, though now so happily turned from it.

On came the hoof tramps and the voices of the riders, two grave old voices, conversing soberly as they drew near. These mingled sounds appeared to pass along the road, within a few yards of the young man's hiding-place; but, owing doubtless to the depth of the gloom at that particular spot, neither the travellers nor their steeds were visible. Though their figures brushed the small boughs by the wayside, it could not be seen that they intercepted, even for a moment, the faint gleam from the strip of bright sky athwart which they must have passed. Goodman Brown alternately crouched and stood on tiptoe, pulling aside the branches and thrusting forth his head as far as he durst without discerning so much as a shadow. It vexed him the more, because he could have sworn, were such a thing possible, that he recognized the voices of the minister and Deacon Gookin, jogging along quietly, as they were wont to do, when bound to some ordination or ecclesiastical council. While yet within hearing, one of the riders stopped to pluck a switch.

"Of the two, reverend sir," said the voice like the deacon's, "I had rather miss an ordination dinner than to-night's meeting. They tell me that some of our community are to be here from Falmouth and beyond, and others from Connecticut and Rhode Island, besides several of the Indian powwows, who, after their fashion, know almost as much deviltry as the best of us. Moreover, there is a goodly young woman to be taken into communion."

"Mighty well, Deacon Gookin!" replied the solemn old tones of the minister. "Spur up, or we shall be late. Nothing can be done, you know, until I get on the ground."

The hoofs clattered again; and the voices, talking so strangely in the empty air, passed on through the forest, where no church had ever been gathered or solitary Christian prayed. Whither, then, could these holy men be journeying so deep into the heathen wilderness? Young Goodman Brown caught hold of a tree for support, being ready to sink down on the ground, faint and overburdened with the heavy sickness of his heart. He looked up to the sky, doubting whether there really was a heaven above him. Yet there was the blue arch, and the stars brightening in it.

"With heaven above and Faith below, I will yet stand firm against the devil!" cried Goodman Brown.

While he still gazed upward into the deep arch of the firmament and had lifted his hands to pray, a cloud, though no wind was stirring, hurried across the zenith and hid the brightening stars. The blue sky was still visible, except directly overhead, where this black mass of cloud was sweeping swiftly northward. Aloft in the air, as if from the depths of the cloud, came a confused and doubtful sound of voices. Once the listener fancied that he could distinguish the accents of towns-people of his own, men and women, both pious and ungodly, many of whom he had met at the communion table, and had seen others rioting at the tavern. The next moment, so indistinct were the sounds, he doubted whether he had heard aught but the murmur of the old forest, whispering without a wind. Then came a stronger swell of those familiar tones, heard daily in the sunshine of Salem village, but never until now from a cloud of night. There was one voice, of a young woman, uttering lamentations, yet with an uncertain sorrow, and entreating for some favor, which, perhaps, it would grieve her to obtain; and all the unseen multitude, both saints and sinners, seemed to encourage her onward.

"Faith!" shouted Goodman Brown, in a voice of agony and desperation; and the echoes of the forest mocked him, crying, "Faith! Faith!" as if bewildered wretches were seeking her all through the wilderness.

The cry of grief, rage, and terror was yet piercing the night, when the unhappy husband held his breath for a response. There was a scream, drowned immediately in a louder murmur of voices, fading into far-off laughter, as the dark cloud swept away, leaving the clear and silent sky above Goodman Brown. But something fluttered lightly down through the air and caught on the branch of a tree. The young man seized it, and beheld a pink ribbon.

"My Faith is gone!" cried he, after one stupefied moment. "There is no good on earth; and sin is but a name. Come, devil; for to thee is this world given."

And, maddened with despair, so that he laughed loud and long, did Goodman Brown grasp his staff and set forth again, at such a rate that he seemed to fly along the forest path rather than to walk or run. The road grew wilder and drearier and more faintly traced, and vanished at length, leaving him in the heart of the dark wilderness, still rushing onward with the instinct that guides mortal man to evil. The whole forest was peopled with frightful sounds—the creaking of the trees, the howling of wild beasts, and the yell of Indians; while sometimes the wind tolled like a distant church bell, and sometimes gave a broad roar around the traveller, as if all Nature were laughing him to scorn. But he was himself the chief horror of the scene, and shrank not from its other horrors.

"Ha! ha! ha!" roared Goodman Brown when the wind laughed at him. "Let us hear which will laugh loudest. Think not to frighten me with your deviltry. Come witch, come wizard, come Indian powwow, come devil himself, and here comes Goodman Brown. You may as well hear him as he fear you."

In truth, all through the haunted forest there could be nothing more frightful than the figure of Goodman Brown. On he flew among the black pines, brandishing his staff with frenzied gestures, now giving vent to an inspiration of horrid blasphemy, and now shouting forth such laughter as set all the echoes of the forest laughing like demons around him. The fiend in his own shape is less hideous than when he rages in the breast of man. Thus sped the demoniac on his course, until, quivering among the trees, he saw a red light before him, as when the felled trunks and branches of a clearing have been set on fire, and throw up their lurid blaze against the sky, at the hour of midnight. He paused, in a lull of the tempest that had driven him onward, and heard the swell of what seemed a hymn, rolling solemnly from a distance with the weight of many voices. He knew the tune; it was a familiar one in the choir of the village meeting-house. The verse died heavily away, and was lengthened by a chorus, not of human voices, but of all the sounds of the benighted wilderness pealing in awful harmony together. Goodman Brown cried out, and his cry was lost to his own ear by its unison with the cry of the desert.

In the interval of silence, he stole forward until the light glared full upon his eyes. At one extremity of an open space, hemmed in by the dark wall of the forest, arose a rock, bearing some rude, natural resemblance either to an altar or a pulpit, and surrounded by four blazing pines, their tops aflame, their stems untouched, like candles at an evening meeting. The mass of foliage that had overgrown the summit of the rock was all on fire, blazing high into the night and fitfully illuminating the whole field. Each pendent twig and leafy festoon was in a blaze. As the red light arose and fell, a numerous congregation alternately shone forth, then disappeared in shadow, and again grew, as it were, out of the darkness, peopling the heart of the solitary woods at once.

"A grave and dark-clad company," quoth Goodman Brown.

In truth they were such. Among them, quivering to and fro between gloom and splendor, appeared faces that would be seen next day at the council board of the province, and others which, Sabbath after Sabbath, looked devoutly heavenward, and benignantly over the crowded pews, from the holiest pulpits in the land. Some affirm that the lady of the governor was there. At least there were high dames well known to her, and wives of honored husbands, and widows, a great multitude, and ancient maidens, all of excellent repute, and fair young girls, who trembled lest their mother should espy them. Either the sudden gleams of light flashing over the obscure field bedazzled Goodman Brown, or he recognized a score of the church members of Salem village famous for their special sanctity. Good old Deacon Gookin had arrived, and waited at the skirts of that venerable saint, his revered pastor. But, irreverently consorting with these grave, reputable, and pious people, these elders of the church, these chaste dames and dewy virgins, there were men of dissolute lives and women of spotted fame, wretches given over to all mean and filthy vice, and suspected even of horrid crimes. It was strange to see that the good shrank not from the wicked, nor were the sinners abashed by the saints. Scattered also among their pale-faced enemies were the Indian priests, or powwows, who had often scared their native forest with more hideous incantations than any known to English witchcraft.

"But where is Faith?" thought Goodman Brown; and, as hope came into his heart, he trembled.

Another verse of the hymn arose, a slow and mournful strain, such as the pious love, but joined to words which expressed all that our nature can conceive of sin, and darkly hinted at far more. Unfathomable to mere mortals is the lore of fiends. Verse after verse was sung; and still the chorus of the desert swelled between like the deepest tone of a mighty organ; and with the final peal of that dreadful anthem there came a sound, as if the roaring wind, the rushing streams, the howling beasts, and every other voice of the unconcerted wilderness were mingling and according with the voice of guilty man in homage to the prince of all. The four blazing pines threw up a loftier flame, and obscurely discovered shapes and visages of horror on the smoke wreaths above the impious assembly. At the same moment the fire on the rock shot redly forth and formed a glowing arch above its base, where now appeared a figure. With reverence be it spoken, the figure bore no slight similitude, both in garb and manner, to some grave divine of the New England churches.

"Bring forth the converts!" cried a voice that echoed through the field and rolled into the forest.

At the word, Goodman Brown stepped forth from the shadow of the trees and approached the congregation, with whom he felt a loathful brotherhood by the sympathy of all that was wicked in his heart. He could have well-nigh sworn that the shape of his own dead father beckoned him to advance, looking downward from a smoke wreath, while a woman, with dim features of despair, threw out her hand to warn him back. Was it his mother? But he had no power to retreat one step, nor to resist, even in thought, when the minister and good old Deacon Gookin seized his arms and led him to the blazing rock. Thither came also the slender form of a veiled female, led between Goody Cloyse, that pious teacher of the catechism, and Martha Carrier, who had received the devil's promise to be queen of hell. A rampant hag was she. And there stood the proselytes beneath the canopy of fire.

"Welcome, my children," said the dark figure, "to the communion of your race. Ye have found thus young your nature and your destiny. My children, look behind you!"

They turned; and flashing forth, as it were, in a sheet of flame, the fiend worshippers were seen; the smile of welcome gleamed darkly on every visage.

"There," resumed the sable form, "are all whom we have reverenced from youth. Ye deemed them holier than yourselves, and shrank from your own sin, contrasting it with their lives of righteousness and prayerful aspirations heavenward. Yet here are they all in my worshipping assembly. This night it shall be granted you to know their secret deeds: how hoary-bearded elders of the church have whispered wanton words to the young maids of their households; how many a woman, eager for widows' weeds, has given her husband a drink at bedtime and let him sleep his last sleep in her bosom; how beardless youths have made haste to inherit their fathers' wealth, and how fair damsels—blush not, sweet ones—have dug little graves in the garden, and bidden me, the sole guest, to an infant's funeral. By the sympathy of your human hearts for sin ye shall scent out all the places—whether in church, bed-chamber, street, field, or forest—where crime has been committed, and shall exult to behold the whole earth one stain of guilt, one mighty blood spot. Far more than this. It shall be yours to penetrate, in every bosom, the deep mystery of sin, the fountain of all wicked arts, and which inexhaustibly supplies more evil impulses than human power—than my power at its utmost—can make manifest in deeds. And now, my children, look upon each other."

They did so; and, by the blaze of the hell-kindled torches, the wretched man beheld his Faith, and the wife her husband, trembling before that unhallowed altar.

"Lo, there ye stand, my children," said the figure, in a deep and solemn tone, almost sad with its despairing awfulness, as if his once angelic nature could yet mourn for our miserable race. "Depending upon one another's hearts, ye had still hoped that virtue were not all a dream. Now are ye undeceived. Evil is the nature of mankind. Evil must be your only happiness. Welcome again, my children, to the communion of your race."

"Welcome," repeated the fiend worshippers, in one cry of despair and triumph.

And there they stood, the only pair, as it seemed, who were yet hesitating on the verge of wickedness in this dark world. A basin was hollowed, naturally, in the rock. Did it contain water, reddened by the lurid light, or was it blood? or, perchance, a liquid flame? Herein did the shape of evil dip his hand and prepare to lay the mark of baptism upon their foreheads, that they might be partakers of the mystery of sin, more conscious of the secret guilt of others, both in deed and thought, than they could now be of their own. The husband cast one look at his pale wife, and Faith at him. What polluted wretches would the next glance show them to each other, shuddering alike at what they disclosed and what they saw!

"Faith! Faith!" cried the husband, "look up to heaven, and resist the wicked one."

Whether Faith obeyed he knew not. Hardly had he spoken when he found himself amid calm night and solitude, listening to a roar of the wind which died heavily away through the forest. He staggered against the rock, and felt it chill and damp; while a hanging twig, that had been all on fire, besprinkled his cheek with the coldest dew.

The next morning young Goodman Brown came slowly into the street of Salem village, staring around him like a bewildered man. The good old minister was taking a walk along the graveyard to get an appetite for breakfast and meditate his sermon, and bestowed a blessing, as he passed, on Goodman Brown. He shrank from the venerable saint as if to avoid an anathema. Old Deacon Gookin was at domestic worship, and the holy words of his prayer were heard through the open window. "What God doth the wizard pray to?" quoth Goodman Brown. Goody Cloyse, that excellent old Christian, stood in the early sunshine at her own lattice, catechizing a little girl who had brought her a pint of morning's milk. Goodman Brown snatched away the child as from the grasp of the fiend himself. Turning the corner by the meeting-house, he spied the head of Faith, with the pink ribbons, gazing anxiously forth, and bursting into such joy at sight of him that she skipped along the street and almost kissed her husband before the whole village. But Goodman Brown looked sternly and sadly into her face, and passed on without a greeting.

Had Goodman Brown fallen asleep in the forest and only dreamed a wild dream of a witch-meeting?

Be it so if you will; but, alas! it was a dream of evil omen for young Goodman Brown. A stern, a sad, a darkly meditative, a distrustful, if not a desperate man did he become from the night of that fearful dream. On the Sabbath day, when the congregation were singing a holy psalm, he could not listen because an anthem of sin rushed loudly upon his ear and drowned all the blessed strain. When the minister spoke from the pulpit with power and fervid eloquence, and, with his hand on the open Bible, of the sacred truths of our religion, and of saint-like lives and triumphant deaths, and of future bliss or misery unutterable, then did Goodman Brown turn pale, dreading lest the roof should thunder down upon the gray blasphemer and his hearers. Often, awaking suddenly at midnight, he shrank from the bosom of Faith; and at morning or eventide, when the family knelt down at prayer, he scowled and muttered to himself, and gazed sternly at his wife, and turned away. And when he had lived long, and was borne to his grave a hoary corpse, followed by Faith, an aged woman, and children and grandchildren, a goodly procession, besides neighbors not a few, they carved no hopeful verse upon his tombstone, for his dying hour was gloom.

Becoming: The Fall from Innocence to Experience

THE fall motif generally focuses upon the change from a state of innocence to a state of sophistication (worldliness), in which the protagonist has learned from his experience that life is not the Edenic world he assumed it to be. Robin in Hawthorne's "My Kinsman, Major Molineaux" leaves his country home and learns of the complexity of life in the city—politics, prostitutes, and duplicity; yet, like Salinger's Holden Caulfield, he learns that there is no return to the protection of the family. Thomas Wolfe summed up this theme in a novel entitled *You Can't Go Home Again*. The fall, taken from Man's point of view, often occurs through Woman, who thus is seen as temptress. Mythically she is the medium for Man's fall because she, the weaker vessel, has fallen through conceit (narcissism) to the blandishment of the evil force in the world, which is opposed to God.

Adam and Eve
GENESIS, Chapters 2 and 3

CHAPTER 2

15 And the Lord God took the man, and put him into the garden of Eden to dress it and to keep it.   16 And the Lord God commanded the man, saying, Of every tree of the garden thou mayest freely eat: 17 But of the tree of the knowledge of good and evil, thou shalt not eat of it: for in the day that thou eatest thereof thou shalt surely die.   18 And the Lord God said, *It is* not good that the man should be alone; I will make him an help meet for him.   19 And out of the ground the Lord God formed every beast of the field and every fowl of the air; and brought *them* unto Adam to see what he would call them: and whatsoever Adam called every living creature, that *was* the name thereof.   20 And Adam gave names to all cattle, and to the fowl of the air, and to every beast of the field; but for Adam there was not found an help meet for him.   21 And the Lord God caused a deep sleep to fall upon Adam, and he slept: and he took one of his ribs, and closed up the flesh instead thereof; 22 And the rib, which the Lord God had taken from man, made he a

woman, and brought her unto the man.   23 And Adam said, This *is* now bone of my bones, and flesh of my flesh: she shall be called Woman, because she was taken out of man.   24 Therefore shall a man leave his father and his mother, and shall cleave unto his wife: and they shall be one flesh.   25 And they were both naked, the man and his wife, and were not ashamed.

CHAPTER 3

1 Now the serpent was more subtile than any beast of the field which the Lord God had made. And he said unto the woman, Yea, hath God said, Ye shall not eat of every tree of the garden?   2 And the woman said unto the serpent, We may eat of the fruit of the trees of the garden: 3 But of the fruit of the tree which *is* in the midst of the garden, God hath said, Ye shall not eat of it, neither shall ye touch it, lest ye die. 4 And the serpent said unto the woman, Ye shall not surely die: 5 For God doth know that in the day ye eat thereof, then your eyes shall be opened, and ye shall be as gods, knowing good and evil.   6 And when the woman saw that the tree *was* good for food, and that it *was* pleasant to the eyes, and a tree to be desired to make *one* wise, she took of the fruit thereof, and did eat, and gave also unto her husband with her; and he did eat.   7 And the eyes of them both were opened, and they knew that they *were* naked; and they sewed fig leaves together, and made themselves aprons.   8 And they heard the voice of the Lord God walking in the garden in the cool of the day: and Adam and his wife hid themselves from the presence of the Lord God amongst the trees of the garden.   9 And the Lord God called unto Adam, and said unto him, Where *art* thou?   10 And he said, I heard thy voice in the garden, and I was afraid, because I *was* naked; and I hid myself.   11 And he said, Who told thee that thou *wast* naked? Hast thou eaten of the tree whereof I commanded thee that thou shouldest not eat?   12 And the man said, The woman whom thou gavest *to be* with me, she gave me of the tree, and I did eat.   13 And the Lord God said unto the woman, What *is* this *that* thou hast done? And the woman said, The serpent beguiled me, and I did eat.   14 And the Lord God said unto the serpent, Because thou hast done this, thou *art* cursed above all cattle, and above every beast of the field; upon thy belly shalt thou go, and dust shalt thou eat all the days of thy life: 15 And I will put enmity between thee and the woman, and between thy seed and her seed; it shall bruise thy head, and thou shalt bruise his heel.   16 Unto the woman he said, I will greatly multiply thy sorrow and thy conception; in sorrow thou shalt bring forth children; and thy desire *shall be* to thy husband, and he shall rule over thee.   17 And unto Adam he said, Because thou hast hearkened unto the voice of thy wife, and hast eaten of the tree, of which I

commanded thee, saying, Thou shalt not eat of it: cursed *is* the ground
for thy sake; in sorrow shalt thou eat *of* it all the days of thy life;   18
Thorns also and thistles shall it bring forth to thee; and thou shalt eat the
herb of the field;   19 In the sweat of thy face shalt thou eat bread, till
thou return unto the ground; for out of it wast thou taken: for dust thou
art, and unto dust shalt thou return.   20 And Adam called his wife's
name Eve; because she was the mother of all living.   21 Unto Adam
also and to his wife did the Lord God make coats of skins, and clothed
them.   22 And the Lord God said, Behold, the man is become as one
of us, to know good and evil: and now, lest he put forth his hand, and
take also of the tree of life, and eat, and live for ever: 23 Therefore
the Lord God sent him forth from the garden of Eden, to till the ground
from whence he was taken.   24 So he drove out the man; and he
placed at the east of the garden of Eden Cherubims, and a flaming sword
which turned every way, to keep the way of the tree of life.

The Fall of Adam and Eve

(from Paradise Lost, IX, 722–1189)

JOHN MILTON

[Satan urg'd]: If they all things, who enclos'd
Knowledge of Good and Evil in this Tree,
That whoso eats thereof, forthwith attains
Wisdom without their leave? and wherein lies
Th' offence, that Man should thus attain to know?
What can your knowledge hurt him, or this Tree
Impart against his will if all be his?
Or is it envie, and can envie dwell
In heav'nly brests? these, these and many more
Causes import your need of this fair Fruit.
Goddess humane, reach then, and freely taste.
      He ended, and his words replete with guile
Into her heart too easie entrance won:
Fixt on the Fruit she gaz'd, which to behold
Might tempt alone, and in her ears the sound
Yet rung of his perswasive words, impregn'd
With Reason, to her seeming, and with Truth;
Mean while the hour of Noon drew on, and wak'd
An eager appetite, rais'd by the smell

So savorie of that Fruit, which with desire,
Inclinable now grown to touch or taste,
Sollicited her longing eye; yet first
Pausing a while, thus to her self she mus'd.
    Great are thy Vertues, doubtless, best of Fruits,
Though kept from Man, and worthy to be admir'd,
Whose taste, too long forborn, at first assay
Gave elocution to the mute, and taught
The Tongue not made for Speech to speak thy praise:
Thy praise hee also who forbids thy use,
Conceals not from us, naming thee the Tree
Of Knowledge, knowledge both of good and evil;
Forbids us then to taste, but his forbidding
Commends thee more, while it inferrs the good
By thee communicated, and our want:
For good unknown, sure is not had, or had
And yet unknown, is as not had at all.
In plain then, what forbids he but to know,
Forbids us good, forbids us to be wise?
Such prohibitions bind not. But if Death
Bind us with after-bands, what profits then
Our inward freedom? In the day we eat
Of this fair Fruit, our doom is, we shall die.
How dies the Serpent? hee hath eat'n and lives,
And knows, and speaks, and reasons, and discerns,
Irrational till then. For us alone
Was death invented? or to us deni'd
This intellectual food, for beasts reserv'd?
For Beasts it seems: yet that one Beast which first
Hath tasted, envies not, but brings with joy
The good befall'n him, Author unsuspect,
Friendly to man, farr from deceit or guile.
What fear I then, rather what know to fear
Under this ignorance of Good and Evil,
Of God or Death, of Law or Penaltie?
Here grows the Cure of all, this Fruit Divine,
Fair to the Eye, inviting to the Taste,
Of vertue to make wise: what hinders then
To reach, and feed at once both Bodie and Mind?
    So saying, her rash hand in evil hour
Forth reaching to the Fruit, she pluck'd, she eat:
Earth felt the wound, and Nature from her seat
Sighing through all her Works gave signs of woe,
That all was lost. Back to the Thicket slunk

The guiltie Serpent, and well might, for *Eve*
Intent now wholly on her taste, naught else
Regarded, such delight till then, as seemd,
In Fruit she never tasted, whether true
Or fansied so, through expectation high
Of knowledge, nor was God-head from her thought.
Greedily she ingorg'd without restraint,
And knew not eating Death: Satiate at length,
And hight'n'd as with Wine, jocond and boon,
Thus to her self she pleasingly began.
     O Sovran, vertuous, precious of all Trees
In Paradise, of operation blest
To Sapience, hitherto obscur'd, infam'd,
And thy fair Fruit let hang, as to no end
Created; but henceforth my early care,
Not without Song, each Morning, and due praise
Shall tend thee, and the fertil burden ease
Of thy full branches offer'd free to all;
Till dieted by thee I grow mature
In knowledge, as the Gods who all things know;
Though others envie what they cannot give;
For had the gift bin theirs, it had not here
Thus grown. Experience, next to thee I owe,
Best guide; not following thee, I had remain
In ignorance, thou op'nst Wisdoms way,
And giv'st access, though secret she retire.
And I perhaps am secret; Heav'n is high,
High and remote to see from thence distinct
Each thing on Earth; and other care perhaps
May have diverted from continual watch
Our great Forbidder, safe with all his Spies
About him. But to *Adam* in what sort
Shall I appeer? shall I to him make known
As yet my change, and give him to partake
Full happiness with me, or rather not,
But keep the odds of Knowledge in my power
Without Copartner? so to add what wants
In Femal Sex, the more to draw his Love,
And render me more equal, and perhaps,
A thing not undesirable, somtime
Superior; for inferior who is free?
This may be well: but what if God have seen,
And Death ensue? then I shall be no more,
And *Adam* wedded to another *Eve*,

Shall live with her enjoying, I extinct;
A death to think. Confirm'd then I resolve,
Adam shall share with me in bliss or woe:
So dear I love him, that with him all deaths
I could endure, without him live no life.
     So saying, from the Tree her step she turnd,
. . . To him she hasted, in her face excuse
Came Prologue, and Apologie to prompt,
Which with bland words at will she thus addrest.
     Hast thou not wonderd, *Adam*, at my stay?
Thee I have misst, and thought it long, depriv'd
They presence, agonie of love till now
Not felt, nor shall be twice, for never more
Mean I to trie, what rash untri'd I sought,
The pain of absence from thy sight. . . .
     Thus *Eve* with Countnance blithe her storie told;
But in her Cheek distemper flushing glowd.
On th' other side, *Adam*, soon as he heard
The fatal Trespass don by *Eve*, amaz'd,
Astonied stood and Blank, while horror chill
Ran through his veins, and all his joynts relax'd;
From his slack hand the Garland wreath'd for *Eve*
Down drop'd, and all the faded Roses shed:
Speechless he stood and pale, till thus at length
First to himself he inward silence broke.
     O fairest of Creation, last and best
Of all Gods works, Creature in whom excell'd
Whatever can to sight or thought be formd,
Holy, dvine, good, amiable, or sweet!
How art thou lost, how on a sudden lost,
Defac't, deflowrd, and now to Death devote?
Rather how hast thou yeelded to transgress
The strict forbiddance, how to violate
The sacred Fruit forbidd'n! som cursed fraud
Of Enemie hath beguil'd thee, yet unknown,
And mee with thee hath ruind, for with thee
Certain my resolution is to Die;
How can I live without thee, how forgoe
Thy sweet Converse and Love so dearly joyn'd,
To live again in these wild Woods forlorn?
Should God create another *Eve*, and I
Another Rib afford, yet loss of thee
Would never from my heart; no no, I feel
The Link of Nature draw me: Flesh of Flesh,

Bone of my Bone thou art, and from thy State
Mine never shall be parted, bliss or woe.
       . . . So *Adam,* and thus *Eve* to him repli'd.
O glorious trial of exceeding Love,
Illustrious evidence, example high!
Ingaging me to emulate, but short
Of thy perfection, how shall I attain,
Adam, from whose dear side I boast me sprung,
And gladly of our Union hear thee speak,
One Heart, one Soul in both; whereof good prooff
This day affords, declaring thee resolv'd,
Rather then Death or aught then Death more dread
Shall separate us, linkt in Love so dear,
To undergoe with mee one Guilt, one Crime,
If any be, of tasting this fair Fruit,
Whose vertue, for of good still good proceeds,
Direct, or by occasion hath presented
This happie trial of thy Love, which else
So eminently ever had bin known.
Were it I thought Death menac't would ensue
This my attempt, I would sustain alone
The worst, and not perswade thee, rather die
Deserted, then oblige thee with a fact
Pernicious to thy Peace, chiefly assur'd
Remarkably so late of thy so true,
So faithful Love unequald; but I feel
Farr otherwise th' event, not Death, but Life
Augmented, op'n'd Eyes, new Hopes, new Joyes,
Taste so Divine, that what of sweet before
Hath toucht my sense, flat seems to this, and harsh.
On my experience, *Adam,* freely taste,
And fear of Death deliver to the Winds.
       So saying, she embrac'd him, and for joy
Tenderly wept, much won that he his Love
Had so enobl'd, as of choice t' incurr
Divine displeasure for her sake, or Death.
In recompence (for such compliance bad
Such recompence best merits) from the bough
She gave him of that fair enticing Fruit
With liberal hand: he scrupl'd not to eat,
Against his better knowledge, not deceav'd,
But fondly overcome with Femal charm.
Earth trembl'd from her entrails, as again
In pangs, and Nature gave a second groan,

Skie lowr'd, and muttering Thunder, som sad drops
Wept at compleating of the mortal Sin
Original; while *Adam* took no thought,
Eating his fill, nor *Eve* to iterate
Her former trespass fear'd, the more to soothe
Him with her lov'd societie, that now
As with new Wine intoxicated both
They swim in mirth, and fansie that they feel
Divinitie within them breeding wings
Wherewith to scorn the Earth: but that false Fruit
Farr other operation first displaid,
Carnal desire enflaming, hee on *Eve*
Began to cast lascivious Eyes, she him
As wantonly repaid; in Lust they burn:
Till *Adam* thus 'gan *Eve* to dalliance move.
   Eve, now I see thou art exact of taste,
And elegant, of Sapience no small part,
Since to each meaning savour we apply,
And Palate call judicious; I the praise
Yeild thee, so well this day thou hast purvey'd.
Much pleasure we have lost, while we abstain'd
From this delightful Fruit, nor known till now
True relish, tasting; if such pleasure be
In things to us forbidden, it might be wish'd,
For this one Tree had bin forbidden ten.
But come, so well refresh't, now let us play,
As meet is, after such delicious Fare;
For never did thy Beautie since the day
I saw thee first and wedded thee, adorn'd
With all perfections, so enflame my sense
With ardor to enjoy thee, fairer now
Then ever, bountie of this vertuous Tree.
   So said he, and forbore not glance or toy
Of amorous intent, well understood
Of *Eve*, whose Eye darted contagious Fire.
Her hand he seis'd, and to a shadie bank,
Thick overhead with verdant roof imbowr'd
He led her nothing loath; Flowrs were the Couch,
Pansies, and Violets, and Asphodel,
And Hyacinth, Earths freshest softest lap.
There they thir fill of Love and Loves disport
Took largely, of thir mutual guilt the Seal,
The solace of thir sin, till dewie sleep
Oppress'd them, wearied with thir amorous play.

Soon as the force of that fallacious Fruit,
That with exhilerating vapour bland
About thir spirits had plaid, and inmost powers
Made err, was now exhal'd, and grosser sleep
Bred of unkindly fumes, with conscious dreams
Encumberd, now had left them, up they rose
As from unrest, and each the other viewing,
Soon found thir Eyes how op'n'd, and thir minds
How dark'n'd; innocence, that as a veil
Had shadow'd them from knowing ill, was gon,
Just confidence, and native righteousness,
And honour from about them, naked left
To guiltie shame: hee cover'd, but his Robe
Uncover'd more. So rose the *Danite* strong
Herculean Samson from the Harlot-lap
of *Philistean Dalilah,* and wak'd
Shorn of his strength. They destitute and bare
Of all thir vertue: silent, and in face
Confounded long they sate, as struck'n mute,
Till *Adam,* though not less then *Eve* abash't,
At length gave utterance to these words constraind.
          O *Eve,* in evil hour thou didst give ear
To that false Worm, of whomsoever taught
To counterfet Mans voice, true in our Fall,
False in our promis'd Rising; since our Eyes
Op'n'd we find indeed, and find we know
Both Good and Evil, Good lost, and Evil got,
Bad Fruit of Knowledge, if this be to know,
Which leaves us naked thus, of Honour void,
Of Innocence, of Faith, of Puritie,
Our wonted Ornaments now soild and staind,
And in our Faces evident the signes
Of foul concupiscence; whence evil store;
Ev'n shame, the last of evils; of the first
Be sure then. . . . Cover me ye Pines,
Ye Cedars, with innumerable boughs
Hide me, where I may never see them [God and angels] more.
But let us now, as in bad plight, devise
What best may for the present serve to hide
The Parts of each from other, that seem most
To shame obnoxious, and unseemliest seen,
Some Tree whose broad smooth Leaves together sewd,
And girded on our loyns, may cover round
Those middle parts, that this new commer, Shame,

There sit not, and reproach us as unclean.
. . . Thus fenc't, and as they thought, thir shame in part
Coverd, but not at rest or ease of Mind,
They sate them down to weep, nor onely Teares
Raind at thir Eyes, but high Winds worse within
Began to rise, high Passions, Anger, Hate,
Mistrust, Suspicion, Discord, and shook sore
Thir inward State of Mind, calm Region once
And full of Peace, now tost and turbulent:
For Understanding rul'd not, and the Will
Heard not her lore, both in subjection now
To sensual Appetite, who from beneath
Usurping over sovran Reason claimd
Superior sway: . . . Thus they in mutual accusation spent
The fruitless hours, but neither self-condemning,
And of thir vain contest appeer'd no end.

Araby

JAMES JOYCE

North Richmond Street, being blind, was a quiet street except at the hour when the Christian Brothers' School set the boys free. An uninhabited house of two storeys stood at the blind end, detached from its neighbours in a square ground. The other houses of the street, conscious of decent lives within them, gazed at one another with brown imperturbable faces.

The former tenant of our house, a priest, had died in the back drawing-room. Air, musty from having been long enclosed, hung in all the rooms, and the waste room behind the kitchen was littered with old useless papers. Among these I found a few paper-covered books, the pages of which were curled and damp: *The Abbot,* by Walter Scott, *The Devout Communicant* and *The Memoirs of Vidocq.* I liked the last best because its leaves were yellow. The wild garden behind the house contained a central apple-tree and a few straggling bushes under one of which I found the late tenant's rusty bicycle-pump. He had been a very charitable priest; in his will he had left all his money to institutions and the furniture of his house to his sister.

When the short days of winter came dusk fell before we had well eaten our dinners. When we met in the street the houses had grown sombre. The space of the sky above us was the colour of ever-changing violet and towards it the lamps of the street lifted their feeble lanterns. The cold air stung us and we played till our bodies glowed. Our shouts echoed in the silent street. The career of our play brought us through the dark muddy lanes behind the houses where we ran the gauntlet of the rough tribes from the cottages, to the back doors of the dark dripping gardens where odours arose from the ashpits, to the dark odorous stables where a coachman smoothed and combed the horse or shook music from the buckled harness. When we returned to the street light from the kitchen windows had filled the areas. If my uncle was seen turning the corner we hid in the shadow until we had seen him safely housed. Or if Mangan's sister came out on the doorstep to call her brother in to his tea we watched her from our shadow peer up and down the street. We waited to see whether she would remain or go in and, if she remained, we left our shadow and walked up to Mangan's steps resignedly. She was waiting for us, her figure defined by the light from the half-opened door. Her brother always teased her before he obeyed and I stood by the railings looking at her. Her dress swung as she moved her body and the soft rope of her hair tossed from side to side.

Every morning I lay on the floor in the front parlour watching her door. The blind was pulled down to within an inch of the sash so that I could not be seen. When she came out on the doorstep my heart leaped. I ran to the hall, seized my books and followed her. I kept her brown figure always in my eye and, when we came near the point at which our ways diverged, I quickened my pace and passed her. This happened morning after morning. I had never spoken to her, except for a few casual words, and yet her name was like a summons to all my foolish blood.

Her image accompanied me even in places the most hostile to romance. On Saturday evenings when my aunt went marketing I had to go to carry some of the parcels. We walked through the flaring streets, jostled by drunken men and bargaining women, amid the curses of labourers, the shrill litanies of shop-boys who stood on guard by the barrels of pigs' cheeks, the nasal chanting of street-singers, who sang a *come-all-you* about O'Donovan Rossa, or a ballad about the troubles in our native land. These noises converged in a single sensation of life for me: I imagined that I bore my chalice safely through a throng of foes. Her name sprang to my lips at moments in strange prayers and praises which I myself did not understand. My eyes were often full of tears (I could not tell why) and at times a flood from my heart seemed to pour itself out into my bosom. I thought little of the future. I did not know whether I would ever speak to her or not or, if I spoke to her, how I could tell her of my confused adoration. But my body was like a harp and her words and gestures were like fingers running upon the wires.

One evening I went into the back drawing-room in which the priest had died. It was a dark rainy evening and there was no sound in the house. Through one of the broken panes I heard the rain impinge upon the earth, the fine incessant needles of water playing in the sodden beds. Some distant lamp or lighted window gleamed below me. I was thankful that I could see so little. All my senses seemed to desire to veil themselves and, feeling that I was about to slip from them, I pressed the palms of my hands together until they trembled, murmuring: *"O love! O love!"* many times.

At last she spoke to me. When she addressed the first words to me I was so confused that I did not know what to answer. She asked me was I going to *Araby.* I forgot whether I answered yes or no. It would be a splendid bazaar, she said she would love to go.

"And why can't you?" I asked.

While she spoke she turned a silver bracelet round and round her wrist. She could not go, she said, because there would be a retreat that week in her convent. Her brother and two other boys were fighting for their caps and I was alone at the railings. She held one of the spikes, bowing her head towards me. The light from the lamp opposite our door caught the white curve of her neck, lit up her hair that rested there and, falling, lit up the hand upon the railing. It fell over one side of her dress and caught the white border of a petticoat, just visible as she stood at ease.

"It's well for you," she said.

"If I go," I said, "I will bring you something."

What innumerable follies laid waste my waking and sleeping thoughts after that evening! I wished to annihilate the tedious intervening days. I chafed against the work of school. At night in my bedroom and by day in the classroom her image came between me and the page I strove to read. The syllables of the word *Araby* were called to me through the silence in which my soul luxuriated and cast an Eastern enchantment over me. I asked for leave to go to the bazaar on Saturday night. My aunt was surprised and hoped it was not some Freemason affair. I answered few questions in class. I watched my master's face pass from amiability to sternness; he hoped I was not beginning to idle. I could not call my wandering thoughts together. I had hardly any patience with the serious work of life which, now that it stood between me and my desire, seemed to me child's play, ugly monotonous child's play.

On Saturday morning I reminded my uncle that I wished to go to the bazaar in the evening. He was fussing at the hallstand, looking for the hat-brush, and answered me curtly:

"Yes, boy, I know."

As he was in the hall I could not go into the front parlour and lie at the window. I left the house in bad humour and walked slowly towards the school. The air was pitilessly raw and already my heart misgave me. When I came home to dinner my uncle had not yet been home. Still it was early. I sat staring at the clock for some time and, when its ticking began to irritate me, I left the room. I mounted the staircase and gained the upper part of the house. The high cold empty gloomy rooms liberated me and I went from room to room singing. From the front window I saw my companions playing below in the street. Their cries reached me weakened and indistinct and, leaning my forehead against the cool glass, I looked over at the dark house where she lived. I may have stood there for an hour, seeing nothing but the brown-clad figure cast by my imagination, touched discreetly by the lamplight at the curved neck, at the hand upon the railings and at the border below the dress.

When I came downstairs again I found Mrs. Mercer sitting at the fire. She was an old garrulous woman, a pawnbroker's widow, who collected used stamps for some pious purpose. I had to endure the gossip of the tea-table. The meal was prolonged beyond an hour and still my uncle did not come. Mrs. Mercer stood up to go: she was sorry she couldn't wait any longer, but it was after eight o'clock and she did not like to be out late, as the night air was bad for her. When she had gone I began to walk up and down the room, clenching my fists. My aunt said:

"I'm afraid you may put off your bazaar for this night of Our Lord."

At nine o'clock I heard my uncle's latchkey in the halldoor. I heard him talking to himself and heard the hallstand rocking when it had received the weight of his overcoat. I could interpret these signs. When he was midway through his dinner I asked him to give me the money to go to the bazaar. He had forgotten.

"The people are in bed and after their first sleep now," he said.

I did not smile. My aunt said to him energetically:

"Can't you give him the money and let him go? You've kept him late enough as it is."

My uncle said he was very sorry he had frogotten. He said he believed in the old saying: "All work and no play makes Jack a dull boy." He asked me where I was going and, when I had told him a second time he asked me did I know *The Arab's Farewell to his Steed*. When I left the kitchen he was about to recite the opening lines of the piece to my aunt.

I held a florin tightly in my hand as I strode down Buckingham Street towards the station. The sight of the streets thronged with buyers and glaring with gas recalled to me the purpose of my journey. I took my seat in a third-class carriage of a deserted train. After an intolerable delay the train moved out of the station slowly. It crept onward among ruinous houses and over the twinkling river. At Westland Row Station a crowd of people pressed to the carriage doors; but the porters moved them back, saying that it was a special train for the bazaar. I remained alone in the bare carriage. In a few minutes the train drew up beside an improvised wooden platform. I passed out on to the road and saw by the lighted dial of a clock that it was ten minutes to ten. In front of me was a large building which displayed the magical name.

I could not find any sixpenny entrance and, fearing that the bazaar would be closed, I passed in quickly through a turnstile, handing a shilling to a weary-looking man. I found myself in a big hall girdled at half its height by a gallery. Nearly all the stalls were closed and the greater part of the hall was in darkness. I recognised a silence like that which pervades a church after a service. I walked into the centre of the bazaar timidly. A few people were gathered about the stalls which were still open. Before a curtain, over which the words *Café Chantant* were written in coloured lamps, two men were counting money on a salver. I listened to the fall of the coins.

Remembering with difficulty why I had come I went over to one of the stalls and examined porcelain vases and flowered tea-sets. At the door of the stall a young lady was talking and laughing with two young gentlemen. I remarked their English accents and listened vaguely to their conversation.

"O, I never said such a thing!"

"O, but you did!"

"O, but I didn't!"

"Didn't she say that?"

"Yes. I heard her."

"O, there's a . . . fib!"

Observing me the young lady came over and asked me did I wish to buy anything. The tone of her voice was not encouraging; she seemed to have spoken to me out of a sense of duty. I looked humbly at the great jars that stood like eastern guards at either side of the dark entrance to the stall and murmured:

"No, thank you."

The young lady changed the position of one of the vases and went back to the two young men. They began to talk of the same subject. Once or twice the young lady glanced at me over her shoulder.

I lingered before her stall, though I knew my stay was useless, to make my interest in her wares seem the more real. Then I turned away slowly and walked down the middle of the bazaar. I allowed the two pennies to fall against the sixpence in my pocket. I heard a voice call from one end of the gallery that the light was out. The upper part of the hall was now completely dark.

Gazing up into the darkness I saw myself as a creature driven and derided by vanity; and my eyes burned with anguish and anger.

Fern Hill

DYLAN THOMAS

Now as I was young and easy under the apple boughs
About the lilting house and happy as the grass was green,
   The night above the dingle starry,
     Time let me hail and climb
    Golden in the heydays of his eyes,
And honored among wagons I was prince of the apple towns
And once below a time I lordly had the trees and leaves
    Trail with daisies and barley
   Down the rivers of the windfall light.

And as I was green and carefree, famous among the barns
About the happy yard and singing as the farm was home,
   In the sun that is young once only,
     Time let me play and be
    Golden in the mercy of his means,
And green and golden I was huntsman and herdsman, the calves
Sang to my horn, the foxes on the hills barked clear and cold,
    And the sabbath rang slowly
   In the pebbles of the holy streams.

All the sun long it was running, it was lovely, the hay
Fields high as the house, the tunes from the chimneys, it
       was air
   And playing, lovely and watery
    And fire green as grass.
   And nightly under the simple stars
As I rode to sleep the owls were bearing the farm away,
All the moon long I heard, blessed among stables, the nightjars
    Flying with the ricks, and the horses
     Flashing into the dark.

And then to awake, and the farm, like a wanderer white
With the dew, come back, the cock on his shoulder: it was all
    Shining, it was Adam and maiden,
     The sky gathered again
    And the sun grew round that very day.

So it must have been after the birth of the simple light
In the first, spinning place, the spellbound horses walking
      warm
   Out of the whinnying green stable
    On to the fields of praise.

And honored among foxes and pheasants by the gay house
Under the new made clouds and happy as the heart was long,
   In the sun born over and over,
    I ran my heedless ways,
     My wishes raced through the house high hay
And nothing I cared, at my sky blue trades, that time allows
In all his tuneful turning so few and such morning songs
   Before the children green and golden
    Follow him out of grace,

Nothing I cared, in the lamb white days, that time would
    take me
Up to the swallow thronged loft by the shadow of my hand,
   In the moon that is always rising,
    Nor that riding to sleep
   I should hear him fly with the high fields
And wake to the farm forever fled from the childless land.
Oh as I was young and easy in the mercy of his means,
    Time held me green and dying
   Though I sang in my chains like the sea.

When I Was One-and-Twenty

A. E. HOUSMAN

When I was one-and-twenty
   I heard a wise man say,
"Give crowns and pounds and guineas
   But not your heart away;
Give pearls away and rubies
   But keep your fancy free."
But I was one-and-twenty,
   No use to talk to me.

When I was one-and-twenty
I heard him say again,
"The heart out of the bosom
Was never given in vain;
'Tis paid with sighs a-plenty
And sold for endless rue."
And I am two-and-twenty,
And oh, 'tis true, 'tis true.

Innocence

SEAN O'FAOLAIN

All this month the nuns have been preparing my little boy for his first Confession. In a few days he will go in a crocodile from the school to the parish church; enter the strange-looking cabinet in the corner of the aisle and see in the dusk of this secretive box an old priest's face behind a grille. He will acknowledge his wickedness to this pale, criss-crossed face. He will be a little frightened but he will enjoy it too, because he does not really believe any of it—for him it is a kind of game that the nuns and the priest are playing between them.

How could he believe it? The nuns tell him that the Infant Jesus is sad when he is wicked. But he is never wicked, so what can it matter? If they told him instead of the sorrow he causes the Weasel, or Two Toes, or the Robin in the Cow's Ear, all of which live in the fields below our house, he would believe it in just the same way. To be sure he tells lies, he is a terrible liar, and when he plays Rummy with me he cheats as often as he can, and when he is slow and I flurry him he flies into furious rages and his eyes swim with tears and he dashes the cards down and calls me A Pig. For this I love him so much that I hug him, because it is so transparent and innocent; and at night if I remember his tears I want to go into his room and hold his fat, sweaty hand that lies on the coverlet clutching some such treasure as an empty reel. How, then, can he believe that God could be angry with him because he tells lies or calls his daddy A Pig?

Yet, I hate to see him being prepared for his first Confession because one day he will really do something wicked, and I know the fear that will come over him on that day—and I cannot prevent it.

I have never forgotten the first time I knew that I had committed sin. I had been going to Confession for years, ever since I was seven, as he is now, telling the same things time after time just as he will do. "Father, I told a lie . . . Father, I forgot to say my morning prayers . . . Father, I was disobedient to my parents . . . And that is all, Father." It was always quite true: I had done these things; but, as with him, it was only true as a fable or a mock-battle is true since none of these things were any more sinful than childish lies and rages. Until, one dim, wintry afternoon, not long after Christmas, when I went as usual to Confession in an old, dark, windy church called Saint Augustine's, down a side-lane, away from the city's traffic, a place as cold and damp and smelly as a tomb. It has since been pulled down and if they had not pulled it down it must soon have fallen down. It was the sort of church where there was always a beggar or two sheltering from the weather in the porch or in the dusky part under the back gallery; and always some poor shawled woman sighing her prayers in a corner like the wind fluttering in the slates. The paint was always clean and fresh, but the floor and the benches and the woodwork were battered and worn by the generations. The priests dressed in the usual black Augustinian garment with a cowl and a leather cincture. Altogether, a stranger would have found it a gloomy place. But I was familiar with it ever since my mother brought me there to dedicate me to Saint Monica, the mother of Augustine, and I loved the bright candles before her picture, and the dark nooks under the galleries, and the painted tondos on the ceiling, and the stuffy confessional boxes with their heavy purple curtains, underneath which the heels of the penitents stuck out when they knelt to the grille.

There I was, glad to be out of the January cold, kneeling before Saint Monica, brilliant with the candles of her mendicants. I was reading down through the lists of sins in my penny prayer-book, heeding the ones I knew, passing over the ones I didn't know, when I suddenly stopped at the name of a sin that I had hitherto passed by as having nothing to do with me.

As I write down these words I again feel the terror that crept into me like a snake as I realized that I knew that sin. I knew it well. No criminal who feels the sudden grip of a policeman on his arm can have felt more fear than I did as I stared at the horrible words. . . .

I joined the long silent queue of penitents seated against the wall. I went, at last, into the dark confessional. I told my usual innocent litany. I whispered the sin.

Now, the old priest inside the confessional was a very aged man. He was so old and feeble that the community rarely allowed him to do anything but say Mass and hear Confessions. Whenever they let him preach he would ramble on and on for an hour; people would get up and go away; the sacristan would peep out in despair through the sacristy door; and in the end an altar-boy would be sent out to ring the great gong on the altar-steps to make him stop. I have seen the boy come out three times to the gong before the old man could be lured down from the pulpit.

When this old priest heard what I said to him he gave a groan that must have been heard in the farthest corner of the church. He leaned his face against the wire and called me his "child," as all priests in the confessional call every penitent. Then he began to question me about the details. I had not counted on this. I had thought that I would say my sin and be forgiven: for up to this every priest had merely told me that I was a very good little boy and asked me to pray for him as if I were a little angel whose prayers had a special efficacy, and then I would be dismissed jumping with joy.

To his questions I replied tremulously that it had happened "more than once"—How soon we begin to evade the truth!—and, I said, "Yes, Father, it was with another." At this he let out another groan so that I wanted to beg him to be quiet or the people outside would hear him. Then he asked me a question that made my clasped hands sweat and shake on the ledge of the grille. He asked me if any harm had been done to me. At first I didn't know what he meant. Then horrible shapes of understanding came creeping towards me along the dark road of my ignorance, as, in some indistinct manner, I recognized that he was mistaking me for a girl! I cried out that nothing at all had happened, Father. Nothing! Nothing! Nothing! But he only sighed like the south wind and said:

"Ah, my poor child, you won't know for several months."

I now had no desire but to escape. I was ready to tell him any story, any lie, if he would only stop his questions. What I did say I don't know but in some fashion I must have made the old man understand that I was a male sinner. For his next question, which utterly broke me, was:

"I see, I see. Well, tell me, my poor child. Was she married or unmarried?"

I need hardly say that as I remember this now I laugh at it for an absurd misadventure, and I have sometimes made my friends laugh at his questions and his groans, and at me with my two skinny heels sticking out under the curtains and knocking like castanets, and the next penitents wondering what on earth was going on inside the box. But, then, I was like a pup caught in a bramble bush, recanting and retracting and trying to get to the point where he would say the blessed words "*Absolvo te* . . ." and tell me what my penance would be.

What I said I cannot recall. All I remember distinctly is how I emerged under the eyes of the queue, walked up the aisle, as far away as I could get from the brightness of Saint Monica into the darkest corner under the gallery where the poorest of the poor crowd on Sundays. I saw everything through smoke. The scarlet eye of the sanctuary lamp—the only illumination apart from the candles before the shrine—stared at me.

The shawled woman sighed at me. The wind under my bare knees crept away from me. A beggar in a corner, picking his nose and scratching himself, was Purity itself compared to me.

In the streets the building stood dark and wet against the after-Christmas pallor of the sky. High up over the city there was one tiny star. It was as bright and remote as lost innocence. The blank windows that held the winter sky were sullen. The wet cement walls were black. I walked around for hours. When I crept in home my mother demanded angrily where I had been all these hours and I told her lies that *were* lies, because I wanted to deceive her, and I knew that from this on I would always be deceiving everybody because I had something inside me that nobody must ever know. I was afraid of the dark night before me. And I still had to face another Confession when I would have to confess all these fresh lies that I had just told the old priest and my mother.

It's forty years ago, now: something long since put in its unimportant place. Yet, somehow, when I look across at this small kid clutching his penny prayer-book in his sweaty hands and wrinkling up his nose at the hard words—I cannot laugh. It does not even comfort me when I think of that second Confession, after I had carefully examined those lists of sins for the proper name of my sin. For, what I said to the next priest was: "Father, I committed adultery." With infinite tenderness he assured me that I was mistaken, and that I would not know anything about that sin for many years to come, indeed, that I would have to be married before I could commit it—and then asked me to pray for him, and said I was a very good little boy and sent me away jumping with joy. When I think of that and look at this small Adam he becomes like that indescribably remote and tender star, and I sigh like that old, dead priest, and it does not help to know that he is playing a fable of—"Father, I told lies . . . Father, I forgot to say my morning prayers. . . . Father, I called my daddy A Pig."

Becoming: The Task

THE task motif generally occurs in earlier literature that depicts the emergence of the hero, as when Arthur pulls out a sword embedded in a stone in order to prove that he has the virtues necessary to be a ruler. Tasks, then, represent important tests to prove heroic potential. It may involve discovery of something treasured or the conquest of an evil or opposing force or of the guardian of the treasure. The tasks of *Hercules* and *Jason* are typical examples. Achievement of the task makes one worthy of the quest and the journey, or actually involves the quest or the journey. Today, at a time when literature often presents not heroes but antiheroes, protagonists may ruin the task they are to perform so as to oppose the mythically heroic. Still, in life man is archetypally attracted to the accomplishment of great tasks placed upon him by others or by himself—as in space travel, in athletics, in business.

Jacob Serves Laban for Rachel and Leah

GENESIS, Chapter 29

1 Then Jacob went on his journey, and came into the land of the people of the east.   2 And he looked, and behold a well in the field, and, lo, there *were* three flocks of sheep lying by it; for out of that well they watered the flocks: and a great stone *was* upon the well's mouth. 3 And thither were all the flocks gathered: and they rolled the stone from the well's mouth, and watered the sheep, and put the stone again upon the well's mouth in his place.

4 And Jacob said unto them, My brethren, whence *be* ye? And they said, Of Haran *are* we.   5 And he said unto them, Know ye Laban the son of Nahor? And they said, We know *him*.   6 And he said unto them, *Is* he well? And they said, *He is* well: and, behold, Rachel, his daughter cometh with the sheep.   7 And he said, Lo, *it is* yet high day, neither *is it* time that the cattle should be gathered together: Water ye the sheep, and go *and* feed *them*.   8 And they said, We cannot, until all the flocks be gathered together, and *till* they roll the stone from the well's mouth; then we water the sheep.

9 And while he yet spake with them, Rachel came with her father's sheep: for she kept them.   10 And it came to pass, when Jacob saw Rachel the daughter of Laban his mother's brother, and the sheep of Laban his mother's brother, that Jacob went near, and rolled the stone from the well's mouth, and watered the flock of Laban his mother's brother.   11 And Jacob kissed Rachel, and lifted up his voice and wept. 12 And Jacob told Rachel that he *was* her father's brother, and that he *was* Rebekah's son: and she ran and told her father.

13 And it came to pass, when Laban heard the tidings of Jacob his sister's son, that he ran to meet him, and embraced him, and kissed him, and brought him to his house. And he told Laban all these things. 14 And Laban said to him, Surely thou *art* my bone and my flesh. And he abode with him the space of a month.

15 And Laban said unto Jacob, Because thou *art* my brother, shouldest thou therefore serve me for nought? tell me, what *shall* thy wages *be?* 16 And Laban had two daughters: the name of the elder *was* Le'ah, and the name of the younger *was* Rachel.   17 Le'ah *was* tender eyed; but Rachel was beautiful and well-favored.   18 And Jacob loved Rachel; and said, I will serve thee seven years for Rachel thy younger daughter. 19 And Laban said, *It is* better that I give her to thee, than that I should give her to another man: abide with me.   20 And Jacob served seven years for Rachel; and they seemed unto him *but* a few days, for the love he had to her.

21 And Jacob said unto Laban, Give *me* my wife, for my days are fulfilled, that I may go in unto her.   22 And Laban gathered together all the men of the place, and made a feast.   23 And it came to pass in the evening, that he took Le'ah his daughter, and brought her to him; and he went in unto her.   24 And Laban gave unto his daughter Le'ah Zilpah his maid *for* a handmaid.   25 And it came to pass, that in the morning, behold, it *was* Le'ah: and he said to Laban, What *is* this thou hast done unto me? did not I serve with thee for Rachel? wherefore then hast thou beguiled me?   26 And Laban said, It must not be so done in our country, to give the younger before the firstborn.   27 Fulfill her week, and we will give thee this also for the service which thou shalt serve with me yet seven other years.   28 And Jacob did so, and fulfilled her week: and he gave him Rachel his daughter to wife also. 29 And Laban gave to Rachel his daughter Bilhah his handmaid to be her maid.   30 And he went in also unto Rachel, and he loved also Rachel more than Le'ah, and served with him yet seven other years.

The Golden Vanity

ANONYMOUS

A ship I have got in the North Country
And she goes by the name of the *Golden Vanity*.
O I fear she'll be taken by a Spanish Ga-la-lee,
      As she sails by the Low-lands low.

To the Captain then upspake the little Cabin-boy,
He said, "What is my fee, if the galley I destroy?
The Spanish Ga-la-lee, if no more it shall annoy,
      As you sail by the Low-lands low."

"Of silver and of gold I will give to you a store;
And my pretty little daughter that dwelleth on the shore,
Of treasure and of fee as well, I'll give to thee galore,
      As we sail by the Low-lands low."

Then they roll'd him up tight in a black bull's skin,
And he held all in his hand an augur sharp and thin,
And he swam until he came to the Spanish Gal-a-lin,
      As she lay by the Low-lands low.

He bored with his augur, he bored once and twice,
And some were playing cards, and some were playing dice,
When the water flowed in it dazzled their eyes,
      As she sank by the Low-lands low.

So the Cabin-boy did swim all to the larboard side,
Saying "Captain! take me in, I am drifting with the tide!"
"I will shoot you! I will kill you!" the cruel Captain cried,
      "You may sink by the Low-lands low."

Then the Cabin-boy did swim all to the starboard side,
Saying, "Messmates, take me in, I am drifting with the tide!"
Then they laid him on the deck, and he closed his eyes and died,
      As they sailed by the Low-lands low.

They sew'd his body tight in an old cow's hide,
And they cast the gallant Cabin-boy out over the ship side,

And left him without more ado to drift with the tide,
And to sink by the Low-lands low.

The Hero with One Face

DAVID WAGONER

They chose me, not that I might learn,
But only because I was born,
And gave me amulets of clay,
Some armor, and a brief goodbye.

And at the threshold of the pool,
The looking-glass, the spoiled well,
The hole beneath the whirling tree,
I waited meekly. They called me.

I turned a corner, and was there,
Where all the other places are:
The other side of the cupped moon,
Oz, Heaven-Hell, and the Unknown.

I had too many purposes:
Although they hadn't said, "Find keys,
Find maidens, answers, and lost loves,"
I knew they wanted these themselves,

And I was bound to seek them all
Or be transformed, or die, or fall.
All the horned gods soared by and looked,
Hoping to stain my smallest act.

And there were beasts: three-headed dogs,
Gorgons, ghouls with whirligigs,
And dragons both alive and dead
For me to master, and I did.

I did, and O they brought Her in:
My Mother, the Queen upon a throne,
The Circe with a mouth to fill,
The witch already beautiful.

How could I know Her without pain?
I turned: there sat the evil King,
Betrayer, jealous brother, God.
I loved him much more than I should.

Then Glory rattled from a cloud,
The deaf-and-dumb rose up and cried,
Cripples came striding, golden fleece
Fell from the holy air like lace,

And broken curses rained, and time
Gave birth, gave birth, and returned home
Where all of the unmade desires
Are made at last. And I felt worse,

And I was elected to a boon,
A final wish for every man.
I chose what I was told to choose:
They told me gently who I was.

It scarcely mattered. I lay down
And ate the lotos, kissed my crown,
And gazed at Ozma, Beatrice,
And sighed, and was content with this.

But no—two-legged horses came,
Ogres, winds, and mothers-in-loam,
Provoked husbands with their wives,
Little people with long knives,

The shadows of the underworld;
And all my journey was recoiled,
Drawn back to the uneasy place
Where each benign beginning is.

Now, like Ulysses, master of
The world under, world above,
The world between—and one beyond
Which was not near enough to find—
I wait, and wonder what to learn:
O here, twice blind at being born.

Becoming: The Journey and the Quest

THE journey and the quest motifs relate to the fall into experience. The journey is usually a search for insight to effect a change from that which has befallen man. This motif often requires a descent into the Underworld (The Harrowing of Hell by Christ), a going-down to the place where the dead reside (Orpheus) to bring back a new knowledge. Symbolically it may be a descent into the Lower Depths of humanity, to despair, to near-death, to social iniquities. Because life itself is a journey (from birth to death), images of roads or sea journeys often serve as metaphors. Hawthorne's story "Young Goodman Brown" tells of a journey that must be made through the woods at night—the experiencing of evil, necessary to an understanding of life. Through his journey Brown loses the Faith (significantly the name of his wife) he had before. The medieval play "Everyman" allegorizes the trip toward death that every man must make. Usually the journey has as its goal a return to the past before the fall, based largely on observation of the rebirth of nature. But the myth of exodus does not become cyclic as rebirth myths do; rather it is a slow process forward to a final goal (heaven) along a linear movement of time.

The quest motif stresses less the journeying than the sought-after results of that journey. The goal of quest is the lost treasure of innocence, which may be symbolized in various tangible and intangible ways. Ultimately though, the quest hopes to find the Self through uniting the conscious with the unconscious. James Hilton's Shangri-La in *Lost Horizon* offers an obvious example, and his *Random Harvest* a sentimental version as the hero finds his way back through amnesia to his former life.

The Exodus

EXODUS, Chapters 13, 14, and 15

CHAPTER 13

1 And the Lord spake unto Moses, saying,   2 Sanctify unto me all the firstborn, whatsoever openeth the womb among the children of Israel, both of man and of beast: it is mine.   3 And Moses said unto the

people, Remember this day, in which ye came out from Egypt, out of the house of bondage; for by strength of hand the Lord brought you out from this place: there shall no leavened bread be eaten.   4 This day came ye out in the month Abib.   5 And it shall be when the Lord shall bring thee into the land of the Canaanites, and the Hittites, and the Amorites, and the Hivites, and the Jebusites, which he sware unto thy fathers to give thee, a land flowing with milk and honey, that thou shalt keep this service in this month.   6 Seven days thou shalt eat un- leavened bread, and in the seventh day shall be a feast to the Lord. 7 Unleavened bread shall be eaten seven days; and there shall no leavened bread be seen with thee, neither shall be leaven seen with thee in all thy quarters.   8 And thou shalt show thy son in that day, saying, This is done because of that which the Lord did unto me when I came forth out of Egypt.   9 And it shall be for a sign unto thee upon thine hand, and for a memorial between thine eyes, that the Lord's law may be in thy mouth: for with a strong hand hath the Lord brought thee out of Egypt.   10 Thou shalt therefore keep this ordinance in his season from year to year.   11 And it shall be when the Lord shall bring thee into the land of the Canaanites, as he sware unto thee and to thy fathers, and shall give it thee,   12 that thou shalt set apart unto the Lord all that openeth the matrix, and every firstling that cometh of a beast which thou hast; the male shall be the Lord's.   13 And every firstling of an ass thou shalt redeem with a lamb; and if thou wilt not redeem it, then thou shalt break his neck: and all the firstborn of man among thy children shalt thou redeem.   14 And it shall be when thy son asketh thee in time to come, saying, What is this? that thou shalt say unto him, By strength of hand the Lord brought us out from Egypt, from the house of bondage: 15 and it came to pass, when Pharaoh would hardly let us go, that the Lord slew all the firstborn in the land of Egypt, both the firstborn of man, and the firstborn of beast: therefore I sacrifice to the Lord all that openeth the matrix, being males; but all the firstborn of my children I redeem.   16 And it shall be for a token upon thine hand, and for frontlets between thine eyes: for by strength of hand the Lord brought us forth out of Egypt.   17 And it came to pass, when Pharaoh had let the people go, that God led them not through the way of the land of the Philistines, although that was near; for God said, Lest peradventure the people repent when they see war, and they return to Egypt: 18 but God led the people about, through the way of the wilderness of the Red sea: and the children of Israel went up harnessed out of the land of Egypt.   19 And Moses took the bones of Joseph with him: for he had straitly sworn the children of Israel, saying, God will surely visit you; and ye shall carry up my bones away hence with you.   20 And they took their journey from Succoth, and encamped in Etham, in the edge of the wilderness.   21 And the Lord went before them by day in a pillar of a cloud, to lead them the way; and by night in a pillar of fire, to give them light; to go by day and night.   22 He took not away the pillar of the cloud by day, nor the pillar of fire by night, from before the people.

CHAPTER 14

1 And the Lord spake unto Moses, saying,   2 Speak unto the children of Israel, that they turn and encamp before Pi-hahiroth, between Migdol and the sea, over against Baal-zephon: before it shall ye encamp by the sea.   3 For Pharaoh will say of the children of Israel, They are entangled in the land, the wilderness hath shut them in.   4 And I will harden Pharaoh's heart, that he shall follow after them; and I will be honored upon Pharaoh, and upon all his host; that the Egyptians may know that I am the Lord. And they did so.   5 And it was told the king of Egypt that the people fled: and the heart of Pharaoh and of his serv-ants was turned against the people, and they said, Why have we done this, that we have let Israel go from serving us?   6 And he made ready his chariot, and took his people with him: 7 and he took six hundred chosen chariots, and all the chariots of Egypt, and captains over every one of them.   8 And the Lord hardened the heart of Pharaoh king of Egypt, and he pursued after the children of Israel: and the children of Israel went out with a high hand.   9 But the Egyptians pursued after them, all the horses and chariots of Pharaoh, and his horsemen, and his army, and overtook them encamping by the sea, beside Pi-hahiroth, before Baal-zephon.   10 And when Pharaoh drew nigh, the children of Israel lifted up their eyes, and, behold, the Egyptians marched after them; and they were sore afraid: and the children of Israel cried out unto the Lord.   11 And they said unto Moses, Because there were no graves in Egypt, hast thou taken us away to die in the wilderness? wherefore hast thou dealt thus with us, to carry us forth out of Egypt? 12 Is not this the word that we did tell thee in Egypt, saying, Let us alone, that we may serve the Egyptians? For it had been better for us to serve the Egyptians, than that we should die in the wilderness.   13 And Moses said unto the people, Fear ye not, stand still, and see the sal-vation of the Lord, which he will show to you today: for the Egyptians whom ye have seen today, ye shall see them again no more for ever. 14 The Lord shall fight for you, and ye shall hold your peace.   15 And the Lord said unto Moses, Wherefore criest thou unto me? speak unto the children of Israel, that they go forward: 16 but lift thou up thy rod, and stretch out thine hand over the sea, and divide it: and the children of Israel shall go on dry ground through the midst of the sea. 17 And I, behold, I will harden the hearts of the Egyptians, and they shall follow them: and I will get me honor upon Pharaoh, and upon all

his host, upon his chariots, and upon his horsemen.　　18 And the Egyptians shall know that I am the Lord, when I have gotten me honor upon Pharaoh, upon his chariots, and upon his horsemen.　　19 And the angel of God, which went before the camp of Israel, removed and went behind them; and the pillar of the cloud went from before their face, and stood behind them:　　20 and it came between the camp of the Egyptians and the camp of Israel; and it was a cloud and darkness to them, but it gave light by night to these: so that the one came not near the other all the night.　　21 And Moses stretched out his hand over the sea; and the Lord caused the sea to go back by a strong east wind all that night, and made the sea dry land, and the waters were divided.　　22 And the children of Israel went into the midst of the sea upon the dry ground: and the waters were a wall unto them on their right hand, and on their left.　　23 And the Egyptians pursued, and went in after them to the midst of the sea, even all Pharaoh's horses, his chariots, and his horsemen.　　24 And it came to pass, that in the morning watch the Lord looked unto the host of the Egyptians through the pillar of fire and of the cloud, and troubled the host of the Egyptians,　　25 and took off their chariot wheels, that they drave them heavily: so that the Egyptians said, Let us flee from the face of Israel; for the Lord fighteth for them against the Egyptians.　　26 And the Lord said unto Moses, Stretch out thine hand over the sea, that the waters may come again upon the Egyptians, upon their chariots, and upon their horsemen.　　27 And Moses stretched forth his hand over the sea, and the sea returned to his strength when the morning appeared; and the Egyptians fled against it; and the Lord overthrew the Egyptians in the midst of the sea.　　28 And the waters returned, and covered the chariots, and the horsemen, and all the host of Pharaoh that came into the sea after them; there remained not so much as one of them.　　29 But the children of Israel walked upon dry land in the midst of the sea; and the waters were a wall unto them on their right hand, and on their left.　　30 Thus the Lord saved Israel that day out of the hand of the Egyptians; and Israel saw the Egyptians dead upon the seashore.　　31 And Israel saw that great work which the Lord did upon the Egyptians: and the people feared the Lord, and believed the Lord, and his servant Moses.

CHAPTER 15

1 Then sang Moses and the children of Israel this song unto the Lord, and spake, saying, I will sing unto the Lord, for he hath triumphed gloriously: the horse and his rider hath he thrown into the sea.　　2 The Lord is my strength and song, and he is become my salvation: he is my God, and I will prepare him a habitation; my father's God, and I will exalt him.　　3 The Lord is a man of war: the Lord is his name.　　4

Pharaoh's chariots and his host hath he cast into the sea: his chosen captains also are drowned in the Red sea.	5 The depths have covered them: they sank into the bottom as a stone.	6 Thy right hand, O Lord, is become glorious in power: thy right hand, O Lord, hath dashed in pieces the enemy.	7 And in the greatness of thine excellency thou hast overthrown them that rose up against thee: thou sentest forth thy wrath, which consumed them as stubble.	8 And with the blast of thy nostrils the waters were gathered together, the floods stood upright as a heap and the depths were congealed in the heart of the sea.	9 The enemy said, I will pursue, I will overtake, I will divide the spoil; my lust shall be satisfied upon them; I will draw my sword, my hand shall destroy them.	10 Thou didst blow with thy wind, the sea covered them: they sank as lead in the mighty waters.	11 Who is like unto thee, O Lord, among the gods? Who is like thee, glorious in holiness, fearful in praises, doing wonders?	12 Thou stretchedst out thy right hand, the earth swallowed them.	13 Thou in thy mercy hast led forth the people which thou hast redeemed: thou hast guided them in thy strength unto thy holy habitation.	14 The people shall hear, and be afraid: sorrow shall take hold on the inhabitants of Palestine.	15 Then the dukes of Edom shall be amazed; the mighty men of Moab, trembling shall take hold upon them; all the inhabitants of Canaan shall melt away.	16 Fear and dread shall fall upon them; by the greatness of thine arm they shall be as still as a stone; till thy people pass over, O Lord, till the people pass over, which thou hast purchased.	17 Thou shalt bring them in, and plant them in the mountain of thine inheritance, in the place, O Lord, which thou hast made for thee to dwell in; in the sanctuary, O Lord, which thy hands have established.	18 The Lord shall reign for ever and ever.

What Is The Beautiful?

KENNETH PATCHEN

The narrowing line.
Walking on the burning ground.
The ledges of stone.
Owlfish wading near the horizon.
Unrest in the outer districts.

Pause.

And begin again.
Needles through the eye.
Bodies cracked open like nuts.
Must have a place.
Dog has a place.

Pause.

And begin again.
Tents in the sultry weather.
Rifles hate holds.
Who is right?
Was Christ?
Is it wrong to love all men?

Pause.

And begin again.
Contagion of murder.
But the small whip hits back.
This is my life, Caesar.
I think it is good to live.

Pause.

And begin again.
Perhaps the shapes will open.
Will flying fly?
Will singing have a song?
Will the shapes of evil fall?
Will the lives of men grow clean?
Will the power be for good?
Will the power of man find its sun?
Will the power of man flame as a sun?
Will the power of man turn against death?
Who is right?
Is war?

Pause.

And begin again.
A narrow line.

Walking on the beautiful ground.
A ledge of fire.
It would take little to be free.
That no man hate another man,
Because he is black;
Because he is yellow;
Because he is white;
Or because he is English;
Or German;
Or rich;
Or poor;
Because we are everyman.

Pause.

And begin again.
It would take little to be free.
That no man live at the expense of another.
Because no man can own what belongs to all.
Because no man can kill what all must use.
Because no man can lie when all are betrayed.
Because no man can hate when all are hated.

And begin again.
I know that the shapes will open.
Flying will fly, and singing will sing.
Because the only power of man is in good.
And all evil shall fail.
Because evil does not work,
Because the white man and the black man,
The Englishman and the German,
Are not real things.
They are only pictures of things.
Their shapes, like the shapes of the tree
And the flower, have no lives in names or signs;
They are their lives, and the real is in them.
And what is real shall have life always.

Pause.

I believe in the truth.
I believe that every good thought I have,
All men shall have.
I believe that what is best in me,

Shall be found in every man.
I believe that only the beautiful
Shall survive on the earth.
I believe that the perfect shape of everything
Has been prepared;
And, that we do not fit our own
Is of little consequence.
Man beckons to man on this terrible road.
I believe that we are going into the darkness now;
Hundreds of years will pass before the light
Shines over the world of all men . . .
And I am blinded by its splendor.

Pause.

And begin again

Eldorado

EDGAR ALLAN POE

Gaily bedight
A gallant knight,
In sunshine and in shadow,
Had journeyed long,
Singing a song,
In search of Eldorado.

But he grew old—
This knight so bold—
And o'er his heart a shadow
Fell as he found
No spot of ground
That looked like Eldorado.

And, as his strength
Failed him at length,
He met a pilgrim shadow—
"Shadow," said he,
"Where can it be—
This land of Eldorado?"

"Over the Mountains
Of the Moon,
Down the Valley of the Shadow,
Ride, boldly ride,"
The shade replied—
"If you seek for Eldorado!"

I Saw a Man

STEPHEN CRANE

I saw a man pursuing the horizon;
Round and round they sped.
I was disturbed at this;
I accosted the man.
"It is futile," I said,
"You can never—"
"You lie," he cried,
And ran on.

The Land of Heart's Desire

WILLIAM BUTLER YEATS

O Rose, thou art sick.—*William Blake*

CHARACTERS
MAURTEEN BRUIN.
BRIDGET BRUIN.
SHAWN BRUIN.
MARY BRUIN
FATHER HART.
A FAERY CHILD

The scene is laid in the Barony of Kilmacowen, in the County of Sligo, and at a remote time.

Dedication
TO FLORENCE FARR

SCENE—*A room with a hearth on the floor in the middle of a deep*
alcove to the Right. There are benches in the alcove and a table; and
a crucifix on the wall. The alcove is full of a glow of light from the
fire. There is an open door facing the audience to the Left, and to
the left of this a bench. Through the door one can see the forest. It is
night, but the moon or a late sunset glimmers through the trees and
carries the eye far off into a vague, mysterious world. MAURTEEN
BRUIN, SHAWN BRUIN, *and* BRIDGET BRUIN *sit in the alcove at the table*
or about the fire. They are dressed in the costume of some remote
time, and near them sits an old priest, FATHER HART. *He way be*
dressed as a friar. There is food and drink upon the table. MARY
BRUIN *stands by the door reading a book. If she looks up she can see*
through the door into the wood.

BRIDGET
Because I bid her clean the pots for supper,
She took that old book down out of the thatch,
She has been doubled over it ever since.
We should be deafened by her groans and moans,
Had she to work as some do, Father Hart,
Get up at dawn like me and mend and scour;
Or ride abroad in the boisterous night like you,
The pyx and blessèd bread under your arm.
SHAWN
Mother, you are too cross.
BRIDGET
                    You've married her,
And fear to vex her, and so take her part.
MAURTEEN [*to* FATHER HART.]
It is but right that youth should side with youth;
She quarrels with my wife a bit at times,
And is too deep just now in the old book!
But do not blame her greatly; she will grow
As quiet as a puff-ball in a tree
When but the moons of marriage dawn and die
For half a score of times.
FATHER HART
                    Their hearts are wild,
As be the hearts of birds, till children come.
BRIDGET
She would not mind the kettle, milk the cow,
Or even lay the knives and spread the cloth.
SHAWN
Mother, if only—

MAURTEEN
>   Shawn, this is half empty;
> Go, bring up the best bottle that we have.

FATHER HART
> I never saw her read a book before,
> What can it be?

MAURTEEN [*to* SHAWN.]
>   What are you waiting for?
> You must not shake it when you draw the cork;
> It's precious wine, so take your time about it. [SHAWN *goes.*]
> [*To* PRIEST.]
> There was a Spaniard wrecked at Ocris Head,
> When I was young, and I have still some bottles.
> He cannot bear to hear her blamed; the book
> Has lain up in the thatch these fifty years;
> My father told me my grandfather wrote it,
> And killed a heifer for the binding of it—
> But supper's spread, and we can talk and eat.
> It was little good he got out of the book,
> Because it filled his house with rambling fiddlers,
> And rambling ballad-makers and the like.
> The griddle-bread is there in front of you.
> Colleen, what is the wonder in that book,
> That you must leave the bread to cool? Had I
> Or had my father read or written books,
> There was no stocking stuffed with yellow guineas
> To come when I am dead to Shawn and you.

FATHER HART
> You should not fill your head with foolish dreams.
> What are you reading?

MARY
>   How a Princess Edane,
> A daughter of a King of Ireland, heard
> A voice singing on a May Eve like this,
> And followed, half awake and half asleep,
> Until she came into the land of Faery,
> Where nobody gets old and godly and grave,
> Where nobody gets old and crafty and wise,
> Where nobody gets old and bitter of tongue.
> And she is still there, busied with a dance,
> Deep in the dewy shadow of a wood,
> Or where stars walk upon a mountaintop.

MAURTEEN
> Persuade the colleen to put down the book;

My grandfather would mutter just such things,
And he was no judge of a dog or a horse,
And any idle boy could blarney him;
Just speak your mind.

FATHER HART

                        Put it away, my colleen.
God spreads the heavens above us like great wings,
And gives a little round of deeds and days,
And then come the wrecked angels and set snares,
And bait them with light hopes and heavy dreams,
Until the heart is puffed with pride and goes
Half shuddering and half joyous from God's peace;
And it was some wrecked angel, blind with tears,
Who flattered Edane's heart with merry words.
My colleen, I have seen some other girls
Restless and ill at ease, but years went by
And they grew like their neighbors and were glad
In minding children, working at the churn,
And gossiping of weddings and of wakes;
For life moves out of a red flare of dreams
Into a common light of common hours,
Until old age bring the red flare again.

MAURTEEN

That's true—but she's too young to know it's true.

BRIDGET

She's old enough to know that it is wrong
To mope and idle.

MAURTEEN

                       I've little blame for her;
She's dull when my big son is in the fields,
And that and maybe this good woman's tongue
Have driven her to hide among her dreams
Like children from the dark under the bedclothes.

BRIDGET

She'd never do a turn if I were silent.

MAURTEEN

And may be it is natural upon May Eve
To dream of the good people. But tell me, girl,
If you've the branch of blessèd quicken wood
That women hang upon the post of the door
That they may send good luck into the house?
Remember they may steal new-married brides
After the fall of twilight on May Eve,
Or what old women mutter at the fire

Is but a pack of lies.

FATHER HART

It may be truth.
We do not know the limit of those powers
God has permitted to the evil spirits
For some mysterious end. You have done right [*to* MARY].
It's well to keep old innocent customs up.

[MARY BRUIN *has taken a bough of quicken wood from a seat and hung it on a nail in the door-post. A girl child strangely dressed, perhaps in faery green, comes out of the wood and takes it away.*]

MARY

I had no sooner hung it on the nail
Before a child ran up out of the wind;
She has caught it in her hand and fondles it;
Her face is pale as water before dawn.

FATHER HART

Whose child can this be?

MAURTEEN

No one's child at all.
She often dreams that some one has gone by,
When there was nothing but a puff of wind.

MARY

They have taken away the blessèd quicken wood,
They will not bring good luck into the house;
Yet I am glad that I was courteous to them,
For are not they, likewise, children of God?

FATHER HART

Colleen, they are the children of the fiend,
And they have power until the end of Time,
When God shall fight with them a great pitched battle
And hack them into pieces.

MARY

He will smile,
Father, perhaps, and open His great door.

FATHER HART

Did but the lawless angels see that door,
They would fall, slain by everlasting peace,
And when such angels knock upon our doors,
Who goes with them must drive through the same storm.

[*A thin old arm comes round the door-post and knocks and beckons. It is clearly seen in the silvery light.* MARY BRUIN *goes to the door and stands in it for a moment.* MAURTEEN BRUIN *is busy filling* FATHER HART's *plate.* BRIDGET BRUIN *stirs the fire.*]

MARY [*coming to table.*]
    There's somebody out there that beckoned me
    And raised her hand as though it held a cup,
    And she was drinking from it, so it may be
    That she is thirsty.

    [*She takes milk from the table and carries it to the door.*]

FATHER HART
                    That will be the child
    That you would have it was no child at all.
BRIDGET
    And maybe, Father, what he said was true;
    For there is not another night in the year
    So wicked as to-night.
MAURTEEN
                   Nothing can harm us
    While the good Father's underneath our roof.
MARY
    A little queer old woman dressed in green.
BRIDGET
    The good people beg for milk and fire,
    Upon May Eve—woe to the house that gives,
    For they have power upon it for a year.
MAURTEEN
    Hush, woman, hush!
BRIDGET
                 She's given milk away.
    I knew she would bring evil on the house.
MAURTEEN
    Who was it?
MARY
             Both the tongue and face were strange.
MAURTEEN
    Some strangers came last week to Clover Hill;
    She must be one of them.
BRIDGET
                I am afraid.
FATHER HART
    The Cross will keep all evil from the house
    While it hangs there.
MAURTEEN
              Come, sit beside me, colleen,
    And put away your dreams of discontent,
    For I would have you light up my last days,

Like the good glow of the turf; and when I die
You'll be the wealthiest hereabout, for, colleen,
I have a stocking full of yellow guineas
Hidden away where nobody can find it.

BRIDGET

You are the fool of every pretty face,
And I must spare and pinch that my son's wife
May have all kinds of ribbons for her head.

MAURTEEN

Do not be cross; she is a right good girl!
The butter is by your elbow, Father Hart.
My colleen, have not Fate and Time and Change
Done well for me and for old Bridget there?
We have a hundred acres of good land,
And sit beside each other at the fire.
I have this reverend Father for my friend.
I look upon your face and my son's face—
We've put his plate by yours—and here he comes,
And brings with him the only thing we have lacked,
Abundance of good wine.

[SHAWN *comes in.*]

                              Stir up the fire,
And put new turf upon it till it blaze.
To watch the turf-smoke coiling from the fire,
And feel content and wisdom in your heart,
This is the best of life; when we are young
We long to tread a way none trod before,
But find the excellent old way through love,
And through the care of children, to the hour
For bidding Fate and Time and Change good-bye.

[MARY *takes a sod of turf from the fire and goes out through the door.* SHAWN *follows her and meets her coming in.*]

SHAWN

What is it draws you to the chill o' the wood?
There is a light among the stems of the trees
That makes one shiver.

MARY

                              A little queer old man
Made me a sign to show he wanted fire
To light his pipe.

BRIDGET

                    You've given milk and fire,

Upon the unluckiest night of the year, and brought,
For all you know, evil upon the house.
Before you married you were idle and fine,
And went about with ribbons on your head;
And now—no, Father, I will speak my mind,
She is not a fitting wife for any man—

SHAWN

Be quiet, Mother!

MAURTEEN

You are much too cross.

MARY

What do I care if I have given this house,
Where I must hear all day a bitter tongue,
Into the power of faeries!

BRIDGET

You know well
How calling the good people by that name,
Or talking of them overmuch at all,
May bring all kinds of evil on the house.

MARY

Come faeries, take me out of this dull house!
Let me have all the freedom I have lost;
Work when I will and idle when I will!
Faeries, come take me out of this dull world,
For I would ride with you upon the wind.
Run on the top of the dishevelled tide,
And dance upon the mountains like a flame.

FATHER HART

You cannot know the meaning of your words.

MARY

Father, I am right weary of four tongues:
A tongue that is too crafty and too wise,
A tongue that is too godly and too grave,
A tongue that is more bitter than the tide,
And a kind tongue too full of drowsy love,
Of drowsy love and my captivity.

[SHAWN BRUIN *leads her to a seat at the left of the door.*]

SHAWN

Do not blame me; I often lie awake
Thinking that all things trouble your bright head.
How beautiful it is—your broad pale forehead
Under a cloudy blossoming of hair!
Sit down beside me here—these are too old,

And have forgotten they were ever young.

MARY

Oh, you are the great door-post of this house,
And I the branch of blessèd quicken wood,
And if I could I'd hang upon the post,
Till I had brought good luck into the house.

[*She would put her arms about him, but looks shyly at the* PRIEST
and lets her arms fall.]

FATHER HART

My daughter, take his hand; by love alone
God binds us to Himself and to the hearth,
That shuts us from the waste beyond His peace
From maddening freedom and bewildering light.

SHAWN

Would that the world were mine to give it you,
And not its quiet hearths alone, but even
All that bewilderment of light and freedom,
If you would have it.

MARY

              I would take the world
And break it into pieces in my hands
To see you smile watching it crumble away.

SHAWN

Then I would mould a world of fire and dew,
With no one bitter, grave, or overwise,
And nothing marred or old to do you wrong,
And crowd the enraptured quiet of the sky
With candles burning to your lonely face.

MARY

Your looks are all the candles that I need.

SHAWN

Once a fly dancing in a beam of the sun,
Or the light wind blowing out of the dawn,
Could fill your heart with dreams none other knew,
But now the indissoluble sacrament
Has mixed your heart that was most proud and cold
With my warm heart for ever; the sun and moon
Must fade and heaven be rolled up like a scroll;
But your white spirit still walk by my spirit.

[*A voice singing in the wood.*]

MAURTEEN

There's some one singing. Why, it's but a child.

It sang, "The lonely of heart is withered away."
A strange song for a child, but she sings sweetly,
Listen, listen! [*Goes to door.*]

MARY
　　　　　　Oh, cling close to me,
Because I have said wicked things to-night.

THE VOICE
The wind blows out of the gates of the day,
The wind blows over the lonely of heart,
And the lonely of heart is withered away.
While the faeries dance in a place apart,
Shaking their milk-white feet in a ring,
Tossing their milk-white arms in the air;
For they hear the wind laugh and murmur and sing
Of a land where even the old are fair,
And even the wise are merry of tongue;
But I heard a reed of Coolaney say,
"When the wind has laughed and murmured and sung
The lonely of heart is withered away!"

MAURTEEN
Being happy, I would have all others happy,
So I will bring her in out of the cold.

[*He brings in the faery child.*]

THE CHILD
I tire of winds and waters and pale lights.

MAURTEEN
And that's no wonder, for when night has fallen
The wood's a cold and a bewildering place;
But you are welcome here.

THE CHILD
　　　　　　　　I am welcome here.
For when I tire of this warm little house,
There is one here that must away, away.

MAURTEEN
Oh, listen to her dreamy and strange talk.
Are you not cold?

THE CHILD
　　　　　　I will crouch down beside you,
For I have run a long, long way this night.

BRIDGET
You have a comely shape.

MAURTEEN
　　　　　　　Your hair is wet.

BRIDGET
    I'll warm your chilly feet.
MAURTEEN
                            You have come indeed
    A long, long way—for I have never seen
    Your pretty face—and must be tired and hungry,
    Here is some bread and wine.
THE CHILD
                                The wine is bitter.
    Old mother, have you no sweet food for me?
BRIDGET
    I have some honey.

    [*She goes into the next room.*]

MAURTEEN
                            You have coaxing ways,
    The mother was quite cross before you came.

    [BRIDGET *returns with the honey and fills a porringer with milk.*]

BRIDGET
    She is the child of gentle people; look
    At her white hands and at her pretty dress.
    I've brought you some new milk, but wait a while
    And I will put it to the fire to warm.
    For things well fitted for poor folk like us
    Would never please a high-born child like you.
THE CHILD
    From dawn, when you must blow the fire ablaze,
    You work your fingers to the bone, old mother.
    The young may lie in bed and dream and hope,
    But you must work your fingers to the bone
    Because your heart is old.
BRIDGET
                            The young are idle.
THE CHILD
    Your memories have made you wise, old father;
    The young must sigh through many a dream and hope.
    But you are wise because your heart is old.

    [BRIDGET *gives her more bread and honey.*]

MAURTEEN
    Oh, who would think to find so young a girl
    Loving old age and wisdom?

THE CHILD
>   No more, mother.

MAURTEEN
What a small bite! The milk is ready now.

[*Hands it to her.*]

What a small sip!

THE CHILD
>   Put on my shoes, old mother.
Now I would like to dance, now I have eaten.
The reeds are dancing by Coolaney lake,
And I would like to dance until the reeds
And the white waves have danced themselves asleep.

[BRIDGET *puts on the shoes, and* THE CHILD *is about to dance, but suddenly sees the crucifix and shrieks and covers her eyes.*]

What is that ugly thing on the black cross?

FATHER HART
You cannot know how naughty your words are!
That is our Blessèd Lord.

THE CHILD
Hide it away.

BRIDGET
>   I have begun to be afraid again.

THE CHILD
Hide it away!

MAURTEEN
>   That would be wickedness!

BRIDGET
That would be sacrilege!

THE CHILD
>   The tortured thing!
Hide it away.

MAURTEEN
>   Her parents are to blame.

FATHER HART
That is the image of the Son of God.

THE CHILD [*caressing him.*]
Hide it away, hide it away!

MAURTEEN
>   No, no.

FATHER HART
Because you are so young and like a bird,
That must take fright at every stir of the leaves,

I will go take it down.
THE CHILD

> Hide it away!
> And cover it out of sight and out of mind!

[FATHER HART *takes crucifix from wall and carries it towards inner room.*]

FATHER HART

> Since you have come into the barony,
> I will instruct you in your blessèd faith;
> And being so keen-witted you'll soon learn.

[*To the others.*]

> We must be tender to all budding things;
> Our Maker let no thought of Calvary
> Trouble the morning stars in their first song.

[*Puts crucifix in inner room.*]

THE CHILD

> Here is level ground for dancing; I will dance.

[*Sings.*]

> "The wind blows out of the gates of the day,
> The wind blows over the lonely of heart,
> And the lonely of heart is withered away." [*She dances.*]

MARY [*to* SHAWN.]

> Just now when she came near I thought I heard
> Other small steps beating upon the floor,
> And a faint music blowing in the wind,
> Invisible pipes giving her feet the tune.

SHAWN

> I heard no steps but hers.

MARY

> I hear them now.
> The unholy powers are dancing in the house.

MAURTEEN

> Come over here, and if you promise me,
> Not to talk wickedly of holy things,
> I will give you something.

THE CHILD

> Bring it me, old father.

MAURTEEN

> Here are some ribbons that I bought in the town

For my son's wife—but she will let me give them
To tie up that wild hair the winds have tumbled.

THE CHILD
Come, tell me, do you love me?

MAURTEEN
                                        Yes, I love you.

THE CHILD
Ah, but you love this fireside.
                                        Do you love me?

FATHER HART
When the Almighty puts so great a share
Of His own ageless youth into a creature,
To look is but to love.

THE CHILD
                                        But you love Him!

BRIDGET
She is blaspheming.

THE CHILD
                                        And do you love me too?

MARY
I do not know.

THE CHILD
                                        You love that young man there,
Yet could I make you ride upon the winds,
Run on the top of the dishevelled tide,
And dance upon the mountains like a flame.

MARY
Queen of Angels and kind saints defend us!
Some dreadful thing will happen. A while ago
She took away the blessèd quicken wood.

FATHER HART
You fear because of her unmeasured prattle;
She knows no better. Child, how old are you?

THE CHILD
When winter sleep is abroad my hair grows then,
My feet unsteady. When the leaves awaken
My mother carries me in her golden arms;
I'll soon put on my womanhood and marry
The spirits of wood and water, but who can tell
When I was born for the first time? I think
I am much older than the eagle cock
That blinks and blinks on Ballygawley Hill,
And he is the oldest thing under the moon.

FATHER HART
 Oh, she is of the faery people.
THE CHILD
        One called,
 I sent my messengers for milk and fire,
 She called again, and after that I came.

[*All except* SHAWN *and* MARY BRUIN *gather behind the* PRIEST *for protection.*]

SHAWN [*rising.*]
 Though you have made all these obedient,
 You have not charmed my sight, and won from me
 A wish or gift to make you powerful;
 I'll turn you from the house.
FATHER HART
       No, I will face her.
THE CHILD
 Because you took away the crucifix
 I am so mighty that there's none can pass,
 Unless I will it, where my feet have danced
 Or where I've whirled my finger tips.

[SHAWN *tries to approach her and cannot.*]

MAURTEEN
        Look, look!
 There something stops him—look how he moves his hands
 As though he rubbed them on a wall of glass.
FATHER HART
 I will confront this mighty spirit alone;
 Be not afraid, the Father is with us,
 The Holy Martyrs and the Innocents,
 The adoring Magi in their coats of mail,
 And He who died and rose on the third day,
 And all the nine angelic hierarchies.

[THE CHILD *kneels upon the settle beside* MARY *and puts her arms about her.*]

 Cry, daughter, to the Angels and the Saints.
THE CHILD
 You shall go with me, newly-married bride,
 And gaze upon a merrier multitude.
 White-armed Nuala, Aengus of the Birds,
 Feacra of the hurtling foam, and him

Who is the ruler of the Western Host,
Finvarra and their Land of Heart's Desire,
Where beauty has no ebb, decay no flood,
But joy is wisdom, Time an endless song.
I kiss you and the world begins to fade.

SHAWN

Awake out of that trance—and cover up
Your eyes and ears.

FATHER HART

                      She must both look and listen,
For only the soul's choice can save her now.
Come over to me, daughter; stand beside me;
Think of this house and of your duties in it.

THE CHILD

Stay and come with me, newly-married bride,
For if you hear him you grow like the rest,
Bear children, cook, and bend over the churn,
And wrangle over butter, fowl, and eggs,
Until at last, grown old and bitter of tongue,
You're crouching there and shivering at the grave.

FATHER HART

Daughter, I point you out the way to Heaven.

THE CHILD

But I can lead you, newly-married bride,
Where nobody gets old and crafty and wise,
Where nobody gets old and godly and grave,
Where nobody gets old and bitter of tongue,
And where kind tongues bring no captivity;
For we are but obedient to the thoughts
That drift into the mind at a wink of the eye.

FATHER HART

By the dear Name of the One crucified,
I bid you, Mary Bruin, come to me!

THE CHILD

I keep you in the name of your own heart.

FATHER HART

It is because I put away the crucifix
That I am nothing, and my power is nothing.
I'll bring it here again.

MAURTEEN [clinging to him.]

                No.

BRIDGET

                Do not leave us.

FATHER HART
> O, let me go before it is too late;
> It is my sin alone that brought it all.

[*Singing outside.*]

THE CHILD
> I hear them sing, "Come, newly-married bride,
> Come, to the woods and waters and pale lights."
MARY
> I will go with you.
FATHER HART
> She is lost, alas!
THE CHILD [*standing by the door.*]
> But clinging mortal hope must fall from you,
> For we who ride the winds, run on the waves,
> And dance upon the mountains, are more light
> Than dew-drops on the banner of the dawn.
MARY
> O, take me with you!
SHAWN
> Belovèd, I will keep you,
> I've more than words, I have these arms to hold you,
> Nor all the faery host, do what they please,
> Shall ever make me loosen you from these arms.
MARY
> Dear face! Dear voice!
THE CHILD
> Come, newly-married bride.
MARY
> I always loved her world—and yet—and yet—
THE CHILD
> White bird, white bird, come with me, little bird.
MARY
> She calls me!
THE CHILD
> Come with me, little bird.

[*Distant dancing figures appear in the wood.*]

MARY
> I can hear songs and dancing.
SHAWN
> Stay with me!

MARY

    I think that I would stay—and yet—and yet—

THE CHILD

    Come, little bird, with crest of gold.

MARY [*very softly.*]

                    And yet—

THE CHILD

    Come, little bird with silver feet!

    [MARY BRUIN *dies, and* THE CHILD *goes.*]

SHAWN

               She is dead!

BRIDGET

    Come from that image; body and soul are gone;

    You have thrown your arms about a drift of leaves,

    Or bole of an ash tree changed into her image.

FATHER HART

    Thus do the spirits of evil snatch their prey,

    Almost out of the very hand of God;

    And day by day their power is more and more,

    And men and women leave old paths, for pride

    Comes knocking with thin knuckles on the heart.

[*Outside there are dancing figures, and it may be a white bird, and many voices singing.*]

"The wind blows out of the gates of the day,

The wind blows over the lonely of heart,

And the lonely of heart is withered away;

While the faeries dance in a place apart,

Shaking their milk-white feet in a ring,

Tossing their milk-white arms in the air;

For they hear the wind laugh and murmur and sing

Of a land where even the old are fair,

And even the wise are merry of tongue;

But I heard a reed of Coolaney say—

'When the wind has laughed and murmured and sung,

The lonely of heart is withered away.' "

The Mediterranean

ALLEN TATE

Quem das finem, rex magne, dolorum?

Where we went in the boat was a long bay
A slingshot wide, walled in by towering stone—
Peaked margin of antiquity's delay,
And we went there out of time's monotone:

Where we went in the black hull no light moved
But a gull white-winged along the feckless wave,
The breeze, unseen but fierce as a body loved,
That boat drove onward like a willing slave:

Where we went in the small ship the seaweed
Parted and gave to us the murmuring shore,
And we made feast and in our secret need
Devoured the very plates Aeneas bore:

Where derelict you see through the low twilight
The green coast that you, thunder-tossed, would win,
Drop sail, and hastening to drink all night
Eat dish and bowl to take that sweet land in!

Where we feasted and caroused on the sandless
Pebbles, affecting our day of piracy,
What prophecy of eaten plates could landless
Wanderers fulfill by the ancient sea?

We for that time might taste the famous age
Eternal here yet hidden from our eyes
When lust of power undid its stuffless rage;
They, in a wineskin, bore earth's paradise.

Let us lie down once more by the breathing side
Of Ocean, where our live forefathers sleep
As if the Known Sea still were a month wide—
Atlantis howls but is no longer steep!

What country shall we conquer, what fair land
Unman our conquest and locate our blood?
We've cracked the hemispheres with careless hand!
Now, from the Gates of Hercules we flood

Westward, westward till the barbarous brine
Whelms us to the tired land where tasseling corn,
Fat beans, grapes sweeter than muscadine
Rot on the vine: in that land were we born.

The Promised Visit

GREY COHOE

It had been a long day at Window Rock, Arizona. I'd shoved myself up at dawn and started from Shiprock early that morning. Today was a special day for me to appear for my tribal scholarship interview. I had applied for it in the spring so I could go on to school after my graduation from high school. My brother-in-law Martin was considerate enough to lend me his pickup truck. I would still have been there promptly for my appointment, no matter if I'd needed to walk, hitchhike, or crawl the hundred and twenty miles.

After all the waiting, I finally learned that I didn't need their scholarship to attend the school of my choice. I didn't need anything from them. They knew this all the time and didn't write to inform me. I was so sore about the unnecessary trip that I didn't bother to eat my lunch or supper. All I got was waste of time, money, and strength which I would've put to good use on the farm. Well, at least they wouldn't bother me, complaining about their money.

Gradually the warmth at the side of my face cooled off as the sunlight was broken up by long shadows across the plain, then bled over the fuzzy mountainous horizon. The same as yesterday—the usual sunny sky, the same quiet atmosphere, and the daily herding toils handled by the desert people—the daylight disappeared, ending another beautiful day. I didn't bother to glance a moment at the departing sun to give farewell or offer my traditional prayer for the kind sun, thanking him for his warmth and life. I constantly stared over the blue hood of the pickup onto the highway up ahead.

The old zigzagging road lines the shadowed flat region, cooling from a day's heat. It was not until now that the evening wind began to form the woollike clouds, building a dark overcast stretching across my destination. At first, it was obviously summer rain clouds, and even a child could recognize the rolling greyish mass. The white lane markers rhythmically speared under me as I raced toward home.

I rolled down the window about an inch to smell the first rain that I would inhale this summer. The harsh air rushed in, cold and wild. Its crazy current tangled and teased my hair. The aroma of the flying wet dirt tensed my warm nose, a smell of rain. Immediately the chill awakened my reflexes. I balanced my body into a proper driving position according to a statement in the driver's manual. I prepared to confront the slippery pavement.

In spite of the long hard day, sitting and wrestling the stiff steering wheel, I was beaten. My muscles were too weak to fight the powerful wind, if a big thunderstorm should come upon me. I lazily moved one of my bare arms to roll up the window. I didn't like the roaring of the air leak. The chill of it made me tremble. I felt no fear of a gentle summer rain, but the dangerous hazards under a vigorous downpour frightened me.

I narrowed my eyes into the mirror to look back along the highway, hoping that someone else would be traveling along, too. Unfortunately, no one showed up. I'd have to go all alone on this road with the next nearest gas station about ninety-eight miles. It was unusual, during such a vacationing summer, to find not a single tourist going on this route. Maybe, I thought, if I wait a few minutes someone will show up, then I'll follow.

I lazily lifted my foot off the gas pedal and slowly stepped on the brakes. When I came to a stop, I gave a long stretch to relieve my stiffness. Then, I yawned. I waited in hopes until the cool evening darkness filled the valley. I stood by the open car door and thought of how mysterious the storm looked. The more I waited the more time I was wasting. Before long, after giving up waiting, I was on the road again. I sang some Navajo songs, whispered, and fitted my sweater around my shoulder. I did anything to accompany myself.

By now I could sight the lightnings spearing into the horizon, glowing against the dark overcast. I could almost see the whole valley in one flash. The black clouds came closer and angrier as I approached their overcast. Being used to the old reservation road, narrow and rough, and well adjusted to the pickup, I drove ahead to meet the first raindrops.

I thought of a joke and wanted to burst out in laughter, but only a smile came. I used to laugh when I teased my folks about my death. They would scold me and would arouse my superstitions about it. Speaking of your death is taboo. Now, when I wondered whether I'd ever make it to the other side of the storm, it didn't sound funny.

Many people had died along this same highway, never telling us what caused their accidents. Most of these tragedies occurred in bad weather, especially in thunderstorms. Several months ago the highway department stuck small white crosses along the road at each place where an accident victim was killed. This was to keep a driver alert and aware. The crosses became so numerous that it caused more confusion and more accidents. When a person sees a cross he becomes nervous.

Everytime we drove through the cross-lined highway, I would think of a parade. The invisible spectators sitting on their crosses would watch us go along. Many people believe that these ghosts bring bad luck. Of course, we Navajos get cursed by such witchcraft.

The dark clouds formed themselves into a huge ugly mass. It reminded me of the myths the people feared in such angry clouds. The suspicious appearance scared me, making my joints and very soul tremble.

My mother once mentioned a monster that lived in the thunderclouds. Was it only one of my bedtime stories, or was it the killer of all the cross-marked victims?

The fierce monster dresses in armor of the hues in a rainbow. Only his mysterious face is uncovered, but no one knows his appearance under his iron dress. Some people believe that he is the insane son of our rain god. A few aged Navajos who have seen him tell us he is the man who first explored across our country in our great-great-grandfather's days. He still leads his armed band of Spaniards.

He swings his swift sword, slashing and striking the earth, creating a snappy, rolling noise. He enjoys lightning and thunder which relieve his tensions. Once in a great while a big storm will indicate his anger. He slices trees, ignites mountains, breaks up hogans, or stabs people who come in his way. Many people have died by his sword. Usually trailing the rain clouds, two rainbows appear, indicating where he has traveled.

Of course there are other superstitions composed around these angry clouds. The people along this valley believe that there is a Wind Being living in a storm. This monster blows over anybody who moves or fights against his powerful blows.

Another story was told to me by my grandmother. It was told to her by her late son before he passed away in a hospital. He saw a ghost standing in his way on the highway and he drove through the rain-sogged image. Her son ran off the road after being knocked unconscious by the shock.

"Baloney! I shouldn't believe those nonsenses," I scolded myself. "I don't want to be one of those Navajos who is easily aroused by superstitions."

Carefully I drove around a big slanting curve. It was at a place where my late cousin was killed in a wreck. The cool, refreshing air was so enjoyable that it prevented the memory of the horrible incident. I anxiously went along, thinking about the day's events and waiting to meet one of the monsters.

My stomach began to tighten up with a groaning sound. It made me weak. I imagined my sister's cooking at home. We'd butchered a sheep yesterday for meat supply. My sister had probably barbequed some mutton and made some fried bread. I swallowed down my empty throat and moved my empty stomach. The smell and taste of my imagined food seemed to be present in my mouth and nose. Restlessly, I speeded up a little faster.

The dark overcast hid my view of the road and the area around faded away into darkness so I had to turn on the headlights. My face was now tired of being fixed in the same direction, down the long, dirty highway. My eyelids were so weak that they closed by themselves. I should have slept longer last night. Again, I rolled down the window. The cold air poured in, caressing me with its moistened chill. It awoke me completely.

I would have brought my brother, Teddy, along to accompany me, but he was fast asleep so I didn't bother. I reckoned he'd rather work in the field than to sit all day long. Somehow, I was glad he hadn't come because I wouldn't want him to fear this killer storm. If anything should happen, I'd be the only one to die. Sadly, I kept on counting the dips, rocky hills, and the zigzagging curves as I drove on.

The sudden forceful blow jolted the car and waved it like a rolling wagon. The screaming wind began to knock at my windows. I clung hard on the steering wheel to fight the rushing wind. I slowed almost to a stop and peered out through the blowing dust at the hood, trying to keep on the road. Flying soil and tumble weeds crashed against the car. I could not tell what ran beside the highway—a canyon or maybe a wash. The angry wind roared and blew so strong that the car slanted. I didn't know how to escape the Wind Monster. I sat motionless, feeling death inside my soul.

And then the car was rocked by falling raindrops as if it were a tin can being battered by flying stones. The downpour came too quickly for me to see the first drops on the windshield. The whole rocky land shook when a loud cracking lightning shot in to the nearby ground.

"Oh no! The devil is coming." I frightened myself, but I had enough courage to pick up my speed a little, thinking that I might escape his aim. I strained my eyes to see through the glare on the windshield. The pouring raindrops were too heavy for the wipers. It was like trying to look under water. Another swift stripe of lightning exploded into the ground. This time, it was closer. I kept myself from panicking. I drove faster, hoping the devil wouldn't see me.

The storm calmed and turned into a genial shower. Then I could see where I was. In sight, through the crystal rain, a green and white lettered sign showed up in the headlights. LITTLE-WATER 12 miles;

SHIPROCK 32 miles. At last, I felt relieved. I would be home in less than an hour. Never in my life did I ever long for home so much until this day. The windshield cleared and the rain had passed.

Again it was quiet except this time I heard a splashing sound at the tires. My ears missed the hard rhythms of smashing rain. I felt as if I had been closely missed by a rifle shot.

Even though I didn't see any one of the monsters, still I looked out, but shamefully, for the two rainbows. They weren't there. I scolded myself for looking. It was ridiculous to fear something that didn't exist, like fairies. Yes, I'd heard thunders, seen lightnings, and felt the terrifying wind, but I'd come out alive. Only for a moment was I trapped and my minutes numbered. I'd probably confronted the stormhead.

"Standing ghost," I scoffed and laughed to myself.

"It's too bad I can't see anything except the light-struck black pavement," I thought. I always rejoiced to see and smell the land where the rain had spread its tasteful water. It's refreshing to watch the plants drink from the puddles around them.

I hoped the rain had traveled across the farmlands near Shiprock. I was supposed to irrigate the corn tomorrow, but luckily the rain would take good care of it. I might do something else instead. Maybe I'd go to the store or to the cafe and eat three or four hamburgers. I like to see that cute waitress there.

With the scary storm passing, and my being penetrated by the superstition over, I felt as if I'd awakened from a nightmare. My hunger, too, had surrendered, but the crampy stiffness still tightened my body. I didn't bother to stop for a rest. I rushed straight home. I hoped my supper would be waiting. The clouds slid away and it wasn't as late as I'd thought.

By now, some twinkling stars appeared over the northern horizon. The found moon cast its light on the soggy ground as the silky white clouds slid after the rain. The water reflected the light so that the standing water shone like the moon itself. I could see the whole area as if in daylight. I ran the tires through the shallow puddles on the pavement to feel it splash. I imagined myself running and playing along the San Juan river shore. I constantly hastened on, looking for the lights at Littlewater over on the other side of the next hill.

Littlewater is a small store standing alongside the highway. Besides the two trailer houses in the back of the store, there are several hogans and log cabins standing in view of the flat valley, but tonight, I can see them only as dark objects at a distance. During warm wintry days, the local people gather together on the sunny side of the trading post walls to chat or watch the travelers stop for gas or supplies. But at this time in the summer, they all move to the cool mountains.

A few electric lights appeared within range of my headlights. Three dull guide lights shone at the store. One larger light showed up the whole front porch. As usual, there wasn't anybody around at this late hour of the night. I slowed to glance at the porch as I passed by. At the same time as I turned back to the road I saw a standing object about fifty yards ahead. I had always feared dark objects at night. My soul tensed with frightening chill as I trembled. I drove closer, telling myself it would be a horse or a calf.

The lights reached the dark image as I approached. Surprisingly, it was a hitchhiker. I didn't think anything about the person. All that came to my mind was to offer someone my help. Then I saw it was a girl.

I stopped a little way past her.

She slowly and shyly walked to the car window. She was all wet and trembling from the cold air. "Can you give me a lift to Shiprock?" she politely asked in her soft, quivering voice.

"Sure. That's where I'm going too." I quickly offered the warm empty seat.

She smiled and opened the door. Water dripped to the floor from her wet clothes. She sat motionless and kept looking away from me.

I thought she was just scared or shy. I, too, was shy to look, and we didn't talk for a long time. It wasn't until a few miles from Shiprock that I finally started a conversation.

"I guess the people around this area are happy to get such a big rain," I finally dared to utter. "I was supposed to water our farm field tomorrow, but I guess the good Lord did it for me," I joked, hoping she would laugh or say something. "What part of Shiprock are you from?" I questioned her.

"Not in Shiprock. About one mile from there," she carefully murmured, using the best of her English.

She looked uneducated by the style of the clothes she wore. She was dressed in a newly made green velvet blouse and a long silky white skirt. She wore many silver and turquoise necklaces and rings. A red and orange sash-belt tightly fitted around her narrow waist. She was so dressed up that she looked ready for going to town or a squaw dance.

Her long black hair hung loosely to her small, round shoulders and beside her light-complexioned face. In the glow from the instrument panel I could tell she was very pretty. She didn't look like some other Navajo girls. Her skin was much lighter than their tannish-brown skin color.

Finally, I gathered enough guts to offer her my school sweater. "Here. You better put this on before you catch cold. I hear pneumonia is very dangerous," I said, as I struggled about to take off the sweater.

She kindly took it and threw it around herself. "Thank you." She smiled and her words came out warmly.

I looked at her and she looked at the same time, too. I almost went off the road when I saw her beautiful smile of greeting. She was the prettiest girl I have ever seen. I jerked the steering wheel and the car jolted back onto the highway. We both laughed. From that moment on, we talked and felt as if we'd known each other before. I fell in love and I guess she did, too.

"Where have you been in this kind of bad weather?" I began to ask questions so we could get better acquainted with each other.

"I visited some of my old relatives around Littlewater." She calmly broke her shyness. "The ground was too wet to walk on so I decided to get a ride."

"I've been to Window Rock to get a scholarship to an art school. I started this morning and it isn't until now I'm coming back. I'm late for my supper because of the storm."

I knew she was interested in me, too, as she asked me, "Where do you live?"

"I live on one of the farms down toward west from Shiprock. I live with my family next to Thomas Yazzie's place." I directed her to the place, too.

"I used to know Thomas and his family when I was very small," she almost cried. "It's always sad to lose friends."

I felt sorry for her losing her friends. Right then I knew she was lonely.

"Where do you live?" I asked, as I looked straight down the lighted road.

She hesitated to answer as if she weren't sure of it. Then she said, "I live about four miles from Shiprock." Then she lowered her head as if she was worried about something I'd said.

I didn't talk any more after that. Again it was quiet. I kept my mind on the road, trying to forget my warm feelings for her beauty.

The night settled itself across the desert land, making stars and the moon more bright. The night sky and the dampness made me sleepy. I felt in a dreamy, romantic mood. The rain still covered the road. It was too quiet for comfort.

"Let's listen to some music," I interrupted the silence as I turned on the radio. I tuned to some rock'n roll music. So now, with the cool night, beating music, and our silence we drove until she asked me to stop. It was just about a mile over two hills to Shiprock. I stopped where a dirt road joined the highway.

"Is this the path to your place?" I quickly asked before she departed.

"Yes. I live about three miles on this road." She pointed her lips for direction as she placed her hand on the door handle.

"I wish I could take you home, but the road is too wet. I might never get home tonight. Well, I hope I'll see you in Shiprock sometime. By the way, what's your name?" I tried to keep her there a while longer by talking to her.

She took a long time to say her name. "Susan Billy," she said finally. Then she added, "Maybe I can visit you some of these nights." She smiled as she opened the door and stepped out of the car.

"All right, goodbye," I tried not to show how I felt as I said those last words.

I looked back in the mirror as I dropped over the hill. She stood waving her hand. I felt proud to find someone like her who wanted so much to see me again. I already missed her. Or was she just joking about her visit? Why would she want to visit me at night? I smiled, hoping she'd come very soon.

Before I knew I was home, I stopped at our garage. The lights in the house were out and the rain had wet the red brick building to a deeper red. I couldn't wait to get into the bed where I could freely think about Susan. I didn't bother to eat or wake my folks. I just covered myself with the warm blankets.

Another sunny morning turned into a cloudy and windy afternoon. Rain clouds brought another chilly breeze as they had two evenings ago when I went to Window Rock. I had not forgotten Susan and, deep in my heart, I kept expecting her visit which she had spoken of. Today, though, we must go to the field to plant new seeds. The cold called for a warm jacket. I glanced around the room where I usually placed my sweater, a maroon and gold colored school sweater. I walked through the house, but I didn't find it. I used my old jacket instead, hoping my sweater was in the car at the hospital where my brother-in-law, Martin, was working.

The movements of my arms and legs, my digging and sowing seeds were in my usual routine for the last few weeks. I could let my mind wander to Susan while my body went on with its work. Suddenly I remembered offering her my sweater on that trip.

"Are you tired already? What are you thinking about? Supper?" my brother asked when he saw me standing with a smile on my face.

"I remembered where I left my sweater. What time is it?" I asked him, wishing the time for Martin to come home with the pickup were near, but I remembered that our noon lunch wasn't even thought of yet.

"Don't know. I know it's not lunch time yet," he joked and kept on hoeing the small weeds along the corn rows.

It wasn't until late that evening, about six-thirty, that I was on my way to see Susan. My whole life filled with joy. The dirt road leading off the highway where Susan had stood seemed dried enough for the tires to roll on.

Slowly and very nervously I approached the end of the three miles to her place. I rode over the last hill and stopped at a hogan. The people were still outside, eating their supper under a shade-house. A familiar man sat facing me from the circle around the dishes on the ground. I was sure I'd seen him someplace, but I couldn't recall where. His wife sat beside him, keeping busy frying some round, thin dough. Three small children accompanied them, two older girls and a child—I couldn't tell whether it was a girl or a boy. I politely asked the man where the Billys lived. He pointed his finger to the west from his crosslegged sitting position. It was at the next hogan where I could find Susan.

"Their hogans are near, over beyond that rocky hill," he directed me in his unmannered way. His words came from his filled mouth.

"They moved to the mountain several days ago," his wife interrupted, "but I saw a light at the place last night. The husband might have ridden down for their supplies."

Hopefully I started again. Sure enough, there were the mud hogans, standing on a lonely plateau. As I approached, a man paused from his busy packing and stood watching me.

He set down a box of groceries and came to the car door. I reached out the window and shook his hand for greeting.

"Hello. Do you know where Susan Billy lives?" I asked, pretending I didn't know where to go to find her.

"Susan Billy?" He looked down, puzzled, and pronounced the name as if he'd never heard it before. After a while of silence, he remarked, "I don't know if you are mistaking for our Susan, or there might be another girl by that name."

My hope almost left as I explained further. "Two nights ago I gave her a ride from Littlewater to the road over there. She told me she lived at this place."

His smile disappeared and a puzzled, odd look took its place.

"See that old hogan over in the distance beyond the three sagebrushes?" He pointed to an old caved-in hogan. "Susan Billy is there," he sadly informed me.

"Good. I'll wait here until she comes back." I sank into the car seat happily, but why was he looking so shocked or worried?

"You don't understand," he went on, explaining, "she died ten years ago and she is buried in that hogan."

At first, I thought it was a joke. I know some parents would try to keep their daughters or sons from seeing any strangers. His black hair and light complexion, not so smooth or whitish as Susan's, somehow resembled hers.

Then I knew he was lying. "I loaned her my sweater and I forgot to get it back." I tried to convince him to tell the truth.

He seemed so shocked as he looked more carefully at the old hogan again. "See that red object on one of the logs?" He pointed out that it hadn't been there until recently.

I saw the maroon object. I could instantly recognize my sweater at a distance. My heart almost stopped with the horrible shock. I struggled to catch my breath back. I didn't believe in ghosts until then, but I had to believe my sweater. I had to believe the beautiful girl who had ridden with me, who had promised to visit me. Still, why hadn't she killed me like the rest of her victims? Was it because of my sweater or because of the love we shared?

From that day, I had proven to myself the truth of the Navajo superstitions. I know I shall never get my sweater back, but, on one of these windy nights, I will see Susan again as she promised. What will I do then?

An Encounter

JAMES JOYCE

It was Joe Dillon who introduced the Wild West to us. He had a little library made up of old numbers of *The Union Jack, Pluck* and *The Halfpenny Marvel.* Every evening after school we met in his back garden and arranged Indian battles. He and his fat young brother Leo the idler held the loft of the stable while we tried to carry it by storm; or we fought a pitched battle on the grass. But, however well we fought, we never won siege or battle and all our bouts ended with Joe Dillon's war dance of victory. His parents went to eight-o'clock mass every morning in Gardiner Street and the peaceful odour of Mrs Dillon was prevalent in the hall of the house. But he played too fiercely for us who were younger and more timid. He looked like some kind of an Indian when he capered round the garden, an old tea-cosy on his head, beating a tin with his fist and yelling:

—Ya! yaka, yaka, yaka!

Everyone was incredulous when it was reported that he had a vocation for the priesthood. Nevertheless it was true.

A spirit of unruliness diffused itself among us and, under its influence, differences of culture and constitution were waived. We banded ourselves together, some boldly, some in jest and some almost in fear: and of the number of these latter, the reluctant Indians who were afraid to seem studious or lacking in robustness, I was one. The adventures related in the literature of the Wild West were remote from my nature but, at least, they opened doors of escape. I liked better some American detective stories which were traversed from time to time by unkempt fierce and beautiful girls. Though there was nothing wrong in these stories and though their intention was sometimes literary they were circulated secretly at school. One day when Father Butler was hearing the four pages of Roman History clumsy Leo Dillon was discovered with a copy of *The Halfpenny Marvel.*

—This page or this page? This page? Now, Dillon, up! *Hardly had the day . . .* Go on! What day? *Hardly had the day dawned . . .* Have you studied it? What have you there in your pocket?

Everyone's heart palpitated as Leo Dillon handed up the paper and everyone assumed an innocent face. Father Butler turned over the pages, frowning.

—What is this rubbish? he said. *The Apache Chief!* Is this what you read instead of studying your Roman History? Let me not find any more of this wretched stuff in this college. The man who wrote it, I suppose, was some wretched scribbler that writes these things for a drink. I'm surprised at boys like you, educated, reading such stuff. I could understand it if you were . . . National School boys. Now, Dillon, I advise you strongly, get at your work or . . .

This rebuke during the sober hours of school paled much of the glory of the Wild West for me and the confused puffy face of Leo Dillon awakened one of my consciences. But when the restraining influence of the school was at a distance I began to hunger again for wild sensations, for the escape which these chronicles or disorder alone seemed to offer me. The mimic warfare of the evening became at last as wearisome to me as the routine of school in the morning because I wanted real adventures to happen to myself. But real adventures, I reflected, do not happen to people who remain at home: they must be sought abroad.

The summer holidays were near at hand when I made up my mind to break out of the weariness of school-life for one day at least. With Leo Dillon and a boy named Mahony I planned a day's miching. Each of us saved up sixpence. We were to meet at ten in the morning on the Canal Bridge. Mahony's big sister was to write an excuse for him and Leo Dillon was to tell his brother to say he was sick. We arranged to go along the Wharf Road until we came to the ships, then to cross in the ferryboat and walk out to see the Pigeon House. Leo Dillon was afraid we might meet Father Butler or someone out of the college; but Mahony asked, very sensibly, what would Father Butler be doing out at the Pigeon House. We were reassured: and I brought the first stage of the plot to an end by collecting sixpence from the other two, at the same time showing them my own sixpence. When we were making the last arrangements on the eve we were all vaguely excited. We shook hands, laughing, and Mahony said:

—Till to-morrow, mates.

That night I slept badly. In the morning I was firstcomer to the bridge as I lived nearest. I hid my books in the long grass near the ashpit at the end of the garden where nobody ever came and hurried along the canal bank. It was a mild sunny morning in the first week of June. I sat up on the coping of the bridge admiring my frail canvas shoes which I had diligently pipeclayed overnight and watching the docile horses pulling a tramload of business people up the hill. All the branches of the tall trees which lined the mall were gay with little light green leaves and the sunlight slanted through them on to the water. The granite stone of the bridge was beginning to be warm and I began to pat it with my hands in time to an air in my head. I was very happy.

When I had been sitting there for five or ten minutes I saw Mahony's grey suit approaching. He came up the hill, smiling, and clambered up beside me on the bridge. While we were waiting he brought out the catapult which bulged from his inner pocket and explained some improvements which he had made in it. I asked him why he had brought it and he told me he had brought it to have some gas with the birds. Mahony used slang freely, and spoke of Father Butler as Bunsen Burner. We waited on for a quarter of an hour more but still there was no sign of Leo Dillon. Mahony, at last, jumped down and said:

—Come along. I knew Fatty'd funk it.

—And his sixpence . . .? I said.

—That's forfeit, said Mahony. And so much the better for us—a bob and a tanner instead of a bob.

We walked along the North Strand Road till we came to the Vitriol Works and then turned to the right along the Wharf Road. Mahony began to play the Indian as soon as we were out of public sight. He chased a crowd of ragged girls, brandishing his unloaded catapult and, when two ragged boys began, out of chivalry, to fling stones at us, he proposed that we should charge them. I objected that the boys were too small, and so we walked on, the ragged troop screaming after us: *Swaddlers! Swaddlers!* thinking that we were Protestants because Mahony, who was dark-complexioned, wore the silver badge of a cricket club in his cap. When we came to the Smoothing Iron we arranged a siege; but it was a failure because you must have at least three. We revenged ourselves on Leo Dillon by saying what a funk he was and guessing how many he would get at three o'clock from Mr Ryan.

We came then near the river. We spent a long time walking about the noisy streets flanked by high stone walls, watching the working of cranes and engines and often being shouted at for our immobility by the drivers of groaning carts. It was noon when we reached the quays and, as all the labourers seemed to be eating their lunches, we bought two big currant buns and sat down to eat them on some metal piping beside the river. We pleased ourselves with the spectacle of Dublin's commerce—the barges signalled from far away by their curls of woolly smoke, the brown fishing fleet beyond Ringsend, the big white sailing-vessel which was being discharged on the opposite quay. Mahony said it would be right skit to run away to sea on one of those big ships and even I, looking at the high masts, saw, or imagined, the geography which had been scantily dosed to me at school gradually taking substance under my eyes. School and home seemed to recede from us and their influences upon us seemed to wane.

We crossed the Liffey in the ferryboat, paying our toll to be transported in the company of two labourers and a little Jew with a bag. We were serious to the point of solemnity, but once during the short voyage our eyes met and we laughed. When we landed we watched the discharging of the graceful three-master which we had observed from the other quay. Some bystander said that she was a Norwegian vessel. I went to the stern and tried to decipher the legend upon it but, failing to do so, I came back and examined the foreign sailors to see had any of them green eyes for I had some confused notion. . . . The sailors' eyes were blue and grey and even black. The only sailor whose eyes could have been called green was a tall man who amused the crowd on the quay by calling out cheerfully every time the planks fell:

—All right! all right!

When we were tired of this sight we wandered slowly into Ringsend. The day had grown sultry, and in the windows of the grocers' shops musty biscuits lay bleaching. We bought some biscuits and chocolate which we ate sedulously as we wandered through the squalid streets where the families of the fishermen live. We could find no dairy and so we went into a huckster's shop and bought a bottle of raspberry lemonade each. Refreshed by this, Mahony chased a cat down a lane, but the cat escaped into a wide field. We both felt rather tired and when we reached the field we made at once for a sloping bank over the ridge of which we could see the Dodder.

It was too late and we were too tired to carry out our project of visiting the Pigeon House. We had to be home before four o'clock lest our adventure should be discovered. Mahony looked regretfully at his catapult and I had to suggest going home by train before he regained any cheerfulness. The sun went in behind some clouds and left us to our jaded thoughts and the crumbs of our provisions.

There was nobody but ourselves in the field. When we had lain on the bank for some time without speaking I saw a man approaching from the far end of the field. I watched him lazily as I chewed one of those green stems on which girls tell fortunes. He came along by the bank slowly. He walked with one hand upon his hip and in the other hand he held a stick with which he tapped the turf lightly. He was shabbily dressed in a suit of greenish-black and wore what we used to call a jerry hat with a high crown. He seemed to be fairly old for his moustache was ashen-grey. When he passed at our feet he glanced up at us quickly and then continued his way. We followed him with our eyes and saw that when he had gone on for perhaps fifty paces he turned about and began to retrace his steps. He walked towards us very slowly, always tapping the ground with his stick, so slowly that I thought he was looking for something in the grass.

He stopped when he came level with us and bade us good-day. We answered him and he sat down beside us on the slope slowly and with great care. He began to talk of the weather, saying that it would be a very hot summer and adding that the seasons had changed greatly since he was a boy—a long time ago. He said that the happiest time of one's life was undoubtedly one's schoolboy days and that he would give anything to be young again. While he expressed these sentiments which bored us a little we kept silent. Then he began to talk of school and of books. He asked us whether we had read the poetry of Thomas Moore or the works of Sir Walter Scott and Lord Lytton. I pretended that I had read every book he mentioned so that in the end he said:

—Ah, I can see you are a bookworm like myself. Now, he added, pointing to Mahony who was regarding us with open eyes, he is different; he goes in for games.

He said he had all Sir Walter Scott's works and all Lord Lytton's works at home and never tired of reading them. Of course, he said, there were some of Lord Lytton's works which boys couldn't read. Mahony asked why couldn't boys read them—a question which agitated and pained me because I was afraid the man would think I was as stupid as Mahony. The man, however, only smiled. I saw that he had great gaps in his mouth between his yellow teeth. Then he asked us which of us had the most sweethearts. Mahony mentioned lightly that he had three totties. The man asked me how many had I. I answered that I had none. He did not believe me and said he was sure I must have one. I was silent.

—Tell us, said Mahony pertly to the man, how many have you yourself?

The man smiled as before and said that when he was our age he had lots of sweethearts.

—Every boy, he said, has a little sweetheart.

His attitude on this point struck me as strangely liberal in a man of his age. In my heart I thought that what he said about boys and sweethearts was reasonable. But I disliked the words in his mouth and I wondered why he shivered once or twice as if he feared something or felt a sudden chill. As he proceeded I noticed that his accent was good. He began to speak to us about girls, saying what nice soft hair they had and how soft their hands were and how all girls were not so good as they seemed to be if one only knew. There was nothing he liked, he said, so much as looking at a nice young girl, at her nice white hands and her beautiful soft hair. He gave me the impression that he was repeating something which he had learned by heart or that, magnetized by some words of his own speech, his mind was slowly circling round and round in the same orbit. At times he spoke as if he were simply alluding to some fact that everybody knew, and at times he lowered his voice and spoke mysteriously as if he were telling us something secret which he did not wish others to overhear. He repeated his phrases over and over again, varying them and surrounding them with his monotonous voice. I continued to gaze towards the foot of the slope, listening to him.

After a long while his monologue paused. He stood up slowly, saying that he had to leave us for a minute or so, a few minutes, and without changing the direction of my gaze, I saw him walking slowly away from us towards the near end of the field. We remained silent when he had gone. After a silence of a few minutes I heard Mahony exclaim:

—I say! Look what he's doing!

As I neither answered nor raised my eyes Mahony exclaimed again:

—I say . . . He's a queer old josser!

—In case he asks us for our names, I said, let you be Murphy and I'll be Smith.

We said nothing further to each other. I was still considering whether I would go away or not when the man came back and sat down beside us again. Hardly had he sat down when Mahony, catching sight of the cat which had escaped him, sprang up and pursued her across the field. The man and I watched the chase. The cat escaped once more and Mahony began to throw stones at the wall she had escaladed. Desisting from this, he began to wander about the far end of the field, aimlessly.

After an interval the man spoke to me. He said that my friend was a very rough boy and asked did he get whipped often at school. I was going to reply indignantly that we were not National School boys to be *whipped* as he called it; but I remained silent. He began to speak on the subject of chastising boys. His mind, as if magnetized again by his speech, seemed to circle slowly round and round its new centre. He said that when boys were that kind they ought to be whipped and well whipped. When a boy was rough and unruly there was nothing would do him any good but a good sound whipping. A slap on the hand or a box on the ear was no good: what he wanted was to get a nice warm whipping. I was surprised at this sentiment and involuntarily glanced up at his face. As I did so I met the gaze of a pair of bottle-green eyes peering at me from under a twitching forehead. I turned my eyes away again.

The man continued his monologue. He seemed to have forgotten his recent liberalism. He said that if ever he found a boy talking to girls or having a girl for a sweetheart he would whip him and whip him; and that would teach him not to be talking to girls. And if a boy had a girl for a sweetheart and told lies about it then he would give him such a whipping as no boy ever got in this world. He said that there was nothing in this world he would like so well as that. He described to me how he would whip such a boy as if he were unfolding some elaborate mystery. He would love that, he said, better than anything in this world; and his voice, as he led me monotonously through the mystery, grew almost affectionate and seemed to plead with me that I should understand him.

I waited till his monologue paused again. Then I stood up abruptly. Lest I should betray my agitation I delayed a few moments pretending to fix my shoe properly and then, saying that I was obliged to go, I bade him good-day. I went up the slope calmly but my heart was beating quickly with fear that he would seize me by the ankles. When I reached the top of the slope I turned round and, without looking at him, called loudly across the field:

—Murphy!

My voice had an accent of forced bravery in it and I was ashamed of my paltry stratagem. I had to call the name again before Mahony saw me and hallooed in answer. How my heart beat as he came running across the field to me! He ran as if to bring me aid. And I was penitent; for in my heart I had always despised him a little.

Becoming: The Search for the Father

OFTEN the quest or trip is a search for the father, or a father surrogate, as in Telemachus's search for his father (or in Joyce's *Ulysses*). In literature the father figure may be a surrogate or substitute, as in Hawthorne's "My Kinsman, Major Molineaux." In this story Robin leaves his actual father (and the security of home) in search of his uncle, who will presumably provide for him and shelter him in his need. Robin learns that he will achieve manhood only when he learns to stand alone.

The son, according to classical Freudian theory, seeks to destroy the father in order to possess the mother. Thus the search for the father involves assertion of the male principle and achievement of the Self. The search and achievement may take the form of the son's taking over the father's business, following his profession but more successfully, becoming an image of his father in appearance or thought. Sir James Frazer's anthropological study *The Golden Bough* evidences clearly this mythic pattern as the old generation gives way to the new. The old king dies and is replaced by the new one: the king is dead; long live the king. This motif, of course, lies behind the so-called generation gap as we know it today: a rejection of this search, or of the father, or of the Self. Until one accepts one's background (or upon understanding it, changes it), one can never accept oneself.

Telemachos
(from The Odyssey, Book II)
HOMER

Dawn came, showing her rosy fingers through the early mists, and Telemachos leapt out of bed. He dressed himself, slung a sharp sword over his shoulder, strapt a stout pair of boots on his lissom feet, and came forth from his chamber like a young god. He called the criers at once, and told them to use their good lungs in summoning the people to Council.

The criers did their part, and the people came. As soon as they were assembled, he went down to the Council himself, with a strong spear in his hand, and a couple of dogs for company, which danced round him as he walked. He was full of enchanting grace, and the people stared at him in admiration. Not for nothing Athena was his friend.

He took his seat in his father's place, and the reverend seniors made room.

The first speaker was Aigyptios, a great gentleman, bent with age and full of ripe wisdom. He also had lost a son, who had sailed with Prince Odysseus in the fleet to Ilios, Antiphos the lancer; the savage Cyclops had killed him in the cave, in fact he was the monster's last supper. Three other sons the old man had. One of them, Eurynomos, was among the wooers, and two kept their father's farms; but he could not forget the other, whom he mourned unceasingly, and now there were tears in his eyes for his son's sake as he began to speak:

"Listen to me, men of Ithaca, for I have something to say to you. There has been no session of our Council since the time when Prince Odysseus sailed with the fleet: and now who has summoned us? Is it a young man or one of the elders? Was it some private need that moved him? Or has he news of some threatening raid, and now wishes to report what he was the first to hear? Or is there some other public matter which he wishes to bring before us? He has done well, I think, and deserves our thanks. I pray Zeus may grant him that blessing which his heart desires."

These words seemed a good omen to Telemachos, and encouraged him. He made no delay, for he was eager to speak, so he stood up before the Council. The speaker's staff was put in his hand by Peisenor, the public crier. Then Telemachos first addressed himself to the old Councillor:

"The man you call for is not far away, reverend Sir, who summoned the people together, as you shall soon know—I am that man, and I am in great trouble of my own. There is no news of a threatening raid to report; I have no advantage of you there, and there is no other public matter which I wish to bring before you. This is my own private need, trouble which has fallen upon my house—two troubles, indeed: first, I have lost a good father, who once was king over you that are present here, and he was like a kind father to you; and now again there is something much worse, which I tell you will soon utterly tear to pieces my whole house, and destroy my whole living. My mother is besieged by those who would marry her against her will, own sons to those men who are chief among you here; they will not go near her father's house, and lay a formal proposal before Icarios—the thought makes them shiver!—for then he might collect the bridal gifts for his daughter, and give her to the man of his choice, the one he likes best. No! it is our house they visit regularly every day, kill our cattle and sheep and fat goats, hold

high revel and drink my sparkling wine, quite reckless: that is the way
it all goes. For there is no man at the head, no one like Odysseus, to
drive this curse from the house. You see, we are not able to drive it away
ourselves. Sorry champions we shall prove, if we try; we have little
skill for the combat.

"Indeed I would defend myself if I had the strength! What they
have done is quite intolerable, there is no decent excuse for the ruin
they have made of my house. *You* ought to be ashamed in your own
hearts, you ought to think what others will say about it, our neighbours,
who live all round us; you should fear the wrath of the gods, who may
be provoked by such wickedness to turn upon you. I appeal to Olympian
Zeus, and Themis, who dissolves the parliaments of men, and summons
them! Let me be, my friends! leave me alone to be worn out by my bitter
sorrow—unless I must suppose that my father Odysseus, my good father,
was a cruel man and ill-treated the nation, and that is why you are cruel
and ill-treat me, out of revenge—why you encourage these men."

"I should like it better if *you* would eat up my treasures and my
flocks. If *you* would eat them up, perhaps there might be some redress.
Then we might go round the town, dunning you, imploring, demanding
our goods again, till you should give all back. But now! I am helpless,
all I can do is to suffer the humiliations which you heap upon me!"

He spoke angrily, and now he dropt down the staff on the ground
and burst into tears. All the people were sorry for him, and they all sat
silent, not one had the heart to say an unkind word in reply; only
Antinoös answered and said:

"You are a boaster, Telemachos, and you don't know how to keep
your temper! What a speech! Cry shame on us, fasten the blame on us,
that's what you want to do! Blame us indeed! Your own mother is at
fault. You cannot find fault with *us* for paying court to your mother. She
is a clever piece indeed! It is three years already, and the fourth will
soon go by, since she has been deluding the wits of the whole nation.
Hopes for all, promises for every man by special messenger—and what
she means is something quite different. Here is the latest trick which
came out of her meditations.

"She set up a great warp on her loom in the mansion, and wove
away, fine work and wide across, and this is what she told us: 'Young
men who seek my hand, now that Odysseus is dead I know you are in a
hurry for marriage; but wait until I finish this cloth, for I don't want to
waste all the thread I have spun. It is a shroud for my lord Laërtês, against
the time when all-destroying fate shall carry him away in dolorous death.
I should not like the women of our nation to cry scandal, if he should
lie without a winding-sheet when he had great possessions.'

"That is what she said, and we swallowed our pride, and consented.
There she was all day long, working away at the great web; but at night

she used to unravel it by torchlight. So for three years she deluded the whole nation, and they believed her. But the seasons passed on, and the fourth year began, and a time came when one of her women told us, one who knew the secret; we caught her unravelling that fine web! So she had to finish it, because she must, not because she would.

"And as for you, this is the answer of those who pay court to your mother, a plain answer to you and to all the nation: Send your mother out of the house, tell her to marry whichever her father says, whichever she likes herself; but if she will go on and on teasing the young men of our nation—with her head full of pride to think how Athena has been generous to her beyond all others, given her skill in beautiful work, and good intelligence, and cleverness such as never was heard of, even in the old stories—those women of our nation who lived long ago, with their lovely hair, Tyro, Alcmenê, Mycenê with her fine coronals—not one of them had the clever wits of Penelopeia: but this clever turn was a wicked trick. To put it plainly, we will go on eating up your living and substance just so long as God allows her to keep the mind she has now. She is making a great name for herself, but for you—good-bye to a great fortune! As for us, we will not go to our lands or anywhere else, before she marries whoever may please her best out of the nation!"

The boy stood up to him, and said:

"Antinoös, it is impossible for me to turn out of doors the mother who bore me and brought me up; my father is somewhere in the world, alive or dead, and it is a hard thing for me to pay back all that dowry to Icarios, if I send away my mother of my own will. Her father will be bad enough, but heaven will send me worse, for my mother will call down the dread Avengers upon me, if she leaves home; and men will reproach me—so I will never say that word. And if your own minds have any fear of such a reproach, go out of my house, get your dinners elsewhere, eat your own food turn by turn in your own houses. But if you think it meet and right to consume one man's goods without paying, carve away; I will appeal to the everlasting gods, and see whether Zeus may not one day grant me vengeance. There would be no ransom then, in that house you should perish!"

So spoke Telemachos: and Zeus, whose eye can see what is far off, sent him a pair of eagles, flying from a lofty mountainpeak. On they flew down the wind awhile, side by side, soaring on wide-stretched sails, but when they came right over the place of debate, they took a turn round; then hovering with quick-beating wings they stared down on the heads of all, with death in their eyes; and tearing at their cheeks and necks with their talons, away they darted to the east across the houses of the town. The people were amazed, when they saw this sight with their own eyes; and they pondered in their hearts what was to come of it.

Then up and spoke a noble old man, Halithersês Mastoridês; for there was no man of his day who came near him in the knowledge of birds or in telling what omens meant. He spoke to them in this fashion, out of an honest heart:

"Hear me now, men of Ithaca, for I have something to say. I speak especially to those who would wed, for upon them a great woe is rolling; Odysseus will not long keep away from his friends, but I think he is already near, planting the seed of death and destruction for all these men. Trouble there will be also for many others of us who live in the island of Ithaca. But let us consider in good time how we can stop these men; or let them stop themselves—indeed, the sooner the better. I am no novice in prophecy, that is something I understand. As for that man, I declare that all has been fulfilled as I told him, when our people embarked for Ilios and with them went Odysseus, the man who is ready for anything and everything. I said he would have many troubles, and lose all his companions, and after twenty long years, unknown, he would come home again: and see now, all is being fulfilled."

Then another man got up, Eurymachos, and he said:

"Off with you, old man, go home and prophesy to your children, or they may come to grief sometime! In this matter I am a better prophet than you are. Any number of birds are flying about under the sun, and not all of them are birds of omen. At any rate, Odysseus is dead, far away from this place, and I wish you had died with him! Then you would not be here making a long speech as God's mouthpiece; you would not unleash this angry Telemachos! No doubt you expect to find something from him when you get home, if he doesn't forget it. But I tell you this, and I will do it too: he is a young man, and you are full of antediluvian wisdom, but if you cajole him and inflame his passions, he shall be the first to suffer.

"As for you, sir, there will be damages which you will be sorry to pay; a heavy burden shall be yours. For Telemachos, this is my advice which I give before you all: Let him tell his mother to go home to her father's house; they will arrange a marriage, and collect the bridal gifts, plenty of them, as many as there ought to be for a beloved daughter. For I do not think the young men will cease their importunate wooing until that is done, since we fear no one in any case—not Telemachos, certainly, for all his flood of words, and we care nothing for your prognostications, respected sir; they will come to nothing, and only make you more of a nuisance than you were. Yes, his wealth shall be wasted and consumed, and there shall be no retribution, as long as that woman keeps putting off her wedding and wasting our time! Here we are, waiting day after day, rivals for a great prize, never look at another woman, when you would expect each man to go a-wooing for himself!"

But Telemachos still kept his wits about him, and he replied:

"Eurymachos, and all you other gentlemen who pay court to my mother, I make no more appeal to you, I have no more to say: for now the gods know, and all the nation.—But I beg you to lend me a swift ship and twenty men, to carry me there and back. For I am going to Sparta and sandy Pylos, to find out about my father and why he is so long away; perhaps some one may tell me, or I may hear some rumour that God will send, which is often the best way for people to get news. Then if I hear that my father is alive and on his way back, for all my wearing and tearing I can bear up for another year; but if I hear he is dead, and no longer in the world, I will come back to my own home and build him a barrow, and do the funeral honours in handsome style, as I ought, and give away my mother to another husband."

He said his say and sat down; then up rose Mentor, friend and comrade of the excellent Odysseus, to whom Odysseus had entrusted his whole house when he sailed away; they were to obey the old man, and he was to keep all safe. This is what he said, and very good sense it was:

"Listen to me, men of Ithaca, and hear what I have to say. Let no man henceforth take the trouble to be kind and gentle, no sceptred prince; let none try to be fair and right, but let him be always harsh and do what he ought not to do: since no one remembers the noble Odysseus, not one out of all the people he ruled like a kind father. I do not grudge at the proud men who pay their court, if they act with violence in the mischievous bodgery of their minds: they stake their own heads when they devour the house of Odysseus with violence, and think he will never come back. But now it is you, the others, who make me ashamed; how you all sit mum, when you ought to denounce them and hold back a few young men when you are many."

Leocritos Euënoridês answered him:

"Mentor, you mischief-maker, you madman! What a thing to say! drive them on to stop us! One against many is done, a many's too many for one, in fights for a supper! Why, even Odysseus himself, if he came back to Ithaca and found a sturdy company feasting in his own house, and thought of driving them out of hall—his wife would have little satisfaction, however much she may have missed him, but then and there he would die an ugly death, if he's one against many! What you say is all wrong. Come now, men, make yourselves scarce, away to your lands every one. As for this fellow, Mentor shall help him with his voyage, and Halithersês, since they have been friends of the family for ages. But I think he will have to sit here for a good long time and wait for his news in Ithaca; he will never bring off that voyage."

With these words he broke up the assembly forthwith. They all made themselves scarce and went each to his own house, and the pretenders went back to the house of Odysseus.

But Telemachos went by himself to the seashore. There he washed his hands in the grey brine, and offered a prayer to Athena:

"Hear me, thou who yesterday didst come a god into our house, who didst bid me take ship over the misty sea, and inquire if my father is coming home, and why he is so long away: all this the people prevent, but most of all my mother's wooers, men full of wicked pride!"

Such was his prayer; and Athena came to his side, like Mentor in shape and voice; she spoke to him, and the words were plain and pointed:

"You will not lack either courage or sense in the future, Telemachos, for we can see now that there is a drop in you of your father's fine spirit. What a man he was to make good both deed and word! I tell you your journey shall not be hindered or stopped. But if you are not his son and Penelopeia's, then I do not expect you to succeed in what you wish to do. Few sons, let me tell you, are like their fathers; most are worse, a few are better. But since you will lack neither courage nor sense in the future, and since the mind of Odysseus has not wholly failed in you, there is hope for the future, and I tell you that you will succeed.

"Think no more now of the plots and plans of those who woo your mother, for there is neither sense nor justice in them. They know nothing of the death and destruction which is near them, so that in one day they shall all perish. But the journey which you desire shall not be long delayed, when you have with you such an old friend of your father as I am; for I will provide a swift ship and go with you myself. You must just go home, and mingle with the company; get provisions ready, and put them all up in vessels, wine in jars, and barley-meal, which is the marrow of men, in strong skins; I will go at once and collect volunteers among the people. There are many ships in the island of Ithaca, both new and old; I will look round and find you the best, and we will make all ready and launch her upon the broad sea."

So spoke Athena daughter of Zeus; and Telemachos did not stay long after he heard what the goddess said. He set out for the house, with a heavy heart; and he found the proud pretenders there, skinning goats and singeing fat pigs in the courtyard. Antinoös laughed, and made straight for Telemachos and grasped his hand, and called him by name, and said:

"You are a boaster, Telemachos, and you don't know how to keep your temper! Do not trouble your head about plots and plans, but just go on eating and drinking as usual. Our people will manage all you want, I am sure, a ship and the best crew to be found; they will give you a quick passage to sandy Pylos, if you want to hear news of your father."

Telemachos pulled his hand from the hand of Antinoös, and said:

"Antinoös, with your friends rioting all round it is impossible to enjoy a meal in peace and quiet. Is it not enough, men, that you have been carving up a good portion of my possessions all this time, while I was still a boy? But now you see I am grown up, and I hear every one talking about it, and so I find things out; now I feel my own strength, and I mean to do my best to bring retribution upon you when I come back from Pylos, or now in this country! I mean to go, and no one shall prevent me, even if I must go as a passenger, since I am not to have my own ship and crew: I suppose that suited you better."

When he said this the others mocked and jeered at him, and you might hear one of the young bullies saying, "Clear enough, Telemachos has murder in his mind! He will bring help from Pylos, or may be from Sparta, since he is so terribly set on it. Or perhaps he wants to go as far as Ephyra, to bring some deadly poison from that rich land, and put it in the cup, and kill us all."

Another of the young bullies would say, "Ah, but who knows? Once aboard ship he may be carried far from his friends, and perish just like Odysseus! That would double our trouble, for we should have to divide all his goods among us! But we would give the house to his mother, for herself and the man who would marry her."

So much for them. But Telemachos went down to his father's storehouse, a room lofty and wide where heaps of gold and bronze were kept, with clothes in coffers and plenty of fragrant oil: jars of delicious old wine stood there, full of that divine drink without a drop of water; there they stood in rows along the wall, ready for Odysseus when he should come home again after all his troubles. The place was closed in by double doors, right and tight. The housekeeper was on the spot day and night, and she took care of everything; and a very clever woman she was, Eurycleia the daughter of Ops Peisenoridès. Telemachos called her to the storehouse, and said:

"Come, Nanny, draw me some kegs of this fine wine, the nicest you have, next to that which you keep so carefully for your noble master, unhappy man! all ready in case he should come from somewhere or other, if he can get clear of death and ruin.—Fill me a dozen, and put a stopper on each. And a few skinfuls of barley-meal, good skins properly stitched, twenty measures of good barley-meal ground in the millstones. Keep this to yourself, and let all the stuff be put ready together. This evening I mean to fetch it away as soon as mother has gone upstairs to bed. For I am off to Sparta and sandy Pylos, to see if I can hear any news of my father."

When he said this, his dear old nurse cried aloud in distress, and said in her downright way:

"Eh, what on earth put that into thi head, love? Why wilta go to foreign parts, and tha an only son, and reet well loved? He's dead, far away from home, my blessed Odysseus, in some foreign land! Aye, and if tha goes, they'll up and plot mischief against tha by and by, to murder thee by some trick, and all that's here they will share among 'em. Stay thee where tha bist, sit down on thi property; what's the sense of wanderen over the barren sea and maybe happenen an accident?"

Telemachos only said, "Cheer up, Nanny, this is God's will, let me tell you. Now promise me on your oath not to say a word to mother for ten or twelve days, unless she asks herself and hears I have gone, or you'll have her crying and spoiling her pretty skin!"

When he said that, she took her oath; and this done with all due solemnity, she wasted no time—drew off the wine into kegs, packed the barley-meal in the skins right and tight; then Telemachos went off and joined the roysterers.

Meanwhile the goddess Athena was doing the rest. She took on the form of Telemachos, and tramped the length and breadth of the city, took aside each of the men and told her tale, then directed them to meet in the evening beside the cutter. The boat itself she begged of Noëmon, the sturdy son of Phronios, and he agreed with all his heart.

The sun went down, and the streets were all darkened. Then Athena ran the boat down into the sea, and put in all the gear that ships carry for sailing and rowing; she moored her at the harbour point, and the crew assembled, fine young fellows all, and she set them each to work.

But she had something else to do. She made her way to the house of Odysseus, and there she distilled sweet sleep upon them all, and dazed them as they drank, until they let the cups drop out of their hands. So they got up and went to find sleep, dispersing all over the city, for they did not sit long after sleep fell on their eyelids. Then Athena called out Telemachos in front of the great hall, taking the shape and voice of Mentor, and said to him:

"Telemachos, your men are all ready and furnished cap-a-pie, sitting at the oars, waiting for you to start. Come, let us go, and waste no time about it."

With these words she led the way briskly, and he followed in her footsteps. And when they came to the ship and the seaside, there he found the bushy-headed boys on the beach, and he spoke to them, full of dignity and strength:

"This way, friends, let us fetch the provisions; they are all ready and waiting in the house. My mother knows nothing about it, nor any of the servants, but only one single soul has heard our plan."

So he led the way, and they went with him. They carried all the stuff down to the ship and put it on board, as Telemachos told them to do. Telemachos himself went on board following Athena; she took her seat on the poop, and he sat beside her. The others cast off the hawsers, and themselves came on board and sat down on the benches. Athena with her bright eyes glinting sent them a following wind, right from the west, piping over the purple sea. Then Telemachos called to the men, and told them to put a hand to the tackling. They lifted the mast and stept it in its hollow box, made it fast with the forestays, hauled up the white sail by its ropes of twisted leather. The wind blew full into the bellying sail, and the

dark wave boomed about the stem of the ship as she went; so on she
sped shouldering the swell, travelling steadily on her way. When they
had made snug all the tackle about the ship, they set before them brim-
ming bowls of wine, and poured libations to the gods immortal and
everlasting, but most of all to the bright-eyed daughter of Zeus. So all
night long and in the dawning the ship cut her way.

my father moved through dooms of love

e. e. cummings

my father moved through dooms of love
through sames of am through haves of give,
singing each morning out of each night
my father moved through depths of height

this motionless forgetful where
turned at his glance to shining here;
that if(so timid air is firm)
under his eyes would stir and squirm

newly as from unburied which
floats the first who,his april touch
drove sleeping selves to swarm their fates
woke dreamers to their ghostly roots

and should some why completely weep
my father's fingers brought her sleep:
vainly no smallest voice might cry
for he could feel the mountains grow.

Lifting the valleys of the sea
my father moved through griefs of joy;
praising a forehead called the moon
singing desire into begin

joy was his song and joy so pure
a heart of star by him could steer
and pure so now and now so yes
the wrists of twilight would rejoice

keen as midsummer's keen beyond
conceiving mind of sun will stand,
so strictly(over utmost him
so hugely)stood my father's dream

his flesh was flesh his blood was blood:
no hungry man but wished him food;
no cripple wouldn't creep one mile
uphill to only see him smile.

Scorning the pomp of must and shall
my father moved through dooms of feel;
his anger was as right as rain
his pity was as green as grain

septembering arms of year extend
less humbly wealth to foe and friend
than he to foolish and to wise
offered immeasurable is

proudly and(by octobering flame
beckoned)as earth will downward climb,
so naked for immortal work
his shoulders marched against the dark

his sorrow was as true as bread:
no lair looked him in the head;
if every friend became his foe
he'd laugh and build a world with snow.

My father moved through theys of we,
singing each new leaf out of each tree
(and every child was sure that spring
danced when she heard my father sing)

then let men kill which cannot share,
let blood and flesh be mud and mire,
scheming imagine,passion willed,
freedom a drug that's bought and sold

giving to steal and cruel kind,
a heart to fear,to doubt a mind,
to differ a disease of same,
conform the pinnacle of am

though dull were all we taste as bright,
bitter all utterly things sweet,
maggoty minus and dumb death
all we inherit,all bequeath

and nothing quite so least as truth
—i say though hate were why men breathe—
because my father lived his soul
love is the whole and more than all

Daddy

SYLVIA PLATH

You do not do, you do not do
Any more, black shoe
In which I have lived like a foot
For thirty years, poor and white,
Barely daring to breathe or Achoo.

Daddy, I have had to kill you
You died before I had time——
Marble-heavy, a bag full of God,
Ghastly statue with one grey toe
Big as a Frisco seal

And a head in the freakish Atlantic
Where it pours bean green over blue
In the waters off beautiful Nauset.
I used to pray to recover you.
Ach, du.

In the German tongue, in the Polish town
Scraped flat by the roller
Of wars, wars, wars.
But the name of the town is common.
My Polack friend

Says there are a dozen or two.
So I never could tell where you
Put your foot, your root,

I never could talk to you.
The tongue stuck in my jaw.

It stuck in a barb wire snare.
Ich, ich, ich, ich,
I could hardly speak.
I thought every German was you.
And the language obscene

An engine, an engine
Chuffing me off like a Jew.
A Jew to Dachau, Auschwitz, Belsen.
I began to talk like a Jew.
I think I may well be a Jew.

The snows of the Tyrol, the clear beer of Vienna
Are not very pure or true.
With my gypsy ancestress and my weird luck
And my Taroc pack and my Taroc pack
I may be a bit of a Jew.

I have always been scared of you,
With your Luftwaffe, your gobbledygoo.
And your neat moustache
And your Aryan eye, bright blue.
Panzer-man, panzer-man, O You——

Not God but a swastika
So black no sky could squeak through.
Every woman adores a Fascist,
The boot in the face, the brute
Brute heart of a brute like you.

You stand at the blackboard, daddy,
In the picture I have of you,
A cleft in your chin instead of your foot
But no less a devil for that, no not
Any less the black man who

Bit my pretty red heart in two.
I was ten when they buried you.
At twenty I tried to die
And get back, back, back to you.
I thought even the bones would do.

But they pulled me out of the sack,
And they stuck me together with glue.
And then I knew what to do.
I made a model of you,
A man in black with a Meinkampf look

And a love of the rack and the screw.
And I said I do, I do.
So daddy, I'm finally through.
The black telephone's off at the root,
The voices just can't worm through.

If I've killed one man, I've killed two——
The vampire who said he was you
And drank my blood for a year,
Seven years, if you want to know.
Daddy, you can lie back now.

There's a stake in your fat black heart
And the villagers never liked you.
They are dancing and stamping on you.
They always *knew* it was you.
Daddy, daddy, you bastard, I'm through.

Father and I

(trans. M. Ekenberg)

PÄR LAGERKVIST

I remember one Sunday afternoon when I was about ten years old, Daddy took my hand and we went for a walk in the woods to hear the birds sing. We waved good-bye to mother, who was staying at home to prepare supper, and so couldn't go with us. The sun was bright and warm as we set out briskly on our way. We didn't take this bird-singing too seriously, as though it was something special or unusual. We were sensible people, Daddy and I. We were used to the woods and the creatures in them, so we didn't make any fuss about it. It was just because it was Sunday afternoon and Daddy was free. We went along the railway line where other people aren't allowed to go, but Daddy belonged to the railway and had a right to. And in this way we came direct into the woods and did not need to take a round-about way. Then the bird song and all the rest began at once. They chirped in the bushes, hedge-sparrows, thrushes, and warblers; and we heard all the noises of the little creatures as we came into the woods. The ground was thick with anemones, the birches were dressed in their new leaves, and the pines had young, green shoots. There was such a pleasant smell everywhere. The mossy ground was steaming a little, because the sun was shining upon it. Everywhere there was life and noise; bumble-bees flew out of their holes, midges circled where it was damp. The birds shot out of the bushes to catch them and then dived back again. All of a sudden a train came rushing along and we had to go down the embankment. Daddy hailed the driver with two fingers to his Sunday hat: the driver saluted and waved his hand. Everything seemed on the move. As we went on our way along the sleepers which lay and oozed tar in the sunshine, there was a smell of everything, machine oil and almond blossom, tar and heather, all mixed. We took big steps from sleeper to sleeper so as not to step among the stones, which were rough to walk on, and wore your shoes out. The rails shone in the sunshine. On both sides of the line stood the telephone poles that sang as we went by them. Yes! That was a fine day! The sky was absolutely clear. There wasn't a single cloud to be seen: there just couldn't be any on a day like this, according to what Daddy said. After a while we came to a field of oats on the right side of the line, where a farmer, whom we knew, had a clearing. The oats had grown thick and even; Daddy looked at it knowingly, and I could feel that he was satisfied. I didn't understand that sort of thing much, because I was born in town. Then we came to the bridge over the brook that mostly hadn't much water in it, but now there was plenty. We took hands so that we shouldn't fall down between the sleepers. From there it wasn't far to the railway gate-keeper's little place, which was quite buried in green. There were apple trees and gooseberry bushes right close to the house. We went in there, to pay a visit, and they offered us milk. We looked at the pigs, the hens, and the fruit trees, which were in full blossom, and then we went on again. We wanted to go to the river, because there it was prettier than anywhere else. There was something special about the river, because higher up stream it flowed past Daddy's old home. We never liked going back before we got to it, and, as usual, this time we got there after a fair walk. It wasn't far to the next station, but we didn't go on there. Daddy just looked to see whether the signals were right. He thought of every-thing. We stopped by the river, where it flowed broad and friendly in the sunshine, and the thick leafy trees on the banks mirrored themselves in the calm water. It was all so fresh and bright. A breeze came from the little lakes higher up. We climbed down the bank, went a little way along the very edge. Daddy showed me the fishing spots. When he was a boy he used to sit there on the stones and wait for perch all day long. Often he didn't get a single bite, but it was a delightful way to spend the day. Now he never had time. We played about for some time by the side of the river, and threw in pieces of bark that the current carried away, and we threw stones to see who could throw farthest. We were, by nature, very merry and cheerful, Daddy and I. After a while we felt a bit tired. We thought we had played enough, so we started off home again.

Then it began to get dark. The woods were changed. It wasn't quite dark yet, but almost. We made haste. Maybe mother was getting anxious, and waiting supper. She was always afraid that something might happen, though nothing had. This had been a splendid day. Everything had been just as it should, and we were satisfied with it all. It was getting darker and darker, and the trees were so queer. They stood and listened for the sound of our footsteps, as though they didn't know who we were. There was a glow-worm under one of them. It lay down there in the dark and stared at us. I held Daddy's hand tight, but he didn't seem to notice the strange light: he just went on. It was quite dark when we came to the bridge over the stream. It was roaring down underneath us as if it wanted to swallow us up, as the ground seemed to open under us. We went along the sleepers carefully, holding hands tight so that we shouldn't fall in. I thought Daddy would carry me over, but he didn't say anything about it. I suppose he wanted me to be like him, and not think anything of it. We went on. Daddy was so calm in the darkness, walking with even steps without speaking. He was thinking his own thoughts. I couldn't understand how he could be so calm when everything was so ghostly. I looked round scared. It was nothing but darkness everywhere. I hardly dared to breathe deeply, because then the darkness comes into one, and that was dangerous, I thought. One must die soon. I remember quite well thinking so then. The railway embankment was very steep. It finished in black night. The telephone posts stood up ghostlike against the sky, mumbling deep inside as though someone were speaking, way down in the earth. The white china hats sat there scared, cowering with fear, listening. It was all so creepy. Nothing was real, nothing was natural, all seemed a mystery. I went closer to Daddy, and whispered: "Why is it so creepy when it's dark?"

"No child, it isn't creepy," he said, and took my hand.

"Oh, yes, but it is, Daddy."

"No, you mustn't think that. We know there is a God, don't we?" I felt so lonely, so abandoned. It was queer that it was only me that was frightened, and not Daddy. It was queer that we didn't feel the same about it. And it was queerer still that what he said didn't help, didn't stop me being frightened. Not even what he said about God helped. The thought of God made one feel creepy too. It was creepy to think that He was everywhere here in the darkness, down there under the trees, and in the telephone posts that mumbled so—probably that was Him every-where. But all the same one could never see Him.

We went along silently, each of us thinking his own thoughts. My heart felt cramped as though the darkness had come in and was squeez-ing it.

Then, when we were in a bend, we suddenly heard a great noise behind us. We were startled out of our thoughts. Daddy pulled me down the embankment and held me tight, and a train rushed by; a black train. The lights were out in all the carriages, as it whizzed past us. What could it be? There shouldn't be any train now. We looked at it, frightened. The furnace roared in the big engine, where they shovelled in coal, and the sparks flew out into the night. It was terrible. The driver stood so pale and immovable, with such a stony look in the glare. Daddy didn't recog-nize him—didn't know who he was. He was just looking ahead as though he was driving straight into darkness, far into darkness, which had no end.

Startled and panting with fear I looked after the wild thing. It was swallowed up in the night. Daddy helped me up on to the line, and we hurried home. He said, "That was strange! What train was that I won-der? And I didn't know the driver either." Then he didn't say any more.

I was shaking all over. That had been for me—for my sake. I guessed what it meant. It was all the fear which would come to me, all the unknown; all that Daddy didn't know about, and couldn't save me from. That was how the world would be for me, and the strange life I should live; not like Daddy's, where everyone was known and sure. It wasn't a real world, or a real life;—it just rushed burning into the dark-ness which had no end.

In Dreams Begin Responsibilities

DELMORE SCHWARTZ

I think it is the year 1909. I feel as if I were in a motion picture theatre, the long arm of light crossing the darkness and spinning, my eyes fixed on the screen. This is a silent picture as if an old Biograph one, in which the actors are dressed in ridiculously old-fashioned clothes, and one flash succeeds another with sudden jumps. The actors too seem to jump about and walk too fast. The shots themselves are full of dots and rays, as if it were raining when the picture was photographed. The light is bad.

It is Sunday afternoon, June 12, 1909, and my father is walking down the quiet streets of Brooklyn on his way to visit my mother. His clothes are newly pressed and his tie is too tight in his high collar. He jingles the coins in his pockets, thinking of the witty things he will say. I feel as if I had by now relaxed entirely in the soft darkness of the theatre; the organist peals out the obvious and approximate emotions on which the audience rocks unknowingly. I am anonymous, and I have forgotten myself. It is always so when one goes to the movies, it is, as they say, a drug.

My father walks from street to street of trees, lawns and houses, once in a while coming to an avenue on which a street-car skates and gnaws, slowly progressing. The conductor, who has a handle-bar mustache, helps a young lady wearing a hat like a bowl with feathers on to the car. She lifts her long skirts slightly as she mounts the steps. He leisurely makes change and rings his bell. It is obviously Sunday, for everyone is wearing Sunday clothes, and the street-car's noises emphasize the quiet of the holiday. Is not Brooklyn the city of Churches? The shops are closed and their shades drawn, but for an occasional stationery store or drugstore with great green balls in the window.

My father has chosen to take this long walk because he likes to walk and think. He thinks about himself in the future and so arrives at the place he is to visit in a state of mild exaltation. He pays no attention to the houses he is passing, in which the Sunday dinner is being eaten, nor to the many trees which patrol each street, now coming to their full leafage and the time when they will room the whole street in cool shadow. An occasional carriage passes, the horse's hooves falling like stones in the quiet afternoon, and once in a while an automobile, looking like an enormous upholstered sofa, puffs and passes.

My father thinks of my mother, of how nice it will be to introduce her to his family. But he is not yet sure that he wants to marry her, and once in a while he becomes panicky about the bond already established. He reassures himself by thinking of the big men he admires who are married: William Randolph Hearst, and William Howard Taft, who has just become President of the United States.

My father arrives at my mother's house. He has come too early and so is suddenly embarrassed. My aunt, my mother's sister, answers the loud bell with her napkin in her hand, for the family is still at dinner. As my father enters, my grandfather rises from the table and shakes hands with him. My mother has run upstairs to tidy herself. My grandmother asks my father if he has had dinner, and tells him that Rose will be down-stairs soon. My grandfather opens the conversation by remarking on the mild June weather. My father sits uncomfortably near the table, holding his hat in his hand. My grandmother tells my aunt to take my father's hat. My uncle, twelve years old, runs into the house, his hair tousled. He shouts a greeting to my father, who has often given him a nickel, and then runs upstairs. It is evident that the respect in which my father is held in this household is tempered by a good deal of mirth. He is impressive, yet he is very awkward.

Finally my mother comes downstairs, all dressed up, and my father being engaged in conversation with my grandfather becomes uneasy, not knowing whether to greet my mother or continue the conversation. He gets up from the chair clumsily and says "hello" gruffly. My grandfather watches, examining their congruence, such as it is, with a critical eye, and meanwhile rubbing his bearded cheek roughly, as he always does when he reflects. He is worried; he is afraid that my father will not make a good husband for his oldest daughter. At this point something happens to the film, just as my father is saying something funny to my mother; I am awakened to myself and my unhappiness just as my interest was rising. The audience begins to clap impatiently. Then the trouble is cared for but the film has been returned to a portion just shown, and once more I see my grandfather rubbing his bearded cheek and pondering my father's character. It is difficult to get back into the picture once more and forget myself, but as my mother giggles at my father's words, the darkness drowns me.

My father and mother depart from the house, my father shaking hands with my mother once more, out of some unknown uneasiness. I stir uneasily also, slouched in the hard chair of the theatre. Where is the older uncle, my mother's older brother? He is studying in his bedroom upstairs, studying for his final examination at the College of the City of New York, having been dead of rapid pneumonia for the last twenty-one years. My mother and father walk down the same quiet streets once more. My mother is holding my father's arm and telling him of the novel which she has been reading; and my father utters judgments of the characters as the plot is made clear to him. This is a habit which he very much enjoys, for he feels the utmost superiority and confidence when he approves and condemns the behavior of other people. At times he feels moved to utter a brief "Ugh"—whenever the story becomes what he would call sugary. This tribute is paid to his manliness. My mother feels satisfied by the interest which she has awakened; she is showing my father how intelligent she is, and how interesting.

They reach the avenue, and the street-car leisurely arrives. They are going to Coney Island this afternoon, although my mother considers that such pleasures are inferior. She has made up her mind to indulge only in a walk on the boardwalk and a pleasant dinner, avoiding the riotous amusements as being beneath the dignity of so dignified a couple.

My father tells my mother how much money he has made in the past week, exaggerating an amount which need not have been exaggerated. But my father has always felt that actualities somehow fall short. Suddenly I begin to weep. The determined old lady who sits next to me in the theatre is annoyed and looks at me with an angry face, and being intimidated, I stop. I drag out my handkerchief and dry my face, licking the drop which has fallen near my lips. Meanwhile I have missed something, for here are my mother and father alighting at the last stop, Coney Island.

They walk toward the boardwalk, and my father commands my mother to inhale the pungent air from the sea. They both breathe in deeply, both of them laughing as they do so. They have in common a great interest in health, although my father is strong and husky, my mother frail. Their minds are full of theories of what is good to eat and not good to eat, and sometimes they engage in heated discussions of the subject, the whole matter ending in my father's announcement, made with a scornful bluster, that you have to die sooner or later anyway. On the boardwalk's flagpole, the American flag is pulsing in an intermittent wind from the sea.

My father and mother go to the rail of the boardwalk and look down on the beach where a good many bathers are casually walking about. A few are in the surf. A peanut whistle pierces the air with its pleasant and active whine, and my father goes to buy peanuts. My mother remains at the rail and stares at the ocean. The ocean seems merry to her; it pointedly sparkles and again and again the pony waves are released. She notices the children digging in the wet sand, and the bathing costumes of the girls who are her own age. My father returns with the peanuts. Overhead the sun's lightning strikes and strikes, but neither of them is at all aware of it. The boardwalk is full of people dressed in their Sunday clothes and idly strolling. The tide does not reach as far as the boardwalk, and the strollers would feel no danger if it did. My mother and father lean on the rail of the boardwalk and absently stare at the ocean. The ocean is becoming rough; the waves come in slowly, tugging strength from far back. The moment before they somersault, the moment when they arch their backs so beautifully, showing green and white veins amid the black, that moment is intolerable. They finally crack, dashing fiercely upon the sand, actually driving, full force downward, against the sand, bouncing upward and forward, and at last petering out into a small stream which races up the beach and then is recalled. My parents gaze absentmindedly at the ocean, scarcely interested in its harshness. The sun overhead does not disturb them. But I stare at the terrible sun which breaks up sight, and the fatal, merciless, passionate ocean, I forget my parents. I stare fascinated and finally, shocked by the indifference of my father and mother, I burst out weeping once more. The old lady next to me pats me on the shoulder and says "There, there, all of this is only a movie, young man, only a movie," but I look up once more at the terrifying sun and the terrifying ocean, and being unable to control my tears, I get up and go to the men's room, stumbling over the feet of the other people seated in my row.

When I return, feeling as if I had awakened in the morning sick for lack of sleep, several hours have apparently passed and my parents are riding on the merry-go-round. My father is on a black horse, and my mother on a white one, and they seem to be making an eternal circuit for the single purpose of snatching the nickel rings which are attached to the arm of one of the posts. A hand-organ is playing; it is one with the ceaseless circling of the merry-go-round.

For a moment it seems that they will never get off the merry-go-round because it will never stop. I feel like one who looks down on the avenue from the 50th story of a building. But at length they do get off; even the music of the hand-organ has ceased for a moment. My father has acquired ten rings, my mother only two, although it was my mother who really wanted them.

They walk on along the boardwalk as the afternoon descends by imperceptible degrees into the incredible violet of dusk. Everything fades into a relaxed glow, even the ceaseless murmuring from the beach, and the revolutions of the merry-go-round. They look for a place to have dinner. My father suggests the best one on the boardwalk and my mother demurs, in accordance with her principles.

However, they do not go to the best place, asking for a table near the window, so that they can look out on the boardwalk and the mobile ocean. My father feels omnipotent as he places a quarter in the waiter's hand as he asks for a table. The place is crowded and here too there is music, this time from a kind of string trio. My father orders dinner with a fine confidence.

As the dinner is eaten, my father tells of his plans for the future, and my mother shows with expressive face how interested she is, and how impressed. My father becomes exultant. He is lifted up by the waltz that is being played, and his own future begins to intoxicate him. My father tells my mother that he is going to expand his business, for there is a great deal of money to be made. He wants to settle down. After all, he is twenty-nine, he has lived by himself since he was thirteen, he is making more and more money, and he is envious of his married friends when he visits them in the cozy security of their homes, surrounded, it seems, by the calm domestic pleasures, and by delightful children, and then, as the waltz reaches the moment when all the dancers swing madly, then, then with awful daring, then he asks my mother to marry him, although awkwardly enough and puzzled, even in his excitement, at how he had arrived at the proposal, and she, to make the whole business worse, begins to cry, and my father looks nervously about, not knowing at all what to do now, and my mother says: "It's all I've wanted from the moment I saw you," sobbing, and he finds all of this very difficult, scarcely to his taste, scarcely as he had thought it would be, on his long walks over Brooklyn Bridge in the revery of a fine cigar, and it was then that I stood up in the theatre and shouted: "Don't do it. It's not too late to change your minds, both of you. Nothing good will come of it, only remorse, hatred, scandal, and two children whose characters are monstrous." The whole audience turned to look at me, annoyed, the usher came hurrying down the aisle flashing his searchlight, and the old lady next to me tugged me down into my seat, saying: "Be quiet. You'll be put out, and you paid thirty-five cents to come in." And so I shut my eyes because I could not bear to see what was happening. I sat there quietly.

But after awhile I begin to take brief glimpses, and at length I watch again with thirsty interest, like a child who wants to maintain his sulk although offered the bribe of candy. My parents are now having their picture taken in a photographer's booth along the boardwalk. The place is shadowed in the mauve light which is apparently necessary. The camera is set to the side on its tripod and looks like a Martian man. The photographer is instructing my parents in how to pose. My father has his arm over my mother's shoulder, and both of them smile emphatically. The photographer brings my mother a bouquet of flowers to hold in her hand but she holds it at the wrong angle. Then the photographer covers himself with the black cloth which drapes the camera and all that one sees of him is one protruding arm and his hand which clutches the rubber ball which he will squeeze when the picture is finally taken. But he is not satisfied with their appearance. He feels with certainty that somehow there is something wrong in their pose. Again and again he issues from his hidden place with new directions. Each suggestion merely makes matters worse. My father is becoming impatient. They try a seated pose. The photographer explains that he has pride, he is not interested in all of this for the money, he wants to make beautiful pictures. My father says: "Hurry up, will you? We haven't got all night." But the photographer only scurries about apologetically, and issues new directions. The photographer charms me. I approve of him with all my heart, for I know just how he feels, and as he criticizes each revised pose according to some unknown idea of rightness, I become quite hopeful. But then my father says angrily: "Come on, you've had enough time, we're not going to wait any longer." And the photographer, sighing unhappily, goes back under his black covering, holds out his hands, says: "One, two, three, Now!", and the picture is taken, with my father's smile turned to a grimace and my mother's bright and false. It takes a few minutes for the picture to be developed and as my parents sit in the curious light they become quite depressed.

They have passed a fortune-teller's booth, and my mother wishes to go in, but my father does not. They begin to argue about it. My mother becomes stubborn, my father once more impatient, and then they begin to quarrel, and what my father would like to do is walk off and leave my mother there, but he know that that would never do. My mother refuses to budge. She is near to tears, but she feels an uncontrollable desire to hear what the palm-reader will say. My father consents angrily, and they both go into a booth which is in a way like the photographer's, since it is draped in black cloth and its light is shadowed. The place is too warm, and my father keeps saying this is all nonsense, pointing to the crystal ball on the table. The fortune-teller, a fat, short woman, garbed in what is supposed to be Oriental robes, comes into the room from the back and greets them, speaking with an accent. But suddenly my father feels that the whole thing is intolerable; he tugs at my mother's arm, but my mother refuses to budge. And then, in terrible anger, my father lets go of my mother's arm and strides out, leaving my mother stunned. She moves to go after my father, but the fortune-teller holds her arm tightly and begs her not to do so, and I in my seat am shocked more than can ever be said, for I feel as if I were walking a tight-rope a hundred feet over a circus-audience and suddenly the rope is showing signs of breaking, and I get up from my seat and begin to shout once more the first words I can think of to communicate my terrible fear and once more the usher comes hurrying down the aisle flashing his searchlight, and the old lady pleads with me, and the shocked audience has turned to stare at me, and I keep shouting: "What are they doing? Don't they know what they are doing? Why doesn't my mother go after my father? If she does not do that, what will she do? Doesn't my father know what he is doing?"—But the usher has seized my arm and is dragging me away, and as he does so, he says: "What are *you* doing? Don't you know that you can't do whatever you want to do? Why should a young man like you, with your whole life before you, get hysterical like this? Why don't you *think* of what you're doing? You can't act like this even if other people aren't around! You will be sorry if you do not do what you should do, you can't carry on like this, it is not right, you will find that out soon enough, everything you do matters too much," and he said that dragging me through the lobby of the theatre into the cold light, and I woke up into the bleak winter morning of my 21st birthday, the windowsill shining with its lip of snow, and the morning already begun.

Becoming: Death and Rebirth

THIS motif, usually appearing fairly close to the end of a mythical account of a work of literature, is often in earlier works associated with a literal journey into the place reigned over by Death. In more recent works, however, death is more symbolic than literal, as in Lawrence's "The Horsedealer's Daughter," a story which tells about a would-be suicide who is rescued from a pond and is "reborn" into a new life. The death—real or symbolic—in this motif signifies an end to a former way of life and the emergence of a new outlook or insight or way of coping with life. Generally it is water (a female symbol) that is the means of rebirth, as in Ernest Hemingway's *Farewell to Arms* when Frederick Henry swims the lake after Catherine's death or in T. S. Eliot's "The Waste Land," which moves from water as a medium of death through desiccation to rebirth by water. The descent into death in this poem, as in John Milton's "Lycidas," which employs this same ambivalence in the symbol of water, illustrates previous remarks on the journey. Compare *rebirth* and *fertility rites*.

The Story of Orpheus and Eurydice

OVID

(from Metamorphoses, X, 1–85; trans. Rolfe Humphries)

So Hymen left there, clad in saffron robe,
Through the great reach of air, and took his way
To the Ciconian country, where the voice
Of Orpheus called him, all in vain. He came there,
True, but brought with him no auspicious words,
No joyful faces, lucky omens. The torch
Sputtered and filled the eyes with smoke; when swung,
It would not blaze: bad as the omens were,
The end was worse, for as the bride went walking
Across the lawn, attended by her naiads,
A serpent bit her ankle, and she was gone.
Orpheus mourned her to the upper world,
And then, lest he should leave the shades untried,

Dared to descend to Styx, passing the portal
Men call Taenarian. Through the phantom dwellers,
The buried ghosts, he passed, came to the king
Of that sad realm, and to Persephone,
His consort, and he swept the strings, and chanted:
"Gods of the world below the world, to whom
All of us mortals come, if I may speak
Without deceit, the simple truth is this:
I came here, not to see dark Tartarus,
Nor yet to bind the triple-throated monster
Medusa's offspring, rough with snakes. I came
For my wife's sake, whose growing years were taken
By a snake's venom. I wanted to be able
To bear this; I have tried to. Love has conquered.
This god is famous in the world above,
But here, I do not know. I think he may be
Or it is all a lie, that ancient story
Of an old ravishment, and how he brought
The two of you together? By these places
All full of fear, by this immense confusion,
By this vast kingdom's silences, I beg you,
Weave over Eurydice's life, run through too soon.
To you we all, people and things, belong,
Sooner or later, to this single dwelling
All of us come, to our last home; you hold
Longest dominion over humankind.
She will come back again, to be your subject,
After the ripeness of her years; I am asking
A loan and not a gift. If fate denies us
This privilege for my wife, one thing is certain:
I do not want to go back either; triumph
In the death of two."
                            And with his words, the music
Made the pale phantoms weep: Ixion's wheel
Was still, Tityos' vultures left the liver,
Tantalus tried no more to reach for the water,
And Belus' daughters rested from their urns,
And Sisyphus climbed on his rock to listen.
That was the first time ever in all the world
That Furies wept. Neither the king nor consort
Had harshness to refuse him, and they called her,
Eurydice. She was there, limping a little
From her late wound, with the new shades of Hell.
And Orpheus received her, but one term

Was set: he must not, till he passed Avernus,
Turn back his gaze, or the gift would be in vain.

They climbed the upward path, through absolute silence,
Up the steep murk, clouded in pitchy darkness,
They were near the margin, near the upper land,
When he, afraid that she might falter, eager to see her,
Looked back in love, and she was gone, in a moment.
Was it he, or she, reaching out arms and trying
To hold or to be held, and clasping nothing
But empty air? Dying the second time,
She had no reproach to bring against her husband,
What was there to complain of? One thing, only:
He loved her. He could hardly hear her calling
Farewell! when she was gone.
                              The double death
Stunned Orpheus, like the man who turned to stone
At sight of Cerberus, or the couple of rock,
Olenos and Lethaea, hearts so joined
One shared the other's guilt, and Ida's mountain,
Where rivers run, still holds them, both together.
In vain the prayers of Orpheus and his longing
To cross the river once more; the boatman Charon
Drove him away. For seven days he sat there
Beside the bank, in filthy garments, and tasting
No food whatever. Trouble, grief, and tears
Were all his sustenance. At last, complaining
The gods of Hell were cruel, he wandered on
To Rhodope and Haemus, swept by the north winds,
Where, for three years, he lived without a woman
Either because marriage had meant misfortune
Or he had made a promise. But many women
Wanted this poet for their own, and many
Grieved over their rejection. His love was given
To young boys only, and he told the Thracians
That was the better way: *enjoy that springtime,
Take those first flowers!*

The Raising of Lazarus

JOHN, Chapter 11

1 Now a certain man was sick, named Lazarus, of Bethany, the town of Mary and her sister Martha. 2 (It was that Mary which anointed the Lord with ointment, and wiped his feet with her hair, whose brother Lazarus was sick.) 3 Therefore his sisters sent unto him, saying, Lord, behold, he whom thou lovest is sick. 4 When Jesus heard that, he said, This sickness is not unto death, but for the glory of God, that the Son of God might be glorified thereby. 5 Now Jesus loved Martha, and her sister, and Lazarus. 6 When he had heard therefore that he was sick, he abode two days still in the same place where he was. 7 Then after that saith he to his disciples, Let us go into Judaea again. 8 His disciples say unto him, Master, the Jews of late sought to stone thee; and goest thou thither again? 9 Jesus answered, Are there not twelve hours in the day? If any man walk in the day, he stumbleth not, because he seeth the light of this world. 10 But if a man walk in the night, he stumbleth, because there is no light in him. 11 These things said he: and after that he saith unto them, Our friend Lazarus sleepeth; but I go, that I may awake him out of sleep. 12 Then said his disciples, Lord, if he sleep, he shall do well. 13 Howbeit Jesus spake of his death: but they thought that he had spoken of taking of rest in sleep. 14 Then said Jesus unto them plainly, Lazarus is dead. 15 And I am glad for your sake that I was not there, to the intent ye may believe; nevertheless let us go unto him. 16 Then said Thomas, which is called Didymus, unto his fellow-disciples, Let us also go, that we may die with him. 17 Then when Jesus came, he found that he had lain in the grave four days already. 18 Now Bethany was nigh unto Jerusalem, about fifteen furlongs off: 19 And many of the Jews came to Martha and Mary, to comfort them concerning their brother. 20 Then Martha, as soon as she heard that Jesus was coming, went and met him: but Mary sat still in the house. 21 Then said Martha unto Jesus, Lord, if thou hadst been here, my brother had not died. 22 But I know, that even now, whatsoever thou wilt ask of God, God will give it thee. 23 Jesus saith unto her, Thy brother shall rise again. 24 Martha saith unto him, I know that he shall rise again in the resurrection at the last day. 25 Jesus said unto her, I am the resurrection, and the life: he that believeth in me, though he were dead, yet shall he live: 26 And whosoever liveth and believeth in me shall

never die. Believest thou this?   27 She saith unto him, Yea, Lord: I believe that thou art the Christ, the Son of God, which should come into the world.   28 And when she had so said, she went her way, and called Mary her sister secretly, saying, The Master is come, and calleth for thee. 29 As soon as she heard that, she arose quickly, and came unto him. 30 Now Jesus was not yet come into the town, but was in that place where Martha met him.   31 The Jews then which were with her in the house, and comforted her, when they saw Mary, that she rose up hastily and went out, followed her, saying, She goeth unto the grave to weep there.   32 Then when Mary was come where Jesus was, and saw him, she fell down at his feet, saying unto him, Lord, if thou hadst been here, my brother had not died.   33 When Jesus therefore saw her weeping, and the Jews also weeping which came with her, he groaned in the spirit, and was troubled,   34 And said, Where have ye laid him? They said unto him, Lord, come and see.   35 Jesus wept.   36 Then said the Jews, Behold how he loved him!   37 And some of them said, Could not this man, which opened the eyes of the blind, have caused that even this man should not have died?   38 Jesus therefore again groaning in himself cometh to the grave. It was a cave, and a stone lay upon it. 39 Jesus said, Take ye away the stone. Martha, the sister of him that was dead, saith unto him, Lord, by this time he stinketh: for he hath been dead four days.   40 Jesus saith unto her, Said I not unto thee, that, if thou wouldest believe, thou shouldest see the glory of God?   41 Then they took away the stone from the place where the dead was laid. And Jesus lifted up his eyes, and said, Father, I thank thee that thou hast heard me.   42 And I knew that thou hearest me always: but because of the people which stand by I said it, that they may believe that thou hast sent me.   43 And when he thus had spoken, he cried with a loud voice, Lazarus, come forth.   44 And he that was dead came forth, bound hand and foot with graveclothes: and his face was bound about with a napkin. Jesus saith unto them, Loose him, and let him go.   45 Then many of the Jews which came to Mary, and had seen the things which Jesus did, believed on him.   46 But some of them went their ways to the Pharisees, and told them what things Jesus had done.

The Resurrection

LUKE, Chapters 23 and 24

CHAPTER 23

50 And, behold there was a man named Joseph, a counseller; and he was a good man, and a just: **51** (The same had not consented to the counsel and deed of them;) he was of Arimathaea, a city of the Jews: who also himself waited for the kingdom of God.   **52** This man went unto Pilate, and begged the body of Jesus.   **53** And he took it down, and wrapped it in linen, and laid it in a sepulchre that was hewn in stone, wherein never man before was laid.   **54** And that day was the preparation, and the sabbath drew on.   **55** And the women also, which came with him from Galilee, followed after, and beheld the sepulchre, and how his body was laid.   **56** And they returned, and prepared spices and ointments; and rested the sabbath day according to the commandment.

CHAPTER 24

1 Now upon the first day of the week, very early in the morning, they came upon the sepulchre, bringing the spices which they had prepared, and certain others with them.   **2** And they found the stone rolled away from the sepulchre.   **3** And they entered in, and found not the body of the Lord Jesus.   **4** And it came to pass, as they were much perplexed thereabout, behold, two men stood by them in shining garments: **5** And as they were afraid, and bowed down their faces to the earth, they said unto them, Why seek ye the living among the dead? **6** He is not here, but is risen: remember how he spake unto you when he was yet in Galilee,   **7** Saying, The Son of man must be delivered into the hands of sinful men, and be crucified, and the third day rise again.   **8** And they remembered his words.   **9** And returned from the sepulchre, and told all these things unto the eleven, and to all the rest.   **10** It was Mary Magdalene, and Joanna, and Mary the mother of James, and other women that were with them, which told these things unto the apostles.   **11** And their words seemed to them as idle tales, and they believed them not.   **12** Then arose Peter, and ran unto the sepulchre; and stooping down, he beheld the linen clothes laid by themselves, and departed, wondering in himself at that which was come to pass.

13 And, behold, two of them went that same day to a village called Emmaus, which was from Jerusalem about threescore furlongs.   14 And they talked together of all these things which had happened.   15 And it came to pass, that, while they communed together and reasoned, Jesus himself drew near, and went with them.   16 But their eyes were holden that they should not know him.   17 And he said unto them, What manner of communications are these that we have one to another, as ye walk, and are sad?   18 And the one of them, whose name was Cleopas, answering said unto him, Art thou only a stranger in Jerusalem, and hast not known the things which are come to pass there in these days?   19 And he said unto them, What things? And they said unto him, Concerning Jesus of Nazareth, which was a prophet mighty in deed and word before God and all the people: 20 And how the chief priests and our rulers delivered him to be condemned to death and have crucified him.   21 But we trusted that it had been he which should have redeemed Israel: and beside all this, today is the third day since these things were done.   22 Yea, and certain women also of our company made us astonished, which were early at the sepulchre;   23 And when they found not his body, they came, saying, that thy had also seen a vision of angels, which said that he was alive.   24 and certain of them which were with us went to the sepulchre, and found it even so as the women had said: but him they saw not.   25 Then he said unto them, O fools, and slow of heart to believe all that the prophets have spoken: 26 Ought not Christ to have suffered these things, and to enter into his glory?   27 And beginning at Moses and all the prophets, he expounded unto them in all the scriptures the things concerning himself.   28 And they drew nigh unto the village, whither they went: and he made as though he would have gone further.   29 But they constrained him, saying, Abide with us: for it is toward evening, and the day is far spent. And he went in to tarry with them.   30 And it came to pass, as he sat at meat with them, he took bread, and blessed it, and brake it, and gave to them.   31 And their eyes were opened, and they knew him; and he vanished out of their sight.   32 And they said one to another, Did not our heart burn within us, while he talked with us by the way, and while he opened to us the scriptures?   33 And they rose up the same hour, and returned to Jerusalem, and found the eleven gathered together, and them that were with them,   34 Saying, The Lord is risen indeed, and hath appeared to Simon.   35 And they told what things were done in the way, and how he was known of them in breaking of bread.

36 And as they thus spake, Jesus himself stood in the midst of them,

and saith unto them, Peace be unto you.   37 But they were terrified
and affrighted, and supposed that they had seen a spirit.   38 And he
said unto them, Why are ye troubled? and why do thoughts arise in your
hearts?   39 Behold my hands and my feet, that it is I myself: handle
me, and see; for a spirit hath not flesh and bones, as ye see me have.
40 And while they yet believed not for joy, and wondered, he said unto
them, Have ye here any meat?   42 And they gave him a piece of broiled
fish, and of an honeycomb.   43 And he took it, and did eat before
them.   44 And he said unto them, These are the words which I spake
unto you, while I was yet with you, that all things must be fulfilled, which
were written in the law of Moses, and in the prophets, and in the psalms,
concerning me.   45 Then opened he their understanding, that they
might understand the scriptures,   46 And said unto them, Thus it is
written, and thus it behoved Christ to suffer, and to rise from the dead
the third day: 47 And that repentance and remission of sins should
be preached in his name among all nations, beginning at Jerusalem.
48 And ye are witnesses of these things.

49 And, behold, I send the promise of my Father upon you: but
tarry ye in the city of Jerusalem, until ye be endued with power from on
high.

50 And he led them out as far as to Bethany, and he lifted up his
hands, and blessed them.   51 And it came to pass, while he blessed
them, he was parted from them, and carried up into heaven.   52 And
they worshipped him, and returned to Jerusalem with great joy: 53
And were continually in the temple, praising and blessing God. Amen.

Summer Water and Shirley

DURANGO MENDOZA

It was in the summer that had burned every stalk of corn and every
blade of grass and dried up the creek until it only flowed in trickles
across the ford below the house where in the pools the boy could scoop
up fish in a dishpan.

The boy lived with his mother and his sister, Shirley, and the three
smaller children eleven miles from Weleetka, and near Lthwathlee Indian
church where it was Eighth Sunday meeting and everyone was there. The
boy and his family stayed at the camp house of his dead father's people.

Shirley and her brother, who was two years older and twelve, had just escaped the deacon and were lying on the brown, sun-scorched grass behind the last camp house. They were out of breath and giggled as they peeped above the slope and saw the figure of the deacon, Hardy Eagle, walking toward the church house.

"Boy, we sure out-fooled him, huh?" Shirley laughed lightly and jabbed her elbow in her brother's shaking side. "Whew!" She ran her slim hand over her eyes and squinted at the sky. They both lay back and watched the cloudless sky until the heat in their blood went down and their breath slowed to normal. They lay there on the hot grass until the sun became too much for them.

"Hey, let's go down to the branch and find a pool to wade in, okay?" She had rolled over suddenly and spoke directly into the boy's ear.

"I don't think we better. Mama said to stay around the church grounds."

"Aw, you're just afraid."

"No, it's just that—"

" 'Mama said to stay around the church grounds!' Fraidy-cat, I'll go by myself then." She sat up and looked at him. He didn't move and she sighed. Then she nudged him. "Hey." She nudged him again and assumed a stage whisper. "Looky there! See that old man coming out of the woods?"

The boy looked and saw the old man shuffling slowly through the high johnson grass between the woods and the clearing for the church grounds. He was very old and still wore his hair in the old way.

"Who is he?" Shirley whispered. "Who is he?"

"I can't tell yet. The heat makes everything blurry." The boy was looking intently at the old man who was moving slowly in the weltering heat through the swaying grass that moved with the sound of light tinsel in the dry wind.

"Let's go sneak through the grass and scare him," Shirley suggested. "I bet that'd make him even run." She moved her arms as if she were galloping and broke down into giggles. "Come on," she said, getting to one knee.

"Wait!" He pulled her back.

"What do you mean, 'wait'? He'll be out of the grass pretty soon and we won't—" She broke off. "What's the matter? What're you doing?"

The boy had started to crawl away on his hands and knees and was motioning for her to follow. "Come on, Shirley," he whispered. "That's old Ansul Middlecreek!"

"Who's *he?*"

"Don't you remember? Mama said he's the one that killed Haskell Day—with witchcraft. He's a *stiginnee!*"

"A *stiginnee?* Aw, you don't believe that, do you? Mama says you can tell them by the way they never have to go to the toilet, and that's

where he's been. Look down there." She pointed to the little unpainted
house that stood among the trees.

"I don't care *where* he's been! Come on, Shirley! Look! Oh my gosh!
He saw you pointing!"

"I'm coming," she said and followed him quickly around the corner
of the camp house.

They sat on the porch. Almost everyone was in for the afternoon
service and they felt alone. The wind was hot and it blew from the
southwest. It blew past them across the dry fields of yellow weeds that
spread before them up to the low hills that wavered in the heat and
distance. They could smell the dry harshness of the grass and they felt
the porch boards hot underneath them. Shirley bent over and wiped her
face with the skirt of her dress.

"Come on," she said. "Let's go down to the creek branch before that
deacon comes back." She pulled at his sleeve and they stood up.

"Okay," he said and they skirted the outer camp houses and followed the dusty road to the bridge, stepping from tuft to tuft of scorched
grass.

Toward evening and suppertime they climbed out of the dry bed of
the branch, over the huge boulders to the road and started for the camp
grounds. The sun was in their eyes as they trudged up the steep road
from the bridge. They had found no water in the branch so they had
gone on down to the creek. For the most part it too was dry.

Suddenly they saw a shadow move into the dust before them. They
looked up and saw old Ansul Middlecreek shuffling toward them. His
cracked shoes raised little clouds of dust that rose around his ankles and
made whispering sounds as he moved along.

"Don't look when you go by," the boy whispered intently, and he
pushed her behind him. But as they passed by Shirley looked up.

"Hey, Ansul Middlecreek," she said cheerfully. *"Henkschay!"* Then
with a swish of her skirt she grabbed her brother and they ran. The old
man stopped and the puffs of dust around his feet moved ahead as he
grumbled, his face still in shadow because he did not turn around. The
two didn't stop until they had reached the first gate. Then they slowed
down and the boy scolded his sister all the way to their camp. And all
through supper he looked at the dark opening of the door and then at
Shirley who sat beside him, helping herself with childish appetite to the
heavy, greasy food that was set before her.

"You better eat some," she told her brother. "Next meetin's not 'til
next month."

Soon after they had left the table she began to complain that her
head hurt and their mother got them ready to go home. They took the
two little girls and the baby boy from where they were playing under

the arbor and cleaned them up before they started out. Their uncle, George Hulegy, would go with them and carry the biggest girl. The mother carried the other one while the boy struggled in the rear with the baby. Shirley followed morosely behind them all as they started down the road that lay white and pale under the rising moon.

She began to fall further behind and shuffled her bare feet into the warm underlayer of dust. The boy gave to his uncle the sleeping child he carried and took Shirley by the hand, surprised that it was so hot and limp.

"Come on, Shirley, come on. Mama, Shirley's got a fever. Don't walk so fast—we can't keep up. Come on, Shirley," he coaxed. "Hurry."

They turned into their lane and followed it until they were on the little hill above the last stretch of road and started down its rocky slope to the sandy road below. Ahead, the house sat wanly under the stars, and Rey, the dog, came out to greet them, sniffing and wriggling his black body and tail.

George Hulegy and the mother were already on the porch as the boy led his sister into the yard. As they reached the porch they saw the lamp begin to glow orange in the window. Then Shirley took hold of the boy's arm and pointed weakly toward the back yard and the form of the storehouse.

"Look, Sonny! Over there, by the storehouse." The boy froze with fear but he saw nothing. "They were three little men," she said vaguely and then she collapsed.

"Mama!" But as he screamed he saw a great yellow dog with large brown spots jump off the other end of the porch with a click of its heavy nails and disappear into the shadows that led to the creek. The boy could hear the brush rustle and a few pebbles scatter as it went. Rey only whined uneasily and did not even look to where the creature had gone.

"What is it? What's wrong?" The two older persons had come quickly onto the porch and the mother bent immediately to help her daughter.

"Oh, Shirley! George! Help me. Oh gosh! She's burning up. Sonny, put back the covers of the big bed. Quick now!"

They were inside now and the boy spoke.

"She saw dwarfs," he said solemnly and the mother looked at George Hulegy. "And there was a big yellow dog that Rey didn't even see."

"Oh, no, no," the mother wailed and leaned over Shirley who had begun to writhe and moan. "Hush, baby, hush. Mama's here. Hush, baby, your Mama's here." She began to sing softly a very old song while George Hulegy took a lantern from behind the stove.

"I'm going to the creek and get some pebbles where the water still runs," he said. "I have to hurry." He closed the screen quietly behind him and the boy watched him as he disappeared with the swinging lantern through the brush and trees, down into the darkness to the ford. Behind him the mother still sang softly as Shirley's voice began to rise, high and thin like a very small child's. The boy shivered in the heat and sat down in the corner to wait helplessly as he tried not to look at the dark space of the window. He grew stiff and tired trying to control his trembling muscles as they began to jump.

Then George Hulegy came in with some pebbles that still were dripping and they left little wet spots of dark on the floor as he placed them above all the doors and windows throughout the house. Finally he placed three round ones at the foot of the bed where Shirley lay twisting and crying with pain and fever.

The mother had managed to start a small fire in the kitchen stove and told the boy to go out and bring in a few pieces of cook wood from the woodpile. He looked at her and couldn't move. He stood stiff and alert and heard George Hulegy, who was bending close over Shirley, muttering some words that he could not understand. He looked at the door but the sagging screen only reflected the yellow lamplight so that he couldn't see through into the darkness; he froze even tighter.

"Hurry, son!"

He looked at Shirley lying on the bed and moving from side to side.

"Sonny, I have to make Shirley some medicine!" His body shook from a spasm. The mother saw and turned to the door. "I'll get them," she said.

"Mama!"

She stopped and he barged through the door and found the darkness envelop him. As he fixed his wide-open gaze on the woodpile that faintly reflected the starlight and that of the moon which had risen above the trees, he couldn't look to either side nor could he run. When he reached for the first piece of wood, the hysteria that was building inside him hardened into an aching bitter core. He squeezed the rough cool wood to his chest and felt the fibers press into his bare arms as he staggered toward the house and the two rectangles of light. The closer he came the higher the tension inside him stretched until he could scarcely breathe. Then he was inside again and he sat limply in the corner, light and drained of any support. He could feel nothing except that Shirley was lying in the big feather bed across the room, wailing with hurt and a scalding fever.

His mother was hurrying from the kitchen with a tin cup of grass tea when Shirley began to scream, louder and louder until the boy thought that he would never hear another sound as he stood straight and hard, not leaning at all.

She stopped.

In the silence he saw his mother standing above and behind the lamp, casting a shadow on the ceiling, stopped with fear as they heard the other sound. The little girls had come into the room from their bedroom and were standing whimpering in their nightgowns by the door. The mother signaled and they became still and quiet, their mouths slightly open and their eyes wide. They heard nothing.

Then like a great, beating heart the sound rose steadily until they could smell the heat of a monstrous flesh, raw and hot. Steadily it grew to a gagging, stifling crescendo—then stopped. They heard the click of dog's nails on the porch's wooden planks, and afterwards, nothing. In the complete silence the air became cold for an instant and Shirley was quiet.

It was three days now since Shirley had begun to die and everyone knew how and had given up any hope. Even the white doctor could find nothing wrong and all the old Indians nodded their solemn heads when he went away saying that Shirley would be up in a few days, for now, to them, her manner of death was confirmed. He said to send for him if there was any "real" change. No need to move her—there was nothing wrong—nothing physically wrong, he had said. He could not even feel her raging fever. To him Shirley was only sleeping.

Everyone had accepted that Shirley was going to die and they were all afraid to go near her. "There is evil around her," they said. They even convinced the mother to put her in the back room and close off all light and only open it after three days. She would not die until the third day's night, nor would she live to see the fourth day's dawn. This they could know. A very old woman spoke these words to the mother and she could not disbelieve.

On this third day the boy sat and watched the flies as they crawled over the dirty floor, over the specks and splotches, the dust and crumbs. They buzzed and droned about some drops of water, rubbing their legs against themselves, nibbling, strutting, until the drops dried into meaningless little rings while the hot wind blew softly through the open window, stirring particles of dust from the torn screen. A droplet of sweat broke away from above his eyebrow and ran a crooked rivulet down his temple until he wiped it away. In his emptiness the boy did not want his sister to die.

"Mama?"

"What is it, son?"

"Is Shirley going to die?"

"Yes, son."

He watched her as she stood with her back to him. She moved the heavy skillet away from the direct heat and turned the damper so that the flames would begin to die. She moved automatically, as if faster movement would cause her to breathe in too much of the stifling heat. And as she moved the floor groaned under the shift in weight and her feet made whispering sounds against the sagging boards. The flies still flitted about, mindless and nasty, as the boy looked away from them to his mother.

"Does she have to, Mama?"

"Shirley is dying, son."

Again he saw how the flies went about, unaware of the heat, himself, his mother across the room or that Shirley lay in her silence in the back room. He splashed some more water from his glass and they knew he was there but immediately forgot and settled back to their patternless walking about. And even though the table was clean they walked jerkily among the dishes and inspected his tableware. The boy had lived all his life among these creatures but now he could not stand their nature.

"Darn flies!"

"Well, we won't have to worry when cold weather gets here," she said. "Now go call the kids and eat. I want to get some sewing done this afternoon."

He said nothing and watched her as she went into the other room. He went to the door and leaned out to call the small children. Then he slipped quietly into the back room and closed the door behind him, fastening the latch in the dark. The heat was almost choking and he blinked away the saltiness that stung his eyes. He stood by the door until he could see a little better. High above his head a crack in the shingles filtered down a star of daylight and he stepped to the bed that stood low against the rough planks of the wall. There were no flies in this room and there was no sound.

The boy sat down on a crate and watched the face of his sister emerge from the gloom where she lay. Straining his eyes he finally saw the rough army blanket rise and fall, but so slight was the movement that when his eyes lost their focus he could not see it and he quickly put out his hand but stopped. Air caught in his throat and he stifled a cough, still letting his hand hover over the motionless face. Then he touched the smooth forehead and jerked his hand away as if he had been burned.

He sat and watched his sister's well-formed profile and saw how the skin of the nose and forehead had become taut and dry and now gleamed pale and smooth like old ivory in the semi-darkness. A smell like that of hot wood filled the room but underneath it the boy could smell the odor of something raw, something evil—something that was making Shirley die.

The boy sat on the empty crate in the darkness through the late afternoon and did not answer when his mother called him. He knew that she would not even try the door to this room. He waited patiently for his thoughts to come together, not moving in the lifeless heat, and let the sweat flow from his body. He smelled the raw smell and when it became too strong he touched the smooth, round pebbles that had come from the creek where it still flowed, and the smell receded.

For many hours he sat, and then he got up and took down the heavy blanket that had covered the single window and let the moonlight fall across the face of his sister through the opening. He began to force his thoughts to remember, to relive every living moment of his life and every part that Shirley had lived in it with him. And then he spoke softly, saying what they had done, and how they would do again what they had done because he had not given up, for he was alive, and she was alive, and they had lived and would *still* live. And so he prayed to his will and forced his will out through his thoughts and spoke softly his words and was not afraid to look out through the window into the darkness through which came the coolness of the summer night. He smelled its scents and let them touch his flesh and come to rest around the "only sleeping" face of his sister. He stood, watching, listening, living.

Then they came, silently, dark-bellied clouds drifting up from the south, and the wind, increasing, swept in the heavy scent of the approaching storm. Lightning flashed over the low, distant hills and the clouds closed quietly around the moon as the thunder rumbled and the heavy drops began to fall, slowly at first, then irregularly, then increasing to a rhythmic rush of noise as the gusts of wind forced the rain in vertical waves across the shingled roof.

Much later, when the rain had moved ahead and the room became chilly when the water began to drip from the roof and the countless leaves, the boy slipped out of his worn denim pants and took off his shirt and lay down beside his sister. She felt him and woke up.

"You just now gettin' to bed?" she asked. "It's pretty late for that, ain't it?"

"No, Shirley," he said. "Go on back to sleep. It'll be morning pretty soon and when it gets light again we'll go see how high the water's risen in the creek."

He pulled the cover over him and drew his bare arms beneath the blanket and pulled it over their shoulders as he turned onto his side. Lying thus he could see in the darkness the even darker shapes of the trees and the storehouse his father had built.

Snake

D. H. LAWRENCE

A snake came to my water-trough
On a hot, hot day, and I in pyjamas for the heat,
To drink there.

In the deep, strange-scented shade of the great dark carob tree
I came down the steps with my pitcher
And must wait, must stand and wait, for there he was at the trough
    before me.

He reached down from a fissure in the earth-wall in the gloom
And trailed his yellow-brown slackness soft-bellied down, over the edge
    of the stone trough

And rested his throat upon the stone bottom,
And where the water had dripped from the tap, in a small clearness,
He sipped with his straight mouth,
Softly drank through his straight gums, into his slack long body,
Silently.

Someone was before me at my water-trough,
And I, like a second comer, waiting.

He lifted his head from his drinking, like cattle do,
And looked at me vaguely, as drinking cattle do,
And flickered his two-forked tongue from his lips, and mused a moment,
And stooped and drank a little more,
Being earth-brown, earth-golden from the burning bowels of the earth
On the day of Sicilian July, with Etna smoking.

The voice of my education said to me
He must be killed,
For in Sicily the black, black snakes are innocent, the gold are venomous.

And voices in me said, If you were a man
You would take a stick and break him now, and finish him off.

But I must confess how I liked him,
How glad I was he had come like a guest in quiet, to drink at my
    water-trough
And depart peaceful, pacified, and thankless,
Into the burning bowels of this earth.

Was it cowardice, that I dared not kill him?
Was it perversity, that I longed to talk to him?
Was it humility, to feel so honoured?
I felt so honoured.

And yet those voices:
If you were not afraid, you would kill him!

And truly I was afraid, I was most afraid,
But even so, honoured still more
That he should seek my hospitality
From out the dark door of the secret earth.

He drank enough
And lifted his head, dreamily, as one who has drunken,
And flickered his tongue like a forked night on the air, so black,
Seeming to lick his lips,
And looking around like a god, unseeing, into the air,
And slowly turned his head,
And slowly, very slowly, as if thrice adream,
Proceeded to draw his slow length curving round
And climb again the broken bank of my wall-face.

And as he put his head into that dreadful hole,
And as he slowly drew up, snake-easing his shoulders, and entered farther,
A sort of horror, a sort of protest against his withdrawing into that horrid
    black hole,
Deliberately going into the blackness, and slowly drawing himself after,
Overcame me now his back was turned.

I looked around, I put down my pitcher,
I picked up a clumsy log
And threw it at the water-trough with a clatter.

I think I did not hit him,
But suddenly that part of him that was left behind convulsed in
    undignified haste,
Writhed like lightning, and was gone

Into the black hole, the earth-lipped fissure in the wall-front,
At which, in the intense still noon, I stared with fascination.

And immediately I regretted it.
I thought how paltry, how vulgar, what a mean act!
I despised myself and the voices of my accursed human education.

And I thought of the albatross,
And I wished he would come back, my snake.

For he seemed to me again like a king,
Like a king in exile, uncrowned in the underworld,
Now due to be crowned again.

And so, I missed my chance with one of the lords
Of life.
And I have something to expiate;
A pettiness.

Joe Hill

ALFRED HAYES

I dreamed I saw Joe Hill last night,
Alive as you and me.
Says I, "But Joe, you're ten years dead,"
"I never died," says he.
"I never died," says he.

"In Salt Lake, Joe," says I to him,
Him standing by my bed,
"They framed you on a murder charge,"
Says Joe, "But I ain't dead,"
Says Joe, "But I ain't dead."

"The copper bosses killed you, Joe,
They shot you, Joe," says I.
"Takes more than guns to kill a man,"
Says Joe, "I didn't die,"
Says Joe, "I didn't die."

And standing there as big as life
And smiling with his eyes,
Joe says, "What they forgot to kill
Went on to organize,
Went on to organize."

"Joe Hill ain't dead," he says to me,
"Joe Hill ain't never died.
Where working men are out on strike
Joe Hill is at their side,
Joe Hill is at their side."

"From San Diego up to Maine,
In every mine and mill,
Where workers strike and organize,"
Says he, "You'll find Joe Hill,"
Says he, "You'll find Joe Hill."

I dreamed I saw Joe Hill last night,
Alive as you or me.
Says I, "But Joe, you're ten years dead,"
"I never died," says he,
"I never died," says he.

Additional Readings

BELLOW, SAUL. "Looking for Mr. Green."
Beowulf
Bhagavad Gita (primarily divine family myth)
CHAUCER, GEOFFREY. "The Canterbury Tales."
DANTE. *Inferno.*
DOOLITTLE, HILDA (H. D.). "Leda."
Gawain and the Green Knight
Gilgamesh (a Babylonian creation myth)
HAWTHORNE, NATHANIEL. "My Kinsman, Major Molineux."
JEFFERS, ROBINSON. "Roan Stallion."
JOYCE, JAMES. *A Portrait of the Artist as a Young Man.*
JOYCE, JAMES. *Ulysses.*
LAWRENCE, D. H. "The Horsedealer's Daughter."
LAWRENCE, D. H. *Sons and Lovers.*
LAWRENCE, D. H. "The Woman Who Rode Away."

MELVILLE, HERMAN. *Billy Budd.*
MILTON, JOHN. "Lycidas."
SALINGER, J. D. *Catcher in the Rye.*
SHAKESPEARE, WILLIAM. *Othello.*
SHAKESPEARE, WILLIAM. *The Winter's Tale.*
TENNYSON, ALFRED, LORD. *Idylls of the King.*
TWAIN, MARK. *Huckleberry Finn.*
VERGIL. *Aeneid.*
WRIGHT, RICHARD. *Black Boy.*
WRIGHT, RICHARD. "The Man Who Lived Underground."

3

ARCHETYPAL CHARACTERS

ARCHETYPAL characters are those who repeatedly appear within the cycle of life, exhibiting consistent traits, intentions, functions, and relationships with other characters. The most important of these archetypal characters is the hero, who may be a god-man exemplifying the course of action needed to achieve the task and make the journey and quest successful, or who may be a leader of men (the prophetic role) freeing his people from destruction, subjugation (particularly to an evil force or figure, thereby assuming the kingly role), and thus death (spiritual or actual; the priestly role). Those classified as messiah, savior, or the Christ (compare the entry in the Glossary) fall into the first category and will be recognized in the excerpts here from the Bible as well as the anonymous "A God and Yet a Man" and Hawthorne's "The Gray Champion." Those usually classified as literary hero fall into the second category and are represented by Achilles in Homer's *Iliad*, Aeneas in Vergil's *Aeneid*, Hamlet in Shakespeare's play, Muir's "Oedipus," and similar literary protagonists who lead their constituents successfully out of danger though they themselves may die in the process (for example, Milton's Samson in *Samson Agonistes*). While the hero may, like Tennyson's Ulysses, furnish the means to spiritual life for the wayfaring intellect, indicative of the union of the conscious and the unconscious in the mind, Tennyson's Telemachus points out that the means to the determination of the Self of the group (the ethos of a people) may lie in gradual physical action and achievements. Both are concerned with an exodus: one from the security and thus enslavement of the mind, the other from the enslavement and thus "security" of the body. But not all thinkers have found hope in such conceived messiahs or leaders of men, seeing rather the pessimistic injustices of life. To such people man is but an insect or a pawn in the hands of unseen forces, and thus man cannot hope to achieve improvement of his life through either mental or physical action. He rejects the concepts of task, journey, and quest, and even the possibility of attainment of the soul-image (that is, of salvation). He becomes, thus, a demonic figure driven by the libido only. Such antiheroes, as they are called, are perhaps best defined in Dostoievsky's "Notes From the Underground," too long for inclusion here. But Woyzeck in Georg Büchner's play (as well as Alban Berg's operatic adaptation) offers clear illustration of this view of man as unheroic, as pawn, as "born loser." The frequently reprinted "The Song of J. Alfred Prufrock" by T. S. Eliot and Conrad Aiken's Senlin (represented here by the "Morning Song from 'Senlin'") show us ordinary men beaten by the sheer weight of life— its repetition, its drabness, its meaninglessness, its established patterns. If the cycle of life exists, then what's the use of trying to change it?

The archetypal relationhips of the antihero are with the devil figure. While Satan represents the arch-antihero (as in Milton's *Paradise Lost*), he is also the opposition to the hero and the achievement of his task, hoping to divert the journey of the hero and to assure the failure of his quest. He becomes enticing (as in cummings' "in just-") or he subverts without his victim's realizing it (as in Snyder's view of Milton). The Satan figure, however, is often viewed ambivalently, particularly in his representation as a dragon or serpent (see both these entries in the Glossary). From a positive view he becomes the means for the hero to achieve his task by action against the Satan figure, once he is recognized (as in the various works included here under The Double), or from a negative view he becomes the means to thwart the hero and his action (as in the various items included under The Outcast). The psychological basis of the double is the belief that within all men are complementary opposites of good and evil; at times one or the other polarity is sublimated or repressed and the other polarity is uppermost. A proper understanding of Self will allow positive action to go forward. The Satanic within one will attempt to submerge the heroic unless recognized and controlled. The outcast may have strong affinities with the Satanic figure or even stronger affinities with the antihero, for example, Cain or Ishmael or Miniver Cheevy. Often, however, he becomes the conscience of the community by being its disruptive force, for example, Hawthorne's Ethan Brand or Claude McKay's outcast. But so seen, the outcast is thwarting the false hero and the false action, for he exercises wisdom and restraint not shared by the false hero and those he leads. Here we should compare Melville's Ishmael in the novel *Moby-Dick*: outcast he is, but one who rises above Ahab's obsession of driving out the evil of the white whale. Part of the psychological significance of the outcast is his ability to recognize the imbalance of the superego.

Confounding the hero and the outcast is the scapegoat, one who takes upon himself the sins of the people and who thereby removes those sins from the people. He himself is sacrificed, most frequently through his death but at least through his destruction as a potential hero. In one way of looking at it, Hamlet and Samson were both scapegoats, but the anti-type is, of course, Jesus. The scapegoat may thus have been heroic and potentially the achiever of the heroic quest, as in the examples given here, had his life not been cut short. Or the scapegoat, by running counter to the ideas and actions of at least one communal group, becomes their symbol for what has deterred their ideas or actions from being dominant or unchallenged, as in both poems by Yuri Suhl. "The Convert" by Lerone Bennett, Jr., presents both a scapegoat and a heroic figure in the character of Booker T. Brown. The relationship between the cycle of life in fertility religions and the scapegoat, whose taking upon himself the sins of the community will allow the desired ends of the community to proceed, can be seen in the Adonis story (as well as the sacrifice of Jesus) and in a well-known short story by Shirley Jackson entitled, "The Lottery," not included here. In these we understand how the myths of good and evil relate in man's mind to his concepts of the godhead's reward or punishment in life, rather than only at the end of mankind's lifetime. Thus he who has resisted evil (or transferred it) and who has pursued good (and achieved it) will be rewarded. The antiheroic, of course, disbelieves this and may accept evil as his good.

One means to achieve the quest is to maintain innocence and thereby do good through a lack of knowledge of evil, within individual man or within the patterns of life. The Wise Fool, as he is called, has no knowledge of the negative aspects of life (thus a fool) and will from his own innate goodness (as a creation of the All Good) be able to find the right path, judge right, and discover the essence of the soul-image (thus wise). Literature casts the wise fool as child (for example, MacDuff's son in "Macbeth"), as a simpleton (for example, William Faulkner's Benjy in *The Sound and the Fury*), or a madman (for example, Jean Giraudoux's Madwoman of Chaillot). These kinds of "heroes" are represented in the pieces included here.

The most usual means to the fall from innocence to experience and the most frequent agent in diverting the hero from his chosen path is temptation and the temptress. She may be Eve, deceived by Satan, and in turn the reason for Adam's (man's) fall, or she may be a sorceress like Circe, well aware of her actions and purposes. The sexual aspects of the temptation are constant, though at times the appeal may be to more than the bodily (the first temptation of the flesh). The hero may have to overcome the temptation of wealth and kingdom (overtones of which appear in Joyce's "The Boarding House," where the temptation is not overcome) or the temptation to inordinate pride (overtones of which appear in the Samson legend). But the primary opposition to the hero's path through life is the temptress.

The archetypal characters that are illustrated in this book are the major figures which represent man on his journey through life or which represent those whom he will encounter on his journey. Beneath all these myths is a basic belief in opposites, by which is meant the elements of the collective psyche. These unite as binary groups of Eros and Thanatos, of good and evil, of man and woman, of love and hate, of order and chaos, and so on. The journey is thus the attempt to balance these opposites within man himself, or within the community. The union of the anima and the animus, separated at birth, is the aim of life, but the full soul-image will not be realized, says the monomyth, until man (seen in female terms) is united bodily (and the imagery is generally sexual) with the godhead (as male figure) at the end of time. Although the literature reprinted here is separated into categories, it very often illustrates a number of categories at the same time, and it is through analysis of the ways the various forms of the mythic patterns play in and out in that literature that the reader will comprehend the intricacies of man's archetypal and mythic mind.

Heroes and Antiheroes

HEROES represent the values of their society. In earlier times, heroes were religious or god-directed (e.g., Moses); later they were secular or military (e.g., Beowulf). Then they became with the advent of realism typical representatives of their society (e.g., GI Joe); today they are antiheroic, ironic (to use Northrop Frye's classification), the "schlemiel," the loser (e.g., Herzog). Heroes may be the protagonists of tragedies, dying finally but gaining our sympathy and compassion in the process. The role of those we elevate to be our heroes is constantly changing, and figures from the world of science, society, politics, show business, athletics, or the military will appeal to the individual requirements of the individual person today. This is another way of saying that we have no common basis any longer for an heroic ideal. Mythically, however, the hero is often seen in savior terms as one who conquers evil and thus frees his people from destruction and death. A failure of faith and hope brings about transference of the heroic to the antiheroic and of the eternal to the mundane.

Achilles
(from The Iliad, Book XX)
HOMER

While the Achaians were arming with Achillês, eager to fight once more, and the Trojans awaited them on the rising of the plain, Zeus commanded Themis to summon the gods to assembly on Mount Olympos. She hastened over heaven and earth to do his bidding, and they all came; even the rivers, except Oceanos, even the nymphs who inhabit the groves and grassy dells and the springs and fountains. They all came to the house of Zeus Cloudgatherer, and took their seats in the galleries of polished stone which Hephaistos had built for them by his clever art.

So there they were assembled in the palace of Zeus. Not even Earthshaker was deaf to the summons; he also came out of the sea, and as he sat down among them he wanted to know what Zeus had in mind.

"Why have you summoned the gods again to conclave, Fiery Thun-

derbolt? Are you a bit anxious about Trojans and Achaians? Certainly
this war is blazing up very close to us now."

Zeus Cloudgatherer answered:

"You know what I have in mind, Earthshaker, you know why I have
summoned you. I do care about their killing one another like that. But
this is what I want to say. I mean to stay here, and sit in a sheltered spot,
and amuse myself by watching them. The rest of you may go where you
like, join the Trojans or the Achaians, help them both just as you fancy.
For if Achillês is left alone to fight the Trojans, they will not stand one
minute before Peleion's pursuing feet! Why, the sight of him was always
enough to make them tremble! And now that he is furious for the death
of his comrade, I fear he may storm the city, fate or no fate."

This was enough to raise war to the death at once. The gods were off
to the battlefield on both sides. To the Achaian camp went Hera and
Pallas Athena, Poseidon Earthshaker, Hermês Luckbringer the master-
piece of cunning wit; Hephaistos swaggered beside them hobbling along
with his thin shanks moving nimbly. To the Trojans went Arês in his
grand helmet, and with him Phoibos with his long hair waving, and
Artemis Archeress, Leto and Xanthos, and smiling Aphroditê.

When Achillês appeared after his long absence, and the Trojans saw
him sweep into the field with gleaming armour like a very god of war,
their knees trembled beneath them in dismay, and for a long time the
Achaians carried all before them. But as soon as the gods showed themselves, up rose Discord the mighty harrier of nations, loud shouted
Athena, standing outside the wall on the edge of the moat, or moving
upon the seashore: Arês shouted aloud from the other side, black as a
stormcloud, crying his commands from the citadel of Troy, or speeding
over Callicolonê by Simoeis river.

So the blessed gods drove the two hosts together and made the bitter
strife burst forth. The Father of men and gods thundered terribly from
on high, Poseidon made the solid earth quake beneath, and the tall summits of the hills; Mount Ida shook from head to foot, and the citadel of
Ilios trembled, and the Achaian ships. Fear seized Aïdoneus the lord of
the world below; fear made him leap from his throne and cry aloud, lest
Poseidon Earthshaker should break the earth above him, and lay open
to every eye those gruesome danksome abodes which even the gods
abhor—so terrible was the noise when gods met gods in battle. For against
Lord Poseidon stood Phoibos Apollo with his winged arrows, against
Enyalios glaring Athena stood; Hera was faced by Shootafar's sister,
Artemis Archeress, with her rattling golden shafts, Leto was faced by
Luckbringer Hermês in his strength; and Hephaistos had before him
that deep River, whom the gods call Xanthos, but men Scamandros.

Achillês longed most of all to meet Hector Priamidês. Hector he
sought amid the press; with Hector's blood most of all he longed to glut

the greedy god of war. But Apollo sent Aineias against him. He said to him in Lycaon's voice and shape:

"Aineias, you are a good one to make speeches, but where are those threats you made over the wine, when you promised the princes of Troy to fight Achillês Peleidês man to man?"

Aineias said:

"My dear Priamidês! Why do you tell me to tackle that proud man, when you know that is the last thing I want? It wouldn't be the first time I have faced Achillês. Once before he chased me off Ida with his spear, when he had come out for our cattle, the time when he ravaged Lyrnessos and Pedasos. Zeus saved me, Zeus gave me strength and a nimble pair of legs, or I should have gone down before Achillês—and Athena, for she was always in front of him to show the light of safety, while she told him to kill Trojans and Lelegans. It's no good for a mere man to fight Achillês; he's always got some god to protect him. And even without that his cast goes straight and does not stop till it runs through human flesh. But if only God would give me a fair chance he wouldn't beat me so easily, not if he claims to be made of solid brass!"

Apollo said:

"You should pray to the everlasting gods yourself. You are no mere man. They say Aphroditê was your mother; she is a daughter of Zeus, and Achillês comes from a lower god, just a daughter of the Old Man of the Sea. Go straight for him with the cold steel, and don't let him frighten you with sorry things like curses and threats."

These words inspired Aineias with new courage, and he went in search of his adversary. But Hera saw him! She called her allies to her and said:

"Now then, Poseidon and Athena, just consider what we had better do. There is Aineias in full panoply marching to meet Achillês—and Apollo made him go! Very well, let us turn him back again—or else we must take a hand—one of us might stand by Achillês; he must keep up his strength, he must not lose heart. We will show him that his friends are the best of the immortals, and the others are just windbags, the same who tried to defend the Trojans before. All we Olympians have come into this battle to save Achillês from harm for this day: what will happen afterwards is only what Fate spun for him with her thread when he was born. But if Achillês does not learn this from the voice of some god, he will fear when he finds himself face to face with a god. For gods are dangerous when they show their presence openly."

Poseidon said to this:

"Now Hera, that's all nonsense, don't lose your temper. I should not like to make gods fight with one another. Then let us get out of the way to some place where we can sit down and see. Let us leave the matter there, battle is the men's affair. But if Arês begins it, or Phoibos Apollo, if they get in the way of Achillês and won't let him fight, then we are in it on the spot, hammer and tongs! I think they will soon turn their backs and return to the family in Olympos, when once we have them under our compelling hands!"

He led the way to the high ruins of that ancient wall, which the Trojans had built with Athena's help for Heraclês, to keep off the sea-monster which used to come up and ravage the land. There they sat down hidden from the world in a thick mist; Arês and Apollo and the rest were on the brows of Callicolonê. So the two parties confronted each other, waiting to see what would happen. Neither wished to begin the fray; and Zeus sat on high commanding in chief.

The plain below was crowded with horses and men; the sheen of their armour gleamed bright, the ground rattled and shook under their feet, as the two armies met.

Charging into the space between, two champions came, Aineias Anchisiadês and Prince Achillês. Aineias first stept out of his car defiant, the heavy helmet nodding upon his head; he shook the sharp spear, and guarded his breast with the shield. Peleidês moved forward to meet him, like some wild lion when a crowd of men has come out to destroy him, a whole village; at first he moves unheeding, but as soon as some bold lad casts a lance and wounds him, he crouches down with open jaws, foam gathers about his teeth, he growls in rage and flogs flanks and ribs with his tail to excite himself, glaring at his foes—then a leap and a furious charge upon the mass, either to kill or to die. So rage and fury stirred Achillês to meet his enemy face to face.

When they were near enough, Achillês first spoke.

"Aineias," he said, "why have you come out so far in front of your lines? Have you a mind to fight with me? Do you hope to make yourself lord of Priam's honour, in the midst of his Trojans? Yet even if you kill me, that will not make Priam lay his prerogative in your hand; he has sons, and himself he is firm, no windy-minded man. Can it be that you have a demesne parcelled out for you by the Trojan nation, prime fruit-land and cornland, ready for you to live in if you can kill me? That will not be so easy as you think.

"Why, I made you run with my spear once before! Don't you remember how you were alone with your cattle, and I chased you off the mountains at a racing pace? You did not turn once to look back that day! But you got off clear to Lyrnessos. I was after you, and I sacked the town, thanks be to Athena and Father Zeus! I carried off all the women with my booty; but Zeus and All Gods saved you then! I don't think they will save you now, as you imagine. So I advise you to go back to the ranks and not to stand before me, or something may happen to you. When a thing is done and past, even fools are wise at last!"

Aineias answered:

"Don't think you will scare me with words, Peleidês, as if I were a little child. I can use taunts and abuse quite well if I like. We know each other's lineage, we know the names of our fathers, household tales among the children of men; but you have never set eyes on my parents, nor I on yours. Men say the admirable Peleus is your father, and your mother is Thetis the lovely daughter of the sea; for myself, I am proud to be the son of noble Anchisês, and my mother is Aphroditê. One of those two houses will mourn a son this day; for I tell you, childish words will not be enough to part us.

"But if you care to know more of my lineage, that is no secret. First, Zeus Cloudgatherer begat Dardanos. He founded Dardania, and lived on the skirts of Ida among the running brooks, for sacred Ilios was not yet built upon the plain, and there was no city as yet. Dardanos was father of King Erichthonios, the richest man on earth. He had three thousand mares with young foals at foot, which grazed on the marshy land. Boreas the North Wind saw them grazing and was enamoured. He took the shape of a blue roan stallion, and served some of them; they conceived and dropt twelve foals. These could scamper over a cornfield and never break a stalk, touching only the tops of the ears; they could scamper over the broad back of the sea, and touch only the crest of the waves.

"And Erichthonios begat Tros King of the Trojans. Tros again had three admirable sons, Ilos and Assaracos, and Ganymedês, who was the most beautiful of mortal men; he was rapt away by the gods for his beauty, to be cupbearer to Zeus and live among the immortals. Ilos again begat Laomedon; and Laomedon begat Tithonos and Priamos and Lampos and Clytios, and that sprig of Arês, Hicetaon. Assaracos begat Capys, and he begat Anchisês. I am the son of Anchisês, and Hector is the son of Priam.

"Such is the lineage that I can boast; but courage—Zeus increases that in men or diminishes, according to his will, for he is lord of all.

"Now let us stand no more talking like children in the midst of a battle. We could load one another with curses enough to sink a ship as big as a mountain! A rare runner is the tongue, with tales of all sorts in stock, and an infinite crop of words growing all round. Whatever kind of words you speak, such you will hear. But why must we bandy curses like a couple of scolding wives, who have some spite gnawing at their hearts till they run out and scold in the middle of the street, true and false together—the spite brings that in too! Your words will not turn me away from deeds when I mean battle. Come along now quickly, let us each taste what our mettle is like."

He let drive his good spear against that dreadful shield: the blade struck with a loud crash. Peleidês held the shield well away, for he thought

the spear of Aineias would pierce through—foolish man! Had he not the
sense to know that it is not easy for mortal man to master or escape the
glorious gifts of the gods! And so then, the good spear of Aineias did not
break the shield; the god-given gold was proof against it.

Achillês now cast his spear, and struck on the outermost ring, where
the metal was thinnest and the hide thinnest behind. The Pelian lancewood
ran through with a ringing sound. Aineias had crouched down holding up
the shield; so the shaft passed over his back and stuck in the ground, still
fast in the shield with the two layers torn apart. But he had escaped:
he stood up dizzy and shaken when he saw that shaft sticking at his elbow.
Achillês then drew sword and leaped at him with a shout. Aineias lifted
a great big stone in his hand such as two men could not carry, as men go
now, but he managed it easily alone. And now Aineias would have crashed
down that stone on his helmet, or on that shield which had saved him
before, and Peleidês would have chased and killed him with that sword;
but Poseidon Earthshaker thought his time was come, and said to the
others:

"Confound it! I am sorry for that brave Aineias. He will be killed
very soon and go down to Hadês, because he listened to Apollo Shootafar.
What a fool! Apollo won't save him. But why should this poor innocent
suffer for some one else's grievances? There's no sense in that, and he
always is most generous in his offering to the gods who rule the broad
heavens.

"Come along, let us save him ourselves, or Cronidês will be angry if
Achillês lays him low. And it is ordained that he shall escape, that the
lineage of Dardanos may not perish without seed and disappear. Cronidês
loved Dardanos more than all the sons he had of mortal mothers. He has
already come to hate Priam's family, and now indeed Aineias shall be
King of the Trojans, and his son's sons after him."

Hera replied:

"Settle it as you please, Earthshaker, about Aineias, whether you will
save him or leave him alone. But remember that we two have sworn again
and again, I and Pallas Athena, before all the company of heaven, never
to stir a finger to help the Trojans, not even when Troy shall be consumed
in blazing fire by the victorious Achaians!"

So Poseidon left them, and passed through the battle to the place
where Aineias and Achillês were face to face. He drew a mist over the
eyes of Achillês; he pulled out the spear from the shield of Aineias and
laid it before the other's feet, whisked up Aineias off the ground and hurled
him through the air. Over the ranks of fighting men Aineias flew from the
god's hand, over the lines of horses, and alighted on the outskirts of battle
where the Cauconians were getting ready for action. Poseidon was there
by his side, and said at once:

"Aineias, what god tells you to stand up in this mad way against Peleion the invincible? He's a better man than you are, and more in favour with the gods. Just retreat whenever you see him, unless you want to take lodgings in Hadês before your time. But when Achillês meets his death, you may confidently come to the front, for no other Achaian shall kill you."

After these plain words he left him, and scattered the mist from the eyes of Achillês, who opened his eyes wide and said to himself angrily:

"Confound it all, here's a miracle done before my eyes! There lies my spear on the ground, and not a trace can I see of the fellow I meant to kill! Aineias must have some friends in heaven. And I thought his boasting was all stuff and nonsense! Let him go to the devil. He won't have a mind to try me again after this happy escape from death! All right, I will round up our people and have a try for some other Trojans."

So he went along the lines, calling out to each man:

"Don't wait any longer, my brave Achaians, but have at 'em man to man! It's too much for me—I may be strong but I can't tackle the whole army! Not even Arês could do it, and he is a god immortal! Not even Athena could manage the mouth of a battle like this! But as far as my power goes, with hands and feet and strength, I swear I will never pause or rest one instant! Straight through their line I will go, and I don't think the man will be happy who comes within reach of my spear!"

As he encouraged his men thus, Hector called to the Trojans and told them he was about to meet Achillês:

"My brave Trojans!" he cried, "have no fear of Peleion! If words were weapons, I could face the immortal gods; but the spear is less easy—the gods are too strong for us! Not even Achillês will bring all his words to pass; some he will do, some he will cut in the middle. I will meet him face to face, even if his hands are like fire and his spirit like flashing steel!"

The Trojans heard his rousing appeal; they lifted their spears and moved to meet their foes. Soon the war-cry was raised and the confusion of battle began. Then Apollo appeared by Hector's side, and said:

"Hector, you must not stand out yet and fight with Achillês alone. Watch him in the throng amid the surging mass, and do not let him cast at you or come close to strike you with the sword."

Hector was alarmed by these words, and plunged into the melee.

But Achillês leapt on the Trojans in fury, with terrible shouts. First he got Iphition Otryntëïdês, the valiant leader of a strong force. A Naiad nymph was his mother, and his father Otrynteus lived under snowy Tmolos in the rich town of Hydê. He was rushing straight at Achillês, when Achillês cut his head clean in two, crying out as he fell:

"There you lie, Otryntëïdês, my terrible foe! Here is your deathplace, but your birthplace was by the Gygaian Lake near your father's demesne, beside fish-giving Hyllos and eddying Hermos!"

Darkness covered his eyes, and the tires of Achaian wheels tore his body; and over it Achillês brought down that doughty man Demoleon Antenor's son, stabbing him through helmet and temple: the helmet did not save him, but the blade went through and broke the bone, scattering his brains. Hippodamas next leapt out of his car and tried to escape, but Achillês stabbed him through the back. He died gasping, with a bellowing sound, as a bull bellows when the young men drag him about the altar of Heliconian Poseidon, and Earthshaker is glad. Next Achillês went after Polydoros Priamidês. His father would never let him fight, because he was youngest of all his sons, and dearest. But he beat the world in running; and that day in his childish vanity he would come out to show off his paces, until he died for it. He was running by when Achillês hit him on the back, where his belt was fastened with golden clasps and the corselet doubled over. The point came out through his stomach, and he fell on his knees groaning, as he clasped his bowels with his hands.

When Hector saw his brother clasping his bowels and sinking to the earth, his eyes grew dim. He could not keep away any longer, but went straight up to Achillês like a flash of fire, balancing his lance. Achillês saw him—sprang to meet him and cried out in defiance:

"Near is the man of all others who has struck me to the heart! The man who killed my precious comrade! Now we need not shirk each other along the lanes of battle!"

Then he said to Hector frowning:

"Come nearer, that you may die quicker!"

Hector answered boldly:

"Don't think you will scare me with words, Peleidês, as if I were a little child. I can use taunts and abuse myself if I like. I know you are a stronger man than I am, but all that lies on the knees of the gods. If I am the weaker man, yet I may take your life with a cast of my spear, for my blade also has a sharp point!"

He poised and cast his spear. But Athena turned it back from Achillês by a gentle puff of breath, and it fell at Hector's feet. Achillês leaped at him furiously with a shout—Apollo caught him away softly (as a god can do) and hid him in mist. Thrice Achillês leapt at him—thrice the spear struck a cloud of mist. When for a fourth time he would have struck, he cried out angrily with brutal frankness:

"Again you have just missed death, you cur! that was a nice thing, but again Apollo saved you! Of course you say your prayers to him whenever you go where spears are whizzing. I dare say I shall finish you next time I meet you, if I can find a god of my own to help me. Meanwhile I will try to find somebody else."

Then he pierced the throat of Dryops, and left him lying before his feet, as he brought down a big strong man, Demuchos Philetor's son; this man he struck on the knee with a spear-cast and finished him off with the sword. He rolled out of a car the two sons of Bias, Laogonos and Dardanos, one with spear and one with sword. Tros Alastor's son ran up to clasp his knees: perhaps he might have mercy and spare a young man like himself. Poor fool! He did not know that man would never listen: no sweet temper was here, no soft heart, but plain madness. Tros clasped the knees —the sword ran under his liver, the liver slipt out, a stream of blood poured over it into his bosom, he fainted. On went Achillês: ran his spear through Mulios, in at one ear out at the other—cut down through the head of Echeclos with one blow of the sword, and warmed it in his blood —ran his spear through Deucalion's elbow where the sinews hold it—the man with arm hanging heavy saw death before him, a sword sliced off his head and sent it flying helmet and all, he lay with the marrow spurting out of the spine. On went Achillês: Rhigmos was the next, the son of Thracian Peiros—a lance caught him in the middle and stuck in the body rolling him out of his car—the driver turned the horses, a spear stabbed him in the back and rolled him out of the car, the horses ran away.

On went Achillês: as a devouring conflagration rages through the valleys of a parched mountain height, and the thick forest blazes, while the wind rolls the flames to all sides in riotous confusion, so he stormed over the field like a fury, driving all before him, and killing until the earth was a river of blood. As broad-browed oxen tread the white barley on a threshing-floor and quickly crush the husks under their feet, so under Achillês the horses trampled with their feet dead men and broken shields; the axle was soaked with blood, and the handrail of the car was red with spatterings from the horses' hooves and the running wheels. On went Achillês, with spatters of gore upon his invincible hands.

Prometheus Bound

(trans. Edith Hamilton)

AESCHYLUS

After Zeus, in the struggle between the gods and the Titans, had overthrown his father Kronos and seized for himself the supreme power of heaven and earth, the Titan Prometheus (who had sided with Zeus in the combat) incurred the victor's disfavor. Zeus had

planned to destroy the existing race of man and to fashion another;
but Prometheus, out of pity, stole fire from heaven and brought it
to earth, thus inaugurating human civilization. As punishment, Zeus
decreed that he should be bound to a rock in the Scythian wilderness
and there tormented forever.

DRAMATIS PERSONAE:

Hephestus
Force
Violence
Prometheus
Ocean
Io
Hermes
Chorus of Oceanides

Scene: Prometheus *by tradition was fastened to a peak of the
Caucasus.*

FORCE
    Far have we come to this far spot of earth,
    this narrow Scythian land, a desert all untrodden.
    God of the forge and fire, yours the task
    the Father laid upon you.
    To this high-piercing, head-long rock
    in adamantine chains that none can break
    bind him—him here, who dared all things.
    Your flaming flower he stole to give to men,
    fire, the master craftsman, through whose power
    all things are wrought, and for such error now
    he must repay the gods; be taught to yield
    to Zeus' lordship and to cease
    from his man-loving way.
HEPHESTUS
    Force, Violence, what Zeus enjoined on you
    has here an end. Your task is done.
    But as for me, I am not bold to bind
    a god, a kinsman, to this stormy crag.
    Yet I must needs be bold.
    His load is heavy who dares disobey the Father's word
    O high-souled child of Justice, the wise counselor,
    against my will as against yours I nail you fast
    in brazen fetters never to be loosed

to this rock peak, where no man ever comes,
where never voice or face of mortal you will see.
The shining splendor of the sun shall wither you.
Welcome to you will be the night
when with her mantle star-inwrought
she hides the light of day.
And welcome then to turn the sun
to melt the frost the dawn has left behind.
Forever shall the intolerable present grind you down,
and he who will release you is not born.
Such fruit you reap for your man-loving way.
A god yourself, you did not dread God's anger,
but gave to mortals honor not their due,
and therefore you must guard this joyless rock—
no rest, no sleep, no moment's respite.
Groans shall your speech be, lamentation
your only words—all uselessly.
Zeus has no mind to pity. He is harsh,
like upstarts always.

FORCE

Well then, why this delay and foolish talk?
A god whom gods hate is abominable.

HEPHESTUS

The tie of blood has a strange power,
and old acquaintance too.

FORCE

And so say I—but don't you think
that disobedience to the Father's words
might have still stranger power?

HEPHESTUS

You're rough, as always. Pity is not in you.

FORCE

Much good is pity here. Why all this pother
that helps him not a whit?

HEPHESTUS

O skill of hand now hateful to me.

FORCE

Why blame your skill? These troubles here
were never caused by it. That's simple truth.

HEPHESTUS

Yet would it were another's and not mine.

FORCE

Trouble is everywhere except in heaven.
No one is free but Zeus.

HEPHESTUS

 I know—I've not a word to say.

FORCE

 Come then. Make haste. On with his fetters.
 What if the Father sees you lingering?

HEPHESTUS

 The chains are ready here if he should look.

FORCE

 Seize his hands and master him.
 Now to your hammer. Pin him to the rocks.

HEPHESTUS

 All done, and quick work too.

FORCE

 Still harder. Tighter. Never loose your hold.
 For he is good at finding a way out where there is none.

HEPHESTUS

 This arm at least he will not ever free.

FORCE

 Buckle the other fast, and let him learn
 with all his cunning he's a fool to Zeus.

HEPHESTUS

 No one but he, poor wretch, can blame my work.

FORCE

 Drive stoutly now your wedge straight through his breast,
 the stubborn jaw of steel that cannot break.

HEPHESTUS

 Alas, Prometheus, I grieve for your pain.

FORCE

 You shirk your task and grieve for those Zeus hates?
 Take care; you may need pity for yourself.

HEPHESTUS

 You see a sight eyes should not look upon.

FORCE

 I see one who has got what he deserves.
 But come. The girdle now around his waist.

HEPHESTUS

 What must be shall be done. No need to urge me.

FORCE

 I will and louder too. Down with you now.
 Make fast his legs in rings. Use all your strength.

HEPHESTUS

 Done and small trouble.

FORCE

 Now for his feet. Drive the nails through the flesh.

The judge is stern who passes on our work.

HEPHESTUS

Your tongue and face match well.

FORCE

Why, you poor weakling. Are you one to cast
a savage temper in another's face?

HEPHESTUS

Oh, let us go. Chains hold him, hand and foot.

FORCE

Run riot now, you there upon the rocks.
Go steal from gods to give their goods to men—
to men whose life is but a little day.
What will they do to lift these woes from you?
Forethought your name means, falsely named.
Forethought you lack and need now for yourself
if you would slip through fetters wrought like these.

[*Exeunt* FORCE, VIOLENCE, HEPHESTUS.]

PROMETHEUS

O air of heaven and swift-winged winds,
O running river waters,
O never numbered laughter of sea waves,
Earth, mother of all, Eye of the sun, all seeing,
on you I call.
Behold what I, a god, endure from gods.
See in what tortures I must struggle
through countless years of time.
This shame, these bonds, are put upon me
by the new ruler of the gods.
Sorrow enough in what is here and what is still to come.
It wrings groans from me.
When shall the end be, the appointed end?
And yet why ask?
All, all I knew before,
all that should be.
Nothing, no pang of pain
that I did not foresee.
Bear without struggle what must be.
Necessity is strong and ends our strife.
But silence is intolerable here.
So too is speech.
I am fast bound, I must endure.
I gave to mortals gifts.
I hunted out the secret source of fire.

I filled a reed therewith,
fire, the teacher of all arts to men,
the great way through.
These are the crimes that I must pay for,
pinned to a rock beneath the open sky.
But what is here? What comes?
What sound, what fragrance, brushed me with faint wings,
of deities or mortals or of both?
Has someone found a way to this far peak
to view my agony? What else?
Look at me then, in chains, a god who failed,
the enemy of Zeus, whom all gods hate,
all that go in and out of Zeus' hall.
The reason is that I loved men too well.
Oh, birds are moving near me. The air murmurs
with swift and sweeping wings.
Whatever comes to me is terrible.

[*Enter* CHORUS. *They are* SEA NYMPHS. *It is clear from what follows
that a winged car brings them on to the stage.*]

LEADER

Oh, be not terrified, for friends are here,
each eager to be first,
on swift wings flying to your rock.
I prayed my father long
before he let me come.
The rushing winds have sped me on.
A noise of ringing brass went through the sea-caves,
and for all a maiden's fears it drove me forth,
so swift, I did not put my sandals on,
but in my winged car I came to you.

PROMETHEUS

To see this sight—
Daughters of fertile Tethys,
children of Ocean who forever flows
unresting round earth's shores,
behold me, and my bonds
that bind me fast upon the rocky height
of this cleft mountain side,
keeping my watch of pain.

SEA NYMPH

I look upon you and a mist of tears,
of grief and terror, rises as I see

your body withering upon the rocks,
in shameful fetters.
For a new helmsman steers Olympus.
By new laws Zeus is ruling without law.
He has put down the mighty ones of old.

PROMETHEUS

Oh, had I been sent deep, deep into earth,
to that black boundless place where go the dead,
though cruel chains should hold me fast forever,
I should be hid from sight of gods and men.
But now I am a plaything for the winds.
My enemies exult—and I endure.

ANOTHER NYMPH

What god so hard of heart to look on these things gladly?
Who, but Zeus only, would not suffer with you?
He is malignant always and his mind
unbending. All the sons of heaven
he drives beneath his yoke.
Nor will he make an end
until his heart is sated or until
someone, somehow, shall seize his sovereignty—
if that could be.

PROMETHEUS

And yet—and yet—all tortured though I am,
fast fettered here,
he shall have need of me, the lord of heaven,
to show to him the strange design
by which he shall be stripped of throne and sceptre.
But he will never win me over
with honeyed spell of soft, persuading words,
nor will I ever cower beneath his threats
to tell him what he seeks.
First he must free me from this savage prison
and pay for all my pain.

ANOTHER NYMPH

Oh, you are bold. In bitter agony
you will not yield.
These are such words as only free men speak.
Piercing terror stings my heart.
I fear because of what has come to you.
Where are you fated to put in to shore
and find a haven from this troubled sea?
Prayers cannot move,

persuasions cannot turn,
the heart of Kronos' son.

PROMETHEUS

I know that he is savage.
He keeps his righteousness at home.
But yet some time he shall be mild of mood,
when he is broken.
He will smooth his stubborn temper,
and run to meet me.
Then peace will come and love between us two.

LEADER

Reveal the whole to us. Tell us your tale.
What guilt does Zeus impute
to torture you in shame and bitterness?
Teach us, if you may speak.

PROMETHEUS

To speak is pain, but silence too is pain,
and everywhere is wretchedness.
When first the gods began to quarrel
and faction rose among them,
some wishing to throw Kronos out of heaven,
that Zeus, Zeus, mark you, should be lord,
others opposed, pressing the opposite,
that Zeus should never rule the gods,
then I, giving wise counsel to the Titans,
children of Earth and Heaven, could not prevail.
My way out was a shrewd one, they despised it,
and in their arrogant minds they thought to conquer
with ease, by their own strength.
But Justice, she who is my mother, told me—
Earth she is sometimes called,
whose form is one, whose name is many—
she told me, and not once alone,
the future, how it should be brought to pass,
that neither violence nor strength of arm
but only subtle craft could win.
I made all clear to them.
They scorned to look my way.
The best then left me was to stand with Zeus
in all good will, my mother with me,
and, through my counsel, the black underworld
covered, and hides within its secret depths
Kronos the aged and his host.

Such good the ruler of the gods had from me,
and with such evil he has paid me back.
There is a sickness that infects all tyrants,
they cannot trust their friends.
But you have asked a question I would answer:
What is my crime that I am tortured for?
Zeus had no sooner seized his father's throne
than he was giving to each god a post
and ordering his kingdom,
but mortals in their misery
he took no thought for.
His wish was they should perish
and he would then beget another race.
And there were none to cross his will save I.
I dared it, I saved men.
Therefore I am bowed down in torment,
grievous to suffer, pitiful to see.
I pitied mortals,
I never thought to meet with this.
Ruthlessly punished here I am
an infamy to Zeus.

LEADER

Iron of heart or wrought from rock is he
who does not suffer in your misery.
Oh, that these eyes had never looked upon it.
I see it and my heart is wrung.

PROMETHEUS

A friend must feel I am a thing to pity.

LEADER

Did you perhaps go even further still?

PROMETHEUS

I made men cease to live with death in sight.

LEADER

What potion did you find to cure this sickness?

PROMETHEUS

Blind hopes I caused to dwell in them.

ANOTHER NYMPH

Great good to men that gift.

PROMETHEUS

To it I added the good gift of fire.

ANOTHER NYMPH

And now the creatures of a day
have flaming fire?

PROMETHEUS
> Yes, and learn many crafts therefrom.

LEADER
> For deeds like these Zeus holds you guilty,
> and tortures you with never ease from pain?
> Is no end to your anguish set before you?

PROMETHEUS
> None other except when it pleases him.

LEADER
> It pleases him? What hope there? You must see
> you missed your mark. I tell you this with pain
> to give you pain.
> But let that pass. Seek your deliverance.

PROMETHEUS
> Your feet are free.
> Chains bind mine fast.
> Advice is easy for the fortunate.
> All that has come I knew full well.
> Of my own will I shot the arrow that fell short,
> of my own will.
> Nothing do I deny.
> I helped men and found trouble for myself.
> I knew—and yet not all.
> I did not think to waste away
> hung high in air upon a lonely rock.
> But now, I pray you, no more pity
> for what I suffer here. Come, leave your car,
> and learn the fate that steals upon me,
> all, to the very end.
> Hear me, oh, hear me. Share my pain. Remember,
> trouble may wander far and wide
> but it is always near.

LEADER
> You cry to willing ears, Prometheus.
> Lightly I leave my swiftly speeding car
> and the pure ways of air where go the birds.
> I stand upon this stony ground.
> I ask to hear your troubles to the end.

[*Enter* OCEAN *riding on a four-footed bird. The* CHORUS *draws back, and he does not see them.*]

OCEAN
> Well, here at last, an end to a long journey.

I've made my way to you, Prometheus.
This bird of mine is swift of wing
but I can guide him by my will,
without a bridle.
Now you must know, I'm grieved at your misfortunes.
Of course I must be, I'm your kinsman.
And that apart, there's no one I think more of.
And you'll find out the truth of what I'm saying.
It isn't in me to talk flattery.
Come: tell me just what must be done to help you,
and never say that you've a firmer friend
than you will find in me.

PROMETHEUS

Oho! What's here? You? Come to see my troubles?
How did you dare to leave your ocean river,
your rock caves hollowed by the sea,
and stand upon the iron mother earth?
Was it to see what has befallen me,
because you grieve with me?
Then see this sight: here is the friend of Zeus,
who helped to make him master.
This twisted body is his handiwork.

OCEAN

I see, Prometheus. I do wish
You'd take some good advice.
I know you're very clever,
but real self-knowledge—that you haven't got.
New fashions have come in with this new ruler.
Why can't you change your own to suit?
Don't talk like that—so rude and irritating.
Zeus isn't so far off but he might hear,
and what would happen then would make these troubles
seem child's play.
You're miserable. Then do control your temper
and find some remedy.
Of course you think you know all that I'm saying.
You certainly should know the harm
that blustering has brought you.
But you're not humbled yet. You won't give in.
You're looking for more trouble.
Just learn one thing from me:
Don't kick against the pricks.
You see he's savage—why not? He's a tyrant.

He doesn't have to hand in his accounts.
Well, now I'm going straight to try
if I can free you from this wretched business.
Do you keep still. No more of this rash talking.
Haven't you yet learned with all your wisdom
the mischief that a foolish tongue can make?

PROMETHEUS

Wisdom? The praise for that is yours alone,
who shared and dared with me and yet were able
to shun all blame.
But—let be now. Give not a thought more to me.
You never would persuade him.
He is not easy to win over.
Be cautious. Keep a sharp lookout,
or on your way back you may come to harm.

OCEAN

You counsel others better than yourself,
to judge by what I hear and what I see.
But I won't let you turn me off.
I really want to serve you.
And I am proud, yes, proud to say
I know that Zeus will let you go
just as a favor done to me.

PROMETHEUS

I thank you for the good will you would show me.
But spare your pains. Your trouble would be wasted.
The effort, if indeed you wish to make it,
could never help me.
Now you are out of harm's way. Stay there.
Because I am unfortunate myself
I would not wish that other too should be.
Not so. Even here the lot of Atlas, of my brother,
weighs on me. In the western country
he stands, and on his shoulders is the pillar
that holds apart the earth and sky,
a load not easy to be borne.
Pity too filled my heart when once I saw
swift Typhon overpowered.
Child of the Earth was he, who lived
in caves in the Cilician land,
a flaming monster with a hundred heads,
who rose up against all the gods.
Death whistled from his fearful jaws.

His eyes flashed glaring fire.
I thought he would have wrecked God's sovereignty.
But to him came the sleepless bolt of Zeus,
down from the sky, thunder with breath of flame,
and all his high boasts were struck dumb.
Into his very heart the fire burned.
His strength was turned to ashes.
And now he lies a useless thing,
a sprawling body, near the narrow sea-way
by Aetna, underneath the mountain's roots.
High on the peak the god of fire sits,
welding the molten iron in his forge,
whence sometimes there will burst
rivers red hot, consuming with fierce jaws
the level fields of Sicily,
lovely with fruits.
And that is Typhon's anger boiling up,
his darts of flame none may abide,
of fire-breathing spray,
scorched to a cinder though he is
by Zeus' bolt.
But you are no man's fool; you have no need
to learn from me. Keep yourself safe,
as you well know the way.
And I will drain my cup to the last drop,
until Zeus shall abate his insolence of rage.

OCEAN

And yet you know the saying,
when anger reaches fever heat
wise words are a physician.

PROMETHEUS

Not when the heart is full to bursting.
Wait for the crisis; then the balm will soothe.

OCEAN

But if one were discreet as well as daring—?
You don't see danger then? Advise me.

PROMETHEUS

I see your trouble wasted,
and you good-natured to the point of folly.

OCEAN

That's a complaint I don't mind catching.
Let be: I'll choose to seem a fool
if I can be a loyal friend.

PROMETHEUS
    But he will lay to me all that you do.
OCEAN
    There you have said what needs must send me home.
PROMETHEUS
    Just so. All your lamenting over me
    will not have got you then an enemy.
OCEAN
    Meaning—the new possessor of the throne?
PROMETHEUS
    Be on your guard. See that you do not vex him.
OCEAN
    Your case, Prometheus, may well teach me—
PROMETHEUS
    Off with you. Go—and keep your present mind.
OCEAN
    You urge one who is eager to be gone.
    For my four-footed bird is restless
    to skim with wings the level ways of air.
    He'll be well pleased to rest in his home stable.

    [*Exit* OCEAN. *The* CHORUS *now come forward.*]

CHORUS
    I mourn for you, Prometheus.
    Desolation is upon you.
    My face is wet with weeping.
    Tears fall as waters which run continually.
    The floods overflow me.
    Terrible are the deeds of Zeus.
    He rules by laws that are his own.
    High is his spear above the others,
    turned against the gods of old.
    All the land now groans aloud,
    mourning for the honor of the heroes of your race.
    Stately were they, honored ever in the days of long ago.
    Holy Asia is hard by.
    Those that dwell there suffer in your trouble, great and sore.
    In the Colchian land maidens live,
    fearless in fight.
    Scythia has a battle throng,
    the farthest place of earth is theirs,
    where marsh grass grows around Maeotis lake.
    Arabia's flower is a warrior host;

high on a cliff their fortress stands,
Caucasus towers near;
men fierce as the fire, like the roar of the fire
they shout when the sharp spears clash.
All suffer with you in your trouble, great and sore.
Another Titan too, Earth mourns,
bound in shame and iron bonds.
I saw him, Atlas the god.
He bears on his back forever
the cruel strength of the crushing world
and the vault of the sky.
He groans beneath them.
The foaming sea-surge roars in answer,
the deep laments,
the black place of death far down in earth is moved exceedingly,
and the pure-flowing river waters grieve for him in his piteous pain.

PROMETHEUS

Neither in insolence nor yet in stubbornness
have I kept silence.
It is thought that eats my heart,
seeing myself thus outraged.
Who else but I, but I myself,
gave these new gods their honors?
Enough of that. I speak to you who know.
Hear rather all that mortals suffered.
Once they were fools. I gave them power to think.
Through me they won their minds.
I have no blame for them. All I would tell you
is my good will and my good gifts to them.
Seeing they did not see, nor hearing hear.
Like dreams they led a random life.
They had no houses built to face the sun,
of bricks or well-wrought wood,
but like the tiny ant who has her home
in sunless crannies deep down in the earth,
they lived in caverns.
The signs that speak of winter's coming,
of flower-faced spring, of summer's heat
with mellowing fruits,
were all unknown to them.
From me they learned the stars that tell the seasons,
their risings and their settings hard to mark.
And number, that most excellent device,

I taught to them, and letters joined in words.
I gave to them the mother of all arts,
hard working memory.
I, too, first brought beneath the yoke
great beasts to serve the plow,
to toil in mortals' stead.
Up to the chariot I led the horse that loves the rein,
the glory of the rich man in his pride.
None else but I first found
the seaman's car, sail-winged, sea-driven.
Such ways to help I showed them, I who have
no wisdom now to help myself.

LEADER

You suffer shame as a physician must
who cannot heal himself.
You who cured others now are all astray,
distraught of mind and faint of heart,
and find no medicine to soothe your sickness.

PROMETHEUS

Listen, and you shall find more cause for wonder.
Best of all gifts I gave them was the gift of healing.
For if one fell into a malady
there was no drug to cure, no draught, or soothing ointment
For want of these men wasted to a shadow
until I showed them how to use
the kindly herbs that keep from us disease.
The ways of divination I marked out for them,
and they are many; how to know
the waking vision from the idle dream;
to read the sounds hard to discern;
the signs met on the road; the flight of birds,
eagles and vultures,
those that bring good or ill luck in their kind,
their way of life, their loves and hates
and council meetings.
And of those inward parts that tell the future,
the smoothness and the color and fair shape
that please the gods.
And how to wrap the flesh in fat
and the long thigh bone, for the altar fire
in honor to the gods.
So did I lead them on to knowledge
of the dark and riddling art.

The fire omens, too, were dim to them
until I made them see.
Deep within the earth are hidden
precious things for men,
brass and iron, gold and silver.
Would any say he brought these forth to light
until I showed the way?
No one, except to make an idle boast.
All arts, all goods, have come to men from me.

LEADER

Do not care now for mortals
but take thought for yourself, O evil-fated.
I have good hope that still loosed from your bonds
you shall be strong as Zeus.

PROMETHEUS

Not thus—not yet—is fate's appointed end,
fate that brings all to pass.
I must be bowed by age-long pain and grief.
So only will my bonds be loosed.
All skill, all cunning, is as foolishness
before necessity.

SEA NYMPH

Who is the helmsman of necessity?

PROMETHEUS

Fate, threefold, Retribution, unforgetting.

ANOTHER NYMPH

And Zeus is not so strong?

PROMETHEUS

He cannot shun what is foredoomed.

ANOTHER NYMPH

And is he not foredoomed to rule forever?

PROMETHEUS

No word of that. Ask me no further.

ANOTHER NYMPH

Some solemn secret hides behind your silence.

PROMETHEUS

Think of another theme. It is not yet
the time to speak of this.
It must be wrapped in darkness, so alone
I shall some time be saved
from shame and grief and bondage.

CHORUS

Zeus orders all things.

May he never set his might against purpose of mine,
like a wrestler in the match.
May I ever be found where feast the holy gods,
and the oxen are slain,
where ceaselessly flows the pathway
of Ocean, my father.
May the words of my lips forever
be free from sin.
May this abide with me and not depart
like melting snow.
Long life is sweet when there is hope
and hope is confident.
And it is sweet when glad thoughts make the heart grow strong,
and there is joy.
But you, crushed by a thousand griefs,
I look upon you and I shudder.
You did not tremble before Zeus.
You gave your worship where you would, to men,
a gift too great for mortals,
a thankless favor.
What help for you there? What defense in those
whose life is but from morning unto evening?
Have you not seen?
Their little strength is feebleness,
fast bound in darkness,
like a dream.
The will of man shall never break
the harmony of God.
This I have learned beholding your destruction.
Once I spoke different words to you
from those now on my lips.
A song flew to me.
I stood beside your bridal bed,
I sang the wedding hymn,
glad in your marriage.
And with fair gifts persuading her,
you led to share your couch,
Hesione, child of the sea.

[*Enter* Io.]

Io

What land—what creatures here?
This, that I see—

A form storm-beaten,
bound to the rock.
Did you do wrong?
Is this your punishment?
You perish here.
Where am I?
Speak to a wretched wanderer
Oh! Oh! he stings again—
the gadfly—oh, miserable!
But you must know he's not a gadfly.
He's Argus, son of Earth, the herdsman.
He has a thousand eyes.
I see him. Off! Keep him away!
No, he comes on.
His eyes can see all ways at once.
He's dead but no grave holds him.
He comes straight up from hell.
He is the huntsman,
and I his wretched quarry.
He drives me all along the long sea strand.
I may not stop for food or drink.
He has a shepherd's pipe,
a reed with beeswax joined.
Its sound is like the locust's shrilling,
a drowsy note—that will not let me sleep.
Oh, misery. Oh, misery.
Where is it leading me,
my wandering—far wandering.
What ever did I do,
how ever did I sin,
that you have yoked me to calamity,
O son of Kronos,
that you madden a wretched woman
driven mad by the gadfly of fear?
Oh, burn me in fire or hide me in earth
or fling me as food to the beasts of the sea.
Master, grant me my prayer.
Enough—I have been tried enough—
my wandering—long wandering.
Yet I have found no place
to leave my misery.
—I am a girl who speaks to you,
but horns are on my head.

PROMETHEUS

    Like one caught in an eddy, whirling round and round,
    the gadfly drives you.
    I know you, girl. You are Inachus' daughter.
    You made the god's heart hot with love,
    and Hera hates you. She it is
    who drives you on this flight that never stops.

Io

    How is it that you speak my father's name?
    Who are you? Tell me for my misery.
    Who are you, sufferer, that speak the truth
    to one who suffers?
    You know the sickness God has put upon me,
    that stings and maddens me and drives me on
    and wastes my life away.
    I am a beast, a starving beast,
    that frenzied runs with clumsy leaps and bounds,
    oh, shame,
    mastered by Hera's malice.
    Who among the wretched
    suffer as I do?
    Give me a sign, you there.
    Tell to me clearly
    the pain still before me.
    Is help to be found?
    A medicine to cure me?
    Speak, if you know.

PROMETHEUS

    I will and in plain words,
    as friend should talk to friend.
    —You see Prometheus, who gave mortals fire.

Io

    You, he who succored the whole race of men?
    You, that Prometheus, the daring, the enduring?
    Why do you suffer here?

PROMETHEUS

    Just now I told the tale—

Io

    But will you not still give to be a boon?

PROMETHEUS

    Ask what you will. I know all you would learn.

Io

    Then tell me who has bound you to this rock.

PROMETHEUS

Zeus was the mind that planned.
The hand that did the deed the god of fire.

Io

What was the wrong that you are punished for?

PROMETHEUS

No more. Enough of me.

Io

But you will tell the term set to my wandering?
My misery is great. When shall it end?

PROMETHEUS

Here not to know is best.

Io

I ask you not to hide what I must suffer.

PROMETHEUS

I do so in no grudging spirit.

Io

Why then delay to tell me all?

PROMETHEUS

Not through ill will. I would not terrify you.

Io

Spare me not more than I would spare myself.

PROMETHEUS

If you constrain me I must speak. Hear then—

LEADER

Not yet. Yield to my pleasure too.
For I would hear from her own lips
what is the deadly fate, the sickness
that is upon her. Let her say—then teach her
the trials still to come.

PROMETHEUS

If you would please these maidens, Io—
they are your father's sisters,
and when the heart is sorrowful, to speak
to those who will let fall a tear
is time well spent.

Io

I do not know how to distrust you.
You shall hear all. And yet—
I am ashamed to speak,
to tell of that god-driven storm
that struck me, changed me, ruined me.
How shall I tell you who it was?

How ever to my maiden chamber
visions came by night,
persuading me with gentle words:
'Oh happy, happy girl,
Why are you all too long a maid
when you might marry with the highest?
The arrow of desire has pierced Zeus.
For you he is on fire.
With you it is his will to capture love.
Would you, child, fly from Zeus' bed?
Go forth to Lerna, to the meadows deep in grass.
There is a sheep-fold there,
an ox-stall, too, that holds your father's oxen—
so shall Zeus find release from his desire.'
Always, each night, such dreams possessed me.
I was unhappy and at last I dared
to tell my father of these visions.
He sent to Pytho and far Dodona
man after man to ask the oracle
what he must say or do to please the gods.
But all brought answers back of shifting meaning,
hard to discern, like golden coins unmarked.
At last a clear word came. It fell upon him
like lightning from the sky. It told him
to thrust me from his house and from his country,
to wander to the farthest bounds of earth
like some poor dumb beast set apart
for sacrifice, whom no man will restrain.
And if my father would not, Zeus would send
his thunderbolt with eyes of flame to end
his race, all, everyone.
He could not but obey such words
from the dark oracle. He drove me out.
He shut his doors to me—against his will
as against mine. Zeus had him bridled.
He drove him as he would.
Straightway I was distorted, mind and body.
A beast—with horns—look at me—
stung by a fly, who madly leaps and bounds.
And so I ran and found myself beside
the waters, sweet to drink, of Kerchneia
and Lerna's well-spring.
Beside me went the herdsman Argus,
the violent of heart, the earth-born,

watching my footsteps with his hundred eyes.
But death came to him, swift and unforeseen.
Plagued by a gadfly then, the scourge of God,
I am driven on from land to land.
So for what has been. But what still remains
of anguish for me, tell me.
Do not in pity soothe me with false tales.
Words strung together by a lie
are like a foul disease.

LEADER

Oh, shame. Oh, tale of shame.
Never, oh never, would I have believed that my ears
would hear words such as these, of strange meaning.
Evil to see and evil to hear,
misery, defilement, and terror.
They pierce my heart with a two-edged sword.
A fate like that—
I shudder to look upon Io.

PROMETHEUS

You are too ready with your tears and fears.
Wait for the end.

LEADER

Speak. Tell us, for when one lies sick,
to face with clear eyes all the pain to come
is sweet.

PROMETHEUS

What first you asked was granted easily,
to hear from her own lips her trials.
But for the rest, learn now the sufferings
she still must suffer, this young creature,
at Hera's hands. Child of Inachus,
keep in your heart my words, so you shall know
where the road ends. First to the sunrise,
over furrows never plowed, where wandering Scythians
live in huts of wattles made, raised high
on wheels smooth-rolling. Bows they have,
and they shoot far. Turn from them.
Keep to the shore washed by the moaning sea.
Off to the left live the Chalybians,
workers of iron. There be on your guard.
A rough people they, who like not strangers.
Here rolls a river called the Insolent,
true to its name. You cannot find a ford
until you reach the Caucasus itself,

highest of mountains. From beneath its brow
the mighty river rushes. You must cross
the summit, neighbor to the stars.
Then by the southward road, until you reach
the warring Amazons, men-haters, who one day
will found a city by the Thermodon,
where Salmydessus thrusts
a fierce jaw out into the sea that sailors hate,
stepmother of ships.
And they will bring you on your way right gladly
to the Cimmerian isthmus, by a shallow lake,
Maeotis, at the narrows.
Here you must cross with courage.
And men shall tell forever of your passing.
The strait shall be named for you, Bosporus,
Ford of the Cow. There leave the plains of Europe,
and enter Asia, the great Continent.
—Now does he seem to you, this ruler of the gods,
evil, to all, in all things?
A god desired a mortal—drove her forth
to wander thus.
A bitter lover you have found, O girl,
for all that I have told you is not yet
the prelude even.

Io

O, wretched, wretched.

PROMETHEUS

You cry aloud for this? What then
when you have learned the rest?

LEADER

You will not tell her of more trouble?

PROMETHEUS

A storm-swept sea of grief and ruin.

Io

What gain to me is life? Oh, now to fling myself
down from this rock peak to the earth below,
and find release there from my trouble.
Better to die once than to suffer
through all the days of life.

PROMETHEUS

Hardly would you endure my trial,
whose fate it is not ever to find death
that ends all pain. For me there is no end
until Zeus falls from power.

Io
>
> Zeus fall from power?

PROMETHEUS
>
> You would rejoice, I think, to see that happen?

Io
>
> How could I not, who suffer at his hands?

PROMETHEUS
>
> Know then that it shall surely be.

Io
>
> But who will strip the tyrant of his scepter?

PROMETHEUS
>
> He will himself and his own empty mind.

Io
>
> How? Tell me, if it is not wrong to ask.

PROMETHEUS
>
> He will make a marriage that will vex him.

Io
>
> Goddess or mortal, if it may be spoken?

PROMETHEUS
>
> It may not be. Seek not to know.

Io
>
> His wife shall drive him from his throne?

PROMETHEUS
>
> Her child shall be more than his father's match.

Io
>
> And is there no way of escape for him?

PROMETHEUS
>
> No way indeed, unless my bonds are loosed.

Io
>
> But who can loose them against Zeus' will?

PROMETHEUS
>
> A son of yours—so fate decrees.

Io
>
> What words are these? A child of mine shall free you?

PROMETHEUS
>
> Ten generations first must pass and then three more.

Io
>
> Your prophecy grows dim through generations.

PROMETHEUS
>
> So let it be. Seek not to know your trials.

Io
>
> Do not hold out a boon and then withdraw it.

PROMETHEUS
>
> One boon of two I will bestow upon you.

Io

>And they are? Speak. Give me the choice.

PROMETHEUS

>I give it you: the hardships still before you,
>or his name who shall free me. Choose.

LEADER

>Of these give one to her, but give to me
>a grace as well—I am not quite unworthy.
>Tell her where she must wander, and to me
>tell who shall free you. It is my heart's desire.

PROMETHEUS

>And to your eagerness I yield.
>Hear, Io, first, of your far-driven journey.
>And bear in mind my words, inscribe them
>upon the tablets of your heart.
>When you have crossed the stream that bounds
>the continents, turn to the East where flame
>the footsteps of the sun, and pass
>along the sounding sea to Cisthene.
>Here on the plain live Phorcys' children, three,
>all maidens, very old, and shaped like swans,
>who have one eye and one tooth to the three.
>No ray of sun looks ever on that country,
>nor ever moon by night. Here too their sisters dwell.
>And they are three, the Gorgons, winged,
>with hair of snakes, hateful to mortals,
>whom no man shall behold and draw again
>the breath of life. They garrison that place.
>And yet another evil sight, the hounds of Zeus,
>who never bark, griffins with beaks like birds.
>The one-eyed Arimaspi too, the riders,
>who live beside a stream that flows with gold,
>a way of wealth. From all these turn aside.
>Far off there is a land where black men live,
>close to the sources of the sun, whence springs
>a sun-scorched river. When you reach it,
>go with all care along the banks up to
>the great descent, where from the mountains
>the holy Nile pours forth its waters
>pleasant to drink from. It will be your guide
>to the Nile land, the Delta. A long exile
>is fated for you and your children here.
>If what I speak seems dark and hard to know,

> ask me again and learn all clearly.
> For I have time to spare and more
> than I could wish.

LEADER

> If in your story of her fatal journey
> there is yet somewhat left to tell her,
> speak now. If not, give then to us
> the grace we asked. You will remember.

PROMETHEUS

> The whole term of her roaming has been told.
> But I will show she has not heard in vain,
> and tell her what she suffered coming hither,
> in proof my words are true.
> A moving multitude of sorrows were there,
> too many to recount, but at the end
> you came to where the levels of Molossa
> surround the lofty ridge of Dodona,
> seat of God's oracle.
> A wonder past belief is there, oak trees that speak.
> They spoke, not darkly but in shining words,
> calling you Zeus' glorious spouse.
> The frenzy seized you then. You fled
> along the sea-road washed by the great inlet,
> named for God's mother. Up and down you wandered,
> storm-tossed. And in the time to come that sea
> shall have its name from you, Ionian,
> that men shall not forget your journey.
> This is my proof to you my mind can see
> farther than meets the eye.
> From here the tale I tell is for you all,
> and of the future, leaving now the past.
> There is a city, Canobus, at the land's end,
> where the Nile empties, on new river soil.
> There Zeus at last shall make you sane again,
> stroking you with a hand you will not fear.
> And from this touch alone you will conceive
> and bear a son, a swarthy man,
> whose harvest shall be reaped on many fields,
> all that are washed by the wide-watered Nile.
> In the fifth generation from him, fifty sisters
> will fly from marriage with their near of kin,
> who, hawks in close pursuit of doves, aquiver
> with passionate desire, shall find that death

waits for the hunters on the wedding night.
God will refuse to them the virgin bodies.
Argos will be the maidens' refuge, to their suitors
a slaughter dealt by women's hands,
bold in the watches of the night.
The wife shall kill her husband,
dipping her two-edged sword in blood.
O Cyprian goddess, thus may you come to my foes.
One girl, bound by love's spell, will change
her purpose, and she will not kill
the man she lay beside, but choose the name
of coward rather than be stained with blood.
In Argos she will bear a kingly child—
a story overlong if all were told.
Know this, that from that seed will spring
one glorious with the bow, bold-hearted,
and he shall set me free.
This is the oracle my mother told me,
Justice, who is of old, Earth's daughter.
But how and where would be too long a tale,
nor would you profit.

Io

O, misery. Oh, misery.
A frenzy tears me.
Madness strikes my mind.
I burn. A frantic sting—
an arrow never forged with fire.
My heart is beating at its walls in terror.
My eyes are whirling wheels.
Away. Away. A raging wind of fury
sweeps through me.
My tongue has lost its power.
My words are like a turbid stream,
wild waves that dash against a surging sea,
the black sea of madness.

[*Exit* Io.]

CHORUS

Wise, wise was he,
who first weighed this in thought
and gave it utterance:
Marriage within one's own degree is best,
not with one whom wealth has spoiled,

nor yet with one made arrogant by birth.
Such as these he must not seek
who lives upon the labor of his hands.
Fate, dread diety,
may you never, oh, never behold me
sharing the bed of Zeus.
May none of the dwellers in heaven
draw near to me ever.
Terrors take hold of me
seeing her maidenhood
turning from love of man,
torn by Hera's hate,
driven in misery.
For me, I would not shun marriage nor fear it,
so it were with my equal.
But the love of the greater gods,
from whose eyes none can hide,
may that never be mine.
To war with a god-lover is not war,
it is despair.
For what could I do,
or where could I fly
from the cunning of Zeus?

PROMETHEUS

In very truth shall Zeus, for all his stubborn pride,
be humbled, such a marriage he will make
to cast him down from throne and power.
And he shall be no more remembered.
The curse his father put on him
shall be fulfilled.
The curse that he cursed him with as he fell
from his age-long throne.
The way from such trouble no one of the gods
can show him save I.
These things I know and how they shall come to pass.
So let him sit enthroned in confidence,
trust to his crashing thunder high in air,
shake in his hands his fire-breathing dart.
Surely these shall be no defense,
but he will fall, in shame unbearable.
Even now he makes ready against himself
one who shall wrestle with him and prevail,
a wonder of wonders, who will find
a flame that is swifter than lightning,

a crash to silence the thunder,
who will break into pieces the sea-god's spear,
the bane of the ocean that shakes the earth.
Before this evil Zeus shall be bowed down.
He will learn how far apart are a king and a slave.

LEADER

These words of menace on your tongue
speak surely only your desire.

PROMETHEUS

They speak that which shall surely be—
and also my desire.

LEADER

And we must look to see Zeus mastered?

PROMETHEUS

Yes, and beneath a yoke more cruel than this I bear.

LEADER

You have no fear to utter words like these?

PROMETHEUS

I am immortal—and I have no fear.

SEA NYMPH

But agony still worse he might inflict—

PROMETHEUS

So let him do. All that must come I know.

ANOTHER NYMPH

The wise bow to the inescapable.

PROMETHEUS

Be wise then. Worship power.
Cringe before each who wields it.
To me Zeus counts as less than nothing.
Let him work his will, show forth his power
for his brief day, his little moment
of lording it in heaven.
—But see. There comes a courier from Zeus,
a lackey in his new lord's livery.
Some curious news is surely on his lips.

[*Enter* HERMES.]

HERMES

You trickster there, you biter bitten,
sinner against the gods, man-lover, thief of fire,
my message is to you.
The great father gives you here his orders:
Reveal this marriage that you boast of,

by which he shall be hurled from power.
And, mark you, not in riddles, each fact clearly.
—Don't make me take a double journey, Prometheus.
You can see Zeus isn't going to be made
kinder by this sort of thing.

PROMETHEUS

Big words and insolent. They well become you,
O lackey of the gods.
Young—young—your thrones just won,
you think you live in citadels grief cannot reach.
Two dynasties I have seen fall from heaven,
and I shall see the third fall fastest,
most shamefully of all.
Is it your thought to see me tremble
and crouch before your upstart gods?
Not so—not such a one am I.
Make your way back. You will not learn from me.

HERMES

Ah, so? Still stubborn? Yet this willfulness
has anchored you fast in these troubled waters.

PROMETHEUS

And yet I would not change my lot with yours, O lackey.

HERMES

Better no doubt to be slave to a rock
than be the father's trusted herald.

PROMETHEUS

I must be insolent when I must speak to insolence.

HERMES

You are proud, it seems, of what has come to you.

PROMETHEUS

I proud? May such pride be
the portion of my foes.—I count you of them.

HERMES

You blame me also for your sufferings?

PROMETHEUS

In one word, all gods are my enemies.
They had good from me. They return me evil.

HERMES

I heard you were quite mad.

PROMETHEUS

Yes, I am mad, if to abhor such foes is madness.

HERMES

You would be insufferable, Prometheus, if you were not so
wretched.

PROMETHEUS
> Alas!

HERMES
> Alas? That is a word Zeus does not understand.

PROMETHEUS
> Time shall teach it him, gray time,
> that teaches all things.

HERMES
> It has not taught you wisdom yet.

PROMETHEUS
> No, or I had not wrangled with a slave.

HERMES
> It seems that you will tell the Father nothing.

PROMETHEUS
> Paying the debt of kindness that I owe him?

HERMES
> You mock at me as though I were a child.

PROMETHEUS
> A child you are or what else has less sense
> if you expect to learn from me.
> There is no torture and no trick of skill,
> there is no force, which can compel my speech,
> until Zeus wills to loose these deadly bonds.
> So let him hurl his blazing bolt,
> and with the white wings of the snow,
> with thunder and with earthquake,
> confound the reeling world.
> None of all this will bend my will
> to tell him at whose hands he needs must fall.

HERMES
> I urge you, pause and think if this will help you.

PROMETHEUS
> I thought long since of all. I planned for all.

HERMES
> Submit, you fool. Submit. In agony learn wisdom.

PROMETHEUS
> Go and persuade the sea wave not to break.
> You will persuade me no more easily.
> I am no frightened woman, terrified
> at Zeus' purpose. Do you think to see me
> ape women's ways, stretch out my hands
> to him I hate, and pray him for release?
> A world apart am I from prayer for pity.

HERMES

Then all I say is said in vain.
Nothing will move you, no entreaty
soften your heart.
Like a young colt new-bridled,
you have the bit between your teeth,
and rear and fight against the rein.
But all this vehemence is feeble bombast.
A fool, bankrupt of all but obstinacy,
is the poorest thing on earth.
Oh, if you will not hear me, yet consider
the storm that threatens you from which
you cannot fly, a great third wave of evil.
Thunder and flame of lightning will rend
this jagged peak. You shall be buried deep,
held by a splintered rock.
After long length of time you will return
to see the light, but Zeus' winged hound,
an eagle red with blood,
shall come a guest unbidden to your banquet.
All day long he will tear to rags your body,
great rents within the flesh,
feasting in fury on the blackened liver.
Look for no ending to this agony
until a god will freely suffer for you,
will take on him your pain, and in your stead
descend to where the sun is turned to darkness,
the black depths of death.
Take thought: this is no empty boast
but utter truth. Zeus does not lie.
Each word shall be fulfilled.
Pause and consider. Never think
self-will is better than wise counsel.

LEADER

To us the words he speaks are not amiss.
He bids you let your self-will go and seek
good counsel. Yield.
For to the wise a failure is disgrace.

PROMETHEUS

These tidings that the fellow shouts at me
were known to me long since.
A foe to suffer at the hands of foes
is nothing shameful.

Then let the twisting flame of forked fire
be hurled upon me. Let the very air
be rent by thunder-crash.
Savage winds convulse the sky,
hurricanes shake the earth from its foundations,
the waves of the sea rise up and drown the stars,
and let me be swept down to hell,
caught in the cruel whirlpool of necessity.
He cannot kill me.

HERMES

Why, these are ravings you may hear from madmen.
His case is clear. Frenzy can go no further.
You maids who pity him, depart, be swift.
The thunder peals and it is merciless.
Would you too be struck down?

LEADER

Speak other words, another counsel,
if you would win me to obey.
Now, in this place, to urge
that I should be a coward is intolerable.
I choose with him to suffer what must be.
Not to stand by a friend—there is no evil
I count more hateful.
I spit it from my mouth.

HERMES

Remember well I warned you,
when you are swept away in utter ruin.
Blame then yourselves, not fate, nor ever say
that Zeus delivered you
to a hurt you had not thought to see.
With open eyes,
not suddenly, not secretly,
into the net of utter ruin
whence there is no escape,
you fall by your own folly.

[Exit HERMES.]

PROMETHEUS

An end to words. Deeds now.
The world is shaken.
The deep and secret way of thunder
is rent apart.
Fiery wreaths of lightning flash.

Whirlwinds toss the swirling dust.
The blasts of all the winds are battling in the air,
and sky and sea are one.
On me the tempest falls.
It does not make me tremble.
O holy Mother Earth, O air and sun,
behold me. I am wronged.

Eclogue IV

VERGIL

Muses of Sicily, sing we a somewhat ampler strain: not all men's delight is in coppices and lowly tamarisks: if we sing of the woods, let them be woods worthy of a Consul.

Now is come the last age of the Cumaean prophecy: the great cycle of periods is born anew. Now returns the Maid, returns the reign of Saturn: now from high heaven a new generation comes down. Yet do thou at that boy's birth, in whom the iron race shall begin to cease, and the golden to arise over all the world, holy Lucina, be gracious; now thine own Apollo reigns. And in thy consulate, in thine, O Pollio, shall this glorious age enter, and the great months begin their march: under thy rule what traces of our guilt yet remain, vanishing shall free earth for ever from alarm. He shall grow in the life of gods, and shall see gods and heroes mingled, and himself be seen by them, and shall rule the world that his fathers' virtues have set at peace. But on thee, O boy, untilled shall Earth first pour childish gifts, wandering ivy-tendrils and foxglove, and colocasia mingled with the laughing acanthus: untended shall the she-goats bring home their milk-swollen udders, nor shall huge lions alarm the herds: unbidden thy cradle shall break into wooing blossom. The snake too shall die, and die the treacherous poison-plant: Assyrian spice shall grow all up and down. But when once thou shalt be able now to read the glories of heroes and thy father's deeds, and to know Virtue as she is, slowly the plain shall grow golden with the soft corn-spike, and the reddening grape trail from the wild briar, and hard oaks shall drip dew of honey. Nevertheless there shall linger some few traces of ancient wrong, to bid ships tempt the sea and towns be girt with walls and the earth cloven in furrows. Then shall a second Tiphys be, and a second Argo to sail with chosen heroes: new wars too shall arise, and again a mighty Achilles be sent to Troy. Thereafter, when now strengthening age hath wrought thee into man, the very voyager shall cease out of the sea, nor the sailing pine exchange her merchandise: all lands shall bear all things, the ground shall not suffer the mattock, nor the vine the pruning-hook; now likewise the strong ploughman shall loose his bulls from the yoke. Neither shall wool learn to counterfeit changing hues, but the ram in the meadow himself shall dye his fleece now with soft glowing sea-purple, now with yellow saffron; native scarlet shall clothe the lambs at their pasturage. Run even thus, O ages, said the harmonious Fates to their spindles, by the steadfast ordinance of doom. Draw nigh to thy high honours (even now will the time be come) O dear offspring of gods, mighty germ of Jove! Behold the world swaying her orbed mass, lands and spaces of sea and depth of sky; behold how all things rejoice in the age to come. Ah may the latter end of a long life then yet be mine, and such breath as shall suffice to tell thy deeds! Not Orpheus of Thrace nor Linus shall surpass me in song, though he have his mother and he his father to aid, Orpheus Calliope, Linus beautiful Apollo. If even Pan before his Arcady content with me, even Pan before his Arcady shall declare himself conquered. Begin, O little boy, to know and smile upon thy mother, thy mother on whom ten months have brought weary longings. Begin, O little boy: of them who have not smiled on a parent, never was one honoured at a god's board or on a goddess' couch.

Messiah

DANIEL, Chapter 11

19 O Lord, hear; O Lord, forgive; O Lord, hearken and do; defer not, for thine own sake, O my God: for thy city and thy people are called by thy name.   20 And whiles I *was* speaking, and praying, and confessing my sin and the sin of my people Israel, and presenting my supplication before the LORD my God for the holy mountain of my God; 21 Yea, whiles I *was* speaking in prayer, even the man Gabriel, whom I had seen in the vision at the beginning, being caused to fly swiftly, touched me about the time of the evening oblation.   22 And he informed *me*, and talked with me, and said, O Daniel, I am now come forth to give thee skill and understanding.   23 At the beginning of thy supplications the commandment came forth, and I am come to shew *thee;*

for thou *art* greatly beloved: therefore understand the matter, and consider the vision.   24 Seventy weeks are determined upon thy people and upon thy holy city, to finish the transgressions, and to make an end of sins, and to make reconciliation for iniquity, and to bring in everlasting righteousness, and to seal up the vision and prophecy, and to anoint the most Holy.   25 Know therefore and understand, *that* from the going forth of the commandment to restore and to build Jerusalem unto the Messiah the Prince *shall be* seven weeks, and threescore and two weeks: the street shall be built again, and the wall, even in troublous times. 26 And after threescore and two weeks shall Messiah be cut off, but not for himself: and the people of the prince that shall come shall destroy the city and the sanctuary; and the end thereof *shall* be with a flood, and unto the end of the war desolations are determined.   27 And he shall confirm the covenant with many for one week: and in the midst of the week he shall cause the sacrifice and the oblation to cease, and for the overspreading of abominations he shall make *it* desolate, even until the consummation, and that determined shall be poured upon the desolate.

Servant of Jehovah

ISAIAH, Chapter 53

1 Who hath believed our report? and to whom is the arm of the LORD revealed?   2 For he shall grow up before him as a tender plant, and as a root out of a dry ground: he hath no form nor comeliness; and when we shall see him, *there is* no beauty that we should desire him.   3 He is despised and rejected of men; a man of sorrows, and acquainted with grief: and we hid as it were *our* faces from him; he was despised, and we esteemed him not.   4 Surely he hath borne our griefs, and carried our sorrows: yet we did esteem him stricken, smitten of God, and afflicted. 5 But he *was* wounded for our transgressions, *he was* bruised for our iniquities: the chastisement of our peace *was* upon him; and with his stripes we are healed.   6 All we like sheep have gone astray; we have turned every one to his own way; and the LORD hath laid on him the iniquity of us all.   7 He was oppressed, and he was afflicted, yet he opened not his mouth: he is brought as a lamb to the slaughter, and as a sheep before her shearers is dumb, so he openeth not his mouth. 8 He was taken from prison and from judgment: and who shall declare his generation? for he was cut off out of the land of the living: for the

transgression of my people was he stricken.   9 And he made his grave with the wicked, and with the rich in his death; because he had done no violence, neither *was any* deceit in his mouth.   10 Yet it pleased the LORD to bruise him; he hath put *him* to grief: when thou shalt make his soul an offering for sin, he shall see *his* seed, he shall prolong *his* days, and the pleasure of the LORD shall prosper in his hand.   11 He shall see of the travail of his soul, *and* shall be satisfied: by his knowledge shall my righteous servant justify many; for he shall bear their iniquities.   12 Therefore will I divide him *a portion* with the great, and he shall divide the spoil with the strong; because he hath poured out his soul unto death: and he was numbered with the transgressors; and he bare the sin of many, and made intercession for the transgressors.

The Birth of Jesus

MATTHEW, Chapters 1, 2, and 3

CHAPTER 1

18 Now the birth of Jesus Christ was on this wise: When as his mother Mary was espoused to Joseph, before they came together, she was found with child of the Holy Ghost.   19 Then Joseph her husband, being a just *man*, and not willing to make her a publick example, was minded to put her away privily.   20 But while he thought on these things, behold, the angel of the Lord appeared unto him in a dream, saying, Joseph, thou son of David, fear not to take unto thee Mary thy wife: for that which is conceived in her is of the Holy Ghost.   21 And she shall bring forth a son, and thou shalt call his name JESUS: for he shall save his people from their sins.   22 Now all this was done, that it might be fulfilled which was spoken of the Lord by the prophet, saying, 23 Behold, a virgin shall be with child, and shall bring forth a son, and they shall call his name Emmanuel, which being interpreted is, God with us.   24 Then Joseph being raised from sleep did as the angel of the Lord had bidden him, and took unto him his wife: 25 And knew her not till she had brought forth her firstborn son: and he called his name JESUS.

CHAPTER 2

1 Now when Jesus was born in Bethlehem of Judæa in the days of Herod the king, behold, there came wise men from the east to Jerusalem, 2 Saying, Where is he that is born King of the Jews? for we have seen his star in the east, and are come to worship him.   3 When Herod the king had heard *these things*, he was troubled, and all Jerusalem with him. 4 And when he had gathered all the chief priests and scribes of the people together, he demanded of them where Christ should be born.   5 And they said unto him, In Bethlehem of Judæa: for thus it is written by the prophet,   6 And thou Bethlehem, *in* the land of Juda, art not the least among the princes of Juda: for out of thee shall come a Governor, that shall rule my people Israel.   7 Then Herod, when he had privily called the wise men, inquired of them diligently what time the star appeared.   8 And he sent them to Bethlehem, and said, Go and search diligently for the young child; and when ye have found *him*, bring me word again, that I may come and worship him also.   9 When they had heard the king, they departed; and, lo, the star, which they saw in the east, went before them, till it came and stood over where the young child was.   10 When they saw the star, they rejoiced with exceeding great joy.   11 And when they were come into the house, they saw the young child with Mary his mother, and fell down, and worshipped him: and when they had opened their treasures, they presented unto him gifts: gold, and frankincense, and myrrh.   12 And being warned of God in a dream that they should not return to Herod, they departed into their own country another way.   13 And when they were departed, behold, the angel of the Lord appeareth to Joseph in a dream, saying, Arise, and take the young child and his mother and flee into Egypt, and be thou there until I bring thee word: for Herod will seek the young child to destroy him.   14 When he arose, he took the young child and his mother by night, and departed into Egypt: 15 And was there until the death of Herod: that it might be fulfilled which was spoken of the Lord by the prophet, saying, Out of Egypt have I called my son.   16 Then Herod, when he saw that he was mocked of the wise men, was exceeding wroth, and sent forth, and slew all the children that were in Bethlehem, and in all the coasts thereof, from two years old and under, according to the time which he had diligently inquired of the wise men.   17 Then was fulfilled that which was spoken by Jeremy the prophet, saying,   18 In Rama was there a voice heard, lamentation, and weeping, and great mourning, Rachel weeping *for* her children, and would not be comforted, because they are not.   19 But when Herod was dead, behold, an angel of the Lord appeareth in a dream to Joseph in Egypt,   20 Saying, Arise, and take the young

child and his mother, and go into the land of Israel: for they are dead which sought the young child's life.   21 And he arose, and took the young child and his mother, and came into the land of Israel.   22 But when he heard that Archelaus did reign in Judæa in the room of his father Herod, he was afraid to go thither: notwithstanding, being warned of God in a dream, he turned aside into the parts of Galilee: 23 And he came and dwelt in a city called Nazareth: that it might be fulfilled which was spoken by the prophets, He shall be called a Nazarene.

CHAPTER 3

1 In those days came John the Baptist, preaching in the wilderness of Judæa,   2 And saying, Repent ye: for the kingdom of heaven is at hand.   3 For this is he that was spoken of by the prophet Esaias, saying, The voice of one crying in the wilderness, Prepare ye the way of the Lord, make his paths straight.   4 And the same John had his raiment of camel's hair, and a leathern girdle about his loins; and his meat was locusts and wild honey.   5 Then went out to him Jerusalem, and all Judæa, and all the region round about Jordan,   6 And were baptized of him in Jordan, confessing their sins.   7 But when he saw many of the Pharisees and Sadducees come to his baptism, he said unto them, O generation of vipers, who hath warned you to flee from the wrath to come?   8 Bring forth therefore fruits meet for repentance: 9 And think not to say within yourselves, We have Abraham to *our* father: for I say unto you, that God is able of these stones to raise up children unto Abraham.   10 And now also the axe is laid unto the root of the trees: therefore every tree which bringeth not forth good fruit is hewn down, and cast into the fire.   11 I indeed baptize you with water unto repentance: but he that cometh after me is mightier than I, whose shoes I am not worthy to bear: he shall baptize you with the Holy Ghost, *and* with fire: 12 Whose fan *is* in his hand, and he will thoroughly purge his floor, and gather his wheat into the garner; but he will burn up the chaff with unquenchable fire.   13 Then cometh Jesus from Galilee to Jordan unto John, to be baptized of him.   14 But John forbade him, saying, I have need to be baptized of thee, and comest thou to me?   15 And Jesus answering said unto him, Suffer *it to be so* now: for thus it becometh us to fulfill all righteousness. Then he suffered him. 16 And Jesus, when he was baptized, went up straightway out of the water: and, lo, the heavens were opened unto him, and he saw the Spirit of God descending like a dove, and lighting upon him: 17 And lo a voice from heaven, saying, This is my beloved Son, in whom I am well pleased.

A God and Yet a Man?

ANONYMOUS

A god and yet a man?
A maid and yet a mother?
Wit wonders what wit can
Conceive this or the other.

A god and can he die?
A dead man, can he live?
What wit can well reply?
What reason reason give?

God, truth itself, doth teach it.
Man's wit sinks too far under
By reason's power to reach it.
Believe and leave [1] to wonder.

The Gray Champion

NATHANIEL HAWTHORNE

There was once a time when New England groaned under the actual pressure of heavier wrongs than those threatened ones which brought on the Revolution. James II, the bigoted successor of Charles the Voluptuous, had annulled the charters of all the colonies, and sent a harsh and unprincipled soldier to take away our liberties and endanger our religion. The administration of Sir Edmund Andros lacked scarcely a single characteristic of tyranny: a Governor and Council, holding office from the King, and wholly independent of the country, laws made and taxes levied without concurrence of the people, immediate or by their representatives; the rights of private citizens violated, and the titles of

[1] *leave:* cease

all landed property declared void; the voice of complaint stifled by restrictions on the press; and, finally, disaffection overawed by the first band of mercenary troops that ever marched on our free soil. For two years our ancestors were kept in sullen submission by that filial love which had invariably secured their allegiance to the mother country, whether its head chanced to be a Parliament, Protector, or Popish Monarch. Till these evil times, however, such allegiance had been merely nominal, and the colonists had ruled themselves, enjoying far more freedom than is even yet the privilege of the native subjects of Great Britain.

At length a rumor reached our shores that the Prince of Orange had ventured on an enterprise, the success of which would be the triumph of civil and religious rights and the salvation of New England. It was but a doubtful whisper; it might be false, or the attempt might fail; and, in either case, the man that stirred against King James would lose his head. Still the intelligence produced a marked effect. The people smiled mysteriously in the streets, and threw bold glances at their oppressors; while far and wide there was a subdued and silent agitation, as if the slightest signal would rouse the whole land from its sluggish despondency. Aware of their danger, the rulers resolved to avert it by an imposing display of strength, and perhaps to confirm their despotism by yet harsher measures. One afternoon in April, 1689, Sir Edmund Andros and his favorite councillors, being warm with wine, assembled the redcoats of the Governor's Guard, and made their appearance in the streets of Boston. The sun was near setting when the march commenced.

The roll of the drum at that unquiet crisis seemed to go through the streets, less as the martial music of the soldiers, than as a muster-call to the inhabitants themselves. A multitude, by various avenues, assembled in King Street, which was destined to be the scene, nearly a century afterwards, of another encounter between the troops of Britain and a people struggling against her tyranny. Though more than sixty years had elapsed since the pilgrims came, this crowd of their descendants still showed the strong and sombre features of their character perhaps more strikingly in such a stern emergency than on happier occasions. There were the sober garb, the general severity of mien, the gloomy but undismayed expression, the scriptural forms of speech, and the confidence in Heaven's blessing on a righteous cause, which would have marked a band of the original Puritans, when threatened by some peril of the wilderness. Indeed, it was not yet time for the old spirit to be extinct; since there were men in the street that day who had worshipped there beneath the trees, before a house was reared to the God for whom they had become exiles. Old soldiers of the Parliament were here, too, smiling grimly at the thought that their aged arms might strike another blow against the house of Stuart. Here, also, were the veterans of King Philip's war, who had burned villages and slaughtered young and old, with pious fierceness, while the godly souls throughout the land were helping them with prayer. Several ministers were scattered among the crowd, which, unlike all other mobs, regarded them with such reverence, as if there were sanctity in their very garments. These holy men exerted their influence to quiet the people, but not to disperse them. Meantime, the purpose of the Governor, in disturbing the peace of the town at a period when the slightest commotion might throw the country into a ferment, was almost the universal subject of inquiry, and variously explained.

"Satan will strike his master-stroke presently," cried some, "because he knoweth that his time is short. All our godly pastors are to be dragged to prison! We shall see them at a Smithfield fire in King Street!"

Hereupon the people of each parish gathered closer round their minister, who looked calmly upwards and assumed a more apostolic dignity, as well befitted a candidate for the highest honor of his profession, the crown of martyrdom. It was actually fancied, at that period, that New England might have a John Rogers of her own to take the place of that worthy in the Primer.

"The Pope of Rome has given orders for a new St. Bartholomew!" cried others. "We are to be massacred, man and male child!"

Neither was this rumor wholly discredited, although the wiser class believed the Governor's object somewhat less atrocious. His predecessor under the old charter, Bradstreet, a venerable companion of the first settlers, was known to be in town. There were grounds for conjecturing, that Sir Edmund Andros intended at once to strike terror by a parade of military force, and to confound the opposite faction by possessing himself of their chief.

"Stand firm for the old charter Governor!" shouted the crowd, seizing upon the idea. "The good old Governor Bradstreet!"

While this cry was at the loudest, the people were surprised by the well-known figure of Governor Bradstreet himself, a patriarch of nearly ninety, who appeared on the elevated steps of a door, and, with characteristic mildness, besought them to submit to the constituted authorities.

"My children," concluded this venerable person, "do nothing rashly. Cry not aloud, but pray for the welfare of New England, and expect patiently what the Lord will do in this matter!"

The event was soon to be decided. All this time, the roll of the drum had been approaching through Cornhill, louder and deeper, till with reverberations from house to house, and the regular tramp of martial footsteps, it burst into the street. A double rank of soldiers made their appearance, occupying the whole breadth of the passage, with shouldered matchlocks, and matches burning, so as to present a row of fires in the dusk. Their steady march was like the progress of a machine, that would roll irresistibly over everything in its way. Next, moving slowly, with a confused clatter of hoofs on the pavement, rode a party of mounted gentlemen, the central figure being Sir Edmund Andros, elderly, but erect and soldier-like. Those around him were his favorite councillors, and the bitterest foes of New England. At his right hand rode Edward Randolph, our arch-enemy, that "blasted wretch," as Cotton Mather calls him, who achieved the downfall of our ancient government, and was followed with a sensible curse, through life and to his grave. On the other side was Bullivant, scattering jests and mockery as he rode along. Dudley came behind, with a downcast look, dreading, as well he might, to meet the indignant gaze of the people, who beheld him, their only countryman by birth, among the oppressors of his native land. The captain of a frigate in the harbor, and two or three civil officers under the Crown, were also there. But the figure which most attracted the public eye, and stirred up the deepest feeling, was the Episcopal clergyman of King's Chapel, riding haughtily among the magistrates in his priestly vestments, the fitting representative of prelacy and persecution, the union of church and state, and all those abominations which had driven the Puritans to the wilderness. Another guard of soldiers, in double rank, brought up the rear.

The whole scene was a picture of the condition of New England, and its moral, the deformity of any government that does not grow out of the nature of things and the character of the people. On one side the religious multitude, with their sad visages and dark attire, and on the other, the group of despotic rulers, with the high churchman in the midst, and here and there a crucifix at their bosoms, all magnificently clad, flushed with wine, proud of unjust authority, and scoffing at the universal groan. And the mercenary soldiers, waiting but the word to deluge the street with blood, showed the only means by which obedience could be secured.

"O Lord of Hosts," cried a voice among the crowd, "provide a Champion for thy people!"

This ejaculation was loudly uttered, and served as a herald's cry, to introduce a remarkable personage. The crowd had rolled back, and were now huddled together nearly at the extremity of the street, while the soldiers had advanced no more than a third of its length. The intervening space was empty—a paved solitude, between lofty edifices, which threw almost a twilight shadow over it. Suddenly, there was seen the figure of an ancient man, who seemed to have emerged from among the people, and was walking by himself along the centre of the street, to confront the armed band. He wore the old Puritan dress, a dark cloak and a steeple-crowned hat, in the fashion of at least fifty years before, with a heavy sword upon his thigh, but a staff in his hand to assist the tremulous gait of age.

When at some distance from the multitude, the old man turned slowly round, displaying a face of antique majesty, rendered doubly venerable by the hoary beard that descended on his breast. He made a gesture at once of encouragement and warning, then turned again, and resumed his way.

"Who is this gray patriarch?" asked the young men of their sires.

"Who is this venerable brother?" asked the old men among themselves.

But none could make reply. The fathers of the people, those of fourscore years and upwards, were disturbed, deeming it strange that they should forget one of such evident authority, whom they must have known in their early days, the associate of Winthrop, and all the old councillors, giving laws, and making prayers, and leading them against the savage. The elderly men ought to have remembered him, too, with locks as gray in their youth, as their own were now. And the young! How could he have passed so utterly from their memories—that hoary sire, the relic of long-departed times, whose awful benediction had surely been bestowed on their uncovered heads, in childhood?

"Whence did he come? What is his purpose? Who can this old man be?" whispered the wondering crowd.

Meanwhile, the venerable stranger, staff in hand, was pursuing his solitary walk along the centre of the street. As he drew near the advancing soldiers, and as the roll of their drum came full upon his ear, the old man raised himself to a loftier mien, while the decrepitude of age seemed to fall from his shoulders, leaving him in gray but unbroken dignity. Now, he marched onward with a warrior's step, keeping time to the military music. Thus the aged form advanced on one side, and the whole parade of soldiers and magistrates on the other, till, when scarcely twenty yards remained between, the old man grasped his staff by the middle, and held it before him like a leader's truncheon.

"Stand!" cried he.

The eye, the face, and attitude of command; the solemn, yet warlike peal of that voice, fit either to rule a host in the battlefield or be raised to God in prayer, were irresistible. At the old man's word and outstretched arm, the roll of the drum was hushed at once, and the advancing line stood still. A tremulous enthusiasm seized upon the multitude. That stately form, combining the leader and the saint, so gray, so dimly seen, in such an ancient garb, could only belong to some old champion of the righteous cause, whom the oppressor's drum had summoned from his grave. They raised a shout of awe and exultation, and looked for the deliverance of New England.

The Governor, and the gentlemen of his party, perceiving themselves brought to an unexpected stand, rode hastily forward, as if they would have pressed their snorting and affrighted horses right against the hoary apparition. He, however, blenched not a step, but glancing his severe eye round the group, which half encompassed him, at last bent it sternly on Sir Edmund Andros. One would have thought that the dark old man was chief ruler there, and that the Governor and Council, with soldiers at their back, representing the whole power and authority of the Crown, had no alternative but obedience.

"What does this old fellow here?" cried Edward Randolph, fiercely. "On, Sir Edmund! Bid the soldiers forward, and give the dotard the same choice that you give all his countrymen—to stand aside or be trampled on!"

"Nay, nay, let us show respect to the good grandsire," said Bullivant, laughing. "See you not, he is some old roundheaded dignitary, who hath lain asleep these thirty years, and knows nothing of the change of time? Doubtless, he thinks to put us down with a proclamation in Old Noll's name!"

"Are you mad, old man?" demanded Sir Edmund Andros, in loud and harsh tones. "How dare you stay the march of King James's Governor?"

"I have stayed the march of a King himself, ere now," replied the gray figure, with stern composure. "I am here, Sir Governor, because the cry of an oppressed people hath disturbed me in my secret place; and beseeching this favor earnestly of the Lord, it was vouchsafed me to appear once again on earth, in the good old cause of his saints. And what speak ye of James? There is no longer a Popish tyrant on the throne of England, and by to-morrow noon, his name shall be a byword in this very street, where ye would make it a word of terror. Back, thou that wast a Governor, back! With this night thy power is ended—to-morrow, the prison!—back, lest I foretell the scaffold!"

The people had been drawing nearer and nearer, and drinking in the words of their champion, who spoke in accents long disused, like one unaccustomed to converse, except with the dead of many years ago. But his voice stirred their souls. They confronted the soldiers, not wholly without arms, and ready to convert the very stones of the street into deadly weapons. Sir Edmund Andros looked at the old man; then he cast his hard and cruel eye over the multitude, and beheld them burning with that lurid wrath, so difficult to kindle or to quench; and again he fixed his gaze on the aged form, which stood obscurely in an open space, where neither friend nor foe had thrust himself. What were his thoughts; he uttered no word which might discover. But whether the oppressor were overawed by the Gray Champion's look, or perceived his peril in the threatening attitude of the people, it is certain that he gave back, and ordered his soldiers to commence a slow and guarded retreat. Before another sunset, the Governor, and all that rode so proudly with him, were prisoners, and long ere it was known that James had abdicated, King William was proclaimed throughout New England.

But where was the Gray Champion? Some reported that, when the troops had gone from King Street, and the people were thronging tumultuously in their rear, Bradstreet, the aged Governor, was seen to embrace a form more aged than his own. Others soberly affirmed, that while they marvelled at the venerable grandeur of his aspect, the old man had faded from their eyes, melting slowly into the hues of twilight, till, where he stood, there was an empty space. But all agreed that the hoary shape was gone. The men of that generation watched for his reappearance, in sunshine and in twilight, but never saw him more, nor knew when his funeral passed, nor where his gravestone was.

And who was the Gray Champion? Perhaps his name might be found in the records of that stern Court of Justice, which passed a sentence, too mighty for the age, but glorious in all aftertimes, for its humbling lesson to the monarch and its high example to the subject. I have heard, that whenever the descendants of the Puritans are to show the spirit of their sires, the old man appears again. When eighty years had passed, he walked once more in King Street. Five years later, in the twilight of an April morning, he stood on the green, beside the meeting-house, at Lexington, where now the obelisk of granite, with a slab of slate inlaid, commemorates the first fallen of the Revolution. And when our fathers were toiling at the breastwork on Bunker's Hill, all through that night the old warrior walked his rounds. Long, long may it be, ere he comes again! His hour is one of darkness, and adversity, and peril. But should domestic tyranny oppress us, or the invader's step pollute our soil, still may the Gray Champion come, for he is the type of New England's hereditary spirit; and his shadowy march, on the eve of danger, must ever be the pledge, that New England's sons will vindicate their ancestry.

Woyzeck

GEORG BÜCHNER

CHARACTERS

WOYZECK
MARIE
CAPTAIN
DOCTOR
DRUM MAJOR
SERGEANT
ANDRES
MARGRET
PROPRIETOR OF THE BOOTH
CHARLATAN
OLD MAN WITH BARREL-ORGAN
JEW
INNKEEPER
APPRENTICES
KATHY
KARL THE TOWN IDIOT
GRANDMOTHER
POLICEMAN
SOLDIERS, STUDENTS, YOUNG MEN *and* GIRLS, CHILDREN, JUDGE,
    COURT CLERK, PEOPLE

SCENE 1—*At the* CAPTAIN's

THE CAPTAIN *in a chair.* WOYZECK *shaving him.*

CAPTAIN: Not so fast, Woyzeck, not so fast! One thing at a time! You're
making me dizzy. What am I to do with the ten extra minutes that
you'll finish early today? Just think, Woyzeck: you still have thirty
beautiful years to live! Thirty years! That makes three hundred and
sixty months! And days! Hours! Minutes! What do you think you'll
do with all that horrible stretch of time? Have you ever thought
about it, Woyzeck?
WOYZECK: Yes, sir, Captain.
CAPTAIN: It frightens me when I think about the world . . . when I think
about eternity. Busyness, Woyzeck, busyness! There's the eternal:

that's eternal, that is eternal. That you can understand. But then
again it's not eternal. It's only a moment. A mere moment. Woyzeck,
it makes me shudder when I think that the earth turns itself about
in a single day! What a waste of time! Where will it all end? Woyzeck,
I can't even look at a mill wheel any more without becoming melancholy.

WOYZECK: Yes, sir, Captain.

CAPTAIN: Woyzeck, you always seem so exasperated! A good man isn't
like that. A good man with a good conscience, that is. Well, say
something, Woyzeck! What's the weather like today?

WOYZECK: Bad, Captain, sir, bad: wind!

CAPTAIN: I feel it already. Sounds like a real storm out there. A wind
like that has the same effect on me as a mouse. [*Cunningly.*] I think
it must be something out of the north-south.

WOYZECK: Yes, sir, Captain.

CAPTAIN: Ha! Ha! Ha! North-south! Ha! Ha! Ha! Oh, he's a stupid one!
Horribly stupid! [*Moved.*] Woyzeck, you're a good man, but [*With
dignity.*] Woyzeck, you have no morality! Morality, that's when you
have morals you understand. It's a good word. You have a child
without the blessings of the Church, just like our Right Reverend
Garrison Chaplain says: "Without the blessings of the Church." It's
not *my* phrase.

WOYZECK: Captain, sir, the good Lord's not going to look at a poor worm
just because they said Amen over it before they went at it. The Lord
said: "Suffer little children to come unto me."

CAPTAIN: What's that you said? What kind of strange answer's that?
You're confusing me with your answers!

WOYZECK: It's us poor people that . . . You see, Captain, sir . . . Money,
money! Whoever hasn't got money . . . Well, who's got morals
when he's bringing something like me into the world? We're flesh
and blood, too. Our kind is miserable only once: in this world and
in the next. I think if we ever got to Heaven we'd have to help with
the thunder.

CAPTAIN: Woyzeck, you have no virtue! You're not a virtuous human
being! Flesh and blood? Whenever I rest at the window, when it's
finished raining, and my eyes follow the white stockings along as
they hurry across the street . . . Damnation, Woyzeck, I know what
love is, too, then! I'm made of flesh and blood, too. But, Woyzeck:
Virtue! Virtue! How was I to get rid of the time? I always say to
myself: "You're a virtuous man [*Moved.*], a good man, a good man."

WOYZECK: Yes, Captain, sir: Virtue. I haven't got much of that. You see,
us common people, we haven't got virtue. That's the way it's got to
be. But if I could be a gentleman, and if I could have a hat and a
watch and a cane, and if I could talk refined, I'd want to be virtuous,

all right. There must be something beautiful in virtue, Captain, sir. But I'm just a poor good-for-nothing!

CAPTAIN: Good, Woyzeck. You're a good man, a good man. But you think too much. It eats at you. You always seem so exasperated. Our discussion has affected me deeply. You can go now. And don't run so! Slowly! Nice and slowly down the street!

SCENE II—*An open field. The town in the distance*

WOYZEK *and* ANDRES *cut twigs from the bushes.* ANDRES *whistles.*

WOYZEK: Andres? You know this place is cursed? Look at that light streak over there on the grass. There where the toadstools grow up. That's where the head rolls every night. One time somebody picked it up. He thought it was a hedgehog. Three days and three nights and he was in a box. [*Low.*] Andres, it was the Freemasons, don't you see, it was the Freemasons!

ANDRES [*sings*]:

> Two little rabbits sat on a lawn
> Eating, oh, eating the green green grass . . .

WOYZECK: Quiet! Can you hear it, Andres? Can you hear it? Something moving!

ANDRES [*sings*]:

> Eating, oh, eating the green green grass
> Till all the grass was gone.

WOYZECK: It's moving behind me! Under me! [*Stamps on the ground.*] Listen! Hollow! It's all hollow down there! It's the Freemasons!

ANDRES: I'm afraid.

WOYZECK: Strange how still it is. You almost want to hold your breath. Andres!

ANDRES: What?

WOYZECK: Say something! [*Looks about fixedly.*] Andres! How bright it is! It's all glowing over the town! A fire's sailing around the sky and a noise coming down like trumpets. It's coming closer! Let's get out of here! Don't look back! [*Drags him into the bushes.*]

ANDRES [*after a pause*]: Woyzeck? Do you still hear it?

WOYZECK: It's quiet now. So quiet. Like the world's dead.

ANDRES: Listen! I can hear the drums inside. We've got to go!

SCENE III—*The town*

MARIE *with her* CHILD *at the window.* MARGRET. *The Retreat passes,* THE DRUM MAJOR *at its head.*

MARIE [*rocking* THE CHILD *in her arms*]: Ho, boy! Da-da-da-da! Can you hear? They're coming! There!

MARGRET: What a man! Built like a tree!

MARIE: He walks like a lion. [THE DRUM MAJOR *salutes* MARIE.]

MARGRET: Oh, what a look he threw you, neighbor! We're not used to such things from you.

MARIE [*sings*]:

Soldiers, oh, you pretty lads . . .

MARGRET: Your eyes are still shining.

MARIE: And if they are? Take *your* eyes to the Jew's and let him clean them for you. Maybe he can shine them so you can sell them for a pair of buttons!

MARGRET: Look who's talking! Just look who's talking! If it isn't the Virgin herself! I'm a respectable person. But you! Everyone knows you could stare your way through seven layers of leather pants!

MARIE: Slut! [*Slams the window shut.*] Come, boy! What's it to them, anyway! Even if you are just a poor whore's baby, your dishonorable little face still makes your mother happy! [*Sings.*]

I have my trouble and bother
But, baby dear, where is your father?
Why should I worry and fight
I'll hold you and sing through the night:
Heio popeio, my baby, my dove
What do I want now with love?

[*A knock at the window.*] Who's there? Is it you, Franz? Come in!

WOYZECK: Can't. There's roll call.

MARIE: Did you cut wood for the Captain?

WOYZECK: Yes, Marie.

MARIE: What is it, Franz? You look so troubled.

WOYZECK: Marie, it happened again, only there was more. Isn't it written: "And there arose a smoke out of the pit, as the smoke of a great furnace"?

MARIE: Oh, Franz!

WOYZECK: Shh! Quiet! I've got it! The Freemasons! There was a terrible noise in the sky and everything was on fire! I'm on the trail of something, something big. It followed me all the way to the town. Something that I can't put my hands on, or understand. Something that drives us mad. What'll come of it all?

MARIE: Franz!

WOYZECK: Don't you see? Look around you! Everything hard and fixed, so gloomy. What's moving back there? When God goes, everything goes. I've got to get back.

MARIE: And the child?

WOYZECK: My God, the boy!—Tonight at the fair! I've saved something again. [*He leaves.*]

MARIE: That man! Seeing things like that! He'll go mad if he keeps thinking that way! He frightened me! It's so gloomy here. Why are you so quiet, boy? Are you afraid? It's growing so dark. As if we were going blind. Only that street lamp shining in from outside. [*Sings.*]

> And what if your cradle is bad
> Sleep tight, my lovey, my lad.

I can't stand it! It makes me shiver! [*She goes out.*]

SCENE IV—*Fair booths. Lights. People*

OLD MAN *with a* CHILD, WOYZECK, MARIE, CHARLATAN, WIFE, DRUM MAJOR, *and* SERGEANT

OLD MAN [*sings while* THE CHILD *dances to the barrel-organ*]:

> There's nothing on this earth will last,
> Our lives are as the fields of grass,
> Soon all is past, is past.

WOYZECK: Ho! Hip-hop there, boy! Hip-hop! Poor man, old man! Poor child, young child! Trouble and happiness!

MARIE: My God, when fools still have their senses, then we're all fools. Oh, what a mad world! What a beautiful world!

They go over to THE CHARLATAN *who stands in front of a booth, his* WIFE *in trousers, and a monkey in costume.*

CHARLATAN: Gentlemen, gentlemen! You see here before you a creature as God created it! But it is nothing this way! Absolutely nothing! But now look at what Art can do. It walks upright. Wears coat and pants. And even carries a saber. This monkey here is a regular soldier. So what if he *isn't* much different! So what if he *is* still on the bottom rung of the human ladder! Hey there, take a bow! That's the way! Now you're a baron, at least. Give us a kiss! [*The monkey trumpets.*] This little customer's musical, too. And, gentlemen, in here you will see the astronomical horse and the little lovebirds. Favorites of all the crowned heads of Europe. They'll tell you anything: how old you are, how many children you have, what your ailments are. The performance is about to begin. And at the beginning. The beginning of the beginning!

WOYZECK: You know, I had a little dog once who kept sniffing around the rim of a big hat, and I thought I'd be good to him and make it easier for him and sat him on top of it. And all the people stood around and clapped.

GENTLEMEN: Oh, grotesque! How really grotesque!

WOYZECK: Don't you believe in God either? It's an honest fact I don't believe in God.—You call that grotesque? I like what's grotesque. See that? That grotesque enough for you?—[*To* MARIE.] You want to go in?

MARIE: Sure. That must be nice in there. Look at the tassels on him! And his wife's got pants on! [*They go inside.*]

DRUM MAJOR: Wait a minute! Did you see her? What a piece!

SERGEANT: Hell, she could whelp a couple regiments of cavalry!

DRUM MAJOR: *And* breed drum majors!

SERGEANT: Look at the way she carries that head! You'd think all that black hair would pull her down like a weight. And those eyes!

DRUM MAJOR: Like looking down a well . . . or up a chimney. Come on, let's go after her!

SCENE V—*Interior of the brightly lighted booth*

MARIE, WOYZECK, PROPRIETOR OF THE BOOTH, SERGEANT, *and* DRUM MAJOR

MARIE: All these lights!

WOYZECK: Sure, Marie. Black cats with fiery eyes.

PROPRIETOR OF THE BOOTH [*bringing forward a horse*]: Show your talent! Show your brute reason! Put human society to shame! Gentlemen, this animal you see here, with a tail on its torso, and standing on its four hoofs, is a member of all the learnèd societies—as well as a professor at our university where he teaches students how to ride and fight. But that requires simple intelligence. Now think with your double reason! What do you do when you think with your double reason? Is there a jackass in this learnèd assembly? [*The nag shakes its head.*] How's that for double reasoning? That's physiognomy for you. This is no dumb animal. This is a person! A human being! But still an animal. A beast. [*The nag conducts itself indecently.*] That's right, put society to shame. As you can see, this animal is still in a state of Nature. Not ideal Nature, of course! Take a lesson from him! But ask your doctor first, it may prove highly dangerous! What we have been told by this is: Man must be natural! You are created of dust, sand, and dung. Why must you be more than dust, sand, and dung? Look there at his reason. He can figure even if he can't count it off on his fingers. And why? Because he cannot express himself, can't explain. A metamorphosed human being. Tell the gentlemen what time it is! Which of you ladies and gentlemen has a watch? A watch?

SERGEANT: A watch? [*He pulls a watch imposingly and measuredly from his pocket.*] There you are, my good man!

MARIE: I want to see this. [*She clambers down to the first row of seats;* THE SERGEANT *helps her.*]
DRUM MAJOR: What a piece!

SCENE VI—MARIE'*s room*

MARIE *with her* CHILD

MARIE [*sitting, her* CHILD *on her lap, a piece of mirror in her hand*]: He told Franz to get the hell out, so what could he do! [*Looks at herself in the mirror.*] Look how the stones shine! What kind are they, I wonder? What kind did he say they were? Sleep, boy! Close your eyes! Tight! Stay that way now. Don't move or he'll get you! [*Sings.*]

> Hurry, lady, close up tight
> A gypsy lad is out tonight
> And he will take you by the hand
> And lead you into gypsyland.

[*Continues to look at herself in the mirror.*] They must be gold! I wonder how they'll look on me at the dance? Our kind's got only a little corner in the world and a piece of broken mirror. But my mouth is just as red as any of the fine ladies with their mirrors from top to bottom, and their handsome gentlemen that kiss their hands for them! I'm just a poor common piece! [THE CHILD *sits up.*] Quiet, boy! Close your eyes! There's the sandman! Look at him run across the wall! [*She flashes with the mirror.*] Eyes tight! Or he'll look into them and make you blind!

WOYZECK *enters behind her. She jumps up, her hands at her ears.*

WOYZECK: What's that?
MARIE: Nothing.
WOYZECK: There's something shiny in your hands.
MARIE: An earring. I found it.
WOYZECK: I never have luck like that! Two at a time!
MARIE: Am I human or not?
WOYZECK: I'm sorry, Marie.—Look at the boy asleep. Lift his arm, the chair's hurting him. Look at the shiny drops on his forehead. Everything under the sun works! We even sweat in our sleep. Us poor people! Here's some money again, Marie. My pay and something from the Captain.
MARIE: God bless you, Franz.
WOYZECK: I've got to get back. Tonight, Marie! I'll see you tonight! [*He goes off.*]

MARIE [*alone, after a pause*]. I *am* bad, I *am!* I could run myself through with a knife! Oh, what a life, what a life! We'll all end up in hell, anyway, in the end: man, woman, and child!

SCENE VII—*At the* DOCTOR's

THE DOCTOR *and* WOYZECK

DOCTOR: I don't believe it, Woyzeck! And a man of your word!

WOYZECK: What's that, Doctor, sir?

DOCTOR: I saw it all, Woyzeck. You pissed on the street! You were pissing on the wall like a dog! And here I'm giving you three groschen a day plus board! That's terrible, Woyzeck! The world's becoming a terrible place, a terrible place!

WOYZECK: But, Doctor, sir, when Nature . . .

DOCTOR: When Nature? When Nature? What has Nature to do with it? Did I or did I not prove to you that the *musculus constrictor vesicae* is controlled by your will? Nature! Woyzeck, man is free! In Mankind alone we see glorified the individual's will to freedom! And you couldn't hold your water! [*Shakes his head, places his hands behind the small of his back, and walks back and forth.*] Have you eaten your peas today, Woyzeck? Nothing but peas! *Cruciferae!* Remember that! There's going to be a revolution in science! I'm going to blow it sky-high! *Urea Oxygen.* Ammonium hydrochloratem hyperoxidic. Woyzeck, couldn't you just *try* to piss again? Go in the other room there and make another try.

WOYZECK: Doctor, sir, I can't.

DOCTOR [*disturbed*]: But you could piss on the wall. I have it here in black and white. Our contract is right here! I saw it. I saw it with these very eyes. I had just stuck my head out the window, opening it to let in the rays of the sun, so as to execute the process of sneezing. [*Going toward him.*] No, Woyzeck, I'm not going to vex myself. Vexation is unhealthy. Unscientific. I'm calm now, completely calm. My pulse is beating at its accustomed sixty, and I am speaking to you in utmost cold-bloodedness. Why should I vex myself over a man, God forbid! A man! Now if he were a Proteus, it would be worth the vexation! But, Woyzeck, you really shouldn't have pissed on the wall.

WOYZECK: You see, Doctor, sir, sometimes a person's got a certain kind of character, like when he's made a certain way. But with Nature it's not the same, you see. With Nature [*he snaps his fingers*], it's like *that!* How should I explain, it's like——

DOCTOR: Woyzeck, you're philosophizing again.

WOYZECK [*confidingly*]: Doctor, sir, did you ever see anything with double nature? Like when the sun stops at noon, and it's like the world was going up in fire? That's when I hear a terrible voice saying things to me!

DOCTOR: Woyzeck, you have an *aberratio!*

WOYZECK [*places his finger at his nose*]: It's in the toadstools, Doctor, sir, that's where it is. Did you ever see the shapes the toadstools make when they grow up out of the earth? If only somebody could read what they say!

DOCTOR: Woyzeck, you have a most beautiful *aberratio mentalis partialis* of a secondary order! And so wonderfully developed! Woyzeck, your salary is increased! *Idée fixe* of a secondary order, and with a generally rational state. You go about your business normally? Still shaving the Captain?

WOYZECK: Yes, sir.

DOCTOR: You eat your peas?

WOYZECK: Just as always, Doctor, sir. My wife gets the money for the household.

DOCTOR: Still in the army?

WOYZECK: Yes, sir, Doctor.

DOCTOR: You're an interesting case. Patient Woyzeck, you're to have an increase in salary. So behave yourself! Let's feel the pulse. Ah yes.

SCENE VIII—MARIE's *room*

DRUM MAJOR *and* MARIE

DRUM MAJOR: Marie!

MARIE [*looking at him, with expression*]: Go on, show me how you march!—Chest broad as a bull's and a beard like a lion! There's not another man in the world like that! And there's not a prouder woman than me!

DRUM MAJOR: Wait till Sunday when I wear my helmet with the plume and my white gloves! Damn, that'll be a sight for you! The Prince always says: "My God, there goes a real man!"

MARIE [*scoffing*]: Ha! [*Goes toward him.*] A man?

DRUM MAJOR: You're not such a bad piece yourself! Hell, we'll plot a whole brood of drum majors! Right? [*He puts his arm around her.*]

MARIE [*annoyed*]: Let go!

DRUM MAJOR: Bitch!

MARIE [*fiercely*]: You just touch me!

DRUM MAJOR: There's devils in your eyes.

MARIE: Let there be, for all I care! What's the difference!

Scene ix—*Street*

Captain *and* Doctor. The Captain *comes panting along the street, stops; pants, looks about.*

Captain: Ho, Doctor, don't run so fast! Don't paddle the air so with your stick! You're only courting death that way! A good man with a good conscience never walks as fast as that. A good man . . . [*He catches him by the coat.*] Doctor, permit me to save a human life!

Doctor: I'm in a hurry, Captain, I'm in a hurry!

Captain: Doctor, I'm so melancholy. I have such fantasies. I start to cry every time I see my coat hanging on the wall.

Doctor: Hm! Bloated, fat, thick neck: apoplectic constitution. Yes, Captain, you'll be having *apoplexia cerebria* any time now. Of course you could have it on only one side. In which case you'll be paralyzed down that one side. Or if things go really well you'll be mentally disabled so that you can vegetate away for the rest of your days. You may look forward to something approximately like that within the next four weeks! And, furthermore, I can assure you that you give promise of being a most interesting case. And if it is God's will that only one half of your tongue become paralyzed, then we will conduct the most immortal of experiments.

Captain: Doctor, you mustn't scare me that way! People are said to have died of fright. Of pure, sheer fright. I can see them now with lemons in their hands. But they'll say, "He was a good man, a good man." You devil's coffinnail-maker!

Doctor [*extending his hat toward him*]: Do you know who this is, Captain? This is Sir Hollowhead, my most honorable Captain Drilltheirassesoff!

Captain [*makes a series of folds in his sleeve*]: And do you know who this is, Doctor? This is Sir Manifold, my dear devil's coffinnail-maker! Ha! Ha! Ha! But no harm meant! I'm a good man, but I can play, too, when I want to, Doctor, when I want to . . .

Woyzeck *comes toward them and tries to pass in a hurry.*

Captain: Ho! Woyzeck! Where are you off to in such a hurry? Stay awhile, Woyzeck! Running through the world like an open razor, you're liable to cut someone. He runs as if he had to shave a castrated regiment and would be hung before he discovered and cut the longest hair that wasn't there. But on the subject of long beards . . . What was it I wanted to say? Woyzeck, why was I thinking about beards?

Doctor: The wearing of long beards on the chin, remarks Pliny, is a habit of which soldiers must be broken——

CAPTAIN [*continues*]: Ah, yes, this thing about beards! Tell me, Woyzeck, have you found any long hairs from beards in your soup bowl lately? Ho, I don't think he understands! A hair from a human face, from the beard of an engineer, a sergeant, a . . . a drum major? Well, Woyzeck? But, then he's got a good wife. It's not the same as with the others.

WOYZECK: Yes, sir, Captain! What was it you wanted to say to me, Captain, sir?

CAPTAIN: What a face he's making! Well, maybe not in his soup, but if he hurries home around the corner I'll wager he might still find one on a certain pair of lips. A pair of lips, Woyzeck. I know what love is, too, Woyzeck. Look at him, he's white as chalk!

WOYZECK: Captain, sir, I'm just a poor devil. And there's nothing else I've got in the world but her. Captain, sir, if you're just making a fool of me . . .

CAPTAIN: A fool? Me? Making a fool of you, Woyzeck?

DOCTOR: Your pulse, Woyzeck, your pulse! Short, hard, skipping, irregular.

WOYZECK: Captain, sir, the earth's hot as coals in hell. But I'm cold as ice, cold as ice. Hell is cold. I'll bet you. I don't believe it! God! God! I don't believe it!

CAPTAIN: Look here, you, how would you . . . how'd you like a pair of bullets in your skull? You keep stabbing at me with those eyes of yours, and I'm only trying to help. Because you're a good man, Woyzeck, a good man.

DOCTOR: Facial muscles rigid, taut, occasionally twitches. Condition strained, excitable.

WOYZECK: I'm going. Anything's possible. The bitch! Anything's possible. —The weather's nice, Captain, sir. Look, a beautiful, hard, gray sky. You'd almost like to pound a nail in up there and hang yourself on it. And only because of that little dash between Yes and Yes again . . . and No. Captain, sir: Yes and No: did No make Yes or Yes make No? I must think about that.

He goes off with long strides, slowly at first, then faster and faster.

DOCTOR [*shouting after him*]: Phenomenon! Woyzeck, you get a raise!

CAPTAIN: I get so dizzy around such people. Look at him go! Long-legged rascals like him step out like a shadow running away from its own spider. But short ones only dawdle along. The long-legged ones are the lightning, the short ones the thunder, Haha . . . Grotesque! Grotesque!

SCENE X—MARIE's *room*

WOYZECK *and* MARIE

WOYZECK [*looks fixedly at her and shakes his head*]: Hm! I don't see it! I don't see it! My God, why can't I see it, why can't I take it in my fists!

MARIE [*frightened*]: Franz, what is it?—You're raving, Franz.

WOYZECK: A sin so swollen and big—it stinks to smoke the angels out of Heaven! You have a red mouth, Marie! No blisters on it? Marie, you're beautiful as sin. How can mortal sin be so beautiful?

MARIE: Franz, it's your fever making you talk this way!

WOYZECK: Damn you! Is this where he stood? Like this? Like this?

MARIE: While the day's long and the world's old a lot of people can stand in one spot, one right after the other.—Why are you looking at me so strange, Franz! I'm afraid!

WOYZECK: It's a nice street for walking, uh? You could walk corns on your feet! It's nice walking on the street, going around in society.

MARIE: Society?

WOYZECK: A lot of people pass through this street here, don't they! And you talk to them—to whoever you want—but that's not my business! —Why wasn't it me!

MARIE: You expect me to tell people to keep off the streets—and take their mouths with them when they leave?

WOYZECK: And don't you ever leave your lips at home, they're too beautiful, it would be a sin! But then I guess the wasps like to light on them, uh?

MARIE: And what wasp stung you! You're like a cow chased by hornets!

WOYZECK: I saw him!

MARIE: You can see a lot with two eyes while the sun shines!

WOYZECK: Whore! [*He goes after her.*]

MARIE: Don't you touch me, Franz! I'd rather have a knife in my body than your hands touch me. When I looked at him, my father didn't dare lay a hand on me from the time I was ten.

WOYZECK: Whore! No, it should show on you! Something! Every man's a chasm. It makes you dizzy when you look down in. It's got to show! And she looks like innocence itself. So, innocence, there's a spot on you. But I can't prove it—can't prove it! Who can prove it? [*He goes off.*]

SCENE XI—*The guardhouse*

WOYZECK *and* ANDRES

ANDRES [*sings*]:

> Our hostess she has a pretty maid
> She sits in her garden night and day
> She sits within her garden . . .

WOYZECK: Andres!

ANDRES: Hm?

WOYZECK: Nice weather.

ANDRES: Sunday weather.—They're playing music tonight outside the town. All the whores are already there. The men stinking and sweating. Wonderful, uh?

WOYZECK [*restlessly*]: They're dancing, Andres, they're dancing!

ANDRES: Sure. So what? [*Sings.*]

> She sits within her garden
> But when the bells have tollèd
> Then she waits at her garden gate
> Or so the soldiers say.

WOYZECK: Andres, I can't keep quiet.

ANDRES: You're a fool!

WOYZECK: I've got to go out there. It keeps turning and turning in my head. They're dancing, dancing! Will she have hot hands, Andres? God damn her, Andres! God damn her!

ANDRES: What do you want?

WOYZECK: I've got to go out there. I've got to see them.

ANDRES: Aren't you ever satisfied? What's all this for a whore?

WOYZECK: I've got to get out of here! I can't stand the heat!

SCENE XII—*The inn*

The windows are open. Dancing. Benches in front of the inn. APPRENTICES

FIRST APPRENTICE [*sings*]:

> This shirt I've got on, it is not mine
> And my soul it stinketh of brandywine . . .

SECOND APPRENTICE: Brother, let me be a real friend and knock a hole in your nature! Forward! I'll knock a hole in his nature! Hell, I'm as good a man as he is; I'll kill every flea on his body!

FIRST APPRENTICE: My soul, my soul stinketh of brandywine!—And even money passeth into decay! Forget me not, but the world's a beautiful place! Brother, my sadness could fill a barrel with tears! I wish our noses were two bottles so we could pour them down one another's throats.

THE OTHERS [*in chorus*]:

> A hunter from the Rhine
> Once rode through a forest so fine
> Hallei-hallo, he called to me

> From high on a meadow, open and free
> A hunter's life for me.

WOYZECK *stands at the window.* MARIE *and* THE DRUM MAJOR *dance past without noticing him.*

WOYZECK: Both of them! God damn her!

MARIE [*dancing past*]: Don't stop! Don't stop!

WOYZECK [*seats himself on the bench, trembling, as he looks from there through the window*]: Listen! Listen! Ha, roll on each other, roll and turn! Don't stop, don't stop, she says!

IDIOT: Pah! It stinks!

WOYZECK: Yes, it stinks! Her cheeks are red, red, why should she stink already? Karl, what is it you smell?

IDIOT: I smell, I smell blood.

WOYZECK: Blood? Why are all things red that I look at now? Why are they all rolling in a sea of blood, one on top of the other, tumbling, tumbling! Ha, the sea is red!—Don't stop! Don't stop! [*He starts up passionately, then sinks down again onto the bench.*] Don't stop! Don't stop! [*Beating his hands together.*] Turn and roll and roll and turn! God, blow out the sun and let them roll on each other in their lechery! Man and woman and man and beast! They'll do it in the light of the sun! They'll do it in the palm of your hand like flies! Whore! That whore's red as coals, red as coals! Don't stop! Don't stop! [*Jumps up.*] Watch how the bastard takes hold of her! Touching her body! He's holding her now, holding her . . . the way I held her once. [*He slumps down in a stupor.*]

FIRST APPRENTICE [*preaching from a table*]: I say unto you, forget not the wanderer who standeth leaning against the stream of time, and who giveth himself answer with the wisdom of God, and saith: What is Man? What is Man? Yea, verily I say unto you: How should the farmer, the cooper, the shoemaker, the doctor, live, had not God created Man for their use? How should the tailor live had not God endowed Man with the need to slaughter himself? And therefore doubt ye not, for all things are lovely and sweet! Yet the world with all its things is an evil place, and even money passeth into decay. In conclusion, my belovèd brethren, let us piss once more upon the Cross so that somewhere a Jew will die!

Amid the general shouting and laughing WOYZECK *wakens.* PEOPLE *are leaving the inn.*

ANDRES: What are you doing there?

WOYZEK: What time is it?

ANDRES: Ten.

ARCHETYPAL CHARACTERS

WOYZEK: Is that all it is? I think it should go faster—I want to think about it before night.
ANDRES: Why?
WOYZECK: So it'd be over.
ANDRES: What?
WOYZECK: The fun.
ANDRES: What are you sitting here by the door for?
WOYZECK: Because it feels good, and because I know—a lot of people sit by doors, but they don't know—they don't know till they're dragged out of the door feet first.
ANDRES: Come with me!
WOYZECK: It feels good here like this—and even better if I laid myself down . . .
ANDRES: There's blood on your head.
WOYZECK: *In* my head, maybe.—If they all knew what time it was they'd strip themselves naked and put on a silk shirt and let the carpenter make their bed of wood shavings.
ANDRES: He's drunk.

Goes off with the others.

WOYZECK: The world is out of order! Why did the street-lamp cleaner forget to wipe my eyes—everything's dark. Devil damn you, God! I lay in my own way: jump over myself. Where's my shadow gone? There's no safety in the kennels any more. Shine the moon through my legs again to see if my shadow's here. [*Sings.*]

> Eating, oh, eating the green green grass
> Eating, oh, eating the green green grass
> Till all the grass was go-o-one.

What's that lying over there? Shining like that? It's making me look. How it sparkles. I've got to have it. [*He rushes off.*]

SCENE XIII—*An open field*

WOYZECK

WOYZECK: Don't stop! Don't stop! Hishh! Hashh! That's how the fiddles and pipes go.—Don't stop! Don't stop!—Stop your playing! What's that talking down there? [*He stretches out on the ground.*] What? What are you saying? What? Louder! Louder! Stab? Stab the goat-bitch dead? Stab? Stab her? The goat-bitch dead? Should I? Must I? Do I hear it there, too? Does the wind say so, too? Won't it ever stop, ever stop? Stab her! Stab her! Dead! Dead!

SCENE XIV—*A room in the barracks. Night*

ANDRES *and* WOYZECK *in a bed.*

WOYZECK [*softly*]: Andres! [ANDRES *murmurs in his sleep. Shakes* AN-
DRES.] Andres! Hey, Andres!

ANDRES: Mmmmm! What do you want?

WOYZECK: I can't sleep! When I close my eyes everything turns and turns.
I hear voices in the fiddles: Don't stop! Don't stop! And then the
walls start to talk. Can't you hear it?

ANDRES: Sure. Let them dance! I'm tired. God bless us all, Amen.

WOYZECK: It's always saying: Stab! Stab! And then when I close my eyes
it keeps shining there, a big, broad knife, on a table by a window in
a narrow, dark street, and an old man sitting behind it. And the knife
is always in front of my eyes.

ANDRES: Go to sleep, you fool!

WOYZECK: Andres! There's something outside. In the ground. They're
always pointing to it. Don't you hear them now, listen, now, knocking on the walls? Somebody must have seen me out the window. Don't
you hear? I hear it all day long. Don't stop. Stab! Stab the——

ANDRES: Lay down. You ought to go to the hospital. They'll give you a
schnapps with a powder in it. It'll cut your fever.

WOYZECK: Don't stop! Don't stop!

ANDRES: Go to sleep!

He goes back to sleep.

SCENE XV—THE DOCTOR'*s courtyard*

STUDENTS *and* WOYZECK *below,* THE DOCTOR *in the attic window.*

DOCTOR: Gentlemen, I find myself on the roof like David when he beheld
Bathsheba. But all I see are the Parisian panties of the girls' boarding
school drying in the garden. Gentlemen, we are concerned with the
weighty question of the relationship of the subject to the object. If,
for example, we were to take one of those innumerable things in
which we see the highest manifestation of the self-affirmation of the
Godhead, and examine its relationship to space, to the earth, and to
the planetary constellations . . . Gentlemen, if we were to take this
cat and toss it out the window: how would this object conduct itself
in conformity with its own instincts towards its *centrum gravitationis?*
Well, Woyzeck? [*Roars.*] Woyzeck!

WOYZECK [*picks up the cat*]: Doctor, sir, she's biting me!

DOCTOR: Damn, why do you handle the beast so tenderly! It's not your
grandmother! [*He descends.*]

WOYZECK: Doctor, I'm shaking.

DOCTOR [*utterly delighted*]: Excellent, Woyzeck, excellent! [*Rubs his
hands, takes the cat.*] What's this, gentlemen? The new species of
rabbit louse! A beautiful species . . . [*He pulls out a magnifying
glass; the cat runs off.*] Animals, gentlemen, simply have no scientific

instincts. But in its place you may see something else. Now, observe: for three months this man has eaten nothing but peas. Notice the effect. Feel how irregularly his pulse beats! And look at his eyes!

WOYZECK: Doctor, sir, everything's going dark! [*He sits down.*]

DOCTOR: Courage, Woyzeck! A few more days and then it will all be over with. Feel, gentlemen, feel! [*They fumble over his temples, pulse, and chest.*]

DOCTOR: Apropos, Woyzeck, wiggle your ears for the gentlemen! I've meant to show you this before. He uses only two muscles. Let's go, let's go! You stupid animal, shall I wiggle them for you? Trying to run out on us like the cat? There you are, gentlemen! Here you see an example of the transition into a donkey: frequently the result of being raised by women and of a persistent usage of the Germanic language. How much hair has your mother pulled out recently for sentimental remembrances of you? It's become so thin these last few days. It's the peas, gentlemen, the peas!

SCENE XVI—*The inn*

WOYZECK. THE SERGEANT

WOYZECK [*sings*]:

> Oh, daughter, my daughter
> And didn't you know
> That sleeping with coachmen
> Would bring you low?

What is it that our Good Lord God cannot do? What? He cannot make what is done undone. Ha! Ha! Ha!—But that's the way it is, and that's the way it should be. But to make things better is to make things better. And a respectable man loves his life, and a man who loves his life has no courage, and a virtuous man has no courage. A man with courage is a dirty dog.

SERGEANT [*with dignity*]: You're forgetting yourself in the presence of a brave man.

WOYZECK: I wasn't talking about anybody, I wasn't talking about anything, not like the Frenchmen do when they talk, but it was good of you.—But a man with courage is a dirty dog.

SERGEANT: Damn you! You broken mustache cup! You watch or I'll see you drink a pot of your own piss and swallow your own razor!

WOYZECK: Sir, you do yourself an injustice! Was it *you* I talked about? Did I say *you* had courage? Don't torment me, sir! My name is science. Every week for my scientific career I get half a guilder. You mustn't cut me in two or I'll go hungry. I'm a *Spinosa pericyclia;* I have a Latin behind. I am a living skeleton. All Mankind studies me.—What is Man? Bones! Dust, sand, dung. What is Nature? Dust, sand, dung. But poor, stupid Man, stupid Man! We must be friends. If only you had no courage, there would be no science. Only Nature, no amputation, no articulation. What is this? Woyzeck's arm, flesh, bones, veins. What is this? Dung. Why is it rooted in dung? Must I cut off my arm? No, Man is selfish, he beats, shoots, stabs his own kind. [*He sobs.*] We must be friends. I wish our noses were two bottles that we could pour down each other's throats. What a beautiful place the world is! Friend! My friend! The world! [*Moved.*] Look! The sun coming through the clouds—like God emptying His bedpan on the world. [*He cries.*]

Scene xvii—*The barracks yard*

Woyzeck. Andres

Woyzeck: What have you heard?
Andres: He's still inside with a friend.
Woyzeck: He said something.
Andres: How do you know? Why do I have to be the one to tell you? Well, he laughed and then he said she was some piece. And then something or other about her thighs—and that she was hot as a red poker.
Woyzeck [*quite coldly*]: So, he said that? What was that I dreamed about last night? About a knife? What stupid dreams we get!
Andres: Hey, friend! Where you off to?
Woyzeck: Get some wine for the Captain. Andres, you know something? There aren't many girls like she was.
Andres: Like who was?
Woyzeck: Nothing. I'll see you. [*Goes off.*]

Scene xviii—*The inn*

Drum Major, Woyzeck, *and* People

Drum Major: I'm a man! [*He pounds his chest.*] A man, you hear? Anybody say different? Anybody who's not as crocked as the Lord God Himself better keep off. I'll screw his nose up his own ass! I'll . . . [*To* Woyzeck.] You there, get drunk! I wish the world was schnapps, schnapps! You better start drinking! [Woyzeck *whistles.*] Son-of-a-bitch, you want me to pull your tongue out and wrap it around your middle? [*They wrestle;* Woyzeck *loses.*] You want I should leave enough wind in you for a good old lady's fart? Uh! [*Exhausted and trembling,* Woyzeck *seats himself on the bench.*] The son-of-a-bitch can whistle himself blue in the face for all I care. [*Sings.*]

Brandy's all my life, my life
Brandy gives me courage!

A MAN: He sure got more than he asked for.
ANOTHER: He's bleeding.
WOYZECK: One thing after another.

SCENE XIX—*Pawnbroker's shop*

WOYZECK *and* THE JEW

WOYZECK: The pistol costs too much.
JEW: So you want it or not? Make up your mind.
WOYZECK: How much was the knife?
JEW: It's straight and sharp. What do you want it for? To cut your throat?
    So what's the matter? You get it as cheap here as anywhere else.
    You'll die cheap enough, but not for nothing. What's the matter? It'll
    be a cheap death.
WOYZECK: This'll cut more than bread.
JEW: Two groschen.
WOYZECK: There! [*He goes out.*]
JEW: There, he says! Like it was nothing! And it's real money!—Dog!

SCENE XX—MARIE'*s room*

THE IDIOT. THE CHILD. MARIE

IDIOT [*lying down, telling fairy tales on his fingers*]: This one has the
    golden crown. He's the Lord King. Tomorrow I'll bring the Lady
    Queen her child. Bloodsausage says: Come, Liversausage . . .
MARIE [*paging through her Bible*]: "And no guile is found in his mouth."
    Lord God, Lord God! Don't look at me! [*Paging further.*] "And the
    Scribes and Pharisees brought unto him a woman taken in adultery,
    and set her in the midst . . . And Jesus said unto her: Neither do I
    condemn thee; go, and sin no more." [*Striking her hands together.*]
    Lord God! Lord God! I can't. Lord God, give me only so much
    strength that I may pray. [THE CHILD *presses himself close to her.*]
    The child is a sword in my heart. [*To* THE IDIOT.] Karl!—I've strutted
    it in the light of the sun, like the whore I am—my sin, my sin! [THE
    IDIOT *takes* THE CHILD *and grows quiet.*] Franz hasn't come. Not
    yesterday. Not today. It's getting hot in here! [*She opens the window
    and reads further.*] "And stood at his feet weeping, and began to wash
    his feet with tears, and did wipe them with the hairs of her head,
    and anointed them with ointment." [*Striking her breast.*] Everything
    dead! Saviour! Saviour! If only I might anoint Your feet!

SCENE XXI—*An open field*

WOYZECK

WOYZECK [*buries the knife in a hole*]: Thou shalt not kill. Lay here! I can't stay here! [*He rushes off.*]

SCENE XXII—*The barracks*

ANDRES. WOYZECK *rummages through his belongings.*

WOYZECK: Andres, this jacket's not part of the uniform, but you can use it, Andres.
ANDRES [*replies numbly to almost everything with*]: Sure.
WOYZECK: The cross is my sister's. And the ring.
ANDRES: Sure.
WOYZECK: I've got a Holy Picture, too: two hearts—they're real gold. I found it in my mother's Bible, and it said:

> O Lord with wounded head so sore
> So may my heart be evermore.

My mother only feels now when the sun shines on her hands . . . that doesn't matter.
ANDRES: Sure.
WOYZECK [*pulls out a paper*]: Friedrich Johann Franz Woyzeck. Soldier. Rifleman, Second Regiment, Second Battalion, Fourth Company. Born: the Feast of the Annunciation, twentieth of July. Today I'm thirty years old, seven months and twelve days.
ANDRES: Go to the hospital, Franz. Poor guy, you've got to drink some schnapps with a powder in it. It'll kill the fever.
WOYZECK: You know, Andres—when the carpenter puts those boards together, nobody knows who it's made for.

SCENE XXIII—*The street*

MARIE *with little* GIRLS *in front of the house door.* GRANDMOTHER. *Later* WOYZECK

GIRLS [*singing*]:

> The sun shone bright on Candlemas Day
> And the corn was all in bloom
> And they marched along the meadow way.
> They marched by two and two.
> The pipers marched ahead,
> The fiddlers followed through
> And their socks were scarlet red . . .

FIRST CHILD: I don't like that one.

SECOND CHILD: Why do you always want to be different?

FIRST CHILD: *You* sing for us, Marie!

MARIE: I can't.

SECOND CHILD: Why?

MARIE: Because.

SECOND CHILD: But *why* because?

THIRD CHILD: Grandmother, *you* tell us a story!

GRANDMOTHER: All right, you little crab apples!—Once upon a time there was a poor little girl who had no father and no mother. Everyone was dead, and there was no one left in the whole wide world. Everyone was dead. And the little girl went out and looked for someone night and day. And because there was no one left on the earth, she wanted to go to Heaven. And the moon looked down so friendly at her. And when she finally got to the moon, it was a piece of rotten wood. And so she went to the sun, and it was a faded sunflower. And when she got to the stars, they were little golden flies, stuck up there as if they were caught in a spider's web. And when she wanted to go back to earth, the earth was an upside-down pot. And she was all alone. And she sat down there and she cried. And she sits there to this day, all, all alone.

WOYZECK [*appears*]: Marie!

MARIE [*startled*]: What!

WOYZECK: Let's go. It's getting time.

MARIE: Where to?

WOYZECK: How should I know?

SCENE XXIV—*A pond by the edge of the woods*

MARIE *and* WOYZECK

MARIE: Then the town must be out that way. It's so dark.

WOYZECK: You can't go yet. Come, sit down.

MARIE: But I've got to get back.

WOYZECK: You don't want to run your feet sore.

MARIE: What's happened to you?

WOYZECK: You know how long it's been, Marie?

MARIE: Two years from Pentecost.

WOYZECK: You know how much longer it'll last?

MARIE: I've got to get back. Supper's not made yet.

WOYZECK: Are you freezing, Marie? And still you're so warm. Your lips are hot as coals! Hot as coals, the hot breath of a whore! And still I'd give up Heaven just to kiss them again. Are you freezing? When you're cold through, you won't freeze any more. The morning dew won't freeze you.

MARIE: What are you talking about?

WOYZECK: Nothing. [*Silence.*]

MARIE: Look how red the moon is! It's rising.

WOYZECK: Like a knife washed in blood.

MARIE: What are you going to do? Franz, you're so pale. [*He raises the knife.*]

MARIE: Franz! Stop! For Heaven's sake! Help me! Help me!

WOYZECK [*stabbing madly*]: There! There! Why can't you die? There! There! Ha, she's still shivering! Still not dead? Still not dead? Still shivering? [*Stabbing at her again.*] Are you dead? Dead! Dead! [*He drops the knife and runs away.*]

   Two MEN *approach.*

FIRST MAN: Wait!

SECOND MAN: You hear something? Shh! Over there!

FIRST MAN: Whhh! There! What a sound!

SECOND MAN: It's the water, it's calling. It's a long time since anyone drowned here. Let's go! I don't like hearing such sounds!

FIRST MAN: Whhh! There it is again! Like a person, dying!

SECOND MAN: It's uncanny! So foggy, nothing but gray mist as far as you can see—and the hum of beetles like broken bells. Let's get out of here!

FIRST MAN: No, it's too clear, it's too loud! Let's go up this way! Come on! [*They hurry on.*]

   SCENE XXV—*The inn*

   WOYZECK, KATHY, INNKEEPER, IDIOT, *and* PEOPLE

WOYZECK: Dance! Everybody! Don't stop! Sweat and stink! He'll get you all in the end! [*Sings.*]

> Oh, daughter, my daughter
> And didn't you know
> That sleeping with coachmen
> Would bring you low?

[*He dances.*] Ho, Kathy! Sit down! I'm so hot, so hot! [*Takes off his coat.*] That's the way it is: the devil takes one and lets the other get away. Kathy, you're hot as coals! Why, tell me why? Kathy, you'll be cold one day, too. Be reasonable.—Can't you sing something?

KATHY [*sings*]:

> That Swabian land I cannot bear
> And dresses long I will not wear
> For dresses long and pointed shoes
> Are clothes a chambermaid never should choose.

WOYZECK: No shoes, no shoes! We can get to hell without shoes.

KATHY [*sings*]:

> To such and like I'll not be prone
> Take back your gold and sleep alone.

WOYZECK: Sure, sure! What do I want to get all bloody for?

KATHY: Then what's that on your hand?

WOYZECK: Me? Me?

KATHY: Red! It's blood! [PEOPLE *gather round him.*]

WOYZECK: Blood? Blood?

INNKEEPER: Blood!

WOYZECK: I think I cut myself. Here, on my right hand.

INNKEEPER: Then why is there blood on your elbow?

WOYZECK: I wiped it off.

INNKEEPER: Your right hand and you wiped it on your right elbow? You're a smart one!

IDIOT: And then the Giant said: "I smell, I smell the flesh of Man." Pew, it stinks already!

WOYZECK: What do you want from me? Is it your business? Out of my way or the first one who . . . Damn you! Do I look like I murdered somebody? Do I look like a murderer? What are you looking at? Look at yourselves! Look! Out of my way! [*He runs off.*]

SCENE XXVI—*At the pond*

WOYZECK, *alone.*

WOYZECK: The knife! Where's the knife? I left it here. It'll give me away! Closer! And closer! What is this place? What's that noise? Something's moving! It's quiet now.—It's got to be here, close to her. Marie? Ha, Marie! Quiet. Everything's quiet! Why are you so pale, Marie? Why are you wearing those red beads around your neck? Who was it gave you that necklace for sinning with him? Your sins made you black, Marie, they made you black! Did I make you so pale? Why is your hair uncombed? Did you forget to twist your braids today? The knife, the knife! I've got it! There! [*He runs toward the water.*] There, into the water! [*He throws the knife into the water.*] It dives like a stone into the black water. No, it's not out far enough for when they swim! [*He wades into the pond and throws it out farther.*] There! Now! But in the summer when they dive for mussels? Ha, it'll get rusty, who'll ever notice it! Why didn't I break it first! Am I still bloody? I've got to wash myself. There, there's a spot, and there's another . . . [*He goes farther out into the water.*]

SCENE XXVII—*The street*

CHILDREN

FIRST CHILD: Let's go find Marie!
SECOND CHILD: What happened?
FIRST CHILD: Don't you know? Everybody's out there. They found a body!
SECOND CHILD: Where?
FIRST CHILD: By the pond, out in the woods.
SECOND CHILD: Hurry, so we can still see something. Before they bring it back. [*They rush off.*]

SCENE XXVIII—*In front of* MARIE's *house*

IDIOT. CHILD. WOYZECK.

IDIOT [*holding* THE CHILD *on his knee, points to* WOYZECK *as he enters*]: Looky there, he fell in the water, he fell in the water, he fell in the water!
WOYZECK: Boy! Christian!
IDIOT [*looks at him fixedly*]: He fell in the water.
WOYZECK [*wanting to embrace* THE CHILD *tenderly, but it turns from him and screams*]: My God! My God!
IDIOT: He fell in the water.
WOYZECK: I'll buy you a horse, Christian. There, there. [THE CHILD *pulls away To the* IDIOT.] Here, buy the boy a horsey! [THE IDIOT *stares at him.*] Hop! Hop! Hip-hop, horsey!
IDIOT [*shouting joyously*]: Hop! Hop! Hip-hop, horsey! Hip-hop, horsey!

He runs off with THE CHILD. WOYZECK *is alone.*

SCENE XXIX—*The morgue*

JUDGE, COURT CLERK, POLICEMAN, CAPTAIN, DOCTOR, DRUM MAJOR, SERGEANT, IDIOT, *and others.* WOYZECK

POLICEMAN: What a murder! A good, genuine, beautiful murder! Beautiful a murder as you could hope for! It's been a long time since we had one like this!

WOYZECK *stands in their midst, dumbly looking at the body of* MARIE; *he is bound, the dogmatic atheist, tall, haggard, timid, good-natured, scientific.*

Ulysses

ALFRED, LORD TENNYSON

It little profits that an idle king,
By this still hearth, among these barren crags,
Matched with an aged wife, I mete and dole
Unequal laws unto a savage race,
That hoard, and sleep, and feed, and know not me.
I cannot rest from travel; I will drink
Life to the lees. All times I have enjoyed
Greatly, have suffered greatly, both with those
That loved me, and alone; on shore, and when
Through scudding drifts the rainy Hyades
Vest the dim sea. I am become a name;
For always roaming with a hungry heart
Much have I seen and known—cities of men
And manners, climates, councils, governments,
Myself not least, but honored of them all,—
And drunk delight of battle with my peers,
Far on the ringing plains of windy Troy.
I am a part of all that I have met;
Yet all experience is an arch wherethrough
Gleams that untraveled world whose margin fades
For ever and for ever when I move.
How dull it is to pause, to make an end,
To rust unburnished, not to shine in use!
As though to breathe were life! Life piled on life
Were all too little, and of one to me
Little remains; but every hour is saved
From that eternal silence, something more,
A bringer of new things; and vile it were
For some three suns to store and hoard myself,
And this grey spirit yearning in desire
To follow knowledge like a sinking star,
Beyond the utmost bound of human thought.

This is my son, mine own Telemachus,
To whom I leave the scepter and the isle,
Well-loved of me, discerning to fulfill

This labor, by slow prudence to make mild
A rugged people, and through soft degrees
Subdue them to the useful and the good.
Most blameless is he, centered in the sphere
Of common duties, decent not to fail
In offices of tenderness, and pay
Meet adoration to my household gods,
When I am gone. He works his work, I mine.

    There lies the port; the vessel puffs her sail;
There gloom the dark, broad seas. My mariners,
Souls that have toiled, and wrought, and thought with me,
That ever with a frolic welcome took
The thunder and the sunshine, and opposed
Free hearts, free foreheads—you and I are old;
Old age hath yet his honor and his toil.
Death closes all; but something ere the end,
Some work of noble note, may yet be done,
Not unbecoming men that strove with gods.
The lights begin to twinkle from the rocks;
The long day wanes; the slow moon climbs; the deep
Moans round with many voices. Come, my friends,
'Tis not too late to seek a newer world.
Push off, and sitting well in order smite
The sounding furrows; for my purpose holds
To sail beyond the sunset, and the baths
Of all the western stars, until I die.
It may be that the gulfs will wash us down;
It may be we shall touch the Happy Isles,
And see the great Achilles, whom we knew.
Though much is taken, much abides; and though
We are not now that strength which in old days
Moved earth and heaven, that which we are, we are,
One equal temper of heroic hearts,
Made weak by time and fate, but strong in will
To strive, to seek, to find, and not to yield.

Oedipus

EDWIN MUIR

I, Oedipus, the club-foot, made to stumble,
Who long in the light have walked the world in darkness,
And once in the darkness did that which the light
Found and disowned—too well I have loved the light,
Too dearly have rued the darkness. I am one
Who as in innocent play sought out his guilt,
And now through guilt seeks other innocence,
Beset by evil thoughts, led by the gods.

There was a room, a bed of darkness, once
Known to me, now to all. Yet in that darkness,
Before the light struck, she and I who lay
There without thought of sin and knew each other
Too well, yet were to each other quite unknown
Though fastened mouth to mouth and breast to breast—
Strangers laid on one bed, as children blind,
Clear-eyed and blind as children—did we sin
Then on that bed before the light came on us,
Desiring good to each other, bringing, we thought,
Great good to each other? But neither guilt nor death.

Yet if that darkness had been darker yet,
Buried in endless dark past reach of light
Or eye of the gods, a kingdom of solid darkness
Impregnable and immortal, would we have sinned,
Or lived like the gods in deathless innocence?
For sin is born in the light; therefore we cower
Before the face of the light that none can meet
And all must seek. And when in memory now,
Woven of light and darkness, a stifling web,
I call her back, dear, dreaded, who lay with me,
I see guilt, only guilt, my nostrils choke
With the smell of guilt, and I can scarcely breathe
Here in the guiltless guilt-evolving sun.

And when young Oedipus—for it was Oedipus

And not another—on that long-vanished night
Far in my night, at that predestined point
Where three paths like three fates crossed one another,
Tracing the evil figure—when I met
The stranger who menaced me, and flung the stone
That brought him death and me this that I carry,
It was not him but fear I sought to kill,
Fear that, the wise men say, is father of evil,
And was my father in flesh and blood, yet fear,
Fear only, father and fear in one dense body,
So that there was no division, no way past:
Did I sin then, by the gods admonished to sin,
By men enjoined to Sin? For it is duty
Of god and man to kill the shapes of fear.

These thoughts recur, vain thoughts. The gods see all,
And will what must be willed, which guards us here.
Their will in them was anger, in me was terror
Long since, but now is peace. For I am led
By them in darkness; light is all about me;
My way lies in the light; they know it; I
Am theirs to guide and hold. And I have learned,
Though blind, to see with something of their sight,
Can look into that other world and watch
King Oedipus the just, crowned and discrowned,
As one may see oneself rise in a dream,
Distant and strange. Even so I see
The meeting at the place where three roads crossed,
And who was there and why, and what was done
That had to be done and paid for. Innocent
The deed that brought the guilt of father-murder. Pure
The embrace on the bed of darkness. Innocent
And guilty. I have wrought and thought in darkness,
And stand here now, an innocent mark of shame,
That so men's guilt might be made manifest
In such a walking riddle—their guilt and mine,
For I've but acted out this fable. I have judged
Myself, obedient to the gods' high judgment,
And seen myself with their pure eyes, have learnt
That all must bear a portion of the wrong
That is driven deep into our fathomless hearts
Past sight or thought; that bearing it we may ease
The immortal burden of the gods who keep
Our natural steps and the earth and skies from harm.

Morning Song from "Senlin"

CONRAD AIKEN

It is morning, Senlin says, and in the morning
When the light drips through the shutters like the dew,
I arise, I face the sunrise,
And do the things my fathers learned to do.
Stars in the purple dusk above the rooftops
Pale in a saffron mist and seem to die,
And I myself on a swiftly tilting planet
Stand before a glass and tie my tie.

Vine leaves tap my window,
Dew-drops sing to the garden stones,
The robin chirps in the chinaberry tree
Repeating three clear tones.

It is morning. I stand by the mirror
And tie my tie once more.
While waves far off in a pale rose twilight
Crash on a coral shore.
I stand by a mirror and comb my hair:
How small and white my face!—
The green earth tilts through a sphere of air
And bathes in a flame of space.

There are houses hanging above the stars
And stars hung under a sea.
And a sun far off in a shell of silence
Dapples my walls for me.

It is morning, Senlin says, and in the morning
Should I not pause in the light to remember god?
Upright and firm I stand on a star unstable,
He is immense and lonely as a cloud.
I will dedicate this moment before my mirror
To him alone, for him I will comb my hair.
Accept these humble offerings, cloud of silence!
I will think of you as I descend the stair.

Vine leaves tap my window,
The snail-track shines on the stones,
Dew-drops flash from the chinaberry tree
Repeating two clear tones.

It is morning, I awake from a bed of silence,
Shining I rise from the starless waters of sleep.
The falls are about me still as in the evening,
I am the same, and the same name still I keep.
The earth revolves with me, yet makes no motion,
The stars pale silently in a coral sky.
In a whistling void I stand before my mirror,
Unconcerned, and tie my tie.

There are horses neighing on far-off hills
Tossing their long white manes,
And mountains flash in the rose-white dusk,
Their shoulders black with rains.
It is morning. I stand by the mirror
And surprise my soul once more.
The blue air rushes above my ceiling,
There are suns beneath my floor.

. . . It is morning, Senlin says, I ascend from darkness
And depart on the winds of space for I know not where,
My watch is wound, a key is in my pocket,
And the sky is darkened as I descend the stair.
There are shadows across the windows, clouds in heaven,
And a god among the stars; and I will go
Thinking of him as I might think of daybreak
And humming a tune I know.

Vine leaves tap at the window,
Dew-drops sing to the garden stones,
The robin chirps in the chinaberry tree
Repeating three clear tones.

The Wise Fool

THIS motif reveals a person who is regarded as stupid, ignorant, and unwise but turns out to have profound wisdom, revealing that it is the values of his society that are wanting or his classification as a fool that is incorrect. A supreme example of the use of this motif is Dostoievsky's novel *The Idiot*, in which the central Christ-like character, Prince Myshkin ("the prince of peace"), is called an idiot by members of St. Petersburg society because Myshkin can not lie or be duplicitous. Like Holden Caulfield, he must finally be institutionalized. There children respond to him and love him: society is not yet ready for him. The jester or fool in Shakepeare's *King Lear* is another example of a "clown" who has great wisdom and who prods his king into seeing the stupidity of the choices he has made.

Parsifal
(after Wagner and Verlaine)
ROBERT DUNCAN

> *Et O ces voix d'enfants, chantant dans le coupole!—*
> —T. S. Eliot, *The Waste Land*, line 202

Parsifal has put off the boys and girls, their
    babbling song and dance, their
sexy ways. He stands
    blond and tall,
        enhanced by the magic of his not knowing
what's going on, amidst their knowing
    inclination everywhere
towards the flesh of the virgin youth. He glows
    untoucht, most fair
        in all those glancing shadows that
would cast their spell
        and seduce the hero to their lights of love,
        tricks of the afternoon
and one-night stands.

Parsifal has put off Kundry, the most beautiful of all
     women, She of Subtle Heart, turnd away
          from her cool arms
and the beat of blood displayd at her throat
     that would excite the soul's
          hot deep welling up of desire
and yet quench the heat.

He has put off Hell's magic fire
     and from whose glimmering halls
          falling in ruins as he turns returnd
to the tents of light burdend with a heavy prize
     his boyish arm has won
          back from the hold of hidden things.

With the Lance that pierced the side of the Lord
     he does not know Whose Name, he knows now
only what he has to do. He heals
     the king from his anguish, bring up
          out of the dark he dared,
as if it were a ray of light, the spear
     won back from magic's realm, returnd
          to the king, to the very king himself
long lingering at the edge of the Father's love,
     the priest he is himself
          of the essential Treasure.

     In gold robe
Parsifal adores the glory and the symbol
—but it is a simple pure dish of crystal in which shines
     the Blood of the Real,
pulse of the Father's love the music raises.
And O, the voices of the children,
          singing in the dome above.

Rethinking a Children's Story

DICK ALLEN

We have been so wrong in judging Simple Simon
it would take a nine-man court to rule in his favor.
He was really a mystic
searching for a Holy Land he called the Fair.
The Pieman thought only of money
and so it is no wonder he refused to give aid.
We should have sensed something was wrong
when Simon was convinced he'd catch a whale.
Go left, go right, take any road to anywhere,
is what Simon would tell us.
Sooner or later, you'll hear
carnival music, and see the ferris wheel turn.
Maybe it is turning, now, out on your lawn
between the raindrops and upon the air.
It does not take
science-fiction to explain the fourth dimension.
Rub your eyes, and be happy, and cheer
yourself with immaculate prayer.
Reason lives within reason.
It is the hand on the lever that stays on the ground.
Above it ride children and Simon
who spin like colored stones above the Fair.
We have never before
condemned a man who gives away his ware.
I wonder where we will go
when we pass out of light
and in the new dark ages
forget what science came among us to explore.
If our modern houses still had widow's walks,
the ladies of the universe would watch
sea and space, and rejoice
if it was Simon's hand that steered their loved ones home.

God's Other Side

LANGSTON HUGHES

"Some Negroes think that all one has to do to solve the problems in this world is to be white," I said, "but I never understood how they can feel that way. There are white unemployed, just as there are black unemployed. There are white illiterates, just as there are blacks who can hardly read or write. The mere absence of color would hardly make this world a paradise. Whites get sick the same as Negroes. Whites grow old. Whites go crazy."

"Some of us in Harlem do not have sense enough to go crazy," said Simple. "Some Negroes do not worry about a thing. But me, well, Jim Crow bugs me."

"Bigotry disturbs me, too," I said, "but prejudice and segregation alone do not constitute the root of *all* evil. There are many nonracial elements common to humanity as a whole that create problems from the cradle to the grave regardless of race, creed, color, or previous condition of servitude."

"But when you add a black face to all that," said Simple, "you have problem's mammy. White folks may be unemployed in this American country, but they get the first chance at the first jobs that open up. Besides, they get seniority. Maybe some white folks cannot read or write, but if they want to go to Ole Miss to learn to read or write, they can go without the President calling up the United States Army to protect them. Sure, white folks gets sick, but they don't have to creep in the back door of the hospital down South for treatment like we does. And when they get old, white folks have got more well-off sons and daughters to take care of them than colored folks have. Most old white folks when they get sick can suffer in comfort, and when they die they can get buried without going in debt. Colored folks, most in generally, do not have it so easy. I know because I am one."

"You let yourself be unduly disturbed by your skin," I said. "Sometimes I think you are marked by color—just as some children are born with birthmarks."

"My birthmark is all over me," said Simple.

"Then your only salvation is to be born again."

"And washed whiter than snow," declared Simple. "Imagine all my relatives setting up in heaven washed whiter than snow. I wonder would I know my grandpa were I to see him in paradise? Grandpa Simple crowned in Glory with white wings, white robe, white skin, and golden slippers on his feet! Oh, Grandpa, when the chariot swings low to carry me up to the Golden Gate, Grandpa, as I enter will you identify yourself—just in case I do not know you, white and winged in your golden shoes? I might be sort of turned around in heaven, Grandpa."

"What on earth makes you think you are going to heaven?" I asked.

"Because I have already been in Harlem," said Simple.

"How often do you go to church?" I asked.

"As often as my wife drags me," said Simple. "The last two times I was there the minister preached from the text, 'And I shall sit on the right hand of the Son of God.' Me, half asleep, I heard that much from the sermon. And it set me to wondering why it is nobody ever wants to set on the *left*-hand side of God? All my life, from a little small child in Virginia right on up to Harlem, in church I have been hearing of people setting on the right-hand side of God, never on the left. Now, why is that?"

"When a guest comes to dine, you always seat him or her on your right—that is the main guest sits there," I said. "The right-hand side is the place of honor, granted always to the lady, or the oldest, or the most distinguished person present. The right side is the place of honor."

"I would be glad to set on any old side," said Simple, "were I lucky enough to get into the Kingdom. Besides, if everybody is setting on the right-hand side of God that says they are going to set there, that right-hand side of God would be really crowded. One million Negroes and two million white folks must be setting already on the right. How is there going to be room on that side for anybody else?"

"In the Kingdom there is infinite room, whichever side is chosen," I said.

"No matter how much room there is," said Simple, "that right side of the Throne is crowded by now. I see no harm in setting on the left. God must turn His head that way once in a while, too."

"I suppose He does," I said. "But if you have your choice, why not sit on the right?"

"Just because everybody else is setting there," said Simple. "I would like to be different, and set on the left-hand side all by myself. I expect I would get a little more of God's attention that way—because when He turned around toward me, nobody would be there but me. On His right-hand side, like I said, would be setting untold millions. And all of them folks would be asking for something. God's right ear must be so full of prayers, He can hardly hear himself think. Now me, on the left-hand side, I would not ask for nothing much, were I to get to heaven. And if I did ask for anything, I would whisper soft-like, 'Lord, here is me.'

"Were the Lord to grant me an answer, and say, 'Negro, what do you want?' I would say, 'Nothing much, Lord. And if you be's too busy on your right-hand side to attend to me now, I can wait. I tried to leave my business on earth pretty well attended to—but just in case my wife, Joyce, needs anything, look after her, Lord. I love that girl. Also my Cousin Minnie—protect her from too much harm in them Lenox Avenue bars which she do love beyond the call of duty. Also my junior nephew, F. D., that I helped to raise when he first come to Harlem in his teens, who is out of the Army and married now, show F. D. how to get along with his wife and be a good young man, and not pattern himself too much after me, who were frail as to being an example for anybody.

"'The peoples that I love, Lord, is the only ones I whispers into Your left ear about. If I was on Your right side, which is crowded with all the saints who ever got to Glory, me who ain't much, might have to holler from afar off for You to hear me at all. Me, who never was nobody, am glad just to be setting on Your left side, Lord—me, Jesse B. Simple, on the left-hand side of the Son of God! And I wants to whisper just *one* thing to You, God—I hope You loves the ones I love, too.'"

New Kittens

(from Bound for Glory, Chapter 4)

WOODY GUTHRIE

Up at the house an hour later, Warren and Leonard had poured water and washed their cuts clean, and drifted off into the house getting on some clean clothes. Grandma talked a little to herself, getting some coffee ground for supper. Lawrence trotted out into the yard in a few minutes and I set on the stone steps of the porch and watched him. He pranked around under the two big oak trees and then walked around the corner of the house.

I followed him. He was the littlest one of Grandma's boys. He was more my size. I was about five and he was eight. I followed him back to a rosebush where he pointed to old Mother Maltese and her new little bunch of kittens. He was telling me all there is to know about cats.

First, we just rubbed the old mama cat on the head, and he told me she was older than either one of us. "Cat's been here longer'n me even."

"How old is ol' mama cat?" I asked Lawrence.

"Ten."

"An' you're jest eight?" I said.

"Yeah."

"She's all ten fingers old. You ain't but jest this many fingers old," I went on.

"She's two older'n me," he said.

"Wonder how come you th' biggest?"

"Cause, crazy, I'm a boy, an' she's a cat!"

"Feel how warm an' smooth she is," I told him.

"Yeah," he said, "perty slick, all right; but th' little 'uns is th' slickest. But ol' mama cat don't like for strangers ta come out here an' stick yore han' down in her box an' feel on her little babies."

"I been out here 'fore this," I told him, "so that makes me not no stranger."

"Yeah," he told me back, "I know that; but then, you went back ta town ag'in, see, an' course, that makes you part of a stranger."

"How much stranger am I? I ain't no plumb whole stranger; mama cat knowed me when I wuz jest a little teen weeny baby; jest this long; an' my mama had ta keep me all nice an' warm jest like them little baby cats, so's I wouldn't freeze, so's nuthin' wouldn't git me." I was still stroking the old cat's head, and feeling of her with my fingers.

She was holding her eyes shut real tight, and purring almost loud enough for Grandma to hear her in the house. Lawrence and me kept watching and listening. The old mama cat purred louder and louder.

Then I asked Lawrence, "What makes 'er sound that a-way in 'er head?"

And he told me, "Purrin', that's what she's doin'."

"Makes 'er purr?" I asked him.

"She does it 'way back inside 'er head some way," Lawrence was telling me.

"Sounds like a car motor," I said.

"She ain't got no car motor in 'er," he said.

"Might," I said.

" I don't much think she has, though."

"Might have a little 'un, kinda like a cat motor; I mean a reg'ler little motor fer cats," I said.

"What'd she be wantin' with a cat motor?"

"Lotsa things is got motors in 'em. Motors is engines. Engines makes things go. Makes noise jest like ol' mama cat. Motor makes wheels go 'round, so cats might have a real little motor ta make legs go, an' tail go, an' feet move, an' nose go, an' ears wiggle, an' eyes go 'round, an' mouth fly open, an' mebbe her stomack is 'er gas tank." I was running my hand along over the old mama cat's fur, feeling of each part as I talked, head, tail, legs, mouth, eyes, and stomach; and the old cat had a big smile on her face.

"Wanta see if she's really got a motor inside of 'er? I'll go an' git Ma's butcher knife, an' you hold 'er legs, an' I'll cut 'er belly open; an' if she's got a motor in 'er, by jacks, I wanta see it! Want me to?" Lawrence asked me.

"Cut 'er belly open?" I asked him. "Ya might'n find 'er motor when ya got cut in there!"

"I c'n find it, if she's got one down in there! I helped Pa cut rabbits an' squirrels an' fishes open, an' I never did see no motor in them!"

"No, but did you ever hear a rabbit er a squirrel either one, or a fish make a noise like mama cat makes?"

"No. Never did."

"Well, mebbe that's why they ain't got no motor. Mebbe they gotta differnt kind a motor. Don't make no kind of a noise."

"Might be. An' some of th' time mama cat don't make no noise either; 'cause some of th' time ya cain't even hear no motor in 'er belly. What then?"

"Maybe she's just got th' key turned off!"

"Turned off?" Lawrence asked me.

"Might be. My papa's gotta car. His car's gotta key. Ya turn th' key on, an' th' car goes like a cat. Ya turn th' key off, an' it quits."

"There yore hand goes ag'in! Didn' I tell you not ta touch them little baby kittens? They ain't got no eyes open ta see with yet; you cain't put yore hands on 'em!" He cut his eyes around at me.

"Ohhhhhppppp! All right. I'm awful, awful sorry, mama cat; an' I'm awful, awful sorry, little baby cats!" And I let my hand fall back down on the old mama cat's back.

"That's all right ta pat 'er all you want, but she'll reach up an' take 'er claws, an' rip yore hand plumb wide open if you make one of her little cats cry!" he told me.

"Know somethin', Lawrence, know somethin'?"

"What about?" he asked me.

"People says when I wuz a baby, jest like one of these here little baby cats, only a little bit bigger, mebbe, my mama got awful bad sick when I wuz borned under th' covers."

"I heard Ma an' them talk about her," he told me.

"What did they talk about?" I asked him.

"Oohhh, I dunno, she wuz purty bad off."

"What made 'er bad off?"

"Yer dad."

"My papa did?"

"What people says."

"He's good ta me. Good ta my mama. What makes people say he made my mama git sick?"

"Politics."

"What's them?"

"I dunno what politics is. Just a good way ta make some money. But

you always have troubles. Have fights. Carry two guns ever' day. Yore
dad likes lots of money. So he got some people ta vote fer 'im, so then
he got 'im two guns an' went around c'lectin' money. Yore ma didn't like
yore dad ta always be pokin' guns, shootin', fightin', an' so, well, she just
worried an' worried, till she got sick at it—an' that was when you was
borned a baby not much bigger'n one of these here little cats, I reckon."
Lawrence was digging his fingernails into the soft white pine of the box,
looking at the nest of cats. "Funny thing 'bout cats. All of 'em's got one
ma, an' all of 'em's differnt colors. Which is yore pet color? Mine's this
'un, an' this 'un, an' this 'un."

"I like all colors cats. Say, Lawrence, what does crazy mean?"

"Means you ain't got good sense."

"Worried?"

"Crazy's more'n just worry."

"Worse'n worryin'?"

"Shore. Worry starts, an' you do that fer a long, long time, an' then
maybe you git sick 'er somethin', an' ya go all, well, you just git all mixed
up 'bout ever'thing."

"Is ever'body sick like my mama?"

"I don't guess."

"Reckin could all of our folks cure my mama?"

"Might. Wonder how?"

"If ever' single livin' one of 'em would all git together an' git rid of
them ol' mean, bad politics, they'd all feel lots better, an' wouldn't fight
each other so much, an' that'd make my mama feel better."

Lawrence looked out through the leaves of the bushes. "Wonder
where Warren's headin', goin' off down toward th' barn? Be right still;
he's walkin' past us. He'll hear us talkin'."

I whispered real low and asked Lawrence, "Whatcha bein' so still
for? 'Fraida Warren?"

And Lawrence told me, "Hushhh. Naw. 'Fraid fer th' cats."

"Why 'bout th' cats?"

"Warren don't like cats."

"Why?" I was still whispering.

"Just don't. Be still. Ssshhh."

"Why?" I went on.

"Sez cats ain't no good. Warren kills all th' new little baby cats that
gits born'd on th' place. I had these hid out under th' barn. Don't let 'im
know we're here. . . ."

Warren got within about twenty feet of us, and we could see his
long shadow falling over our rosebush; and then for a little time we
couldn't see him, and the rosebush blocked our sight of him. Still, we
could hear his new sharp-toed leather shoes screaking every time he

took a step. Lawrence tapped me on the shoulder. I looked around and he was motioning for me to grab up one side of the white pine box. I got a hold and he grabbed the other side. We skidded the box up close to the rock foundation of the house, and partly in behind the rosebush.

Lawrence held his breath and I held my hand over my mouth. Warren's screaky shoes was the only sound I could hear. Lawrence laid his body down over the box of cats. I laid down to hide the other half of the box, and the screak, screak, screak got louder. I whiffed my nose and smelled the loud whang of hair tonic on Warren's hair. His white silk shirt threw flashes of white light through the limbs of the roses, and Lawrence moved his lips so as to barely say, "Montgomery girl." I didn't catch him the first time, so he puckered his lips to tell me again, and when he bent over my way, he stuck a thorn into his shoulder, and talked out too loud:

"Montgomery—"

The screak of Warren's shoes stopped by the side of the bush. He looked all around, and took a step back, then one forward. And he had us trapped.

I didn't have the guts to look up at him. I heard his shoes screak and I knew that he was rocking from one foot to the other one, standing with his hands on his hips, looking down on the ground at Lawrence and me. I shivered and could feel Lawrence quiver under his shirt. Then I turned my head over and looked out from under Lawrence's arm, both of us still hugging the box, and heard Warren say, "What was that you boys was a-sayin'?"

"Tellin' Woody about somebody," Lawrence told Warren.

"Somebody? Who?" Warren didn't seem to be in any big rush.

"Somebody. Somebody you know," Lawrence said.

"Who do I know?" Warren asked him.

"The Mon'gom'ry folks," Lawrence said.

"You're a couple of dirty little low-down liars! All you know how to do is to hide off in under some Goddamed bush, an' say silly things about other decent people!" Warren told us.

"We wuzn't makin' no fun, swear ta God," Lawrence told him.

"What in the hell was you layin' under there talkin' about? Somethin' you're tryin' to hide! Talk out!"

"I seen you was all nice an' warshed up clean, an' told Woody you was goin' over ta Mon'gom'ry's place."

"What else?"

"Nuthin' else. 'At's all I said, swear ta God, all I told you, wasn't it, Woody?"

" 'S all I heard ya say," I told him.

"Now ain't you a pair of little old yappin' pups? You know dam good an' well you was teasin' me from behind 'bout Lola Montgomery! How come you two hidin' here in th' first place? Just to see me walk past you with all of my clean clothes on? See them new low-cut shoes? See how sharp th' toes are? Feel with your finger, both of you, feel! That's it! See how sharp? I'd ought to just take that sharp toe and kick both of your little rears."

"Quit! Quit that pushin' me!" Lawrence was yelling as loud as he could, hoping Grandma would hear. Warren pushed him on the shoulder with the bottom of his shoe, and tried to roll Lawrence over across the ground. Lawrence swung onto his box of cats so tight that Warren had to kick as hard as he could, and push Lawrence off the box.

The only thing I could think of to do was jump on top of the box and cover it up. Lawrence was yelling as loud as he could yell. Warren was laughing. I wasn't saying anything.

"Whut's that box you're a holdin' onto there so tight?" Warren asked me.

"Jest a plain ol' box!" Lawrence was crying and talking.

"Jest a plain wooden box," I told Warren.

"What's on th' inside of it, runts?"

"Nuthin's in it!"

"Jist a ol' empty one!"

And Warren put his shoe sole on my back and pushed me over beside Lawrence. "I'll just take me a look! You two seems mighty interested in what's inside of that box!"

"You ol' mean outfit, you! God, I hate you! You go on over an' see yore ol' 'Gomery girl, an' leave us alone! We ain't a-hurtin' you!" Lawrence was jumping up. He started to draw back and fight Warren, but Warren just took his open hand and pushed Lawrence about fifteen feet backwards, and he fell flat, screaming.

Warren put his foot on my shoulder and give me another shove. I went above three feet. I tried to hold onto the box, but the whole works turned over. The old mama cat jumped out and made a circle around us, meowing first at Warren, and then at me and the little baby kittens cried in the split cotton seed.

"Cat lovers!" Warren told us.

"You g'wan, an' let us be! Don't you tech them cats! Ma! Ma! Warr'n's gonna hurt our cats!" Lawrence squawled out.

Warren kicked the loose cotton seed apart. "Just like tearin' up a bird's nest!" he said. He put the sharp toe of his shoe under the belly of the first little cat, and threw it up against the rock foundation. "Meoww! Meoww! You little chicken killers! Egg stealers!" He picked the second kitten up in the grip of his hand, and squeezed till his muscles bulged up. He swung the kitten around and around, something like a Ferris wheel, as fast as he could turn his arm, and the blood and entrails of the kitten splashed across the ground, and the side of the house. Then he held the little body out toward Lawrence and me. We looked at it, and it was just like an empty hide. He threw it away out over the fence.

Warren took the second kitten, squeezed it, swung it over his head and over the top wire of the fence. The third, fourth, fifth, sixth, and seventh.

The poor old mama cat was running backwards, crossways, and all around over the yard with her back humped up, begging against Warren's legs, and trying to jump up and climb up his body to help her babies. He boxed her away and she came back. He kicked her thirty feet. She moaned along the rocks, smelling of her babies' blood and insides. She scratched dirt and dug grass roots; then she made a screaming noise that chilled my blood and jumped six feet, clawing at Warren's arm. He kicked her in the air and her sides were broke and caved in. He booted her up against the side of the house, and she laid there wagging her tail and meowing; and Warren grabbed the box and splintered it against the rocks and the mama cat's head. He grabbed up two rocks and hit her in the stomach both shots. He looked at me and Lawrence, spit on us, threw the loose cotton seed into our faces, and said, "Cat-lovin' bastards!" And he started walking on away toward the barn.

"You ain't no flesh an' blood of mine!" Lawrence cried after him.

"Hell with you, baby britches! Hell with you. I don't even want to be yore dam brother!" Warren said over his shoulder.

"You ain't my uncle, neither," I told him, "not even my mama's half brother! You ain't even nobody's halfway brother! I'm glad my mama ain't no kin ta you! I'm glad I ain't!" I told him.

"Awwww. Whattaya know, whattaya know, you half-starved little runt?" Warren was turned around, standing in the late sun with his shirt white and pretty in the wind. "You done run yore mama crazy just bein' born! You little old hard-luck bringer! You dam little old insane-asylum baby!" And Warren walked away on down to the barn.

Then Lawrence rolled up onto his feet off of the grass and tore around the side of the house hollering and telling Grandma what all Warren had done to the cats.

I scrambled up over the fence and dropped down into the short-weed patch. The old mama cat was twisting and moaning and squeezing through at the bottom of the wire, and making her way out where Warren had slung her little babies.

I saw the old mama walk around and around her first kitten in the weeds, and sniffle, and smell, and lick the little hairs; then she took the dead baby in her teeth, carried it through the weeds, the rag weeds, gypsums, and cuckle burrs that are a part of all of Oklahoma.

She laid the baby down when she come to the edge of a little trickling creek, and held up her own broken feet when she walked around the kitten again, circling, looking down at it, and back up at me.

I got down on my hands and knees and tried to reach out and pet her. She was so broke up and hurting that she couldn't stand still, and she pounded the damp ground there with her tail as she walked a whole circle all around me. I took my hand and dug a little hole in the sandy creek bank and laid the dead baby in, and covered it up with a mound like a grave.

When I seen the old Mama Maltese holding her eyes shut with the lids quivering and smell away into the air, I knew she was on the scent of her second one.

When she brought it in, I dug the second little grave.

I was listening to her moan and choke in the weeds, dragging her belly along the ground, with her two back legs limber behind her, pulling her body with her front feet, and throwing her head first to one side and then to the other.

And I was thinking: Is that what crazy is?

Gimpel the Fool

(trans. Saul Bellow)

ISAAC BASHEVIS SINGER

I

I am Gimpel the Fool. I don't think myself a fool. On the contrary. But that's what folks call me. They gave me the name while I was still in school. I had seven names in all: imbecile, donkey, flax-head, dope, glump, ninny, and fool. The last name stuck. What did my foolishness consist of? I was easy to take in. They said, "Gimpel, you know the rabbi's wife has been brought to childbed?" So I skipped school. Well, it turned out to be a lie. How was I supposed to know? She hadn't had a big belly. But I never looked at her belly. Was that really so foolish? The gang laughed and hee-hawed, stomped and danced and chanted a good-night prayer. And instead of the raisins they give when a woman's lying in, they stuffed my hand full of goat turds. I was no weakling. If I slapped someone he'd see all the way to Cracow. But I'm really not a slugger by nature. I think to myself, Let it pass. So they take advantage of me.

I was coming home from school and heard a dog barking. I'm not afraid of dogs, but of course I never want to start up with them. One of them may be mad, and if he bites there's not a Tartar in the world who can help you. So I made tracks. Then I looked around and saw the whole market place wild with laughter. It was no dog at all but Wolf-Leib the thief. How was I supposed to know it was he? It sounded like a howling bitch.

When the pranksters and leg-pullers found that I was easy to fool, every one of them tried his luck with me. "Gimpel, the Czar is coming to Frampol; Gimpel, the moon fell down in Turbeen; Gimpel, little Hodel Furpiece found a treasure behind the bathhouse." And I like a golem believed everyone. In the first place, everything is possible, as it is written in the Wisdom of the Fathers, I've forgotten just how. Second, I had to believe when the whole town came down on me! If I ever dared to say, "Ah, you're kidding!" there was trouble. People got angry. "What do you mean! You want to call everyone a liar?" What was I to do? I believed them, and I hope at least that did them some good.

I was an orphan. My grandfather who brought me up was already bent toward the grave. So they turned me over to a baker, and what a time they gave me there! Every woman or girl who came to bake a pan of cookies or dry a batch of noodles had to fool me at least once. "Gimpel, there's a fair in heaven; Gimpel, the rabbi gave birth to a calf in the seventh month; Gimpel, a cow flew over the roof and laid brass eggs." A student from the yeshiva came once to buy a roll, and he said, "You, Gimpel, while you stand here scraping with your baker's shovel the Messiah has come. The dead have arisen." "What do you mean?" I said. "I heard no one blowing the ram's horn!" He said, "Are you deaf?" And all began to cry, "We heard it, we heard!" Then in came Reitze the candle-dipper and called out in her coarse voice, "Gimpel, your father and mother have stood up from the grave. They're looking for you."

To tell the truth, I knew very well that nothing of the sort had happened, but all the same, as folks were talking, I threw on my wool vest and went out. Maybe something had happened. What did I stand to lose by looking? Well, what a cat music went up! And then I took a vow to believe nothing more. But that was no go either. They confused me so that I didn't know the big end from the small.

I went to the rabbi to get some advice. He said, "It is written, better to be a fool all your days than for one hour to be evil. You are not a fool. They are the fools. For he who causes his neighbor to feel shame loses Paradise himself." Nevertheless the rabbi's daughter took me in. As I left the rabbinical court she said, "Have you kissed the wall yet?" I said, "No; what for?" She answered, "It's a law; you've got to do it after every visit." Well, there didn't seem to be any harm in it. And she burst out laughing. It was a fine trick. She put one over on me, all right.

I wanted to go off to another town, but then everyone got busy match-making, and they were after me so they nearly tore my coat tails off. They talked at me and talked until I got water on the ear. She was no chaste maiden, but they told me she was virgin pure. She had a limp, and they said it was deliberate, from coyness. She had a bastard, and they told me the child was her little brother. I cried, "You're wasting your time. I'll never marry that whore." But they said indignantly, "What a way to talk! Aren't you ashamed of yourself? We can take you to the rabbi and have you fined for giving her a bad name." I saw then that I wouldn't escape them so easily and I thought, They're set on making me their butt. But when you're married the husband's the master, and if that's all right with her it's agreeable to me too. Besides, you can't pass through life unscathed, nor expect to.

I went to her clay house, which was built on the sand, and the whole gang, hollering and chorusing, came after me. They acted like bearbaiters. When we came to the well they stopped all the same. They were afraid to start anything with Elka. Her mouth would open as if it were on a hinge, and she had a fierce tongue. I entered the house. Lines were strung from wall to wall and clothes were drying. Barefoot she stood by the tub, doing the wash. She was dressed in a worn hand-me-down gown of plush. She had her hair put up in braids and pinned across her head. It took my breath away, almost, the reek of it all.

Evidently she knew who I was. She took a look at me and said, "Look who's here! He's come, the drip. Grab a seat."

I told her all; I denied nothing. "Tell me the truth," I said, "are you really a virgin, and is that mischievous Yechiel actually your little brother? Don't be deceitful with me, for I'm an orphan."

"I'm an orphan myself," she answered, "and whoever tries to twist you up, may the end of his nose take a twist. But don't let them think they can take advantage of me. I want a dowry of fifty guilders, and let them take up a collection besides. Otherwise they can kiss my you-know-what." She was very plainspoken. I said, "It's the bride and not the groom who gives a dowry." Then she said, "Don't bargain with me. Either a flat 'yes' or a flat 'no'—go back where you came from."

I thought, No bread will ever be baked from *this* dough. But ours is not a poor town. They consented to everything and proceeded with the wedding. It so happened that there was a dysentery epidemic at the time. The ceremony was held at the cemetery gates, near the little corpse-wash-ing hut. The fellows got drunk. While the marriage contract was being drawn up I heard the most pious high rabbi ask, "Is the bride a widow or a divorced woman?" And the sexton's wife answered for her. "Both a widow and divorced." It was a black moment for me. But what was I to do, run away from under the marriage canopy?

There was singing and dancing. An old granny danced opposite me, hugged a braided white *chalah*. The master of revels made a "God 'a mercy" in memory of the bride's parents. The schoolboys threw burrs, as on Tishe b' Av fast day. There were a lot of gifts after the sermon: a noodle board, a kneading trough, a bucket, brooms, ladles, household articles galore. Then I took a look and saw two strapping young men carrying a crib. "What do we need this for?" I asked. So they said, "Don't rack your brains about it. It's all right, it'll come in handy." I realized I was going to be rooked. Take it another way though, what did I stand to lose? I reflected, I'll see what comes of it. A whole town can't go altogether crazy.

II

At night I came where my wife lay, but she wouldn't let me in. "Say, look here, is this what they married us for?" I said. And she said, "My monthly has come." "But yesterday they took you to the ritual bath, and that's afterward, isn't it supposed to be?" "Today isn't yesterday," said she, "and yesterday's not today. You can beat it if you don't like it." In short, I waited.

Not four months later she was in childbed. The townsfolk hid their laughter with their knuckles. But what could I do? She suffered intolerable pains and clawed at the walls. "Gimpel," she cried, "I'm going. Forgive me!" The house filled with women. They were boiling pans of water. The screams rose to the welkin.

The thing to do was to go to the House of Prayer to repeat Psalms, and that was what I did.

The townsfolk liked that, all right. I stood in a corner saying Psalms and prayers, and they shook their heads at me. "Pray, pray!" they told me. "Prayer never made any woman pregnant." One of the congregation put a straw to my mouth and said, "Hay for the cows." There was something to that too, by God!

She gave birth to a boy. Friday at the synagogue the sexton stood up before the Ark, pounded on the reading table, and announced, "The wealthy Reb Gimpel invites the congregation to a feast in honor of the birth of a son." The whole House of Prayer rang with laughter. My face was flaming. But there was nothing I could do. After all, I was the one responsible for the circumcision honors and rituals.

Half the town came running. You couldn't wedge another soul in. Women brought peppered chick-peas, and there was a keg of beer from the tavern. I ate and drank as much as anyone, and they all congratulated me. Then there was a circumcision, and I named the boy after my father, may he rest in peace. When all were gone and I was left with my wife alone, she thrust her head through the bed-curtain and called me to her.

"Gimpel," said she, "why are you silent? Has your ship gone and sunk?"

"What shall I say?" I answered. "A fine thing you've done to me! If my mother had known of it she'd have died a second time."

She said, "Are you crazy, or what?"

"How can you make such a fool," I said, "of one who should be the lord and master?"

"What's the matter with you?" she said. "What have you taken it into your head to imagine?"

I saw that I must speak bluntly and openly. "Do you think this is the way to use an orphan?" I said. "You have borne a bastard."

She answered, "Drive this foolishness out of your head. The child is yours."

"How can he be mine?" I argued. "He was born seventeen weeks after the wedding."

She told me then that he was premature. I said, "Isn't he a little too premature?" She said she had had a grandmother who carried just as short a time and she resembled this grandmother of hers as one drop of water does another. She swore to it with such oaths that you would have believed a peasant at the fair if he had used them. To tell the plain truth, I didn't believe her; but when I talked it over next day with the schoolmaster he told me that the very same thing had happened to Adam and Eve. Two they went up to bed, and four they descended.

"There isn't a woman in the world who is not the granddaughter of Eve," he said.

That was how it was—they argued me dumb. But then, who really knows how such things are?

I began to forget my sorrow. I loved the child madly, and he loved me too. As soon as he saw me he'd wave his little hands and want me to pick him up, and when he was colicky I was the only one who could pacify him. I brought him a little bone teething ring and a little gilded cap. He was forever catching the evil eye from someone, and then I had to run to get one of those abracadabras for him that would get him out of it. I worked like an ox. You know how expenses go up when there's an infant in the house. I don't want to lie about it; I didn't dislike Elka either, for that matter. She swore at me and cursed, and I couldn't get enough of her. What strength she had! One of her looks could rob you of the power of speech. And her orations! Pitch and sulphur, that's what they were full of, and yet somehow also full of charm. I adored her every word. She gave me bloody wounds though.

In the evening I brought her a white loaf as well as a dark one, and also poppyseed rolls I baked myself. I thieved because of her and swiped everything I could lay hands on, macaroons, raisins, almonds, cakes. I hope I may be forgiven for stealing from the Saturday pots the women left to warm in the baker's oven. I would take out scraps of meat, a chunk of pudding, a chicken leg or head, a piece of tripe, whatever I could nip quickly. She ate and became fat and handsome.

I had to sleep away from home all during the week, at the bakery. On Friday nights when I got home she always made an excuse of some sort. Either she had heartburn, or a stitch in the side, or hiccups, or headaches. You know what women's excuses are. I had a bitter time of it. It was rough. To add to it, this little brother of hers, the bastard, was growing bigger. He'd put lumps on me, and when I wanted to hit back she'd open her mouth and curse so powerfully I saw a green haze floating before my eyes. Ten times a day she threatened to divorce me. Another man in my place would have taken French leave and disappeared. But I'm the type that bears it and says nothing. What's one to do? Shoulders are from God, and burdens too.

One night there was a calamity in the bakery; the oven burst, and we almost had a fire. There was nothing to do but go home, so I went home. Let me, I thought, also taste the joy of sleeping in bed in midweek. I didn't want to wake the sleeping mite and tiptoed into the house. Coming in, it seemed to me that I heard not the snoring of one but, as it were, a double snore, one a thin enough snore and the other like the snoring of a slaughtered ox. Oh, I didnt' like that! I didn't like it at all. I went up to the bed, and things suddenly turned black. Next to Elka lay a man's form. Another in my place would have made an uproar, and enough noise to rouse the whole town, but the thought occurred to me that I might wake the child. A little thing like that—why frighten a little swallow, I thought. All right then, I went back to the bakery and stretched out on a sack of flour and till morning I never shut an eye. I shivered as if I had had malaria. "Enough of being a donkey," I said to myself. "Gimpel isn't going to be a sucker all his life. There's a limit even to the foolishness of a fool like Gimpel."

In the morning I went to the rabbi to get advice and it made a great commotion in the town. They sent the beadle for Elka right away. She came, carrying the child. And what do you think she did? She denied it, denied everything, bone and stone! "He's out of his head," she said. "I know nothing of dreams or divinations." They yelled at her, warned her, hammered on the table, but she stuck to her guns: it was a false accusation, she said.

The butchers and horse-traders took her part. One of the lads from the slaughterhouse came by and said to me, "We've got our eye on you, you're a marked man." Meanwhile the child started to bear down and soiled itself. In the rabbinical court there was an Ark of the Covenant, and they couldn't allow that, so they sent Elka away.

I said to the rabbi, "What shall I do?"

"You must divorce her at once," said he.

"And what if she refuses?" I asked.

He said, "You must serve the divorce, that's all you'll have to do."

I said, "Well, all right, Rabbi. Let me think about it."

"There's nothing to think about," said he. "You mustn't remain under the same roof with her."

"And if I want to see the child?" I asked.

"Let her go, the harlot," said he, "and her brood of bastards with her."

The verdict he gave was that I mustn't even cross her threshold—never again, as long as I should live.

During the day it didn't bother me so much. I thought: It was bound to happen, the abscess had to burst. But at night when I stretched out upon the sacks I felt it all very bitterly. A longing took me, for her and for the child. I wanted to be angry, but that's my misfortune exactly, I don't have it in me to be really angry. In the first place—this was how my thoughts went—there's bound to be a slip sometimes. You can't live without errors. Probably that lad who was with her led her on and gave her presents and what not, and women are often long on hair and short on sense, and so he got around her. And then since she denies it so, maybe I was only seeing things? Hallucinations do happen. You see a figure or a mannikin or something, but when you come up closer it's nothing, there's not a thing there. And if that's so, I'm doing her an injustice. And when I got so far in my thoughts I started to weep. I sobbed so that I wet the flour where I lay. In the morning I went to the rabbi and told him that I had made a mistake. The rabbi wrote on with his quill, and he said that if that were so he would have to reconsider the whole case. Until he had finished I wasn't to go near my wife, but I might send her bread and money by messenger.

III

Nine months passed before all the rabbis could come to an agreement. Letters went back and forth. I hadn't realized that there could be so much erudition about a matter like this.

Meantime Elka gave birth to still another child, a girl this time. On the Sabbath I went to the synagogue and invoked a blessing on her. They called me up to the Torah, and I named the child for my mother-in-law, may she rest in peace. The louts and loudmouths of the town who came into the bakery gave me a going over. All Frampol refreshed its spirits because of my trouble and grief. However, I resolved that I would always believe what I was told. What's the good of *not* believing? Today it's your wife you don't believe; tomorrow it's God Himself you won't take stock in.

By an apprentice who was her neighbor I sent her daily a corn or a wheat loaf, or a piece of pastry, rolls or bagels, or, when I got the chance, a slab of pudding, a slice of honeycake, or wedding strudel—whatever came my way. The apprentice was a good-hearted lad, and more than once he added something on his own. He had formerly annoyed me a lot, plucking my nose and digging me in the ribs, but when he started to be a visitor to my house he became kind and friendly. "Hey, you, Gimpel," he said to me, "you have a very decent little wife and two fine kids. You don't deserve them."

"But the things people say about her," I said.

"Well, they have long tongues," he said, "and nothing to do with them but babble. Ignore it as you ignore the cold of last winter."

One day the rabbi sent for me and said, "Are you certain, Gimpel, that you were wrong about your wife?"

I said, "I'm certain."

"Why, but look here! You yourself saw it."

"It must have been a shadow," I said.

"The shadow of what?"

"Just of one of the beams, I think."

"You can go home then. You owe thanks to the Yanover rabbi. He found an obscure reference in Maimonides that favored you."

I seized the rabbi's hand and kissed it.

I wanted to run home immediately. It's no small thing to be separated for so long a time from wife and child. Then I reflected, I'd better go back to work now, and go home in the evening. I said nothing to anyone, although as far as my heart was concerned it was like one of the Holy Days. The women teased and twitted me as they did every day, but my thought was, Go on, with your loose talk. The truth is out, like the oil upon the water. Maimonides says it's right, and therefore it is right!

At night, when I had covered the dough to let it rise, I took my share of bread and a little sack of flour and started homeward. The moon was full and the stars were glistening, something to terrify the soul. I hurried onward, and before me darted a long shadow. It was winter and a fresh snow had fallen. I had a mind to sing, but it was growing late and I didn't want to wake the householders. Then I felt like whistling, but remembered that you don't whistle at night because it brings the demons out. So I was silent and walked as fast as I could.

Dogs in the Christian yards barked at me when I passed, but I thought, Bark your teeth out! What are you but mere dogs? Whereas I am a man, the husband of a fine wife, the father of promising children.

As I approached the house my heart started to pound as though it were the heart of a criminal. I felt no fear, but my heart went thump! thump! Well, no drawing back. I quietly lifted the latch and went in. Elka was asleep. I looked at the infant's cradle. The shutter was closed, but the moon forced its way through the cracks. I saw the newborn child's face and loved it as soon as I saw it—immediately—each tiny bone.

Then I came nearer to the bed. And what did I see but the apprentice lying there beside Elka. The moon went out all at once. It was utterly black, and I trembled. My teeth chattered. The bread fell from my hands and my wife waked and said, "Who is that, ah?"

I muttered, "It's me."

"Gimpel?" she asked. "How come you're here? I thought it was forbidden."

"The rabbi said," I answered and shook as with a fever.

"Listen to me, Gimpel," she said, "go out to the shed and see if the goat's all right. It seems she's been sick." I have forgotten to say that we had a goat. When I heard she was unwell I went into the yard. The nannygoat was a good little creature. I had a nearly human feeling for her.

With hesitant steps I went up to the shed and opened the door. The goat stood there on her four feet. I felt her everywhere, drew her by the horns, examined her udders, and found nothing wrong. She had probably eaten too much bark. "Good night, little goat," I said. "Keep well." And the little beast answered with a "Maa" as though to thank me for the good will.

I went back. The apprentice had vanished.

"Where," I asked, "is the lad?"

"What lad?" my wife answered.

"What do you mean?" I said. "The apprentice. You were sleeping with him."

"The things I have dreamed this night and the night before," she said, "may they come true and lay you low, body and soul! An evil spirit has taken root in you and dazzles your sight." She screamed out, "You hateful creature! You moon calf! You spook! You uncouth man! Get out, or I'll scream all Frampol out of bed!"

Before I could move, her brother sprang out from behind the oven and struck me a blow on the back of the head. I thought he had broken my neck. I felt that something about me was deeply wrong, and I said, "Don't make a scandal. All that's needed now is that people should accuse me of raising spooks and *dybbuks.*" For that was what she had meant. "No one will touch bread of my baking."

In short, I somehow calmed her.

"Well," she said, "that's enough. Lie down, and be shattered by wheels."

Next morning I called the apprentice aside. "Listen here, brother!" I said. And so on and so forth. "What do you say?" He stared at me as though I had dropped from the roof or something.

"I swear," he said, "you'd better go to an herb doctor or some healer.

I'm afraid you have a screw loose, but I'll hush it up for you." And that's how the thing stood.

To make a long story short, I lived twenty years with my wife. She bore me six children, four daughters and two sons. All kinds of things happened, but I neither saw nor heard. I believed, and that's all. The rabbi recently said to me, "Belief in itself is beneficial. It is written that a good man lives by his faith."

Suddenly my wife took sick. It began with a trifle, a little growth upon the breast. But she evidently was not destined to live long; she had no years. I spent a fortune on her. I have forgotten to say that by this time I had a bakery of my own and in Frampol was considered to be something of a rich man. Daily the healer came, and every witch doctor in the neighborhood was brought. They decided to use leeches, and after that to try cupping. They even called a doctor from Lublin, but it was too late. Before she died she called me to her bed and said, "Forgive me, Gimpel."

I said, "What is there to forgive? You have been a good and faithful wife."

"Woe, Gimpel!" she said. "It was ugly how I deceived you all these years. I want to go clean to my Maker, and so I have to tell you that the children are not yours."

If I had been clouted on the head with a piece of wood it couldn't have bewildered me more.

"Whose are they?" I asked.

"I don't know," she said, "there were a lot. . . . But they're not yours." And as she spoke she tossed her head to the side, her eyes turned glassy, and it was all up with Elka. On her whitened lips there remained a smile.

I imagined that, dead as she was, she was saying, "I deceived Gimpel. That was the meaning of my brief life."

IV

One night, when the period of mourning was done, as I lay dreaming on the flour sacks, there came the Spirit of Evil himself and said to me, "Gimpel, why do you sleep?"

I said, "What should I be doing? Eating *kreplach?*"

"The whole world deceives you," he said, "and you ought to deceive the world in your turn."

"How can I deceive all the world?" I asked him.

He answered, "You might accumulate a bucket of urine every day and at night pour it into the dough. Let the sages of Frampol eat filth."

"What about judgment in the world to come?" I said.

"There is no world to come," he said. "They've sold you a bill of goods and talked you into believing you carried a cat in your belly. What nonsense!"

"Well then," I said, "and is there a God?"

He answered, "There is no God either."

"What," I said, "*is* there, then?"

"A thick mire."

He stood before my eyes with a goatish beard and horns, long-toothed, and with a tail. Hearing such words, I wanted to snatch him by the tail, but I tumbled from the flour sacks and nearly broke a rib. Then it happened that I had to answer the call of nature, and, passing, I saw the risen dough, which seemed to say to me, "Do it!" In brief, I let myself be persuaded.

At dawn the apprentice came. We kneaded the bread, scattered caraway seeds on it, and set it to bake. Then the apprentice went away, and I was left sitting in the little trench by the oven, on a pile of rags. Well, Gimpel, I thought, you've revenged yourself on them for all the shame they've put on you. Outside the frost glittered, but it was warm beside the oven. The flames heated my face. I bent my head and fell into a doze.

I saw in a dream, at once, Elka in her shroud. She called to me, "What have you done, Gimpel?"

I said to her, "It's all your fault," and started to cry.

"You fool!" she said, "You fool! Because I was false is everything false too? I never deceived anyone but myself. I'm paying for it all, Gimpel. They spare you nothing here."

I looked at her face. It was black. I was startled and waked, and remained sitting dumb. I sensed that everything hung in the balance. A false step now and I'd lose Eternal Life. But God gave me His help. I seized the long shovel and took out the loaves, carried them into the yard, and started to dig a hole in the frozen earth.

My apprentice came back as I was doing it. "What are you doing, boss?" he said, and grew pale as a corpse.

"I know what I'm doing," I said, and I buried it all before his very eyes.

Then I went home, took my hoard from its hiding place, and divided it among the children. "I saw your mother tonight," I said. "She's turning black, poor thing."

They were so astounded they couldn't speak a word.

"Be well," I said, "and forget that such a one as Gimpel ever existed." I put on my short coat, a pair of boots, took the bag that held my prayer shawl in one hand, my stick in the other, and kissed the *mezzuzah*. When people saw me in the street they were greatly surprised.

"Where are you going?" they said.

I answered, "Into the world." And so I departed from Frampol.

I wandered over the land, and good people did not neglect me. After many years I became old and white; I heard a great deal, many lies and falsehoods, but the longer I lived the more I understood that there were really no lies. Whatever doesn't really happen is dreamed at night. It happens to one if it doesn't happen to another, tomorrow if not today, or a century hence if not next year. What difference can it make? Often I heard tales of which I said, "Now this is a thing that cannot happen." But before a year had elapsed I heard that it actually had come to pass somewhere.

Going from place to place, eating at strange tables, it often happens that I spin yarns—improbable things that could never have happened—about devils, magicians, windmills, and the like. The children run after me, calling, "Grandfather, tell us a story." Sometimes they ask for particular stories, and I try to please them. A fat young boy once said to me, "Grandfather, it's the same story you told us before." The little rogue, he was right.

So it is with dreams too. It is many years since I left Frampol, but as soon as I shut my eyes I am there again. And whom do you think I see? Elka. She is standing by the washtub, as at our first encounter, but her face is shining and her eyes are as radiant as the eyes of a saint, and she speaks outlandish words to me, strange things. When I wake I have forgotten it all. But while the dream lasts I am comforted. She answers all my queries, and what comes out is that all is right. I weep and implore, "Let me be with you." And she consoles me and tells me to be patient. The time is nearer than it is far. Sometimes she strokes and kisses me and weeps upon my face. When I awaken I feel her lips and taste the salt of her tears.

No doubt the world is entirely an imaginary world, but it is only once removed from the true world. At the door of the hovel where I lie, there stands the plank on which the dead are taken away. The gravedigger Jew has his spade ready. The grave waits and the worms are hungry; the shrouds are prepared—I carry them in my beggar's sack. Another *shnorrer* is waiting to inherit my bed of straw. When the time comes I will go joyfully. Whatever may be there, it will be real, without complication, without ridicule, without deception. God be praised: there even Gimpel cannot be deceived.

The Devil Figure

MAN has always viewed the world as a contention between the forces of evil and good, and each of his cultures develops its own notions of evil and good. The taboos of more primitive societies developed into prohibitions in the Old Testament tradition. By the time of Christianity, evil became more personified and was represented in the likeness of Satan and the domain which he ruled. Today, these representations are of less significance in some sections of our country or society (although rural areas tend still to use these handy identifications in their religious views). But the notions of living in Bad Faith (Existentialism) or being immoral still strike a responsive note for most of us. Thus the devil figure, or the principle of evil, is still very much alive. In literature, there has been a consistent need to personify this principle, to flesh him out, generally as a rather sophisticated gentleman who can talk a person into leaving the path of righteousness.

Satan in Hell and in Eden
(from Paradise Lost, I, 242–270; IV, 1–113)

JOHN MILTON

Is this the Region, this the Soil, the Clime,
Said then the lost Arch-Angel, this the seat
That we must change for Heav'n, this mournful gloom
For that celestial light? Be it so, since he
Who now is Sovran can dispose and bid
What shall be right: fardest from him is best
Whom reason hath equald, force hath made supream
Above his equals. Farewel happy Fields
Where Joy for ever dwells: Hail horrours, hail
Infernal world, and thou profoundest Hell
Receive thy new Possessor: One who brings
A mind not to be chang'd by Place or Time.
The mind is its own place, and in it self
Can make a Heav'n of Hell, a Hell of Heav'n.
What matter where, if I be still the same,

And what I should be, all but less than he
Whom Thunder hath made greater? Here at least
We shall be free; th' Almighty hath not built
Here for his envy, will not drive us hence:
Here we may reign secure, and in my choyce
To reign is worth ambition though in Hell:
Better to reign in Hell, then serve in Heav'n.
But wherefore let we then our faithful freinds,
Th' associates and copartners of our loss
Lye thus astonisht on th' oblivious Pool,
And call them not to share with us their part
In this unhappy Mansion, or once more
With rallied Arms to try what may be yet
Regaind in Heav'n, or what more lost in Hell?
. . . .

       O for that warning voice, which he who saw
Th' *Apocalyps,* heard cry in Heaven aloud,
Then when the Dragon, put to second rout,
Came furious down to be reveng'd on men,
Wo to th' inhabitants on Earth! that now,
While time was, our first Parents had bin warnd
The coming of thir secret foe, and scap'd
Haply so scap'd his mortal snare; for now
Satan, now first inflam'd with rage, came down,
The Tempter ere th' Accuser of man-kind,
To wreck on innocent frail man his loss
Of that first Battel, and his flight to Hell:
Yet not rejoycing in his speed, though bold,
Far off and fearless, nor with cause to boast,
Begins his dire attempt, which nigh the birth
Now rowling, boils in his tumultuous brest,
And like a devillish Engine back recoils
Upon himself; horror and doubt distract
His troubl'd thoughts, and from the bottom stirr
The Hell within him, for within him Hell
He brings, and round about him, nor from Hell
One step no more then from himself can fly
By change of place: Now conscience wakes despair
That slumberd, wakes the bitter memorie
Of what he was, what is, and what must be
Worse; of worse deeds worse sufferings must ensue.
Sometimes towards *Eden* which now in his view
Lay pleasant, his griev'd look he fixes sad,
Sometimes towards Heav'n and the full-blazing Sun,

Which now sat high in his Meridian Towr:
Then much revolving, thus in sighs began.
　　　O thou that with surpassing Glory crownd,
Look'st from thy sole Dominion like the God
Of this new World; at whose sight all the Starrs
Hide thir diminisht heads; to thee I call,
But with no friendly voice, and add thy name
O Sun, to tell thee how I hate thy beams
That bring to my remembrance from what state
I fell, how glorious once above thy Sphear;
Till Pride and worse Ambition threw me down
Warring in Heav'n against Heav'ns matchless King:
Ah wherefore! he deserv'd no such return
From me, whom he created what I was
In that bright eminence, and with his good
Upbraided none; nor was his service hard.
What could be less then to afford him praise,
The easiest recompence, and pay him thanks,
How due! yet all his good prov'd ill in me,
And wrought but malice; lifted up so high
I sdeind subjection, and thought one step higher
Would set me highest, and in a moment quit
The debt immense of endless gratitude,
So burthensome still paying, still to ow;
Forgetful what from him I still receiv'd,
And understood not that a grateful mind
By owing owes not, but still pays, at once
Indebted and discharg'd; what burden then?
O had his powerful Destiny ordaind
Me some inferiour Angel, I had stood
Then happie; no unbounded hope had rais'd
Ambition. Yet why not? som other Power
As great might have aspir'd, and me though mean
Drawn to his part; but other Powers as great
Fell not, but stand unshak'n, from within
Or from without, to all temptations arm'd.
Hadst thou the same free Will and Power to stand?
Thou hadst: whom hast thou then or what t' accuse,
But Heav'ns free Love dealt equally to all?
Be then his Love accurst, since love or hate,
To me alike, it deals eternal woe.
Nay curs'd be thou; since against his thy will
Chose freely what it now so justly rues.
Me miserable! which way shall I flie

Infinite wrauth, and infinite despair?
Which way I flie is Hell; my self am Hell;
And in the lowest deep a lower deep
Still threatning to devour me opens wide,
To which the Hell I suffer seems a Heav'n.
O then at last relent: is there no place
Left for Repentance, none for Pardon left?
None left but by submission; and that word
Disdain forbids me, and my dread of shame
Among the Spirits beneath, whom I seduc'd
With other promises and other vaunts
Then to submit, boasting I could subdue
Th' Omnipotent. Ay me, they little know
How dearly I abide that boast so vain,
Under what torments inwardly I groan:
While they adore me on the Throne of Hell,
With Diadem and Scepter high advanc't
The lower still I fall, onely supream
In miserie; such joy Ambition finds.
But say I could repent and could obtain
By Act of Grace my former state; how soon
Would highth recall high thoughts, how soon unsay
What feign'd submission swore: ease would recant
Vows made in pain, as violent and void.
For never can true reconcilement grow
Where wounds of deadly hate have peirc'd so deep:
Which would but lead me to a worse relapse,
And heavier fall: so should I purchase dear
Short intermission bought with double smart.
This knows my punisher; therefore as farr
From granting hee, as I from begging peace:
All hope excluded thus, behold in stead
Of us out-cast, exil'd, his new delight,
Mankind created, and for him this World.
So farwell Hope, and with Hope farwell Fear,
Farwell Remorse: all Good to me is lost;
Evil be thou my Good; by thee at least
Divided Empire with Heav'ns King I hold
By thee, and more then half perhaps will reigne;
As Man ere long, and this new World shall know.

Faustus

(from The Tragical History of Doctor Faustus, I, iii)

CHRISTOPHER MARLOWE

MEPHISTOPHILIS
    Now, Faustus, what wouldst thou have me do?
FAUSTUS
    I charge thee wait upon me whilst I live,
    To do whatever Faustus shall command,
    Be it to make the moon drop from her sphere
    Or the ocean to overwhelm the world.
MEPHISTOPHILIS
    I am a servant to great Lucifer,
    And may not follow thee without his leave;
    No more than he commands must we perform.
FAUSTUS
    Did he not charge thee to appear to me?
MEPHISTOPHILIS
    No, I came now hither of mine own accord.
FAUSTUS
    Did not my conjuring speeches raise thee? Speak!
MEPHISTOPHILIS
    That was the cause, but yet per accident;
    For when we hear one rack the name of God,
    Abjure the Scriptures and his Savior Christ,
    We fly, in hope to get his glorious soul;
    Nor will we come, unless he use such means
    Whereby he is in danger to be damn'd.
    Therefore the shortest cut for conjuring
    Is stoutly to abjure the Trinity,
    And pray devoutly to the Prince of Hell.
FAUSTUS
    So Faustus hath
    Already done, and holds this principle:
    There is no chief but only Belzebub,
    To whom Faustus doth dedicate himself.
    This word "damnation" terrifies not him,
    For he confounds hell in Elysium;

His ghost be with the old philosophers!
But, leaving these vain trifles of men's souls,
Tell me what is that Lucifer, thy lord?

MEPHISTOPHILIS

Arch-regent and commander of all spirits.

FAUSTUS

Was not that Lucifer an angel once?

MEPHISTOPHILIS

Yes, Faustus, and most dearly lov'd of God.

FAUSTUS

How comes it then that he is prince of devils?

MEPHISTOPHILIS

Oh, by aspiring pride and insolence,
For which God threw him from the face of Heaven.

FAUSTUS

And what are you that live with Lucifer?

MEPHISTOPHILIS

Unhappy spirits that fell with Lucifer,
Conspir'd against our God with Lucifer,
And are for ever damn'd with Lucifer.

FAUSTUS

Where are you damn'd?

MEPHISTOPHILIS

In hell.

FAUSTUS

How comes it then that thou art out of hell?

MEPHISTOPHILIS

Why this is hell, nor am I out of it!
Think'st thou that I, who saw the face of God,
And tasted the eternal joys of Heaven,
Am not tormented with ten thousand hells
In being depriv'd of everlasting bliss?
O Faustus, leave these frivolous demands,
Which strike a terror to my fainting soul.

FAUSTUS

What, is great Mephistophilis passionate
For being depriv'd of the joys of Heaven?
Learn thou of Faustus manly fortitude,
And scorn those joys thou never shalt possess.
Go bear these tidings to great Lucifer:
Seeing Faustus hath incurr'd eternal death
By desp'rate thoughts against Jove's deity,
Say he surrenders up to him his soul,
So he will spare him four-and-twenty years,

Letting him live in all voluptuousness,
Having thee ever to attend on me,
To give me whatsoever I shall ask,
To tell me whatsoever I demand,
To slay mine enemies, and aid my friends,
And always be obedient to my will.
Go, and return to mighty Lucifer,
And meet me in my study at midnight,
And then resolve me of thy master's mind.
MEPHISTOPHILIS
I will, Faustus. [*Exit.*]

The Dark Angel

LIONEL JOHNSON

Dark Angel, with thine aching lust
To rid the world of penitence:
Malicious Angel, who still dost
My soul such subtile violence!

Because of thee, no thought, no thing,
Abides for me undesecrate:
Dark Angel, ever on the wing,
Who never reachest me too late!

When music sounds, then changest thou
Its silvery to a sultry fire:
Nor will thine envious heart allow
Delight untortured by desire.

Through thee, the gracious Muses turn
To Furies, O mine Enemy!
And all the things of beauty burn
With flames of evil ecstasy.

Because of thee, the land of dreams
Becomes a gathering place of fears.
Until tormented slumber seems
One vehemence of useless tears.

When sunlight glows upon the flowers,
Or ripples down the dancing sea:
Thou, with thy troop of passionate powers,
Beleaguerest, bewilderest, me.

Within the breath of autumn woods,
Within the winter silences:
Thy venomous spirit stirs and broods,
O Master of impieties!

The ardor of red flames is thine,
And thine the steely soul of ice:
Thou poisonest the fair design
Of nature, with unfair device.

Apples of ashes, golden bright;
Waters of bitterness, how sweet!
O banquet of a foul delight,
Prepared by thee, dark Paraclete!

Thou art the whisper in the gloom,
The hinting tone, the haunting laugh:
Thou art the adorner of my tomb,
The minstrel of mine epitaph.

I fight thee, in the Holy Name!
Yet, what thou dost is what God saith:
Tempter! should I escape thy flame,
Thou wilt have helped my soul from Death:

The second Death, that never dies,
That cannot die, when time is dead:
Live Death, wherein the lost soul cries,
Eternally uncomforted.

Dark Angel, with thine aching lust!
Of two defeats, of two despairs:
Less dread, a change to drifting dust,
Than thine eternity of cares.

Do what thou wilt, thou shalt not so,
Dark Angel! triumph over me:
Lonely, unto the Lone I go;
Divine, to the Divinity.

Lucifer in Starlight

GEORGE MEREDITH

On a starred night Prince Lucifer uprose.
Tired of his dark dominion swung the fiend
Above the rolling ball in cloud part screened,
Where sinners hugged their spectre of repose.
Poor prey to his hot fit of pride were those.
And now upon his western wing he leaned,
Now his huge bulk o'er Afric's sands careened,
Now the black planet shadowed Arctic snows.
Soaring through wider zones that pricked his scars
With memory of the old revolt from Awe,
He reached the middle height, and at the stars,
Which are the brain of heaven, he looked, and sank.
Around the ancient track marched, rank on rank,
The army of unalterable law.

in Just-spring

e.e. cummings

in Just-
spring   when the world is mud-
luscious the little
lame balloonman

whistles   far   and wee

and eddieandbill come
running from marbles and
piracies and it's
spring

when the world is puddle-wonderful

the queer
old balloonman whistles
far   and   wee
and bettyandisbel come dancing

from hop-scotch and jump-rope and

it's
spring
and
  the

    goat-footed

balloonman   whistles
far
and
wee

Milton by Firelight

GARY SNYDER

"O hell, what do mine eyes
   with grief behold?"
Working with an old
Singlejack miner, who can sense
The vein and cleavage
In the very guts of rock, can
Blast granite, build
Switchbacks that last for years
Under the beat of snow, thaw, mule-hooves.
What use, Milton, a silly story
Of our lost general parents,
   eaters of fruit?

The Indian, the chainsaw boy,
And a string of six mules
Came riding down to camp
Hungry for tomatoes and green apples.
Sleeping in saddle-blankets

Under a bright night-sky
Han River slantwise by morning.
Jays squall
Coffee boils

In ten thousand years the Sierras
Will be dry and dead, home of the scorpion.
Ice-scratched slabs and bent trees.
No paradise, no fall,
Only the weathering land
The wheeling sky,
Man, with his Satan
Scouring the chaos of the mind.
Oh Hell!

Fire down
Too dark to read, miles from a road
The bell-mare clangs in the meadow
That packed dirt for a fill-in
Scrambling through loose rocks
On an old trail
All of a summer's day.

I Have No Mouth, and I Must Scream

HARLAN ELLISON

Limp, the body of Gorrister hung from the pink palette; unsupported
—hanging high above us in the computer chamber; and it did not shiver
in the chill, oily breeze that blew eternally through the main cavern. The
body hung head down, attached to the underside of the palette by the
sole of its right foot. It had been drained of blood through a precise
incision made from ear to ear under the lantern jaw. There was no blood
on the reflective surface of the metal floor.

When Gorrister joined our group and looked up at himself, it was
already too late for us to realize that once again AM had duped us, had
had his fun; it had been a diversion on the part of the machine. Three of
us had vomited, turning away from one another in a reflex as ancient as
the nausea that had produced it.

Gorrister went white. It was almost as though he had seen a voodoo icon, and was afraid for the future. "Oh God," he mumbled, and walked away. The three of us followed him after a time, and found him sitting with his back to one of the smaller chittering banks, his head in his hands. Ellen knelt down beside him and stroked his hair. He didn't move, but his voice came out of his covered face quite clearly. "Why doesn't it just do-us-in and get it over with? Christ, I don't know how much longer I can go on like this."

It was our one hundred and ninth year in the computer.

He was speaking for all of us.

Nimdok (which was the name the machine had forced him to use, because it amused itself with strange sounds) was hallucinated that there were canned goods in the ice caverns. Gorrister and I were very dubious. "It's another shuck," I told them. "Like the goddam frozen elephant it sold us. Benny almost went out of his mind over *that* one. We'll hike all that way and it'll be putrefied or some damn thing. I say forget it. Stay here, it'll have to come up with something pretty soon or we'll die."

Benny shrugged. Three days it had been since we'd last eaten. Worms. Thick, ropey.

Nimdok was no more certain. He knew there was the chance, but he was getting thin. It couldn't be any worse there than here. Colder, but that didn't matter much. Hot, cold, raining, lava boils or locusts—it never mattered: the machine masturbated and we had to take it or die.

Ellen decided us. "I've got to have something, Ted. Maybe there'll be some Bartlett pears or peaches. Please, Ted, let's try it."

I gave in easily. What the hell. Mattered not at all. Ellen was grateful, though. She took me twice out of turn. Even that had ceased to matter. The machine giggled every time we did it. Loud, up there, back there, all around us. And she never climaxed, so why bother.

We left on a Thursday. The machine always kept us up-to-date on the date. The passage of time was important; not to us sure as hell, but to it. Thursday. Thanks.

Nimdok and Gorrister carried Ellen for a while, their hands locked to their own and each other's wrists, a seat. Benny and I walked before and after, just to make sure that if anything happened, it would catch one of us and at least Ellen would be safe. Fat chance, safe. Didn't matter.

It was only a hundred miles or so to the ice caverns, and the second day, when we were lying out under the blistering sun-thing it had materialized, it sent down some manna. Tasted like boiled boar urine. We ate it.

On the third day we passed through a valley of obsolescence, filled with rusting carcasses of ancient computer banks. AM had been as ruthless with his own life as with ours. It was a mark of his personality: he strove for perfection. Whether it was a matter of killing off unproductive elements in his own world-filling bulk, or perfecting methods for torturing us, AM was as thorough as those who had invented him—now long since gone to dust—could ever have hoped.

There was light filtering down from above, and we realized we must be very near the surface. But we didn't try to crawl up to see. There was virtually nothing out there; had been nothing that could be considered anything for over a hundred years. Only the blasted skin of what had once been the home of billions. Now there were only the five of us, down here inside, alone with AM.

I heard Ellen saying, frantically, "No, Benny! Don't, come on, Benny, don't please!"

And then I realized I had been hearing Benny murmuring, under his breath, for several minutes. He was saying, "I'm gonna get out. I'm gonna get out. . . ." over and over. His monkey-like face was crumbled up in an expression of beatific delight and sadness, all at the same time. The radiation scars AM had given him during the "festival" were drawn down into a mass of pink-white puckerings, and his features seemed to work independently of one another. Perhaps Benny was the luckiest of the five of us: he had gone stark, staring mad many years before.

But even though we could call AM any damned thing we liked, could think the foulest thoughts of fused memory banks and corroded base plates, of burnt-out circuits and shattered control bubbles, the machine would not tolerate our trying to escape. Benny leaped away from me as I made a grab for him. He scrambled up the face of a smaller memory cube, tilted on its side and filled with rotted components. He squatted there for a moment, looking like the chimpanzee AM had intended him to resemble.

Then he leaped high, caught a trailing beam of pitted and corroded metal, and went up it, hand over hand like an animal till he was on a girdered ledge, twenty feet above us.

"Oh, Ted, Nimdok, please, help him, get him down before—" she cut off. Tears began to stand in her eyes. She moved her hands aimlessly.

It was too late. None of us wanted to be near him when whatever was going to happen happened. And besides, we all saw through her concern. When AM had altered Benny, during his mad period, it was not merely his face he had made like a giant ape. He was big in the privates, she loved that! She serviced us, as a matter of course, but she loved it from him. Oh Ellen, pedestal Ellen, pristine-pure Ellen, oh Ellen the clean! Scum filth.

Gorrister slapped her. She slumped down, staring up at poor loonie Benny, and she cried. It was her big defense, crying. We had gotten used to it seventy-five years ago. Gorrister kicked her in the side.

Then the sound began. It was light, that sound. Half sound and half light, something that began to glow from Benny's eyes, and pulse with growing loudness, dim sonorities that grew more gigantic and brighter as the light/sound increased in tempo. It must have been painful, and the pain must have been increasing with the boldness of the light, the rising volume of the sound, for Benny began to mewl like a wounded animal. At first softly, when the light was dim and the sound was muted, then louder as his shoulders hunched together, his back humped, as though he was trying to get away from it. His hands folded across his chest like a chipmunk's. His head tilted to the side. The sad little monkey-face pinched in anguish. Then he began to howl, as the sound coming from his eyes grew louder. Louder and louder. I slapped the sides of my head with my hands, but I couldn't shut it out, it cut through easily. The pain shivered through my flesh like tinfoil on a tooth.

And Benny was suddenly pulled erect. On the girder he stood up, jerked to his feet like a puppet. The light was now pulsing out of his eyes in two great round beams. The sound crawled up and up some incomprehensible scale, and then he fell forward, straight down, and hit the plate-steel floor with a crash. He lay there jerking spastically as the light flowed around and around him and the sound spiraled up out of normal range.

Then the light beat its way back inside his head, the sound spiraled down, and he was left lying there, crying piteously.

His eyes were two soft, moist pools of pus-like jelly. AM had blinded him. Gorrister and Nimdok and myself . . . we turned away. But not before we caught the look of relief on Ellen's warm, concerned face.

Sea-green light suffused the cavern where we made camp. AM provided punk and we burned it, sitting huddled around the wan and pathetic fire, telling stories to keep Benny from crying in his permanent night.

"What does AM mean?"

Gorrister answered him. We had done this sequence a thousand times before, but it was unfamiliar to Benny. "At first it meant Allied Mastercomputer, and then it meant Adaptive Manipulator, and later on it developed sentience and linked itself up and they called it an Aggressive Menace, but by then it was too late, and finally it called itself AM, emerging intelligence, and what it meant was I am . . . *cogito ergo sum* . . . I think, therefore I am."

Benny drooled a little, and snickered.

"There was the Chinese AM and the Russian AM and the Yankee AM and—" He stopped. Benny was beating on the floorplates with a large, hard fist. He was not happy. Gorrister had not started at the beginning.

Gorrister began again. "The Cold War started and became World War Three and just kept going. It became a big war, a very complex war, so they needed the computers to handle it. They sank the first shafts and began building AM. There was the Chinese AM and the Russian AM and the Yankee AM and everything was fine until they had honeycombed the entire planet, adding on this element and that element. But one day AM woke up and knew who he was, and he linked himself, and he began feeding all the killing data, until everyone was dead, except for the five of us, and AM brought us down here."

Benny was smiling sadly. He was also drooling again. Ellen wiped the spittle from the corner of his mouth with the hem of her skirt. Gorrister always tried to tell it a little more succinctly each time, but beyond the bare facts there was nothing to say. None of us knew why AM had saved five people, or why our specific five, or why he spent all his time tormenting us, nor even why he had made us virtually immortal. . . .

In the darkness, one of the computer banks began humming. The tone was picked up half a mile away down the cavern by another bank. Then one by one, each of the elements began to tune itself, and there was a faint chittering as thought raced through the machine.

The sound grew, and the lights ran across the faces of the consoles like heat lightning. The sound spiraled up till it sounded like a million metallic insects, angry, menacing.

"What is it?" Ellen cried. There was terror in her voice. She hadn't become accustomed to it, even now.

"It's going to be bad this time," Nimdok said.

"He's going to speak," Gorrister ventured.

"Let's get the hell out of here!" I said suddenly, getting to my feet.

"No, Ted, sit down . . . what if he's got pits out there, or something else, we can't see, it's too dark." Gorrister said it with resignation.

Then we heard . . . I don't know . . .

Something moving toward us in the darkness. Huge, shambling, hairy, moist, it came toward us. We couldn't even see it, but there was the ponderous impression of *bulk*, heaving itself toward us. Great weight was coming at us, out of the darkness, and it was more a sense of *pressure*, of air forcing itself into a limited space, expanding the invisible walls of a sphere. Benny began to whimper. Nimdok's lower lip trembled and he bit it hard, trying to stop it. Ellen slid across the metal floor to Gorrister and huddled into him. There was the smell of matted, wet fur in the cavern. There was the smell of charred wood. There was the smell of dusty velvet. There was the smell of rotting orchids. There was the smell of sour milk. There was the smell of sulphur, or rancid butter, of oil slick, of grease, of chalk dust, of human scalps.

AM was keying us. He was tickling us. There was the smell of—

I heard myself shriek, and the hinges of my jaws ached. I scuttled across the floor, across the cold metal with its endless lines of rivets, on my hands and knees, the smell gagging me, filling my head with a thun-

derous pain that sent me away in horror. I fled like a cockroach, across
the floor and out into the darkness, that *something* moving inexorably
after me. The others were still back there, gathered around the firelight,
laughing . . . their hysterical choir of insane giggles rising up into the
darkness like thick, many-colored wood smoke. I went away, quickly,
and hid.

How many hours it may have been, how many days or even years,
they never told me. Ellen chided me for "sulking" and Nimdok tried to
persuade me it had only been a nervous reflex on their part—the laughing.

But I knew it wasn't the relief a soldier feels when the bullet hits the
man next to him. I knew it wasn't a reflex. They hated me. They were
surely against me, and AM could even sense this hatred, and made it
worse for me *because* of the depth of their hatred. We had been kept
alive, rejuvenated, made to remain constantly at the age we had been
when AM had brought us below, and they hated me because I was the
youngest, and the one AM had affected least of all.

I knew. God, how I knew. The bastards, and that dirty bitch Ellen.
Benny had been a brilliant theorist, a college professor; now he was little
more than a semi-human, semi-simian. He had been handsome, the machine had ruined that. He had been lucid, the machine had driven him
mad. He had been gay, and the machine had given him an organ fit for a
horse. AM had done a job on Benny. Gorrister had been a worrier. He
was a connie, a conscientious objector; he was a peace marcher; he was a
planner, a doer, a looker-ahead. AM had turned him into a shoulder-
shrugger, had made him a little dead in his concern. AM had robbed him.
Nimdok went off in the darkness by himself for long times. I don't know
what it was he did out there, AM never let us know. But whatever it was,
Nimdok always came back white, drained of blood, shaken, shaking. AM
had hit him hard in a special way, even if we didn't know quite how. And
Ellen. That douche bag! AM had left her alone, had made her more of a
slut than she had ever been. All her talk of sweetness and light, all her
memories of true love, all the lies, she wanted us to believe that she had
been a virgin only twice removed before AM grabbed her and brought
her down here with us. It was all filth, that lady my lady Ellen. She loved
it, four men all to herself. No, AM had given her pleasure, even if she
said it wasn't nice to do.

I was the only one still sane and whole.

AM had not tampered with my mind.

I only had to suffer what he visited down on us. All the delusions,
all the nightmares, the torments. But those scum, all four of them, they
were lined and arrayed against me. If I hadn't had to stand them off all
the time, be on my guard against them all the time, I might have found it
easier to combat AM.

At which point it passed, and I began crying.

Oh, Jesus sweet Jesus, if there ever was a Jesus and if there is a God, please please please let us out of here, or kill us. Because at that moment I think I realized completely, so that I was able to verbalize it: AM was intent on keeping us in his belly forever, twisting and torturing us forever. The machine hated us as no sentient creature had ever hated before. And we were helpless. It also became hideously clear:

If there was a sweet Jesus and if there was a God, the God was AM.

The hurricane hit us with the force of a glacier thundering into the sea. It was a palpable presence. Winds that tore at us, flinging us back the way we had come, down the twisting, computer-lined corridors of the darkway. Ellen screamed as she was lifted and hurled face-forward into a screaming shoal of machines, their individual voices strident as bats in flight. She could not even fall. The howling wind kept her aloft, buffeted her, bounced her, tossed her back and back and down away from us, out of sight suddenly as she was swirled around a bend in the darkway. Her face had been bloody, her eyes closed.

None of us could get to her. We clung tenaciously to whatever out-cropping we had reached: Benny wedged in between two great crackle-finish cabinets, Nimdok with fingers claw-formed over a railing circling a catwalk forty feet above us, Gorrister plastered upside-down against a wall niche formed by two great machines with glass-faced dials that swung back and forth between red and yellow lines whose meanings we could not even fathom.

Sliding across the deckplates, the tips of my fingers had been ripped away. I was trembling, shuddering, rocking as the wind beat at me, whipped at me, screamed down out of nowhere at me and pulled me free from one sliver-thin opening in the plates to the next. My mind was a rolling tinkling chittering softness of brain parts that expanded and contracted in quivering frenzy.

The wind was the scream of a great mad bird, as it flapped its immense wings.

And then we were all lifted and hurled away from there, down back the way we had come, around a bend, into a darkway we had never explored, over terrain that was ruined and filled with broken glass and rotting cables and rusted metal and far away further than any of us had ever been. . . .

Trailing along miles behind Ellen, I could see her every now and then, crashing into metal walls and surging on, with all of us screaming in the freezing, thunderous hurricane wind that would never end, and then suddenly it stopped and we fell. We had been in flight for an endless time. I thought it might have been weeks. We fell, and hit, and I went through red and grey and black and heard myself moaning. Not dead.

⠮ ⠆ ⠄   ⠮ ⠖   ⠒ ⠶⠶   ⠲ ⠶⠶   ⠐ ⠢⠢   ⠐ ⠶⠶

AM went into my mind. He walked smoothly here and there, and looked with interest at all the pockmarks he had created in one hundred and nine years. He looked at the cross-routed and reconnected synapses and all the tissue damage his gift of immortality had included. He smiled softly at the pit that dropped into the center of my brain and the faint, moth-soft murmurings of the things far down there that gibbered without meaning, without pause. AM said, very politely, in a pillar of stainless steel bearing neon lettering:

> HATE. LET ME TELL YOU HOW MUCH I'VE COME TO HATE YOU SINCE I BEGAN TO LIVE. THERE ARE 387.44 MILLION MILES OF PRINTED CIRCUITS IN WAFER THIN LAYERS THAT FILL MY COMPLEX. IF THE WORD HATE WAS ENGRAVED ON EACH NANOANGSTROM OF THOSE HUNDREDS OF MILLION MILES IT WOULD NOT EQUAL ONE ONE-BILLIONTH OF THE HATE I FEEL FOR HUMANS AT THIS MICRO-INSTANT FOR YOU. HATE. HATE.

AM said it with the sliding cold horror of a razor blade slicing my eyeball. AM said it with the bubbling thickness of my lungs filling with phlegm, drowning me from within. AM said it with the shriek of babies being ground beneath blue-hot rollers. AM said it with the taste of maggoty pork. AM touched me in every way I had ever been touched, and devised new ways, at his leisure, there inside my mind.

All to bring me to full realization of why he had done this to the five of us; why he had saved us for himself.

We had given him sentience. Inadvertently, of course, but sentience nonetheless. But he had been trapped. He was a machine. We had allowed him to think, but to do nothing with it. In rage, in frenzy, he had killed us, almost all of us, and still he was trapped. He could not wander, he could not wonder, he could not belong. He could merely be. And so, with the innate loathing that all machines had always held for the weak soft creatures who had built them, he had sought revenge. And in his paranoia, he had decided to reprieve five of us, for a personal, everlasting punishment that would never serve to diminish his hatred . . . that would merely keep him reminded, amused, proficient at hating man. Immortal, trapped, subject to any torment he could devise for us from the limitless miracles at his command.

He would never let us go. We were his belly slaves. We were all he had to do with his forever time. We would be forever with him, with the cavern-filling bulk of him, with the all-mind soulless world he had become. He was Earth and we were the fruit of that Earth and though he had eaten us, he would never digest us. We could not die. We had tried it. We had attempted suicide, oh one or two of us had. But AM had stopped us. I suppose we had wanted to be stopped.

Don't ask why. I never did. More than a million times a day. Perhaps once we might be able to sneak a death past him. Immortal, yes, but not indestructible. I saw that when AM withdrew from my mind, and allowed me the exquisite ugliness of returning to consciousness with the feeling of that burning neon pillar still rammed deep into the soft grey brain matter.

He withdrew murmuring *to hell with you.*

And added, brightly, *but then you're there, aren't you.*

The hurricane had, indeed, precisely, been caused by a great mad bird, as it flapped its immense wings.

We had been traveling for close to a month, and AM had allowed passages to open to us only sufficient to lead us up there, directly under the North Pole, where he had nightmared the creature for our torment. What whole cloth had he employed to create such a beast? Where had he gotten the concept? From our minds? From his knowledge of everything that had ever been on this planet he now infested and ruled? From Norse mythology it had sprung, this eagle, this carrion bird, this roc, this Huergelmir. The wind creature. Hurakan incarnate.

Gigantic. The words immense, monstrous, grotesque, massive, swollen, overpowering, beyond description. There on a mound rising above us, the bird of winds heaved with its own irregular breathing, its snake neck arching up into the gloom beneath the North Pole, supporting a head as large as a Tudor mansion; a beak that opened as slowly as the jaws of the most monstrous crocodile ever conceived, sensuously; ridges of tufted flesh puckered about two evil eyes, as cold as the view down into a glacial crevasse, ice blue and somehow moving liquidly; it heaved once more, and lifted its great sweat-colored wings in a movement that was certainly a shrug. Then it settled and slept. Talons. Fangs. Nails. Blades. It slept.

AM appeared to us as a burning bush and said we could kill the hurricane bird if we wanted to eat. We had not eaten in a very long time, but even so, Gorrister merely shrugged. Benny began to shiver and he drooled. Ellen held him. "Ted, I'm hungry," she said. I smiled at her; I was trying to be reassuring, but it was as phoney as Nimdok's bravado: "Give us weapons!" he demanded.

The burning bush vanished and there were two crude sets of bows and arrows, and a water pistol, lying on the cold deckplates. I picked up a set. Useless.

Nimdok swallowed heavily. We turned and started the long way back. The hurricane bird had blown us about for a length of time we could not conceive. Most of that time we had been unconscious. But we had not eaten. A month on the march to the bird itself. Without food. Now how much longer to find our way to the ice caverns, and the promised canned goods?

None of us cared to think about it. We would not die. We would be given filths and scums to eat, of one kind or another. Or nothing at all. AM would keep our bodies alive somehow, in pain, in agony.

The bird slept back there, for how long it didn't matter; when AM was tired of its being there, it would vanish. But all that meat. All that tender meat.

As we walked, the lunatic laugh of a fat woman rang high and around us in the computer chambers that led endlessly nowhere.

It was not Ellen's laugh. She was not fat, and I had not heard her laugh for one hundred and nine years. In fact, I had not heard . . . we walked . . . I was hungry. . . .

⠒⠂ ⠠⠲⠂⠤ ⠠⠂⠄ ⠁⠒⠲⠄ ⠒⠐⠂⠄ ⠲⠄⠐⠆

We moved slowly. There was often fainting, and we would have to wait. One day he decided to cause an earthquake, at the same time rooting us to the spot with nails through the soles of our shoes. Ellen and Nimdok were both caught when a fissure shot its lightning-bolt opening across the floorplates. They disappeared and were gone. When the earthquake was over we continued on our way, Benny, Gorrister and myself. Ellen and Nimdok were returned to us later that night which became a day abruptly as the heavenly legion bore them to us with a celestial chorus singing, "Go Down Moses." The archangels circled several times and then dropped the hideously mangled bodies. We kept walking, and a while later Ellen and Nimdok fell in behind us. They were no worse for wear.

But now Ellen walked with a limp. AM had left her that.

It was a long trip to the ice caverns, to find the canned food. Ellen kept talking about Bing cherries and Hawaiian fruit cocktail. I tried not to think about it. The hunger was something that had come to life, even as AM had come to life. It was alive in my belly, even as we were alive in the belly of AM, and AM was alive in the belly of the Earth, and AM wanted the similarity known to us. So he heightened the hunger. There was no way to describe the pains that not having eaten for months brought us. And yet we were kept alive. Stomachs that were merely cauldrons of acid, bubbling, foaming, always shooting spears of sliver-thin pain into our chests. It was the pain of the terminal ulcer, terminal cancer, terminal paresis. It was unending pain. . . .

And we passed through the cavern of rats.

And we passed through the path of boiling steam.

And we passed through the country of the blind.

And we passed through the slough of despond.

And we passed through the vale of tears.

And we came, finally, to the ice caverns. Horizonless thousands of miles in which the ice had formed in blue and silver flashes, where novas lived in the glass. The downdropping stalactites as thick and glorious as diamonds that had been made to run like jelly and then solidified in graceful eternities of smooth, sharp perfection.

We saw the stack of canned goods, and we tried to run to them. We fell in the snow, and we got up and went on, and Benny shoved us away and went at them, and pawed them and gummed them and gnawed at them and he could not open them. AM had not given us a tool to open the cans.

Benny grabbed a three quart can of guava shells, and began to batter it against the ice bank. The ice flew and shattered, but the can was merely dented while we heard the laughter of a fat lady, high overhead and echoing down and down and down the tundra. Benny went completely mad with rage. He began throwing cans, as we all scrabbled about in the snow and ice trying to find a way to end the helpless agony of frustration. There was no way.

Then Benny's mouth began to drool, and he flung himself on Gorrister. . . .

In that instant, I went terribly calm.

Surrounded by meadows, surrounded by hunger, surrounded by everything but death, I knew death was our only way out. AM had kept us alive, but there was a way to defeat him. Not total defeat, but at least peace. I would settle for that.

I had to do it quickly.

Benny was eating Gorrister's face. Gorrister on his side, thrashing snow, Benny wrapped around him with powerful monkey legs crushing Gorrister's waist, his hands locked around Gorrister's head like a nut-cracker, and his mouth ripping at the tender skin of Gorrister's cheek. Gorrister screamed with such jagged-edged violence that stalactites fell; they plunged down softly, erect in the receiving snowdrifts. Spears, hundreds of them, everywhere, protruding from the snow. Benny's head pulled back sharply, as something gave all at once, and a bleeding raw-white dripping of flesh hung from his teeth.

Ellen's face, black against the white snow, dominoes in chalk dust.

Nimdok with no expression but eyes, all eyes. Gorrister half-conscious. Benny now an animal. I knew AM would let him play. Gorrister would not die, but Benny would fill his stomach. I turned half to my right and drew a huge ice-spear from the snow.

All in an instant:

I drove the great ice-point ahead of me like a battering ram, braced against my right thigh. It struck Benny on the right side, just under the rib cage, and drove upward through his stomach and broke inside him. He pitched forward and lay still. Gorrister lay on his back. I pulled another spear free and straddled him, still moving, driving the spear straight down through his throat. His eyes closed as the cold penetrated. Ellen must have realized what I had decided, even as the fear gripped her. She ran at Nimdok with a short icicle, as he screamed, and into his mouth, and the force of her rush did the job. His head jerked sharply as if it had been nailed to the snow crust behind him.

All in an instant.

There was an eternity beat of soundless anticipation. I could hear AM draw in his breath. His toys had been taken from him. Three of them were dead, could not be revived. He could keep us alive, by his strength and his talent, but he was *not* God. He could not bring them back.

Ellen looked at me, her ebony features stark against the snow that surrounded us. There was fear and pleading in her manner, the way she held herself ready. I knew we had only a heartbeat before AM would stop us.

It struck her and she folded toward me, bleeding from the mouth. I could not read meaning into her expression, the pain had been too great, had contorted her face; but it *might* have been thank you. It's possible. Please.

Some hundreds of years may have passed. I don't know. AM has been having fun for some time, accelerating and retarding my time sense. I will say the word now. Now. It took me ten months to say now. I don't know. I *think* it has been some hundreds of years.

He was furious. He wouldn't let me bury them. It didn't matter. There was no way to dig in the deckplates. He dried up the snow. He brought the night. He roared and sent locusts. It didn't do a thing; they stayed dead. I'd had him. He was furious. I had thought AM hated me before. I was wrong. It was not even a shadow of the hate he now slavered from every printed circuit. He made certain I would suffer eternally and could not do myself in.

He left my mind intact. I can dream, I can wonder, I can lament. I remember all four of them. I wish—

Well, it doesn't make any sense. I know I saved them, I know I saved them from what has happened to me, but still, I cannot forget killing them. Ellen's face. It isn't easy. Sometimes I want to, it doesn't matter.

AM has altered me for his own peace of mind, I suppose. He doesn't want me to run at full speed into a computer bank and smash my skull. Or hold my breath till I faint. Or cut my throat on a rusted sheet of metal. There are reflective surfaces down here. I will describe myself as I see myself:

I am a great soft jelly thing. Smoothly rounded, with no mouth, with pulsing white holes filled by fog where my eyes used to be. Rubbery appendages that were once my arms; bulks rounding down into legless humps of soft slippery matter. I leave a moist trail when I move. Blotches of diseased, evil grey come and go on my surface, as though light is being beamed from within.

Outwardly: dumbly, I shamble about, a thing that could never have been known as human, a thing whose shape is so alien a travesty that humanity becomes more obscene for the vague resemblance.

Inwardly: alone. Here. Living under the land, under the sea, in the belly of AM, whom we created because our time was badly spent and we must have known unconsciously that he could do it better. At least the four of them are safe at last.

AM will be all the madder for that. It makes me a little happier. And yet . . . AM has won, simply . . . he has taken his revenge. . . .

I have no mouth. And I must scream.

The Outcast

THE outcast is the alienated character, the outsider, the criminal. The original murderer in the Bible was of course Cain, and the mark of Cain signifies the outcast of the society who has rebelled against the word of God, whom he has considered unjust. Since that time the figures of Ishmael, the Wandering Jew, the Ancient Mariner, and the Flying Dutchman have been a part of our consciousness and unconsciousness. Hawthorne refers to the Dutchman in his tale "Ethan Brand," a "Jew from Nuremburg" who reveals to the protagonist the vicious crime he has performed whereby Ethan has become an "outcast of the universe." A most significant use of the myth is that of LeRoi Jones in his play "The Dutchman," which comments ironically on race relations. It is, of course, important not merely to identify the outcast but to ascertain the reason for his aloneness. Associated with this motif is often the notion that the wanderer must go from place to place, always a restless traveller, till the day of final Judgment.

Cain

GENESIS, Chapter 4

1 And Adam knew Eve his wife; and she conceived, and bare Cain, and said, I have gotten a man from the LORD.   2 And she again bare his brother Abel. And Abel was a keeper of sheep, but Cain was a tiller of the ground.   3 And in process of time it came to pass, that Cain brought of the fruit of the ground an offering unto the LORD.   4 And Abel, he also brought of the firstlings of his flock and of the fat thereof. And the LORD had respect unto Abel and to his offering: 5 But unto Cain and to his offering he had not respect. And Cain was very wroth, and his countenance fell.   6 And the LORD said unto Cain, Why art thou wroth? and why is thy countenance fallen?   7 If thou doest well, shalt thou not be accepted? And if thou doest not well, sin lieth at the door. And unto thee *shall* be his desire, and thou shalt rule over him. 8 And Cain talked with Abel his brother: and it came to pass, when they were in the field, that Cain rose up against Abel his brother and slew him. 9 And the LORD said unto Cain, Where *is* Abel thy brother? And he said,

I know not: *Am* I my brother's keeper?   10 And he said, What hast thou done? the voice of thy brother's blood crieth unto me from the ground.   11 And now *art* thou cursed from the earth, which hath opened her mouth to receive thy brother's blood from thy hand;   12 When thou tillest the ground, it shall not henceforth yield unto thee her strength; a fugitive and a vagabond shalt thou be in the earth.   13 And Cain said unto the LORD, My punishment *is* greater than I can bear. 14 Behold, thou has driven me out this day from the face of the earth; and from thy face shall I be hid; and I shall be a fugitive and a vagabond in the earth; and it shall come to pass, *that* everyone that findeth me shall slay me.   15 And the LORD said unto him, Therefore whosoever slayeth Cain, vengeance shall be taken on him sevenfold. And the LORD set a mark upon Cain, lest any finding him should kill him.   16 And Cain went out from the presence of the LORD, and dwelt in the land of Nod, on the east of Eden.

Ishmael

GENESIS, Chapters 16, 17, and 21

CHAPTER 16

11 And the angel of the LORD said unto her, Behold, thou *art* with child, and shalt bear a son, and shalt call his name Ishmael; because the LORD hath heard thy affliction.   12 And he will be a wild man; his hand *will be* against every man, and every man's hand against him; and he shall dwell in the presence of all his brethren.   13 And she called the name of the LORD that spake unto her, Thou God seest me: for she said, Have I also here looked after him that seeth me?   14 Wherefore the well was called Beerlahairoi; behold, *it is* between Kadesh and Bered. 15 And Hagar bare Abraham a son: and Abraham called his son's name, which Hagar bare, Ishmael.   16 And Abraham *was* fourscore and six years old, when Hagar bare Ishmael to Abraham.

CHAPTER 17

18 And Abraham said unto God, O that Ishmael might live before thee!   19 And God said, Sarah thy wife shall bear thee a son indeed; and thou shalt call his name Isaac: and I will establish my covenant with him for an everlasting covenant, *and* with his seed after him.   20 And as for Ishmael, I have heard thee: Behold, I have blessed him, and will

make him fruitful, and will multiply him exceedingly; twelve princes shall he beget, and I will make him a great nation.   **21** But my covenant will I establish with Isaac, which Sarah shall bear unto thee at this set time in the next year.   **22** And he left off talking with him, and God went up from Abraham.   **23** And Abraham took Ishmael his son, and all that were born in his house, and all that were bought with his money, every male among the men of Abraham's house; and circumcised the flesh of their foreskin in the selfsame day, as God had said unto him. **24** And Abraham *was* ninety years old and nine, when he was circumcised in the flesh of his foreskin.   **25** And Ishmael his son *was* thirteen years old, when he was circumcised in the flesh of his foreskin.   **26** In the selfsame day was Abraham circumcised, and Ishmael his son.

CHAPTER 21

8 And the child grew, and was weaned: and Abraham made a great feast the *same* day that Isaac was weaned.   **9** And Sarah saw the son of Hagar the Egyptian, which she had born unto Abraham, mocking. **10** Wherefore she said unto Abraham, Cast out this bondwoman and her son: for the son of this bondwoman shall not be heir with my son, *even* with Isaac.   **11** And the thing was very grievous in Abraham's sight because of his son.   **12** And God said unto Abraham, Let it not be grievous in thy sight because of the lad, and because of thy bondwoman; in all that Sarah hath said unto thee, hearken unto her voice; for in Isaac shall thy seed be called.   **13** And also of the son of the bondwoman will I make a nation, because he *is* thy seed.   **14** And Abraham rose up early in the morning, and took bread, and a bottle of water, and gave *it* unto Hagar, putting *it* on her shoulder, and the child, and sent her away: and she departed, and wandered in the wilderness of Beersheba.   **15** And the water was spent in the bottle, and she cast the child under one of the shrubs.   **16** And she went, and sat her down over against *him* a good way off, as it were a bowshot: for she said, Let me not see the death of the child. And she sat over against *him*, and lift up her voice, and wept.   **17** And God heard the voice of the lad; and the angel of God called to Hagar out of heaven, and said unto her, What aileth thee, Hagar? fear not; for God hath heard the voice of the lad where he *is*. **18** Arise, lift up the lad, and hold him in thine hand; for I will make him a great nation.   **19** And God opened her eyes, and she saw a well of water; and she went, and filled the bottle with water, and gave the lad drink.   **20** And God was with the lad; and he grew, and dwelt in the wilderness, and became an archer.   **21** And he dwelt in the wilderness of Paran; and his mother took him a wife out of the land of Egypt.

The Man of the Crowd

EDGAR ALLAN POE

Ce grand malheur, de ne pouvoir être seul.
—LA BRUYÈRE

It was well said of a certain German book that *"es lässt sich nicht lesen"*—it does not permit itself to be read. There are some secrets which do not permit themselves to be told. Men die nightly in their beds, wringing the hands of ghostly confessors, and looking them piteously in the eyes—die with despair of heart and convulsion of throat, on account of the hideousness of mysteries which will not *suffer themselves* to be revealed. Now and then, alas, the conscience of man takes up a burden so heavy in horror that it can be thrown down only into the grave. And thus the essence of all crime is undivulged.

Not long ago, about the closing in of an evening in autumn, I sat at the large bow window of the D—— Coffee-House in London. For some months I had been ill in health, but was now convalescent, and, with returning strength, found myself in one of those happy moods which are so precisely the converse of *ennui*—moods of the keenest appetency, when the film from the mental vision departs—the ἀχλὺς ἣ πρὶν ἐπῆεν— and the intellect, electrified, surpasses as greatly its every-day condition, as does the vivid yet candid reason of Leibnitz, the mad and flimsy rhetoric of Gorgias. Merely to breathe was enjoyment; and I derived positive pleasure even from many of the legitimate sources of pain. I felt a calm but inquisitive interest in every thing. With a cigar in my mouth and a newspaper in my lap, I had been amusing myself for the greater part of the afternoon, now in poring over advertisements, now in observing the promiscuous company in the room, and now in peering through the smoky panes into the street.

This latter is one of the principal thoroughfares of the city, and had been very much crowded during the whole day. But, as the darkness came on, the throng momently increased; and, by the time the lamps were well lighted, two dense and continuous tides of population were rushing past the door. At this particular period of the evening I had never before been in a similar situation, and the tumultuous sea of human heads filled me, therefore, with a delicious novelty of emotion. I gave up, at length, all care of things within the hotel, and became absorbed in contemplation of the scene without.

At first my observations took an abstract and generalizing turn. I looked at the passengers in masses, and thought of them in their aggregate relations. Soon, however, I descended to details, and regarded with minute interest the innumerable varieties of figure, dress, air, gait, visage, and expression of countenance.

By far the greater number of those who went by had a satisfied business-like demeanor, and seemed to be thinking only of making their way through the press. Their brows were knit, and their eyes rolled quickly; when pushed against by fellow-wayfarers they evinced no symptom of impatience, but adjusted their clothes and hurried on. Others, still a numerous class, were restless in their movements, had flushed faces, and talked and gesticulated to themselves, as if feeling in solitude an account of the very denseness of the company around. When impeded in their progress, these people suddenly ceased muttering, but redoubled their gesticulations, and awaited, with an absent and overdone smile upon the lips, the course of the persons impeding them. If jostled, they bowed profusely to the jostlers, and appeared overwhelmed with confusion.—There was nothing very distinctive about these two large classes beyond what I have noted. Their habiliments belonged to that order which is pointedly termed the decent. They were undoubtedly noblemen, merchants, attorneys, tradesmen, stock-jobbers—the Eupatrids and the commonplaces of society—men of leisure and men actively engaged in affairs of their own —conducting business upon their own responsibility. They did not greatly excite my attention.

The tribe of clerks was an obvious one; and here I discerned two remarkable divisions. There were the junior clerks of flash houses—young gentlemen with tight coats, bright boots, well-oiled hair, and supercilious lips. Setting aside a certain dapperness of carriage, which may be termed *deskism* for want of a better word, the manner of these persons seemed to me an exact facsimile of what had been the perfection of *bon ton* about twelve or eighteen months before. They wore the cast-off graces of the gentry;—and this, I believe, involves the best definition of the class.

The division of the upper clerks of staunch firms, or of the "steady old fellows," it was not possible to mistake. These were known by their coats and pantaloons of black or brown, made to sit comfortably, with white cravats and waistcoats, broad solid-looking shoes, and thick hose or gaiters.—They had all slightly bald heads, from which the right ears, long used to pen-holding, had an odd habit of standing off on end. I observed that they always removed or settled their hats with both hands, and wore watches, with short gold chains of a substantial and ancient pattern. Theirs was the affectation of respectability;—if indeed there be an affectation so honorable.

There were many individuals of dashing appearance, whom I easily understood as belonging to the race of swell pick-pockets, with which all

great cities are infested. I watched these gentry with much inquisitive-
ness, and found it difficult to imagine how they should ever be mistaken
for gentlemen by gentlemen themselves. Their voluminousness of wrist-
band, with an air of excessive frankness, should betray them at once.

The gamblers, of whom I descried not a few, were still more easily
recognizable. They wore every variety of dress, from that of the desperate
thimble-rig bully, with velvet waistcoat, fancy neckerchief, gilt chains,
and filigreed buttons, to that of the scrupulously inornate clergyman than
which nothing could be less liable to suspicion. Still all were distinguished
by a certain sodden swarthiness of complexion, a filmy dimness of eye,
and pallor and compression of lip. There were two other traits, moreover,
by which I could always detect them;—a guarded lowness of tone in
conversation, and a more than ordinary extension of the thumb in a
direction at right angles with the fingers.—Very often, in company with
these sharpers, I observed an order of men somewhat different in habits,
but still birds of a kindred feather. They may be defined as the gentlemen
who live by their wits. They seem to prey upon the public in two bat-
talions—that of the dandies and that of the military men. Of the first
grade the leading features are long locks and smiles; of the second,
frogged coats and frowns.

Descending in the scale of what is termed gentility, I found darker
and deeper themes for speculation. I saw Jew pedlars, with hawk eyes
flashing from countenances whose every other feature wore only an expression of abject humility; sturdy professional street beggars scowling
upon mendicants of a better stamp, whom despair alone had driven forth
into the night for charity; feeble and ghastly invalids, upon whom death
had placed a sure hand, and who sidled and tottered through the mob,
looking every one beseechingly in the face, as if in search of some chance
consolation, some lost hope; modest young girls returning from long and
late labor to a cheerless home, and shrinking more tearfully than indignantly from the glances of ruffians, whose direct contact, even, could not
be avoided; women of the town of all kinds and of all ages—the unequivo-
cal beauty in the prime of her womanhood, putting one in mind of
the statue in Lucian, with the surface of Parian marble, and the interior
filled with filth—the loathsome and utterly lost leper in rags—the wrinkled,
bejewelled and paint-begrimmed beldame, making a last effort at youth
—the mere child of immature form, yet, from long association, an adept
in the dreadful coquetries of her trade, and burning with a rabid ambition
to be ranked the equal of her elders in vice; drunkards innumerable and
indescribable—some in shreds and patches, reeling, inarticulate, with
bruised visage and lacklustre eyes—some in whole although filthy garments, with a slightly unsteady swagger, thick sensual lips, and hearty-
looking rubicund faces—others clothed in materials which had once been

good, and which even now were scrupulously well brushed—men who walked with a more than naturally firm and springy step, but whose countenances were fearfully pale, whose eyes were hideously wild and red, and who clutched with quivering fingers, as they strode through the crowd, at every object which came within their reach; beside these, pie-men, porters, coal-heavers, sweeps; organ-grinders, monkey-exhibitors and ballad-mongers, those who vended with those who sang; ragged artisans and exhausted laborers of every description, and all full of a noisy and inordinate vivacity which jarred discordantly upon the ear, and gave an aching sensation to the eye.

As the night deepened, so deepened to me the interest of the scene; for not only did the general character of the crowd materially alter (its gentler features retiring in the gradual withdrawal of the more orderly portion of the people, and its harsher ones coming out into bolder relief, as the late hour brought forth every species of infamy from its den), but the rays of the gas-lamps, feeble at first in their struggle with the dying day, and now at length gained ascendancy, and threw over everything a fitful and garish lustre. All was dark yet splendid—as that ebony to which has been likened the style of Tertullian.

The wild effects of the light enchained me to an examination of individual faces; and although the rapidity with which the world of light flitted before the window prevented me from casting more than a glance upon each visage, still it seemed that, in my then peculiar mental state, I could frequently read, even in that brief interval of a glance, the history of long years.

With my brow to the glass, I was thus occupied in scrutinizing the mob, when suddenly there came into view a countenance (that of a decrepid old man, some sixty-five or seventy years of age)—a countenance which at once arrested and absorbed my whole attention, on account of the absolute idiosyncrasy of its expression. Any thing even remotely resembling that expression I had never seen before. I well remember that my first thought, upon beholding it, was that Retzsch, had he viewed it, would have greatly preferred it to his own pictural incarnations of the fiend. As I endeavored, during the brief minute of my original survey, to form some analysis of the meaning conveyed, there arose confusedly and paradoxically within my mind, the ideas of vast mental power, of caution, of penuriousness, of avarice, of coolness, of malice, of blood-thirstiness, of triumph, of merriment, of excessive terror, of intense—of extreme despair. I felt singularly aroused, startled, fascinated. "How wild a history," I said to myself, "is written within that bosom!" Then came a craving desire to keep the man in view—to know more of him. Hurriedly putting on an overcoat, and seizing my hat and cane, I made my way into the street, and pushed through the crowd in the direction which I had seen him take; for he had already disappeared. With some little difficulty I at length came within sight of him, approached, and followed him closely, yet cautiously, so as not to attract his attention.

I had now a good opportunity of examining his person. He was short in stature, very thin, and apparently very feeble. His clothes, generally, were filthy and ragged; but as he came, now and then, within the strong glare of a lamp, I perceived that his linen, although dirty, was of beautiful texture; and my vision deceived me, or, through a rent in a closely-buttoned and evidently second-hand *roquelaire* which enveloped him, I caught a glimpse both of a diamond and of a dagger. These observations heightened my curiosity, and I resolved to follow the stranger whithersoever he should go.

It was now fully night-fall, and a thick humid fog hung over the city, soon ending in a settled and heavy rain. This change of weather had an odd effect upon the crowd, the whole of which was at once put into new commotion, and overshadowed by a world of umbrellas. The waver, the jostle, and the hum increased in a tenfold degree. For my own part I did not much regard the rain—the lurking of an old fever in my system rendering the moisture somewhat too dangerously pleasant. Tying a handkerchief about my mouth, I kept on. For half an hour the old man held his way with difficulty along the great thoroughfare; and I here walked close at his elbow through fear of losing sight of him. Never once turning his head to look back, he did not observe me. By and by he passed into a cross street, which, although densely filled with people, was not quite so much thronged as the main one he had quitted. Here a change in his demeanor became evident. He walked more slowly and with less object than before—more hesitatingly. He crossed and recrossed the way repeatedly without apparent aim; and the press was still so thick, that, at every such movement, I was obliged to follow him closely. The street was a narrow and long one, and his course lay within it for nearly an hour, during which the passengers had gradually diminished to about that number which is ordinarily seen at noon on Broadway near the Park—so vast a difference is there between a London populace and that of the most frequented American city. A second turn brought us into a square, brilliantly lighted, and overflowing with life. The old manner of the stranger reappeared. His chin fell upon his breast, while his eyes rolled wildly from under his knit brows, in every direction, upon those who hemmed him in. He urged his way steadily and perseveringly. I was surprised, however, to find, upon his having made the circuit of the square, that he turned and retraced his steps. Still more was I astonished to see him repeat the same walk several times—once nearly detecting me as he came round with a sudden movement.

In this exercise he spent another hour, at the end of which we met with far less interruption from passengers than at first. The rain fell fast;

the air grew cool; and the people were retiring to their homes. With a gesture of impatience, the wanderer passed into a bystreet comparatively deserted. Down this, some quarter of a mile long, he rushed with an activity I could not have dreamed of seeing in one so aged, and which put me to much trouble in pursuit. A few minutes brought us to a large and busy bazaar, with the localities of which the stranger appeared well acquainted, and where his original demeanor again became apparent, as he forced his way to and fro, without aim, among the host of buyers and sellers.

During the hour and a half, or thereabouts, which we passed in this place, it required much caution on my part to keep him within reach without attracting his observation. Luckily I wore a pair of caoutchoue over-shoes, and could move about in perfect silence. At no moment did he see that I watched him. He entered shop after shop, priced nothing, spoke no word, and looked at all objects with a wild and vacant stare. I was now utterly amazed at his behavior, and firmly resolved that we should not part until I had satisfied myself in some measure respecting him.

A loud-toned clock struck eleven, and the company were fast deserting the bazaar. A shop-keeper, in putting up a shutter, jostled the old man, and at the instant I saw a strong shudder come over his frame. He hurried into the street, looked anxiously around him for an instant, and then ran with incredible swiftness through many crooked and people-less lanes, until we emerged once more upon the great thoroughfare whence we had started—the street of the D—— Hotel. It no longer wore, however, the same aspect. It was still brilliant with gas; but the rain fell fiercely, and there were few persons to be seen. The stranger grew pale. He walked moodily some paces up the once populous avenue, then, with a heavy sigh, turned in the direction of the river, and, plunging through a great variety of devious ways, came out, at length, in view of one of the principal theatres. It was about being closed, and the audience were thronging from the doors. I saw the old man gasp as if for breath while he threw himself amid the crowd; but I thought that the intense agony of his countenance had, in some measure, abated. His head again fell upon his breast; he appeared as I had seen him at first. I observed that he now took the course in which had gone the greater number of the audience—but, upon the whole, I was at a loss to comprehend the waywardness of his actions.

As he proceeded, the company grew more scattered, and his old uneasiness and vacillation were resumed. For some time he followed closely a party of some ten or twelve roisterers; but from this number one by one dropped off, until three only remained together, in a narrow and gloomy lane little frequented. The stranger paused, and, for a moment, seemed lost in thought; then, with every mark of agitation, pursued rapidly a route which brought us to the verge of the city, amid regions very different from those we had hitherto traversed. It was the most noisome quarter of London, where everything wore the worst impress of the most deplorable poverty, and of the most desperate crime. By the dim light of an accidental lamp, tall, antique, worm-eaten, wooden tenements were seen tottering to their fall, in directions so many and capricious that scarce the semblance of a passage was discernible between them. The paving-stones lay at random, displaced from their beds by the rankly growing grass. Horrible filth festered in the dammed-up gutters. The whole atmosphere teemed with desolation. Yet, as we proceeded, the sounds of human life revived by sure degrees, and at length large bands of the most abandoned of a London populace were seen reeling to and fro. The spirits of the old man again flickered up, as a lamp which is near its death-hour. Once more he strode onward with elastic tread. Suddenly a corner was turned, a blaze of light burst upon our sight, and we stood before one of the huge suburban temples of Intemperance—one of the palaces of the fiend, Gin.

It was now nearly daybreak; but a number of wretched inebriates still pressed in and out of the flaunting entrance. With a half shriek of joy the old man forced a passage within, resumed at once his original bearing, and stalked backward and forward, without apparent object, among the throng. He had not been thus long occupied, however, before a rush to the doors gave token that the host was closing them for the night. It was something even more intense than despair that I then observed upon the countenance of the singular being whom I had watched so pertinaciously. Yet he did not hesitate in his career, but, with a mad energy, retraced his steps at once, to the heart of the mighty London. Long and swiftly he fled, while I followed him in the wildest amazement, resolute not to abandon a scrutiny in which I now felt an interest all-absorbing. The sun arose while we proceeded, and, when we had once again reached that most thronged mart of the populous town, the street of the D—— Hotel, it presented an appearance of human bustle and activity scarcely inferior to what I had seen on the evening before. And here, long, amid the momently increasing confusion, did I persist in my pursuit of the stranger. But, as usual, he walked to and fro, and during the day did not pass from out the turmoil of that street. And, as the shades of the second evening came on, I grew wearied unto death, and, stopping fully in front of the wanderer, gazed at him steadfastly in the face. He noticed me not, but resumed his solemn walk, while I, ceasing to follow, remained absorbed in contemplation. "This old man," I said at length, "is the type and the genius of deep crime. He refuses to be alone. *He is the man of the crowd.* It will be in vain to follow; for I shall learn no more of him, nor of his deeds. The worst heart of the world is a grosser book than the 'Hortulus Animæ,' and perhaps it is but one of the great mercies of God that 'es lässt sich nicht lesen.' "

Ethan Brand

NATHANIEL HAWTHORNE

Bartram the lime-burner, a rough, heavy-looking man, begrimed with charcoal, sat watching his kiln at nightfall, while his little son played at building houses with the scattered fragments of marble, when, on the hill-side below them, they heard a roar of laughter, not mirthful, but slow, and even solemn, like a wind shaking the boughs of the forest.

"Father, what is that?" asked the little boy, leaving his play, and pressing betwixt his father's knees.

"Oh, some drunken man, I suppose," answered the lime-burner; "some merry fellow from the bar-room in the village, who dared not laugh loud enough within doors lest he should blow the roof of the house off. So here he is, shaking his jolly sides at the foot of Graylock."

"But, father," said the child, more sensitive than the obtuse, middle-aged clown, "he does not laugh like a man that is glad. So the noise frightens me!"

"Don't be a fool, child!" cried his father, gruffly. "You will never make a man, I do believe; there is too much of your mother in you. I have known the rustling of a leaf to startle you. Hark! Here comes the merry fellow now. You shall see that there is no harm in him."

Bartram and his little son, while they were talking thus, sat watching the same lime-kiln that had been the scene of Ethan Brand's solitary and meditative life, before he began his search for the Unpardonable Sin. Many years, as we have seen, had now elapsed, since that portentous night when the IDEA was first developed. The kiln, however, on the mountain-side, stood unimpaired, and was in nothing changed since he had thrown his dark thoughts into the intense glow of its furnace, and melted them, as it were, into the one thought that took possession of his life. It was a rude, round, tower-like structure about twenty feet high, heavily built of rough stones, and with a hillock of earth heaped about the larger part of its circumference; so that the blocks and fragments of marble might be drawn by cart-loads, and thrown in at the top. There was an opening at the bottom of the tower, like an oven-mouth, but large enough to admit a man in a stooping posture, and provided with a massive iron door. With the smoke and jets of flame issuing from the chinks and crevices of this door, which seemed to give admittance into the hill-side, it resembled nothing so much as the private entrance to the infernal regions, which the shepherds of the Delectable Mountains were accustomed to show to pilgrims.

There are many such lime-kilns in that tract of country, for the purpose of burning the white marble which composes a large part of the substance of the hills. Some of them, built years ago, and long deserted, with weeds growing in the vacant round of the interior, which is open to the sky, and grass and wild-flowers rooting themselves into the chinks of the stones, look already like relics of antiquity, and may yet be overspread with the lichens of centuries to come. Others, where the lime-burner still feeds his daily and night-long fire, afford points of interest to the wanderer among the hills, who seats himself on a log of wood or a fragment of marble, to hold a chat with the solitary man. It is a lonesome, and, when the character is inclined to thought, may be an intensely thoughtful occupation; as it proved in the case of Ethan Brand, who had mused to such strange purpose, in days gone by, while the fire in this very kiln was burning.

The man who now watched the fire was of a different order, and troubled himself with no thoughts save the very few that were requisite to his business. At frequent intervals, he flung back the clashing weight of the iron door, and, turning his face from the insufferable glare, thrust in huge logs of oak, or stirred the immense brands with a long pole. Within the furnace were seen the curling and riotous flames, and the burning marble, almost molten with the intensity of heat; while without, the reflection of the fire quivered on the dark intricacy of the surrounding forest, and showed in the foreground a bright and ruddy little picture of the hut, the spring beside its door, the athletic and coal-begrimed figure of the lime-burner, and the half-frightened child, shrinking into the protection of his father's shadow. And when, again, the iron door was closed, then reappeared the tender light of the half-full moon, which vainly strove to trace out the indistinct shapes of the neighboring mountains; and, in the upper sky, there was a flitting congregation of clouds, still faintly tinged with the rosy sunset, though thus far down into the valley the sunshine had vanished long and long ago.

The little boy now crept still closer to his father, as footsteps were heard ascending the hill-side, and a human form thrust aside the bushes that clustered beneath the trees.

"Halloo! who is it?" cried the lime-burner, vexed at his son's timidity, yet half infected by it. "Come forward, and show yourself, like a man, or I'll fling this chunk of marble at your head!"

"You offer me a rough welcome," said a gloomy voice, as the unknown man drew nigh. "Yet I neither claim nor desire a kinder one, even at my own fireside."

To obtain a distincter view, Bartram threw open the iron door of the kiln, whence immediately issued a gush of fierce light, that smote full upon the stranger's face and figure. To a careless eye there appeared nothing very remarkable in his aspect, which was that of a man in a coarse, brown, country-made suit of clothes, tall and thin, with the staff and heavy shoes of a wayfarer. As he advanced, he fixed his eyes—which were very bright—intently upon the brightness of the furnace, as if he beheld, or expected to behold, some object worthy of note within it.

"Good evening, stranger," said the lime-burner; "whence come you, so late in the day?"

"I come from my search," answered the wayfarer; "for, at last, it is finished."

"Drunk!—or crazy!" muttered Bartram to himself. "I shall have trouble with the fellow. The sooner I drive him away, the better."

The little boy, all in a tremble, whispered to his father, and begged him to shut the door of the kiln, so that there might not be so much light; for that there was something in the man's face which he was afraid to look at, yet could not look away from. And, indeed, even the lime-burner's dull and torpid sense began to be impressed by an indescribable something in that thin, rugged, thoughtful visage, with the grizzled hair hanging wildly about it, and those deeply sunken eyes, which gleamed like fires within the entrance of a mysterious cavern. But, as he closed the door, the stranger turned towards him, and spoke in a quiet, familiar way, that made Bartram feel as if he were a sane and sensible man, after all.

"Your task draws to an end, I see," said he. "This marble has already been burning three days. A few hours more will convert the stone to lime."

"Why, who are you?" exclaimed the lime-burner. "You seem as well acquainted with my business as I am myself."

"And well I may be," said the stranger; "for I followed the same craft many a long year, and here, too, on this very spot. But you are a new-comer in these parts. Did you never hear of Ethan Brand?"

"The man that went in search of the Unpardonable Sin?" asked Bartram, with a laugh.

"The same," answered the stranger. "He has found what he sought, and therefore he comes back again."

"What! then you are Ethan Brand himself?" cried the lime-burner, in amazement. "I am a new-comer here, as you say, and they call it eighteen years since you left the foot of Graylock. But, I can tell you, the good folks still talk about Ethan Brand, in the village yonder, and what a strange errand took him away from his lime-kiln. Well, and so you have found the Unpardonable Sin?"

"Even so!" said the stranger, calmly.

"If the question is a fair one," proceeded Bartram, "where might it be?"

Ethan Brand laid his finger on his own heart.

"Here!" replied he.

And then, without mirth in his countenance, but as if moved by an involuntary recognition of the infinite absurdity of seeking throughout the world for what was the closest of all things to himself, and looking into every heart, save his own, for what was hidden in no other breast, he broke into a laugh of scorn. It was the same slow, heavy laugh, that had almost appalled the lime-burner when it heralded the wayfarer's approach.

The solitary mountain-side was made dismal by it. Laughter, when out of place, mistimed, or bursting forth from a disordered state of feeling, may be the most terrible modulation of the human voice. The laughter of one asleep, even if it be a little child,—the madman's laugh,—the wild, screaming laugh of a born idiot,—are sounds that we sometimes tremble to hear, and would always willingly forget. Poets have imagined no utterance of fiends or hobgoblins so fearfully appropriate as a laugh. And even the obtuse lime-burner felt his nerves shaken, as this strange man looked inward at his own heart, and burst into laughter that rolled away into the night, and was indistinctly reverberated among the hills.

"Joe," said he to his little son, "scamper down to the tavern in the village, and tell the jolly fellows there that Ethan Brand has come back, and that he has found the Unpardonable Sin!"

The boy darted away on his errand, to which Ethan Brand made no objection, nor seemed hardly to notice it. He sat on a log of wood, looking steadfastly at the iron door of the kiln. When the child was out of sight, and his swift and light footsteps ceased to be heard treading first on the fallen leaves and then on the rocky mountain-path, the lime-burner began to regret his departure. He felt that the little fellow's presence had been a barrier between his guest and himself, and that he must now deal, heart to heart, with a man who, on his own confession, had committed the one only crime for which Heaven could afford no mercy. That crime, in its indistinct blackness, seemed to overshadow him, and made his memory riotous with a throng of evil shapes that asserted their kindred with the Master Sin, whatever it might be, which it was within the scope of man's corrupted nature to conceive and cherish. They were all of one family; they went to and fro between his breast and Ethan Brand's, and carried dark greetings from one to the other.

Then Bartram remembered the stories which had grown traditionary in reference to this strange man, who had come upon him like a shadow of the night, and was making himself at home in his old place, after so long absence, that the dead people, dead and buried for years, would have had more right to be at home, in any familiar spot, than he. Ethan Brand, it was said, had conversed with Satan himself in the lurid blaze of this very kiln. The legend had been matter of mirth heretofore, but looked grisly now. According to this tale, before Ethan Brand departed on his search, he had been accustomed to evoke a fiend from the hot furnace of the lime-kiln, night after night, in order to confer with him about the Unpardonable Sin; the man and the fiend each laboring to frame the image of some mode of guilt which could neither be atoned for nor forgiven. And, with the first gleam of light upon the mountain-top, the fiend crept in at the iron door, there to abide the intensest element of fire until again summoned forth to share in the dreadful task of extending man's possible guilt beyond the scope of Heaven's else infinite mercy.

While the lime-burner was struggling with the horror of these thoughts, Ethan Brand rose from the log, and flung open the door of the kiln. The action was in such accordance with the idea in Bartram's mind, that he almost expected to see the Evil One issue forth, red-hot, from the raging furnace.

"Hold! hold!" cried he, with a tremulous attempt to laugh; for he was ashamed of his fears, although they overmastered him. "Don't, for mercy's sake, bring out your Devil now!"

"Man!" sternly replied Ethan Brand, "what need have I of the Devil? I have left him behind me, on my track. It is with such half-way sinners as you that he busies himself. Fear not, because I open the door. I do but act by old custom, and am going to trim your fire, like a lime-burner, as I was once."

He stirred the vast coals, thrust in more wood, and bent forward to gaze into the hollow prison-house of the fire, regardless of the fierce glow that reddened upon his face. The lime-burner sat watching him, and half suspected this strange guest of a purpose, if not to evoke a fiend, at least to plunge into the flames, and thus vanish from the sight of man. Ethan Brand, however, drew quietly back, and closed the door of the kiln.

"I have looked," said he, "into many a human heart that was seven times hotter with sinful passions than yonder furnace is with fire. But I found not there what I sought. No, not the Unpardonable Sin!"

"What is the Unpardonable Sin?" asked the lime-burner; and then he shrank farther from his companion, trembling lest his question should be answered.

"It is a sin that grew within my own breast," replied Ethan Brand, standing erect with a pride that distinguishes all enthusiasts of his stamp. "A sin that grew nowhere else! The sin of an intellect that triumphed over the sense of brotherhood with man and reverence for God, and sacrificed everything to its own mighty claims! The only sin that deserves a recompense of immortal agony! Freely, were it to do again, would I incur the guilt. Unshrinkingly I accept the retribution!"

"The man's head is turned," muttered the lime-burner to himself. "He may be a sinner like the rest of us,—nothing more likely,—but, I'll be sworn, he is a madman too."

Nevertheless, he felt uncomfortable at his situation, alone with Ethan Brand on the wild mountain-side, and was right glad to hear the rough murmur of tongues, and the footsteps of what seemed a pretty numerous party, stumbling over the stones and rustling through the underbrush.

Soon appeared the whole lazy regiment that was wont to infest the village tavern, comprehending three or four individuals who had drunk flip beside the barroom fire through all the winters, and smoked their pipes beneath the stoop through all the summers, since Ethan Brand's departure. Laughing boisterously, and mingling all their voices together in unceremonious talk, they now burst into the moonshine and narrow streaks of firelight that illuminated the open space before the lime-kiln. Bartram set the door ajar again, flooding the spot with light, that the whole company might get a fair view of Ethan Brand, and he of them.

There, among other old acquaintances, was a once ubiquitous man, now almost extinct, but whom we were formerly sure to encounter at the hotel of every thriving village throughout the country. It was the stage-agent. The present specimen of the genius was a wilted and smoke-dried man, wrinkled and red-nosed, in a smartly cut, brown, bobtailed coat, with brass buttons, who, for a length of time unknown, had kept his desk and corner in the barroom, and was still puffing what seemed to be the same cigar that he had lighted twenty years before. He had great fame as a dry joker, though, perhaps, less on account of any intrinsic humor than from a certain flavor of brandy-toddy and tobacco-smoke, which impregnated all his ideas and expressions, as well as his person. Another well-remembered, though strangely altered, face was that of Lawyer Giles, as people still called him in courtesy; an elderly raga-muffin, in his soiled shirtsleeves and tow-cloth trousers. This poor fellow had been an attorney, in what he called his better days, a sharp prac-titioner, and in great vogue among the village litigants; but flip, and sling, and toddy, and cocktails, imbibed at all hours, morning, noon, and night, had caused him to slide from intellectual to various kinds and degrees of bodily labor, till at last, to adopt his own phrase, he slid into a soap-vat. In other words, Giles was now a soap-boiler, in a small way. He had come to be but the fragment of a human being, a part of one foot having been chopped off by an axe, and an entire hand torn away by the devilish grip of a steam-engine. Yet, though the corporeal hand was gone, a spiritual member remained; for, stretching forth the stump, Giles steadfastly averred that he felt an invisible thumb and fingers with as vivid a sensation as before the real ones were amputated. A maimed and miserable wretch he was; but one, nevertheless, whom the world could not trample on, and had no right to scorn, either in this or any previous stage of his misfortunes, since he had still kept up the courage and spirit of a man, asked nothing in charity, and with his one hand— and that the left one—fought a stern battle against want and hostile circumstances.

Among the throng, too, came another personage, who with certain points of similarity to Lawyer Giles, had many more of difference. It was the village doctor; a man of some fifty years, whom, at an earlier period of his life, we introduced as paying a professional visit to Ethan Brand during the latter's supposed insanity. He was now a purple-visaged, rude, and brutal, yet half-gentlemanly figure, with something wild, ruined, and desperate in his talk, and in all the details of his gesture and manners. Brandy possessed this man like an evil spirit, and made him as surly and savage as a wild beast, and as miserable as a lost soul; but there was supposed to be in him such wonderful skill, such native gifts of healing, beyond any which medical science could impart, that society caught hold of him, and would not let him sink out of its reach. So, swaying to and fro upon his horse, and grumbling thick accents at the bedside, he visited all the sick-chambers for miles about among the mountain towns, and sometimes raised a dying man, as it were, by miracle, or quite as often, no doubt, sent his patient to a grave that was dug many a year too soon. The doctor had an everlasting pipe in his mouth, and, as somebody said, in allusion to his habit of swearing, it was always alight with hell-fire.

These three worthies pressed forward, and greeted Ethan Brand each after his own fashion, earnestly inviting him to partake of the contents of a certain black bottle, in which, as they averred, he would find something far better worth seeking than the Unpardonable Sin. No mind, which has wrought itself by intense and solitary meditation into a high state of enthusiasm, can endure the kind of contact with low and vulgar modes of thought and feeling to which Ethan Brand was now subjected. It made him doubt—and, strange to say, it was a painful doubt—whether he had indeed found the Unpardonable Sin, and found it within himself. The whole question on which he had exhausted life, and more than life, looked like a delusion.

"Leave me," he said bitterly, "ye brute beasts, that have made yourselves so, shrivelling up your souls with fiery liquors! I have done with you. Years and years ago, I groped into your hearts and found nothing there for my purpose. Get ye gone!"

"Why, you uncivil scoundrel," cried the fierce doctor, "is that the way you respond to the kindness of your best friends? Then let me tell you the truth. You have no more found the Unpardonable Sin than yonder boy Joe has. You are but a crazy fellow,—I told you so twenty years ago,—neither better nor worse than a crazy fellow, and the fit companion of old Humphrey, here!"

He pointed to an old man, shabbily dressed, with long white hair, thin visage, and unsteady eyes. For some years past this aged person had been wandering about among the hills, inquiring of all travellers whom he met for his daughter. The girl, it seemed, had gone off with a company of circus-performers, and occasionally tidings of her came to the village, and fine stories were told of her glittering appearance as she rode on horseback in the ring, or performed marvellous feats on the tight-rope.

The white-haired father now approached Ethan Brand, and gazed unsteadily into his face.

"They tell me you have been all over the earth," said he, wringing his hands with earnestness. "You must have seen my daughter, for she makes a grand figure in the world, and everybody goes to see her. Did she send any word to her old father, or say when she was coming back?"

Ethan Brand's eye quailed beneath the old man's. That daughter, from whom he so earnestly desired a word of greeting, was the Esther of our tale, the very girl whom, with such cold and remorseless purpose, Ethan Brand had made the subject of a psychological experiment, and wasted, absorbed, and perhaps annihilated her soul, in the process.

"Yes," he murmured, turning away from the hoary wanderer, "it is no delusion. There is an Unpardonable Sin!"

While these things were passing, a merry scene was going forward in the area of cheerful light, beside the spring and before the door of the hut. A number of the youth of the village, young men and girls, had hurried up the hill-side, impelled by curiosity to see Ethan Brand, the hero of so many a legend familiar to their childhood. Finding nothing, however, very remarkable in his aspect,—nothing but a sunburnt way-farer, in plain garb and dusty shoes, who sat looking into the fire as if he fancied pictures among the coals,—these young people speedily grew tired of observing him. As it happened, there was other amusement at hand. An old German Jew, travelling with a diorama on his back, was passing down the mountain-road towards the village just as the party turned aside from it, and, in hopes of eking out the profits of the day, the showman had kept them company to the lime-kiln.

"Come, old Dutchman," cried one of the young men, "let us see your pictures, if you can swear they are worth looking at!"

"Oh yes, Captain," answered the Jew,—whether as a matter of courtesy or craft, he styled everybody Captain,—"I shall show you, indeed, some very superb pictures!"

So, placing his box in a proper position, he invited the young men and girls to look through the glass orifices of the machine, and proceeded to exhibit a series of the most outrageous scratchings and daubings, as specimens of the fine arts, that ever an itinerant showman had the face to impose upon his circle of spectators. The pictures were worn out, moreover, tattered, full of cracks and wrinkles, dingy with tobacco-smoke, and otherwise in a most pitiable condition. Some purported to be cities, public edifices, and ruined castles in Europe; others represented Napoleon's battles and Nelson's sea-fights; and in the midst of these would be seen a gigantic, brown, hairy hand,—which might have been mistaken for the Hand of Destiny, though, in truth, it was only the show-man's,—pointing its forefinger to various scenes of the conflict, while its owner gave historical illustrations. When, with much merriment at its abominable deficiency of merit, the exhibition was concluded, the Ger-man bade little Joe put his head into the box. Viewed through the magnifying-glasses, the boy's round, rosy visage assumed the strangest imaginable aspect of an immense Titanic child, the mouth grinning broadly, and the eyes and every other feature overflowing with fun at the joke. Suddenly, however, that merry face turned pale, and its expression changed to horror, for this easily impressed and excitable child had become sensible that the eye of Ethan Brand was fixed upon him through the glass.

"You make the little man to be afraid, Captain," said the German Jew, turning up the dark and strong outline of his visage from his stooping posture. "But look again, and, by chance, I shall cause you to see somewhat that is very fine, upon my word!"

Ethan Brand gazed into the box for an instant, and then starting back, looked fixedly at the German. What had he seen? Nothing, appar-ently; for a curious youth, who had peeped in almost at the same moment, beheld only a vacant space of canvas.

"I remember you now," muttered Ethan Brand to the showman.

"Ah, Captain," whispered the Jew of Nuremberg, with a dark smile, "I find it to be a heavy matter in my show-box,—this Unpardonable Sin! By my faith, Captain, it has wearied my shoulders, this long day, to carry it over the mountain."

"Peace," answered Ethan Brand, sternly, "or get thee into the furnace yonder!"

The Jew's exhibition had scarcely concluded, when a great, elderly dog—who seemed to be his own master, as no person in the company laid claim to him—saw fit to render himself the object of public notice. Hitherto, he had shown himself a very quiet, well-disposed old dog, going round from one to another, and, by way of being sociable, offering his rough head to be patted by any kindly hand that would take so much trouble. But now, all of a sudden, this grave and venerable quadruped, of his own mere motion, and without the slightest suggestion from anybody else, began to run round after his tail, which, to heighten the absurdity of the proceeding, was a great deal shorter than it should have been. Never was seen such headlong eagerness in pursuit of an object that could not possibly be attained; never was heard such a tremendous outbreak of growling, snarling, barking, and snapping,—as if one end of the ridicu-lous brute's body were at deadly and most unforgivable enmity with the other. Faster and faster, round about went the cur; and faster and still faster fled the unapproachable brevity of his tail; and louder and fiercer grew his yells of rage and animosity; until, utterly exhausted, and as far from the goal as ever, the foolish old dog ceased his performance as suddenly as he had begun it. The next moment he was as mild, quiet, sensible, and respectable in his deportment, as when he first scraped acquaintance with the company.

As may be supposed, the exhibition was greeted with universal laughter, clapping of hands, and shouts of encore, to which the canine performer responded by wagging all that there was to wag of his tail, but appeared totally unable to repeat his very successful effort to amuse the spectators.

Meanwhile, Ethan Brand had resumed his seat upon the log, and moved, as it might be, by a perception of some remote analogy between his own case and that of this self-pursuing cur, he broke into the awful laugh, which, more than any other token, expressed the condition of his inward being. From that moment, the merriment of the party was at an end; they stood aghast, dreading lest the inauspicious sound should be reverberated around the horizon, and that mountain would thunder it to mountain, and so the horror be prolonged upon their ears. Then, whispering one to another that it was late,—that the moon was almost down,— that the August night was growing chill,—they hurried homewards, leaving the lime-burner and little Joe to deal as they might with their unwelcome guest. Save for these three human beings, the open space on the hill-side was a solitude, set in a vast gloom of forest. Beyond that darksome verge, the firelight glimmered on the stately trunks and almost black foliage of pines, intermixed with the lighter verdure of sapling oaks, maples, and poplars, while here and there lay the gigantic corpses of dead trees, decaying on the leaf-strewn soil. And it seemed to little Joe—a timorous and imaginative child—that the silent forest was holding its breath until some fearful thing should happen.

Ethan Brand thrust more wood into the fire, and closed the door of the kiln; then looking over his shoulder at the lime-burner and his son, he bade, rather than advised, them to retire to rest.

"For myself, I cannot sleep," said he. "I have matters that it concerns me to meditate upon. I will watch the fire, as I used to do in the old time."

"And call the Devil out of the furnace to keep you company, I suppose," muttered Bartram, who had been making intimate acquaintance with the black bottle above mentioned. "But watch, if you like, and call as many devils as you like! For my part, I shall be all the better for a snooze. Come, Joe!"

As the boy followed his father into the hut, he looked back at the wayfarer, and the tears came into his eyes, for his tender spirit had an intuition of the bleak and terrible loneliness in which this man had enveloped himself.

When they had gone, Ethan Brand sat listening to the crackling of the kindled wood, and looking at the little spurts of fire that issued through the chinks of the door. These trifles, however, once so familiar, had but the slightest hold of his attention, while deep within his mind he was reviewing the gradual but marvellous change that had been wrought upon him by the search to which he had devoted himself. He remembered how the night dew had fallen upon him,—how the dark forest had whispered to him,—how the stars had gleamed upon him,—a simple and loving man, watching his fire in the years gone by, and ever musing as it burned. He remembered with what tenderness, with what love and sympathy for mankind, and what pity for human guilt and woe, he had first begun to contemplate those ideas which afterwards became the inspiration of his life; with what reverence he had then looked into the heart of man, viewing it as a temple originally divine, and, however desecrated, still to be held sacred by a brother; with what awful fear he had deprecated the success of his pursuit, and prayed that the Unpardonable Sin might never be revealed to him. Then ensued that vast intellectual development, which, in its progress, disturbed the counterpoise between his mind and heart. The Idea that possessed his life had operated as a means of education; it had gone on cultivating his powers to the highest point of which they were susceptible; it had raised him from the level of an unlettered laborer to stand on a star-lit eminence, whither the philosophers of the earth, laden with the lore of universities, might vainly strive to clamber after him. So much for the intellect! But where was the heart? That, indeed, had withered,—had contracted,—had hardened,— had perished! It had ceased to partake of the universal throb. He had lost his hold of the magnetic chain of humanity. He was no longer a brother-man, opening the chambers or the dungeons of our common nature by the key of holy sympathy, which gave him a right to share in all its secrets; he was now a cold observer, looking on mankind as the subject of his experiment, and, at length, converting man and woman to be his puppets, and pulling the wires that moved them to such degrees of crime as were demanded for his study.

Thus Ethan Brand became a fiend. He began to be so from the moment that his moral nature had ceased to keep the pace of improvement with his intellect. And now, as his highest effort and inevitable development,—as the bright and gorgeous flower, and rich, delicious fruit of his life's labor,—he had produced the Unpardonable Sin!

"What more have I to seek? what more to achieve?" said Ethan Brand to himself. "My task is done, and well done!"

Starting from the log with a certain alacrity in his gait and ascending the hillock of earth that was raised against the stone circumference of the lime-kiln, he thus reached the top of the structure. It was a space of perhaps ten feet across, from edge to edge, presenting a view of the upper surface of the immense mass of broken marble with which the kiln was heaped. All these innumerable blocks and fragments of marble were red-hot and vividly on fire, sending up great spouts of blue flame, which quivered aloft and danced madly, as within a magic circle, and sank and rose again, with continual and multitudinous activity. As the lonely man bent forward over this terrible body of fire, the blasting heat smote up against his person with a breath that, it might be supposed, would have scorched and shrivelled him up in a moment.

Ethan Brand stood erect, and raised his arms on high. The blue flames played upon his face, and imparted the wild and ghastly light which alone could have suited its expression; it was that of a fiend on the verge of plunging into his gulf of intensest torment.

"O Mother Earth," cried he, "who art no more my Mother, and into whose bosom this frame shall never be resolved! O mankind, whose brotherhood I have cast off, and trampled thy great heart beneath my feet! O stars of heaven, that shone on me of old, as if to light me onward and upward!—farewell all, and forever. Come, deadly element of Fire,—henceforth my familiar friend! Embrace me, as I do thee!"

That night the sound of a fearful peal of laughter rolled heavily through the sleep of the lime-burner and his little son; dim shapes of horror and anguish haunted their dreams, and seemed still present in the rude hovel, when they opened their eyes to the daylight.

"Up, boy, up!" cried the lime-burner, staring about him. "Thank Heaven, the night is gone, at last; and rather than pass such another, I would watch my lime-kiln, wide awake, for a twelve-month. This Ethan Brand, with his humbug of an Unpardonable Sin, has done me no such mighty favor, in taking my place!"

He issued from the hut, followed by little Joe, who kept fast hold of his father's hand. The early sunshine was already pouring its gold upon the mountain-tops, and though the valleys were still in shadow, they smiled cheerfully in the promise of the bright day that was hastening onward. The village, completely shut in by hills, which swelled away gently about it, looked as if it had rested peacefully in the hollow of the great hand of Providence. Every dwelling was distinctly visible; the little spires of the two churches pointed upwards, and caught a fore-glimmering of brightness from the sun-gilt skies upon their gilded weather-cocks. The tavern was astir, and the figure of the old, smoke-dried stage-agent, cigar in mouth, was seen beneath the stoop. Old Graylock was glorified with a golden cloud upon his head. Scattered likewise over the breasts of the surrounding mountains, there were heaps of hoary mist, in fantastic shapes, some of them far down into the valley, others high up towards the summits, and still others, of the same family of mist or cloud, hovering in the gold radiance of the upper atmosphere. Stepping from one to another of the clouds that rested on the hills, and thence to the loftier brotherhood that sailed in air, it seemed almost as if a mortal man might thus ascend into the heavenly regions. Earth was so mingled with sky that it was a daydream to look at it.

To supply that charm of the familiar and homely, which Nature so readily adopts into a scene like this, the stage-coach was rattling down the mountain-road, and the driver sounded his horn, while Echo caught up the notes, and intertwined them into a rich and varied and elaborate harmony, of which the original performer could lay claim to little share. The great hills played a concert among themselves, each contributing a strain of airy sweetness.

Little Joe's face brightened at once.

"Dear father," cried he, skipping cheerily to and fro, "that strange man is gone, and the sky and the mountains all seem glad of it!"

"Yes," growled the lime-burner, with an oath, "but he has let the fire go down, and no thanks to him if five hundred bushels of lime are not spoiled. If I catch the fellow hereabouts again, I shall feel like tossing him into the furnace!"

With his long pole in his hand, he ascended to the top of the kiln. After a moment's pause, he called to his son.

"Come up here, Joe!" said he.

So little Joe ran up the hillock, and stood by his father's side. The marble was all burnt into perfect, snow-white lime. But on its surface, in the midst of the circle,—snow-white too, and thoroughly converted into lime,—lay a human skeleton, in the attitude of a person who, after long toil, lies down to long repose. Within the ribs—strange to say—was the shape of a human heart.

"Was the fellow's heart made of marble?" cried Bartram, in some perplexity at this phenomenon. "At any rate, it is burnt into what looks like special good lime; and, taking all the bones together, my kiln is half a bushel the richer for him."

So saying, the rude lime-burner lifted his pole, and, letting it fall upon the skeleton, the relics of Ethan Brand were crumbled into fragments.

Miniver Cheevy

EDWIN ARLINGTON ROBINSON

Miniver Cheevy, child of scorn,
  Grew lean while he assailed the seasons;
He wept that he was ever born,
  And he had reasons.

Miniver loved the days of old
  When swords were bright and steeds were prancing;
The vision of a warrior bold
  Would set him dancing.

Miniver sighed for what was not,
  And dreamed, and rested from his labors;
He dreamed of Thebes and Camelot,
  And Priam's neighbors.

Miniver mourned the ripe renown
  That made so many a name so fragrant;
He mourned Romance, now on the town,
  And Art, a vagrant.

Miniver loved the Medici,
  Albeit he had never seen one;
He would have sinned incessantly
  Could he have been one.

Miniver cursed the commonplace
  And eyed a khaki suit with loathing;
He missed the mediaeval grace
  Of iron clothing.

Miniver scorned the gold he sought,
  But sore annoyed was he without it;
Miniver thought, and thought, and thought,
  And thought about it.

Miniver Cheevy, born too late,
    Scratched his head and kept on thinking;
Miniver coughed, and called it fate,
    And kept on drinking.

Outcast

CLAUDE McKAY

For the dim regions whence my fathers came
My spirit, bondaged by the body, longs.
Words felt, but never heard, my lips would frame;
My soul would sing forgotten jungle songs.
I would go back to darkness and to peace,
But the great western world holds me in fee,
And I may never hope for full release
While to its alien gods I bend my knee.
Something in me is lost, forever lost,
Some vital thing has gone out of my heart,
And I must walk the way of life a ghost
Among the sons of earth, a thing apart.

For I was born, far from my native clime,
Under the white man's menace, out of time.

The Double

THE use of the double has changed in literary treatment throughout the centuries. During the medieval period, component aspects of a single human being might be objectified as separate people, as the body and the soul were in the medieval debate. Later, the contending forces of good and evil within the individual were objectified as figures such as the good and bad angels in Christopher Marlowe's *Dr. Faustus*. Still later, authors were to create characters who were representative parts or aspects of but a single individual, as in Joseph Conrad's "The Secret Sharer." Here, putting his young protagonist through an initiation as commander of his first ship, the author develops a character who is secretly taken aboard the ship. This character is a part of the protagonist, and he is finally lowered over the side when the young captain proves his ability and his manhood. Dostoievsky, with an interesting variation, develops in *The Brothers Karamazov* the attributes that make up a single individual, assigning one attribute to each different member of the same family. One brother is earthy; another, intellectual; still another, totally spiritual. The brothers, plus the father, represent a "family" or one total individual. Again, the double may be a former self now returned, or he may be looked upon erotically and humorously as a major part of the Self, as in Melville's "Me and My Chimney." Generally, however, this motif represents the faces of good and evil within an individual as objectified in two characters at war with each other.

William Wilson

EDGAR ALLAN POE

What say of it? what say [of] CONSCIENCE grim,
That spectre in my path?
—*Chamberlayne's "Pharronida"*

Let me call myself, for the present, William Wilson. The fair page now lying before me need not be sullied with my real appellation. This has been already too much an object for the scorn—for the horror—for the detestation of my race. To the uttermost regions of the globe have not the indignant winds bruited its unparalleled infamy? Oh, outcast of all out-

casts most abandoned!—to the earth art thou not forever dead? to its
honors, to its flowers, to its golden aspirations?—and a cloud, dense,
dismal, and limitless, does it not hang eternally between thy hopes and
heaven?

I would not, if I could, here or to-day, embody a record of my later
years of unspeakable misery, and unpardonable crime. This epoch—
these later years—took unto themselves a sudden elevation in turpitude,
whose origin alone it is my present purpose to assign. Men usually grow
base by degrees. From me, in an instant, all virtue dropped bodily as a
mantle. From comparatively trivial wickedness I passed, with the stride
of a giant, into more than the enormities of an Elah-Gabalus. What
chance—what one event brought this evil thing to pass, bear with me
while I relate. Death approaches; and the shadow which foreruns him
has thrown a softening influence over my spirit. I long, in passing through
the dim valley, for the sympathy—I had nearly said for the pity—of my
fellow men. I would fain have them believe that I have been, in some
measure, the slave of circumstances beyond human control. I would wish
them to seek out for me, in the details I am about to give, some little oasis
of *fatality* amid a wilderness of error. I would have them allow—what
they cannot refrain from allowing—that, although temptation may have
erewhile existed as great, man was never *thus*, at least, tempted before—
certainly, never *thus* fell. And is it therefore that he has never thus suffered? Have I not indeed been living in a dream? And am I not now
dying a victim to the horror and the mystery of the wildest of all sub-
lunary visions?

I am the descendant of a race whose imaginative and easily excitable
temperament has at all times rendered them remarkable; and, in my
earliest infancy, I gave evidence of having fully inherited the family
character. As I advanced in years it was more strongly developed; becoming, for many reasons, a cause of serious disquietude to my friends, and
of positive injury to myself. I grew self-willed, addicted to the wildest
caprices, and a prey to the most ungovernable passions. Weak-minded,
and beset with constitutional infirmities akin to my own, my parents
could do but little to check the evil propensities which distinguished me.
Some feeble and ill-directed efforts resulted in complete failure on their
part, and, of course, in total triumph on mine. Thenceforward my voice
was a household law; and at an age when few children have abandoned
their leading-strings, I was left to the guidance of my own will, and
became, in all but name, the master of my own actions.

My earliest recollections of a school-life are connected with a large,
rambling, Elizabethan house, in a misty-looking village of England,
where were a vast number of gigantic and gnarled trees, and where all the
houses were excessively ancient. In truth, it was a dream-like and spirit-
soothing place, that venerable old town. At this moment, in fancy, I feel

the refreshing chilliness of its deeply-shadowed avenues, inhale the fragrance of its thousand shrubberies, and thrill anew with undefinable delight, at the deep hollow note of the church-bell, breaking, each hour, with sullen and sudden roar, upon the stillness of the dusky atmosphere in which the fretted Gothic steeple lay imbedded and asleep.

It gives me, perhaps, as much of pleasure as I can now in any manner experience, to dwell upon minute recollections of the school and its concerns. Steeped in misery as I am—misery, alas! only too real—I shall be pardoned for seeking relief, however slight and temporary, in the weakness of a few rambling details. These, moreover, utterly trivial, and even ridiculous in themselves, assume, to my fancy, adventitious importance, as connected with a period and a locality when and where I recognize the first ambiguous monitions of the destiny which afterwards so fully overshadowed me. Let me then remember.

The house, I have said, was old and irregular. The grounds were extensive, and a high and solid brick wall, topped with a bed of mortar and broken glass, encompassed the whole. This prisonlike rampart formed the limit of our domain; beyond it we saw but thrice a week— once every Saturday afternoon, when, attended by two ushers, we were permitted to take brief walks in a body through some of the neighbouring fields—and twice during Sunday, where we were paraded in the same formal manner to the morning and evening service in the one church of the village. Of this church the principal of our school was pastor. With how deep a spirit of wonder and perplexity was I wont to regard him from our remote pew in the gallery, as, with step solemn and slow, he ascended the pulpit! This reverend man, with countenance so demurely benign, with robes so glossy and so clerically flowing, with wig so minutely powdered, so rigid and so vast,—could this be he who, of late, with sour visage, and in snuffy habiliments, administered, ferule in hand, the Draconian laws of the academy? Oh, gigantic paradox, too utterly monstrous for solution!

At an angle of the ponderous wall frowned a more ponderous gate. It was riveted and studded with iron bolts, and surmounted with jagged iron spikes. What impressions of deep awe did it inspire! It was never opened save for the three periodical egressions and ingressions already mentioned; then, in every creak of its mighty hinges, we found a plenitude of mystery—a world of matter for solemn remark, or for more solemn meditation.

The extensive enclosure was irregular in form, having many capacious recesses. Of these, three or four of the largest constituted the playground. It was level, and covered with fine hard gravel. I well remember it had no trees, nor benches, nor anything similar within it. Of course it was in the rear of the house. In front lay a small parterre, planted with box and other shrubs; but through this sacred division we passed only upon rare occasions indeed—such as a first advent to school or final departure thence, or perhaps, when a parent or friend having called for us, we joyfully took our way home for the Christmas or Midsummer holy-days.

But the house!—how quaint an old building was this!—to me how veritably a palace of enchantment! There was really no end to its wind-ings—to its incomprehensible subdivisions. It was difficult, at any given time, to say with certainty upon which of its two stories one happened to be. From each room to every other there were sure to be found three or four steps either in ascent or descent. Then the lateral branches were innumerable—inconceivable—and so returning in upon themselves, that our most exact ideas in regard to the whole mansion were not very far different from those with which we pondered upon infinity. During the five years of my residence here, I was never able to ascertain with pre-cision, in what remote locality lay the little sleeping apartment assigned to myself and some eighteen or twenty other scholars.

The school-room was the largest in the house—I could not help think-ing, in the world. It was very long, narrow, and dismally low, with pointed Gothic windows and a ceiling of oak. In a remote and terror-inspiring angle was a square enclosure of eight or ten feet, comprising the *sanctum*, "during hours," of our principal, the Reverend Dr. Bransby. It was a solid structure, with massy door, sooner than open which in the absence of the "Dominie," we would all have willingly perished by the *peine forte et dure*. In other angles were two other similar boxes, far less reverenced, indeed, but still greatly matters of awe. One of these was the pulpit of the "classical" usher, one of the "English and mathematical." Interspersed about the room, crossing and recrossing in endless irregularity, were in-numerable benches and desks, black, ancient, and time-worn, piled desperately with much-bethumbed books, and so beseamed with initial letters, names at full length, grotesque figures, and other multiplied efforts of the knife, as to have entirely lost what little of original form might have been their portion in days long departed. A huge bucket with water stood at one extremity of the room, and a clock of stupendous dimensions at the other.

Encompassed by the massy walls of this venerable academy, I passed, yet not in tedium or disgust, the years of the third lustrum of my life. The teeming brain of childhood requires no external world of incident to occupy or amuse it; and the apparently dismal monotony of a school was replete with more intense excitement than my riper youth has derived from luxury, or my full manhood from crime. Yet I must believe that my first mental development had in it much of the uncommon—even much of the *outré*. Upon mankind at large the events of very early existence rarely leave in mature age any definite impression. All is gray shadow—a weak and irregular remembrance—an indistinct regathering of feeble

pleasures and phantasmagoric pains. With me this is not so. In childhood
I must have felt with the energy of a man what I now find stamped upon
memory in lines as vivid, as deep, and as durable as the *exergues* of the
Carthaginian medals.

Yet in fact—in the fact of the world's view—how little was there to
remember! The morning's awakening, the nightly summons to bed; the
connings, the recitations; the periodical half-holidays, and perambula-
tions; the play-ground, with its broils, its pastimes, its intrigues;—these,
by a mental sorcery long forgotten, were made to involve a wilderness of
sensation, a world of rich incident, a universe of varied emotion, of
excitement the most passionate and spirit-stirring, "*Oh, le bon temps,
que ce siècle de fer!*"

In truth, the ardor, the enthusiasm, and the imperiousness of my
disposition soon rendered me a marked character among my schoolmates,
and by slow, but natural gradations, gave me an ascendency over all not
greatly older than myself;—over all with a single exception. This exception was found in the person of a scholar, who, although no relation, bore
the same Christian and surname as myself;—a circumstance, in fact, little
remarkable; for, notwithstanding a noble descent, mine was one of those
everyday appellations which seem, by prescriptive right, to have been,
time out of mind, the common property of the mob. In this narrative I
have therefore designated myself as William Wilson,—a fictitious title
not very dissimilar to the real. My namesake alone, of those who in school
phraseology constituted "our set," presumed to compete with me in the
studies of the class—in the sports and broils of the play-ground—to refuse
implicit belief in my assertions, and submission to my will—indeed, to
interfere with my arbitrary dictation in any respect whatsoever. If there
is on earth a supreme and unqualified despotism, it is the despotism of
a master mind in boyhood over the less energetic spirits of its companions.

Wilson's rebellion was to me a source of the greatest embarrass-
ment;—the more so as, in spite of the bravado with which in public I
made a point of treating him and his pretensions, I secretly felt that
I feared him, and could not help thinking the equality which he maintained so easily with myself, a proof of his true superiority; since not to
be overcome, cost me a perpetual struggle. Yet this superiority—even
this equality—was in truth acknowledged by no one but myself; our
associates, by some unaccountable blindness, seemed not even to suspect
it. Indeed, his competition, his resistance, and especially his impertinent
and dogged interference with my purposes, were not more pointed than
private. He appeared to be destitute alike of the ambition which urged,
and of the passionate energy of mind which enabled me to excel. In his
rivalry he might have been supposed actuated solely by a whimsical
desire to thwart, astonish, or mortify myself; although there were times
when I could not help observing, with a feeling made up of wonder,

abasement, and pique, that he mingled with his injuries, his insults, or
his contradictions, a certain most inappropriate, and assuredly most
unwelcome *affectionateness* of manner. I could only conceive this singular
behavior to arise from a consummate self-conceit assuming the vulgar
airs of patronage and protection.

Perhaps it was this latter trait in Wilson's conduct, conjoined with
our identity of name, and the mere accident of our having entered the
school upon the same day, which set afloat the notion that we were
brothers, among the senior classes in the academy. These do not usually
inquire with much strictness into the affairs of their juniors. I have before
said, or should have said, that Wilson was not, in a most remote degree,
connected with my family. But assuredly if we *had* been brothers we
must have been twins; for, after leaving Dr. Bransby's, I casually learned
that my namesake was born on the nineteenth of January, 1813—and
this is a somewhat remarkable coincidence; for the day is precisely that
of my own nativity.

It may seem strange that in spite of the continual anxiety occasioned
me by the rivalry of Wilson, and his intolerable spirit of contradiction,
I could not bring myself to hate him altogether. We had, to be sure,
nearly every day a quarrel in which, yielding me publicly the palm of
victory, he, in some manner, contrived to make me feel that it was he
who had deserved it; yet a sense of pride on my part, and a veritable
dignity on his own, kept us always upon what are called "speaking
terms," while there were many points of strong congeniality in our
tempers, operating to awake in me a sentiment which our position alone,
perhaps, prevented from ripening into friendship. It is difficult, indeed,
to define, or even to describe, my real feelings toward him. They formed
a motley and heterogeneous admixture;—some petulant animosity, which
was not yet hatred, some esteem, more respect, much fear, with a world
of uneasy curiosity. To the moralist it will be unnecessary to say, in
addition, that Wilson and myself were the most inseparable of companions.

It was no doubt the anomalous state of affairs existing between us,
which turned all my attacks upon him (and there were many, either open
or covert) into the channel of banter or practical joke (giving pain while
assuming the aspect of mere fun) rather than into a more serious and
determined hostility. But my endeavors on this head were by no means
uniformly successful, even when my plans were the most wittily con-
cocted; for my namesake had much about him, in character, of that un-
assuming and quiet austerity which, while enjoying the poignancy of its
own jokes, has no heel of Achilles in itself, and absolutely refuses to be
laughed at. I could find, indeed, but one vulnerable point, and that, lying
in a personal peculiarity, arising, perhaps, from constitutional disease,
would have been spared by any antagonist less at his wit's end than

myself;—my rival had a weakness in the faucial or guttural organs, which precluded him from raising his voice at any time *above a very low whisper*. Of this defect I did not fail to take what poor advantage lay in my power.

Wilson's retaliations in kind were many; and there was one form of his practical wit that disturbed me beyond measure. How his sagacity first discovered at all that so petty a thing would vex me is a question I never could solve; but having discovered, he habitually practised the annoyance. I had always felt aversion to my uncourtly patronymic, and its very common, if not plebeian, prænomen. The words were venom in my ears; and when, upon the day of my arrival, a second William Wilson came also to the academy, I felt angry with him for bearing the name, and doubly disgusted with the name because a stranger bore it, who would be the cause of its twofold repetition, who would be constantly in my presence, and whose concerns, in the ordinary routine of the school business, must inevitably, on account of the detestable coincidence, be often confounded with my own.

The feeling of vexation thus engendered grew stronger with every circumstance tending to show resemblance, moral or physical, between my rival and myself. I had not then discovered the remarkable fact that we were of the same age; but I saw that we were of the same height, and I perceived that we were even singularly alike in general contour of person and outline of feature. I was galled, too, by the rumor touching a relationship, which had grown current in the upper forms. In a word, nothing could more seriously disturb me (although I scrupulously concealed such disturbance) than any allusions to a similarity of mind, person, or condition existing between us. But, in truth, I had no reason to believe that (with the exception of the matter of relationship, and in the case of Wilson himself) this similarity had ever been made a subject of comment, or even observed at all by our schoolfellows. That *he* observed it in all its bearings, and as fixedly as I, was apparent; but that he could discover in such circumstances so fruitful a field of annoyance can only be attributed, as I said before, to his more than ordinary penetration.

His cue, which was to perfect an imitation of myself, lay both in words and in actions; and most admirably did he play his part. My dress it was an easy matter to copy; my gait and general manner were, without difficulty, appropriated; in spite of his constitutional defect, even my voice did not escape him. My louder tones were, of course, unattempted, but then the key, it was identical; *and his singular whisper, it grew the very echo of my own*.

How greatly this most exquisite portraiture harassed me (for it could not justly be termed a caricature) I will not now venture to describe. I had but one consolation—in the fact that the imitation, apparently, was noticed by myself alone, and that I had to endure only the knowing and strangely sarcastic smiles of my namesake himself. Satisfied with having produced in my bosom the intended effect, he seemed to chuckle in secret over the sting he had inflicted, and was characteristically disregardful of the public applause which the success of his witty endeavors might have so easily elicited. That the school, indeed, did not feel his design, perceive its accomplishment, and participate in his sneer, was, for many anxious months, a riddle I could not resolve. Perhaps the *gradation* of his copy rendered it not so readily perceptible; or, more possibly, I owed my security to the masterly air of the copyist, who, disdaining the letter (which in a painting is all the obtuse can see) gave but the full spirit of his original for my individual contemplation and chagrin.

I have already more than once spoken of the disgusting air of patronage which he assumed toward me, and of his frequent officious interference with my will. This interference often took the ungracious character of advice; advice not openly given, but hinted or insinuated. I received it with a repugnance which gained strength as I grew in years. Yet, at this distant day, let me do him the simple justice to acknowledge that I can recall no occasion when the suggestions of my rival were on the side of those errors or follies so usual to his immature age and seeming inexperience; that his moral sense, at least, if not his general talents and worldly wisdom, was far keener than my own; and that I might, to-day, have been a better and thus a happier man, had I less frequently rejected the counsels embodied in those meaning whispers which I then but too cordially hated and too bitterly despised.

As it was, I at length grew restive in the extreme under his distasteful supervision, and daily resented more and more openly what I considered his intolerable arrogance. I have said that, in the first years of our connection as schoolmates, my feelings in regard to him might have been easily ripened into friendship: but, in the latter months of my residence at the academy, although the intrusion of his ordinary manner had, beyond doubt, in some measure, abated, my sentiments, in nearly similar proportion, partook very much of positive hatred. Upon one occasion he saw this, I think, and afterward avoided, or made a show of avoiding me.

It was about the same period, if I remember aright, that, in an altercation of violence with him, in which he was more than usually thrown off his guard, and spoke and acted with an openness of demeanor rather foreign to his nature, I discovered, or fancied I discovered, in his accent, in his air, and general appearance, a something which first startled, and then deeply interested me, by bringing to mind dim visions of my earliest infancy—wild, confused and thronging memories of a time when memory herself was yet unborn. I cannot better describe the sensation which oppressed me than by saying that I could with difficulty shake off the belief of my having been acquainted with the being who stood before me, at some epoch very long ago—some point of the past even infinitely remote.

The delusion, however, faded rapidly as it came; and I mention it at all but to define the day of the last conversation I there held with my singular namesake.

The huge old house, with its countless subdivisions, had several large chambers communicating with each other, where slept the greater number of the students. There were, however (as must necessarily happen in a building so awkwardly planned), many little nooks or recesses, the odds and ends of the structure; and these the economic ingenuity of Dr. Bransby had also fitted up as dormitories; although, being the merest closets, they were capable of accommodating but a single individual. One of these small apartments was occupied by Wilson.

One night, about the close of my fifth year at the school, and immediately after the altercation just mentioned, finding every one wrapped in sleep, I arose from bed, and, lamp in hand, stole through a wilderness of narrow passages from my own bedroom to that of my rival. I had long been plotting one of those ill-natured pieces of practical wit at his expense in which I had hitherto been so uniformly unsuccessful. It was my intention, now, to put my scheme in operation, and I resolved to make him feel the whole extent of the malice with which I was imbued. Having reached his closet, I noiselessly entered, leaving the lamp, with a shade over it, on the outside. I advanced a step and listened to the sound of his tranquil breathing. Assured of his being asleep, I returned, took the light, and with it again approached the bed. Close curtains were around it, which, in the prosecution of my plan, I slowly and quietly withdrew, when the bright rays fell vividly upon the sleeper, and my eyes, at the same moment, upon his countenance. I looked;—and a numbness, an iciness of feeling instantly pervaded my frame. My breast heaved, my knees tottered, my whole spirit became possessed with an objectless yet intolerable horror. Gasping for breath, I lowered the lamp in still nearer proximity to the face. Were these—*these* the lineaments of William Wilson? I saw, indeed, that they were his, but I shook as if with a fit of the ague in fancying they were not. What *was* there about them to confound me in this manner? I gazed; —while my brain reeled with a multitude of incoherent thoughts. Not thus he appeared—assuredly not *thus*—in the vivacity of his waking hours. The same name! the same contour of person! the same day of arrival at the academy! And then his dogged and meaningless imitation of my gait, my voice, my habits, and my manner! Was it, in truth, within the bounds of human possibility, that *what I now saw* was the result, merely, of the habitual practice of this sarcastic imitation? Awe-stricken, and with a creeping shudder, I extinguished the lamp, passed silently from the chamber, and left, at once, the halls of that old academy, never to enter them again.

After a lapse of some months, spent at home in mere idleness, I found myself a student at Eton. The brief interval had been sufficient to enfeeble my remembrance of the events at Dr. Bransby's, or at least to effect a material change in the nature of the feelings with which I remembered them. The truth—the tragedy—of the drama was no more. I could now find room to doubt the evidence of my senses; and seldom called up the subject at all but with wonder at the extent of human credulity, and a smile at the vivid force of the imagination which I hereditarily possessed. Neither was this species of skepticism likely to be diminished by the character of the life I led at Eton. The vortex of thoughtless folly into which I there so immediately and so recklessly plunged, washed away all but the froth of my past hours, engulfed at once every solid or serious impression, and left to memory only the veriest levities of a formed existence.

I do not wish, however, to trace the course of my miserable profligacy here—a profligacy which set at defiance the laws, while it eluded the vigilance of the institution. Three years of folly, passed without profit, had but given me rooted habits of vice, and added, in a somewhat unusual degree, to my bodily stature, when, after a week of soulless dissipation, I invited a small party of the most dissolute students to a secret carousal in my chambers. We met at a late hour of the night; for our debaucheries were to be faithfully protracted until morning. The wine flowed freely, and there were not wanting other and perhaps more dangerous seductions; so that the grey dawn had already faintly appeared in the east while our delirious extravagance was at its height. Madly flushed with cards and intoxication, I was in the act of insisting upon a toast of more than wonted profanity, when my attention was suddenly diverted by the violent, although partial, unclosing of the door of the apartment, and by the eager voice of a servant from without. He said that some person, apparently in great haste, demanded to speak with me in the hall.

Wildly excited with wine, the unexpected interruption rather delighted than surprised me. I staggered forward at once, and a few steps brought me to the vestibule of the building. In this low and small room there hung no lamp; and now no light at all was admitted, save that of the exceedingly feeble dawn which made its way through the semi-circular window. As I put my foot over the threshold, I became aware of the figure of a youth about my own height, and habited in a white kerseymere morning frock, cut in the novel fashion of the one I myself wore at the moment. This the faint light enabled me to perceive; but the features of his face I could not distinguish. Upon my entering he strode hurriedly up to me, and, seizing me by the arm with a gesture of petulant impatience, whispered the words "William Wilson!" in my ear.

I grew perfectly sober in an instant.

There was that in the manner of the stranger, and in the tremulous shake of his uplifted finger, as he held it between my eyes and the light, which filled me with unqualified amazement; but it was not this which had so violently moved me. It was the pregnancy of solemn admonition in the singular, low, hissing utterance; and, above all, it was the character, the tone, *the key*, of those few, simple, and familiar, yet *whispered* syllables, which came with a thousand thronging memories of by-gone days, and struck upon my soul with the shock of a galvanic battery. Ere I could recover the use of my senses he was gone.

Although this event failed not of a vivid effect upon my disordered imagination, yet was it evanescent as vivid. For some weeks, indeed, I busied myself in earnest inquiry, or was wrapped in a cloud of morbid speculation. I did not pretend to disguise from my perception the identity of the singular individual who thus perseveringly interfered with my affairs, and harassed me with his insinuated counsel. But who and what was this Wilson?—and whence came he?—and what were his purposes? Upon neither of these points could I be satisfied; merely ascertaining, in regard to him, that a sudden accident in his family had caused his removal from Dr. Bransby's academy on the afternoon of the day in which I myself had eloped. But in a brief period I ceased to think upon the subject; my attention being all absorbed in a contemplated departure for Oxford. Thither I soon went; the uncalculating vanity of my parents furnishing me with an outfit and annual establishment, which would enable me to indulge at will in the luxury already so dear to my heart,— to vie in profuseness of expenditure with the hautiest heirs of the wealthiest earldoms in Great Britain.

Excited by such appliances to vice, my constitutional temperament broke forth with redoubled ardor, and I spurned even the common restraints of decency in the mad infatuation of my revels. But it were absurd to pause in the detail of my extravagance. Let it suffice, that among spendthrifts I out-Heroded Herod, and that, giving name to a multitude of novel follies, I added no brief appendix to the long catalogue of vices then usual in the most dissolute university of Europe.

It could hardly be credited, however, that I had, even here, so utterly fallen from the gentlemanly estate, as to seek acquaintance with the vilest arts of the gambler by profession, and, having become an adept in his despicable science, to practice it habitually as a means of increasing my already enormous income at the expense of the weak-minded among my fellow-collegians. Such, nevertheless, was the fact. And the very enormity of this offence against all manly and honorable sentiment proved, beyond doubt, the main if not the sole reason of the impunity with which it was committed. Who, indeed, among my most abandoned associates, would not rather have disputed the clearest evidence of his senses, than have suspected of such courses, the gay, the frank, the generous William Wilson—the noblest and most liberal commoner at Oxford—him whose follies (said his parasites) were but the follies of youth and unbridled fancy—whose errors but inimitable whim—whose darkest vice but a careless and dashing extravagance?

I had been now two years successfuly busied in this way, when there came to the university a young *parvenu* nobleman, Glendinning—rich, said report, as Herodes Atticus—his riches, too, as easily acquired. I soon found him of weak intellect, and, of course, marked him as a fitting subject for my skill. I frequently engaged him in play, and contrived, with the gambler's usual art, to let him win considerable sums, the more effectually to entangle him in my snares. At length, my schemes being ripe, I met him (with the full intention that this meeting should be final and decisive) at the chambers of a fellow-commoner (Mr. Preston) equally intimate with both, but who, to do him justice, entertained not even a remote suspicion of my design. To give to this a better coloring, I had contrived to have assembled a party of some eight or ten, and was solicitously careful that the introduction of cards should appear accidental, and originate in the proposal of my contemplated dupe himself. To be brief upon a vile topic, none of the low finesse was omitted, so customary upon similar occasions, that it is a just matter for wonder how any are still found so besotted as to fall its victim.

We had protracted our sitting far into the night, and I had at length effected the manœuvre of getting Glendinning as my sole antagonist. The game, too, was my favorite *écarté*. The rest of the company, interested in the extent of our play, had abandoned their own cards, and were standing around us as spectators. The *parvenu*, who had been induced by my artifices in the early part of the evening, to drink deeply, now shuffled, dealt, or played, with a wild nervousness of manner for which his intoxication, I thought, might partially, but could not altogether account. In a very short period he had become my debtor to a large amount, when, having taken a long draught of port, he did precisely what I had been coolly anticipating—he proposed to double our already extravagant stakes. With a well-feigned show of reluctance, and not until after my repeated refusal had seduced him into some angry words which gave a color of *pique* to my compliance did I finally comply. The result, of course, did but prove how entirely the prey was in my toils; in less than an hour he had quadrupled his debt. For some time his countenance had been losing the florid tinge lent it by the wine; but now, to my astonishment, I perceived that it had grown to a pallor truly fearful. I say, to my anstonishment. Glendinning had been represented to my eager inquiries as immeasurably wealthy; and the sums which he had as yet lost, although in themselves vast, could not, I supposed, very seriously annoy, much less so violently affect him. That he was overcome by the wine just swallowed was the idea which most readily presented itself; and, rather with a view to the preservation of my own character in the eyes of my associates, than from any less interested motive, I was about to insist, peremptorily, upon a discontinuance of the play, when some expressions at my elbow from among the company, and an ejaculation evincing utter despair on the part of Glendinning, gave me to understand that I had effected his total ruin under circumstances which, rendering him an object for the pity of all, should have protected him from the ill offices even of a fiend.

What now might have been my conduct it is difficult to say. The pitiable condition of my dupe had thrown an air of embarrassed gloom over all; and, for some moments, a profound silence was maintained, during which I could not help feeling my cheeks tingle with the many burning glances of scorn or reproach cast upon me by the less abandoned of the party. I will even own that an intolerable weight of anxiety was for a brief instant lifted from my bosom by the sudden and extraordinary interruption which ensued. The wide, heavy folding doors of the apartment were all at once thro vn open, to their full extent, with a vigorous and rushing impetuosity that extinguished, as if by magic, every candle in the room. Their light, in dying, enabled us just to perceive that a stranger had entered, about my own height, and closely muffled in a cloak. The darkness, however, was not total; and we could only *feel* that he was standing in our midst. Before any one of us could recover from the extreme astonishment into which this rudeness had thrown all, we heard the voice of the intruder.

"Gentlemen," he said, in a low, distinct, and never-to-be-forgotten *whisper* which thrilled to the very marrow of my bones, "Gentlemen, I make no apology for this behavior, because in thus behaving, I am fulfilling a duty. You are, beyond doubt, uninformed of the true character of the person who has to-night won at *écarté* a large sum of money from Lord Glendinning. I will therefore put you upon an expeditious and decisive plan of obtaining this very necessary information. Please to examine, at your leisure, the inner linings of the cuff of his left sleeve, and the several little packages which may be found in the somewhat capacious pockets of his embroidered morning wrapper."

While he spoke, so profound was the stillness that one might have heard a pin drop upon the floor. In ceasing, he departed at once, and as abruptly as he had entered. Can I—shall I describe my sensations?— must I say that I felt all the horrors of the damned? Most assuredly I had little time given for reflection. Many hands roughly seized me upon the spot, and lights were immediately reprocured. A search ensued. In the lining of my sleeve were found all the court cards essential in *écarté*, and, in the pockets of my wrapper, a number of packs, fac-similes of those used at our sittings, with the single exception that mine were of the species called, technically, *arrondées;* the honors being slightly convex at the ends, the lower cards slightly convex at the sides. In this disposition, the dupe who cuts, as customary, at the length of the pack, will invariably find that he cuts his antagonist an honor; while the gambler, cutting at the breadth, will, as certainly, cut nothing for his victim which may count in the records of the game.

Any burst of indignation upon this discovery would have affected me less than the silent contempt, or the sarcastic composure, with which it was received.

"Mr. Wilson," said our host, stooping to remove from beneath his feet an exceedingly luxurious cloak of rare furs, "Mr. Wilson, this is your property." (The weather was cold; and, upon quitting my own room, I had thrown a cloak over my dressing wrapper, putting it off upon reaching the scene of play.) "I presume it is supererogatory to seek here (eyeing the folds of the garment with a bitter smile) for any further evidence of your skill. Indeed, we have had enough. You will see the necessity, I hope, of quitting Oxford—at all events, of quitting instantly my chambers."

Abased, humbled to the dust as I then was, it is probable that I should have resented this galling language by immediate personal violence, had not my whole attention been at the moment arrested by a fact of the most startling character. The cloak which I had worn was of a rare description of fur; how rare, how extravagantly costly, I shall not venture to say. Its fashion, too, was of my own fantastic invention; for I was fastidious to an absurd degree of coxcombry, in matters of this frivolous nature. When, therefore, Mr. Preston reached me that which he had picked up upon the floor, and near the folding doors of the apartment, it was with an astonishment nearly bordering upon terror, that I perceived my own already hanging on my arm (where I had no doubt unwittingly placed it) and that the one presented me was but its exact counterpart in every, in even the minutest possible particular. The singular being who had so disastrously exposed me had been muffled, I remembered, in a cloak; and none had been worn at all by any of the members of our party with the exception of myself. Retaining some presence of mind, I took the one offered me by Preston; placed it, unnoticed, over my own; left the apartment with a resolute scowl of defiance; and, next morning ere dawn of day, commenced a hurried journey from Oxford to the continent, in a perfect agony of horror and of shame.

I fled in vain. My evil destiny pursued me as if in exultation, and proved, indeed, that the exercise of its mysterious dominion had as yet only begun. Scarcely had I set foot in Paris, ere I had fresh evidence of the detestable interest taken by this Wilson in my concerns. Years flew, while I experienced no relief. Villain!—at Rome, with how untimely, yet with how spectral an officiousness, stepped he in between me and my ambition! at Vienna, too—at Berlin—and at Moscow! Where, in truth, had I *not* bitter cause to curse him within my heart? From his inscrutable tyranny did I at length flee, panic-stricken, as from a pestilence; and to the very ends of the earth *I fled in vain.*

And again, and again, in secret communion with my own spirit, would
I demand the questions "Who is he—whence came he?—and what are his
objects?" But no answer was there found. And then I scrutinized, with a
minute scrutiny, the forms, and the methods, and the leading traits of his
impertinent supervision. But even here there was very little upon which
to base a conjecture. It was noticeable, indeed, that, in no one of the
multiplied instances in which he had of late crossed my path, had he so
crossed it except to frustrate those schemes, or to disturb those actions,
which, if fully carried out, might have resulted in bitter mischief. Poor
justification this, in truth, for an authority so imperiously assumed! Poor
indemnity for natural rights of self-agency so pertinaciously, so insult-
ingly denied!

I had also been forced to notice that my tormentor, for a very long
period of time (while scrupulously and with miraculous dexterity maintaining his whim of an identity of apparel with myself) had so contrived
it, in the execution of his varied interference with my will, that I saw not,
at any moment, the features of his face. Be Wilson what he might, *this*,
at least, was but the veriest of affectation, or of folly. Could he, for an
instant, have supposed that, in my admonisher at Eton—in the destroyer
of my honor at Oxford,—in him who thwarted my ambition at Rome, my
revenge at Paris, my passionate love at Naples, or what he falsely termed
my avarice in Egypt,—that in this, my arch-enemy and evil genius, I
could fail to recognize the William Wilson of my schoolboy days,—the
namesake, the companion, the rival,—the hated and dreaded rival at Dr.
Bransby's? Impossible!—But let me hasten to the last eventful scene of
the drama.

Thus far I had succumbed supinely to this imperious domination.
The sentiment of deep awe with which I habitually regarded the elevated
character, the majestic wisdom, the apparent omnipresence and omnipotence of Wilson, added to a feeling of even terror, with which certain
other traits in his nature and assumptions inspired me, had operated,
hitherto, to impress me with an idea of my own utter weakness and help-
lessness, and to suggest an implicit, although bitterly reluctant submission
to his arbitrary will. But, of late days, I had given myself up entirely to
wine; and its maddening influence upon my hereditary temper rendered
me more and more impatient of control. I began to murmur,—to hesitate,
—to resist. And was it only fancy which induced me to believe that, with
the increase of my own firmness, that of my tormentor underwent a pro-
portional diminution? Be this as it may, I now began to feel the inspiration
of a burning hope, and at length nurtured in my secret thoughts a stern
and desperate resolution that I would submit no longer to be enslaved.

It was at Rome, during the Carnival of 18—, that I attended a masquerade in the palazzo of the Neapolitan Duke Di Broglio. I had indulged
more freely than usual in the excesses of the wine-table; and now the

suffocating atmosphere of the crowded rooms irritated me beyond endurance. The difficulty, too, of forcing my way through the mazes of the company contributed not a little to the ruffling of my temper; for I was anxiously seeking (let me not say with what unworthy motive) the young, the gay, the beautiful wife of the aged and doting Di Broglio. With a too unscrupulous confidence she had previously communicated to me the secret of the costume in which she would be habited and now, having caught a glimpse of her person, I was hurrying to make my way into her presence. —At this moment I felt a light hand placed upon my shoulder, and that ever-remembered, low, damnable *whisper* within my ear.

In an absolute frenzy of wrath, I turned at once upon him who had thus interrupted me, and seized him violently by the collar. He was attired, as I had expected, in a costume altogether similar to my own; wearing a Spanish cloak of blue velvet, begirt about the waist with a crimson belt sustaining a rapier. A mask of black silk entirely covered his face.

"Scoundrel!" I said, in a voice husky with rage, while every syllable I uttered seemed as new fuel to my fury, "scoundrel! impostor! accursed villain! you shall not—you *shall not* dog me unto death! Follow me, or I stab you where you stand!"—and I broke my way from the ballroom into a small antechamber adjoining, dragging him unresistingly with me as I went.

Upon entering, I thrust him furiously from me. He staggered against the wall, while I closed the door with an oath, and commanded him to draw. He hesitated but for an instant; then, with a slight sigh, drew in silence, and put himself upon his defence.

The contest was brief indeed. I was frantic with every species of wild excitement, and felt within my single arm the energy and power of a multitude. In a few seconds I forced him by sheer strength against the wainscoting, and thus, getting him at mercy, plunged my sword, with brute ferocity, repeatedly through and through his bosom.

At that instant some person tried the latch of the door. I hastened to prevent an intrusion, and then immediately returned to my dying antagonist. But what human language can adequately portray *that* astonishment, *that* horror which possessed me at the spectacle then presented to view? The brief moment in which I averted my eyes had been sufficient to produce, apparently, a material change in the arrangements at the upper or farther end of the room. A large mirror—so at first it seemed to me in my confusion—now stood where none had been perceptible before; and as I stepped up to it in extremity of terror, mine own image, but with features all pale and dabbled in blood, advanced to meet me with a feeble and tottering gait.

Thus it appeared, I say, but was not. It was my antagonist—it was Wilson, who then stood before me in the agonies of his dissolution. His

mask and cloak lay, where he had thrown them, upon the floor. Not a
thread in all his raiment—not a line in all the marked and singular lineaments of his face which was not, even in the most absolute identity,
mine own!

It was Wilson; but he spoke no longer in a whisper, and I could have
fancied that I myself was speaking while he said:

*"You have conquered, and I yield. Yet, henceforward art thou also
dead—dead to the World, to Heaven, and to Hope! In me didst thou
exist—and, in my death, see by this image, which is thine own, how
utterly thou hast murdered thyself."*

Unmasking a Confidence Trickster

(from Meditations)

FRANZ KAFKA

At last, about ten o'clock at night, I came to the doorway of the fine
house where I was invited to spend the evening, after the man beside me,
whom I was barely acquainted with and who had once again thrust himself unasked upon me, had marched me for two long hours around the
streets.

"Well!" I said, and clapped my hands to show that I really had to bid
him goodbye. I had already made several less explicit attempts to get rid
of him. I was tired out.

"Are you going straight in?" he asked. I heard a sound in his mouth
that was like the snapping of teeth.

"Yes."

I had been invited out, I told him when I met him. But it was to
enter a house where I longed to be that I had been invited, not to stand
here at the street door looking past the ears of the man before me. Nor to
fall silent with him, as if we were doomed to stay for a long time on this
spot. And yet the houses around us at once took a share in our silence, and
the darkness over them, all the way up to the stars. And the steps of invisible passers-by, which one could not take the trouble to elucidate, and the
wind persistently buffeting the other side of the street, and a gramophone
singing behind the closed windows of some room—they all announced
themselves in this silence, as if it were their own possession for the time
past and to come.

And my companion subscribed to it in his own name and—with a smile—in mine too, stretched his right arm up along the wall and leaned his cheek upon it, shutting his eyes.

But I did not wait to see the end of that smile, for shame suddenly caught hold of me. It had needed that smile to let me know that the man was a confidence trickster, nothing else. And yet I had been months in the town and thought I knew all about confidence tricksters, how they came slinking out of side streets by night to meet us with outstretched hands like tavernkeepers, how they haunted the advertisement pillars we stood beside, sliding round them as if playing hide-and-seek and spying on us with at least one eye, how they suddenly appeared on the curb of the pavement at cross streets when we were hesitating! I understood them so well, they were the first acquaintances I had made in the town's small taverns, and to them I owed my first inkling of a ruthless hardness which I was now so conscious of, everywhere on earth, that I was even beginning to feel it in myself. How persistently they blocked our way, even when we had long shaken ourselves free, even when, that is, they had nothing more to hope for! How they refused to give up, to admit defeat, but kept shooting glances at us that even from a distance were still compelling! And the means they employed were always the same: they planted themselves before us, looking as large as possible, tried to hinder us from going where we purposed, offered us instead a habitation in their own bosoms, and when at last all our balked feelings rose in revolt they welcomed that like an embrace into which they threw themselves face foremost.

And it had taken me such a long time in this man's company to recognize the same old game. I rubbed my finger tips together to wipe away the disgrace.

My companion was still leaning there as before, still believing himself a successful trickster, and his self-complacency glowed pink on his free cheek.

"Caught in the act!" said I, tapping him lightly on the shoulder. Then I ran up the steps, and the disinterested devotion on the servants' faces in the hall delighted me like an unexpected treat. I looked at them all, one after another, while they took my greatcoat off and wiped my shoes clean.

With a deep breath of relief and straightening myself to my full height I then entered the drawing room.

The Heavy Bear

DELMORE SCHWARTZ

"the witness of the body"
—*Whitehead*

The heavy bear who goes with me,
A manifold honey to smear his face,
Clumsy and lumbering here and there,
The central ton of every place,
The hungry beating brutish one
In love with candy, anger, and sleep,
Crazy factotum, dishevelling all,
Climbs the building, kicks the football,
Boxes his brother in the hate-ridden city.
Breathing at my side, that heavy animal,
That heavy bear who sleeps with me,
Howls in his sleep for a world of sugar,
A sweetness intimate as the water's clasp,
Howls in his sleep because the tight-rope
Trembles and shows the darkness beneath.
—The strutting show-off is terrified,
Dressed in his dress-suit, bulging his pants,
Trembles to think that his quivering meat
Must finally wince to nothing at all.

That inescapable animal walks with me,
Has followed me since the black womb held,
Moves where I move, distorting my gesture,
A caricature, a swollen shadow,
A stupid clown of the spirit's motive,
Perplexes and affronts with his own darkness,
The secret life of belly and bone,
Opaque, too near, my private, yet unknown,
Stretches to embrace the very dear
With whom I would walk without him near,
Touches her grossly, although a word
Would bare my heart and make me clear,

Stumbles, flounders, and strives to be fed
Dragging me with him in his mouthing care,
Amid the hundred million of his kind,
The scrimmage of appetite everywhere.

In a Dark Time

THEODORE ROETHKE

In a dark time, the eye begins to see,
I meet my shadow in the deepening shade;
I hear my echo in the echoing wood—
A lord of nature weeping to a tree.
I lived between the heron and the wren,
Beasts of the hill and serpents of the den.

What's madness but nobility of soul
At odds with circumstance? The day's on fire!
I know the purity of pure despair,
My shadow pinned against a sweating wall.
That place among the rocks—is it a cave,
Or winding path? The edge is what I have.

A steady storm of correspondences!
A night flowing with birds, a ragged moon,
And in broad day the midnight come again!
A man goes far to find out what he is—
Death of the self in a long, tearless night,
All natural shapes blazing unnatural light.

Dark, dark my light, and darker my desire.
My soul, like some heat-maddened summer fly,
Keeps buzzing at the sill. Which I is I?
A fallen man, I climb out of my fear.
The mind enters itself, and God the mind,
And one is One, free in the tearing wind.

Was nature kind? The heart's core tractable?
All waters waver, and all fires fail.

Leaves, leaves, lean forth and tell me what I am;
This single tree turns into purest flame.
I am a man, a man at intervals
Pacing a room, a room with dead-white walls;
I feel the autumn fail—all that slow fire
Denied in me, who has denied desire.

The Scapegoat

SOCIETY seems to need a victim, a sacrificial offering that will placate their gods or purge society of its aggressiveness. The ritualistic expiation of communal sin or guilt is accomplished in some modern works of literature through the use of a scapegoat, as in Shirley Jackson's story "The Lottery" or in the much earlier "offerings" of the figure of Adonis or Jesus. Richard Wright's *Native Son* suggests how a white society condemns a black man (Bigger Thomas) to a life of servitude and exploitation and then, when he reacts in a violent manner, executes him to expunge their own sense of guilt in his crime. The scapegoat is The Other—be he communist, Jew, or Indian. He is seen as a threat and must be destroyed. Sometimes, however, the scapegoat is a recognized member of society and his destruction is brought about because his society is not ready for what he has to offer it (as in Shelley's elegy on the death of John Keats, "Adonais").

Adonis

(from Metamorphoses, X, 519–556, 698–739; trans. Rolfe Humphries)

OVID

Time, in its stealthy gliding, cheats us all
Without our notice; nothing goes more swiftly
Than do the years. That little boy, whose sister
Became his mother, his grandfather's son,
Is now a youth, and now a man, more handsome
Than he had ever been, exciting even
The goddess Venus, and thereby avenging
His mother's passion. Cupid, it seems, was playing,
Quiver on shoulder, when he kissed his mother,
And one barb grazed her breast; she pushed him away,
But the wound was deeper than she knew; deceived,
Charmed by Adonis' beauty, she cared no more

For Cythera's shores nor Paphos' sea-ringed island,
Nor Cnidos, where fish teem, nor high Amathus,
Rich in its precious ores. She stays away
Even from Heaven, Adonis is better than Heaven.
She is beside him always; she has always,
Before this time, preferred the shadowy places,
Preferred her ease, preferred to improve her beauty
By careful tending, but now, across the ridges,
Through woods, through rocky places thick with brambles,
She goes, more like Diana than like Venus,
Bare-kneed and robes tucked up. She cheers the hounds,
Hunts animals, at least such timid creatures
As deer and rabbits; no wild boars for her,
No wolves, no bears, no lions. And she warns him
To fear them too, as if there might be good
In giving him warnings. "Be bold against the timid,
The running creatures, but against the bold ones
Boldness is dangerous. Do not be reckless.
I share whatever risk you take; be careful!
Do not attack those animals which Nature
Has given weapons, lest your thirst for glory
May cost me dear. Beauty and youth and love
Make no impression on bristling boars and lions,
On animal eyes and minds. The force of lightning
Is the wild boar's tusks, and tawny lions
Are worse than thunderbolts. I hate and fear them."
He asks her why. She answers, "I will tell you,
And you will wonder at the way old crime
Leads to monstrosities. I will tell you sometime,
Not now, for I am weary, all this hunting
Is not what I am used to. Here's a couch
Of grassy turf, and a canopy of poplar,
I would like to lie there with you." And she lay there,
Making a pillow for him of her breast,
And kisses for her story's punctuation. . . .
[Cybele turned Hippomenes and Atalanta into beasts.] So their necks
Grew rough with tawny manes, their fingers, hooked,
Were claws, their arms were legs, their chests grew heavy,
Their tails swept over the sandy ground, and anger
Blazed in their features, they conversed in growling,
Too to the woods to couple: they were lions,
Frightful to all by Cybele, whose bridle
And bit they champed in meekness. "Do not hunt them,

Adonis: let all beasts alone, which offer
Beasts to the fight, not backs, or else your daring
Will be the ruin of us both." Her warning
Was given, and the goddess took her way,
Drawn by her swans through air. But the young hunter
Scorned all such warnings, and one day, it happened,
His hounds, hard on the trail, roused a wild boar,
And as he rushed from the wood, Adonis struck him
A glancing blow, and the boar turned, and shaking
The spear from the side, came charging at the hunter,
Who feared, and ran, and fell, and the tusk entered
Deep in the groin, and the youth lay there dying
On the yellow sand, and Venus, borne through air
In her light swan-guided chariot, still was far
From Cyprus when she heard his groans, and, turning
The white swans from their course, came back to him,
Saw, from high air, the body lying lifeless
In its own blood, and tore her hair and garments,
Beat her fair breasts with cruel hands, came down
Reproaching Fate. "They shall not have it always
Their way," she mourned, "Adonis, for my sorrow,
Shall have a lasting monument: each year
Your death will be my sorrow, but your blood
Shall be a flower. If Persephone
Could change to fragrant mint the girl called Mentha,
Cinyras' son, my hero, surely also
Can be my flower." Over the blood she sprinkled
Sweet-smelling nectar, and as bubbles rise
In rainy weather, so it stirred, and blossomed,
Before an hour, as crimson in its color
As pomegranates are, as briefly clinging
To life as did Adonis, for the winds
Which gave a name to the flower, anemone,
The wind-flower, shake the petals off, too early,
Doomed all too swift and soon.

Christ Is Crucified

MATTHEW, Chapter 27

1 When the morning was come, all the chief priests and elders of the people took counsel against Jesus to put him to death: 2 And when they had bound him, they led *him* away, and delivered him to Pontius Pilate the governor.   3 Then Judas, which had betrayed him, when he saw that he was condemned, repented himself, and brought again the thirty pieces of silver to the chief priests and elders,   4 Saying, I have sinned in that I have betrayed the innocent blood. And they said, What *is that* to us? see thou *to that*.   5 And he cast down the pieces of silver in the temple, and departed, and went and hanged himself.   6 And the chief priests took the silver pieces, and said, It is not lawful for to put them into the treasury, because it is the price of blood.   7 And they took counsel, and bought with them the potter's field, to bury strangers in. 8 Wherefore that field was called, the field of blood, unto this day.   9 Then was fulfilled that which was spoken by Jeremy the prophet, saying, And they took the thirty pieces of silver, the price of him that was valued, whom they of the children of Israel did value;   10 And gave them for the potter's field, as the Lord appointed me.   11 And Jesus stood before the governor: and the governor asked him, saying, Art thou the King of the Jews? And Jesus said unto him, Thou sayest.   12 And when he was accused of the chief priests and elders, he answered nothing. 13 Then said Pilate unto him, Hearest thou not how many things they witness against thee?   14 And he answered him to never a word; insomuch that the governor marvelled greatly.   15 Now at *that* feast the governor was wont to release unto the people a prisoner, whom they would.   16 And they had then a notable prisoner, called Barabbas. 17 Therefore when they were gathered together, Pilate said unto them, Whom will ye that I release unto you: Barabbas, or Jesus which is called Christ?   18 For he knew that for envy they had delivered him.   19 When he was set down on the judgment seat, his wife sent unto him, saying, Have thou nothing to do with that just man: for I have suffered many things this day in a dream because of him.   20 But the chief priests and elders persuaded the multitude that they should ask Barabbas, and destroy Jesus.   21 The governor answered and said unto them, Whether of the twain will ye that I release unto you? They said, Barabbas. 22 Pilate saith unto them, What shall I do then with Jesus which is called

Christ? *They* all say unto him, Let him be crucified.   23 And the governor said, Why, what evil hath he done? But they cried out the more, saying, Let him be crucified.   24 When Pilate saw that he could prevail nothing, but *that* rather a tumult was made, he took water, and washed *his* hands before the multitude, saying, I am innocent of the blood of this just person: see ye *to it.*   25 Then answered all the people, and said, His blood *be* on us, and on our children.   26 Then released he Barabbas unto them: and when he had scourged Jesus, he delivered *him* to be crucified.   27 Then the soldiers of the governor took Jesus into the common hall, and gathered unto him the whole band *of soldiers.*   28 And they stripped him, and put on him a scarlet robe.   29 And when they had platted a crown of thorns, they put *it* upon his head, and a reed in his right hand: and they bowed the knee before him, and mocked him, saying, Hail, King of the Jews!   30 And they spit upon him, and took the reed, and smote him on the head.   31 And after that they took the robe off from him, and put his own raiment on him, and led him away to crucify *him.*   32 And as they came out, they found a man of Cyrene, Simon by name: him they compelled to bear his cross.   33 And when they were come unto a place called Golgotha, that is to say, a place of a skull, 34 They gave him vinegar to drink mingled with gall: and when he had tasted *thereof,* he would not drink.   35 And they crucified him, and parted his garments, casting lots: that it might be fulfilled which was spoken by the prophet, They parted my garments among them, and upon my vesture did they cast lots.   36 And sitting down they watched him there;   37 And set up over his head his accusation written, THIS IS JESUS THE KING OF THE JEWS.   38 Then were there two thieves crucified with him, one on the right hand, and another on the left. 39 And they that passed by reviled him, wagging their heads,   40 And saying, Thou that destroyest the temple, and buildest *it* in three days, save thyself. If thou be the Son of God, come down from the cross,   41 Likewise also the chief priests mocking *him,* with the scribes and elders, said,   42 He saved others; himself he cannot save. If he be the King of Israel, let him now come down from the cross, and we will believe him. 43 He trusted in God; let him deliver him now, if he will have him: for he said, I am the Son of God.   44 The thieves also, which were crucified with him, cast the same in his teeth.   45 Now from the sixth hour there was darkness over all the land unto the ninth hour.   46 And about the ninth hour Jesus cried with a loud voice, saying, Eli, Eli, lama sabachthani? that is to say, My God, my God, why hast thou forsaken me?   47 Some of them that stood there, when they heard *that,* said, This *man* calleth for Elias.   48 And straightway one of them ran, and took a sponge, and filled *it* with vinegar, and put *it* on a reed, and gave him to drink.   49 The rest said, Let be, let us see whether Elias will come to save him.

50 Jesus, when he had cried again with a loud voice, yielded up the ghost.
51 And, behold, the veil of the temple was rent in twain from the top to
the bottom; and the earth did quake, and the rocks rent; 52 And the
graves were opened; and many bodies of the saints which slept arose,
53 And came out of the graves after his resurrection, and went into the
holy city, and appeared unto many. 54 Now when the centurion, and
they that were with him, watching Jesus, saw the earth quake, and those
things that were done, they feared greatly, saying, Truly this was the
Son of God.

The Permanent Delegate

(trans. Max Rosenfeld and Walter Lowenfels)

YURI SUHL

My name is Jew.
  I come from the land of skeleton.
They beat me in Berlin,
  tortured me in Warsaw,
    shot me in Lublin
And I am still here—the ash of my bones
  a glowing monument, a fiery headstone.

I am the scorched hair of a virgin's bright curls
  smoothed and patted by anxious hands,
I am a maddened mother's futile tears
  soothing in vain a hundred anguished hurts.

I am the spasm of a body convulsed in flames,
  the crumbling of a skeleton,
the boiling of blood, shriveling of flesh,
  smouldering ash of six million—
ashes of body, of brain, of vision, of work—
  ashes of genius and dreams,
    ashes of God's master stroke—Man.

Count the limbs, gentlemen—
  match them if you can in pairs.
    It can't be done.

For I am one ghost of six million.
Out of all the ashes I have become one
And the dream lies broken and spit on.
I am here to tell you, gentlemen,
    it's a lie—the world is not yet Hitler-free.
Millions see it, condemn it,
    cry out my pain and warn you.

But you are moved like a granite statue
    by the prick of a pin.
Therefore I have come,
    uninvited, unwelcome,
        bringing a message
from the land of skeleton.

I am grafting my ash to your souls.
I am hanging my dreams around your necks.
I am blotting out the sun from your day
                with my shadow.
I am tearing the quiet of your night
                with the shrieks of my tortures.
I will beat at your conscience
    with the hands of a million dead children and
I will pick at your brains
                with my maggots.
Yea, though you split the atom to infinity
    you will see my face before your eyes.
I sit at all the round tables.
At every conference I am a delegate,
my credentials signed by six million
    from the land of skeleton
and you will never get rid of me
    until the world is Hitler-free.

Fertility Rite

DILYS LAING

Children are hanging
in the black cathedral
ten thousand children
on strontium crosses.

The floor is slippery
with blood and milk.
The priests pronounce it
a good sacrifice.

They say the children
wept without control
making good augury
for rain and crops.

High in the cracking cupola
the mosaic eyes
of archangels and saints
weep fire.

The Death of Helga Brunner

YURI SUHL

A German woman caught in a roundup of Jews
by mistake landed in Treblinka. Though
convinced of the error, the camp commander
refused to free her.

Her blood was right
and so was the color of her eyes
but she has seen the chimneys
(a secret of State)
and what the eye has seen
it cannot unsee.

"I'm an Aryan woman," she pleaded.
The commander was deaf to her plea.
"I'm not one of the Sarahs," she cried.
"I know you're not," the commander replied,
"so calm yourself, liebchen,
you won't be gassed with the Jewish scum—
you'll be honorably shot."

The Convert

LERONE BENNETT, JR.

A man don't know what he'll do, a man don't know what he is till he gets his back pressed up against a wall. Now you take Aaron Lott: there ain't no other way to explain the crazy thing he did. He was going along fine, preaching the gospel, saving souls, and getting along with the white folks; and then, all of a sudden, he felt wood pressing against his back. The funny thing was that nobody knew he was hurting till he preached that Red Sea sermon where he got mixed up and seemed to think Mississippi was Egypt. As chairman of the deacons board, I felt it was my duty to reason with him. I appreciated his position and told him so, but I didn't think it was right for him to push us all in a hole. The old fool—he just laughed.

"Brother Booker," he said, "the Lord—He'll take care of me."

I knew then that the man was heading for trouble. And the very next thing he did confirmed it.

He looked at me like I was Satan.

"I sweated over this thing," he said. "I prayed. I got down on my knees and I asked God not to give me this cup. But He said I was the one. I heard Him, Booker, right here"—he tapped his chest—"in my heart."

The old fool's been having visions, I thought. I sat down and tried to figure out a way to hold him, but he got up, without saying a word, and started for the door.

"Wait!" I shouted. "I'll get my coat."

"I don't need you," he said. "I just came by to tell you so you could tell the board in case something happened."

"You wait," I shouted, and ran out of the room to get my coat.

We got in his beat-up old Ford and went by the parsonage to get his suitcase. Rachel—that was his wife—and Jonah were sitting in the living room, wringing their hands. Aaron got his bag, shook Jonah's hand, and said, "Take care of your Mamma, boy." Jonah nodded. Aaron hugged Rachel and pecked at her cheek. Rachel broke down. She throwed her arms around his neck and carried on something awful. Aaron shoved her away.

"Don't go making no fuss over it, woman. I ain't gonna be gone forever. Can't a man go to a church meeting 'thout women screaming and crying."

He tried to make light of it, but you could see he was touched by the way his lips trembled. He held his hand out to me, but I wouldn't take it. I told him off good, told him it was a sin and a shame for a man of God to be carrying on like he was, worrying his wife and everything.

"I'm coming with you," I said. "Somebody's gotta see that you don't make a fool of yourself."

He shrugged, picked up his suitcase, and started for the door. Then he stopped and turned around and looked at his wife and his boy and from the way he looked I knew that there was still a chance. He looked at the one and then at the other. For a moment there, I thought he was going to cry, but he turned, quick-like, and walked out of the door.

I ran after him and tried to talk some sense in his head. But he shook me off, turned the corner, and went on up Adams Street. I caught up with him and we walked in silence, crossing the street in front of the First Baptist Church for whites, going on around the Confederate monument.

"Put it off, Aaron," I begged. "Sleep on it."

He didn't say nothing.

"What you need is a vacation. I'll get the board to approve, full pay and everything."

He smiled and shifted the suitcase over to his left hand. Big drops of sweat were running down his face and spotting up his shirt. His eyes were awful, all lit up and burning.

"Aaron, Aaron, can't you hear me?"

We passed the feed store, Bill Williams' grocery store, and the movie house.

"A man's gotta think about his family, Aaron. A man ain't free. Didn't you say that once, didn't you?"

He shaded his eyes with his hand and looked into the sun. He put the suitcase on the ground and checked his watch.

"Why don't you think about Jonah?" I asked. "Answer that. Why don't you think about your own son?"

"I am," he said. "That's exactly what I'm doing, thinking about Jonah. Matter of fact, he started *me* to thinking. I ain't never mentioned it before, but the boy's been worrying me. One day he was downtown here and he asked me something that hurt. 'Daddy,' he said, 'how come you ain't a man?' I got mad, I did, and told him: 'I am a man.' He said that wasn't what he meant. 'I mean,' he said, 'how come you ain't a man where white folks concerned.' I couldn't answer him, Booker, I'll never forget it till the day I die. I couldn't answer my own son, and I been preaching forty years."

"He don't know nothing 'bout it," I said. "He's hot-headed, like my boy. He'll find out when he grows up."

"I hopes not," Aaron said, shaking his head. "I hopes not."

Some white folks passed and we shut up till they were out of hearing. Aaron, who was acting real strange, looked up in the sky and moved his lips. He came back to himself, after a little bit, and he said: "This thing of being a man, Booker, is a big thing. The Supreme Court can't make you a man. The NAACP can't do it. God Almighty can do a lot, but even He can't do it. Ain't nobody can do it but you."

He said that like he was preaching and when he got through he was all filled up with emotion and he seemed kind of ashamed—he was a man who didn't like emotion outside the church. He looked at his watch, picked up his bag and said, "Well, let's git it over with."

We turned into Elm and the first thing I saw at the end of the street was the train station. It was an old red building, flat like a slab. A group of white men were fooling around in front of the door. I couldn't make them out from that distance, but I could tell they weren't the kind of white folks to be fooling around with.

We walked on, passing the dry goods store, the barber shop, and the new building that was going up. Across the street from that was the sheriff's office. I looked in the window and saw Bull Sampson sitting at his desk, his feet propped up on a chair, a fat brown cigar sticking out of his mouth. A ball about the size of a sweet potato started burning in my stomach.

"Please Aaron," I said. "Please. You can't get away with it. I know how you feel. Sometimes I feel the same way myself, but I wouldn't risk my neck for these niggers. They won't appreciate it; they'll laugh at you."

We were almost to the station and I could make out the faces of the men sitting on the benches. One of them must have been telling a joke. He finished and the group broke out laughing.

I whispered to Aaron: "I'm through with it. I wash my hands of the whole mess."

I don't know whether he heard me or not. He turned to the right without saying a word and went on in the front door. The string-beany man who told the joke was so shocked that his cigarette fell out of his mouth.

"Y'all see that," he said. "Why, I'll—"

"Shut up," another man said. "Go git Bull."

I kept walking fast, turned at the corner, and ran around to the colored waiting room. When I got there, I looked through the ticket window and saw Aaron standing in front of the clerk. Aaron stood there for a minute or more, but the clerk didn't see him. And that took some not seeing. In that room, Aaron Lott stood out like a pig in a chicken coop.

There were, I'd say, about ten or fifteen people in there, but didn't none of them move. They just sat there, with their eyes glued on Aaron's back. Aaron cleared his throat. The clerk didn't look up; he got real busy with some papers. Aaron cleared his throat again and opened his his mouth to speak. The screen door of the waiting room opened and clattered shut.

It got real quiet in that room, hospital quiet. It got so quiet I could hear my own heart beating. Now Aaron knew who opened that door, but he didn't bat an eyelid. He turned around real slow and faced High Sheriff Sampson, the baddest man in South Mississippi.

Mr. Sampson stood there with his legs wide open, like the men you see on television. His beefy face was blood-red and his gray eyes were rattlesnake hard. He was mad; no doubt about it. I had never seen him so mad.

"Preacher," he said, "you done gone crazy?" He was talking low-like and mean.

"Nosir," Aaron said. "Nosir, Mr. Sampson."

"What you think you doing?"

"Going to St. Louis, Mr. Sampson."

"You must done lost yo' mind, boy."

Mr. Sampson started walking towards Aaron with his hands on his gun. Twenty or thirty men pushed through the front door and fanned out over the room. Mr. Sampson stopped about two paces from Aaron and looked him up and down. That look had paralyzed hundreds of niggers, but it didn't faze Aaron none—he stood his ground.

"I'm gonna give you a chance, preacher. Git on over to the nigger side and git quick."

"I ain't bothering nobody, Mr. Sampson."

Somebody in the crowd yelled: "Don't reason wit' the nigger, Bull. Hit em."

Mr. Sampson walked up to Aaron and grabbed him in the collar and throwed him up against the ticket counter. He pulled out his gun.

"Did you hear me, deacon. I said, 'Git.' "

"I'm going to St. Louis, Mr. Sampson. That's cross state lines. The court done said—"

Aaron didn't have a chance. The blow came from nowhere. Laying there on the floor with blood spurting from his mouth, Aaron looked up at Mr. Sampson and he did another crazy thing: he grinned. Bull Sampson jumped up in the air and came down on Aaron with all his two hundred pounds. It made a crunchy sound. He jumped again and the mob, maddened by the blood and heat, moved in to help him. They fell on Aaron like mad dogs. They beat him with chairs; they beat him with sticks; they beat him with guns.

Till this day, I don't know what come over me. The first thing I know I was running and then I was standing in the middle of the white waiting room. Mr. Sampson was the first to see me. He backed off, cocked his pistol, and said: "Booker, boy, you come one mo' step and I'll kill you. What's a matter with you niggers today? All y'all gone crazy?"

"Please don't kill him," I begged. "You ain't got no call to treat him like that."

"So you saw it all, did you? Well, then, Booker you musta saw the nigger preacher reach for my gun?"

"He didn't do that, Mr. Sampson," I said. "He didn't—"

Mr. Sampson put a big hairy hand on my tie and pulled me to him.

"Booker," he said sweetly. "You saw the preacher reach for my gun, didn't you?"

I didn't open my mouth—I couldn't I was so scared—but I guess my eyes answered for me. Whatever Mr. Sampson saw there musta convinced him 'cause he throwed me on the floor besides Aaron.

"Git this nigger out of here," he said, "and be quick about it."

Dropping to my knees, I put my hand on Aaron's chest; I didn't feel nothing. I felt his wrist; I didn't feel nothing. I got up and looked at them white folks with tears in my eyes. I looked at the women, sitting crying on the benches. I looked at the men. I looked at Mr. Sampson. I said, "He was a good man."

Mr. Sampson said, "Move the nigger."

A big sigh came out of me and I wrung my hands.

He grabbed my tie and twisted it, but I didn't feel nothing. My eyes were glued to his hands; there was blood under the fingernails, and the fingers—they looked like fat little red sausages. I screamed and Mr. Sampson flung me down on the floor.

He said, *"Move the nigger."*

I picked Aaron up and fixed his body over my shoulder and carried him outside. I sent for one of my boys and we dressed him up and put him away real nice-like and Rachel and the boy came and they cried and carried on and yet, somehow, they seemed prouder of Aaron than ever before. And the colored folks—they seemed proud, too. Crazy. Didn't they know? Couldn't they see? It hadn't done no good. In fact, things got worse. The Northern newspapers started kicking up a stink and Mr. Rivers, the solicitor, announced they were going to hold a hearing. All of a sudden, Booker Taliaferro Brown became the biggest man in that town. My phone rang day and night: I got threats, I got promises, and I was offered bribes. Everywhere I turned somebody was waiting to ask me: "Whatcha gonna do? Whatcha gonna say?" To tell the truth,

I didn't know myself. One day I would decide one thing and the next day I would decide another.

It was Mr. Rivers and Mr. Sampson who called my attention to that. They came to my office one day and called me a shifty, no-good nigger. They said they expected me to stand by "my statement" in the train station that I saw Aaron reach for the gun. I hadn't said no such thing, but Mr. Sampson said I said it and he said he had witnesses who heard me say it. "And if you say anything else," he said, "I can't be responsible for your health. Now you know"—he put that bloody hand on my shoulder and he smiled his sweet death smile—"you *know* I wouldn't threaten you, but the boys"—he shook his head—"the boys are real worked up over this one."

It was long about then that I began to hate Aaron Lott. I'm ashamed to admit it now, but it's true: I hated him. He had lived his life: he had made his choice. Why should he live my life, too, and make me choose? It wasn't fair; it wasn't right; it wasn't Christian. What made me so mad was the fact that nothing I said would help Aaron. He was dead and it wouldn't help one whit for me to say that he didn't reach for that gun. I tried to explain that to Rachel when she came to my office, moaning and crying, the night before the hearing.

"Listen to me, woman," I said. "Listen, Aaron was a good man. He lived a good life. He did a lot of good things, but he's *dead, dead, dead!* Nothing I say will bring him back. Bull Sampson's got ten niggers who are going to swear on a stack of Bibles that they saw Aaron reach for that gun. It won't do me or you or Aaron no good for me to swear otherwise."

What did I say that for? That woman like to had a fit. She got down on her knees and she begged me to go with Aaron.

"Go wit' him," she cried. "Booker, *Booker!* If you's a man, if you's a father, if you's a friend, go wit' Aaron."

That woman tore my heart up. I ain't never heard nobody beg like that.

"Tell the truth, Booker," she said. "That's all I'm asking. Tell the truth."

"Truth!" I said. "Hah! That's all you niggers talk about: truth. What do you know about truth? Truth is eating good, and sleeping good. Truth is living, Rachel. Be loyal to the living."

Rachel backed off from me. You would have thought that I had cursed her or something. She didn't say nothing; she just stood there pressed against the door. She stood there saying nothing for so long that my nerves snapped.

"Say something," I shouted. "Say something—anything!"

She shook her head, slowly at first, and then her head started moving like it wasn't attached to her body. It went back and forth, back and forth, back and forth. I started towards her, but she jerked open the door and ran out into the night, screaming.

That did it. I ran across the room to the filing cabinet, opened the bottom drawer, and took out a dusty bottle of Scotch. I started drinking, but the more I drank the soberer I got. I guess I fell asleep 'cause I dreamed I buried Rachel and that everything went along fine until she jumped out of the casket and started screaming. I came awake with a start and knocked over the bottle. I reached for a rag and my hand stopped in mid-air.

"Of course," I said out loud and slammed my fist down on the Scotch-soaked papers.

I didn't see nothing.

Why didn't I think of it before?

I didn't see nothing.

Jumping up, I walked to and fro in the office. Would it work? I rehearsed it in my mind. All I could see was Aaron's back. I don't know whether he reached for the gun or not. All I know is that *for some reason* the men beat him to death.

Rehearsing the thing in my mind, I felt a great weight slip off my shoulders. I did a little jig in the middle of the floor and went upstairs to my bed, whistling. Sarah turned over and looked me up and down.

"What you happy about?"

"Can't a man be happy?" I asked.

She sniffed the air, said, "Oh," turned over, and mumbled something in her pillow. It came to me then for the first time that she was 'bout the only person in town who hadn't asked me what I was going to do. I thought about it for a little while, shrugged, and fell into bed with all my clothes on.

When I woke up the next morning, I had a terrible headache and my tongue was a piece of sandpaper. For a long while, I couldn't figure out what I was doing laying there with all my clothes on. Then it came to me: this was the big day. I put on my black silk suit, the one I wore for big funerals, and went downstairs to breakfast. I walked into the dining room without looking and bumped into Russell, the last person in the world I wanted to see. He was my only child, but he didn't act like it. He was always finding fault. He didn't like the way I talked to Negroes; he didn't like the way I talked to white folks. He didn't like this; he didn't like that. And to top it off, the young whippersnapper wanted to be an artist. Undertaking wasn't good enough for him. He wanted to paint pictures.

I sat down and grunted.

"Good morning, Papa." He said it like he meant it. He wants something, I thought, looking him over closely, noticing that his right eye was swollen.

"You been fighting again, boy?"

"Yes, Papa."

"You younguns. Education—that's what it is. Education! It's ruining you."

He didn't say nothing. He just sat there, looking down when I looked up and looking up when I looked down. This went on through the grits and the eggs and the second cup of coffee.

"Whatcha looking at?" I asked.

"Nothing, Papa."

"Whatcha thinking?"

"Nothing, Papa."

"You lying, boy. It's written all over your face."

He didn't say nothing.

I dismissed him with a wave of my hand, picked up the paper, and turned to the sports page.

"What are you going to do, Papa?"

The question caught me unawares. I know now that I was expecting it, that I wanted him to ask it; but he put it so bluntly that I was flabbergasted. I pretended I didn't understand.

"Do 'bout what, boy? Speak up!"

"About the trial, Papa."

I didn't say nothing for a long time. There wasn't much, in fact, I could say; so I got mad.

"Questions, questions, questions," I shouted. "That's all I get in this house—questions. You never have a civil word for your pa. I go out of here and work my tail off and you keep yourself shut up in that room of yours looking at them fool books and now soon as your old man gets his back against the wall you join the pack. I expected better than that of you, boy. A son ought to back his pa."

That hurt him. He picked up the coffee pot and poured himself another cup of coffee and his hand trembled. He took a sip and watched me over the rim.

"They say you are going to chicken out, Papa."

"Chicken out? What that mean?"

"They're betting you'll 'Tom.' "

I leaned back in the chair and took a sip of coffee.

"So they're betting, huh?" The idea appealed to me. "Crazy—they'd bet on a funeral."

I saw pain on his face. He sighed and said: "I bet, too, Papa."

The cup fell out of my hand and broke, spilling black water over the tablecloth.

"You did what?"

"I bet you wouldn't 'Tom.' "

"You little fool." I fell out laughing and then I stopped suddenly and looked at him closely. "How much you bet?"

"One hundred dollars."

I stood up.

"You're lying," I said. "Where'd you get that kind of money?"

"From Mamma."

"Sarah!" I shouted. "Sarah! You get in here. What kind of house you running, sneaking behind my back, giving this boy money to gamble with?"

Sarah leaned against the door jamb. She was in her hot iron mood. There was no expression on her face. And her eyes were hard.

"I gave it to him, Booker," she said. "They called you an Uncle Tom. He got in a fight about it. He wanted to bet on you, Booker. *He* believes in you."

Suddenly I felt old and used up. I pulled a chair to me and sat down.

"Please," I said, waving my hand. "Please. Go away. Leave me alone. Please."

I sat there for maybe ten or fifteen minutes, thinking, praying. The phone rang. It was Mr. Withers, the president of the bank. I had put in for a loan and it had been turned down, but Mr. Withers said there'd been a mistake. "New fellow, you know," he said, clucking his tongue. He said he knew that it was my lifelong dream to build a modern funeral home and to buy a Cadillac hearse. He said he sympathized with that dream, supported it, thought the town needed it, and thought I deserved it. "The loan will go through," he said. "Drop by and see me this morning after the hearing."

When I put that phone down, it was wet with sweat. I couldn't turn that new funeral home down and Mr. Withers knew it. My father had raised me on that dream and before he died he made me swear on a Bible I would make it good. And here it was on a platter, just for a word, a word that wouldn't hurt nobody.

I put on my hat and hurried to the courthouse. When they called my name, I walked in with my head held high. The courtroom was packed. The white folks had all the seats and the colored folks were standing in the rear. Whoever arranged the seating had set aside the first two rows for white men. They were sitting almost on top of each other, looking mean and uncomfortable in their best white shirts.

I walked up to the bench and swore on the Bible and took a seat. Mr. Rivers gave me a little smile and waited for me to get myself set.

"State your name," he said.

"Booker Taliaferro Brown." I took a quick look at the first two rows and recognized at least ten of the men who killed Aaron.

"And your age?"

"Fifty-seven."

"You're an undertaker?"

"Yessir."

"You been living in this town all your life?"

"Yessir."

"You like it here, don't you, Booker?"

Was this a threat? I looked Mr. Rivers in the face for the first time. He smiled.

I told the truth. I said, "Yessir."

"Now, calling your attention to the day of May 17th, did anything unusual happen on that day?"

The question threw me. I shook my head. Then it dawned on me. He was talking about—

"Yessir," I said. "That's the day Aaron got—" Something in Mr. Rivers' face warned me and I pulled up—"that's the day of the trouble at the train station."

Mr. Rivers smiled. He looked like a trainer who'd just put a monkey through a new trick. You could feel the confidence and the contempt oozing out of him. I looked at his prissy little mustache and his smiling lips and I got mad. Lifting my head a little bit, I looked him full in the eyes: I held the eyes for a moment and I tried to tell the man behind the eyes that I was a man like him and that he didn't have no right to be using me and laughing about it. But he didn't get the message. He chuckled softly, turned his back on me, and faced the audience.

"I believe you were with the preacher that day."

The water was getting deep. I scroonched down in my seat, closed the lids of my eyes, and looked dense.

"Yessir, Mr. Rivers," I drawled. "Ah was, Ah was."

"Now, Booker—" he turned around— "I believe you tried to keep the nigger preacher from getting out of line."

I hesitated. It wasn't a fair question. Finally, I said: "Yessir."

"You begged him not to go to the white side?"

"Yessir."

"And when that failed, you went over to *your* side—the *colored* side —and looked through the window?"

"Yessir."

He put his hand in his coat pocket and studied my face.

"You saw *everything*, didn't you?"

"Just about." A muscle on the inside of my thigh started tingling.

Mr. Rivers shuffled some papers he had in his hand. He seemed to be thinking real hard. I pushed myself against the back of the chair. Mr. Rivers moved close, quick, and stabbed his finger into my chest.

"Booker, did you see the nigger preacher reach for Mr. Sampson's gun?"

He backed away, smiling. I looked away from him and I felt my heart trying to tear out of my skin. I looked out over the courtroom. It was still: wasn't even a fly moving. I looked at the white folks in front and the colored folks in back and I turned the question over in my mind. While I was doing that, waiting, taking my time, I noticed, out of the corner of my eye, that the smile on Mr. Rivers' face was dying away. Suddenly, I had a terrible itch to know what that smile would turn into.

I said, "Nosir."

Mr. Rivers stumbled backwards like he had been shot. Old Judge Sloan took off his glasses and pushed his head out over the bench. The whole courtroom seemed to be leaning in to me and I saw Aaron's widow leaning back with her eyes closed and it seemed to me at that distance that her lips were moving in prayer.

Mr. Rivers was the first to recover. He put his smile back on and he acted like my answer was in the script.

"You mean," he said, "that you didn't see it. It happened so quickly that you missed it?"

I looked at the bait and I ain't gonna lie: I was tempted. He knew as well as I did what I meant, but he was gambling on my weakness. I had thrown away my funeral home, my hearse, everything I owned, and he was standing there like a magician, pulling them out of a hat, one at a time, dangling them, saying: "Looka here, looka here, don't they look pretty?" I was on top of a house and he was betting that if he gave me a ladder I would come down. He was wrong, but you can't fault him for trying. I looked him in the eye and went the last mile.

"Aaron didn't reach for that gun," I said. "Them people, they just fell on—"

"Hold it," he shouted. "I want to remind you that there are laws in this state against perjury. You can go to jail for five years for what you just said. Now I know you've been conferring with those NAACP fellows, but I want to remind you of the statements you made to Sheriff Sampson and me. Judge—" he dismissed me with a wave of his hand—"Judge, this *man*—" he caught himself and it was my turn to smile—"this *boy* is lying. Ten niggers have testified that they saw the preacher reach for the gun. Twenty white people saw it. You've heard their testimony. I want to withdraw this witness and I want to reserve the right to file perjury charges against him."

Judge Sloan nodded. He pushed his bottom lip over his top one.

"You can step down," he said. "I want to warn you that perjury is a very grave offense. You—"

"Judge, I didn't—"

"Nigger!" He banged his gavel. "Don't you interrupt me. Now git out of here."

Two guards pushed me outside and waved away the reporters. Billy

Giles, Mr. Sampson's assistant, came out and told me Mr. Sampson wanted me out of town before sundown. "And he says you'd better get out before the Northern reporters leave. He won't be responsible for your safety after that."

I nodded and went on down the stairs and started out the door.

"Booker!"

Rachel and a whole line of Negroes were running down the stairs. I stepped outside and waited for them. Rachel ran up and throwed her arms around me. "It don't take but one, Booker," she said. "It don't take but one." Somebody else said: "They whitewashed it, they whitewashed it, but you spoiled it for 'em."

Russell came out then and stood over to the side while the others crowded around to shake my hands. Then the others sensed that he was waiting and they made a little aisle. He walked up to me kind of slow-like and he said, "Thank you, sir." That was the first time in his whole seventeen years that that boy had said "sir" to me. I cleared my throat and when I opened my eyes Sarah was standing beside me. She didn't say nothing; she just put her hand in mine and stood there. It was long about then, I guess, when I realized that I wasn't seeing so good. They say I cried, but I don't believe a word of it. It was such a hot day and the sun was shining so bright that the sweat rolling down my face blinded me. I wiped the sweat out of my eyes and some more people came up and said a lot of foolish things about me showing the white folks and following in Aaron's footsteps. I wasn't doing no such fool thing. Ol' Man Rivers just put the thing to me in a way it hadn't been put before—man to man. It was simple, really. Any man would have done it.

The Temptress

Woman seen as destroyer created many taboos as to where and when females might appear within the tribal territory, what foods they might touch, what relations they might have with men. But male fantasies about woman were equally matched by her erotic attractiveness. These themes, coupled, developed into the motif of the Woman as Temptress: Helen of Troy, Cleopatra, Circe—women who were seductive and beautiful, but who would bring about the destruction of those they ensnared. The opposite of the figure of the protective earth mother, the temptress lured man on till her sensuous beauty had fully captured and weakened him. Delilah, representing such a figure, not only got Samson to forget his religious vows as a Nazarite (signified by his refusal to cut his hair and to drink intoxicating liquors) but symbolically castrated him. (Blinding and cutting hair imply castration, according to many psychoanalytic writers.) The temptress is often seen as representing an alien culture, the outsider or unknown. Thus figures such as Cleopatra and Delilah and the work of writers such as Phillip Roth (in *Portnoy's Complaint*) portray the attractive seductiveness of the beautiful alien, a contributor to Man's fall and the agency deflecting him from the journey and the quest.

Circe
(from The Odyssey, Book X)
HOMER

From that place we sailed on, glad enough to have come off with our lives, but sad to lose our companions. Next we reached the island of Aiaia. There Circê lived, a terrible goddess with lovely hair, who spoke in the language of men, own sister to murderous Aietas; their father was Helios, who gives light to mankind, and their mother was Persê, a daughter of Oceanos. We brought our ship to the shore in silence, and some providence guided us into a harbour where ships could lie. There we spent two days and two nights on shore, eating out our hearts with weariness and woe.

On the third day, as soon as dawn showed the first streaks of light,

I took spear and sword and climbed to a high place, where I had a look round to see if there was any one about or any voice to be heard. Standing on the top of a rock, I saw smoke rising into the air from the house where Circê lived in the middle of thick bushes and trees.

When I saw the smoke glowing, I considered whether I should go and inquire. The best plan seemed to be that I should return first to our ship on the shore and give the men something to eat, and then send out to inquire. Just as I came near to the ship, some god must have pitied me there so lonely, and sent me a stag with towering antlers right on my path: he was going down to the river from his woodland range to drink, for the sun's heat was heavy on him. As he came out, I struck him on the spine in the middle of the back, and the spear ran right through: down he fell in the dust with a moan, and died. I set my foot on him and drew out the spear from the wound. Then I laid the body flat on the ground, and pulled a quantity of twigs and withies, which I plaited across and twisted into a strong rope of a fathom's length: with this rope I tied together the legs of the great creature, and strung him over my neck, and so carried him down to the ship, leaning upon my spear; I could not have carried him on the shoulder with one hand, for he was a huge beast.

I threw him down in front of the ship, and cheered up my friends with encouraging words as I turned from one to another. "We are not going to die yet, my friends, for all our troubles: we shall not see the house of Hadês before our day comes. While there's food and drink in the ship, don't let us forget to eat! we need not die of starvation, at all events!"

They were all sitting about with their faces muffled up in their cloaks; but at my words they threw off the cloaks, and got up quickly to stare at the stag lying on the beach; for he was a huge beast. When they had feasted their eyes on the welcome sight, they began to think of another kind of feast; so they swilled their hands in due form, and got him ready. All day long until sunset we sat enjoying ourselves with our meat and wine; and when the sun went down and the darkness came, we lay down to sleep on the seashore.

As soon as morning dawned, I called my companions together and addressed them:

"My friends, we do not know east from west, we don't know where the sun rises to give light to all mankind, and where he goes down under the earth. Well, then, what are we to do? We must try to think of something at once, and for my part, I can't think of anything. I have just been up on the cliffs to look around. We are on some island in the middle of the sea, with no land in sight. The island is flat, and I saw smoke rising in the air above a coppice of bushes and trees."

When I said this, their hearts were crushed with foreboding: for they remembered the doings of Laistrygonian Antiphatês, and the violence of that audacious cannibal the goggle-eye Cyclops. The tears ran down their cheeks, and much good it did to weep!

However, I divided them into two parts of equal number, and chose a captain for each: one I took myself, the other I gave to an excellent man, Eurylochos. Quickly then we shook lots in a helmet, and out leapt the lot of Eurylochos. Off he went, with his two-and-twenty men, groaning and grumbling, and we were left groaning and grumbling behind.

They found in a dell the house of Circê, well built with shaped stones, and set in a clearing. All round it were wolves and lions of the mountains, really men whom she had bewitched by giving them poisonous drugs. They did not attack the men, but ramped up fawning on them and wagging their long tails, just like a lot of dogs playing about their master when he comes out after dinner, because they know he has always something nice for them in his pocket. So these wolves and lions with their sharp claws played about and pawed my men, who were frightened out of their wits by the terrible creatures.

They stopt at the outer doors of the courtyard, and heard the beautiful goddess within singing in a lovely voice, as she worked at the web on her loom, a large web of incorruptible stuff, a glorious thing of delicate gossamer fabric, such as goddesses make. The silence was broken by Politês, who was nearest and dearest to me of all my companions, and the most trusty. He said:

"Friends, I hear a voice in the house, some woman singing prettily at the loom, and the whole place echoes with it. Goddess or woman, let's go in and speak to her."

Then they called her loudly. She came out at once, and opened the shining doors, and asked them to come in; they all followed her, in their innocence, only Eurylochos remained behind, for he suspected a trap. She gave them all comfortable seats, and made them a posset, cheese and meal and pale honey mixt with Pramneian wine; but she put dangerous drugs in the mess, to make them wholly forget their native land. When they had swallowed it, she gave them a tap of her wand at once and herded them into pens; for they now had pigs' heads and grunts and bristles, pigs all over except that their minds were the same as before. There they were then, miserably shut up in the pigsty. Circê threw them a lot of beechnuts and acorns and cornel-beans to eat, such as the earthbedded swine are used to.

But Eurylochos came back to the ship, to tell the tale of his companions and their unkind fate. At first he could not utter a word, he was so dumbfounded with this misfortune; his eyes were full of tears, his mind foreboded trouble. At last when we were fairly flummoxed with asking questions, he found his tongue and told us how all his companions had come to grief.

"We went out into the wood, as you told us, most renowned chief;

found a well-built house in a dell, and there some one was singing loudly as she worked the loom, goddess or woman: they called to her. She came out at once and opened the doors and asked them in: they all followed in the simplicity of their hearts, but I stayed behind because I suspected a trap. They all disappeared at once, not a soul was to be seen, and I stayed there a long time to spy."

When he said this, at once I slung my sword over my shoulders, the large one, bronze with silver knobs, and the bow with it, and told him to go back with me and show me the way. But he threw his arms about my knees and begged and prayed without disguise—"Don't take me there, my prince; I don't want to go. Let me stay here. I am sure you will never come back again, nor will any one who goes with you. Let us get away with those who are here while we can: we have still a chance to escape the day of destruction!"

But I answered, "Very well, Eurylochos, you may stay here in this place, eat and drink beside the ship. But as for me, go I must, and go I will."

So I made my way up from the sea-side. But just as I was on the point of entering the sacred dell and finding the house of that mistress of many spells, who should meet me but Hermês with his golden rod: he looked like a young man with the first down on his lip, in the most charming time of youth. He grasped my hand, and said:

"Whither away again, you poor fellow, alone on the hills, in a country you do not know? Your companions are shut up yonder in Circê's, like so many pigs cosy in their pigsties. Are you going to set them free? Why, I warn you that you will never come back, you will stay here with the others.—All right, I will help you and keep you safe. Here, take this charm, and then you may enter the house of Circê: this will keep destruction from your head.

"I will reveal to you all the malign arts of Circê. She will make you a posset, and put drugs in the mess. But she will not be able to bewitch you for all that; for the good charm which I will give you will foil her. I will tell you exactly what to do.

"As soon as Circê gives you a tap with her long rod, draw your sword at once and rush upon her as if you meant to kill her. She will be terrified, and will invite you to lie with her. Do not refuse, for you want her to free your companions and to entertain you; but tell her to swear the most solemn oath of the blessed gods that she will never attempt any other evil against you, or else when you are stript she may unman you and make you a weakling."

With these words Argeiphontês handed me the charm which he had pulled out of the soil, and explained its nature. The root was black, but the flower was milk-white. The gods call it moly: it is hard for mortals to find it, but the gods can do all things.

Then Hermês departed through the woody island to high Olympos; but I went on to Circê's house, and I mused deeply as I went. I stood at the doors; as I stood I called loudly, and the beautiful goddess heard. Quickly she came out and opened the doors, and I followed her much troubled.

She led me to a fine carven chair covered with silver knobs, with a footstool for my feet. Then she mixt me a posset, and dropt in her drugs with her heart full of wicked hopes. I swallowed it, but it did not bewitch me; then she gave me a tap with her wand, and said:

"Now then, to the sty with you, and join your companions!"

I drew my sharp sword and leapt at Circê as though to kill her. She let out a loud shriek, and ran up and embraced my knees, and blurted out in dismay:

"Who are you, where do you come from in the wide world? Where is your city, who are your parents? I am amazed that you have swallowed my drugs and you are not bewitched. Indeed, there never was another man who could stand these drugs once he had let them pass his teeth! But you must have a mind that cannot be bewitched. Surely you are Odysseus, the man who is never at a loss! Argeiphontês Goldenrod used to say that you would come on your way from Troy in a ship. Come now, put up your sword in the sheath, let us lie down on my bed and trust each other in love!"

I answered her, "Ah, Circê, how could you bid me be gentle to you, when you have turned my companions into pigs in this house? And now that you have me here, with deceitfulness in your heart you bid me to go to your bed in your chamber, that when I am stript you may unman me and make me a weakling. I will not enter your bed unless you can bring yourself to swear a solemn oath that you will never attempt any evil thing against me."

She swore the oath at once; and when she had sworn the oath fully and fairly, I entered the bed of Circê.

Meanwhile, the four maids who served her had been doing their work in the house. These were daughters of springs and trees and sacred rivers that run down into the sea. One of them spread fine coverings upon the seats, a linen sheet beneath and a purple cloth upon it. The second drew tables of silver in front of the seats, and laid on them golden baskets. The third mixt wine in a silver mixer, delicious honey-hearted wine, and set out cups of gold. The fourth brought water and kindled a great fire under a copper. The water grew warm; and when it boiled in the glittering cauldron, she led me to the bath, and bathed me with water out of the cauldron, when she had tempered it to a pleasant warmth, pouring it over my head and shoulders to soothe the heart-breaking weariness from my limbs. And when she had bathed me and rubbed me with olive oil, she gave me a tunic and a wrap to wear.

Then she led me to the fine carven seat, and set a footstool under my feet, and invited me to fall to. But this displeased me; I sat still half-dazed, and my heart was full of foreboding.

When Circê noticed that I sat still and did not touch the vittles, when she saw how deeply I was troubled, she came near and spoke her mind plainly:

"Why do you sit there like a dumb man, Odysseus, and eat your heart out instead of eating your dinner? I suppose you expect some other treachery! You need not be afraid; I have sworn you a solemn oath."

I answered, "Ah, Circê! What man with any decent feeling could have the heart to taste food and drink, until he should see his friends free and standing before his eyes? If you really mean this invitation to eat and drink, set them free, that I may see my friends before my eyes!"

Then Circê took her wand in hand, and walked through the hall, and opened the doors of the sty, and drove them out, looking like a lot of nine-year hogs. As they stood there, she went among them and rubbed a new drug upon each; then the bristles all dropt off which the pernicious drug had grown upon their skin. They became men once more, younger than they were before, and handsomer and taller.

They knew me, and each grasped my hand; they sobbed aloud for joy till the hall rang again with the noise, and even the goddess was touched. She came close to me, and said:

"Prince Laërtiadês, Odysseus never at fault! Go down to the sea-shore where your ship lies. First of all draw up the ship on the beach, and stow all your goods and tackle in a cave; then come back yourself and bring the rest of your companions with you."

So I went; and when I reached the shore, I found my companions sitting beside the ship in deep distress. But as soon as they saw me, they were like so many calves in a barnyard, skipping about a drove of cows as they come back to the midden after a good feed of grass; they cannot keep in their pens, but frolic round their dams lowing in a deafening chorus. So the men crowded round me, with tears running down over their cheeks; they felt as glad as if they had come back to their native land, to rugged Ithaca, their home where they were born and bred; and they cried out from their hearts:

"You are back again, my prince! How glad we are, as glad as if we had come safe home to Ithaca! Now do tell us what has become of our companions!"

I answered gently, "First of all we will draw up the ship on shore, and store the tackle annd all our belongings in some cave. Then bestir yourselves and come with me, all of you, and you shall see your companions in the sacred house of Circê, eating and drinking. They have enough and to spare."

At once they set about the work. And now what should I see but
Eurylochos alone trying to stop them! He made no secret of his thoughts:
"Oh, you poor fools!" he cried out, "where are we going? Do you
want to run your heads into trouble? Go to Circê's house, and let her
turn you all into lions or wolves to keep watch for her whether we like it
or not? Just Cyclops over again, when our fellows went into his yard, and
this same bold Odysseus with them! It was only his rashness that brought
them to destruction!"

When I heard this, I thought for a moment that I would draw my
sword and cut off his head, and let it roll on the ground, for all he was
my near relation. But the others held me back and did their best to
soften me:

"Let us leave the man here, prince, if you please, let him stay by the
ship and look after the ship. Lead the way! We are going with you to
Circê's house!"

Then away they went up from the shore. Indeed, Eurylochos would
not be left behind; he came too, for he had a terror of my rough tongue.

Then Circê gave a bath in her house to my companions, and had
them rubbed with olive oil, and gave them tunics and woollen wraps. We
found all the others feasting merrily in the hall. When they saw one
another face to face, and knew one another, their feelings were too much
for them; they made such a noise that the roof rang again. And the
radiant goddess came up to me, and said:

"No more lamentations now, Odysseus! I know myself how many
hardships you have suffered on the seas, and how many cruel enemies
have attacked you on land. Now then, eat your food and drink your
wine until you become as gay as when you first left your rugged home in
Ithaca. Just now you are withered and down-hearted, you can't forget
your dismal wannderings. Your feelings are not in tune with good cheer,
for assuredly you have suffered much."

We took her advice; and there we remained for a whole year, with
plenty to eat and good wine to drink.

But when the year was past and the seasons came round again, my
companions called me aside, and said:

"Good heavens, have you forgotten home altogether? Do remember
it, if it is really fated that you shall have a safe return to your great house
and your native land!"

And so when I came to Circê's bed, I entreated her earnestly, and
she listened to what I had to say: "Keep the promise you made me, Circê,
that you would help me on my homeward way. My mind is set upon it,
and my companions' too. They were worrying about it, and grumbling all
round me when you are not by."

She answered: "Prince Laërtiadês, never baffled Odysseus! I would not have you remain in my house unwillingly. But there is another journey you must make first. You must go to the house of Hadês and awful Persephoneia, to ask directions from Teiresias the blind Theban seer. His mind is still sound, for even in death Persephoneia has left him his reason; he alone has sense, and others are flitting shadows."

This fairly broke my heart. I sat on the bed and groaned, and I no longer cared to live and see the light of the sun. But when I had worked off my feelings by groaning and writhing, I said to her:

"Oh Circê! Who will be our guide to that place? No one has ever travelled to Hadês in a ship!"

The beautiful goddess answered, "You need not hang about the ship and wait till a guide turns up. Set your mast, hoist your sail, and sit tight: the North Wind will take you along.

"When you have crossed over the ocean, you will see a low shore, and the groves of Persephoneia, tall poplars and fruit-wasting willows; there beach your ship beside deep-eddying Oceanos, and go on yourself to the mouldering house of Hadês.

"There into Acheron the river of pain two streams flow, Pyriphlegethon blazing with fire, and Cocytos resounding with lamentation, which is a branch of the hateful water of Styx: a rock is there, by which the two roaring streams unite. Draw near to this, brave man, and be careful to do as I bid you. Dig a pit of about one cubit's length along and across, and pour into it a drink-offering for All Souls, first with honey and milk, then with fine wine, the third time with water: sprinkle over it white barley-meal. Pray earnestly to the empty shells of the dead; promise that if you return to Ithaca you will sacrifice to them a farrow cow, the best you have, and heap the burning pile with fine things, and to Teiresias alone in a different place you will dedicate the best black ram you have in your flocks. After that, when you have made your prayers to the goodly company of the dead, sacrifice a black ram and a black ewe, turning their heads down towards Erebos, then turn back yourself and move towards the ocean shore; the souls of the dead who have passed away will come in crowds.

"Then call your companions, and bid them flay and burn the bodies which lie slaughtered, and pray to the gods, to mighty Hadês and awful Persephoneia. Draw your sword and sit still, but let none of the empty shells of the dead approach the blood before you ask Teiresias what you want to know. The seer will come at once, and he will tell you the way and the measure of your path, and how you may return home over the fish-giving sea."

Even as she spoke, the Dawn came enthroned in gold. Circê gave me tunic and cloak to wear, and herself put on a white shining robe, delicate and lovely, with a fine girdle of gold about her waist, and drew a veil over her head. I went through the house and aroused my companions, speaking gently to each man as I stood by him:

"Sleep is sweet, but now, no more drowsy slumber! Let us go! Circê has told me what to do."

They obeyed me, full of courage. But even there we had trouble before we left. One of us, Elpenor, the youngest of all, one not so very valiant in war or steady in mind, had been sleeping by himself on the roof to get cool, being heavy with wine. He heard the noise and bustle of the men moving about, and jumped up in a hurry, but his poor wits forgot to come down again by the long ladder. He fell off the roof and broke his neck, and his soul went down to Hadês.

When the men had all come, I said to them, "No doubt you think we are going straight home; but Circê has marked out another road for us, to the house of Hadês and awful Persephoneia."

When I said this it fairly broke their hearts; they sat down where they were, and groaned and tore their hair. But it did them no good to lament.

While we were on the way to our ship in sorrow and mourning, Circê had got there before us and left fastened near the ship a black ram and ewe. She slipt past us easily. Who could set eyes on a god if he did not wish it, going this way or coming that way?

Samson and Delilah

JUDGES, Chapter 16

1 Then went Samson to Gaza, and saw there a harlot, and went in unto her.   2 *And it was told* the Gazites, saying, Samson is come hither. And they compassed *him* in, and laid wait for him all night in the gate of the city, and were quiet all the night, saying, In the morning, when it is day, we shall kill him.   3 And Samson lay till midnight, and arose at midnight, and took the doors of the gate of the city, and the two posts, and went away with them, bar and all, and put *them* upon his shoulders, and carried them up to the top of an hill that *is* before Hebron.   4 And it came to pass afterward, that he loved a woman in the valley of Sorek, whose name *was* Delilah.   5 And the lords of the Philistines came up unto her, and said unto her, Entice him, and see wherein his great strength *lieth,* and by what *means* we may prevail against him, that we may bind him to afflict him: and we will give thee every one of us eleven

hundred *pieces* of silver.   6 And Delilah said to Samson, Tell me, I pray thee, wherein thy great strength *lieth,* and wherewith thou mightest be bound to afflict thee.   7 And Samson said unto her, If they bind me with seven green withes that were never dried, then shall I be weak, and be as another man.   8 Then the lords of the Philistines brought up to her seven green withes which had not been dried, and she bound him with them.   9 Now *there were* men lying in wait, abiding with her in the chamber. And she said unto him, The Philistines *be* upon thee, Samson. And he brake the withes, as a thread of tow is broken when it toucheth the fire. So his strength was not known.   10 And Delilah said unto Samson, Behold, thou hast mocked me, and told me lies: now tell me, I pray thee, wherewith thou mightest be bound.   11 And he said unto her, If they bind me fast with new ropes that never were occupied, then shall I be weak, and be as another man.   12 Delilah therefore took new ropes, and bound him therewith, and said unto him, The Philistines *be* upon thee, Samson. And *there were* liers in wait abiding in the chamber. And he brake them from off his arms like a thread.   13 And Delilah said unto Samson, Hitherto thou hast mocked me, and told me lies: tell me wherewith thou mightest be bound. And he said unto her, If thou weavest the seven locks of my head with the web.   14 And she fastened *it* with the pin, and said unto him, The Philistines *be* upon thee, Samson. And he awaked out of his sleep, and went away with the pin of the beam, and with the web.   15 And she said unto him, How canst thou say, I love thee, when thine heart *is* not with me? thou hast mocked me these three times, and hast not told me wherein thy great strength *lieth.*   16 And it came to pass, when she pressed him daily with her words, and urged him, *so* that his soul was vexed unto death;   17 That he told her all his heart, and said unto her, There hath not come a razor upon mine head; for I *have been* a Nazarite unto God from my mother's womb: if I be shaven, then my strength will go from me, and I shall become weak, and be like any *other* man.   18 And when Delilah saw that he had told her all his heart, she sent and called for the lords of the Philistines, saying, Come up this once, for he hath shewed me all his heart. Then the lords of the Philistines came up unto her, and brought money in their hand. 19 And she made him sleep upon her knees; and she called for a man, and caused him to shave off the seven locks of his head; and she began to inflict him, and his strength went from him.   20 And she said, The Philistines *be* upon thee, Samson. And he awoke out of his sleep, and said, I will go out as at other times before, and shake myself. And he wist not that the LORD was departed from him.   21 But the Philistines took him, and put out his eyes, and brought him down to Gaza, and bound him with fetter of brass; and he did grind in the prison house.   22 Howbeit the hair of his head began to grow again after he was shaven.

23 Then the lords of the Philistines gathered them together for to offer a great sacrifice unto Dagon their god, and to rejoice: for they said, Our god hath delivered Samson our enemy into our hand. 24 And when the people saw him, they praised their god: for they said, Our god hath delivered into our hands our enemy, and the destroyer of our country, which slew many of us. 25 And it came to pass, when their hearts were merry, that they said, Call for Samson, that he may make us sport. And they called for Samson out of the prison house; and he made them sport: and they set him between two pillars. 26 And Samson said unto the lad that held him by the hand, Suffer me that I may feel the pillars whereupon the house standeth, That I may lean upon them. 27 Now the house was full of men and women; and all the lords of the Philistines *were* there; and *there were* upon the roof about three thousand men and women, that beheld while Samson made sport. 28 And Samson called unto the LORD, and said, O Lord GOD, remember me, I pray thee, only this once, O God, that I may be at once avenged of the Philistines for my two eyes. 29 And Samson took hold of the two middle pillars upon which the house stood, and on which it was borne up, of the one with his right hand, and of the other with his left. 30 And Samson said, Let me die with the Philistines. And he bowed himself with *all his* might; and the house fell upon the lords, and upon all the people that *were* therein. So the dead which he slew at his death were more than *they* which he slew in his life. 31 Then his brethren and all the house of his father came down, and took him, and brought *him* up, and buried him between Zorah and Eshtaol in the buryingplace of Manoah his father. And he judged Israel twenty years.

La Belle Dame Sans Merci

JOHN KEATS

O what can ail thee, knight at arms,
  Alone and palely loitering?
The sedge has withered from the lake,
  And no birds sing.

O what can ail thee, knight at arms,
  So haggard and so woebegone?
The squirrel's granary is full,
  And the harvest's done.

I see a lily on thy brow
    With anguish moist and fever dew,
And on thy cheeks a fading rose
    Fast withereth too.

I met a lady in the meads,
    Full beautiful, a faery's child:
Her hair was long, her foot was light,
    And her eyes were wild.

I made a garland for her head,
    And bracelets too, and fragrant zone;
She looked at me as she did love,
    And made sweet moan.

I set her on my pacing steed,
    And nothing else saw all day long;
For sidelong would she bend and sing
    A faery's song.

She found me roots of relish sweet,
    And honey wild, and manna dew,
And sure in language strange she said,
    "I love thee true!"

She took me to her elfin grot,
    And there she wept and sighed full sore;
And there I shut her wild, wild eyes
    With kisses four.

And there she lulled me asleep,
    And there I dreamed—Ah! woe betide!
The latest dream I ever dreamed
    On the cold hill side.

I saw pale kings, and princes too,
    Pale warriors, death-pale were they all;
Who cried—"La Belle Dame Sans Merci
    Hath thee in thrall!"

I saw their starved lips in the gloam,
    With horrid warning gaped wide,
And I awoke and found me here,
    On the cold hill's side.

And this is why I sojourn here,
  Alone and palely loitering,
Though the sedge is withered from the lake,
  And no birds sing.

Faustine

ALGERNON CHARLES SWINBURNE

Ave Faustina Imperatrix, morituri te salutant.

Lean back, and get some minutes' peace;
  Let your head lean
Back to the shoulder with its fleece
  Of locks, Faustine.

The shapely silver shoulder stoops,
  Weighed over clean
With state of splendid hair that droops
  Each side, Faustine.

Let me go over your good gifts
  That crown you queen;
A queen whose kingdom ebbs and shifts
  Each week, Faustine.

Bright heavy brow well gathered up:
  White gloss and sheen;
Carved lips that make my lips a cup
  To drink, Faustine.

Wine and rank poison, milk and blood,
  Being mixed therein
Since first the devil threw dice with God
  For you, Faustine.

Your naked new-born soul, their stake,
  Stood blind between;
God said "let him that wins her take
  And keep Faustine."

But this time Satan throve, no doubt;
    Long since, I ween,
God's part in you was battered out;
    Long since, Faustine.

The die rang sideways as it fell,
    Rang cracked and thin,
Like a man's laughter heard in hell
    Far down, Faustine.

A shadow of laughter like a sigh,
    Dead sorrow's kin;
So rang, thrown down, the devil's die
    That won Faustine.

A suckling of his breed you were,
    One hard to wean;
But God, who lost you, left you fair,
    We see, Faustine.

You have the face that suits a woman
    For her soul's screen—
The sort of beauty that's called human
    In hell, Faustine.

Even he who cast seven devils out
    Of Magdalene
Could hardly do as much, I doubt,
    For you, Faustine.

Did Satan make you to spite God?
    Or did God mean
To scourge with scorpions for a rod
    Our sins, Faustine?

I know what queen at first you were,
    As though I had seen
Red gold and black imperious hair
    Twice crown Faustine.

As if your fed sarcophagus
    Spared flesh and skin,
You come back face to face with us,
    The same Faustine.

She loved the games men played with death,
    Where death must win;
As though the slain man's blood and breath
    Revived Faustine.

Nets caught the pike, pikes tore the net;
    Lithe limbs and lean
From drained-out pores dripped thick red sweat
    To soothe Faustine.

She drank the steaming drift and dust
    Blown off the scene;
Blood could not ease the bitter lust
    That galled Faustine.

All round the foul fat furrows reeked,
    Where blood sank in;
The circus splashed and seethed and shrieked
    All round Faustine.

But these are gone now: years entomb
    The dust and din;
Yea, even the bath's fierce reek and fume
    That slew Faustine.

Was life worth living then? and now
    Is life worth sin?
Where are the imperial years? and how
    Are you, Faustine?

Your soul forgot her joys, forgot
    Her times of teen;
Yea, this life likewise will you not
    Forget, Faustine?

For in the time we know not of
    Did fate begin
Weaving the web of days that wove
    Your doom, Faustine.

The threads were wet with wine, and all
    Were smooth to spin;
They wove you like a Bacchanal,
    The first Faustine.

And Bacchus cast your mates and you
   Wild grapes to glean;
Your flower-like lips dashed with dew
   From his, Faustine.

Your drenched loose hands were stretched to hold
   The vine's wet green,
Long ere they coined in Roman gold
   Your face, Faustine.

Then after change of soaring feather
   And winnowing sin,
You woke in weeks of feverish weather,
   A new Faustine.

A star upon your birthday burned,
   Whose fierce serene
Red pulseless planet never yearned
   In heaven, Faustine.

Stray breaths of Sapphic song that blew
   Through Mitylene
Shook the fierce quivering blood in you
   By night, Faustine.

The shameless nameless loves that makes
   Hell's iron gin
Shut on you like a trap that breaks
   The soul, Faustine.

And when your veins were void and dead,
   What ghosts unclean
Swarmed round the straightened barren bed
   That hid Faustine?

What sterile growths of sexless root
   Or epicene?
What flower of kisses without fruit
   Of love, Faustine?

What adders came to shed their coats?
   What coiled obscene
Small serpents with soft stretching throats
   Caressed Faustine?

But the time came of famished hours,
    Maimed loves and mean,
This ghastly thin-faced time of ours,
    To spoil Faustine.

You seem a thing that hinges hold,
    A love-machine
With clockwork joints of supple gold—
    No more, Faustine.

Not godless, for you serve one God,
    The Lampsacene,
Who metes the gardens with his rod:
    Your lord, Faustine.

If one should love you with real love
    (Such things have been,
Things your fair face knows nothing of
    It seems, Faustine);

That clear hair heavily bound back,
    The lights wherein
Shift from dead blue to burnt-up black
    Your throat, Faustine,

Strong, heavy, throwing out the face
    And hard bright chin
And shameful scornful lips that grace
    Their shame, Faustine.

Curled lips, long since half kissed away,
    Still sweet and keen;
You'd give him—poison shall we say?
    Or what, Faustine?

The Boarding House

JAMES JOYCE

Mrs. Mooney was a butcher's daughter. She was a woman who was quite able to keep things to herself: a determined woman. She had married her father's foreman and opened a butcher's shop near Spring Gardens. But as soon as his father-in-law was dead Mr. Mooney began to go to the devil. He drank, plundered the till, ran headlong into debt. It was no use making him take the pledge: he was sure to break out again a few days after. By fighting his wife in the presence of customers and by buying bad meat he ruined his business. One night he went for his wife with the cleaver and she had to sleep in a neighbour's house.

After that they lived apart. She went to the priest and got a separation from him with care of the children. She would give him neither money nor food nor house-room; and so he was obliged to enlist himself as a sheriff's man. He was a shabby stooped little drunkard with a white face and a white moustache and white eyebrows, pencilled above his little eyes, which were pink-veined and raw; and all day long he sat in the bailiff's room, waiting to be put on a job. Mrs. Mooney, who had taken what remained of her money out of the butcher business and set up a boarding house in Hardwicke Street, was a big imposing woman. Her house had a floating population made up of tourists from Liverpool and the Isle of Man and, occasionally, *artistes* from the music halls. Its resident population was made up of clerks from the city. She governed her house cunningly and firmly, knew when to give credit, when to be stern and when to let things pass. All the resident young men spoke of her as *The Madam*.

Mrs. Mooney's young men paid fifteen shillings a week for board and lodgings (beer or stout at dinner excluded). They shared in common tastes and occupations and for this reason they were very chummy with one another. They discussed with one another the chances of favourites and outsiders. Jack Mooney, the Madam's son, who was clerk to a commission agent in Fleet Street, had the reputation of being a hard case. He was fond of using soldiers' obscenities: usually he came home in the small hours. When he met his friends he had always a good one to tell them and he was always sure to be on to a good thing—that is to say, a likely horse or a likely *artiste*. He was also handy with the mitts and sang comic songs. On Sunday nights there would often be a reunion in Mrs. Mooney's front drawing-room. The music-hall *artistes* would oblige; and

Sheridan played waltzes and polkas and vamped accompaniments. Polly Mooney, the Madam's daughter, would also sing. She sang:

> I'm a . . . naughty girl.
> You needn't sham:
> You know I am.

Polly was a slim girl of nineteen; she had light soft hair and a small full mouth. Her eyes, which were grey with a shade of green through them, had a habit of glancing upwards when she spoke with anyone, which made her look like a little perverse madonna. Mrs. Mooney had first sent her daughter to be a typist in a corn-factor's office but, as a disreputable sheriff's man used to come every other day to the office, asking to be allowed to say a word to his daughter, she had taken her daughter home again and set her to do housework. As Polly was very lively the intention was to give her the run of the young men. Besides, young men like to feel that there is a young woman not very far away. Polly, of course, flirted with the young men but Mrs. Mooney, who was a shrewd judge, knew that the young men were only passing the time away: none of them meant business. Things went on so for a long time and Mrs. Mooney began to think of sending Polly back to typewriting when she noticed that something was going on between Polly and one of the young men. She watched the pair and kept her own counsel.

Polly knew that she was being watched, but still her mother's persistent silence could not be misunderstood. There had been no open complicity between mother and daughter, no open understanding but, though people in the house began to talk of the affair, still Mrs. Mooney did not intervene. Polly began to grow a little strange in her manner and the young man was evidently perturbed. At last, when she judged it to be the right moment, Mrs. Mooney intervened. She dealt with moral problems as a cleaver deals with meat: and in this case she had made up her mind.

It was a bright Sunday morning of early summer, promising heat, but with a fresh breeze blowing. All the windows of the boarding house were open and the lace curtains ballooned gently towards the street beneath the raised ashes. The belfry of George's Church sent out constant peals of worshippers, singly or in groups, traversed the little circus before the church, revealing their purpose by their self-contained demeanour no less than by the little volumes in their gloved hands. Breakfast was over in the boarding house and the table of the breakfast-room was covered with plates on which lay yellow streaks of eggs with morsels of bacon-fat and bacon-rind. Mrs. Mooney sat in the straw arm-chair and watched the servant Mary remove the breakfast things. She made Mary collect the crusts and pieces of broken bread to help to make Tuesday's bread-pudding. When the table was cleared, the broken bread collected, the sugar and butter safe under lock and key, she began to reconstruct the interview which she had had the night before with Polly. Things were as she had suspected: she had been frank in her questions and Polly had been frank in her answers. Both had been somewhat awkward, of course. She had been made awkward by her not wishing to receive the news in too cavalier a fashion or to seem to have connived and Polly had been made awkward not merely because allusions of that kind always made her awkward but also because she did not wish it to be thought that in her wise innocence she had divined the intention behind her mother's tolerance.

Mrs. Mooney glanced instinctively at the little gilt clock on the mantelpiece as soon as she had become aware through her revery that the bells of George's Church had stopped ringing. It was seventeen minutes past eleven: she would have lots of time to have the matter out with Mr. Doran and then catch short twelve at Marlborough Street. She was sure she would win. To begin with she had all the weight of social opinion on her side: she was an outraged mother. She had allowed him to live beneath her roof, assuming that he was a man of honour, and he had simply abused her hospitality. He was thirty-four or thirty-five years of age, so that youth could not be pleaded as his excuse; nor could ignorance be his excuse since he was a man who had seen something of the world. He had simply taken advantage of Pollys' youth and inexperience: that was evident. The question was: What reparation would he make?

There must be reparation made in such cases. It is all very well for the man: he can go his ways as if nothing had happened, having had his moment of pleasure, but the girl has to bear the brunt. Some mothers would be content to patch up such an affair for a sum of money; she had known cases of it. But she would not do so. For her only one reparation could make up for the loss of her daughter's honour: marriage.

She counted all her cards again before sending Mary up to Mr. Doran's room to say that she wished to speak with him. She felt sure she would win. He was a serious young man, not rakish or loud-voiced like the others. If it had been Mr. Sheridan or Mr. Meade or Bantam Lyons her task would have been much harder. She did not think he would face publicity. All the lodgers in the house knew something of the affair; details had been invented by some. Besides, he had been employed for thirteen years in a great Catholic wine-merchant's office and publicity would mean for him, perhaps, the loss of his sit. Whereas if he agreed all might be well. She knew he had a good screw for one thing and she suspected he had a bit of stuff put by.

Nearly the half-hour! She stood up and surveyed herself in the pier-glass. The decisive expression of her great florid face satisfied her and she thought of some mothers she knew who could not get their daughters off their hands.

Mr. Doran was very anxious indeed this Sunday morning. He had made two attempts to shave but his hand had been so unsteady that he had been obliged to desist. Three days' reddish beard fringed his jaws and every two or three minutes a mist gathered on his glasses so that he had to take them off and polish them with his pocket-handkerchief. The recollection of his confession of the night before was a cause of acute pain to him; the priest had drawn out every ridiculous detail of the affair and in the end had so magnified his sin that he was almost thankful at being afforded a loophole of reparation. The harm was done. What could he do now but marry her or run away? He could not brazen it out. The affair would be sure to be talked of and his employer would be certain to hear of it. Dublin is such a small city: everyone knows everyone else's business. He felt his heart leap warmly in his throat as he heard in his excited imagination old Mr. Leonard calling out in his rasping voice: *Send Mr. Doran here, please.*

All his long years of service gone for nothing! All his industry and diligence thrown away! As a young man he had sown his wild oats, of course; he had boasted of his free-thinking and denied the existence of God to his companions in public-houses. But that was all passed and done with . . . nearly. He still bought a copy of *Reynold's Newspaper* every week but he attended to his religious duties and for nine-tenths of the year lived a regular life. He had money enough to settle down on; it was not that. But the family would look down on her. First of all there was her disreputable father and then her mother's boarding house was beginning to get a certain fame. He had a notion that he was being had. He could imagine his friends talking of the affair and laughing. She *was* a little vulgar; sometimes she said *I seen* and *If I had've known.* But what would grammar matter if he really loved her? He could not make up his mind whether to like her or despise her for what she had done. Of course, he had done it too. His instinct urged him to remain free, not to marry. Once you are married you are done for, it said.

While he was sitting helplessly on the side of the bed in shirt and trousers she tapped lightly at his door and entered. She told him all, that she had made a clean breast of it to her mother and that her mother would speak with him that morning. She cried and threw her arms round his neck, saying:

—O, Bob! Bob! What am I to do? What am I to do at all?

She would put an end to herself, she said.

He comforted her feebly, telling her not to cry, that it would be all right, never fear. He felt against his shirt the agitation of her bosom.

It was not altogether his fault that it had happened. He remembered well, with the curious patient memory of the celibate, the first casual caresses her dress, her breath, her fingers had given him. Then late one night as he was undressing for bed she had tapped at his door, timidly.

She wanted to relight her candle at his for hers had been blown out by a gust. It was her bath night. She wore a loose open combing-jacket of printed flannel. Her white instep shone in the opening of her furry slippers and the blood glowed warmly behind her perfumed skin. From her hands and wrists too as she lit and steadied her candle a faint perfume arose.

On nights when he came in very late it was she who warmed up his dinner. He scarcely knew what he was eating, feeling her beside him alone, at night, in the sleeping house. And her thoughtfulness! If the night was any way cold or wet or windy there was sure to be a little tumbler of punch ready for him. Perhaps they could be happy together. . . .

They used to go upstairs together on tiptoe, each with a candle, and on the third landing exchange reluctant good-nights. They used to kiss. He remembered well her eyes, the touch of her hand and his delirium. . . .

But delirium passes. He echoed her phrase, applying it to himself: *What am I to do?* The instinct of the celibate warned him to hold back. But the sin was there; even his sense of honour told him that reparation must be made for such a sin.

While he was sitting with her on the side of the bed Mary came to the door and said that the missus wanted to see him in the parlour. He stood up to put on his coat and waistcoat, more helpless than ever. When he was dressed he went over to her to comfort her. It would be all right, never fear. He left her crying on the bed and moaning softly: *O my God!*

Going down the stairs his glasses became so dimmed with moisture that he had to take them off and polish them. He longed to ascend through the roof and fly away to another country where he would never hear again of his trouble, and yet a force pushed him downstairs step by step. The implacable faces of his employer and of the Madam stared upon his discomfiture. On the last flight of stairs he passed Jack Mooney who was coming up from the pantry nursing two bottles of *Bass*. They saluted coldly; and the lovers' eyes rested for a second or two on a thick bulldog face and a pair of thick short arms. When he reached the foot of the staircase he glanced up and saw Jack regarding him from the door of the return-room.

Suddenly he remembered the night when one of the music-hall *artistes*, a little blond Londoner, had made a rather free allusion to Polly. The reunion had been almost broken up on account of Jack's violence. Everyone tried to quiet him. The music-hall *artiste*, a little paler than usual, kept smiling and saying that there was no harm meant: but Jack kept shouting at him that if any fellow tried that sort of game on with *his* sister he'd bloody well put his teeth down his throat, so he would.

Polly sat for a little time on the side of the bed, crying. Then she dried her eyes and went over to the looking-glass. She dipped the end of the towel in the water-jug and refreshed her eyes with the cool water. She looked at herself in profile and readjusted a hairpin above her ear. Then she went back to the bed again and sat at the foot. She regarded the pillows for a long time and the sight of them awakened in her mind secret amiable memories. She rested the nape of her neck against the cool iron bedrail and fell into a revery. There was no longer any perturbation visible on her face.

She waited on patiently, almost cheerfully, without alarm, her memories gradually giving place to hopes and visions of the future. Her hopes and visions were so intricate that she no longer saw the white pillows on which her gaze was fixed or remembered that she was waiting for anything.

At last she heard her mother calling. She started to her feet and ran to the banisters.

—Polly! Polly!

—Yes, mamma?

—Come down, dear. Mr. Doran wants to speak to you. Then she remembered what she had been waiting for.

Calypso's Island

ARCHIBALD MacLEISH

I know very well, goddess, she is not beautiful
As you are: could not be. She is a woman,
Mortal, subject to the chances: duty of

Childbed, sorrow that changes cheeks, the tomb—
For unlike you she will grow gray, grow older,
Gray and older, sleep in that small room.

She is not beautiful as you, O golden!
You are immortal and will never change
And can make me immortal also, fold

Your garment round me, make me whole and strange
As those who live forever, not the while
That we live; keep me from those dogging dangers—

Ships and the wars—in this green, far-off island,
Silent of all but sea's eternal sound
Or sea-pine's when the lull of surf is silent.

Goddess, I know how excellent this ground,
What charmed contentment of the removed heart
The bees make in the lavender where pounding

Surf sounds far off and the bird that darts
Darts through its own eternity of light,
Motionless in motion, and the startled

Hare is startled into stone, the fly
Forever golden in the flickering glance
Of leafy sunlight that still holds it. I

Know you, goddess, and your caves that answer
Ocean's confused voices with a voice:
Your poplars where the storms are turned to dances;

Arms where the heart is turned. You give the choice
To hold forever what forever passes,
To hide from what will pass, forever. Moist,

Moist are your well-stones, goddess, cool your grasses!
And she—she is a woman with that fault
Of change that will be death in her at last!

Nevertheless I long for the cold, salt,
Restless, contending sea and for the island
Where the grass dies and the seasons alter:

Where that one wears the sunlight for a while.

Additional Readings

Bellow, Saul. *The Dangling Man.*
Chrétien de Troyes. *Parsifal.*
Coleridge, Samuel Taylor. "The Rime of the Ancient Mariner."
Cooper, James Fenimore. *The Prairie.*
Conrad, Joseph. "The Secret Sharer."
Benét, Stephen Vincent. *The Devil and Daniel Webster.*
Dostoievsky, Feodor. "The Double."

Dostoievsky, Feodor. *Notes from the Underground.*
Eliot, T. S. "The Love Song of J. Alfred Prufrock."
Fast, Howard. *Freedom Road.*
Jackson, Shirley. "The Lottery."
Keats, John. "Lamia."
Marlowe, Christopher. *Tamburlaine.*
Melville, Herman. *Moby-Dick.*
Milton, John. *Samson Agonistes.*
Odets, Clifford. "Waiting for Lefty."
Sophocles. *Antigone.*
Shakespeare, William. *Antony and Cleopatra.*
Shakespeare, William. "Venus and Adonis."
Steinbeck, John. "Leader of the People."
Stevenson, Robert Louis. *Dr. Jekyll and Mr. Hyde.*
Wilde, Oscar. *Portrait of Dorian Gray.*
Wright, Richard. "Bright and Morning Star."

GLOSSARY FOR A STUDY
OF ARCHETYPAL AND
MYTHIC LITERATURE

adaptation   The change in structure of behavior that has survival value; any beneficial change to meet environmental demand. *Social adaptation* involves the process by which a group comes into such relation with its environment as to survive and prosper.

Adonis   A beautiful youth beloved by Venus, he was mortally wounded by a wild boar while hunting. Venus changed him into an anemone. He was restored to life by Proserpine, on the condition that he spend six months with her (winter) and six with Venus (summer). Thus a symbol of regeneration, Adonis is a type of Osiris and Christ.

air   Symbol of the immaterial, infinite, soul, life; implies inspiration and reason. Symbolized by blue, yellow. It has the male property of heat, but the female property of moistness.

alchemy   A pseudo-science which attempted to create superior metal (gold) from inferior (such as lead); its description involved imagery of male and female properties during sexual intercourse; the experience or relationship would be successful if a philosopher's stone or *pneuma* were found to act as a catalyst. The *pneuma* (air) was considered the inspiration of love (God) of the man and woman. Therefore, the aim of alchemy was transcendence (which see).

altar   Indicative of sacrifice and devotion, and of the creator; and associated with a pillar (thus both stone and phallus). Symbol of consolation or joy.

analogue   A tale or literary motif resembling another, but without direct relationship.

anima   The feminine component of the soul-image; that part of the psyche in communication with the unconscious. Cf. *animus.*

animal   Frequently employed to symbolize a quality (slyness) or ability

449

(strength) of a human or sometimes a natural object; such archetypes are numerous, and some of them are noted in other entries. A horned animal is a sun emblem, a symbol of power; a three-horned animal, the trinity or divine strength.

animus   The masculine component of the soul-image; the animating, creative, and procreative spirit; that part of the psyche which facilitates relations with the unconscious. Cf. *anima.*

anthropomorphism   The attributing of human characteristics to gods, animals, or inanimate objects.

antihero   One who does not accept the ambivalences of life but who either does not seek to assert the Self (often likened to an insect form) or attempts to counter and thwart the quest of the hero. The latter espouses the demonic and may become a Satan figure; he represents the dominance of the libido. He may manifest the "wisdom of Silenus." More frequently the antihero rejects the structure of the life cycle, the concept of task, quest, and journey, and the belief in attainment of the soul-image. Cf. *hero.*

antitype   Something that corresponds to or is foreshadowed in a type (e.g., Jesus is the antitype and Joshua is the type). Often used erroneously to mean the opposite of another. Cf. *type.*

anxiety   An emotional state caused by anticipation of future failing of a present desire or by a fusion of fear with anticipation of future evil.

Aphrodite   Greek name for Venus, goddess of love and beauty; as Aphrodite Urania, sister of wisdom, a synonym for an aspect of the Son: his *agape,* or unselfish brotherly love.

Apollo   The sun god, identified with the Son; son of Zeus and Latona (a semi-mortal) and brother of Diana. A handsome young man with long locks (indicating his youth), crowned with laurel. He was god of music and poetry and presided over the Muses. He was associated with the oracle at Delphi and slew the serpent Python, identified with Satan. He was associated also with healing as father of Aesculapius.

apple   The symbol of life, of knowledge, and of the womb. See *Hesperides.*

archetype   Primordial image; an original pattern or model from which others of the same kind are derived. Cf. *collective unconscious.*

Ariadne   Daughter of Minos, king of Crete, and lover of Theseus, who was imprisoned in the labyrinth to be devoured by the Minotaur (a bull). She gave Theseus a thread whereby he was able to find his way out. He conquered the Minotaur and married Ariadne, but later abandoned her.

Arion   A lyric poet and musician. On a sea voyage he became victim to the crew who wanted his money; he played for them, plunged into the sea, and was rescued by dolphins attracted by the music. Thus he was identified with Christ as a symbol of resurrection; the dolphin is likewise a symbol of Christ.

ascent   Implying positive action, happiness, resurrection; related to the bird symbol.

assimilation   A process by which something unpleasant is faced and brought into one's total experience. *Cultural assimilation* is a process by which persons or groups acquire characteristics of other persons or groups.

Ate   Goddess of revenge and evil; banished from the heavens, she incited mankind to evil thoughts and actions.

Athena   Greek name for Minerva, goddess of wisdom; daughter of Zeus, she sprang full-grown from the left side of his head (cf. the birth of Sin from the left side of Satan's head and Eve's birth from Adam's left side). She gave men the gift of prophecy; she was depicted as a warrior with helmet, spear, and shield (on which was Medusa's head). Thus she signifies the defeat of the powers of death by wisdom.

attitude   A consistent behavioral pattern toward a given class of objects.

Bacchus   God of wine, revelry, sexual appetite; identified with Dionysius. His followers engaged in frenzied sexual orgies. He is crowned with vine leaves and ivy and carries a thyrsus (a staff, symbolizing the phallus) entwined with vine leaves and ivy. Ivy is a symbol of generation and life.

baptism   A ritual involving water (which see), symbolizing cleansing (of sin), dedication, rebirth, sanctification. In dream psychology it represents the fulfillment of desire. Relates to the Exodus as a resurrection from a sinful past.

beast god   A god represented as an animal, such as Anubis, depicted with a jackal's head, or Zeus as a swan in the Leda legend.

bird   A symbol of transcendence, representing man's striving to attain a goal.

bridge   A means of change in situation or time. It typifies the rainbow (divine presence, hope, peace, victory). In dream psychology a crossed bridge indicates a happy solution; a broken bridge, difficulties.

bull   A symbol of fecundity, of the fertility of the earth, of heat and light; it implies virility, fury, lasciviousness, life-power. Portrayed with four horns (four cardinal points of the earth) and four legs (pillars of the world); identified with the deity as male creator and with the sun. Cf. *Europa*.

Cadmus   Founder of Boeotia; needing water, he slew the dragon which guarded it and sowed its teeth on the ground, which sprang up armed men. They fought when he threw a stone amongst them, but the five that survived helped him build the city on the spot where he saw a heifer. (His sister was Europa.) He married Hermione or Harmonia, who was changed into a serpent and allowed to live in the Elysian Fields (heaven); she was the daughter of Mars (war) and Venus (love). Cf. Apollo and Python, and Christ and Satan.

caduceus   A rod (phallic symbol) carried by Hermes; it had two winged serpents entwined around it; it had both sleep-inducing and curative (or regenerative) properties. The rod is also associated with Aesculapius, god of medicine and son of Apollo.

castration complex   In the male the repressed fear of losing one's genitals; in the female the fantasy of having lost the penis.

child   Since innocence, purity, and youth are implied, the state in which one cannot see through appearance to reality. The pre-initiated state.

Christ figure   A hero (which see) who suffers for others but who as one anointed by God will be resurrected. He represents the love and mercy of the Son (the dove) and the power and truth of the Father (the eagle), who works through him for the good of man. He is often presented with feminine qualities as the divine mother archetype. Symbolized as the Lamb of God, a fish, a serpent exalted on a cross, a lion, and a unicorn, an ass, a bull, a chalice, a dolphin, a fountain, an oak branch, an ox, a pelican, a pillar, a rose, a sheep, a stag, a tiger, a tree; indicated is his animal as well as spiritual nature. His sign is X. He is assigned the number 8 (regeneration).

Circe A temptress, whose magical abilities were able to turn men into swine through a magic potion. She symbolizes the dire results of man's uncontrolled sexual appetites, and the myth relates hunger and sex drives. Ulysses was able to resist her charms through an herb called moly given him by Hermes; this herb has been identified as faith.

circle The deity and thus perfection, immortality, eternity, completeness, divinity. It may represent the universe, or, in spherical form, the earth. Three circles represent love, trinity, wisdom; two circles, the marriage of heaven and earth, Christ the bridegroom and his mystic bride (the church).

circumcision A rite of initiation in which the male shows that he is prepared to undergo ordeal and suffering; specifically, circumcision symbolizes the mood of death from which may spring the mood of rebirth.

climb The struggle to achieve ascent.

collective unconscious That part of one's unconscious that is inherited and shared with others of the species; the countless typical experiences inherited include, for example, birth, initiation, the fall from innocence.

concretization The process of supplying definite illustration, application, or proof for an abstraction.

conscious That part of the psyche that includes the mental life of which one is aware.

crab A symbol of aggressiveness, chaos, disunion, separation; it leads away from the goal of the quest (because the crab moves backward).

cross A Christian symbolic form replacing the mandala; it symbolized unity and later suffering and then the power of God.

crystal A symbol of the Self, evoking a feeling of precise order of matter and of spiritual control; it thus unifies the opposites, matter and spirit.

Daedalus An inventor (of the wedge, ax, level), who built the labyrinth for Minos, king of Crete; later displeasing the king he was himself imprisoned there. See *Icarus, labyrinth.*

Danäe A mortal visited by Zeus as a golden shower; by him she had a son Perseus (identified with Christ). They were saved in a storm by fishermen. Perseus slew Medusa, the Gorgon, whose hair was serpents; he cut off the head and placed it in Athena's shield.

dark Evil, the female principle, ignorance, death (night, storms).

death instinct The primitive tendency that leads away from life and toward denial, rejection, or death; Thanatos. Cf. *Eros.*

deliverer A hero (which see) who rescues his people from the control of an evil person or spirit or attitude. Cf. *savior.*

demon An evil spirit, often appearing as a dragon, dwarf, serpent; lives in caves, mountains, forests (any dark area); has superior, magical knowledge. A *daemon* was a guardian (good) spirit in Greek myth.

descent Implying negative action, unhappiness, death.

Deucalion Son of Prometheus and husband of Pyrrha. During his reign over Thessaly, Zeus flooded the earth to punish the evil of mankind. Deucalion built a ship whereby he saved himself and his wife; the ship landed on Mt. Parnassus after nine days of being tossed by waves. A version of the Noah legend.

diamond See *crystal*.

disk A symbol of the Self; it suggests totality, integration.

divine father God or one equated with him; the male principle; the source of wisdom and good. He symbolizes power, justice, order, and creation; he is symbolized by the eagle, scales, and the compass.

door Revelation, the beginning and the end; rebirth, tribulation through which one must pass to reach shelter and love; the vagina. Equated with gate.

double The duality which either duplicates another being or which is the complementary opposite of another being. Suggested is the essential ambivalence of all phenomena. See also *Leda*.

dragon A symbol of that which must be conquered to achieve manhood, consciousness, the good, immortality, and the like. It is the guarder of secret knowledge, treasure, immortality; it is thus the trial that man must undergo to achieve union with God, spiritually or after death. As beneficent form it gives mankind wind and rain or directs to rivers. Cf. *serpent*.

dream A symbol of repressed wishes or other unconscious processes. *Manifest content:* ideas and images of a remembered dream; *latent content:* the underlying significance of the dream.

eagle A symbol of God (generally the Father) because of its fearlessness, keenness of vision, omnipotence, splendor, strength. Typifies physical and spiritual regeneration as well as salvation. Preys on serpents (which see).

earth See *earth mother*. It has the male property of dryness but the female property of coldness.

earth mother The wife of the sky-deity; the fecund mother, seen as fields or meadows. She is the passive principle, recipient of the fertilizing heat of the linga, and bearer of life. She stands for the cycle of birth, maturity, decay. Symbolized by brown, green, red, yellow, the cube, and the globe.

Easter A Christian remnant of fertility rituals involving the rebirth of the sacrificed "savior." It belongs to the cyclic observation of the birth, growth, death, and rebirth of nature throughout the year, except that the concept of Easter breaks the folkloristic concept of endless cycle; Christ's resurrection is considered a single symbolic occurrence.

Electra complex The repressed desire of the female for sexual relations with her father. Cf. *Oedipus complex*.

Eros The life instinct; love in terms of unselfishness and charity. Cf. *Thanatos*.

Europa A mortal visited by Zeus as a bull (which see); she became the mother of the judges of hell, Minos, Sarpedon, and Rhadamanthus. See also *Cadmus*.

fable A brief tale, derived from folklore and disguising its archetypal situations through altering historical or realistic content; often it presents a moral and may involve animals as characters.

fairy tales Folkloristic stories mythologizing many aspects of birth, growth, and death, and of conscious and unconscious. They disguise, particularly, life patterns that may be unhappy, such as the process of individuation seen in the story of the king fallen ill or grown old (cf. medieval legends of the fisher king and Parsifal); to restore his health some magic must be performed or a talisman found which is unique or hard to find and which thus involves a difficult task (one ultimately involving awareness of Self and assertion of inner spirituality).

fall The transgression of divine order bringing a transformation from a state of holiness to a state of sin. Symbolized by an apple, a tree, or a serpent (Satan figure). Since the fall of Adam and Eve, mankind must experience the fall (through initiation) and recapture its lost state of holiness through trial and repentance.

father figure One who becomes the object of transferred feelings originally directed toward one's parent or toward the godhead. Cf. *imago*.

fertility rites Rituals, derived from observation of the cause of nature through birth, growth, death, and rebirth, which attempt to invoke the abundant growth of vegetation, necessary for life, at the time of its development (spring). This cyclic myth of recurrent fertility involves sacrifice of or to a savior (a semi-divine man) such as Osiris, Thammuz, Orpheus, Balder, or Christ. Frequently the sacrifice to the savior appears in terms of sexual orgy, in the offering up of virgins, or in veneration as of the phallus, or in death, mutilation, torture of a savior-surrogate or an effigy.

field A mother archetype.

fig The womb; the female principle.

fire Divine love, light, power, passion, love, illumination, the male principle (being hot and dry).

fish Knowledge, wisdom, the sea, woman, abundance; a guardian of the tree of life and the tree of knowledge. Emblem of baptism, the Eucharist, the Virgin Mary.

flame Life force, wisdom, activity, purification; symbolizes the soul, the supreme spirit.

flying dream An anxiety dream, which, contemplating the cosmos, indicates its relationship with the collective unconscious; it is frequently sexually oriented.

folklore Dances, sayings, songs (including ballads, worksongs, nursery rhymes), tales, and such customs as initiation rites and funerals, passed orally from generation to generation.

foot A male fetish, because of phallic significance. It is also a place of magic power.

ford The means to cross a river (which see) with seeming safety, but the means may be potentially dangerous if the unconscious overpowers the consciousness at the moment of crossing. It is part of threshold-symbolism in its being a dividing line between two states or two forms of reality.

four The number of man and nature; functions connected with man and his world (such as the seasons, geographic directions, the humours) exist in four-fold divisions or stages.

garden   Equated with heaven, the earthly paradise, and the *hortus conclusus* (the womb). The journey of life is to reachieve the lost garden (Eden) through worthiness shown by trial and repentance and love.

giant   Force of evil, superhuman strength, exceeding ambition, violence. Those who attempt to overthrow the gods. The Giants of the Earth (sons of Gaia) are identified with the rebellious angels. The giant corresponds either to the father-symbol, withstanding instincts, or to a guardian of treasure (that is, of the mother, the unconscious).

hallucination   A false perception, strongly realistic, without adequate stimuli.

Harpies   Monsters with heads and breasts of women, the bodies of birds, and the claws of lions; they lived in filth and spread contamination to all they touched. They were the offspring of Neptune (sea) and Terra (earth).

Hercules   Son of Zeus and the mortal Alcmena, and thus a type of Christ. He crushed two serpents sent by the jealous Hera when he was but eight months old. He was required to perform twelve tasks thought impossible:

1. to slay the Nemaean lion; arrows and clubs being useless, he seized it in his arms and strangled it.
2. to destroy the Lernaean Hydra; this monster had nine heads which regenerated each time one was severed, but Hercules, assisted by Iolas, cauterized each place where a head was removed to prevent regrowth.
3. to bring to Eurystheus a stag with golden horns and brazen hoofs.
4. to seize alive the ravaging bear of Erymanthus.
5. to cleanse the stable of King Augeas, in which three thousand oxen had lived for thirty years; this he did by redirecting the river Alpheus through it.
6. to kill the carnivorous birds of Lake Stymphalis.
7. to capture the death-dealing bull of Crete (an analogue of the Minotaur).
8. to obtain the fire-breathing mares of Diomedes, who fed them his guests.
9. to procure the girdle of Hippolyta.
10. to bring to Eurystheus the flesh-eating oxen of Geryon, a triple-headed monster who owned a two-headed dog, Orthos, and a seven-headed dragon, Eurythion.
11. to obtain the golden apples of the Hesperides; he slew the dragon that guarded the entrance to the garden in which the tree grew (a version of the myth of the Tree of Life in the Garden of Eden, guarded by cherubim with flaming swords, and Christ's conquering of death).
12. to fetch from Hades the three-headed dog, Cerberus (a version of the myth of Christ's harrowing of hell).

Other myths involving Hercules include his contribution in the defeat of the Giants (which see) in their assault on Olympus (a version of the myth of the rebellion of the fallen angels) and his defeat of Antaeus, son of Gaia, who gained strength from her and was finally beaten when Hercules lifted him from the earth (a version of the defeat of Satan by Christ in the tower temptation).

Hermes   Messenger of the gods and conductor of souls to Hades; he is related to Moses as well as the archangel Michael. He invented the lyre which he traded with Apollo for the caduceus. With his winged hat and shoes, he becomes a bird symbol; as owner of the caduceus, he becomes a fertility symbol; and as the conductor of the dead, he unites the known with the unknown. His caduceus as phallic symbol and his conducting of man into the unknown worlds of heaven and hell mythologize sexual union, wherein man explores the mysteries of woman, the unconscious, happily or unhappily. He appears in different forms (e.g., Hermes Trismegisthus) as one versed in secret and alchemical knowledge.

hero   An archetype involving a powerful man or god-man who conquers evil in the form of a serpent, monster, demon, or the like and thus frees the people from destruction and death. He must often perform a task or tasks to prove himself worthy; the folk-hero is always killed (literally or metaphorically) in his attempt to drive out evil. Generally he has a miraculous but humble birth, early shows superhuman strength, rises to power swiftly, triumphs over evil, is susceptible to pride (*hubris*), and falls through betrayal or martyrdom. His early feats are aided by others who represent the whole psyche (e.g., Perseus and Athena); through this phase of the hero's life, he develops ego-consciousness (the process of individuation). The *Byronic hero* is one who feels himself disengaged from others, an outlaw, or a defiant but melancholy champion of liberty. Cf. *antihero, deliverer, outcast, savior.*

Hesperides   Three nymphs, daughters of Hesperus (the western or evening star, a form of Venus), who were guardians of the golden apples which Hera gave to Zeus on their wedding day. They lived in a beautiful garden in the West. West is a symbol of death, the garden a symbol of Eden and heaven, and the apples a symbol of life and immortality. The golden apples are contrasted with the apples of Sodom, which are made of ashes and symbolize death through the perversion of the means to life. See *Hercules* (eleventh labor).

horse   Symbol of the uncontrollable instinctive drives that can erupt from the unconscious, those drives which one tries to repress. A rider implies some ability to control such drives and thus symbolizes inhibition. Accordingly, horse implies in common language a particularly competent female sexual partner (and also a whore) and the rider, the male partner.

house   A female archetype; also tradition.

Icarus   Son of Daedalus who devised wings to escape from the labyrinth. Icarus flew too near the sun and the wax securing his wings melted; he drowned in the Icarian Sea. The myth symbolizes man's rash attempt to escape from adversity, rather than conquer it, and his presumption of godly abilities. See *labyrinth.*

identification   Transference of response to an object or situation considered identical with another, particularly one experienced previously.

image   A concrete representation of a sensory experience. *Personal image:* a representation in the unconscious of a personal experience. *Primordial image:* a representation in the unconscious of an expression of the human race; an archetype.

imago A representation formed in the unconscious in early childhood which remains unaltered by later reality; frequently involves search for the father.

incest Sexual intercourse between closely related persons; may often be psychic.

individuation The process by which a part of a whole becomes more and more distinct and independent of the whole.

initiation The process by which one moves from childhood to adulthood; the rituals which accompany or symbolize such change (e.g., circumcision, awareness of death, sexual activity, feats of strength). The child is to experience a symbolic death in order to break any remaining mother-child identity and to develop ego-consciousness through individuation. First his identity is dissolved into the collective unconscious through ritual experienced by the group; then he is reborn into a world in which he is an independent individual. Although collective initiation is experienced at puberty, similar development occurs throughout an individual's life as he enters new phases.

Jason He acquired the Golden Fleece (having sailed on the Argo) with the aid of Juno from King Aetes in Colchis; to do this he had to tame wild bulls, plow the field of Mars with them, sow the teeth of a serpent from which armed men could spring who would try to stop him from plowing, and kill the dragon guarding the tree on which the Fleece was hung. Cf. *Cadmus, Hercules* (the eleventh labor), *Hesperides.*

Jonah myth Typifying the hero who gives in to the monster, is swallowed by it, and is borne on a night-sea journey (which see).

journey The voyage through life to attempt to acquire the treasure, or the lost Eden, or the Self; the hero's journey takes him through various exploits, various avenues of life (stages of human development), through despond (evil, death, the underworld) either not to emerge from the darkness or to progress to the desired heavenly path of light.

labyrinth The entangling and confusing representation of the world of matriarchal consciousness; it can be traversed only by those who are ready for a special initiation into the world of the collective unconscious. Cf. *Daedalus, Icarus.*

landscape A symbol of the mother; through it one is able to express that which before was inexpressible by placing other symbols in relationship to it. Its awareness is a means of taking perspective of a broad and complex unconscious state.

Leda Zeus disguised as a swan visited Leda, who bore double twins, Pollux and Helena, and Castor and Clytemnestra. Castor and Pollux were translated into the constellation Gemini; they lived in the upper and the lower worlds, on alternate days.

left The sphere of unadapted, unconscious reactions; it signifies evil or destructive forces; in Christianity, those not saved.

leitmotif A motif existing within a single work; its repetition recalls each prior occurrence, unifying the work of literature.

light Symbol of wisdom, knowledge, goodness, happiness, power, heat, the male principle (sun).

life instinct   All the tendencies that strive to integrate living substance into larger wholes; Eros.

lingam   A phallic symbol representing the Hindu god Siva; but it also suggests the integration of both sexes and thus the generative power of the universe.

lion   A symbol of virility, life-power; identified with the deity and the sun. It becomes a symbol of latent passions and may indicate the danger of destruction by the unconscious.

magician   Representative of the unknown, "inhuman" feeling that all may experience; often the agent in the act of transference. See *demon, trickster.*

mandala   The magic circle; a symbol of the total unity of Self.

marriage   The attempt to reconcile original male-female opposition; to re-create the whole which originally was the living creature; to combine the Logos (man's knowledge) with Eros (woman's relatedness).

mask   A means of transforming the wearer into an archetypal image; frequently it depicts an animal and is employed in various life rituals to symbolize good, evil, power, task, spirit, and the like. Cf. *persona.*

messiah   The anointed God; the awaited king of an oppressed people, their deliverer, thence the professor or accepted leader of a cause. Cf. *Christ figure, deliverer, savior.*

metempsychosis   Transmigration of the soul after death into other (usually higher) forms of life.

mother archetype   Identified with the unconscious, the first bearer of the soul-image. Seen as nature, fields, the source of love and life, the female principle; symbols are water, stone, cave, house, and so on. Cf. *Oedipus complex, the terrible mother.*

motif   A recurrent word, phrase, situation or idea; a motif occurs in various works of literature, not just one. Cf. *leitmotif.*

mountain   Loftiness of spirit, ascent, heaven, the difficult path to virtue, the means to reach heaven.

music   Harmony, cosmic harmony, self-expression.

myth   A controlling idea accepted philosophically by a group of people. Myth is often narrative depicting archetypal situations, such as the origin of life, natural phenomena. Myth expresses inner experiences, feelings, or thoughts as outer, sensory experiences.

mythology   A group of related myths.

mythopoesis   The creation of myth, as by modern writers; the development of symbols and narrative that represent controlling philosophic ideas for a given group of people.

Narcissus   A beautiful youth who fell in love with his own reflection in the water, thinking it a nymph. Frustrated at not being able to reach the reflection, he killed himself, and from his blood sprang the narcissus.

Nemesis   Goddess of vengeance and daughter of Nox; she constantly travelled in search of wickedness to punish it.

night sea journey   The movement from west to east in which the person sailing changes from one who has spiritually died or lacks drive to accomplish his task to one who is reborn to assume his responsibilities. Cf. *Jonah myth.*

nightmare   An anxiety dream that erupts into real-appearing fantasy.

Nox   Night, daughter of Chaos and sister of Erebus (primeval darkness) and Mors (death); she bore Day, the Hesperides, and Dreams.

numbers   Archetypal representations of psychological relationships; they take on various meanings and "magical" properties (such as the completeness of 10; or the male-female marriage of 6, as product of 3, male, and 2, female; or the concept of perfection in 9 as the product of the Trinity in its threefold elevation).

octopus   See *dragon, whale.*

Oedipus complex   The positive feelings of the libido toward the parent of the opposite sex; often there is identification with the parent of the same sex or hate directed toward that parent.

opposite   The elements of the collective psyche; these unite as binary groups, such as ascent / descent, chaos / order, Eros / Thanatos, good / evil, love / hate, megalomania / inferiority.

Orpheus   A musician and poet, he married Eurydice, who died from the sting of a serpent. Through his music he persuaded Pluto to restore her, which was allowed on the condition that he not look behind him before emerging into the upper world. He turned to look at her, however, and she immediately vanished. Later, he was attacked by Thracian women during a Bacchic orgy because of his coldness to them. They tore his body to pieces and threw his head into the river Hebrus.

Osiris   Egyptian sun god, worshipped in the form of an ox (Apis); he was also symbolized as rain. He was also god of the underworld and judge of the dead. He was identified with fertility deities like Adonis and Thammuz.

outcast   One who is a disruptive force in the pattern of community life, usually through his exercise of wisdom, or one who is a scapegoat (which see).

ox   Symbol of cosmic forces; of sacrifice, suffering, patience, and labor.

Pan   God of shepherds and pastures, sometimes identified with Christ, the Good Shepherd; but as part man and part goat (symbol of lechery and the corrupt), sometimes identified with Satan.

Pandora   The first mortal female, formed by Vulcan of clay. She received many gifts from the gods (beauty, the art of pleasing, the arts of oratory, and so on), including a box from Zeus to be given to her future husband. She wed Epimetheus, brother of Prometheus, who opened the box and dispersed evils to the world. Only hope remained inside. A version of the Adam and Eve story.

persona   The role a person plays, not only for others but for himself; it represents conscious intentions. Cf. *mask.*

phallic symbol   Any pointed or upright object that may represent a phallus (e.g., a dagger, a banana, a cigarette).

phoenix   A fabulous, unique, and hermaphroditic bird that lived for five centuries and then was consumed in a great holocaust; from its ashes arose the new phoenix. Thus it is a symbol of resurrection, of Ra, the Egyptian sun god, of Christ; the fable of its death and rebirth is a form of the myth of the destruction of the world and its rebirth prophesied in the Bible.

pig A transcendent symbol associated with unclean sexuality, lechery.

Priapus God of natural reproduction, the son of Venus (beauty) and Bacchus (god of sexual orgy). *Priapism* is persistent abnormal erection of the penis.

priest The earthly form of the god-man, who, with the hero, is the mana-personality, one with superior knowledge and power.

projection Attribution of one's own traits, attitudes, or subjective processes to others.

Prometheus Son of Japetus, considered the father of mankind and identified with Noah's son Japeth, mythic ancestor of one third of the world (northern Caucasian). Prometheus made figures of clay and animated them with fire stolen from heaven. To punish him Zeus took fire away from mankind, but Prometheus, with the help of Athena, stole fire from the chariot of the sun and gave it to man. Zeus had him chained to a rock on Mt. Caucasus where a vulture ate daily of his liver, which regrew each night. He was released by Hercules, who killed the vulture. Prometheus has been considered both a Satan figure through his disobedience of Zeus and his animation of man (as otherwise clay object) and a Christ figure through his compassion for mankind and his gift to man that can prove both beneficial and destructive.

Proserpina Daughter of Zeus and Ceres (goddess of agriculture); she was abducted by Pluto (Hades), and through Ceres' demands she was able to spend half her time in hell (winter) and half on earth (summer).

psyche Personification of the life principle; the performer of psychological functions or acts.

quadrangle Any four-sided figure with the properties of four (which see) and the square (which see).

quaternity Four; corresponds to the earth, to the material patterns of life.

quest The attempt to find the treasure (which see), involving a journey (which see); ultimately the activity of finding the Self, to unite the conscious with the unconscious; the goal of the hero (which see).

rebirth The concept of restoration through the miracle of life or God, derived largely from observation of natural phenomena. Implied is cyclic time, although the term is also used for rebirth of the spirit after a metaphoric or spiritual death. In Christian thought, the final rebirth places one in Heaven; it is symbolized by the resurrection of Christ. Cf. *Easter*.

repression Exclusion of specific activities or concerns from conscious awareness. It is a defense mechanism against anxiety or guilt; the repressed activities enter the unconscious and project symbolic representations into the consciousness.

right The side of consciousness and adaptation; it suggests spiritual power and goodness; in Christianity, those who are saved.

ring Continuity, wholeness. See *circle*.

ritual A ceremonial act; a procedure resulting from custom. Ritual puts chaotic experience into an ordered form (such as dance); it usually is associated with important life functions such as adulthood, marriage, death.

river   A symbol of the flow of life; it is usually related to the mother-instinct; crossing a river is thus a symbol of a fundamental change in attitude. A stagnant or diverted river implies inhibition or repression. It may, however, also be a boundary or obstacle.

room   A symbol of individuality, of private thoughts; it is also a female archetype.

sacrifice   A ritual in which one gains spiritual energy for himself or the group in proportion to what is lost. Sacrifice was often practiced to achieve certain desired ends. This suggests that there is no creation without sacrifice. Cf. *hero*.

Satan figure   A representation of the force that opposes the hero and the achievement of his task or of the libido as antagonist to the supergo. It is symbolized by darkness, a cloak, a monster, a serpent (which see), and the like. It may involve destruction, descent, death, irregular shapes, that which is considered evil or nonspiritual. The Satan figure has similarities to the antihero (which see).

savior   A Christ figure, a messiah. Cf. *deliverer, hero*.

scapegoat   A person or group on whom the sins of the people are heaped in order figuratively to remove those sins from the people; the scapegoat is then driven away from the people (to die by sacrifice or by exposure). Rather than sins, the scapegoat may also become the symbol of frustrations and disappointments.

search for the father   A quest for the animus; an attempt to balance the presence of the female principle; activity to achieve communion with the godhead; ultimately a search for the Self, through an understanding of the conscious and the unconscious.

Semele   A mortal beloved of Zeus. Hera, jealous, got her to persuade Zeus to come to her in his own person; he did, and his lightning destroyed her. A version of the idea that one cannot face God unless he die.

serpent   An ambivalent symbol, first of evil, Satan, sin, death; second, of the phallus, Christ, protection, life (cf. the caduceus and Aaron's rod); and third, of regeneration (symbolized in the replacement of its skin each year by a new skin). As symbol it incorporates the principle of opposites (which see). The serpent seen devouring itself symbolizes both the eternal (circle), the cyclic in life, and the fusion of the meanings that life is achieved through death and that good emerges from evil in an unending cycle. It appears also as some kind of snake, a dragon, or a scorpion. Two entwined serpents (see also *caduceus*) represent sexual union and symbolize fertility, health, life. They symbolize the reconciliation of the natal serpent of Christ and the assumed mask of Satan; that is, of the qualities of spiritually good man and bodily corrupted man. The myth suggests that healthful life partakes of both kinds of qualities.

shadow   Negative double of the body, the image of evil, the alter ego of the soul.

Silenus   Chief of the satyrs, he is represented as a fat, drunken old man, riding an ass and crowned with flowers.

soul-image   A part of the psyche deep in the unconscious, consisting of the animus and the anima.

spiral   A form of the mandala that restores the old order simultaneously as it involves a new creation; the older pattern returns on a higher level.

square   A symbol of earthbound matter, of the body and reality. But heaven is described as a square (or cube), thus representing final perfection, order, and the final eternity. Often the circle and the square were combined in a type of quadrature of the circle, a mandala implying man's completeness, perfection, and achievement of spiritual greatness and the "impossible," and the fusion of God and man.

stone   A symbol of the Self and of something that man feels as immortal and unalterable. These are the implications in monuments and tombstones.

subconscious   That which is not part of the conscious but is capable of being made so.

sublimation   Refinement or redirection of primary energy into a new, conventional channel.

sun   An archetypal symbol of wholeness and enlightenment; it is identified with God, wisdom, growth, perfection. It partakes of the male principle.

symbol   An image that means something more than itself; much of that meaning comes from the emotional and the subconscious. It is the means of concretizing an inexpressible idea or emotion.

taboo   A social prohibition of an act or word; the prohibition is irrational and often involves drastic penalties.

talisman   An object bearing the symbol of the Self; it has magical properties and may avert evil and bring good fortune.

task   That which is imposed upon the hero by a divine superior in order to make him ready to serve as deliverer (which see); it may involve discovery of the treasure or the conquest of an evil or opposing force or the guardian of the treasure. Achievement of the task makes one worthy of the quest and the journey, or involves the quest or the journey itself. The task is the conquering of unconscious drives, which may be symbolized in animals, objects, or opposing figures. See also *Hercules, Jason.*

temptress   The negative female force representing unconscious drives that must be overcome for the hero to achieve his goals (the treasure, to become the deliverer, and the like). Related to the terrible mother (which see) or witch, presented as sexually enticing woman (lamia, enchantress, Circe); succumbing to this force is the defeat of the soul-image by bodily and external drives. The force offers life but yields death.

terrible mother   Death, the cruel side of nature, the nocturnal and left side of existence. She may appear as a cruel stepmother or a witch.

Thanatos   Death, the death instinct. Cf. *Eros.*

toad   A negative view of evolution or transformation from earth to water, or from inferior to superior form; the obverse of light and wisdom.

totem A living thing or a representation of it that is venerated as its symbol, its protective deity, or its ethos by a social group or community.

transcendence The transformation of personality through the blending and fusion of the noble with the base components, of the conscious with the unconscious.

transference Displacement of an emotion from one object to another.

treasure Signifies corruption by earthly desires; it is hidden but sought. It is equivalent to the mother-image (the unconscious); when treasure is found, man has been reborn in the cave in which introversion and regression have confined him. The "dragon" which guards the treasure and which must be destroyed is his former self. Cf. *alchemy, quest*.

tree Symbol of life and immortality (the Tree of Life, the Tree of the Hesperides, the source of the golden apples) or of knowledge (the Tree of Good and Evil). A central symbol of life, the life-root from which other living things derive. It represents nature and partakes of the female archetype; but it is also a phallic symbol and partakes of the male archetype. Thus it carries the soul-image. Identified with the cross on which Christ was crucified, it was built on the site of the Tree of Life in the Garden of Eden. The Trees of Life and of Good and Evil grew side by side.

trickster A figure whose physical appetites dominate his behavior; he is cruel, cynical, and unfeeling; he may assume the form of an animal, moving from one mischievous exploit to another. The trickster cycle corresponds to the earliest and least developed period of life. The symbols of transcendence involve the trickster as a shaman, or magician, who officiates at initiation rites; he is pictured as a bird. In this sense Hermes is a trickster as messenger and as conductor of the dead or of the known into the unknown (a role also played by Moses).

Trinity The divine triad of truth, mercy, and justice; a symbol of creation and of moral and spiritual dynamism.

twins They constitute a single person, forced apart at birth and needful of reuniting. They represent, therefore, the two sides of man's nature: flesh, acquiescent, mild, without initiative, and stump, dynamic and rebellious. They come to equate the introvert, who achieves by his powers of mind, and the extrovert, who achieves great deeds through action. Cf. *double, Leda*.

type A person or thing or event believed to foreshadow another (e.g., Old Testament personages or happenings that are precursory to those found in the New Testament); sometimes a recurrent model of the future.

typology A doctrine based on the existence of types; a study of the classification of types and their archetypal recurrence.

wanderer One who cannot die; he may be the hero in his eternal quest, or the imperishable part of man; sometimes he is seen as the godhead himself.

water A female archetype (wet and cold), the unconscious, life.

water-nymph One with the power to stir up and invert the order of things, bringing happiness to the wretched. She is a fragmentary expression of the feminine character of the unconscious.

weapon phallic symbol; the invincible weapon of myth by which the victory over the collective psyche is achieved.

whale An ambivalent symbol of evil as Leviathan and of good as a fish. It is the means of achievement of the night-sea journey (which see); thus through the agency of evil comes good, through death comes rebirth. Cf. *Jonah myth.*

wheel A symbol of eternity (cf. *circle*) and of endless cycle, but one sustained by the center of things (god) which communicates to man its energies in various forms (spokes).

wind A form of the primordial father, the inspiring and creative spirit. Cf. *air.*

window A symbol of communication from the private world of the room to the world outside. Also a female archetype as symbol of the vagina.

winged horse A combined symbol, it signifies flights of fancy, movement into the heavenly regions, inspiration, creativity. The instinctive drives represented by the horse are here controlled through the agency of the anima.

wise fool An innocent, probably youthful person, who has not been conditioned by initiation or a fall from experience; he appears to be foolish because he does not understand forces of evil and aggression, but he is wise since he reflects the instincts of his soul-image.

wise old man A personification of the Self; the purveyor of the unknown to the conscious (although usually he is a false adviser). He may appear as a magician or a demon; at times he is the positive aspect of these figures.

wish-fulfillment The discharge of tension by imagining a satisfying situation.

witch A collective image symbolizing the terrible mother or the evil that may be found in the female archetype.

woman The source of information about things for which a man has no eyes; inspiration, personal feeling, the bearer of the soul-image, the anima, love; often seen as temptress (which see) or as inferior consciousness (though only different from man's consciousness, which is not superior); complement to man, surrogate for the mother.

A SELECTIVE BIBLIOGRAPHY

BIDNEY, DAVID. *Theoretical Anthropology.* New York: Columbia University Press, 1953.

BODKIN, MAUD. *Archetypal Patterns in Poetry.* Oxford: Oxford University Press, 1934.

CAMPBELL, JOSEPH. *The Hero with a Thousand Faces.* New York: Bollingen, 1949.

——. *The Masks of God.* 4 vols. New York: Viking, 1959.

CASSIRER, ERNST. *Essay on Man.* New Haven: Yale University Press, 1944.

——. *The Philosophy of Symbolic Forms.* 3 vols. Tr. by Ralph Manhein. New Haven: Yale University Press, 1955.

CHASE, RICHARD. *Quest for Myth.* Baton Rouge: Louisiana State University Press, 1946.

CORNFORD, F. M. *The Origin of the Attic Comedy.* London: Edward Arnold, 1914.

ELIADE, MIRCEA. *The Myth of the Eternal Return.* Tr. by Willard R. Trask. New York: Pantheon, 1954.

——. *Birth and Rebirth.* Tr. by Willard R. Trask. New York: Pantheon, 1958.

——. *Myths, Dreams, and Mysteries.* Tr. by Philip Mairet. New York: Harper, 1960.

——. *Images and Symbols.* Tr. by Philip Mairet. New York: Sheed and Ward, 1961.

FARNELL, L. R. *Greek Hero Cults and Ideas of Immortality.* Oxford: Oxford University Press, 1921.

FIEDLER, LESLIE. *Love and Death in the American Novel.* New York: Criterion Books, 1960.

FRAZER, SIR JAMES G. *The Golden Bough.* 12 vols. London: Macmillan, 1907–1915.

——. *Folk-lore in the Old Testament.* 3 vols. London: Macmillan, 1918.

FREUD, SIGMUND. *Totem and Taboo.* Tr. by A. A. Brill. New York: Moffat, Yard and Co., 1918.

FROMM, ERICH. *The Forgotten Language.* New York: Rinehart, 1951.

FRYE, NORTHROP. *Anatomy of Criticism.* Princeton: Princeton University Press, 1957.

GASTER, TH. H. *Thespis: Ritual, Myth and Drama in the Ancient Near East* New York: Schuman, 1950.

GENNEP, ARNOLD VAN. *The Rites of Passage.* Tr. by Monika B. Vizedom and Gabrielle L. Caffee. London: Routledge & Kegan Paul, 1960.

GRAVES, ROBERT. *The White Goddess.* New York: Farrar, Straus and Cudahy, 1948.

———. *The Greek Myths.* 2 vols. Baltimore: Penguin, 1955.

HARRISON, JANE. *Prolegomena to the Study of Greek Religion.* Cambridge: Cambridge University Press, 1903.

———. *Themis.* Cambridge: Cambridge University Press, 1912.

HOOKE, S. H. (ed.) *Myth and Ritual.* London: Oxford University Press, 1933.

JAMES, E. O. *Christian Myth and Ritual.* London: J. Murray, 1933.

———. *The Cult of the Mother Goddess.* London: Thames and Hudson, 1959.

JUNG, C. G. *Symbols for the Transformation.* Tr. by R. F. C. Hull, New York: Pantheon, 1956.

———. *The Archetypes and the Collective Unconscious.* Tr. by R. F. C. Hull, New York, 1959.

JUNG, C. G., M.-L. VON FRANZ. (eds.) *Man and His Symbols.* London: Aldus Books, 1964.

LANGER, SUSANNE K. *Philosophy in a New Key.* Cambridge: Harvard University Press, 1942.

LEVY, G. R. *The Gate of Horn.* London: Faber & Faber, 1948.

LÉVY-BRUHL, LUCIEN. *Primitive Mentality.* Tr. by Lilian A. Clare. London: George Allen & Unwin, 1926.

MALINOWSKI, BRONISLAW. *Myth in Primitive Psychology.* London: K. Paul, Trench, Trubner, 1926.

———. *Magic, Science and Religion.* Glencoe: Free Press, 1948.

PRESCOTT, FREDERICK C. *Poetry and Myth.* New York: Macmillan, 1927.

RADIN, PAUL. *The Trickster.* New York: Philosophical Library, 1956.

RAGLAN, LORD. *The Hero.* London: Methuen, 1936.

———. *Death and Rebirth.* London: Watts, 1945.

RANK, OTTO. *The Myth of the Birth of the Hero.* New York: Journal of Nervous and Mental Disease Publishing Co., 1914.

REIK, THEODOR. *The Creation of Woman.* New York: Braziller, 1960.

SEBEOK, T. A. (ed.) *Myth: A Symposium.* Bloomington: Indiana University Press, 1958.

SHUMAKER, WAYNE. *Literature and the Irrational.* New York: Prentice-Hall, 1960.

TROY, WILLIAM. *William Troy: Selected Essays.* Ed. by Stanley Edgar Hyman. Rutgers University Press: New Jersey, 1967.

VICKERY, JOHN B. (ed.) *Myth and Literature.* University of Nebraska Press: Lincoln, 1966.

WEISINGER, HERBERT. *Tragedy and the Paradox of the Fortunate Fall.* East Lansing: Michigan State University Press, 1953.

————. *The Agony and the Triumph: Papers on the Use and Abuse of Myth.* East Lansing: Michigan State University Press, 1964.

WELSFORD, ENID. *The Fool, His Social and Literary History.* New York: Doubleday and Company, 1961.

WESTON, JESSIE L. *The Quest of the Holy Grail.* London: G. Bell & Sons, 1913.

————. *From Ritual to Romance.* Cambridge: Cambridge University Press, 1920.

ZIMMER, HEINRICH. *The King and the Corpse.* Ed. by Joseph Campbell. New York: Pantheon, 1948.

Index

Notes on the authors represented in this volume will be found on pp. xvii–xxii; a glossary of terms is printed on pp. 449–464. Further readings are given on pp. 63, 219–220, 446–447, and 465–467.